THE
YALOM
READER

THE
YALOM
READER

*Selections from the Work
of a Master Therapist
and Storyteller*

IRVIN D. YALOM

BasicBooks
A Subsidiary of Perseus Books, L.L.C.

Published by BasicBooks,
A Subsidiary of Perseus Books, L.L.C.

FIRST EDITION

Designed by Elliott Beard

Library of Congress Cataloging-in-Publication Data

Yalom, Irvin D., 1931–
    The Yalom reader : selections from the work of a master therapist and storyteller / by Irvin D. Yalom ; edited by Ben Yalom. — 1st ed.
        p.   cm.
    Includes index.
    ISBN 0-465-03610-4
    1. Psychotherapy and literature.   2. Group psychotherapy.
3. Existential psychotherapy.   I. Yalom, Ben.   II. Title.
    RC480.5.Y34   1997
    616.89—dc21   97-21790

98 99 00 01 02 ❖/RRD 10 9 8 7 6 5 4 3 2

To Marilyn, wife, lover, editor.
Soulmate for fifty years—and not nearly long enough

Contents

PART III

ON WRITING   267

Introduction

When Basic Books, my publisher for the past three decades, first proposed this book, I shuddered. I had always thought an anthology to be a posthumous collection of a writer's work. Or, if not *posthumous,* then a retrospective—a collection compiled at the very end of one's writing career. So it seemed to me that the proposal was just one more life stage marker, another melancholy reminder of aging—like retiring from Stanford University; developing senile plaques and aching knees; saying farewell to tennis; watching my children marry, settle into professions, and have children themselves.

Gradually, however, I warmed to the idea of a reader-cum-retrospective because I thought it offered a curtain call for many beloved, long-forgotten works. Eagerly I blew the dust off old files and reread my darling articles concerning such things as the hypnotic treatment of plantar warts, postpartum blues, aggression in voyeurism, LSD, Hemingway, organic brain diseases of senility, family therapy for ulcerative colitis. But it did not take long to realize that I might be the sole interested reader of such an arcane, disconnected, and often outdated collection. Consequently, I put them away (except for the Hemingway article—that stayed) and saw the wisdom in the publisher's view that the sensible raison d'être of such a reader would be to chart the arc of my writing career as it has progressed, over thirty years, from research reports in professional journals to fiction.

My early books were texts of psychotherapy. My most recent works are novels of psychotherapy. Hence, I have two sets of readers: psychotherapists who have been assigned my textbooks during their formal training, and lay readers, casually interested in psychotherapy, who are drawn to the storytelling format of my later work. I hope in these pages to introduce each of these audiences to the other pole of my work—to expose, in a gentle fashion, the lay reader to a more theoretical, empirically based view of psychotherapy and, on the other hand, to instill in practicing therapists a greater appreciation of the centrality of narrative in the process of psychotherapy.

This volume has three parts, reflecting my major interests: (1) group psychotherapy, (2) existential psychotherapy, and (3) writing. From the beginning, in my effort to understand, illuminate, and teach psychotherapy, I have been fascinated with two major therapy approaches: group therapy and existential therapy. I was first trained to think as a medical scientist, and my group therapy texts were informed, whenever possible, by empirical research. Later, as I explored the field of existential therapy, it became apparent that empirical research had less to offer: questions surrounding the deep subjective responses to the human condition do not lend themselves to empirical investigation. Consequently much of my work in existential therapy is informed primarily by philosophical investigation—my own and that of others.

Part III of this volume, "On Writing," chronicles the powerful interest in narrative that has lurked behind all my professional writing, has inserted itself from time to time in my texts, and ultimately, in later years, has taken over altogether.

Although I can trace my attraction to literature to my earliest years, there was a specific moment in my education that brought home to me the power of narrative. In my first two years of medical school I had performed well enough in my basic science classes. A diligent student, I was always near the top of my class but performed mechanically with no *passion* for any part of a scientific medical curriculum. As a third-year student I took a psychiatry clerkship and was assigned my first patient. Though I've long since forgotten her name, I remember her well: a young, depressed, freckled-faced lesbian with long red braids carelessly bound with thick rubber bands.

I was extremely uncomfortable in our initial meeting. It was obvious to both of us that I knew next to nothing about psychiatry. Perhaps that was a help; she was highly distrustful of my field (rightly so—those were the days when homosexual acts were illegal, and she would have been officially diagnosed as a sexual deviant). And not only was I ignorant about psychotherapy: I also knew nothing at all about lesbians aside from one titillating passage in Proust where Swann spied on two women making love.

What could I possibly offer her? All I could do, I ultimately decided, was to allow her to be my guide and to explore her world as best I could. Her previous experience with men had been horrendous, and I was the first of my sex to listen, respectfully and attentively, to her. Her story touched me. I thought about her often between our meetings, and over the weeks we developed a tender, even loving, relationship. She seemed to improve rapidly. How much of her improvement was real? How much of it was a reward for listening and caring? I never knew.

All psychiatric students were asked to present a case at the weekly case conference. When my turn came I looked around the room in terror at my audience of psychiatric faculty as well as several luminaries of the Boston Psychoanalytic Institute. Finally I screened them out of mind, gulped, and began. That was forty years ago. I remember little of the conference aside from the stillness and deep silence in the conference room as I told them about my meetings with my patient and the development of our loving feelings toward each another. No one moved or took notes, and in the ensuing discussion, each participant psychiatrist seemed oddly at a loss for words. To my astonishment many offered lavish, even embarrassing, praise for my presentation; others simply commented that my presentation spoke for itself and nothing more needed to be said.

My experience in that conference was an epiphany—a moment of sudden, deep, clarifying insight. How had I evoked such interest from that distinguished audience? Certainly not by displaying any grasp of theory. Nor by describing a course of systematic effective therapy. No, what I had done was something quite different: *I had conveyed the essence of my patient and our relationship in the form of an interesting story.* I had always known how to tell stories and now I believed I had found a way to put that ability to good use. I walked out of that conference forty years ago certain that psychiatry was my calling. And certain, too, that in some manner, as yet unknown, my particular contribution to psychiatry would be as a storyteller.

Aside from the many section introductions and three new essays on narrative, the text of this volume is excerpted from published books and articles and edited for brevity, readability, and continuity. I have been blessed with the opportunity to work on this project with my son, Ben Yalom, a writer and editor *extraordinaire*. He has edited this volume from inception to finish, and I am deeply indebted to him for his expert advice in the organization of this volume, for the content of the introductions, and for the selection and editing of the excerpts. I am also grateful to my publishers at Basic Books: Joann Miller for suggesting this volume, and Gail Winston and John Donatich for supporting the project to the finish.

Note to the Text

Shaded boxes are used throughout this volume to denote new text written to introduce and accompany the excerpted material within.

PART I

GROUP THERAPY

I was fortunate to have had my psychiatric training at Johns Hopkins University, where I came under the tutelage of Jerome Frank, a pioneer in group therapy and an eminent psychotherapy researcher and theoretician. Not only did Dr. Frank encourage his psychiatric residents to conduct groups, but he permitted us to observe his groups through a postage stamp sized two way mirror. Both his daring in having his work observed and the two-way mirror were innovations at that time. After a few months of observation I began leading groups for outpatients and inpatients, and over the next thirty-five years I led a great variety of groups: brief and long-term dynamic outpatient groups; inpatient groups; conjoint family groups; multiple family groups; groups for cancer patients, families of cancer patients, AIDS patients, bereaved spouses, bereaved parents, anorexic patients, alcoholics, adult children of alcoholics, sexual deviants, imprisoned murderers, schizophrenic patients, and sexually abused women; and therapy/training groups for corporate CEOs, teachers, hospital staff for chronic patients, psychiatric residents, psychology interns, medical students, psychiatric nurses, and psychotherapists in private practice.

My clinical group experience coupled with research findings—my own and those of others—long ago persuaded me of the great power of therapy groups. Yet the majority of clinicians persistently resist practicing group therapy. Over many years I have written, lectured, and given workshops in an attempt to diminish that resistance.

Why is there so much resistance? Certainly it is not based on rational professional inquiry. A very persuasive body of research has demonstrated, project by project, or through meta-analysis, that patients do as well in the group format as in the individual format, or better. The resistance comes from other sources. There are economic concerns (too many therapists, too few patients) and practical concerns (organizing and maintaining a group in private practice requires considerable energy and a wide referral base); sometimes uninformed and unprepared patients find the idea of a group frightening and choose the individual format for its presumed safety and comfort; there is ingrained professional prejudice—the analytic one-to-one model has held sway for many decades, and older therapists are loath to desert it for the scarier prospects of leading a group; and, finally, some therapists have personal fears and prefer the role of authoritarian medical practitioner to the more egalitarian, transparent role required of the group therapist.

One of the very few positive aspects of the contemporary economic revolution in the delivery of mental health care today is that this resistance, which has limited the use of group therapy and has withstood all the persuasive research evidence demonstrating its effectiveness, may be simply mandated away on the basis of economic concerns. Managed health care will inevitably make greater use of therapy groups in the future. Therapy groups have always been a more efficient form of therapy (from the standpoint of manpower required), though I wish to make it clear that economic expediency has never, in my view, been the raison d'être of group therapy. The arena of the psychotherapy group offers, as I hope to demonstrate in this collection, unique opportunities in therapy: groups are not a diluted individual therapy but instead offer possibilities for therapeutic changes that are unavailable in individual therapy.

Early in my career I had a good deal of contact with encounter groups, as a member, leader, and researcher. With two colleagues, Morton Lieberman and Matthew Miles, I conducted a large project researching the process and outcome of ten models of group leadership in eighteen different encounter groups, and we eventually published our findings in a research monograph, *Encounter Groups: First Facts*. This is the one book that I have not excerpted in this volume (the language is too uncompromisingly technical), but the research it describes, coupled with my personal experience with encounter group leadership technology, has had a significant influence on the model of group therapy I ultimately evolved.

This section of the reader consists of three chapters: the first examines the therapeutic factors in group psychotherapy; the second presents the here-and-now, a core concept in my approach to group psychotherapy; and the third reviews therapy with specialized groups.

CHAPTER 1

The Therapeutic Factors:
What It Is That Heals

INTRODUCTION

This chapter, as well as the next, is drawn from *The Theory and Practice of Group Psychotherapy*, by far my most widely read book. Approximately six hundred thousand copies have been printed in the United States and abroad, where it has been translated into several foreign languages. After the publication of the first edition in 1970, the textbook required continued care and maintenance: each subsequent edition (the second, third, and fourth editions appeared at approximately eight-year intervals) demanded two years of concentrated work. Between editions it was necessary to stay abreast of the professional literature, to monitor new developments in the field, and to keep careful records of any of my own group therapy meetings that might serve a pedagogical purpose.

When I first began writing the text, my primary audience, I am chagrined to say, was the Stanford University promotion committee. Beginning with two middle chapters, I wrote a labored and detailed critical analysis of the world research literature on the selection of patients for group therapy and the composition of therapy groups. Shortly after finishing those chapters I was notified that I had been promoted and granted academic tenure. Immediately thereafter I radically changed my audience and my writing approach: I put the promotion committee out of my mind; I eliminated all jargon, all detailed research analysis, and all unnecessarily complex theoretical structures; and I wrote with only one purpose in mind—to interest and to educate the group therapy student.

The Theory and Practice of Group Psychotherapy begins with a survey of the wide scope of group therapy practice. There is no single group therapy; there are many group therapies. In the previous pages I offered a list of the different types of groups I have led in my career; although the list may seem long and varied, it represents only a small fraction of the types of therapy groups to be found in contemporary clinical practice. Each of these groups has its own ambiance, its own flavor, methods, technical problems and procedures. How, then, to write a text that will speak to all group leaders and all clinical therapy groups?

My pedagogical strategy in the textbook was to focus on the common denominators of therapy groups: to ignore the variegated and often exotic trappings of various group approaches and to focus, instead, on the question central to all—how do groups really help? The answer to this question—the various "therapeutic factors" ("curative factors," I labeled them in the first two editions)—constitutes the spine of the textbook. I describe twelve of these therapeutic factors in the first few chapters and from them derive the basic rules of leadership procedure and technique. In other words, I take the position that once we identify the basic healing factors in therapy, we can, with assurance, know how therapists should proceed: *they should do whatever is necessary to facilitate the emergence and maturation of these therapeutic factors.*

The first selection—edited from the first four chapters of *The Theory and Practice of Group Psychotherapy*—discusses the derivation and meaning of the therapeutic factors.

THE THERAPEUTIC FACTORS

How does group therapy help patients? A naive question. But if we can answer it with some measure of precision and certainty, we will have at our disposal a central organizing principle by which to approach the most vexing and controversial problems of psychotherapy.

I suggest that therapeutic change is an enormously complex process that occurs through an intricate interplay of human experiences, which I will refer to as "therapeutic factors." From my perspective, natural lines of cleavage divide the therapeutic experience into eleven primary factors. The distinctions among these factors are arbitrary; though I discuss them singly, they are interdependent and neither occur nor function separately. Keeping this in mind, we can view them as providing a cognitive map. This grouping of the therapeutic factors is not set in cement: other clinicians and researchers have arrived at a different, and also arbitrary, cluster of factors. No explanatory system can encompass all of therapy.

The inventory of therapeutic factors I propose issues from my clinical experience, from the experience of other therapists, from the views of the successfully treated group patient, and from relevant systematic research. None of these sources is beyond doubt, however; neither group members nor group leaders are entirely objective, and our research methodology is often crude and inapplicable.

From the group therapists we obtain a variegated and internally inconsistent inventory of therapeutic factors. Therapists, by no means disinterested or unbiased observers, have invested considerable time and energy in mastering a certain therapeutic approach. Their answers will be determined largely by their particular school of conviction. Even among therapists who share the same ideology and speak the same language, there may be no consensus about why patients improve. The history of psychotherapy abounds in healers who were effective, but not for the reasons they supposed. At other times we therapists throw up our hands in bewilderment. Who has not had a patient who made vast improvement for entirely obscure reasons?

Patients at the end of a course of group therapy can supply data about the therapeutic factors they considered most and least helpful; or, during therapy, they can supply evaluations of the significant aspects of each group meeting. Yet we know that the completeness and accuracy of the patients' evaluations will be limited. Will they not, perhaps, focus primarily on superficial factors and neglect some profound healing forces that may be beyond their awareness? Will their responses not be influenced by a variety of factors difficult to control? For example, their views may be distorted by the nature of their relationship to the therapist or to the group. (One team of researchers demonstrated that when patients were interviewed four years after the conclusion of therapy, they were far more apt to comment on unhelpful or harmful aspects of their group experience than when interviewed immediately at its termination.)[1]

Research has also shown, for example, that the therapeutic factors valued by patients may differ greatly from those cited by their therapists or by group observers.[2] Furthermore, many confounding factors influence the patient's evaluation of the therapeutic factors: for example, the length of time in treatment and the level of a patient's functioning,[3] the type of group (that is, whether outpatient, inpatient, day hospital, brief therapy),[4] the age and the diagnosis of a patient,[5] and the ideology of the group leader.[6] Another factor that complicates the search for common therapeutic factors is the extent to which different group patients perceive and experience the same event in different ways.[7] Any given experience may be important or helpful to some members and inconsequential or even harmful to others.

Despite these limitations, patients' reports are a rich and relatively untapped source of information. After all, it is *their* experience, theirs alone, and the farther we move from the patients' experience, the more inferential are our conclusions. To be sure, there are aspects of the process of change that operate outside a patient's awareness, but it does not follow that we should disregard what patients *do* say.

In addition to therapists' views and patients' reports, there is a third important method of evaluating the therapeutic factors: the systematic research approach. The most common research strategy by far is to correlate in-therapy variables with outcome in therapy. By discovering which variables are significantly related to successful outcome, one can establish a reasonable base from which to begin to delineate the therapeutic factors. However, there are many inherent problems in this approach: the measurement of outcome is itself a methodological morass, and the selection and measurement of the in-therapy variables are equally problematic. (Generally the accuracy of the measurement is directly proportional to the triviality of the variable. It is easy, for example, to measure a variable such as "verbal activity"—the number of words spoken by each patient. But it is extraordinarily difficult to examine insight: one can measure the incidence of interpretive statements offered by the therapist, but how is one to determine the meaningfulness to the patient of each statement?)

I have drawn from all these methods to derive the therapeutic factors discussed in this book. Still, I do not regard these conclusions as definitive; rather, I offer them as provisional guidelines that may be tested and deepened by other clinical researchers. For my part, I am satisfied that they derive from the best available evidence at this time and that they constitute the basis of an effective approach to therapy.

Instillation of Hope

The instillation and maintenance of hope is crucial in any psychotherapy. Not only is hope required to keep the patient in therapy so that other therapeutic factors may take effect, but faith in a treatment mode can in itself be therapeutically effective. Several research inquiries have demonstrated that pretherapy high expectation of help is significantly correlated with a positive therapy outcome.[8] Consider also the massive data documenting the efficacy of faith healing and placebo treatment—therapies mediated entirely through hope and conviction.

Group therapists can capitalize on this factor by doing whatever we can to increase patients' belief and confidence in the efficacy of the group mode. This task begins before the group starts, in the pregroup orientation in which the therapist reinforces positive expectations, removes negative preconceptions, and presents a lucid and powerful explanation of the group's healing properties.

Group therapy not only draws from the general ameliorative effects of positive expectations but also benefits from a source of hope that is unique to the group format. Therapy groups invariably contain individuals who are at different points along a coping-collapse continuum. Each member thus has considerable contact with others—often individuals with similar problems—who have improved as a result of therapy. I have often heard patients remark at the end of their group therapy how important it was for them to have observed the improvement of others.

Research substantiates that it is also vitally important that therapists believe in themselves and in the efficacy of their group.[9] I sincerely believe that I am able to help every motivated patient who is willing to work in the group for at least six months. In my initial meetings with patients individually, I share this conviction with them and attempt to imbue them with my optimism.

Many of the self-help groups place heavy emphasis on the instillation of hope.[10] A major part of Recovery, Inc. (for current and former psychiatric patients), and Alcoholics Anonymous meetings is dedicated to testimonials. At each meeting, members of Recovery, Inc., give accounts of potentially stressful incidents in which they avoided tension by the application of Recovery, Inc., methods, and successful Alcoholics Anonymous members tell their stories of downfall and then rescue by AA. One of the great strengths of Alcoholics Anonymous is the fact that the leaders are all ex-alcoholics—living inspirations to the others. Similarly, substance-abuse treatment programs commonly mobilize hope in patients by using recovered drug addicts as group leaders. Members are inspired and expectations raised by contact with those who have trod the same path and found the way back.

Universality

Many patients enter therapy with the disquieting thought that they are unique in their wretchedness, that they alone have certain frightening or unacceptable problems, thoughts, impulses, and fantasies. Of course, there is a core of truth to this notion, since most patients have had an unusual constellation of severe life stresses and are periodically flooded by frightening material that has leaked from the unconscious.

To some extent this is true for all of us, but many patients, because of their extreme social isolation, have a heightened sense of uniqueness. Their interpersonal difficulties preclude the possibility of deep intimacy. In everyday life they neither learn about others' analogous feelings and experiences nor avail themselves of the opportunity to confide in, and ultimately to be validated and accepted by, others.

In the therapy group, especially in the early stages, the disconfirmation of a patient's feelings of uniqueness is a powerful source of relief. After hearing other members disclose concerns similar to their own, patients report feeling more in touch with the world and describe the process as a "welcome to the human race" experience. Simply put, the phenomenon finds expression in the cliché "We're all in the same boat," or perhaps more cynically, "Misery loves company."

There is no human deed or thought that is fully outside the experience of other people. I have heard group members reveal such acts as incest, burglary, embezzlement, murder, attempted suicide, and fantasies of an even more desperate nature. Invariably, I have observed other group members reach out and embrace these very acts as within the realm of their own possibilities. Long ago Freud noted that the staunchest taboos (against incest and patricide) were constructed precisely because these very impulses are part of the human being's deepest nature.

Nor is this form of aid limited to group therapy. Universality plays a role in individual therapy also, although in that format less of an opportunity for consensual validation exists. Once I reviewed with a patient his 600-hour experience in individual analysis with another therapist. When I asked what he recalled as the most significant event in his therapy, he described an incident when he was profoundly distressed about his feelings toward his mother. Despite strong concurrent positive sentiments, he was beset with death wishes for her—he stood to inherit a sizable estate. His analyst, at one point, commented simply, "That seems to be the way we're built." That artless statement offered considerable relief and furthermore enabled the patient to explore his ambivalence in great depth.

Despite the complexity of human problems, certain common denominators are clearly evident, and the members of a therapy group soon perceive their similarities. An example is illustrative: for many years I asked members of T-groups or "process groups" to engage in a "top-secret" task. They were to write, anonymously, on a slip of paper the one thing they would be most disinclined to share with the group. The secrets prove to be startlingly similar, with a couple of major themes predominating. The most common secret is a deep conviction of basic inadequacy—a feeling that one is basically incompetent, that one glides through life on a sleek intellectual bluff. Next in frequency is a deep sense of interpersonal alienation—that, despite appearances, one really does not, or cannot, care for or love another person. The third most frequent category is some variety of sexual secret. These chief concerns of nonpatients are qualitatively the same in individuals seeking professional help. Almost invariably, our patients experience deep concern about their sense of worth and their ability to relate to others.

Some specialized groups composed of individuals for whom secrecy has been an especially important and isolating factor place a particularly great emphasis on universality. For example, short-term structured groups for bulimic patients build into their protocol a strong requirement for self-disclosure, especially disclosure about attitudes toward body image and detailed accounts of each patient's eating rituals and purging practices. With rare exceptions, patients express great relief at discovering that they are not alone, that others share the same dilemmas and life experiences.[11]

Members of sexual abuse groups, too, profit enormously from the experience of universality. An integral part of these groups is the intimate sharing, often for the first time in each member's life, of the details of the abuse and the ensuing internal devastation. Members can encounter others who have suffered similar violations as children, who were not responsible for what happened to them, and who have also suffered deep feelings of shame, guilt, rage, and uncleanliness.[12]

In multicultural groups, therapists may need to pay particular attention to this therapeutic fact. Cultural minorities in a predominantly Caucasian group may feel excluded because of different attitudes toward disclosure, interaction, and affective expression. Therapists must help the group move past a focus on concrete cultural differences to transcultural responses to human situations and tragedies that all of us share.[13]

Universality, like the other therapeutic factors, does not have sharp borders; it merges with other therapeutic factors. As patients perceive their similarity to others and share their deepest concerns, they benefit further from the accompanying catharsis and from ultimate acceptance by other members.

Imparting Information

Under the general rubric of imparting information, I include didactic instruction about mental health, mental illness, and general psychodynamics given by the therapists, as well as advice, suggestions, or direct guidance from either the therapist or other patients.

Most patients, at the conclusion of successful interactional group therapy, have learned a great deal about psychic functioning, the meaning of symptoms, interpersonal and group dynamics, and the process of psychotherapy. Generally, the educational process is implicit; most group therapists do not offer explicit didactic instruction in interactional group therapy. Over the past decade, however, many group therapy approaches have made formal instruction, or psycho-education, an important part of the program.

For example, Recovery, Inc., the nation's oldest and largest self-help program for current and former psychiatric patients, is basically organized along didactic lines.[14] Founded in 1937 by the late Abraham Low, this organization had almost 1,000 operating groups by 1993, with an annual attendance of over 275,000. Membership is voluntary, and the leaders spring from the membership. Though there is no formal professional guidance, the conduct of the meetings has been highly structured by Dr. Low; parts of his textbook, *Mental Health Through Will Training,* are read aloud and discussed at every meeting.[15] Psychological illness is explained on the basis of a few simple principles, which the members memorize. For example: the neurotic symptom is distressing but not dangerous; tension intensifies and sustains the symptom and should be avoided; the use of free will is the solution to the nervous patient's dilemmas.

Many other self-help groups strongly emphasize the imparting of information. Groups such as Adult Survivors of Incest, Parents Anonymous, Gamblers Anonymous, Make Today Count (for cancer patients), Parents Without Partners, and Mended Hearts encourage the exchange of information among members and often invite experts to address the group.[16]

Recent group therapy literature abounds with descriptions of specialized groups for patients who have some specific disorder or face some definitive life crisis—for example, obesity,[17] bulimia,[18] adjustment after divorce,[19] rape,[20] self-image adjustment after mastectomy,[21] and chronic pain.[22]

In addition to offering mutual support, these groups generally build in a cognitive therapy approach by offering explicit instruction about the nature of a patient's illness or life situation and examining patients' misconceptions and self-defeating responses to their illness. For example, the leaders of a group for patients with panic disorders describe the physiologic cause of panic disorders: heightened stress and arousal increase the flow of adrenaline, which may result in hyperventilation, shortness of breath, and dizziness; this in turn is misinterpreted by the patient ("I'm dying; I'm going crazy"), which only exacerbates the vicious cycle. The therapists discuss the benign nature of panic attacks and offer group members instruction, first, in how to bring on a mild attack, and then in how to prevent it. The leaders pay special attention to providing detailed instruction in proper breathing techniques and progressive muscular relaxation.

Leaders of groups for HIV-positive patients offer considerable illness-related medical information, correct irrational fears (for example, greatly exaggerated fears about infectiousness), and give advice about telling others about one's condition, fashioning a different, less guilt-provoking lifestyle, and seeking both professional and nonprofessional help.[23]

Leaders of bereavement groups may provide information about the natural cycle of bereavement to help members realize that there is a sequence of pain through which they are progressing and there will be a natural, almost inevitable, subsiding to their distress. Leaders may help patients anticipate, for example, the acute anguish they will feel with each significant date (holidays, anniversaries, birthdays) during the first year of bereavement.

Didactic instruction has thus been employed in a variety of fashions in group therapy: to transfer information, to alter sabotaging thought patterns, to structure the group, to explain the process of illness. Often such instruction functions as the initial binding force in the group, until other therapeutic factors become operative. In part, however, explanation and clarification function as effective therapeutic agents in their own right. Human beings have always abhorred uncertainty and through the ages have sought to order the universe by providing explanations, primarily religious or scientific. The explanation of a phenomenon is the first step toward its control. If a volcanic eruption is caused by a displeased god, then at least there is hope of pleasing the god.

Frieda Fromm-Reichman underscores the role of uncertainty in producing anxiety.[24] She points out that being aware that one is not one's own helmsman, that one's perceptions and behavior are controlled by irrational forces, is in itself an important source of anxiety. Jerome Frank, in a post–World War II study of Americans' reactions to an unfamiliar South Pacific disease (schistosomiasis), demonstrated that anxiety stemming from uncertainty often creates more havoc than the disease itself.[25]

And so it is with psychiatric patients: fear and anxiety that stem from uncertainty of the source, meaning, and seriousness of psychiatric symptoms may so compound the total dysphoria that effective exploration becomes vastly more difficult. Didactic instruction, through its provision of structure and explanation, has intrinsic value and deserves a place in our repertoire of therapeutic instruments.

Unlike explicit didactic instruction from the therapist, direct advice from the members occurs without exception in every therapy group. In dynamic interactional therapy groups, it is invariably part of the early life of the group and occurs with such regularity that it can be used to estimate a group's age. If I observe a group in which the patients with some regularity say things like, "I think you ought to _____," or "What you should do is _____," or "Why don't you _____?" then I can be reasonably certain either that the group is young or that it is an older group facing some difficulty that has impeded its development or effected temporary regression. Advice giving is common in early interactional group therapy, but it is rare that a specific suggestion for some problem will directly benefit any patient. Indirectly, however, advice giving serves a purpose; the *process,* rather than the *content* of the advice, may be beneficial, implying and conveying, as it does, mutual interest and caring.

Advice-giving or advice-seeking behavior is often an important clue in the elucidation of interpersonal pathology. The patient who, for example, continuously pulls advice and suggestions from others, ultimately only to reject them and frustrate others, is well known to group therapists as the "help-rejecting complainer" or the "yes . . . but" patient.[26] Some patients may bid for attention and nurturance by asking for suggestions about a problem that either is insoluble or has already been solved. Other patients soak up advice with an unquenchable thirst, yet never reciprocate to others who are equally needy. Some group members are so intent on preserving a high-status role in the group or a facade of cool self-sufficiency that they never ask directly for help; some are so anxious to please that they never ask for anything for themselves; some are excessively effusive in their gratitude; others never acknowledge the gift but take it home, like a bone, to gnaw on privately.

Other types of groups, noninteractionally focused, make explicit and effective use of direct suggestions and guidance. For example, behavior-shaping groups, partial hospitalization groups (preparing patients for autonomous living), communicational skills groups, Recovery, Inc., and Alcoholics Anonymous all proffer considerable direct advice. A communicational skills group for chronic psychiatric patients reports excellent results with a structured group program that includes focused feedback, videotape playback, and problem-solving projects.[27] AA makes use of guidance and slogans: for example, patients are asked to remain abstinent for only the next twenty-four hours—"one day at a time." Recovery, Inc., teaches members how to spot symptoms, how to erase and retrace, how to rehearse and reverse, how to apply willpower effectively.

Is some advice better than others? Researchers who studied a behavior-shaping group of male sex offenders noted not only that advice was common but that it was differentially useful. The least effective form of advice was a direct suggestion; most effective were more systematic, operationalized instructions or a series of alternative suggestions about how to achieve a desired goal.[28]

Altruism

There is an old Hasidic story of a rabbi who had a conversation with the Lord about Heaven and Hell. "I will show you Hell," said the Lord, and led the rabbi into a room containing a group of famished, desperate people sitting around a large, circular table. In the center of the table rested an enormous pot of stew, more than enough for everyone. The smell of the stew was delicious and made the rabbi's mouth water. Yet no one ate. Each diner at the table held a very long-handled spoon— long enough to reach the pot and scoop up a spoonful of stew, but too long to get the food into one's mouth. The rabbi saw that their suffering was indeed terrible and bowed his head in compassion. "Now I will show you Heaven," said the Lord, and they entered another room, identical to the first—same large, round table, same enormous pot of stew, same long-handled spoons. Yet there was gaiety in the air: everyone appeared well nourished, plump, and exuberant. The rabbi could not understand and looked to the Lord. "It is simple," said the Lord, "but it requires a certain skill. You see, the people in this room have learned to feed each other!"

In therapy groups, too, patients receive through giving, not only as part of the reciprocal giving-receiving sequence but also from the intrinsic act of giving. Psychiatric patients beginning therapy are demoralized and possess a deep sense of having nothing of value to offer others. They have long considered themselves as burdens, and the experience of finding that they can be of importance to others is refreshing and boosts self-esteem.

And, of course, patients are enormously helpful to one another in the group therapeutic process. They offer support, reassurance, suggestions, insight; they share similar problems with one another. Not infrequently group members will accept observations from another member far more readily than from the group therapist. To many patients, the therapist remains the paid professional; but the other members represent the real world: they can be counted on for spontaneous and truthful reactions and feedback. Looking back over the course of therapy, almost all patients credit other members as having been important in their improvement. Sometimes they cite their explicit support and advice, sometimes their simply having been present and allowing their fellow patients to grow as a result of a facilitative, sustaining relationship.

Altruism is a venerable therapeutic factor in other systems of healing. In primitive cultures, for example, a troubled person is often given the task of preparing a feast or performing some type of service for the community.[29] Altruism plays an important part in the healing process at Catholic shrines such as Lourdes, where the sick pray not only for themselves but for one another. Warden Duffy, a legendary figure at San Quentin Prison, once claimed that the best way to help a man is to let him help you. People need to feel they are needed and useful. It is commonplace for ex-alcoholics to continue their AA contacts for years after achieving complete sobriety; many members have related the story of downfall and subsequent reclamation at least a thousand times.

Neophyte group members do not at first appreciate the healing impact of other members. In fact, many prospective candidates resist the suggestion of group therapy with the question, "How can the blind lead the blind?" or "What can I possibly get from others as confused as I? We'll end up pulling one another down." Such resistance is best worked through by exploring a patient's critical self-evaluation. Generally, a patient who deplores the prospect of getting help from other patients is really saying, "I have nothing of value to offer anyone."

There is another, more subtle benefit inherent in the altruistic act. Many patients who complain of meaninglessness are immersed in a morbid self-absorption, which takes the form of obsessive introspection or a teeth-gritting effort to actualize oneself. I agree with Victor Frankl that a sense of life meaning ensues but cannot be deliberately, self-consciously pursued: it is always a derivative phenomenon that materializes when we have transcended ourselves, when we have forgotten ourselves and become absorbed in someone (or something) outside ourselves.[30] The therapy group implicitly teaches its members that lesson and provides a new counter-solipsistic perspective.

The Corrective Recapitulation of
the Primary Family Group

The great majority of patients who enter groups—with the exception of those suffering from post-traumatic stress syndrome or from some medical or environmental stress—have a background of a highly unsatisfactory experience in their first and most important group: the primary family. The therapy group resembles a family in many aspects: there are authority/parental figures, peer siblings, deep personal revelations, strong emotions, and deep intimacy as well as hostile, competitive feelings. In fact, therapy groups are often led by a male and female therapy team in a deliberate effort to simulate the parental configuration as closely as possible. Once the initial discomfort is overcome, it is inevitable that, sooner or later, the members will interact with leaders and other members in modes reminiscent of the way they once interacted with parents and siblings.

There is an enormous variety of patterns: some members become helplessly dependent upon the leaders, whom they imbue with unrealistic knowledge and power; others blindly defy the leaders, who are perceived as infantilizing and controlling; others are wary of the leaders, whom they believe attempt to strip members of their individuality; some members try to split the co-therapists in an attempt to incite parental disagreements and rivalry; some compete bitterly with other members, hoping to accumulate units of attention and caring from the therapists; others expend energy in a search for allies among the other patients, in order to topple the therapists; still others neglect their own interests in a seemingly selfless effort to appease the leaders and the other members.

Obviously, similar phenomena occur in individual therapy, but the group provides a vastly greater number and array of recapitulative possibilities. In one of my groups, Betty, a patient who had been silently pouting for a couple of meetings, bemoaned the fact that she was not in one-to-one therapy. She claimed she was inhibited because she knew the group could not satisfy her needs. She knew she could speak freely of herself in a private conversation with the therapist or with any one of the members. When pressed, Betty expressed her irritation that others were favored over her in the group. In a recent meeting, another member had been welcomed warmly upon returning from a vacation, whereas her return from a vacation went largely unnoticed by the group. Furthermore, another patient was praised for offering an important interpretation to a member, whereas she had made a similar statement weeks ago that had gone unnoticed. For some time, too, she had noticed her growing resentment at sharing the group time; she was impatient while waiting for the floor and irritated whenever attention was shifted away from her.

Was Betty right? Was group therapy the wrong treatment for her? Absolutely not! These very criticisms—which had roots stretching down into her early relationships with her siblings—did not constitute valid objections to group therapy. Quite the contrary: the group format was particularly valuable for her, since it allowed her envy and her craving for attention to surface. In individual therapy—where the therapist attends to the patient's every word and concern, and the patient is expected to use up all the allotted time—these particular conflicts might emerge belatedly, if at all.

What is important, though, is not only that early familial conflicts are relived but that they are relived correctively. Growth-inhibiting relationships must not be permitted to freeze into the rigid, impenetrable system that characterizes many family structures. Instead, fixed roles must be constantly explored and challenged, and ground rules for investigating relationships and testing new behavior must be constantly encouraged. For many patients, then, working out problems with therapists and other members is also working through unfinished business from long ago.

Development of Socializing Techniques

Social learning—the development of basic social skills—is a therapeutic factor that operates in all therapy groups, although the nature of the skills taught and the explicitness of the process vary greatly depending on the type of group therapy. There may be explicit emphasis on the development of social skills in, for example, groups preparing hospitalized patients for discharge or adolescent groups. Group members may be asked to role-play approaching a prospective employer or asking someone out on a date.

In other groups, social learning is more indirect. Members of dynamic therapy groups, which have ground rules encouraging open feedback, may obtain considerable information about maladaptive social behavior. A patient may, for example, learn about a disconcerting tendency to avoid looking at the person with whom he or she is conversing; about others' impressions of his or her haughty, regal attitude; or about a variety of other social habits that, unbeknownst to the patient, have been undermining social relationships. For individuals lacking intimate relationships, the group often represents the first opportunity for accurate interpersonal feedback. One patient, for example, who had been aware for years that others either avoided or curtailed social contact with him, learned in the therapy group that his obsessive inclusion of minute, irrelevant details in his social conversation was exceedingly off-putting. Years later he told me that one of the most important events of his life was when a group member (whose name he had long since forgotten) told him: "When you talk about your feelings, I like you and want to get closer; but when you start talking about facts and details, I want to get the hell out of the room!"

Frequently senior members of a therapy group acquire highly sophisticated social skills: they are attuned to process; they have learned how to be helpfully responsive to others; they have acquired methods of conflict resolution; they are less likely to be judgmental and more capable of experiencing and expressing accurate empathy. These skills cannot but help to serve these patients well in future social interactions.

Imitative Behavior

Patients during individual psychotherapy may, in time, sit, walk, talk, and even think like their therapists. There is considerable evidence that group therapists influence the communicational patterns in their groups by modeling certain behaviors, for example, self-disclosure or support.[31] In groups the imitative process is more diffuse: patients may model themselves on aspects of the other group members as well as of the therapist.[32] The importance of imitative behavior in the therapeutic process is difficult to gauge, but social psychological research suggests that therapists may have underestimated it. Bandura, who has long claimed that social learning cannot be adequately explained on the basis of direct reinforcement, has experimentally demonstrated that imitation is an effective therapeutic force.[33] For example, he has successfully treated a large number of individuals with snake phobias by asking them to observe him handling a snake. In group therapy it is not uncommon for a patient to benefit by observing the therapy of another patient with a similar problem constellation—a phenomenon generally referred to as *vicarious* or *spectator* therapy.[34]

Imitative behavior generally plays a more important role in the early stages of a group than in its later stages, as members look for more senior members or therapists with whom to identify.[35] Even if imitative behavior is, in itself, short-lived, it may help to unfreeze the individual enough to experiment with new behavior, which in turn can launch an adaptive spiral. In fact, it is not uncommon for patients throughout therapy to "try on," as it were, bits and pieces of other people and then relinquish them as ill fitting. This process may have solid therapeutic impact; finding out what we are not is progress toward finding out what we are.

Catharsis

Catharsis has always assumed an important role in the therapeutic process, though the rationale behind its use has varied considerably. For centuries, patients have been purged to cleanse them of excessive bile, evil spirits, and infectious toxins (the word itself is derived from the Greek root, "to clean"). Since Breuer and Freud's 1895 treatise on the treatment of hysteria,[36] many therapists have attempted to help patients rid themselves of suppressed, choked affect. What Freud and subsequently all dynamic psychotherapists have learned is that catharsis is not enough. After all, we have emotional experiences, sometimes very intense ones, all our lives without their leading to change.

The data support this conclusion. Although the research into the patient's appraisal of the therapeutic factors reveals the importance of catharsis, the research also suggests important qualifications. In a study of 210 participants in encounter groups, my colleagues and I found that catharsis was necessary to good outcome but not sufficient for it.[37] Members who cited the sole importance of catharsis were, in fact, more likely to have had a negative experience in the group. Those who had a growth experience characteristically coupled catharsis with some form of cognitive learning.

Similar conclusions emerged from a study in which my colleagues and I administered a sixty-item Q-sort to patients who had a successful group therapy experience. Ventilation, in and of itself, was not deemed highly useful by patients. *Effective* catharsis was linked to other factors. For one thing, it was part of an interpersonal process: group members did not express emotions in a closet—they did so in a social context. The same is true in individual therapy. When a patient weeps in my office I am, of course, interested in the reasons for weeping, but I am often more interested in how it felt for that patient to weep at that time, in my presence. I invariably inquire about this and often the discussion leads us into important areas such as trust, shame, or fear of judgment. In addition catharsis is intricately related to cohesiveness. Catharsis is more helpful once supportive group bonds have formed. Freedman and Hurley show that catharsis is more valued late rather than early in the course of the group.[38] Conversely, strong expression of emotion enhances the development of cohesiveness: members who express strong feelings toward one another and work honestly with these feelings will develop close mutual bonds. In groups of patients dealing with loss, McCallum, Piper, and Morin found that expressions of positive affect were associated with positive outcomes, and increased throughout the course of short-term groups. The expression of negative affect, on the other hand, was therapeutic only when it occurred in the context of genuine attempts to understand oneself or other group members.[39]

In summary, then, the open expression of affect is, without question, vital to the group therapeutic process; in its absence, a group would degenerate into a sterile academic exercise. Yet it is only part of the process and must be complemented by other factors.

One last point. The intensity of emotional expression is highly relative and must be appreciated not from the leader's perspective but from that of each member's experiential world. A seemingly muted expression of emotion may, for a highly constricted individual, represent an event of considerable intensity. On many occasions I have witnessed students who, after viewing a videotape of a group meeting, complain about the session being muted and boring, whereas the members themselves experienced the session as highly intense and charged.

Existential Factors

Successful group therapy patients consider existential factors to be significant in their improvement. In my Q-sort study three existentially oriented items were heavily weighted by patients: (1) *recognizing that no matter how close I get to other people, I must still face life alone;* (2) *facing the basic issues of my life and death, and thus living my life more honestly and being less caught up in trivialities; (3) learning that I must take the ultimate responsibility for the way I live my life no matter how much guidance and support I get from others.*[40]

Such factors play a paramount role in specialized groups where patients are starkly confronted with existential issues—for example, groups of patients with life-threatening illness or groups of bereaved patients. But if the leader has a highly developed sensibility to these issues, they will play an important role in any psychotherapy group. Members learn there is a limit to the guidance they can get from others. They learn that they must bear ultimate responsibility for the autonomy of their group and their life. They learn that there is a basic isolation in existence that cannot be breached: everyone is thrown into the world alone, and must die alone. Still, despite this, there is a deep comfort from relating intimately to other fellow travelers in the world. The basic encounter provides presence and a "being with" in the face of harsh existential facts of life.*

Group Cohesiveness**

Group cohesiveness and interpersonal learning are of greater power and complexity than any of the other therapeutic factors examined thus far, and for this reason I discuss them in considerably greater detail in the sections that follow.

Over the past thirty years, a vast number of controlled studies of psychotherapy outcome have been performed. One particularly rigorous review of 475 controlled studies concluded that the average person who receives psychotherapy is better off at the end of it than 80 percent of people who do not, and that the outcome from group therapy is virtually identical to that of individual therapy.[41] Other reviews of rigorous

*Existential issues are discussed more fully in chapters 3 and 4 of the present volume.

**Group cohesiveness and interpersonal learning are of greater power and complexity than any of the other therapeutic factors examined thus far, and for this reason I discuss them in considerably greater detail in the sections that follow.

research support the effectiveness of group therapy, both in an absolute sense and in comparison to other psychotherapies.[42]

So what is it that makes for successful therapy? After all, not all psychotherapy is successful, and there is evidence that treatment may be for better or for worse: though most therapists help their patients, some therapists make some patients worse.[43] Although many factors are involved, *a sine qua non for effective therapy outcome is a proper therapeutic relationship.*[44] The best research evidence available overwhelmingly supports the conclusion that successful therapy is mediated by a relationship between therapist and patient that is characterized by trust, warmth, empathic understanding, and acceptance.[45]

Furthermore, it has long been established that the quality of the relationship is independent of the individual therapist's school of conviction. Experienced and effective clinicians from different schools (Freudian, nondirective, gestalt, transactional analytic, encounter, psychodrama) resemble one another (and differ from nonexperts in their own school) in their conception of the ideal therapeutic relationship and in the nature of the relationship they themselves establish with their patients.[46] It has also been demonstrated that the warm, cohesive quality of the relationship is no less important in the more impersonal, behavioral, or systems-oriented forms of psychotherapy.[47] The nature of the relationship has proved to be so critical in individual psychotherapy that we are compelled to ask whether relationship plays an equally critical role in group psychotherapy. But it is obvious that *the group therapy analogue of the patient-therapist relationship in individual therapy must be a broader concept: it must encompass the patient's relationship not only to the group therapist but to the other group members and to the group as a whole.* At the risk of courting semantic confusion, I refer to all these factors under the term *group cohesiveness.*

Cohesiveness is a widely researched basic property of groups. Several hundred research articles exploring cohesiveness have been written, many with widely varying definitions. In general, however, there is agreement that groups differ from one another in the amount of "groupness" present. Those with a greater sense of solidarity, or "we-ness," value the group more highly and will defend it against internal and external threats. Such groups have a higher rate of attendance, participation, and mutual support and will defend the group standards much more than groups with less esprit de corps.

Cohesiveness is a complex and abstruse variable that has defied researchers and resisted precise definition. A recent comprehensive and thoughtful review concluded that cohesiveness "is like dignity: everyone can recognize it but apparently no one can describe it, much less measure it."[48] The problem is that cohesiveness refers to overlapping dimensions. On the one hand, there is a group phenomenon—the total esprit de corps; on the other hand, there is the individual member cohesiveness (or, more strictly, the individual's attraction to the group).[49]

There are, in fact, many methods of measuring cohesiveness,[50] and a precise definition depends upon the method employed. Cohesiveness may be broadly defined as the resultant of all the forces acting on all the members to remain in the group[51] or, more simply, the attractiveness of a group for its members.[52] It refers to the condition of members feeling warmth and comfort in the group, feeling they belong, valuing the group and feeling, in turn, that they are valued and unconditionally accepted and supported by other members.[53]

Group esprit de corps and individual cohesiveness are interdependent: in fact, group cohesiveness is often computed simply by summing the individual members' level of attraction to the group. Newer methods of measuring group cohesiveness from raters' evaluations of group climate make for greater quantitative precision but do not negate the fact that the group esprit de corps remains a function and a summation of the individual members' sense of belongingness.[54] Keep in mind, however, that group members are differentially attracted to the group and that cohesiveness is not fixed—once achieved, forever held—but instead fluctuates greatly during the course of the group.[55] Recent research has differentiated between the individual's sense of belonging and his or her appraisal of total group engagement—how well the entire group is working. It is not infrequent for an individual to feel "that this group works well, but I'm not part of it."[56]

It is essential to note that group cohesiveness is more than a potent therapeutic force in its own right. Perhaps even more important, it is a necessary precondition for other therapeutic factors to function optimally. When, in individual therapy, we say that it is the relationship that heals, we do not mean that love or loving acceptance is enough; we mean that an ideal therapist-patient relationship creates conditions in which the necessary risk taking, catharsis, and intrapersonal and interpersonal exploration may unfold. It is the same for group therapy: cohesiveness is necessary for other group therapeutic factors to operate.

Although I have discussed the therapeutic factors separately, they are, to a great degree, interdependent. Catharsis and universality, for example, are not complete processes. It is not the sheer process of ventilation that is important; it is not only the discovery of others' problems similar to one's own and the ensuing disconfirmation of one's wretched uniqueness that are important. It is the affective sharing of one's inner world *and then the acceptance by others* that seem of paramount importance. To be accepted by others brings into question the patient's belief that he or she is basically repugnant, unacceptable, or unlovable. The group will accept an individual, provided that the individual adheres to the group's procedural norms, regardless of his or her past life experiences, transgressions, or social failings. Deviant lifestyles, history of prostitution, sexual perversion, heinous criminal offenses—all can be accepted by the therapy group, so long as norms of nonjudgmental acceptance and inclusiveness are established early in the group.

For the most part, the disturbed interpersonal skills of psychiatric patients have limited their opportunities for affective sharing and acceptance in intimate relationships. Furthermore, patients' convictions that their impulses and fantasies are abhorrent have limited their interpersonal sharing even more. I have known many isolated patients for whom the group represented their only deeply human contact. After just a few sessions, they have a deeper sense of being at home in the group than anywhere else. Later, even years afterward, when most other recollections of the group have faded from memory, they may still remember the warm sense of belonging and acceptance.

As one successful patient, looking back over two and a half years of therapy, put it, "The most important thing in it was just having a group there, people that I could always talk to, that wouldn't walk out on me. There was so much caring and hating and loving in the group, and I was a part of it. I'm better now and have my own life, but it's sad to think that the group's not there anymore."

Some patients internalize the group: "It's as though the group is sitting on my shoulder, watching me. I'm forever asking, 'What would the group say about this or that?'" Often therapeutic changes persist and are consolidated because, even years later, the members are disinclined to let the group down.[57]

Group membership, acceptance, and approval are of the utmost importance in the individual's developmental sequence. The importance of belonging to childhood peer groups, adolescent cliques, sororities or fraternities, or the proper social "in" group can hardly be overestimated. Nothing seems to be of greater importance for the self-esteem and well-being of the adolescent, for example, than to be included and accepted in some social group, and nothing is more devastating than exclusion.[58]

Most psychiatric patients, however, have an impoverished group history; never before have they been valuable and integral to a group. For these patients, the sheer successful negotiation of a group experience may in itself be curative.

Thus, in a number of ways, members of a therapy group come to mean a great deal to one another. The therapy group, at first perceived as an artificial group that does not count, may in fact come to count very much. I have known groups to experience together severe depressions, psychoses, marriage, divorce, abortions, suicide, career shifts, sharing of innermost thoughts, and incest (sexual activity among the group members). I have seen a group physically carry one of its members to the hospital and seen many groups mourn the death of members. Relationships are often cemented by moving or hazardous adventures. How many relationships in life are so richly layered?

Along with the many positive aspects described above, other elements, such as anger and hostility, play a crucial role in the life of the group. Once the group is able to deal constructively with conflict in the group, therapy is enhanced in many ways. I already mentioned the importance of catharsis, of risk taking, of gradually exploring previously avoided or unknown parts of oneself and recognizing that the anticipated dreaded catastrophe is chimerical. Many patients are desperately afraid of anger—their own and that of others. A highly cohesive group permits working through these fears.

It is important for patients to realize that their anger is not lethal.

Both they and others can and do survive an expression of their impatience, irritability, or even outright rage. It is also important for some patients to have the experience of weathering an attack. In the process, as J. Frank suggests, one may become better acquainted with the reasons for one's position and learn to withstand pressure from others.[59] Conflict may also enhance self-disclosure, as each opponent tends to reveal more and more to clarify his or her position. As members are able to go beyond the mere statement of position, as they begin to understand the other's experiential world, past and present, and view the other's position from their own frame of reference, they may begin to understand that the other's point of view may be as appropriate for that person as their own is for themselves. The coming to grips with, working through, and eventual resolution of extreme dislike or hatred of another person is an experience of great therapeutic power. A clinical illustration demonstrates many of these points.

Susan, a forty-six-year-old very proper school principal, and Jean, a twenty-one-year-old high school dropout, were locked into a vicious struggle. Susan despised Jean because of her libertine lifestyle and what she imagined to be sloth and promiscuity. Jean was enraged by Susan's judgmentalism, her sanctimoniousness, her embittered spinsterhood, her closed posture to the world. Fortunately, both women were deeply committed members of the group. (Fortuitous circumstances played a part here. Jean had been a core member of the group for a year and then married and went abroad for three months. Just at that time Susan became a member and, during Jean's absence, became heavily involved in the group.)

Both had had considerable past difficulty in tolerating and expressing anger. Over a four-month period, they interacted heavily, at times in pitched battles. For example, Susan erupted sanctimoniously when she found out that Jean was obtaining food stamps illegally; and Jean, learning of Susan's virginity, ventured the opinion that she was a curiosity, a museum piece, a mid-Victorian relic. Much good group work was done. Jean and Susan, despite their conflict, never broke off communication. They learned a great deal about each other and eventually realized the cruelty of their mutual judgmentalism. Finally, they could both understand how much each meant for the other on both a personal and a symbolic level. Jean desperately wanted Susan's approval; Susan deeply envied Jean for the freedom she had never permitted herself. In the working-through process, both fully experienced their rage; they encountered and then accepted previously unknown parts of themselves. Ultimately, they developed an empathic understanding and then an acceptance of each other. Neither could possibly have tolerated the extreme discomfort of the conflict were it not for the strong cohesion that, despite the pain, bound them to the group.

Interpersonal Learning

From whatever perspective we study human society—whether we scan humanity's broad evolutionary history or scrutinize the development of the single individual—we are at all times obliged to consider the human being in the matrix of his or her interpersonal relationships. Humans have always lived in groups that have been characterized by intense and persistent relationships among members. Interpersonal behavior has clearly been adaptive in an evolutionary sense: without deep, positive, reciprocal interpersonal bonds, neither individual nor species survival would have been possible.

All modern American schools of dynamic psychotherapy are interpersonally based and draw heavily, though implicitly, on the American neo-Freudian theorists Karen Horney, Erich Fromm, and especially and most systematically, Harry Stack Sullivan and his interpersonal theory of psychiatry.[60]

Sullivan contends that the personality is almost entirely the product of interaction with other significant human beings. The need to be closely related to others is as basic as any biological need and is, in the light of the prolonged period of helpless infancy, equally necessary to survival. *The developing child, in the quest for security, tends to cultivate and to stress those traits and aspects of the self that meet with approval, and will squelch or deny those that meet with disapproval.* Eventually the individual develops a concept of the self (*self-dynamism*) based on these perceived appraisals of significant others.

Sullivan suggests that the proper focus of research in mental health is the study of processes that involve or go on between people.[61] Mental disorder, or psychiatric symptomatology in all its varied manifestations, should be translated into interpersonal terms and treated accordingly. "Mental disorder" refers to interpersonal processes that are either inadequate to the social situation or excessively complex because of the introduction of illusory persons into the situations.[62] Accordingly, psychiatric treatment should be directed toward *the correction of interpersonal distortions,* thus enabling the individual to lead a more abundant life, to participate collaboratively with others, to obtain interpersonal satisfactions in the context of realistic, mutually satisfying interpersonal relationships: "One achieves mental health to the extent that one becomes aware of one's interpersonal relationships."[63] Psychiatric cure is the "expanding of the self to such final effect that the patient as known to himself is much the same person as the patient behaving to others."[64]

These ideas   that therapy is broadly interpersonal, both in its goals and in its means—are exceedingly germane to group therapy. That does not mean that all, or even most, patients entering group therapy ask explicitly for help in their interpersonal relationships. Yet I have observed that the therapeutic goals of patients, somewhere between the third and the sixth months of group therapy, often undergo a shift. Their initial goal, relief of suffering, is modified and eventually replaced by new goals, usually interpersonal in nature. Goals may change from wanting relief from anxiety or depression to wanting to learn to communicate with others, to be more trusting and honest with others, to learn to love.

The goal shift from relief of suffering to change in interpersonal functioning is an essential early step in the dynamic therapeutic process. It is important in the thinking of the therapist as well. Therapists cannot, for example, treat depression per se: depression offers no effective therapeutic handhold. It is necessary, first, to translate depression into interpersonal terms and then to treat the underlying interpersonal pathology.

The theory of interpersonal relationships has become so much an integral part of the fabric of psychiatric thought that it needs no further underscoring. People need people—for initial and continued survival, for socialization, for the pursuit of satisfaction. No one transcends the need for human contact.

For instance, the outcasts—those individuals thought to be so inured to rejection that their interpersonal needs have become heavily calloused—have compelling social needs. I once had an experience in a prison that provided me with a forceful reminder of the ubiquitous nature of this human need. An untrained psychiatric technician consulted me about his therapy group, composed of twelve inmates. The members of the group were all hardened recidivists, whose offenses ranged from pedophilia to murder. The group, he complained, was sluggish and persisted in focusing on extraneous, extragroup material. I agreed to observe his group and suggested that first he obtain some sociometric information by asking each member privately to rank-order everyone in the group for general popularity. (I had hoped that the discussion of this task would induce the group to turn its attention upon itself.) Although we had planned to discuss these results before the next group session, unexpected circumstances forced us to cancel our presession consultation.

During the next group meeting, the therapist, enthusiastic but professionally inexperienced and insensitive to interpersonal needs, announced that he had decided simply to read aloud the results of the popularity poll. Hearing this, the group members grew agitated and fearful. They made it clear that they did not wish to know the results. Several members spoke so vehemently of the devastating possibility that they might appear at the bottom of the list that the therapist quickly and permanently abandoned his plan of reading the list aloud.

I suggested an alternative plan for the next meeting: each member would indicate whose vote he cared about most and then explain his choice. This device, also, was too threatening, and only one-third of the members ventured a choice. Nevertheless, the group shifted to an interactional level and developed a degree of tension, involvement, and exhilaration previously unknown. These men had received the ultimate message of rejection from society at large: they were imprisoned, segregated, and explicitly labeled as outcasts. To the casual observer, they seemed hardened, indifferent to the subtleties of interpersonal approval and disapproval. Yet they cared, and cared deeply.

The need for acceptance by and interaction with others is no different among people at the opposing pole of human fortunes—those who occupy the ultimate realms of power, renown, or wealth. I once worked with an enormously wealthy woman whose major issues revolved around the wedge that money created between herself and others. Did anyone value her for herself rather than her money? Was she continually being exploited by others? To whom could she complain of the burdens of a forty-million-dollar fortune? The secret of her wealth kept her isolated from others.

Every group therapist has, I am sure, encountered patients who profess indifference to or detachment from the group. They proclaim: "I don't care what they say or think or feel about me; they're nothing to me; I have no respect for the other members," or words to that effect. My experience has been that if I can keep such patients in the group long enough, other sentiments inevitably surface. They are concerned at a very deep level about the group. One patient who maintained her indifferent posture for many months was once invited to ask the group her secret question, the one question she would like most of all to place before the group. To everyone's astonishment, this seemingly aloof, detached woman posed this question: "How can you put up with me?"

Many patients anticipate meetings with great eagerness or with anxiety; some feel too shaken afterward to drive home or to sleep that night; many have imaginary conversations with the group during the week. Moreover, this engagement with other members is often long lived; I have known many patients who think and dream about the group members months, even years, after the group has ended.

In short, people do not feel indifferent toward others in their group for long. And patients do not quit the therapy group because of boredom. Believe scorn, contempt, fear, discouragement, shame, panic, hatred! Believe any of these! But never believe indifference!

The Group as Social Microcosm

A freely interactive group with few structural restrictions will, in time, develop into a social microcosm of the participant members. Given enough time, group members will begin to be themselves: they will interact with the group members as they interact with others in their social sphere, will create in the group the same interpersonal universe they have always inhabited. In other words, patients will, over time, automatically and inevitably begin to display their maladaptive interpersonal behavior in the therapy group. There is no need for them to describe or give a detailed history of their pathology: they will sooner or later enact it before the group members' eyes.

This concept is of paramount importance in group therapy and constitutes a keystone upon which rests the entire approach to such therapy. It is widely accepted by clinicians, although each therapist's perception and interpretation of group events and descriptive language will be determined by his or her school of conviction. Thus, Freudians may see patients manifesting their oral, sadistic, or masochistic needs in their relationship to other members; object-relations theorists may focus on the patients' manifesting the defenses of splitting, projective identification, idealization, devaluation; correctional workers may see conning, exploitative behavior; whereas students of Horney may see the detached, resigned person putting energies into acting noncommittal and indifferent, or the arrogant-vindictive person struggling to prove himself or herself right by proving others wrong.

The important point is that, regardless of the type of conceptual spectacles worn by the therapist-observer, each member's interpersonal style will eventually appear in his or her transactions in the group. The development of the ability to identify and put to therapeutic advantage maladaptive interpersonal behavior as seen in the social microcosm of the small group is one of the chief tasks of a training program for group psychotherapists. Some clinical examples may make these principles more graphic.*

---

*In order to ensure each patient's right to privacy, I have altered certain facts, such as name, occupation, and age. In addition, the interaction described in the text is not verbatim but has been reconstructed from detailed clinical notes taken after each therapy meeting.

Valerie, a twenty-seven-year-old musician, sought therapy with me primarily because of severe marital discord of several years' standing. She had had considerable, unrewarding individual and hypnotic uncovering therapy. Her husband, she reported, was an alcoholic who was reluctant to engage her socially, intellectually, or sexually. Now the group could have, as some groups do, investigated her marriage interminably. The members might have taken a complete history of the courtship, of the evolution of the discord, of her husband's pathology, of her reasons for marrying him, of her role in the conflict; they might have given advice for new behavior or for a trial or permanent separation.

But all this historical, problem-solving activity would have been in vain: this entire line of inquiry not only disregards the unique potential of therapy groups but is also based on the highly questionable premise that a patient's account of a marriage is even reasonably accurate. Groups that function in this manner fail to help the protagonist and also suffer demoralization because of the ineffectiveness of a problem solving, historical group therapy approach. Let us instead observe Valerie's behavior as it unfolds in the here-and-now of the group.

Valerie's group behavior was flamboyant. First, there was her grand entrance, always five or ten minutes late. Bedecked in fashionable but flashy garb, she would sweep in, sometimes throwing kisses, and immediately begin talking, oblivious to whether some other member was in the midst of a sentence. Here was narcissism in the raw! Her worldview was so solipsistic that it did not take in the possibility that life could have been going on in the group before her arrival.

After very few meetings, Valerie began to give gifts: to an obese female member, a copy of a new diet book; to a woman with strabismus, the name of a good ophthalmologist; to an effeminate gay patient, a subscription to Field and Stream *magazine (to masculinize him); to a twenty-four-year-old virginal male, an introduction to a promiscuous divorced friend of hers. Gradually it became apparent that the gifts were not duty-free. For example, she pried into the relationship between the young man and her divorced friend and insisted on serv-*

ing as a go-between, thus exerting considerable control over both individuals.

Her efforts to dominate soon colored all of her interactions in the group. I became a challenge to her, and she made various efforts to control me. By sheer chance, a few months previously I had seen her sister in consultation and referred her to a competent therapist, a clinical psychologist. In the group Valerie congratulated me for the brilliant tactic of sending her sister to a psychologist; I must have divined her deep-seated aversion to psychiatrists. Similarly, on another occasion, she responded to a comment from me, "How perceptive you were to have noticed my hands trembling."

The trap was set! In fact, I had neither "divined" her sister's alleged aversion to psychiatrists (I had simply referred her to the best therapist I knew), nor noted Valerie's trembling hands. If I silently accepted her undeserved tribute, then I would enter into a dishonest collusion with Valerie; if, on the other hand, I admitted my insensitivity either to the trembling of the hands or to the sister's aversion, then in a sense I would also be bested. She would control me either way! In such situations, the therapist has only one real option: to change the frame and to comment upon the process—the nature and the meaning of the entrapment.

Valerie vied with me in many other ways. Intuitive and intellectually gifted, she became the group expert on dream and fantasy interpretation. On one occasion she saw me between group sessions to ask whether she could use my name to take a book out of the medical library. On one level the request was reasonable: the book (on music therapy) was related to her profession; furthermore, having no university affiliation, she was not permitted to use the library.

However, in the context of the group process, the request was complex in that she was testing limits; granting her request would have signaled to the group that she had a special and unique relationship with me. I clarified these considerations to her and suggested further discussion in the next session. Following this perceived rebuttal, however, she called the three male members of the group at home and, after swearing them to secrecy, arranged to see them. She engaged in sexual relations with two; the third, a gay man, was not interested in *her sexual advances but she launched a mighty seduction attempt nonetheless.*

The following group meeting was horrific. Extraordinarily tense and unproductive, it demonstrated the axiom that if something important in the group is being actively avoided, then nothing else of import gets talked about either. *Two days later Valerie, overcome with anxiety and guilt, asked for an individual session with me and made a full confession. It was agreed that the whole matter should be discussed in the next group meeting.*

Valerie opened the next meeting with the words: "This is confession day! Go ahead, Charles!" and then later, "Your turn, Louis." Each man performed as she bade him and, later in the meeting, received from her a critical evaluation of his sexual performance. A few weeks later, Valerie let her estranged husband know what had happened, and he sent threatening messages to all three men. That was the last straw! The members decided they could no longer trust her and, in the only such instance I have known, voted her out of the group. (She continued her therapy by joining another group.) The saga does not end here, but perhaps I have gone far enough to illustrate the concept of the group as social microcosm.

Let us summarize. The first step was that Valerie clearly displayed her interpersonal pathology *in the group*. Her narcissism, her need for adulation, her need to control, her sadistic relationship with men—the entire tragic behavioral scroll—unrolled in the here-and-now of therapy. The next step was reaction and feedback. The men expressed their deep humiliation and anger at having to "jump through a hoop" for her and at receiving "grades" for their sexual performance. They drew away from her. They began to reflect: "I don't want a report card every time I have sex. It's controlling, like sleeping with my mother! I'm beginning to understand more about your husband moving out!" and so on. The others in the group, the female members and the therapists, shared the men's feelings about the wantonly destructive course of Valerie's behavior—destructive for the group as well as for herself.

Most important of all, she had to deal with this fact: she had joined a group of troubled individuals who were eager to help one another and whom she grew to like and respect; yet, in the course of several weeks, she had so poisoned her environment that, against her conscious wishes, she became a pariah, an outcast from a group that had had the potential to be very helpful to her. Facing and working through these issues in her subsequent therapy group enabled her to make substantial personal changes and to employ much of her considerable potential constructively in her later relationships and endeavors.

Ron, a forty-eight-year-old attorney who was separated from his wife, entered therapy because of depression, anxiety, and intense feelings of loneliness. His relationships, with both men and women, were highly problematic. He yearned for a close male friend but had not had one since high school. His current relationships with men assumed one of two forms: either he and the other man related in a highly competitive, antagonistic fashion, which veered dangerously close to combativeness, or he assumed an exceedingly dominant role and soon found the relationship empty and dull.

His relationships with women had always followed a predictable sequence: instant attraction, a crescendo of passion, a rapid withering. His love for his wife had decayed years ago and he was currently in the midst of a painful divorce.

Intelligent and highly articulate, Ron immediately assumed a position of great influence in the group. He offered a continuous stream of useful and thoughtful observations to the other members, yet kept his own pain and his own needs well concealed. He requested nothing and accepted nothing from me or my co-therapist. In fact, each time I set out to interact with Ron, I felt myself bracing for battle. His antagonistic resistance was so great that for months my major interaction with him consisted of repeatedly requesting him to examine his reluctance to experience me as someone who could offer help.

"Ron," I asked, giving it my best shot, "let's understand what's happening. You have many areas of unhappiness in your life. I'm an experienced therapist, and you come to me for help. You come regu-

larly, you never miss a meeting, you pay me for my services, yet you systematically prevent me from helping. Either you so hide your pain that I find little to offer you, or when I do extend some help, you reject it in one fashion or another. Reason dictates that we should be allies, working together to help you. How does it come about that we are adversaries?"

But even that failed to alter our relationship. Ron seemed bemused and speculated that I might be identifying one of my problems rather than his. His relationship with the other group members was characterized by his insistence on seeing them outside the group. He systematically arranged for some extragroup activity with each of the members. He was a pilot and took some members flying, others sailing, others to lavish dinners; he gave legal advice to some and became romantically involved with one of the female members; and (the final straw) he invited my co-therapist, a female psychiatric resident, for a skiing weekend.

Furthermore, he refused to examine his behavior or to discuss these extragroup meetings in the group, even though the pregroup preparation had emphasized to all the members that such unexamined, undiscussed extragroup meetings generally sabotage therapy.

After a meeting in which we strongly pressured him to examine the meaning of the extragroup invitations, especially the skiing invitation to my co-therapist, he left the session confused and shaken. On his way home, Ron unaccountably began to think of the legend of Robin Hood, his favorite childhood story, which he had not thought about for decades.

Following an impulse, he drove directly to the nearest public library to sit in a small child's chair in the children's section and read the story one more time. In a flash, the meaning of his behavior was illuminated! Why had the Robin Hood legend always fascinated and delighted him? Because Robin Hood rescued people, especially women, from tyrants!

That motif had played a powerful role in his interior life beginning with the Oedipal struggles in his own family. Later, in early adulthood, he built up a successful law firm by first assisting in a partner-

ship and then enticing his boss's employees to work for him. He had often been most attracted to women who were attached to some powerful man. Even his motives for marrying were blurred: he could not distinguish between love for his wife and desire to rescue her from a tyrannical father.

The first stage of interpersonal learning is pathology display. *Ron's characteristic modes of relating to both men and women unfolded vividly in the microcosm of the group. His major interpersonal motif was to struggle with and to vanquish other men. He competed openly and, because of his intelligence and his great verbal skills, soon procured the dominant role in the group. He then began to mobilize the other members in the final conspiracy: the unseating of the therapist. He formed close alliances through extragroup meetings and through placing other members in his debt by offering favors. Next he endeavored to capture "my women"—first the most attractive female member and then my co-therapist.*

Not only was Ron's interpersonal pathology displayed in the group, but so also were its adverse, self-defeating consequences. His struggles with men resulted in the undermining of the very reason he had come to therapy: to obtain help. In fact, the competitive struggle was so powerful that any help I extended to him was experienced not as help but as defeat, a sign of weakness.

Furthermore, the microcosm of the group revealed the consequences of his actions on the texture of his relationship with his peers. In time the other members became aware that Ron did not really relate to them. He only appeared *to relate but, in actuality, was using them as a way of relating to me, the powerful and feared male in the group. The others soon felt used, felt the absence of a genuine desire in Ron to know them, and gradually began to distance themselves from him. Only after Ron was able to understand and to alter his intense and distorted ways of relating to me was he able to turn to and relate in good faith to the other members of the group.*

The idea of the social microcosm is, I believe, sufficiently clear: if the group is so conducted that the members can behave in an unguarded, unself-conscious manner, they will, most vividly, re-create and display their pathology in the group. *Furthermore, in the* in vivo *drama of the group meeting, the trained observer has a unique opportunity to understand the dynamics of each patient's behavior.*

CHAPTER 2

The Therapist Working in the Here-and-Now

INTRODUCTION

I have chosen the following excerpt (from chapter 6 of *The Theory and Practice of Group Psychotherapy*) for a number of reasons. As the last selection indicates, I value the entire range of therapeutic factors, but I place particular importance on *interpersonal learning* (and its accompanying here-and-now focus). In some groups this therapeutic factor plays little role (for example, in Alcoholics Anonymous, cognitive therapy groups, psychoeducational groups, cancer support groups), but in groups that have goals of both symptom alleviation *and* change in relationship patterns, interpersonal learning is of crucial importance. I believe that the here-and-now focus is the power cell of the small dynamic group, and whenever I am called to consult about a stalled or lifeless therapy group, I find, almost invariably, that the problems emanate from the therapists' failing to make proper use of the here-and-now.

I include this section to underscore the importance of the here-and-now and to delineate the techniques of the therapist which harvest the here-and-now approach. This is the area of group psychotherapy where I have made my most original contributions—it is the signature of my particular approach to therapy, both individual and group therapy.

Another reason for stressing the material in this selection is that group members and therapists do not naturally and automatically develop a here-and-now focus: it doesn't just happen on its own; it is a learned skill and has to be taught explicitly. We are not used to operating in the here-and-now. It does not occur elsewhere in our experience. In fact, it is precisely the here-and-now focus that distinguishes the effective therapy group from the group without trained therapeutic leadership—the leaderless, or self-help, group.

One additional point about the section entitled "Process Commentary: A Theoretical Overview." I have generally stressed that my interests in group psychotherapy and existential psychotherapy are separate and discrete: not only do the therapies have different formats (existential psychotherapy generally takes place in a one-to-one setting) but they operate from different frames of reference. Group therapists make the assumption that their patients fall into despair because of their inability to establish and maintain stabilizing and intimate relationships with others. Existentially oriented therapists make a fundamentally different assumption about the source of dysphoria—namely, that patients fall into despair as a result of a confrontation with the brute facts of the human condition (more about this in Part II).

The process commentary excerpt demonstrates one of the ways in which these two streams of thought, existential and interpersonal, come together to work synergistically by incorporating the existential concepts of personal freedom and responsibility assumption into the group process.

THE THERAPIST:
WORKING IN THE HERE-AND-NOW

The major difference between an outpatient therapy group that hopes to effect extensive and enduring behavioral and characterological change and such groups as AA, Recovery, Inc., psychoeducational groups, weight-reduction groups, and cancer support groups is that the therapy group strongly emphasizes the importance of the here-and-now experience.

The here-and-now focus, to be effective, consists of two symbiotic tiers, neither of which has therapeutic power without the other. The first tier is an *experiencing* one: the members live in the here-and-now; they develop strong feelings toward the other group members, the therapist, and the group. These here-and-now feelings become the major discourse of the group. The thrust is ahistoric: *the immediate events in the meeting take precedence over events both in the current outside life and in the distant past of the members.* This focus greatly facilitates the development and emergence of each member's social microcosm. It facilitates feedback, catharsis, meaningful self-disclosure, and acquisition of socializing techniques. The group becomes more vital, and all of the members (not only the one who is working that session) become intensely involved in the meeting.

But the here-and-now focus rapidly reaches the limits of its usefulness without the second tier, which is the *illumination of process.* If the powerful therapeutic factor of interpersonal learning is to be set in motion, the group must recognize, examine, and understand process. It must examine itself; it must study its own transactions; it must transcend pure experience and apply itself to the integration of that experience.

Thus, the effective use of the here-and-now requires two steps: the group lives in the here-and-now, and it also doubles back on itself; it performs a self-reflective loop and examines the here-and-now behavior that has just occurred.

If the group is to be effective, both aspects of the here-and-now are essential. If only the first—the experiencing of the here-and-now—is present, the group experience will still be intense, members will feel deeply involved, emotional expression may be high, and members will finish the group agreeing, "Wow, that was a powerful experience!" Yet it will also prove to be an evanescent experience: members will have no cognitive framework that will permit them to retain the group experience, to generalize from it, and to transfer their learning from the group to situations back home.

If, on the other hand, only the second part of the here-and-now—the examination of process—is present, then the group loses its liveliness and meaningfulness. It degenerates into a sterile intellectual exercise. This is the error made by overly formal, aloof, rigid therapists. Accordingly, the therapist has two discrete functions in the here-and-now: to steer the group into the here-and-now and to facilitate the self-reflective loop (or process commentary).

Definition of Process

The term *process* has a highly specialized meaning in many fields, including law, anatomy, sociology, anthropology, psychoanalysis, and descriptive psychiatry. In interactional psychotherapy, also, process has a specific technical meaning: it refers to the nature of the relationship between interacting individuals.

It is useful to contrast process with content. Imagine two individuals in a discussion. The content of that discussion consists of the explicit words spoken, the substantive issues, the arguments advanced. The process is an altogether different matter. When we ask about process, we ask, "What do these explicit words, the style of the participants, the nature of the discussion, tell about the interpersonal relationship of the participants?"

Therapists who are process-oriented are concerned not primarily with the verbal content of a patient's utterance, but with the "how" and the "why" of that utterance, especially insofar as the how and the why illuminate aspects of the patient's relationship to other people. Thus, therapists focus on the *metacommunicational* aspects of the message and wonder why, *from the relationship aspect,* a patient makes a statement at a certain time in a certain manner to a certain person.

Metacommunication refers to the communication about the communication. Consider, for example, this transaction: during a lecture, a student raises her hand and asks what the date of Freud's death was. The lecturer replies, "1938," only to have the student inquire, "But, sir, wasn't it 1939?" Obviously the student's motivation was not a quest for information. (A question ain't a question if you know the answer.) The metacommunication? Most likely the student wished to demonstrate her knowledge, or to humiliate the lecturer.

Frequently, in the group therapy setting, the understanding of

process becomes more complex; we search for the process not only behind a simple statement but behind a sequence of statements made by a
patient or several patients. The group therapist endeavors to understand what a particular sequence reveals about the relationship between
one patient and the other group members, or between clusters or cliques
of members, or between the members and the leader, or, finally, between the group as a whole and its primary task.

Some clinical vignettes may further clarify the concept.

*Early in the course of a group therapy meeting, Burt, a tenacious, intense,
bulldog-faced graduate student, exclaimed to the group in general and to
Rose (an unsophisticated, astrologically inclined cosmetologist and mother of
four) in particular, "Parenthood is degrading!" This provocative statement
elicited considerable response from the group, all of whom possessed parents,
and many of whom were parents. The free-for-all that followed consumed
the remainder of the group session.*

Burt's statement can be viewed strictly in terms of *content*. In fact,
this is precisely what occurred in the group; the members engaged Burt
in a debate over the virtues versus the dehumanizing aspects of parenthood—a discussion that was affect-laden but intellectualized and
brought none of the members closer to their goals in therapy. Subsequently, the group felt discouraged about the meeting and angry with
themselves and with Burt for having dissipated a meeting.

On the other hand, the therapist might have considered the process
of Burt's statement from any one of a number of perspectives:

1. Why did Burt attack Rose? What was the interpersonal process
between them? In fact, the two had had a smoldering conflict for many
weeks, and in the previous meeting Rose had wondered why, if Burt
was so brilliant, he was still, at the age of thirty-two, a student. Burt had
viewed Rose as an inferior being who functioned primarily as a mam-
mary gland; once, when she had been absent, he referred to her as a
brood mare.

2. Why was Burt so judgmental and intolerant of nonintellectuals?
Why did he always have to maintain his self-esteem by standing on the
carcass of a vanquished or humiliated adversary?

3. Assuming that Burt's chief intent was to attack Rose, why did he proceed so indirectly? Is this characteristic of Burt's expression of aggression? Or is it characteristic of Rose that no one dares, for some unclear reason, to attack her directly?

4. Why did Burt, through an obviously provocative and indefensible statement, set himself up for a universal attack by the group? Although the words were different, this was a familiar melody for the group and for Burt, who had on many previous occasions placed himself in this position. Was it possible that Burt was most comfortable when relating to others in this fashion? He once stated that he had always loved a fight; indeed, he glowed with anticipation at the appearance of a quarrel in the group. His early family environment was distinctively a fighting one. Was fighting, then, a form (perhaps the only available form) of involvement for Burt?

5. The process may be considered from the even broader perspective of the entire group. Other relevant events in the life of the group must be considered. For the past two months, the session had been dominated by Kate, a deviant, disruptive, and partially deaf member who had, two weeks previously, dropped out of the group with the face-saving proviso that she would return when she obtained a hearing aid. Was it possible that the group needed a Kate, and that Burt was merely filling the required role of scapegoat? Through its continual climate of conflict, through its willingness to spend an entire session discussing in nonpersonal terms a single theme, was the group avoiding something— possibly an honest discussion of members' feelings concerning Kate's rejection by the group or their guilt or fear of a similar fate? Or were they perhaps avoiding the anticipated perils of self-disclosure and intimacy?

Was the group saying something to the therapist through Burt (and through Kate)? For example, Burt may have been bearing the brunt of an attack really aimed at the co-therapists but displaced from them. The therapists—aloof figures with a proclivity for rabbinical pronouncements—had never been attacked or confronted by the group. Surely there were strong, avoided feelings toward the therapists, which may have been further fanned by their failure to support Kate and by their complicity through inactivity in her departure from the group.

Which one of these many process observations is correct? Which one could the therapist have employed as an effective intervention? The answer is, of course, that any and all may be correct. They are not mutually exclusive; each views the transaction from a slightly different vantage point. By clarifying each of these in turn, the therapist could have focused the group on many different aspects of its life. Which one, then, should the therapist have chosen?

The therapist's choice should be based on one primary consideration: the needs of the group. Where was the group at that particular time? Had there been too much focus on Burt of late, leaving the other members feeling bored, uninvolved, and excluded? In that case, the therapist might best have wondered aloud what the group was avoiding. The therapist might have reminded the group of previous sessions spent in similar discussions that left them dissatisfied, or might have helped one of the members verbalize this point by inquiring about the member's inactivity or apparent uninvolvement in the discussion. If the group communications had been exceptionally indirect, the therapist might have commented on the indirectness of Burt's attacks or asked the group to help clarify, via feedback, what was happening between Burt and Rose. If, as in this group, an important group event was being strongly avoided (Kate's departure), then it should be pointed out. In short, the therapist must determine what he or she thinks the group needs most at a particular time and help it move in that direction.

In another group, Saul sought therapy because of his deep sense of isolation. He was particularly interested in a group therapeutic experience because of his feeling that he had never been a part of a primary group. Even in his primary family, he had felt himself an outsider. He had been a spectator all his life, pressing his nose against cold windowpanes, gazing longingly at warm, convivial groups within.

At Saul's fourth therapy meeting, another member, Barbara, began the meeting by announcing that she had just broken up with a man who had been very important to her. Barbara's major reason for being in therapy had been her inability to sustain a relationship with a man, and she was profoundly distressed in the meeting. Barbara had an extremely poignant way of describing her pain, and the group was swept along with her feelings. Everyone in the group was very moved; I noted silently that Saul, too, had tears in his eyes.

The group members (with the exception of Saul) did everything in their power to offer Barbara support. They passed Kleenex; they reminded her of all her assets; they reassured Barbara that she had made a wrong choice, that the man was not good enough for her, that she was "lucky to be rid of that jerk."

Suddenly Saul interjected, "I don't like what's going on here in the group today, and I don't like the way it's being led" (a thinly veiled allusion to me, I thought). He went on to explain that the group members had no justification for their criticism of Barbara's ex-boyfriend. They didn't really know what he was like. They could see him only through Barbara's eyes, and probably she was presenting him in a distorted way. (Saul had a personal ax to grind on this matter, having gone through a divorce a couple of years previously. His wife had attended a women's support group, and he had been the "jerk" of that group.)

Saul's comments, of course, changed the entire tone of the meeting. The softness and support disappeared. The room felt cold; the warm bond among the members was broken. Everyone was on edge. I felt justifiably reprimanded. Saul's position was technically correct: the group was probably wrong to condemn Barbara's ex-boyfriend.

So much for the content. Now examine the process of this interaction. First, note that Saul's comment had the effect of putting him outside the group. The rest of the group was caught up in a warm, supportive atmosphere from which he excluded himself. Recall his chief complaint that he was never a member of a group, but always the outsider. The meeting provided an in vivo demonstration of how that came to pass. In his fourth group meeting, Saul had, kamikaze-style, attacked and voluntarily ejected himself from a group he wished to join.

A second issue had to do not with what Saul said but with what he did not say. In the early part of the group, everyone except Saul had made warm supportive statements to Barbara. I had no doubt but that Saul felt supportive of her. The tears in his eyes indicated that. Why had he chosen to be silent? Why did he always choose to respond from his critical self and not from his warmer, more supportive self?

The examination of the process of this interaction led us to some very important issues for Saul. Obviously it was difficult for him to express the softer, affectionate part of himself. He feared being vulnerable and exposing his dependent cravings. He feared losing himself, his precious individuality, by be-

coming a member of a group. Behind the aggressive, ever-vigilant, hard-nosed defender of honesty (honesty of expression of negative but not positive sentiments) there is always the softer, submissive child thirsting for acceptance and love.

In another group, Kevin, an overbearing business executive, opened the meeting by asking the other members—housewives, teachers, clerical workers, and shopkeepers—for help with a problem: he had received "downsizing" orders. He had to cut his staff immediately by 50 percent—to fire twenty out of his staff of forty.

The content of the problem was intriguing, and the group spent forty-five minutes discussing such aspects as justice versus mercy: that is, whether one retains the most competent workers or workers with the largest families or those who would have the greatest difficulty in finding other jobs. Despite the fact that most of the members engaged animatedly in the discussion, which involved important problems in human relations, the therapist strongly felt that the session was unproductive: the members remained in safe territory, and the discussion could have appropriately occurred at a dinner party or any other social gathering. Furthermore, as time passed, it became abundantly clear that Kevin had already spent considerable time thinking through all aspects of this problem, and no one was able to provide him with novel approaches or suggestions.

The continued focus on content was unrewarding and eventually frustrating for the group. The therapists began to wonder about process—what this content revealed about the nature of Kevin's relationship to the other members. As the meeting progressed, Kevin, on two occasions, let slip the amount of his salary (which was more than double that of any other member). In fact, the overall interpersonal effect of Kevin's presentation was to make others aware of his affluence and power.

The process became even more clear when the therapists recalled the previous meetings in which Kevin had attempted, in vain, to establish a special kind of relationship with one of the therapists (he had sought some technical information on psychological testing for personnel). Furthermore, in the preceding meeting, Kevin had been soundly attacked by the group for his fundamentalist religious convictions, which he used to criticize others' behavior but not his own propensity for extramarital affairs and compulsive lying. At that meeting, he had also been termed "thick-skinned" because of his appar-

ent insensitivity to others. One other important aspect of Kevin's group be-havior was his dominance; almost invariably, he was the most active, central figure in the group meetings.

With this information about process, a number of alternatives were avail-able. The therapists might have focused on Kevin's bid for prestige, especially following his loss of face in the previous meeting. Phrased in a nonaccusatory manner, a clarification of this sequence might have helped Kevin become aware of his desperate need for the group members to respect and admire him. At the same time, the self-defeating aspects of his behavior could have been pointed out. Despite his efforts to the contrary, the group had come to resent and, at times, even to scorn him. Perhaps, too, Kevin was attempting to disclaim the appellation of thick-skinned by sharing with the group in melodramatic fashion the personal agony he experienced in deciding how to cut his staff. The style of the intervention would have depended on Kevin's degree of defensiveness: if he had seemed particularly brittle or prickly, then the therapists might have underscored how hurt he must have been at the previous meeting. If Kevin had been more open, the therapists might have asked him directly what type of response he would have liked from the others.

Other therapists might have preferred to interrupt the content discussion and ask the group what Kevin's question had to do with last week's session. Still another alternative would be to call attention to an entirely different type of process by reflecting on the group's apparent willingness to permit Kevin to occupy center stage in the group week after week. By encouraging the members to discuss their response to his monopolization, the therapist could have helped the group initiate an exploration of their relationship to Kevin.

Process Focus: The Power Source of the Group

Process focus is not just one of many possible procedural orientations; on the contrary, it is indispensable and a common denominator to all ef-fective interactional groups. One so often hears words to this effect: "No matter what else may be said about experiential groups (therapy groups, encounter groups, and so on), one cannot deny that they are potent—that they offer a compelling experience for participants." Why are these groups potent? Precisely because they encourage process exploration! The process focus is the power cell of the group!

A process focus is the one truly unique feature of the experiential group; after all, there are many socially sanctioned activities in which one can express emotions, help others, give and receive advice, confess and discover similarities between oneself and others. But where else is it permissible, in fact encouraged, to comment, in depth, on here-and-now behavior, on the nature of the immediately current relationship between people? Possibly only in the parent–young child relationship, and even then the flow is unidirectional. The parent, but not the child, is permitted process comments: "Don't look away when I talk to you!"; "Be quiet when someone else is speaking"; "Stop saying, 'I dunno.'"

But process commentary among adults is taboo social behavior; it is considered rude or impertinent. Positive comments about another's immediate behavior often denote a seductive or flirtatious relationship. When an individual comments negatively about another's manners, gestures, speech, physical appearance, we can be certain that the battle is bitter and the possibility of conciliation chancy.

The Therapist's Tasks in the Here-and-Now

In the first stage of the here-and-now focus, the activating phase, the therapist's task is to move the group into the here-and-now. By a variety of techniques, group leaders steer the group members away from discussion of outside material and focus their energy on their relationships with one another. Group therapists expend more time and effort on this task early in the course of the group. As the group progresses, the members come to value the here-and-now and will themselves focus on it and, by a variety of means, encourage their fellow members to do likewise.

It is altogether another matter with the second phase of the here-and-now orientation, process illumination. Forces prevent members from fully sharing that task with the therapist. One who comments on process sets himself or herself apart from the other members and is viewed with suspicion, as "not one of us." When a group member makes observations about what is happening in the group, the others often respond resentfully about the presumptuousness of elevating oneself above the others. If a member comments, for example, that "nothing is happening today," or that "the group is stuck," or that "no one is self-revealing," or that "there seem to be strong feelings toward the therapist," then that member is courting danger. The response of the other members is predictable. They will challenge the challenging member: "*You* make something happen today," or "you reveal *yourself*," or "*you* talk about *your* feelings to the therapist." Only the therapist is relatively exempt from that charge. Only the therapist has the right to suggest that others work, or that others reveal themselves, without having to engage personally in the act he or she suggests.

Throughout the life of the group, the members are involved in a struggle for positions in the hierarchy of dominance. At times, the conflict around control and dominance is flagrant; at other times, quiescent. But it never vanishes. Some members strive nakedly for power; others strive subtly; others desire it but are fearful of assertion; others always assume an obsequious, submissive posture. Statements by members that suggest that they place themselves above or outside the group generally evoke responses that emerge from the dominance struggle rather than from consideration of the content of the statement. Even therapists are not entirely immune to evoking this response; some patients are inordinately sensitive to being controlled or manipulated by the therapist. They find themselves in the paradoxical position of applying to the therapist for help and being unable to accept help because all statements by the therapist are viewed through spectacles of distrust. This is a function of the specific pathology of some patients (and it is, of course, good grist for the therapeutic mill). It is not a universal response of the entire group.

The therapist is an *observer-participant* in the group. The observer status affords the objectivity necessary to store information, to make observations about sequences or cyclical patterns of behavior, to connect events that have occurred over long periods of time. Therapists act as the group historian. Only they are permitted to maintain a temporal perspective; only they remain immune from the charge of not being one of the group, of elevating themselves above the others. It is also only the therapists who keep in mind the original goals of the patient and the relationship between these goals and the events that gradually unfold in the group.

Two patients, Tim and Marjorie, had a sexual affair that eventually came to light in the group. The other members reacted in various ways but none so condemnatory nor so vehemently as Diana, a forty-five-year-old nouveau-moralist, who criticized them both for breaking group rules: Tim, for "being too intelligent to act like such a fool," Marjorie for her "irresponsible disregard for her husband and child," and the Lucifer therapist (me) who "just sat there and let it happen." I eventually pointed out that, in her formidable moralistic broadside, some individuals had been obliterated, that the Marjorie and Tim with all their struggles and doubts and fears whom Diana had known for so long had suddenly been replaced by faceless one-dimensional stereotypes. Furthermore, I was the only one to recall, and to remind the group, of the reasons (expressed at the first group meeting) why Diana had sought therapy: namely, that she needed help in dealing with her rage toward a nineteen-year-old, rebellious, sexually awakening daughter who was in the midst of a search for her identity and autonomy! From there it was but a short step for the group, and then for Diana herself, to understand that her conflict with her daughter was being played out in the here-and-now of the group.

There are many occasions when the process is obvious to all the members in the group but they cannot comment on it simply because the situation is too hot: they are too much a part of the interaction to separate themselves from it. In fact, often, even at a distance, the therapist too feels the heat and is wary about naming the beast.

One neophyte therapist, when leading an experiential group of pediatric oncology nurses (a support group intended to help members decrease the stress experienced in their work), learned through collusive glances between members in the first meeting that there was considerable unspoken tension between the young, progressive nurses and the older, conservative nursing supervisors in the group. The therapist felt that the issue, reaching deep into taboo regions of the authority-ridden nursing profession, was too sensitive and potentially explosive to touch. His supervisor assured him that it was too important an issue to leave unexplored and that he should broach it, since it was highly unlikely that anyone else in the group could do what he dared not.

In the next meeting, the therapist broached the issue in a manner that is almost invariably effective in minimizing defensiveness: he stated his own dilemma about the issue. He told the group that he sensed a hierarchical struggle between the junior nurses and the powerful senior nurses, but that he was hesitant to bring it up lest the younger nurses either deny it or so attack the supervisors that the latter would suffer injury or decide to scuttle the group. His comment was enormously helpful and plunged the group into an open and constructive exploration of a vital issue.

I do not mean that only the leader should make process comments. Other members are entirely capable of performing this function; in fact, there are times when their process observations will be more readily accepted than those of the therapists. What is important is that they not engage in this function for defensive reasons—for example, to avoid the patient role or in any other way to distance themselves from or elevate themselves above the other members.

Thus far in this discussion I have, for pedagogical reasons, overstated two fundamental points that I must now qualify. Those points are: (1) the here-and-now approach is an ahistoric one, and (2) there is a sharp distinction between here-and-now experience and here-and-now process illumination.

Strictly speaking, an ahistoric approach is an impossibility: every process comment refers to an act already belonging to the past. (Sartre once said, "Introspection is retrospection.") Not only does process commentary involve behavior that has just transpired, but it frequently refers to cycles of behavior or repetitive acts that have occurred in the group over weeks or months. Thus, the past events of the therapy group are a part of the here-and-now and an integral part of the data on which process commentary is based.

Often it is helpful to ask patients to review their past experiences in the group. If a patient feels that she is exploited every time she trusts someone or reveals herself, I often inquire about her history of experiencing that feeling in this group. Other patients, depending upon the relevant issues, may be encouraged to discuss such experiences as the times they have felt most close to others, most angry, most accepted, or most ignored.

My qualification of the ahistoric approach goes even further. No group can maintain a total here-and-now approach. There will be frequent excursions into the "then-and-there"—that is, into personal history and into current life situations. In fact, these excursions are so inevitable that one becomes curious when they do not occur. It is not that the group doesn't deal with the past; it is what is done with the past: the crucial task is not to uncover, to piece together, and to understand the past, *but to use the past for the help it offers in understanding (and changing) the individual's mode of relating to the others in the present.*

Summary

The effective use of the here-and-now focus requires two steps: experience in here-and-now and process illumination. The combination of these two steps imbues an experiential group with compelling potency.

The therapist has different tasks in each step. First, the group must be plunged into the here-and-now experience; second, the group must be helped to understand the process of the here-and-now experience: that is, what the interaction conveys about the nature of the members' relationships to one another.

The first step, here-and-now activation, becomes part of the group norm structure; ultimately the group members will assist the therapist in this chore.

The second step, process illumination, is more difficult. There are powerful injunctions against process commentary in everyday social intercourse which the therapist must overcome. The task of process commentary, to a great extent, remains the responsibility of the therapist and consists, as I will discuss shortly, of a wide and complex range of behavior—from labeling single behavioral acts, to juxtaposing several acts, to combining acts over time into a pattern of behavior, to pointing out the undesirable consequences of a patient's behavioral patterns, to more complex inferential explanations or interpretations about the meaning and motivation of such behavior.

Techniques of Here-and-Now Activation

Each therapist must develop techniques consonant with his or her style. Indeed, therapists have a more important task than mastering a technique: they must fully comprehend the strategy and theoretical foundations upon which all effective technique must rest.

I suggest that you *think* here-and-now. When you grow accustomed to thinking of the here-and-now, you automatically steer the group into the here-and-now. Sometimes I feel like a shepherd herding a flock into an ever-tightening circle. I head off errant strays—forays into personal historical material, discussions of current life situations, intellectualisms—and guide them back into the circle. Whenever an issue is raised in the group, I think, "How can I relate this to the group's primary task? How can I make it come to life in the here-and-now?" *I am relentless in this effort, and I begin it in the very first meeting of the group.*

Consider a typical first meeting of a group. After a short, awkward pause, the members generally introduce themselves and proceed, often with help from the therapist, to tell something about their life problems, why they have sought therapy, and perhaps, the type of distress they suffer. I generally intervene at some convenient point well into the meeting and remark to the effect that "We've done a great deal here today so far. Each of you has shared a great deal about yourself, your pain, your reasons for seeking help. But I have a hunch that something else is also going on, and that is that you're sizing one another up, each arriving at some impressions of the other, each wondering how you'll fit in with the others. I wonder now if we could spend some time discussing what each of us has come up with thus far." Now this is no subtle, artful, shaping statement: it is a heavy-handed, explicit directive. Yet I find that most groups respond favorably to such clear guidelines.

The therapist moves the focus from outside to inside, from the abstract to the specific, from the generic to the personal. If a patient describes a hostile confrontation with a spouse or roommate, the therapist may, at some point, inquire, "If you were to be angry like that with anyone in the group, with whom would it be?" or "With whom in the group can you foresee getting into the same type of struggle?" If a patient comments that one of his problems is that he lies, or that he stereotypes people, or that he manipulates groups, the therapist may inquire, "What is the main lie you've told in the group thus far?" or "Can you describe the way you've stereotyped some of us?" or "To what extent have you manipulated the group thus far?"

If a patient complains of mysterious flashes of anger or suicidal compulsions, the therapist may urge the patient to signal to the group the very moment such feelings occur during the session, so that the group can track down and relate these experiences to events in the session.

In each of these instances, the therapist can deepen interaction by encouraging further responses from the others. For example, "How do you feel about the perception of your ridiculing him? Can you imagine doing that? Do you, at times, feel judgmental in the group? Does this resonate with feelings that you are indeed influential, angry, too tactful?" Even simple techniques of asking patients to speak directly to one another, to use second-person pronouns ("you") rather than third-person pronouns, and to look at one another are very useful.

Easier said than done! These suggestions are not always heeded. To some patients, they are threatening indeed, and the therapist must here, as always, employ good timing and attempt to experience what the patient is experiencing. Search for methods that lessen the threat. Begin by focusing on positive interaction: "Toward whom in the group do you feel most warm?" "Who in the group is most like you?" or "Obviously, there are some strong vibes, both positive and negative, going on between you and John. I wonder what you most envy about him? And what parts of him do you find most difficult to accept?"

Sometimes it is easier for group members to work in tandem or in small subgroups. For example, if they learn that there is another member with similar fears or concerns, then the subgroup of two (or more) members can, with less threat, discuss their here-and-now concerns.[1]

Using the conditional and subjunctive tenses provides safety and distance and often is miraculously facilitative. I use them frequently when I encounter initial resistance. If, for example, a patient says, "I don't have any response or feelings at all about Mary today. I'm just feeling too numb and withdrawn," I often say something like, "If you were not numb or withdrawn today, what might you feel about Mary?" The patient generally answers readily: the once-removed position affords a refuge and encourages the patient to answer honestly and directly. Similarly, the therapist might inquire, "If you were to be angry at someone in the group, at whom would it be?" or "If you were to go on a date with Albert (another group member), what kind of experience might it be?"

The therapist must often give instruction in the art of requesting and offering feedback. One important principle to teach patients is to avoid global questions and observations. Questions such as "Am I boring?" or "Do you like me?" are not usually productive. A patient learns a great deal more by asking, "What do I do that causes you to tune out?" "When are you most and least attentive to me?" or "What parts of me or aspects of my behavior do you like least and most?" In the same vein, feedback such as "You're OK," or "a nice guy" is far less useful than "I feel closer to you when you're willing to be honest with your feelings, like in last week's meeting when you said you were attracted to Mary but feared she would scorn you. I feel most distant from you when you're impersonal and start analyzing the meaning of every word said to you, like you did early in the meeting today." (These comments, incidentally, have equal applicability in individual therapy.)

Resistance occurs in many forms. Often it appears in the cunning guise of total equality. Patients, especially in early meetings, often respond to the therapist's here-and-now urgings by claiming that they feel exactly the same toward all the group members: that is, they say that they feel equally warm toward all the members, or no anger toward any, or equally influenced or threatened by all. Do not be misled. Such claims are never true. Guided by your sense of timing, push the inquiry further and help members to differentiate one from the other. Eventually they will disclose that they do have slight differences of feeling toward some of the members. These slight differences are important and are often the vestibule to full interactional participation. I explore the slight differences (no one ever said they had to be enormous); sometimes I suggest that the patient hold up a magnifying glass to these differences and describe what he or she then sees and feels. Often resistance is deeply ingrained, and considerable ingenuity is required, as in the following case study.

Claudia resisted participation on a here-and-now level for months. Keep in mind that resistance is not usually conscious obstinacy but more often stems from sources outside of awareness. Sometimes the here-and-now task is so unfamiliar and uncomfortable to the patient that it is not unlike learning a new language; one has to attend with maximal concentration in order not to slip back into one's habitual remoteness.

Claudia's typical mode of relating to the group was to describe some pressing current life problem, often one of such crisis proportions that the group members felt trapped. First, they felt compelled to deal immediately with the precise problem Claudia presented; second, they had to tread cautiously because she explicitly informed them that she needed all her resources to cope with the crisis and could not afford to be shaken up by interpersonal confrontation. "Don't push me right now," she might say, "I'm just barely hanging on." Efforts to alter this pattern were unsuccessful, and the group members felt discouraged in dealing with Claudia. They cringed when she brought in problems to the meeting.

One day she opened the group with a typical gambit. After weeks of searching she had obtained a new job, but she was convinced that she was going to fail and be dismissed. The group dutifully, but warily, investigated the situation. The investigation met with many of the familiar, treacherous obstacles that generally block the path of work on outside problems. There seemed to be no objective evidence that Claudia was failing at work. She seemed, if anything, to be trying too hard, working eighty hours a week. The evidence, Claudia insisted, simply could not be appreciated by anyone not there at work with her: the glances of her supervisor, the subtle innuendoes, the air of dissatisfaction toward her, the general ambiance in the office, the failure to live up to her (self-imposed and unrealistic) sales goals. Could Claudia be believed? She was a highly unreliable observer; she always downgraded herself and minimized her accomplishments and strengths.

The therapist moved the entire transaction into the here-and-now by asking, "Claudia, it's hard for us to determine whether you are, in fact, failing at your job. But let me ask you another question: What grade do you think you deserve for your work in the group, and what do each of the others get?"

Claudia, not unexpectedly, awarded herself a "D" and staked her claim for at least eight more years in the group. She awarded all the other members substantially superior grades. The therapist replied by awarding Claudia a "B" for her work in the group and then went on to point out the reasons: her commitment to the group, perfect attendance, willingness to help others, great efforts to work despite anxiety and often disabling depression.

Claudia laughed it off; she tried to brush off the incident as a gag or a therapeutic ploy. But the therapist held firm and insisted that he was entirely serious. Claudia then insisted that the therapist was wrong, and pointed out his many failings in the group (one of which was, ironically, the avoidance of the here-and-now). However, Claudia's disagreement with the therapist was incompatible with her long-held, frequently voiced, total confidence in the therapist. (Claudia had often invalidated the feedback of other members in the group by claiming that she trusted no one's judgment except the therapist's.)

The intervention was enormously useful and transferred the process of Claudia's evaluation of herself from a secret chamber lined with the distorting mirrors of her self-perception to the open, vital arena of the group. No longer was it necessary for the members to accept Claudia's perception of her boss's glares and subtle innuendoes. The boss (the therapist) was there in the group. The transaction, in its entirety, was entirely visible to the group.

I never cease to be awed by the rich, subterranean lode of data that exists in every group and in every meeting. Beneath each sentiment expressed there are layers of invisible, unvoiced ones. But how to tap these riches? Sometimes after a long silence in a meeting, I express this very thought: "There is so much information that could be valuable to us all today if only we could excavate it. I wonder if we could, each of us, tell the group about some thoughts that occurred to us in this silence, which we thought of saying but didn't." The exercise is more effective, incidentally, if you participate personally, even start it going. For example, "I've been feeling on edge in the silence, wanting to break it, not wanting to waste time, but on the other hand feeling irritated that it always has to be me doing this work for the group." Or, "I've been feeling torn between wanting to get back to the struggle between you and me, Mike. I feel uncomfortable with this much tension and anger, but I don't know yet how to help understand and resolve it."

When I feel there has been a particularly great deal unsaid in a meeting, I have often used, with success, a technique such as this: "It's now six o'clock and we still have half an hour left, but I wonder if you each would imagine that it's already six-thirty and that you're on your way home. What disappointments would you have about the meeting today?"

Many of the observations the therapist makes may be highly inferential. Objective accuracy is not the issue; as long as you persistently direct the group from the nonrelevant, from the then-and-there, to the here-and-now, you are operationally correct. If a group spends time in an unproductive meeting discussing dull, boring parties, and the therapist wonders aloud if the members are indirectly referring to the present group session, there is no way of determining with any certainty whether they in fact are. Correctness in this instance must be defined relativistically and pragmatically. By shifting the group's attention from then-and-there to here-and-now material, the therapist performs a service to the group—a service that, consistently reinforced, will ultimately result in a cohesive, interactional atmosphere maximally conducive to therapy. Following this model, the effectiveness of an intervention should be gauged by its success in focusing the group on itself.

Often, when activating the group, the therapist performs two simultaneous acts: steers the group into the here-and-now and, at the same time, interrupts the content flow in the group. Not infrequently, some members will resent or feel rejected by the interruption, and the therapist must attend to these feelings for they, too, are part of the here-and-now. This consideration often makes it difficult for the therapist to intervene. Early in our socialization process we learn not to interrupt, not to change the subject abruptly. Furthermore, there are times in the group when everyone seems keenly interested in the topic under discussion. Even though the therapist is certain that the group is not working, it is not easy to buck the group current. Social psychological small group research strongly documents the compelling force of group pressure. To take a stand opposite to the perceived consensus of the group requires considerable courage and conviction.

My experience is that the therapist faced with this type of dilemma can increase the patient's receptivity by expressing both sets of feelings to the group. For example, "Mary, I feel very uncomfortable as you talk. I'm having a couple of strong feelings. One is that you're into something that is very important and painful for you, and the other is that Ben [a new member] has been trying hard to get into the group for the last few meetings and the group seems unwelcoming. This didn't happen when other new members entered the group. Why do you think it's happening now?" Or, "Warren, I had two reactions as you started talking. The first is that I'm delighted you feel comfortable enough now in the group to participate, but the other is that it's going to be hard for the group to respond to what you're saying because it's very abstract and far removed from you personally. I'd be much more interested in how you've been feeling about the group these past few weeks. Which meetings, which issues, have you been most tuned in to? What reactions have you had to the various members?"

There are, of course, many more activating procedures. But my goal in this chapter is not to offer a compendium of techniques. Quite the contrary. I describe techniques only to illuminate the underlying principle of here-and-now activation. These techniques, or group gimmicks, are servants, not masters. To use them injudiciously, to fill voids, to jazz up the group, to acquiesce to the members' demands that the leader lead, is seductive but not constructive for the group.

Group research offers corroborative evidence. In one group project, the activating techniques (structured exercises) of sixteen different leaders were studied and correlated with outcome.[2] There were two important relevant findings:

1. The more structured exercises the leader used, the more competent did members (at the end of the thirty-hour group) deem the leader to be.
2. The more structured exercises used by the leader, the less positive were the results (measured at a six-month follow-up).

In other words, members desire leaders who lead, who offer considerable structure and guidance. They equate a large number of structured exercises with competence. Yet this is a confusion of form and substance: too much structure, too many activating techniques, is counterproductive.

Overall, group leader activity correlates with outcome in a curvilinear fashion (too much or too little activity led to unsuccessful outcome). Too little leader activity results in a floundering group. Too much activation by a leader results in a dependent group that persists in looking to the leader to supply too much.

Remember that sheer acceleration of interaction is not the purpose of these techniques. The therapist who moves too quickly—using gimmicks to make interactions, emotional expression, and self-disclosure too easy—misses the whole point. Resistance, fear, guardedness, distrust—in short, everything that impedes the development of satisfying interpersonal relations—must be permitted expression. The goal is to create not a slick-functioning, streamlined social organization, but one that functions well enough and engenders sufficient trust for the unfolding of each member's social microcosm. Working through the resistances to change is the key to the production of change. Thus, the therapist wants to go not around obstacles but through them. Ormont puts it nicely when he points out that though we urge patients to engage deeply in the here-and-now, we expect them to fail, to default on their contract. In fact, we want them to default because we hope, through the nature of their failure, to identify, and ultimately dispel, each member's particular resistances to intimacy—including each member's resistance style (for example, detachment, fighting, diverting, self-absorption, distrust) and each member's underlying fears of intimacy (for example, impulsivity, abandonment, merger, vulnerability).[3]

Techniques of Process Illumination

As soon as patients have been successfully steered into a here-and-now interactional pattern, the group therapist must attend to turning this interaction to therapeutic advantage. This task is complex and consists of several stages:

1. Patients must first recognize what they are doing with other people (ranging from simple acts to complex patterns unfolding over a long time).

2. They must then appreciate the impact of this behavior on others and how it influences others' opinion of them, and consequently the impact of the behavior on their own self-regard.

3. They must decide whether they are satisfied with their habitual interpersonal style.

4. They must exercise the will to change.

Even when therapists have helped patients transform intent into decision and decision into action, their task is not complete. They must then help solidify change and transfer it from the group setting into patients' larger lives.

Each of these stages may be facilitated by some specific cognitive input by the therapist, and I will describe each step in turn. First, however, I must discuss several prior and basic considerations: How does the therapist recognize process? How can the therapist help the members to assume a process orientation? How can the therapist increase the receptivity of the patient to his or her process commentary?

Recognition of Process

Before therapists can help patients understand process, they themselves must obviously learn to recognize it. The experienced therapist does this naturally and effortlessly, observing the group proceedings from a perspective that permits a continuous view of the process underlying the content of the group discussion. This difference in perspective is the major difference in role between the patient and the therapist in the group.

Consider a group meeting in which a patient, Karen, discloses much heavy, deeply personal material. The group is moved by her account and devotes much time to listening, to helping her elaborate more fully, and to offering her support. The group therapist shares in these activities but entertains many other thoughts as well. For example, the therapist may wonder why, of all the members, it is invariably Karen who reveals first and most. Why does Karen so often put herself in the role of the group patient whom all the members must nurse? Why must she always display herself as vulnerable? And why today? And that last meeting! So much conflict! After such a meeting, one might have expected Karen to be angry. Instead, she shows her throat. Is she avoiding giving expression to her rage?

At the end of a session in another group, Jay, a young, rather fragile patient, had, amid considerable emotional upheaval, revealed that he was gay—his very first step out of the closet. At the next meeting the group urged him to continue. He attempted to do so but, overcome with emotion, blocked and hesitated. Just then, with indecent alacrity, Vicky filled the gap, saying, "Well, if no one else is going to talk, I have a problem."

Vicky, an aggressive forty-year-old cabdriver, who sought therapy be-
cause of social loneliness and bitterness, proceeded to discuss in endless detail
a complex situation involving an unwelcome visiting aunt. For the experi-
enced, process-oriented therapist, the phrase "I have a problem" is a double
entendre. Far more trenchantly than her words, Vicky's behavior says, "I
have a problem," and her problem is manifest in her insensitivity to Jay, who,
after months of silence, had finally mustered the courage to speak.

It is not easy to tell the beginning therapist how to recognize process;
the acquisition of this perspective is one of the major tasks in your education. And it is an interminable task: throughout your career, you learn
to penetrate ever more deeply into the substratum of group discourse.
This deeper vision increases the keenness of a therapist's interest in the
meeting. Generally, beginning students who observe meetings find
them far less meaningful, complex, and interesting than does the experienced therapist.

Certain guidelines, though, may facilitate the neophyte therapist's
recognition of process. Note the simple nonverbal sense data available.[4]
Who chooses to sit where? Which members sit together? Who chooses
to sit close to the therapist? Far away? Who sits near the door? Who
comes to the meeting on time? Who is habitually late? Who looks at
whom when speaking? Do some members, while speaking to another
member, look at the therapist? If so, then they are relating not to one
another but instead to the therapist through their speech to the others.
Who looks at his watch? Who slouches in her seat? Who yawns? Do
the members pull their chairs away from the center at the same time as
they are verbally professing great interest in the group? Are coats kept
on? When in a single meeting or in the sequence of meetings are they
removed? How quickly do the group members enter the room? How
do they leave it?

Sometimes the process is clarified by attending *not only to what is said*
but to what is omitted: the female patient who offers suggestions, advice,
or feedback to the male patients but never to the other women in the
group; the group that never confronts or questions the therapist; the
topics (for example, the taboo trio: sex, money, death) that are never
broached; the patient who is never attacked; the one who is never sup-

ported; the one who never supports or inquires—all these omissions are part of the transactional process of the group.

In one group, for example, Sonia stated that she felt others disliked her. When asked who, she selected Eric, a detached, aloof man who habitually related only to those people who could be of use to him. Eric immediately bristled, "Why me? Tell me one thing I've said to you that makes you pick me." Sonia stated, "That's exactly the point. You have no use for me. You've never said anything to me. Not a question, not a greeting. Nothing. I just don't exist for you." Eric, much later, when completing therapy, cited this incident as a particularly powerful and illuminating instruction.

Physiologists commonly study the function of a hormone by removing the endocrine gland that manufactures it and observing the changes in the hormone-deficient organism. Similarly, in group therapy, we may learn a great deal about the role of a particular member by observing the here-and-now process of the group when that member is absent. For example, if the absent member is aggressive and competitive, the group may feel liberated. Other patients, who had felt threatened or restricted in the missing member's presence, may suddenly blossom into activity. If, on the other hand, the group has depended on the missing member to carry the burden of self-disclosure or to coax other members into speaking, then it will feel helpless and threatened when that member is absent. Often this absence elucidates interpersonal feelings that previously were entirely out of the group members' awareness, and the therapist may, with profit, encourage the group to discuss these feelings toward the absent member both at that time and later in his or her presence.

Similarly, a rich supply of data about feelings toward the therapist often emerges in a meeting in which the leader is absent. One leader led an experiential training group of mental health professionals composed of one woman and twelve men. The woman, though she habitually took the chair closest to the door, felt reasonably comfortable in the group until a leaderless meeting was scheduled when the therapist was out of town. At that meeting the group discussed sexual feelings and experiences far more blatantly than ever before, and the woman had terrifying fantasies of the group locking the door and raping her. She realized how the therapist's presence had offered her safety against fears of unrestrained sexual behavior by the other members and against the emergence of her own sexual fantasies. (She realized, too, the meaning of her occupying the seat nearest the door!)

Search in every possible way to understand the relationship messages in any communication. Look for incongruence between verbal and non-verbal behavior. Be especially curious when there is something arrhythmic about a transaction: when, for example, the intensity of a response seems disproportionate to the stimulus statement; or when a response seems to be off target or to make no sense. At these times look for several possibilities: for example, *parataxic distortion* (the responder is experiencing the sender unrealistically), or *metacommunications* (the responder is responding, accurately, not to the manifest content but to another level of communication), or *displacement* (the responder is reacting not to the current transaction but to feelings stemming from previous transactions).

Common Group Tensions

Remember that certain tensions are always present, to some degree, in every therapy group. Consider, for example, such tensions as the struggle for dominance, the antagonism between mutually supportive feelings and sibling rivalrous ones, between greed and selfless efforts to help the other, between the desire to immerse oneself in the comforting waters of the group and the fear of losing one's precious individuality, between the wish to get better and the wish to stay in the group, between the wish that others improve and the fear of being left behind. Sometimes these tensions are quiescent for months until some event wakens them and they erupt into plain view.

Do not forget these tensions. They are always there, always fueling the hidden motors of group interaction. The knowledge of these tensions often informs the therapist's recognition of process. Consider, for example, one of the most powerful covert sources of group tension: the struggle for dominance. Earlier in this chapter, I described an intervention where the therapist, in an effort to steer a patient into the here-and-now, gave her a grade for her work in the group. The intervention was effective for that particular patient. Yet that was not the end of the story: there were later repercussions on the rest of the group. In the next meeting, two patients asked the therapist to clarify some remark he had made to them at a previous meeting. The remarks had been so supportive in nature and so straightforwardly phrased that the therapist was puzzled at the request for clarification. Deeper investigation revealed that the two patients, and later others, too, were requesting grades from the therapist.

In another experiential group of mental health professionals at several levels of training, the leader was deeply impressed at the group skills of Stewart, one of the youngest, most inexperienced members. The leader expressed his fantasy that Stewart was a plant, that he could not possibly be just beginning his training, since he conducted himself like a veteran with ten years' group experience. The comment evoked a flood of tensions. It was not easily forgotten by the group and, for months to come, was periodically revived and angrily discussed. With his comment, the therapist placed the kiss of death on Stewart's brow, since thereafter the group systematically challenged and deskilled him. It is likely that the therapist who makes a positive evaluation of one member will evoke feelings of sibling rivalry.

The struggle for dominance fluctuates in intensity throughout the group. It is much in evidence at the beginning of the group as members jockey for position in the pecking order. Once the hierarchy is established, the issue may become quiescent, with periodic flare-ups: for example, when some member, as part of his or her therapeutic work, begins to grow in assertiveness and to challenge the established order.

When new members enter the group, especially aggressive members who do not know their place, who do not respectfully search out and honor the rules of the group, you may be certain that the struggle for dominance will rise to the surface.

In one group a veteran member, Betty, was much threatened by the entrance of a new, aggressive woman, Rena. A few meetings later, when Betty discussed some important material concerning her inability to assert herself, Rena attempted to help by commenting that she, herself, used to be like that, and then she presented various methods she had used to overcome it. Rena reassured Betty that if she continued to talk about it openly in the group she, too, would gain considerable confidence. Betty's response was silent fury of such magnitude that several meetings passed before she could discuss and work through her feelings. To the uninformed observer, Betty's response would appear puzzling; but in the light of Betty's seniority in the group and Rena's vigorous challenge to that seniority, her response was entirely predictable. She responded not to Rena's manifest offer of help but instead to Rena's metacommunication: "I'm more advanced than you, more mature, more knowledgeable about the process of psychotherapy, and more powerful in this group despite your longer presence here."

Process Commentary: A Theoretical Overview

It is not easy to discuss, in a systematic way, the actual practice of process illumination. How can one propose crisp, basic guidelines for a procedure of such complexity and range, such delicate timing, so many linguistic nuances? I am tempted to beg the question by claiming that herein lies the art of psychotherapy: it will come as you gain experience; you cannot, in a systematic way, come to it. To a degree, I believe this to be so. Yet I also believe that it is possible to blaze crude trails, to provide the clinician with general principles that will accelerate education without limiting the scope of artistry.

The approach I take in this section closely parallels the approach I use to clarify the basic therapeutic factors in group therapy. Here the issue is not how group therapy helps but how process illumination leads to change. The issue is complex and requires considerable attention, but the length of this discussion should not suggest that the interpretive function of the therapist takes precedence over other tasks.

First, let me proceed to view in a dispassionate manner the entire range of interpretive comments. I ask of each the simplistic but basic question, "How does this interpretation, this process-illuminating comment, help a patient to change?" Such an approach, consistently followed, reveals a set of basic operational patterns.

I begin by considering a series of process comments that a therapist made to a male patient over several months of group therapy:

1. You are interrupting me.
2. Your voice is tight, and your fists are clenched.

3. Whenever you talk to me, you take issue with me.

4. When you do that, I feel threatened and sometimes frightened.

5. I think you feel very competitive with me and are trying to devalue me.

6. I've noticed that you've done the same thing with all the men in the group. Even when they try to approach you helpfully, you strike out at them. Consequently, they see you as hostile and threatening.

7. In the three meetings when there were no women present in the group, you were more approachable.

8. I think you're so concerned about your sexual attractiveness to women that you view men only as competitors. You deprive yourself of the opportunity of ever getting close to a man.

9. Even though you always seem to spar with me, there seems to be another side to it. You often stay after the group to have a word with me; you frequently look at me in the group. And there's that dream you described three weeks ago about the two of us fighting and then falling to the ground in an embrace. I think you very much want to be close to me, but somehow you've got closeness and homosexuality entangled and you keep pushing me away.

10. You are lonely here and feel unwanted and uncared for. That rekindles so many of your bad feelings of unworthiness.

11. What's happened in the group now is that you've distanced yourself, estranged yourself, from all the men here. Are you satisfied with that? (Remember that one of your major goals when you started the group was to find out why you haven't had any close men friends and to do something about that.)

Note, first of all, that the comments form a progression: they start with simple observations of single acts and proceed to a description of feelings evoked by an act, to observations about several acts over a period of time, to the juxtaposition of different acts, to speculations about the patient's intentions and motivations, to comments about the unfortunate repercussions of his behavior, to the inclusion of more inferential data (dreams, subtle gestures), to calling attention to the similarity between the patient's behavioral patterns in the here-and-now and in his outside social world.

In this progression, the comments become more inferential. They begin with sense-data observations and gradually shift to complex generalizations based on sequences of behavior, interpersonal patterns, fantasy, and dream material. As the comments become more complex and more inferential, their author becomes more removed from the other person—in short, more a therapist process-commentator. Members often make some of the earlier statements to one another but rarely make the ones at the end of the sequence.

There is, incidentally, an exceptionally sharp barrier between comments 4 and 5. The first four statements issue from the experience of the commentator. They are the commentator's observations and feelings; the patient can devalue or ignore them but cannot deny them, disagree with them, or take them away from the commentator. The fifth statement ("I think you feel very competitive with me and are trying to devalue me") is much more likely to evoke defensiveness and to close down constructive interactional flow. This genre of comment is intrusive; it is a guess about the other's intention and motivation and is often rejected unless an important trusting, supportive relationship has been previously established. If members in a young group make many "type 5" comments to one another, they are not likely to develop a constructive therapeutic climate.[5]

But how does this series (or any series of process comments) help the patient change? In making these process comments, the group therapist initiates change by escorting the patient through the following sequence:

1. Here is what your behavior is like. Through feedback and later through self-observation, members learn to see themselves as seen by others.

2. Here is how your behavior makes others feel. Members learn about the impact of their behavior on the feelings of other members.

3. Here is how your behavior influences the opinions others have of you. Members learn that, as a result of their behavior, others value them, dislike them, find them unpleasant, respect them, avoid them, and so on.

4. Here is how your behavior influences your opinion of yourself. Building on the information gathered in the first three steps, patients formulate self-evaluations; they make judgments about their self-worth

and their lovability. (Recall Sullivan's aphorism that the self-concept is largely constructed from reflected self-appraisals.)

Once this sequence has been developed and is fully understood by the patient, once patients have a deep understanding that their behavior is not in their own best interests, that relationships to others and to themselves are a result of their own actions, then they have come to a crucial point in therapy: they have entered the antechamber of change. The therapist is now in a position to pose a question that initiates the real crunch of therapy. The question, presented in a number of ways by the therapist but rarely in direct form, is: Are you satisfied with the world you have created? This is what you do to others, to others' opinion of you, and to your opinion of yourself—are you satisfied with your actions?

When the inevitable negative answer arrives, the therapist embarks on a many-layered effort to transform a sense of personal dissatisfaction into a decision to change and then into the act of change. In one way or another, the therapist's interpretive remarks are designed to encourage the act of change. Only a few psychotherapy theoreticians (for example, Otto Rank, Rollo May, Silvano Arieti, Leslie Farber, Allen Wheelis, and myself)[6] include the concept of will in their formulations, yet it is, I believe, implicit in most interpretive systems. I discuss the role of will in psychotherapy in great detail elsewhere, and I refer interested readers to that publication.[7] For now, broad brush strokes are sufficient.

The intrapsychic agency that initiates an act, that transforms intention and decision into action, is will. Will is the primary responsible mover within the individual. Although modern analytic metapsychology has chosen to emphasize the irresponsible movers of our behavior (that is, unconscious motivations and drives),[8] it is difficult to do without the idea of will in our understanding of change. We cannot bypass it under the assumption that it is too nebulous and too elusive, and consequently consign it to the black box of the mental apparatus, to which the therapist has no access.

Knowingly or unknowingly, every therapist assumes that each patient possesses the capacity to change through willful choice. The therapist, using a variety of strategies and tactics, attempts to escort the patient to a crossroads where he or she can choose, choose willfully in the best interests of his or her own integrity. The therapist's task is not to create will or to infuse it into the patient. That, of course, you cannot do. What you can do is to help remove encumbrances from the bound or stifled will of the patient.

The concept of will provides a useful construct for understanding the procedure of process illumination. The interpretive remarks of the therapist can all be viewed in terms of how they bear on the patient's will. The most common and simplistic therapeutic approach is exhortative: "Your behavior is, as you yourself now know, counter to your best interests. You are not satisfied. This is not what you want for yourself. Damn it, change!"

The expectation that the patient will change is simply an extension of the moral philosophical belief that if one knows the good (that is, what is, in the deepest sense, in one's best interest), one will act accordingly. In the words of St. Thomas Aquinas: "Man, insofar as he acts willfully, acts according to some imagined good."[9] And, indeed, for some individuals this knowledge and this exhortation are sufficient to produce therapeutic change.

However, patients with significant and well-entrenched psychopathology generally need much more than exhortation. The therapist, through interpretive comments, then proceeds to exercise one of several other options that help patients to disencumber their will. The therapist's goal is to guide patients to a point where they accept one, several, or all of the following basic premises:

1. Only I can change the world I have created for myself.
2. There is no danger in change.
3. To attain what I really want, I must change.
4. I can change; I am potent.

Each of these premises, if fully accepted by a patient, can be a powerful stimulant to willful action. Each exerts its influence in a different way. Though I will discuss each in turn, I do not wish to imply a sequential pattern. Each, depending on the need of the patient and the style of the therapist, may be effective independently of the others.

"Only I can change the world I have created for myself."

Behind the simple group therapy sequence I have described (seeing one's own behavior and appreciating its impact on others and on oneself), there is a mighty overarching concept, one whose shadow touches every part of the therapeutic process. That concept is responsibility. Though it is rarely discussed explicitly, it is woven into the fabric of most psychotherapeutic systems. Responsibility has many meanings— legal, religious, ethical. I use it in the sense that a person is "responsible for" by being the "basis of," the "cause of," the "author of" something.

One of the most fascinating aspects of group therapy is that everyone is born again, born together in the group. Each member starts off on an equal footing. In the view of the others (and, if the therapist does a good job, in the view of oneself), each gradually scoops out and shapes a life space in the group. Each member, in the deepest sense of the concept, is responsible for this space and for the sequence of events that will occur to him or her in the group. The patient, having truly come to appreciate this responsibility, must then accept, too, that there is no hope for change unless he or she changes. Others cannot bring change, nor can change bring itself. One is responsible for one's past and present life in the group (as well as in the outside world) and similarly and totally responsible for one's future.

Thus, the therapist helps the patient to understand that the interpersonal world is arranged in a generally predictable and orderly fashion, that it is not that the patient cannot change but that he or she will not change, that the patient bears the responsibility for the creation of his or her world, and therefore the responsibility for its transmutation.

"There is no danger in change."

These efforts may not be enough. The therapist may tug at the therapeutic cord and learn that patients, even after being thus enlightened, still make no significant therapeutic movement. In this case, therapists apply additional therapeutic leverage by helping patients face the paradox of continuing to act contrary to their basic interests. In a number of ways therapists must pose the question, "How come? Why do you continue to defeat yourself?"

A common method of explaining "How come?" is to assume that there are obstacles to the patient's exercising willful choice, obstacles that prevent patients from seriously considering altering their behavior. The presence of the obstacle is generally inferred; the therapist makes an "as if" assumption: "You behave as if you feel there were some considerable danger that would befall you if you were to change. You fear to act otherwise for fear that some calamity will befall you." The therapist helps the patient clarify the nature of the imagined danger, and then proceeds, in several ways, to detoxify, to disconfirm the reality of this danger.

The patient's reason may be enlisted as an ally. The process of identifying and naming the fantasized danger may, in itself, enable one to understand how far removed one's fears are from reality. Another approach is to encourage the patient, in carefully calibrated doses, to commit the dreaded act in the group. The fantasized calamity does not, of course, ensue, and the dread is gradually extinguished.

For example, suppose a patient avoids any aggressive behavior because at a deep level he fears that he has a dammed-up reservoir of homicidal fury and must be constantly vigilant lest he unleash it and eventually face retribution from others. An appropriate therapeutic strategy is to help the patient express aggression in small doses in the group: pique at being interrupted, irritation at members who are habitually late, anger at the therapist for charging him money, and so on. Gradually, the patient is helped to relate openly to the other members and to demythologize himself as a homicidal being. Although the language and the view of human nature are different, this is precisely the same approach to change used in systematic desensitization—a major technique of behavior therapy.

"To attain what I really want, I must change."

Another explanatory approach used by many therapists to deal with a patient who persists in behaving counter to his or her best interests is to consider the payoffs of that patient's behavior. Though the behavior of the patient sabotages many of his or her mature needs and goals, at the same time it satisfies another set of needs and goals. In other words, the patient has conflicting motivations that cannot be simultaneously

satisfied. For example, a male patient may wish to establish mature heterosexual relationships; but at another, often unconscious, level, he may
wish to be nurtured, to be cradled endlessly, to assuage castration anxiety by a maternal identification, or, to use an existential vocabulary, to
be sheltered from the terrifying freedom of adulthood.

Obviously, the patient cannot satisfy both sets of wishes: he cannot
establish an adult heterosexual relationship with a woman if he also says
(and much more loudly), "Take care of me, protect me, nurse me, let
me be a part of you."

It is important to clarify this paradox for the patient. The therapist
tries to help the patient understand the nature of his conflicting desires,
to choose between them, to relinquish those that cannot be fulfilled except at enormous cost to his integrity and autonomy. Once the patient
realizes what he really wants (as an adult), and that his behavior is designed to fulfill opposing growth-retarding needs, he gradually concludes: To attain what I really want, I must change.

"I can change; I am potent."

Perhaps the major therapeutic approach to the question, "How
come?" ("How come you act in ways counter to your best interests?") is
to offer explanation, to attribute meaning to the patient's behavior. The
therapist says, in effect, "You behave in certain fashions because ... ,"
and the "because" clause generally involves motivational factors outside
the patient's awareness. It is true that the previous two options I have
discussed also proffer explanation but—and I will clarify this shortly—
the purpose of the explanation (the nature of the leverage exerted on
will) is quite different in each of these approaches.

What type of explanation does the therapist offer the patient? And
which explanations are correct, and which incorrect? Which "deep"?
Which "superficial"? It is at this juncture that the great metapsycholog-
ical controversies of the field arise, since the nature of therapists' explanations are a function of the ideological school to which they belong. I
think we can sidestep the ideological struggle by keeping a fixed gaze
on the function of the interpretation, on the relationship between explanation and the final product: change. After all, our goal is change. Self-
knowledge, derepression, analysis of transference, and self-actualization

all are worthwhile, enlightened pursuits; all are related to change, preludes to change, cousins and companions to it; and yet they are not synonymous with change.

Explanation provides a system by which we can order the events in our lives into some coherent and predictable pattern. To name something, to place it into a logical (or paralogical) causal sequence, is to experience it as being under our control. No longer is our behavior or our internal experience frightening, inchoate, out of control; instead, we behave (or have a particular inner experience) because . . . . The "because" offers us mastery (or a sense of mastery that, phenomenologically, is tantamount to mastery). It offers us freedom and effectance. As we move from a position of being motivated by unknown forces to a position of identifying and controlling these forces, we move from a passive, reactive posture to an active, acting, changing posture.

If we accept this basic premise—that a major function of explanation in psychotherapy is to provide the patient with a sense of personal mastery—it follows that the value of an explanation should be measured by this criterion. To the extent that it offers a sense of potency, a causal explanation is valid, correct, or "true." Such a definition of truth is completely relativistic and pragmatic. It argues that no explanatory system has hegemony or exclusive rights, that no system is the correct one.

Therapists may offer the patient any of several interpretations to clarify the same issue; each may be made from a different frame of reference, and each may be "true." Freudian, interpersonal object relations, self psychology, existential, transactional analytic, Jungian, gestalt, transpersonal, cognitive, behavioral explanations—all of these may be true simultaneously. None, despite vehement claims to the contrary, have sole rights to the truth. After all, they are all based on imaginary, as-if structures. They all say, "You are behaving (or feeling) as if such and such a thing were true." The superego, the id, the ego; the archetypes; the masculine protest; the internalized objects; the self object; the grandiose self and the omnipotent object; the parent, child, and adult ego state—none of these really exists. They are all fictions, all psychological constructs created for semantic convenience. They justify their existence only by virtue of their explanatory powers.

Do we therefore abandon our attempts to make precise, thoughtful interpretations? Not at all. We only recognize the purpose and function of the interpretation. Some may be superior to others, not because they are deeper but because they have more explanatory power, are more credible, provide more mastery, and are therefore more useful. Obviously, interpretations must be tailored to the recipient. In general, they are more effective if they make sense, if they are logically consistent with sound supporting arguments, if they are bolstered by empirical observation, if they are consonant with a patient's frame of reference, if they "feel" right, if they somehow "click" with the internal experience of the patient, and if they can be generalized and applied to many analogous situations in the life of the patient. Higher order interpretations generally offer a novel explanation to the patient for some large pattern of behavior (as opposed to a single trait or act). The novelty of the therapist's explanation stems from his or her unusual frame of reference, which permits an original synthesis of data. Indeed, often the data is material that has been generally overlooked by the patient or is out of his or her awareness.

If pushed, to what extent am I willing to defend this relativistic thesis? When I present this position to students, they respond with such questions as: Does that mean that an astrological explanation is also valid in psychotherapy? These questions make me uneasy, but I have to respond affirmatively. If an astrological or shamanistic or magical explanation enhances a sense of mastery and leads to inner personal change, then it is a valid explanation. There is much evidence from cross-cultural psychiatric research to support this position; the explanation must be consistent with the values and with the frame of reference of the human community in which the patient dwells. In most primitive cultures, it is often only the magical or the religious explanation that is acceptable, and hence valid and effective.[10] Psychoanalytic revisionists make an analogous point and argue that reconstructive attempts to capture historical "truth" are futile; it is far more important to the process of change to construct plausible, meaningful, personal narratives.[11]

An interpretation, even the most elegant one, has no benefit if the patient does not hear it. Therapists should take pains to review their evidence with the patient and present the explanation clearly. (If they cannot, it is likely that the explanation is rickety or that they themselves do not understand it. The reason is not, as has been claimed, that the therapist is speaking directly to the patient's unconscious.)

Do not always expect the patient to accept an interpretation. Sometimes the patient hears the same interpretation many times until one day it seems to "click." Why does it click that one day? Perhaps the patient just came across some corroborating data from new events in the environment or from the surfacing in fantasy or dreams of some previously unconscious material. Sometimes a patient will accept from another member an interpretation that he or she would not accept from the therapist. (Patients are clearly capable of making interpretations as useful as those of the therapists, and members are receptive to these interpretations provided the other member has accepted the patient role and does not offer interpretations to acquire prestige, power, or a favored position with the leader.)

The interpretation will not click until the patient's relationship to the therapist is just right. For example, a patient who feels threatened and competitive with the therapist is unlikely to be helped by any interpretation (except one that clarifies the transference). Even the most thoughtful interpretation will fail because the patient may feel defeated or humiliated by the proof of the therapist's superior perceptivity. An interpretation becomes maximally effective only when it is delivered in a context of acceptance and trust.

CHAPTER 3

Group Therapy with
Specialized Groups

*Hospitalized Patients, Patients Addicted to
Alcohol, the Terminally Ill,
the Bereaved*

INTRODUCTION

Earlier I addressed the problem of writing a textbook that could be responsive to the enormous variety of highly specialized therapy groups. My first basic strategy was to delineate the therapeutic factors common to all groups. My second strategic decision was to forgo any attempt to describe therapeutic procedures appropriate for each of the specialized groups. Because the number of specialized groups has proliferated so greatly, it is no longer possible to address each type separately. Even if that *were* possible, it would not represent good pedagogy. A far better approach, it seemed to me, would be to teach, in great depth, a prototypic form of group therapy and then offer students a set of principles to enable them to adapt this standard group approach to any specialized clinical situation.

I selected as the prototypic group the intensive long-term heterogeneous outpatient group (that is, a group consisting of members with a wide variety of clinical complaints meeting for approximately six months or more and attempting not only to ameliorate symptoms but to change personality or modes of interpersonal relating). Even though the contemporary field is dominated by briefer groups with more limited goals, I selected this group as my model for several reasons: it is a venerable group and has generated a considerable body of research and clinical reflection; furthermore, the therapy required to lead this group is sophisticated and complex. Students who become adept clinicians in such groups will be well positioned to fashion a therapeutic approach for any clinical population.

When attempting to design an appropriate therapy for a specialized population, the clinician's first step is to appraise all relevant aspects of the clinical situation: for example, the nature of the patients' problems, the patients' motivation, the time frame available (length and frequency of meetings, overall duration of therapy), the availability and training of co-therapists, physical surroundings, and the availability for collaboration of concurrent individual therapists. Once the treatment environment is appraised, the clinician must then differentiate between immutable and arbitrary conditions. Next the therapist must set about influencing arbitrary restraints so as to create the optimal conditions for therapy. Following that the therapist must set therapy goals which are realistic and achievable within the existing clinical constraints. Finally the therapist must modify his or her standard therapy techniques to achieve what is possible.

The specialized groups described in the following selections—groups of hospitalized psychiatric patients, alcoholics, individuals with cancer, the spousally bereaved—demonstrate the process of customizing therapy to fit the demands of the clinical situation. The first selection—about groups on the psychiatric hospital ward—describes this process most explicitly.

PART I

GROUP THERAPY WITH
HOSPITALIZED PATIENTS

There are few situations more inhospitable to the therapy group than the psychiatric inpatient setting. During my tenure as medical director of the Stanford University Hospital psychiatric ward, I led a daily inpatient group for five years and became highly sensitized to the logistical difficulties faced by the group therapist. For starters, let me mention that over a five-year period I rarely had the identical group for two straight days (in other words, at least one member had been discharged or a new member admitted), and I almost never had the same group for three straight days. Obviously the traditional practice of building group cohesiveness over a period of weeks and months was no longer pertinent. A new approach had to be devised. During this time I visited many other hospital group programs, experimented with a number of treatment models, conducted process and outcome research on the groups, and ultimately wrote the book from which this selection is taken, *Inpatient Group Psychotherapy*.

The inpatient therapy group is of importance not only because it requires such radical modification of technique but also because it represents, numerically, the most significant form of specialized group. Every day tens of thousands of hospitalized psychiatric patients attend a variety of groups offered by most psychiatric wards in the country.

The selections from *Inpatient Group Psychotherapy* summarize aspects of the environment—the clinical facts of life—of the inpatient ward that have particular relevance for the group therapist, and then proceed to discuss the strategies and techniques of leadership that are consonant with that environment. Finally I describe the beginning phases of a group designed for higher level inpatients.

Clinical Setting of the Inpatient Group

The contemporary acute psychiatric ward is a radically different clinical set-
ting and demands a radical modification of group therapy technique. Let me
begin this discussion by examining the stark clinical facts of life that the
inpatient group therapist must face:

1: There is considerable patient turnover. The average length of
   stay is one to three weeks. There is generally a new patient in the
   group almost every meeting.

2: Many patients attend the group meeting just for a single meeting
   or two. There is no time to work on termination. Some member
   terminates almost every meeting, and a focus on termination
   would consume all the group time.

3: There is great heterogeneity of psychopathology: patients with
   psychosis, neurosis, characterological disturbance, substance
   abuse, adolescent problems, major affective disorders, and
   anorexia nervosa are all present in the same group.

4: All the patients are acutely uncomfortable; they strive toward resolution of psychosis or acute despair rather than toward personal
   growth or self-understanding. As soon as a patient is out of an
   acute crisis, he or she is discharged.

5: There are many unmotivated patients in the group: they may be
   psychologically unsophisticated; they do not want to be there;
   they may not agree that they need therapy; they often are not paying for therapy; they may have little curiosity about themselves.

6: The therapist has no time to prepare or screen patients.

7: The therapist often has no control over group composition.

8: There is little therapist stability. Many of the therapists have rotating schedules and generally cannot attend all of the meetings
   of the group.

9: Patients see their therapist in other roles throughout the day on
   the ward.

10: Group therapy is only one of many therapies in which the patient participates; some of these other therapies are with some of the same patients in the group and often with the same therapist.

11: There is often little sense of cohesion in the group; not enough time exists for members to learn to care for or trust one another.

12: There is not time for gradual recognition of subtle interpersonal patterns, or for "working through," and no opportunity to focus on transfer of learning to the situation at home.

Strategies and Techniques of Leadership

Inpatient clinical exigencies demand that group therapists modify their approach toward such structural issues as composition, frequency, duration and size of meetings, goals of therapy, extragroup socializing, and confidentiality.

Let us now examine the implications of these clinical facts of life for the inpatient group therapist's basic strategy. The strategies and techniques discussed here are generally applicable to all forms of inpatient group therapy.

The Single-Session Time Frame

Outpatient group therapists have a longitudinal time frame: they build cohesiveness over many sessions.

On the inpatient unit, the rapid turnover of group membership, the brief duration of hospitalization, and the changing composition from one meeting to the next all dictate a fundamental shift in the therapist's time frame. Rarely does the group have two consecutive sessions with identical membership. Indeed, many members will attend only a single session.

Inpatient group therapists cannot work within a longitudinal time frame; instead, *they must consider the life of the group to last a single session.* This necessity suggests that they must attempt to do as much effective work as possible for as many patients as possible during each group session. The single-session time frame dictates that inpatient group therapists strive for efficiency. They have no time to build the group, no time to let things develop, no time for gradual working through. Whatever they are going to do, they must do in one session, and they must do it quickly.

These considerations demand a *high level of activity*—far higher than is common or appropriate in long-term outpatient group psychotherapy. Inpatient group therapists must structure and activate the group; they must call on members; they must actively support members; they must interact personally with patients. There is no place in inpatient group therapy for the passive, inactive therapist.

Structure

Nor is there a place in inpatient group psychotherapy for the nondirective leader! Many outpatient group therapists prefer to provide relatively little structure to the procedure of therapy; instead, one permits the group members to search for their own direction, and one studies the varying responses of the group members to the ambiguity of the therapy situation. But, as we have seen, the time frame of the inpatient group therapist does not permit this luxury.

The outpatient group therapist also can depend upon a stable group membership to provide a durable norm skeleton for the group. But, as I also have discussed, the inpatient group therapist cannot depend on that source of structure; instead, the therapist himself must provide a norm structure.

Furthermore, the nature of the psychopathology confronting the inpatient group psychotherapist demands structure. The vast majority of patients on an inpatient unit are confused, frightened, and disorganized; they crave and require some externally imposed structure. The last thing a confused patient needs is to be thrust into an enigmatic, anxiety-provoking situation. Numerous clinical observers have noted that confused patients feel deeply threatened by being placed on wards that themselves appear confused.

Keep in mind the experience of a confused patient who enters a psychiatric unit for the first time: he or she is surrounded by large numbers of deeply troubled, irrationally behaving patients; the new patient's mental acuity may be obtunded by medication; he or she is introduced to a bewilderingly large staff whose specific roles are often undifferentiated; because many staff members are wearing street clothes, the new patient may confuse them with patients; furthermore, since the staff is often on a complex rotating schedule, the patient's sense of external constancy becomes even further eroded.

An externally imposed structure is the first step to a sense of internal structure. A patient's anxiety is relieved when he or she perceives a clear external structure and is provided with some clear, firm expectations for his or her own behavior.

Modes of Structure

Group leaders provide structure for the group by delineating clear spatial and temporal boundaries; by adopting a lucid, decisive, but flexible personal style; by providing an explicit orientation and preparation for the patient; and by developing a consistent, coherent group procedure.

Spatial and Temporal Boundaries   Consistent, well-delineated spatial boundaries beget a sense of inner stability. It is important that the group meet in a room of appropriate size—a room that provides comfort but is not cavernous. I prefer to meet in a room that is largely filled by the group circle. It is exceptionally important that the group meet in a clearly delineated space, *preferably in a room that has a closed door.* Because of space limitations, many groups have to meet in a very large general activity room or in a hallway without clear demarcation. It is my experience that such settings place these groups at a considerable disadvantage, and it is preferable to find a room off the ward than to meet in a space whose boundaries are incomplete or unclear.

The ideal seating arrangement for the group is a circle. Therapists should avoid a seating arrangement in which any member of the group cannot see every other member (for example, three or four patients sitting in a row on a long couch). Such an arrangement will invariably discourage the member-to-member interaction so vital to the therapy group and will, instead, encourage the patients to address the therapist rather than each other.

The therapist should endeavor to have as few interruptions in the group's time as possible. All late arrivals and premature departures of members during a meeting should be discouraged. In the ideal situation, of course, all members are present at the beginning of the meeting, and there are no interruptions whatsoever until its conclusion. Debriefing interviews with patients make it clear that patients invariably resent interruptions caused by latecomers. The therapist must model promptness and be on time for each meeting. The more disorganized patients will often need reminding and escort service into the room. If patients are napping, the staff should awaken them at least ten to fifteen minutes prior to the meeting.

In higher level groups I have, for many years, preferred a policy of not permitting latecomers (regardless of their excuse) to enter the session. Once the door is closed, the group space is inviolable. Naturally some resentment is experienced by members who come three or four minutes late and are not allowed to enter, but the advantages far outweigh the disadvantages. The therapist demonstrates to the patients that he or she values the group's time and wishes to make maximal use of it. The great majority of the group members will appreciate the decision not to allow latecomers to enter, and the patient denied entrance will sulk briefly but invariably be prompt the following day.

It is also desirable that the members of the meeting not leave early. Dealing with early "bolters" is more complex than dealing with latecomers, since highly anxious patients (especially those with claustrophobic tendencies) are likely to become more anxious if they perceive that they will not be permitted to leave the room. Therefore, the therapist is well advised simply to express the hope that members can stay the full meeting. The therapist who, before a meeting starts, sees any clearly hyperactive and agitated patients should inquire whether they feel able to sit in the group for the duration of the meeting. If the answer is no, the therapist may suggest that they not attend the group that day but, instead, return the next day when they feel more settled. In lower level groups patients may frequently have to leave early but should be supported for the time they have been able to remain in the group.

A prompt ending of the group is rarely problematic, since space demands on most inpatient units are heavy, and the room is usually needed for some other activity. On the whole, this limitation is for the good. Occasionally the end of a session may find the group in the midst of a crucial issue which absolutely demands that the session be extended for a few minutes. Generally, however, a prompt ending is as important as a prompt beginning to create a sense of consistent structure for the patients.

Personal Style   The therapist's style of communication greatly contributes to the amount of structure the group provides to patients. Acutely troubled, frightened, and confused patients are reassured by a therapist who is firm, explicit, and decisive yet who, at the same time, shares with them the reasons for his or her actions.

In inpatient groups it is almost invariably an error for therapists to be as nondirective in the face of some major, disruptive event as they might be in an outpatient group. Patients are too frightened, too much in crisis, too highly stressed to be able to deal effectively with such events. They are reassured and experience the group environment as immeasurably safer if the therapist is able to act firmly and decisively in such instances. If, for example, a manic patient is veering out of control, nothing is to be gained by allowing the patient to continue on that course: he or she will not feel better as a result of the runaway behavior, and the rest of the group will feel irritated at the patient and cheated of their therapy time. The therapist's stance must be firm and decisive. You may suggest to the manic patient that it is time to be quiet and to work on learning to listen to others; or if the patient has insufficient inner control, you may have to ask the patient to leave the group.

Patients will be much relieved by such firm intervention by the therapist. Occasionally some patients might feel concerned or threatened by a therapist's decisive behavior; but this response is often ameliorated by a process discussion of the incident and of the therapist's response. Often it is good modeling for the therapist to comment on any of his or her own contradictory feelings. For example, you may comment on having felt uncomfortable at silencing a patient and concerned about having thereby possibly hurt that patient, but mention also your strong feeling that it was the best thing to do for the patient and for the group. It is often advisable to solicit feedback from the group. Do the group members feel you are being too strict or too stern? Do they feel you as rejecting? Do they have some relief when you intervene?

Therapists must feel assured that they have a coherent, cognitive framework for the group's goals and procedures—a framework and an assurance that they convey to the patients. It is not feasible or clinically useful to be explicit about every benefit of the group format: some therapeutic mechanisms are rendered less effective if made absolutely explicit (such as the raising of self-esteem by group acceptance). Furthermore, some therapeutic factors (such as altruism and universality) require a degree of spontaneity and are less effective if explicitly orchestrated. Nonetheless, there are many benefits of the group that can be lucidly described. The leader who shares, in an understandable way, the theoretical rationale underlying his or her actions, not only provides useful structure to the patients but also enlists them as allies in the therapeutic work.

Patients who have developed a clear picture of the group goals and of the task necessary to approach them are more likely to invest themselves in the work of therapy. Research corroborates that patients report high levels of satisfaction with a group session if they feel that the meeting dealt with important, relevant issues and progressed toward clearly formulated goals.

Orientation and Preparation   The first minutes of the group provide an opportunity for the therapist to create considerable structure for the session. The therapist provides an official beginning to the group and launches the meeting on its way. It is a time to introduce, orient, and prepare the new members for group therapy. Even if there are no new members, it is a time nonetheless to restate briefly the goals of the group and its procedure. The provision of external structure, as I have stressed, promotes the acquisition of internal structure; and the beginning of the group is the place to begin building that structure. If observers are viewing the group, the therapist should always so inform the patients at the very outset of the meeting.

A typical orientation in a higher level group session where a new member is present might begin with addressing the new member thus:

"John, I'm Irv Yalom,* and this is the afternoon therapy group which meets daily for one hour and fifteen minutes beginning at two o'-clock. My co-therapist is ————, and she will be here four of the five

---

*There is great variation around the country about how patients and therapists address one another. In the informal climate of California, most group patients and therapists address one another by first name.

meetings for the next four weeks. On the fifth day another psychiatric nurse will take her place. The purpose of this group is to help members to understand their problems better and to learn more about the way they communicate and relate to others. People come into the hospital with many different kinds of important problems, but one thing that most individuals have in common here is some unhappiness about the way that some of their important relationships are going. There are, of course, many other important problems that people have, but those are best worked on in some of your other forms of therapy. What groups do best of all is to help people understand more about their relationships with others. One of the ways that we will try to work on relationships is to focus on them in this group and especially to focus on the relationships that may go on between people in this room. The better your communication becomes with each of the people here, the better will your communication become with people in your outside life.

"It's important to know that observers are present almost every day to watch the group through this one-way mirror. [I point toward the mirror and also toward the microphone, in an attempt to orient the patient as clearly as possible to his spatial surroundings.] The observers will usually be medical students or other members of the ward staff. No one else will be allowed to observe the group without my checking that out with you before the group starts.

"We begin our meetings by going around the group and checking with each person and asking each to say something about the kinds of problems they're having in their lives that they'd like to try to work on in the group. After the go-round we then try to work on as many of these problems as possible. In the last ten minutes of the group, we stop our discussion and check in with everyone here about how they feel about the meeting and about the kinds of leftover feelings that should be looked at before the group ends."

Such an introduction serves a number of functions: it provides some temporal, spatial, and procedural structure; it breaks the ice of the meeting; it serves as a formal beginning; and it also constitutes a brief preparation for group psychotherapy.

Group Therapy Preparation   A compelling body of research literature demonstrates that if the patient is systematically prepared by the therapist for group therapy, then the patient's course in the therapy process will be facilitated. In long-term outpatient therapy groups, it is standard practice for therapists to prepare a patient for the impending group therapy experience in individual session(s) prior to the patient's entry into the group.

In the hustle and bustle of inpatient work, there is no time for the luxury of lengthy preparation. Consequently, group therapists have to prepare patients for group therapy in any way possible during the brief time available. It is often advisable for the therapist to share the task of preparation and orientation with some of the members. The therapist may, for example, ask one of the older members to tell the new member(s) about the purpose and procedure of the group. The therapist then may ask some of the other patients whether there are any additional points they want to contribute; and if the therapist feels there are still some points that have not been stated, he or she can then state them. This approach increases not only the participation of members but also their tendency to experience the meeting and the procedure of the meeting as their own rather than something that is imposed upon them.

Patients who come from the lower socioeconomic levels of society, and are unsophisticated about psychotherapy, particularly profit from an intensive preparation. A researcher systematically prepared such patients admitted to an acute psychiatric ward and compared their progress in the therapy group with similar patients who were not systematically prepared. Data from the first five group sessions demonstrated that the prepared patients worked much more effectively: they volunteered more, communicated more frequently, engaged in self-exploration more frequently, initiated more statements in the group.

One important function of the preparation is that it helps to eliminate discrepancies in expectations between therapists and patients. A study of patient and staff expectations on one inpatient ward demonstrated that patients expected that the staff would approve of their seeking advice, whereas the staff hoped instead for more self-direction on the part of the patients. Such a discrepancy between the patients' and the staff's expectations will invariably breed confusion and impede the formation of a therapeutic alliance. It is absolutely essential in short-term therapy that patients be given explicit procedural directions.

Explicit preparation for the group also reduces the patients' apprehension and makes it more possible for them to participate in the group without crippling anxiety. It is to be expected that patients will be anxious in a therapy group. Individuals with lifelong disabilities in interpersonal relationships will invariably be stressed by a therapy session that urges them to discuss their relationships to others with great candor. Most concur that a certain degree of anxiety is necessary for therapeutic growth; anxiety increases vigilance and motivation to work in the group. But too much anxiety freezes the group work. Primary anxiety—the anxiety stemming from a patient's psychological disorder—will be an inevitable accompaniment of group work, and there is little the leader can do to ameliorate it in the initial stages of the session. But the leader can do a great deal to prevent secondary anxiety—anxiety that stems from the patient's being thrown into an ambiguous therapy situation.

A Consistent, Coherent Group Procedure   Clarity and structure are so important that many clinicians prefer highly structured, explicitly programmed groups. One ward has instituted a procedure in which patients go through a series of "step groups," each of which is designed to teach a specific set of behavioral skills. For example, the most elementary group emphasizes good eye contact, learning to listen and understand others, and so on. The next step teaches patients to ask open-ended questions, to make questions into statements, to reflect feelings. The next step teaches learning to give and accept feedback, and to self-disclose. Clinicians using such programs report that they are far more effective than unstructured groups. My impression is that a heavily structured approach is particularly indicated for groups of more poorly functioning patients.

Structure is as important to a therapist as it is to the patients. Leading a group is anxiety provoking. The therapist is exposed to many powerful and often primitive emotions. There are many patients vying for the leader's sole attention; and the leader will inevitably disappoint and frustrate some of them, who may then respond angrily and ungratefully. Group therapy with psychotic patients particularly is intrinsically anxiety provoking. The work is slow, often unrewarding, and generally perplexing. Furthermore, group therapists are exposed. No secret therapy sessions behind closed doors for them: their work is painfully visible to large numbers of people.

One of the fabled definitions of psychotherapy is attributed to Harry

Stack Sullivan: "A situation in which two people meet together, one of whom is less anxious than the other." The therapist who falls prey to these many sources of anxiety may violate Sullivan's law, become more anxious than the patient, and, by definition, cease to be therapeutically effective.

Ambiguity is as anxiety provoking for the therapist as for the patient, and the therapist's chief defense against the anxiety intrinsic to the practice of psychotherapy is the sense of structure provided by a therapeutic model. It is less important *which* model than that there *be* a model. By developing a cognitive framework that permits an ordering of all the inchoate events of therapy, the therapist experiences a sense of inner order and mastery—a sense that, if deeply felt, is automatically conveyed to patients and generates in them a corresponding sense of clarity and mastery.

Are there any disadvantages in providing structure? Indeed, there are! Providing too much structure is as harmful as providing too little. Although patients desire and require considerable structuring by the therapist, excessive structure may retard their therapeutic growth. If the leader does everything for patients, they will do too little for themselves. Thus, in the early stages of therapy, structure provides reassurance to the frightened and confused patient; but persistent and rigid structure, over the long run, can infantilize the patient and delay assumption of autonomy.

Thus, group leaders face a dilemma. On the one hand, they must provide structure; but, on the other hand, they must not provide so much structure that patients will not learn to use their own resources. The basic task of the therapist is to *augment the advantages* of structuring the group and to *minimize the disadvantages*. There is a solution to this dilemma—*the leader must structure the group in a fashion that facilitates each patient's autonomous functioning.*

Support

Short-term hospitalization is effective only if it is coupled with effective aftercare therapy. One of the major goals of the inpatient therapy group program is to increase the desire in patients to continue therapy after they have left the hospital. In fact, if the therapy group does nothing else but encourage the patient to pursue post-hospital psychotherapy, especially group psychotherapy, it will have been an effective intervention.

Thus, it is imperative that patients perceive the therapy group as a positive, supportive experience, one that they will wish to continue in the future. The therapist must create in the group an atmosphere that is perceived as constructive, warm, and supportive. Patients must feel safe in the group. They must learn to trust the group. They must experience the group as a place where they will be heard, accepted, and understood.

The inpatient therapy group is not the place for confrontations, criticism, or the expression and examination of anger. There is considerable clinical consensus that, if the inpatient therapy group is to accomplish its goals, these sentiments must be avoided. There will be patients who may need a certain degree of confrontation. For example, sociopathic or manipulative individuals do not often profit from a therapeutic approach that is continuously supportive and empathic; but it is far better that the group therapist "miss" these patients than run the risk of making the group feel unsafe to the majority of patients.

A vast body of research literature demonstrates conclusively that, both in individual and in group therapy, positive outcome is positively correlated with a supportive and empathic relationship with the therapist.

Not only does considerable empirical evidence support the importance of a positive, nonjudgmental, accepting therapist-patient relationship, but there are numerous retrospective views of psychotherapy in which patients underscore the importance of a therapist's liking them, valuing them, and noticing and reinforcing their positive characteristics.

In a therapy group situation, the therapist's personal support takes on an added dimension. Not only does the therapist interact with his or her own person upon each of the members of the group, but the therapist's actions shape the norms (the code, or the unwritten rules) that influence how all the members behave. Therapists create norms in many ways: they explicitly set certain rules, they reinforce certain types of behavior in the group and extinguish others (either through explicit disagreement or discouragement or implicitly by inattention to certain types of comment). But one of the most important modes through which therapists shape the norms of the group is through their own behavior upon which patients pattern themselves.

Despite the enormously important role that "support" plays in the ultimate outcome of psychotherapy, relatively little attention is given to it in conceptualizations of psychotherapy or in training programs. Support is often taken for granted; it may be considered superficial; it is often assumed that "of course" therapists will be supportive to their patients. Many therapists conclude that support is equivalent to paying compliments, and that such a simple act hardly needs any detailed discussion in therapy training.

Support is *not* something that therapists "of course" provide. As a matter of fact, many intensive training programs in psychotherapy unwittingly extinguish the therapist's natural proclivities to support the patient. Therapists become pathology sniffers—experts in the detection of weaknesses. In extreme form this tendency results in the therapist's regarding positive qualities with suspicion: kindness, generosity, diligence, moral responsibility—all may be approached in a reductionistic fashion and be interpreted as psychopathology. Furthermore, therapists are so sensitized to transferential and countertransferential issues that they hold themselves back from engaging in basically human supportive behavior with their patients. I remember vividly a heated discussion I heard twenty years ago in an analytic conference about the pros and cons of the therapist's helping a patient (an old lady) on and off with her overcoat! Therefore, learning how to give support in inpatient group therapy often entails a degree of "unlearning" of professionally taught postures and attitudes toward patients which obstruct the therapist's natural human inclinations to provide support.

The Higher Level Inpatient Therapy Group: A Working Model

Higher level groups are the most complex of the inpatient groups to lead and require that the leader be trained in basic group therapy techniques. In this section I will describe one possible structure for a higher level group. Keep in mind that this structure augments, but is not a replacement for, fundamental training in group therapy. The group may be led either by a single therapist or by co-therapists. The co-therapy format makes the group less demanding for the therapists, provides an excellent medium for training neophyte therapists by pairing one with an experienced therapist, and often is more fun for therapists. By no means, however, is the co-therapy model a requirement; the group can be led effectively by a single competent therapist.

One basic blueprint of a seventy-five-minute session is:

1. Orientation and preparation	3 to 5 minutes
2. Agenda go-round (each member formulates a personal agenda for that meeting)	20 to 30 minutes
3. Work on the agendas (the group attempts to "fill" as many agendas as possible)	20 to 35 minutes
4. Therapists' and observers' discussion of the meetings (if there are observers behind a one-way mirror, they enter the room and, together with the therapist, discuss the group in front of the patients)	10 minutes
5. The patients' response to the summary discussion	10 minutes*

Orientation and Preparation

Earlier I presented a detailed illustrative example of the initial statement that the therapist makes for each session. If there are new patients present, as there usually are, the orientation must be more detailed than if one is simply reminding the more experienced members of the basic structure and purpose of the group.

The basic plan of the opening statement is to provide a basic orientation to the members, then to describe the purpose of the group, and finally, to clarify the procedure that the group will follow.

In the *basic orientation statement,* the therapist reminds the patient about the time of the meeting, about its length, and about the presence

---

*Only the first two phases of the blueprint are covered here. For a more exhaustive discussion, please refer to my book *Inpatient Group Psychotherapy* (New York: Basic Books, 1983).

of observers, if any, and may review some basic ground rules of the group (for example, the necessity of arriving punctually or rules about smoking).

The *purpose of the group* must be presented to each patient in extremely lucid terms. New members are always anxious and often confused, and the therapist cannot err in the direction of being too coherent and too explicit. As the sample introduction indicates, the therapist makes a short statement about the importance of working on relationships with other people and asserts that the investigation and improvement of interpersonal relationships is what groups can do best and will be the focus of this group. Furthermore, the therapist lets it be known that the group will be able to be most effective by helping people understand as much as they can about the relationships they have toward one another in the room.

The therapist then outlines the *basic procedure* of the group, describing briefly the five phases of the group I have just described and being especially careful to inform new members of the presence of observers in the room or behind the mirror who, toward the end of the session, will discuss the meeting with the leader(s). The therapist then sets the stage for the next step by commenting that each session begins with a *go-round,* in which the therapist touches base with each person, asking what he or she would like to work on in the group that day. The work must be appropriate and able to be achieved in the therapy group time.

This short statement about the agenda leaves new patients very perplexed and often anxious. The therapist does well simply to reassure them and to let them know it is the therapist's job to help each person formulate an agenda and that the group will begin by letting the new patients participate last.

The Agenda Go-Round

It is important to launch a meeting with some structured vehicle that permits the therapist to make some contact, however brief, with each member in the group. In groups with a stable composition—for example, long-term outpatient groups—the therapist has considerable information at his or her disposal about each of the members of the group and generally requires only a short time to determine the point of urgency for a particular group session. In the rapid change of the inpatient group, the therapist is often confronted with individuals about whom he or she has little information. A structured "go-round" allows the therapist to scan the group quickly, to make contact with each person in the room, and to obtain a bird's-eye view of the work possible for the group that day.

Furthermore, a structured exercise at the onset of an inpatient meeting conveys a clear message to each patient that activity and participation by each is expected. If the therapist allows the group to start on its own, there will almost invariably be a period of silence, confusion, icebreaking ritualistic comments, and casting about for some useful or convenient topic for conversation.

What type of initial structured go-round is preferable? Many options exist. The most obvious one, used by many group leaders, is to ask each patient to describe briefly why he or she is in the hospital. It may be argued that this form of go-round is a "no-nonsense" approach, since it focuses directly upon the life crisis and the ensuing decompensation that brought the patient into the hospital.

But there are many disadvantages in such an opening gambit. For one thing, a patient's perceived reasons for entering the hospital are often several steps removed from the work one can do in a therapy group. Patients may be in the hospital because of substance abuse or because of some external event (for example, the loss of a job, the malfeasance of another, the loss of a lover) or because of some other externalized complaint (for example, a psychosomatic ailment, ideas of reference, or hallucinations) or because of some primary biological disturbance (such as major affective disturbances). To concentrate on these reasons for admission emphasizes the then-and-there and makes it more difficult for patients to use the resources of the group. Often the reasons for hospitalization are complex, and not infrequently most of a session may be consumed in an investigation of the admission stories of the new members. Furthermore, it becomes repetitious for older members to continue to restate their reasons for entering.

Another commonly used initial go-round is for the therapist simply to ask each patient to state something about the way he or she is feeling that day. This tack accomplishes the task of touching base with each patient and obtaining a sense of the overall emotional state of the members of the group, but it often steers the group into a cul-de-sac: it neither provides a blueprint for the remainder of the meeting nor orients patients toward the changing of dysphoric feelings.

In my opinion, a highly effective way of beginning a meeting is to ask each patient to formulate a brief personal agenda for the meeting. The agenda identifies some area in which the patient desires change. The agenda is most effective if it is both realistic and doable in the group meeting that day. I urge the members to formulate an agenda that focuses on interpersonal issues and, if possible, on those that in some way relate to one or more members of the group meeting in that session.

The very best agendas are those that reflect some issue that is of core importance to the individual's functioning, that is interpersonal in nature and may be worked on in the here-and-now of the group. Some examples of agendas that lead to useful, effective work in the group:

1: "My problem is trust. I feel if I open up and be honest about myself, other people, especially men, will ridicule me. I feel that way, for example, about Mike and John [two other members of the group that day]."

2: "I feel like other people consider me a nuisance. I think I talk too much and want to find out if that's true."

3: "I put up a wall around myself. I want to approach others and make friends, but I'm shy. Consequently, I stay alone in my room all day. I feel I have some common interest with Joe and Helen [two other members], but I'm scared to death to talk to them."

Later in this discussion of the agenda go-round I will give many other examples of agendas; but, for the moment, consider these three. Each deals with a concern that is central to the individual speaking. (Note, however, that in none of these three instances was the problem stated in the agenda the actual precipitating cause for hospitalization. The first patient was an anorexic; the second, a young alcoholic; and the third had made a serious suicide attempt.) Furthermore, each of these three agendas expressed an interpersonal concern. Last, each had a here-and-now component: that is, each concern could be examined in the context of that patient's relationship with others in the group that day.

The Advantages of the Agenda Go-Round

The major advantage of the agenda exercise is that it offers the therapist an ideal solution to the dilemma of having either too much structure or too little. The exercise provides a structure for the meeting but simultaneously encourages patients to assume autonomous behavior. Each patient is urged to say, in effect, "Here is what I want to change about myself. Here is what I choose to work on today."

The agenda provides the leader with a wide-angle-lens view of the group work that can be done that day. He or she quickly makes an appraisal of which patient wants to do what type of work and which goals intersect with the goals of others. Furthermore, the agenda serves the function of initiating interaction between members.

The agenda encourages patients to assume a more active posture in psychotherapy. Often the agenda exercise is exceptionally useful in their ongoing therapy once they leave the hospital. Patients are encouraged to state their needs explicitly and straightforwardly—a particularly therapeutic exercise for those patients who habitually ask for help in indirect and self-destructive ways—for example, through self-mutilation or other self-destructive acts. (As I shall emphasize later, not all agendas can or will be filled or even addressed during the meeting; but for many patients, the formulation—not the completion—of the agenda is the key therapeutic task.) The agenda task teaches patients to ask explicitly for something for themselves. It helps them understand what therapy can do and their responsibility for using or not using therapy. They realize very clearly—and this is a point I shall discuss at length—that if they formulate an inadequate agenda, they are unlikely to profit from the meeting.

Helping Patients to Formulate Their Agendas

The formulation of an agenda is not an effortless, automatic task. Patients do not do it easily, and the therapist must devote considerable effort to help them in this task.

For one thing, the great majority of patients have considerable difficulty understanding precisely *what* the therapist wants and *why*. The task must be explained to patients simply and lucidly. The therapist may give examples of possible agendas and painstakingly help each member shape his or her own. The therapist must also explain to patients *why* he or she wants an agenda by stating the advantages of the agenda format.

Agenda formation requires three steps, and the therapist must escort most patients, especially in their first meeting, through each of the three steps:

1: The patient must identify some important personal aspect that he or she wishes to change. Moreover, the task must be realistic; that is, the aspect must be amenable to change and appropriate for a therapy group approach.

2: The patient must attempt to shape his or her complaint into interpersonal terms.

3: The patient must transform that interpersonal complaint into one that has here-and-now ramifications.

These remarks about agenda shaping may be made clearer by clinical illustrations.

Consider a meeting in which a new woman member offers as her agenda item: "I'm depressed and what I want to work on in this group is getting over my depression." This agenda will lead to no useful work in the group. First of all, it is unrealistic. The time frame for the agenda must be *a single meeting;* that is, the agenda must refer to a task that can be accomplished in one session. This particular patient had been depressed for years; how could a single therapy group meeting possibly alleviate that depression? Furthermore, the agenda is too vague; it is not specific and not consonant with the explicit activities of the group. Groups cannot work on "depression": there is no toehold; it is interpersonal problems, not symptoms, that constitute the currency of dynamic psychotherapy.

When helping a patient transform an unrealistic agenda, such as this one, into an appropriate working agenda, it is important to acknowledge the importance of the patient's agenda. After all, in this patient's experience it *is* her depression that is the key reason for her being in the hospital. But the therapist must help the patient to obtain a more realistic perspective on the therapy of the depression. For example, one might say, "Being depressed is the pits, and of course you want to feel better. That's *the* goal, and a very appropriate goal, for your entire course of therapy. To alleviate your depression, however, weeks, even months, of therapy will be required. The important task for today is, How to begin? What can you work on in this group now? What groups can do best is to help people understand what goes wrong in their relationships with one another. What would you like to change in the way that you live with or relate to other people? Your relationships to people, in a way that may not yet be clear to you, are closely related to your depression. If you will begin to work on your ways of relating to others, I feel strongly that ultimately, not in a day, you will begin to experience much less pain in your life."

The therapist must acknowledge the patient's distress but try to place it in the perspective of the work of the group. Thus, the therapist might say, "This must feel devastating to you. I can see how the pain of what has happened must dwarf everything else in your mind now and make it hard to pay attention to other things. But distressing as your loss of job and the problems of finding another must be, I do not see how the group can specifically help you with that. It sounds like an issue you could best work on in your individual therapy or in your work with a vocational counselor or an occupational therapist. Let's see how *this* group could help you. What could you work on here that might be helpful to you?"

Most likely the patient will insist that he wants to work on the job loss or might conclude that there is nothing the group can offer him. The therapist's task at this time is to search for some interpersonal component of the patient's problems. In such a situation I begin to sift silently through a number of interpersonal hunches: "Does this man's interpersonal style have anything to do with his losing his job? Or perhaps his obsequious, self-denigrating manner creates obstacles in applying for and obtaining another job. He doesn't seem to acknowledge his pain. I wonder what he does to get help for his feelings of distress. Does he ever get any support from others? Can he ask for help? Who helps him? He seems very down on himself. I wonder what it feels like for him to tell us about his failure. I wonder if there's someone in the group he feels especially ashamed to tell."

By investigating some of these interpersonal leads, the therapist can generally help a patient relinquish an unrealistic agenda and arrive at one appropriate to the group.

In this clinical example, Harvey, a paranoid schizophrenic crop duster, was admitted to the hospital because of his bizarre, self-destructive behavior. He claimed that his only problem was vertigo (not a good thing for a crop duster to have!), and declined to participate in the agenda task. His admission to the psychiatric ward was a mistake, Harvey claimed; he belonged on a medical ward.

The therapist responded, "It's unfortunate that you were admitted to the wrong ward. But as long as you're here, why not take advantage of what we've got to offer? You know, I often consider this ward a postgraduate course in self-discovery. There are dozens of expensive courses in the community in self-exploration or personal growth. You can never learn too much about yourself. All of us keep learning and growing. We've got expert instructors in this group. You're paying for it anyway, it's all gravy. Why not take advantage of the opportunity?"

Harvey was disarmed by this approach. He opined that it made good sense, and stated that he guessed he could work on why people so often accused him of lecturing to them.

By using such strategic approaches, the therapist is able, without too much difficulty, to help shape each patient's agenda into interpersonal language. The interpersonal agendas vary widely, but the great majority are expressed in one of the following formulations:

1. I'm lonely; there is no one in my life.

2. I want to communicate better with people.

3. I want to be able to express my feelings and not hold everything inside.

4. I want to be able to assert myself, to say no, and not to feel overpowered by others.

5. I want to be able to get closer to others and to make friends.

6. I want to be able to trust others, I've been hurt so often in my life.

7. I want some feedback about how I come across to others.

8. I want to be able to express my anger.

Transforming the Interpersonal Agenda into a Here-and-Now Agenda

Recall that the agenda task consists of three steps: (1) identification of a personal area that the patient wishes to change; (2) transformation of the complaint into interpersonal terms; (3) statement of the agenda in here-and-now terms.

The list of agendas I have just cited satisfied the first two criteria. The therapist has one remaining task: *to help members transform these general interpersonal agendas into specific agendas involving other members of the group.*

Once this basic principle is grasped, the technical work is straightforward. Let us reconsider each of the eight agendas I have listed and examine some approaches the therapist may take to shape them into here-and-now agendas.

1. I'm lonely; there is no one in my life.

"Can you think and talk about the way you are lonely here in the hospital? From whom have you cut yourself off in this group? Perhaps a good agenda might be to try to find out how and why you've made yourself lonely here."

2. I want to communicate better with people.

"With whom in this room is your communication good? With whom is it not entirely satisfactory? With whom here in this room would you like to improve your communication? Is there some 'unfinished business' between yourself and anyone else in this group?"

3. I want to be able to express my feelings and not hold everything inside.

"Would you be willing to express the feelings you have here in the group today as they occur? For example, I wonder if you'd be willing to describe some feelings you've had toward an issue or some person so far today as we've been going around the room doing these agenda go-rounds?"

4. I want to be able to assert myself, to say no, and not to feel overpowered by others.

"Would you be willing to try that today? Would you try to say one thing that you'd ordinarily suppress? Would you select the people in the group today that most overwhelm you, and see if you might be able to explore some of your feelings about that? Would you like to ask something for yourself? How much time would you like for yourself later in the group today?"

5. I want to be able to get closer to others and to make friends.

"With whom here in this room would you like to get closer? I wonder whether a useful agenda might not be to try and explore what keeps you away from trying to get close to these people. Would you try some different way of approaching them today? Would you like feedback from them on how you create distance?"

6. I want to be able to trust others, I've been hurt so often in my life.

"Would you try to explore that with members of this group? Who in this room do you particularly trust? Why? What is there about them? Which people in the room might seem somewhat difficult for you to trust? Why? What is there about them? What do you have to fear from anyone here in this group? In which ways do I threaten you? What do you have to fear from me?"

7. I want some feedback about how I come across to others.

"Why do you want the feedback? [Try to tie it in with some important aspect of the patient's problems with living.] What aspect of yourself would you like some feedback about? From whom here in the room do you especially want some feedback today?"

8. I want to be able to express my anger.

Work on this particular agenda is delicate. It is advisable to steer clear, so far as possible, of overt conflict in the group. One approach to such an agenda is as follows: "Expressing anger is scary to an awful lot of people and it may be too much to try and express a lot of anger here in the group. However, one problem that many people have with anger is that they let it build up inside of them until the sheer amount of it gets to be very frightening. Perhaps one way you might be able to work on it here is to try and let some of the negative feelings out while they're still in a stage of slight irritation or annoyance, before they build up to real anger. I wonder, then, if you would try in the group today to express slighter feelings of annoyance or irritation just as you first perceive them to be forming. For example, would you be willing to talk about some annoyance that you've had with me or with the way I've been leading the group thus far today? Would it be all right with you if I were to check back with you at other points during the group today to see what annoyance you've experienced?"

The therapist's responses to each of these agendas are designed to guide the patient into here-and-now exploration. Each response represents, of course, only one of many possible interventions; and each therapist must construct a repertoire of interventions that are consonant with his or her personal style. Let us consider general strategies upon which specific techniques must rest.

Help Guide Patients from the General to the Specific   Help the members be exceedingly specific with their complaints and with their feelings toward other people. Interact with others. Address others explicitly and by name. Once a member is specific and names someone else (for example, "I want to get closer to Mary, but I feel put off by her"), then the stage is well set for the next phase of the meeting because almost certainly Mary's interest will be kindled, and she will inquire of that patient at some point in the meeting, "What do I do that puts you off?"

Be Gentle but Persistent   Nag the patients. Encourage, cajole, persuade them to formulate a workable agenda. This may be mildly irritating to them, but in the long run it has a high yield. Repeatedly, in debriefing research interviews, patients commented that, though they may have been annoyed during a meeting, they ultimately appreciated the persistence of the therapist. It is necessary to be gentle with patients who are having a difficult time understanding the task. Supply agendas for them, if necessary, in their first meeting or two. Avoid any comments that might injure sensitive feelings.

One useful technique to decrease a patient's irritation is to allow him or her to monitor the procedure. Check in with the patient and ask, on more than one occasion, "Am I nagging you too much?" Or, "Am I pressing you too hard?" Thus you allow the patient to have a sense of controlling the interaction and of being able to terminate it when he or she really wishes to.

Help Patients Differentiate One Another   One of the most common modes of resistance to interacting with others is the reluctance to differentiate one person from another. Thus, a woman patient may say she feels isolated in life and yet will decline to differentiate the group members sufficiently to say that she feels slightly closer to one person than to another. As true interpersonal exploration and all the ensuing interpersonal learning cannot really begin until individuals start to differentiate one from the other, it is important to stress this task. The therapist may underscore the problem and comment that the failure to differentiate between people is another way of staying distant and unengaged—precisely the patterns patients are trying to change.

Strive for Some Commitment   Even a very small commitment in the agenda statement provides important therapeutic leverage. For example, if one patient comments that he or she is intimidated by others, obtain a commitment from this patient to name some of the people who most and least intimidate him or her in the group. Or, if one patient states an agenda of wanting to learn to express feelings, then attempt to extract a commitment from that patient to express in this meeting at least one or two feelings that he or she usually suppresses. Or, if one patient frames an agenda of wanting to learn how to ask for things for herself, then attempt to extract a commitment that that patient will ask for some specified amount of time (even three or four minutes) for herself in the group that day. Or, if one says that he wants to reveal more of himself, obtain a commitment to disclose some personal data that the group has not known before. Each of these commitments represents "credit" in the bank upon which the therapist can draw later in the session.

Be Positive and Constructive   Do not foment conflict in the group. In the agenda go-round, therapists help to avoid conflict and facilitate the development of a trusting, constructive atmosphere by starting with positive feelings. If, for example, if a patient states that his problem centers on being unable to feel close to others, then the therapist best facilitates investigation of this area by beginning the exploration of the positive side of the spectrum. Ask, for example, "With whom do you feel most close in the group?" or, "With whom is your communication good?" Once safety has been established, you can gently move to the more problematic areas with such questions as: "With whom do you experience some blocks in communication?" The general strategy consists of starting on the far side of anger and cautiously inching up on it until you find an optimal area for therapeutic work.

Transform Resistance into Agenda Work   Not infrequently patients will seem unalterably resistant to the agenda task. They may be too depressed, too demoralized, or too convinced that they cannot change and would be better off dead. In such instances, it is always important to locate and ally oneself with the healthy part of the patient, the part that wants to live. One of the advantages of making the higher level group optional is that the therapist can always assume that the part of the patient that decided to come to the group that day is striving for growth.

The agenda go-round may be construed as an exercise in helping individuals to get their needs met. By accentuating that aspect of the agenda, the therapist circumvents resistance and forges a therapeutic alliance. Exhortations to "ask for something for yourself," "get your own needs met," "be more selfish," or "learn to value yourself and take care of yourself more" are basically highly supportive to the patient. They all suggest that the therapist feels strongly that the patient is worthwhile and deserving of care and attention. Therefore, agenda pressure by the therapist need not evoke defensiveness. Rarely will patients object to being considered too selfless, too unselfish, or too giving. Nor will patients take umbrage at a therapist who exhorts them to ask for more for themselves.

Occasionally the resistance stems from problems in the therapeutic relationship. For example, a patient may resist the agenda task as part of his or her overall struggle to defeat the therapist. Such trends are relatively easy to determine and generally will be reflected in the patient's posture toward many therapeutic activities in the ward. If the conflict is considerable, you may first have to clarify the patient-therapist relationship. The therapist is, you may point out, easy to defeat, but the patient's is a Pyrrhic victory: its losses far outweigh its gains. Why be an adversary? After all, you, the therapist, are there to help. Why and whence the conflict?

"Final Product" Agendas: Clinical Examples

Fully formed agendas vary widely in detail, general content, and form; and it is neither possible nor necessary to present an exhaustive list of them. Representative agendas drawn from group meetings may, however, illustrate the texture of a workable agenda:

1: "Rick talked about being gay in the group yesterday, and I have a lot of feelings about that which I didn't share."

2: "Would you [addressing the men in the group] still talk to me and care about me if I didn't have my eye makeup on?"

3: "I've been annoyed about Steve's [another member of the group] 'hyper' behavior. I'm afraid that I hurt his feelings when I mentioned it this morning."

4: "I want to know how my rocking affects everyone in the group."

5: "I've been told I'm not real. Yesterday you two [pointing out two members of the group] said you could take me for one of the staff. I want to find out what that's all about."

6: "I've got to find out why I'm so scared to talk in groups, especially in front of people [designating three members] my own age."

7: "In a group this morning someone told me that I blend into the woodwork. Is that the way you see me, too? If so, I want to work on that."

8: "I want to be able to deal with my anger toward the men in the group."

9: "I need to learn how to talk about my sexual feelings in front of other people."

10: "People think I'm weird because I'm phobic about touching anything. I felt really bad about being laughed at yesterday for playing cards with gloves on. I want to explain to everyone what it's like to have these kinds of fears."

11: "I said some crazy things in the community meeting this morning and I'm very upset about having talked like that. What do you all here feel about me after this morning?"

12: "I want to know whether there's something about me or the way I behave that would make a man want to rape me."

These are "final product" agendas. They have been fully processed and shaped by the therapist and are far different from what patients started out with. For example, the last three agendas were offered by patients who had each been in the group for over twelve meetings. Each agenda is the product of considerable therapeutic evolution. The last agenda was formulated by a patient who, during her first several meetings, declined to talk at all about the fact that she had been raped. Finally, after learning to trust the group and hearing other patients talk about having been sexually assaulted, she was willing to discuss that and, only with much therapeutic work, was able finally in this agenda item to confront the possibility that she, *unlike most rape victims,* may unwittingly have played some significant role in what had happened to her.

Resistance to the Agenda Task: Responsibility Assumption

Earlier I remarked that forming an agenda is difficult for patients simply on a cognitive level. Many patients have difficulty comprehending the relevance and the mechanics of the task, and thus far I have concentrated on methods the therapist can use to help overcome these cognitive difficulties. But there is a second reason that patients find the agenda task troublesome; this reason has deeper roots and offers a more obstinate impediment to therapy. The very nature of the agenda task reaches deep into many patients' psychopathology and evokes fierce resistance. Thus, despite the most lucid instructions, some patients may be unable to comprehend the task, refuse to engage in it, develop considerable anxiety during it, or, for reasons that are unclear to them, be angry at the entire exercise.

In order to formulate a coherent strategy to overcome this resistance, the therapist requires some understanding of its source. At both a conscious and an unconscious level, patients balk at the agenda because the task confronts them with "responsibility." The therapist who is to understand fully the nature of the resistance must understand the concept of responsibility—the subtext of the agenda task.

Responsibility refers to "authorship." To be aware of one's responsibility means to be aware of creating one's own self, destiny, life predicament, feelings, and, if such be the case, one's own suffering.

The individual avoids facing responsibility because awareness of one's responsibility is deeply frightening. Consider its implications. If it is true that it is we, ourselves, who give the world significance, who create, through our own choices, our lives and our destinies, if it is true that there are no external references whatsoever and that there is no grand design in the universe, then it is also true that the world is not always as it had seemed to us. Instead of a world design around us and solid ground beneath us, we have to face the utter loneliness of self-creation and the terror of groundlessness.

There are many clinical modes that patients use to avoid knowledge of responsibility: one may displace responsibility for one's life upon others through externalization, placing the blame for what has gone wrong upon some external figure or force; one may deny responsibility by considering oneself as an "innocent victim" of events that one has oneself (unwittingly) set into motion; one may deny responsibility by being temporarily "out of one's mind"; one may avoid autonomous behavior and choice in different ways; one may behave in a way that elicits "taking over" behavior from others; one may develop a compulsive disorder in which one experiences one's actions as out of one's control.

An important initial step in the therapy of patients with all of these clinical disorders is to help them appreciate the individual's role in creating his or her own distress. In fact, if a patient will not accept such responsibility and persists in blaming others, either other individuals or other forces, for his or her dysphoria, no effective therapy is possible. Consequently, responsibility assumption is a crucial first step in therapy, but it is a step that meets much resistance: at an unconscious level, the patient resists responsibility awareness because of anxiety about groundlessness that invariably accompanies full awareness of responsibility.

There is another source of anxiety in responsibility assumption. If patients become aware that they are responsible for their current life predicaments, they also veer close to appreciating the extent to which they have been responsible for the course of their past lives as well. For many patients that awareness incurs considerable pain: as one looks back upon the wreckage of one's life, upon all one's unfulfilled potential, all of the possibilities never examined or taken, then one becomes flooded with guilt—not guilt in its traditional sense, which is related to what one has done to others, but guilt from an existential sense, which refers to what one has done to one's own life.

Thus, the simple act of forming an agenda is not so simple after all; it confronts patients with issues that have roots steeped in anxiety, roots reaching down to the very foundations of their existence. Consider the steps a patient must take in the proper formation of the agenda.

Realizing That There Is Something about Oneself One Must Change

It is an extraordinarily important step for a patient to realize that there is something about himself or herself that he or she must change. Indeed, for some patients who externalize to an extensive degree, it is an entirely sufficient goal of the acute inpatient psychotherapy group. Patients who regard their problems as "out there"—that is, unfair treatment by employers, abandonment by a treacherous mate, or victimization by fate—cannot begin the change process until they come to terms with their own personal role in their life predicament. Otherwise, why change? It would make more sense for therapy to be directed toward changing not oneself but the offending other party. As long as patients remain in an externalizing mode, the psychological help that they can accept is limited to such modes as commiseration, support, problem solving, advice, and suggestions.

Hospitalized patients who externalize considerably constitute a relatively large percentage of the inpatient population. They represent such diverse clinical entities as psychophysiological disorders, paranoid disorders, involuntarily hospitalization, and substance abuse.

Identifying Some Specific Aspect of Oneself
One Would Like to Change

The identification of some specific piece of work is an important focusing task for each patient. Many patients are so demoralized and so
overwhelmed by the shambles of their lives that they despair of change.
To force oneself to identify a starting point, to commit oneself to a discrete task, often inspires hope and combats confusion.

Communicating One's Wishes to Others

It is an exceedingly important step for patients to learn to communicate their wishes to others, and one that addresses a very important facet
of many patients' psychopathology. It brings home to them that others
cannot read their mind; that others cannot know their wishes automatically; that they have to state their wishes aloud or those wishes will
never be known, much less gratified.

The awareness that one must communicate one's wishes is important because it leads to the insight (distasteful though it may be) that we
are truly alone, that there is no omniscient servant looking over us, that
we will not change unless we change ourselves. The agenda format
brings this insight home via another route as well: patients, after attending many meetings, gradually comprehend that, if they do not formulate an agenda, they will derive little benefit from the meeting. After
even a couple of meetings, patients know perfectly well what type of
agenda gets attention and results in effective work. At some level of
awareness, the agenda initiates an internal dialogue in which patients
are forced to come to grips with their unwillingness to change.

Agenda work with a depressed woman patient illustrates some of
these issues. She felt defeated and self-contemptuous and stated the following agenda: "I feel like an absolute failure. Today what I want from
the group is simply support. I need lots of strokes from people."

The therapist urged her to stretch farther: "What kind of strokes
would you like? What would you like to hear them say to you?"

Now, of course, this line of questioning is highly irritating. It's annoying to be required to state what positive things one wants people to
say to one spontaneously. The patient's reply reflected exasperation. She
snapped, "If I have to tell them what to say, then it doesn't count!"

Yet at another level it counts very much that the patient not only expressed her pain but identified precisely what would make her feel better. This is a giant stride on the road to learning how to become her own mother and father—and, for this patient as for a substantial number of others, that is the major goal of psychotherapy.

Agenda Formation: The Completion of the Task

There is tremendous variation in the types of agenda formulated by members. The agendas are a function of many factors, including the composition of the group that day, its stability, and its size. If the group is relatively stable, and all the members present have formulated agendas in previous meetings, the agenda go-round may be completed quickly. By no means does this indicate that the members will use the same agenda every day. Occasionally an individual will work on the same agenda for several days in a row, but generally agendas will change to some degree: an individual may change focus because of the presence of different members in the group or because the previous day's work opened up different vistas. If there are many new members in a meeting, the agenda go-round will consume much more time. If the group is large, less time will have to be spent on each agenda.

A well-conducted agenda go-round results in a banquet of clinical material which should launch the group into productive use of the remaining time. Consider the following meeting of nine patients:

In approximately twenty-five minutes, an energetic, supportive therapist helped the members formulate these "finished" agendas:

1: "I was a battered child. I've got a lot of feelings about that I haven't worked out. I've never talked about that with other people, and I would like the group to try and help me talk about it."

2: "I have some unfinished business with you [the group leader] left over from yesterday's meeting, and I'd like to talk about that today."

3: "I've got to learn how to identify my feelings. I think I've got to do it alone, but I want to try to talk about feelings that come up during the meeting."

4: "I've got to learn how to take more risks with others and assert myself more, especially with the other men here."

5: "I'm feeling very vulnerable and hurt, and I want to work on that in the group. I'd like to be able to tell all the people in the group about all the various ways I hurt."

6: "I've got some strong feelings about a conversation I had earlier with Mike [another patient in the group] this morning, and I'd like to try to work on those."

7: "I don't have the energy to state an agenda today." The therapist pressed her by asking a question that is usually effective: "If you were to have the energy to state an agenda, what do you think it would be?" The patient went on to say, "I think I'd like to ask for feedback from the other people in the group, especially from the men, since I usually seem to antagonize men for some reason."

8: "I want to talk about the feelings I have about my physical appearance. It's got to do with my size. I'm so big and tall that everyone seems to feel they can lean on me for help."

9: A new patient: "I'm in the hospital because my psychiatrist [a woman] left town for a few weeks. I'm in love with her and I want to marry her, and I'd like to work on that in the group." The therapist inquired about how the group could help him, because, after all, his psychiatrist wasn't present in the group. Was it possible to work on something more relevant to the group? The patient then stated that he was developing somewhat similar feelings toward one of the women in the group and perhaps he could talk about those feelings.

With this beginning the therapist should have no difficulty leading a rich and productive group meeting. There is so much material that therapists must focus their energy on addressing as many agendas as possible.

PART 2

GROUP THERAPY WITH PATIENTS ADDICTED TO ALCOHOL

The group treatment of alcoholics is daunting. Traditional group approaches have long proven so ineffective that most professional group leaders have abandoned attempts to lead such groups. Obviously, a highly specialized approach is required for this population. The following article describes my attempt to employ a disciplined group interactional approach with alcoholics. It is a tricky matter to use a here-and-now approach with alcoholic patients: the intensity of the focus invariably arouses anxiety, and alcoholics often respond to anxiety by turning back to alcohol. Consequently, it was necessary—and this is the heart of the article—to develop a series of techniques that would diminish anxiety but still permit the group to maintain an interactional focus. Some of these techniques, for example, writing a candid summary of the session and mailing it to the members before the next meeting, proved so useful that I incorporated them into my work with many other types of groups. "Group Therapy and Alcoholism" has had a long, active life and has been reprinted and distributed numerous times to classes of alcoholic counselors.

Group Therapy and Alcoholism

(excerpted from *An. of the N.Y. Acad. of Sciences*, 233:85–103, 1974)

I have occasionally attempted to treat alcoholics in therapy groups composed of patients with a wide variety of problems, and like most group therapists, I have ended up discouraged, resolving each time to leave alcoholics to Alcoholics Anonymous. Recently, however, with the encouragement of the National Institute of Alcohol Abuse and Alcoholism, I decided to make a very earnest attempt to apply my group skills to the therapy of alcoholic patients. Although there is a vast literature on the treatment of alcoholics in groups, there have been few, if any, systematic attempts to utilize dynamic interactional group therapy methods with alcoholic patients. In this paper I shall describe my efforts to apply some basic principles of interactional group therapy to the treatment of the alcoholic patient.

I planned to conduct the alcoholic therapy group as a complement to and not a substitute for Alcoholics Anonymous. The task of the therapy group, as I conceptualized it, was not to help individuals attain sobriety but to help them work through the underlying personality conflicts that produce the alcoholic compulsion. I specifically planned to focus on the interpersonal pathology that underlies all maladaptive behavior, including alcoholism. The group's task was to help members overcome feelings of self-contempt, loneliness, alienation, and disengagement; to understand and alter abrasive, maladaptive, self-defeating styles of self-presentation; and to help members involve themselves meaningfully in the peopled world.

Structure of the Group

The Initial Interview   The usual purpose of individual interviews before a patient begins group therapy is twofold: first, the therapist attempts to arrive at a decision as to whether a specific patient is a suitable candidate for group therapy in general and for the specific group the therapist is leading. Second, he attempts to prepare the patient for the group therapy experience which lies ahead. My co-therapist and I had decided in advance to accept all comers, and therefore made no effort to screen patients. Indeed, we suspended our ordinary clinical judgment and accepted some patients whom we would never have considered suitable for a therapy group.

There is ample evidence to indicate that proper pregroup orientation leads to greater patient satisfaction, increased group cohesiveness, and an increased level of interpersonal exploration. We attempted to make the initial interview the beginning of therapy both by conveying to the patient that it was his responsibility to decide what changes he would like to make in himself, as well as by modeling the honesty and candor that we expected of everyone in the group. For example, I told them quite openly that I had had a great deal of experience in group therapy but relatively little experience with alcoholic patients. Since the group experience would benefit both the patients and myself, there was to be a two-way contract. I would provide what group therapy skills I had, while they would enlighten me on the problems of alcoholism. My co-therapist, who was a professionally trained therapist as well as a recovered alcoholic and an active AA member, helped enormously to bridge the gap between the alcoholic patients and myself, the nonalcoholic professional.

We interviewed and accepted eight patients. Three of the patients had long-term sobriety (from one to three years); two had shorter term sobriety (from four to twelve months); one patient had sobriety for only about one month; and two patients were actively drinking. One patient, who was desperately ill and drinking very heavily, came to a single meeting. He was replaced in three to four weeks by another member, who was also an active drinker. At the beginning of their group experience, all but three members were actively involved in AA. As the group progressed the other members began to participate occasionally in AA.

Certain important issues arose during the initial interviews. These may be most clearly illustrated by briefly presenting two examples:

Ken, a 50-year-old divorced musician, had been sober for two years after having been an extremely heavy drinker for the previous five. He was an exceedingly active member of AA, attending approximately five meetings a week and totally orienting his very limited social life around AA. He had considerable difficulty in formulating any goals for himself in therapy, insisting that he had achieved considerable tranquillity and comfort in the life he had shaped for himself. He insisted that he desired no personal changes and had no urgent problems upon which he wanted to work. We suspected that he viewed this group as one more AA-like meeting to fill his lonely life. We would never have accepted Ken for an ordinary therapy group: his level of denial was extraordinarily high, but seemed to be an effective defense. We doubted whether we could offer him anything better than his defense mechanisms, which apparently provided him with unshakable tranquillity. We worried too that without this mechanism of denial, Ken might sink into a serious depression; yet it was not possible to engage Ken in serious therapeutic work without undermining denial. My co-therapist's immediate response to me was "Leave him be. Let's not rock this boat." We decided to express these concerns quite candidly to Ken and warn him that, were he to go into the group, he might experience more discomfort than he had for years.

Another, quite different problem was personified by Donna. Donna had had several years of sobriety and was an active, militant AA member. Her career goal was to become a professional counselor for alcoholics. We distrusted her reasons for entering the group. She stated that she wanted to learn something about professional psychotherapeutic methods which would be helpful to her in her work, but she also explicitly stated that she hated psychiatrists and psychologists and regarded us in many ways as "murderers" of alcoholics. This sentiment was so strong that I had good reason to believe she wanted to come into the group to act as a type of policeman or watchdog to protect the other patients from me. When I insisted that she describe some area in which she wished to change, she evaded me by the rather ingenious ploy of stating that her chief problem was her extreme distrust of professionals. Perhaps, she said, through her work in the group, she might be able to overcome this mistrust. I had a strong sense of being conned, but I squelched my doubts and decided, on an experimental basis, to accept her also. Ultimately this proved unwise: she attended approximately eight or nine sessions and then finally left the group. Not only was she unbenefited, but she clearly fettered the group by parroting AA slogans, refusing to reveal herself, and constantly challenging and undermining the therapists. It was only afterwards that we found out that one of her chief reasons for continuing in the group was her strong sexual feelings toward one of the other members, whom she had known previously in AA.

Another patient, Bill, not only was actively drinking but was in a stage of severe deterioration (had no money, no home) and was approaching some serious physical complications of his drinking. Again, we had little hope of helping Bill in the group, but I had hoped that after starting him in the group we might be able to steer him into AA. He was much too sick, however, attended only one meeting, and shortly thereafter was hospitalized by his physician.

The other patients had a wide range of problems: low self-esteem, loneliness, depression, inability to find work, and a constant struggle with the desire to drink. Many were extremely nonintrospective, conceptualized their problems concretely, and expected advice or solutions from other members and especially from the therapists. They were removed from their feelings, denying, circumstantial, fragile, dependent, restricted interpersonally, and unable to deal with the feelings that were aroused during the meeting. Perhaps I would have considered only one or two at most of the eight patients as suitable for the typical outpatient groups operating in our clinic. It was truly a challenge of the first magnitude.

The early meetings were so labored, tense, and circumstantial that I used them as contrast groups for my group therapy students. By observing and contrasting the alcohol therapy group and an outpatient neurotic therapy group, they could arrive at a clearer picture of honest interpersonal exploration and a dedicated here-and-now orientation. However, by the sixteenth meeting the alcoholic group had changed so much that this type of comparison was no longer possible. The group became intense, hard working, and interactional. I could not possibly have imagined at the onset that this group would have progressed to such a level in the short space of fifteen meetings. Let me now describe some of the methods by which this transformation occurred.

Strategy and Tactics of the Group Leader   Many of the techniques that I used in this group were similar to those that I use in all my group therapy. However, because of the very unusual types of problems presented by this group of alcoholic patients, a number of very specific interventional techniques were required, which I shall describe in context.

We structured the initial session much more than usual by suggesting that the members go around the room and discuss aloud their therapeutic contract, that is, the goals that each of them had in therapy. From the very first moment of the life of the group, we began to guide members in a variety of ways to interact directly with other members of the group and to explore these interactions. For example, I pointed out to one member that he was speaking to Ken but looking at me, and I suggested that the group members look directly at one another when they speak. I pointed out that when one member would speak to Dave he would impersonalize the transaction by avoiding the second person pronoun "you" and referring to him instead by name or by the third person pronoun. We tried to direct members into an immediate focus, reiterating our belief that the group as a whole could not fully appreciate issues and persons outside the group, despite their crucial importance for individual group members. We urged them to talk about how they felt toward the people within the group. A typical question: "Ted, to whom do you feel closest in the group, to whom do you feel most distant?" It is best always to word questions in as nonthreatening a way as possible. For example, I do not ask the members of the group whom they dislike most of all but instead inquire about those aspects of each person they find it most difficult to accept. We focus at first on more positive aspects of their relationships. We are relentless in noting when the group seems to be moving away from the here-and-now.

The leader should strive to transfer the responsibility of the content and direction of the meetings onto the members. In other words the therapist should aim to help the group become self-monitoring. If they discuss some abstract, intellectualized issue, it generally doesn't take very long to observe that many of the members are not so intensely involved as they are when speaking about themselves. In these situations I usually ask certain people about their reactions at that specific moment; how do they feel about what's happening in the group? Generally some members will comment that they feel less engaged at that moment than previously. I try to help them understand which material seems to be most relevant and important for them. One method of doing this is via videotape playback. Each meeting was videotaped and began with a ten-minute playback of important segments of the previous meeting. We ask the group to identify which sections of the meeting seem to be most involved or most important and what sections are least so.

Whenever there is the slightest hint that members of the group are being talked about, it is my reflex as a leader to help the members be specific, to name names. For example, the group was discussing the fact that Bill, an intoxicated member present in the first meeting, was quite disruptive. One of the members said she didn't mind a drunk in the group; in fact she felt the group needed a disruptive influence because things were ordinarily too peaceful and kind in the group. My response at this point was to ask her, "Who in this room are the ringleaders of the peace and calm movement?" When she mentioned two members, the others agreed that these two were always kind and understanding, and that at times it was difficult to know if they ever had negative feelings.

As early as the fifth meeting, the self-monitoring process began to take hold. By that time, when a member indicated he wanted to talk about an article he had read in the newspaper that he considered relevant to his condition, members in the group started to chuckle at his penchant for moving things away from a personal level, and they effectively prevented him from distancing the group.

It is important for the leader to supply cognitive bridges for the members so that they appreciate the rationale of the here-and-now orientation. In this particular instance one of the members asked why we wanted him to show anger. What good does destructive behavior ever do? He described the cruelty of his father, how he was brutalized as a child, and how he decided early to eliminate anger from his life. We provided a cognitive bridge by recalling for him that his original goals in the group consisted largely of his desire to be able to assert himself and to prevent others from exploiting him. We noted that he avoided any type of anger to the point that any form of self-assertive behavior was stifled. He did not accept this interpretation and responded with, "Well, may I ask you a question then?" I immediately pointed out that he was repeating the pattern: Why, of all the people in the group, was it only he who had to ask permission to ask a question? It was quite obvious that everyone was free to say what he or she wished in the group. He then became annoyed with me and said that he was not sure he could trust me and demanded to know what was in this for me. I responded openly by telling him about my desire to help the members of the group while learning more about alcoholism, and I confessed to enjoying certain benefits from a government grant on alcoholism. I also let him know that as a result of his confronting me, I felt closer to him; his approaching me, even in anger, had decreased the distance between us.

Another example of here-and-now training: One member was silent and obviously uncomfortable in a meeting. She had, since the group began, found it very hard to share personal feelings in the group. When I asked her about her present state of mind, she said, as she always did, that she was experiencing some diffuse apprehension and anxiety. Usually this ended the discussion, but in one meeting we escorted her into the here-and-now by saying, "Joan, I know that you're experiencing your fear now as generalized and diffuse, but let us help you make it more specific. If you were going to be afraid of anyone in the group, who would it be? Who in the group frightens you the most or has the most potential for frightening?" This soon moved Joan into an extremely important area for her, that is, her fear of the therapist and of one of the other members who, because of previous group therapy experience, appeared more sophisticated than the others. Joan was enabled to discuss her great investment of pride in her intellect and her desperate fear of looking stupid, of saying the wrong thing, and of being judged adversely.

At one point, Ted, who was extremely impersonal and "intellectualized," commented that he really didn't know Sally very well. My response at this juncture was to ask, "Ted, could you try to think of a question which you could ask Sally that might help you know her better or feel closer to her?" Thus, in a number of ways we gradually made it clear to the members that the group was an experimental society—a society which had a time-limited but deep intimacy, and furthermore a society which dispensed with the normal rules of social etiquette and encouraged members to ask questions of one another that they would never dream of asking in conventional social intercourse.

Another member's problems were demonstrated by his behavior during the sessions. He was always left out of the group and would never ask for help for himself, and consequently the therapists found themselves searching for ways to give him the floor. When we asked about his past or his current life crises, he could discuss these problems but would not personally relate to anyone in the group. When he described how his domineering mother and sister ruled his life, we attempted to relate this to the present session by asking, "Of all the women in the group, who could you imagine dominating you like your mother or your sister?" By helping him to interact in this manner with other members, we brought his past and his outside world to life within the group. We were careful to reinforce him or other members making their first forays into the here-and-now by such direct statements as "that sounds good" or "it's good to hear you be so direct."

Obviously we are asking something quite different of the members than is requested by AA, which not only does not encourage direct interaction but implicitly discourages it. Our relationship to AA, then, is a complex one; we encourage joint membership, yet we work on very different operational models. Indeed, we expend much effort helping members unlearn the ritualized AA models of group interaction.

The Group Dilemma   The first half-dozen meetings were spent in this interactional training procedure. During this phase the group moved relatively slowly and the members required considerable explicit training. Additional factors impeded the pace of the group. For example, the group was unlike the typical outpatient therapy group in that an unceasing staccato of crises seemed to be beating on the door. At almost every meeting some member was facing an important life crisis. One patient lost his business and considered filing for bankruptcy; another was fired from her job; another was enmeshed in a complicated, explosive, extramarital affair; two had episodes of extreme marital discord, and another patient's brother died suddenly. The drinking members each went on a binge, during which they phoned to report they were too ill to come to the meeting; we urged them to attend, but they were so distracted and tremulous they could scarcely contain themselves. Almost every meeting began with a crisis report, and the therapists grew concerned by the evolving group norm, which predicated that a member could ask for the group's attention only if he had a major crisis to present; indeed some members seemed forced into silence by this informal rule. The therapists dealt with this development vigorously by commenting explicitly on what was happening in the group and by facing the members with the decision of whether they wanted a crisis intervention group, whether they wished to forgo other kinds of work, and whether they wished members not in crisis to remain silent about moderate nondramatic discomfort.

After considerable evolution the group gradually assumed a work-oriented posture. By the twelfth meeting, however, another major development occurred; it became very clear that the group was facing a difficult dilemma, which can best be appreciated in this description of a pivotal meeting.

In the two or three previous meetings, one member, Arlene, had become increasingly hostile and dominating. She began to shut out other members, became competitive with one of the therapists, and on a number of occasions presented such long monologues about her personal difficulties that she consumed 50 percent of the group time. In the last meeting she was "working" (as a therapist) with one of the members on some traumatic events in that member's past. When a couple of the men tried to contribute to the discussion, she cut them both off and made it explicit that she considered their contributions to be irrelevant and unhelpful. In the week between meetings, one of these men, Ken (the member who professed tranquillity and a two-year sobriety before the group began), called to say he had decided to leave the group. He had been feeling consistently "uptight" since the last meeting when he had been put down by Arlene, and he felt he had nothing to offer to anyone in the group; for the first time in two years he was experiencing the type of discomfort that in the past had led to drinking. He said that he simply couldn't afford to have that degree of anxiety; he wasn't going to permit the group to push him into alcohol. Ted, the other man who had been attacked by Arlene, was similarly affected and stated that he had been terribly anxious all week long and that if he ever went home from the group feeling like that again, he would never return. Another member's sister called to say that he had been out on a binge, and when we called him, he said that he was too shaky and too ill to return to the group the next week. We encouraged him and Ken to return. In that particular meeting, the two men, with the help of the therapists, faced the source of their anxiety, that is, their anger toward Arlene and her extreme hostility toward them. They did this with much trepidation since both of them were individuals who found it extraordinarily difficult to express anger. After an extremely tempestuous meeting, the two men felt better, but Arlene went home and for the first time in approximately six weeks she began drinking again. When she reported this to the group the next week, the two men were overwhelmed with guilt at having been responsible for Arlene's drinking, and so things went.

This sequence of events was enough to make the therapists realize the group had reached a crisis point and required some drastic intervention. We decided to change our tactics and to move into a much more structured format, which I shall describe shortly. It became clear that we had the option of leaving certain members with their pregroup defenses of avoidance, suppression, and denial, which provided tranquillity but resulted in a massive restriction of intrapersonal and interpersonal exploration, or of helping them move into a self-exploratory posture, which would disturb tranquillity and possibly even cause "eruptions" of drinking, but which might permit them to attain a richer life. This dilemma posed itself more starkly for the AA members than for the drinking non-AA members, who had so little stability that their psychological risk was not as great. As the tension level rose in the group, we were forced to find a number of different ways to moderate the amount of anxiety present. I believe that conflict and anxiety are absolutely essential if change is to occur in the group therapeutic process. The dilemma, however, is that the alcoholic patients in the group are capable of tolerating only small degrees of anxiety before resorting to old, well-ingrained patterns of anxiety relief, especially alcohol and avoidance (leaving the group).

Anxiety-Reducing Tactics

The group had a dual attitude toward the professional leader: both distrust for the nonalcoholic professional and extreme dependency. I decided to make use of this attitude by imposing considerable structure on the group. It was my long-term strategy to build into the structure a method by which they could recognize and alter some of their unrealistic expectations of the leader.

Agenda   In a number of ways the therapists began to provide more explicit leadership. We started the particular crisis meeting that I have just described by putting an agenda on the blackboard and telling the group that, regardless of whatever else we discussed that day, we considered it imperative to cover these issues: (1) Ken's anxiety and his desire to leave the group; (2) Ted's similar anxiety; (3) Arlene's anger and domination of the group and the response this generated in other members; (4) Sally's recent alcoholic lapse and the persistent avoidance of this subject by the rest of the group; (5) the competition between Arlene and the co-therapist.

For the next several months we began every session in a similar fashion. As the group moved on to a new level of functioning, the need for an agenda became less; however, without question it proved to be an extremely valuable structuring technique during the time of crisis. Examples of agenda items from other meetings were: leftover feelings from the last meeting between X and Y; the death of one member's brother, which he had not been willing to discuss in the group; secrets shared by some members in extragroup meetings; the tendency of the group members not to ask a specific member about his current drinking; undiscussed sexual feelings; and the leader's concerns that the previous meeting had been too rough on a certain person.

Didactic Instruction   A structuring device which we used with considerable success was an occasional didactic interlude. We began to go to the blackboard once or twice during a meeting to clarify in diagrammatic form some aspect of the dynamics that were occurring in the group. For example, I sketched out the series of interactions beginning with Arlene's castigation of Ken and Ted, which resulted in their anger at her, which quickly changed into anxiety and then into a desire to leave the group. With our prompting, this anger and anxiety was expressed but resulted in Arlene's resumption of drinking, which then resulted in even greater anxiety and guilt on their part. The clarification of this sequence helped them to understand the dilemma more clearly and helped Arlene understand the bind in which she placed Ken and Ted. We tried to pose alternatives; for example, Ken had two traditional ways of dealing with anxiety—to relieve the anxiety by drinking or to avoid anger- and anxiety-provoking incidents by withdrawal. Although the second method, the one he had been using for the past couple of years, operated satisfactorily, he paid a rather heavy price for his avoidance; the price was isolation, since he increasingly tended to avoid intimate relationships with other people lest they led to discomfort. We then suggested an alternative for Ken: to face, even temporarily, the anger and to express it under the tempered, optimal conditions in the group.

On another occasion Allen, who had good reason to be annoyed with Ted, said to him, "I understand your feelings; three years ago I was in the same place ... " At that point several members grinned and we stopped Allen by asking whether he knew why they had grinned. In response to his bafflement, the therapists sketched out Allen's interaction on the blackboard, noting that he transmitted, at the same time, two opposing messages. The first message was one of concern; he was genuinely trying to be helpful to the other. The second, and the one that prompted the grinning, was "You're three years behind me," or "I'm better and significantly more mature than you."

Another diagram related to intrapersonal functioning. One member of the group described the despair she felt when sober: during those periods she would become more aware of all the things that she was not doing in life, and she would grow increasingly hateful of herself. When we explored the expectations she had for herself, it was quite obvious that they were extraordinarily unrealistic. She wanted to make major social changes in the structure of the country, acts that have been impossible even for a Cabinet officer. I diagrammed Karen Horney's schema of the real and the idealized selves and underscored the extensive "shoulds" she placed on herself. Her idealized image was a highly unrealistic and unattainable one, and yet whenever she noted the discrepancy between what she was and what she demanded she should be, she responded with self-hatred. In the past she responded by turning to alcohol (which blunted her awareness of the discrepancy between her real and idealized selves) to attempt to diminish the pain of self-intolerance caused by placing tyrannical demands upon herself. We suggested that another method might be to explore and to reappraise the highly unrealistic nature of her idealized image. It turned out that this same schema was applicable to several of the other members. A caveat: the therapist must not confuse the means with the end. The means is simply to reduce anxiety by providing some type of cognitive structuring so the patient may participate, without crippling anxiety, in the intensive group experience and benefit from one or several of the mechanisms of change described above. Too often zealots of any specific system take it too seriously, forget the universal mechanisms of change, and expend their energy on converting patients to their conceptual framework.

Summaries for Patients   The most successful method we found to modulate the anxiety of the group was the dictated summary. After each group therapy meeting, it is my practice to dictate an extremely detailed summary of the meeting for my own research interests. When the alcohol therapy group appeared to be going into crisis, I decided on a form of feedback that I have never attempted before (and to the best of my knowledge has not been reported by other group therapists). I decided to use a special summary, similar but not identical to my own summary, which I then distributed to the patients before the next meeting. For the first couple of weeks, the patients came fifteen to twenty minutes early to read the summary immediately before the session. They soon began to value the summary so much that they asked to receive it earlier in the week to have more time to digest it; I then began mailing the summary approximately three to four days before the meeting. The general structure of the summary is a three- to five-page double-spaced narrative of the meeting. I tried to present an objective account of the meeting and to review each person's contributions to it.

The summary gives therapists a medium to convey an enormous amount of information to the patients. They can make editorial comments or present feelings or opinions about events in the group. These may be restatements of comments they made in the group, observations that they did not feel it timely to report during the meeting, or afterthoughts. The summary may be used to reinforce certain kinds of behavior. For example, when Ken expressed anger in the group, we pointed out how pleased we and the other members were to see him express himself so freely. We often expressed our concern over specific events: for example, after one meeting that had been particularly upsetting for one of the members, we wondered in the summary if he would choose to miss the next meeting or even terminate therapy. Such predictions were usually reassuring and often prevented impulsive antitherapeutic decisions. We supported individuals in need of support. For example, Arlene, who came under considerable attack for her abrasiveness, was praised in the summary for her risk taking, which, although soliciting much anger, was nonetheless very helpful to the group; if everyone could be as honest as Arlene, we pointed out, the group would move more quickly. The summary made explicit certain important implicit themes, such as the members' reluctance to ask Wayne whether or not he was still drinking, because of their sensitivity to his intense shame. We pointed out the dilemma for the group: that they did not wish to embarrass or threaten Wayne, but that if they continued to protect him, they would isolate him and prevent him from benefiting from the group.

We attempted to increase cohesiveness by indicating in the summary similarities between members of the group. We made guesses why certain silent members were blocking. We openly discussed some of the dilemmas we as therapists faced, such as the group dilemma, that is, that although it was necessary for conflict to develop, we were distressed when members confessed they were driven to the point of wanting to take a drink. We repeated some of the more didactic interpretations made in the meeting so the members would have time to assimilate them the second time around. We wondered whether or not certain people were being ignored. We expressed our concern about people who were not present at the meeting. We wondered about the previously good relationship between two members, which seemed to be going sour. We attempted to take some of the sting out of attacks on certain members. We tried to present some of the interpretations in a lighthearted way so that they could be more easily accepted.

There are times when we hesitate to make an interpretation to a patient during a particular session because he seems so fragile; however, we find it feasible to make the interpretation in the summary, where we speak openly of the reasons for having avoided the issue during the meeting. For example, when Arlene (who had been drinking during the week and was very shaky) made an effort to clarify exactly what she had said the previous week but did so by once again cutting off the other members and taking up too much time, we felt it would have been poor timing to point this out in the group. However, the summary provided an excellent opportunity to make that kind of statement. Our written formulations increased the security of the members, convincing them that someone really knew what was going on in the meeting; someone appeared to be in charge of this seemingly runaway wild beast of a group. By specifying which of the meetings or sections of meetings we considered good or poor, we used the summaries to help the group learn to monitor itself.

An important use of the summary was to help the members of the group view the leaders more realistically. I talked about my feelings of helplessness when certain members expected me to be able to see through everything and to provide a near-magical solution. As the meetings progressed, I gradually became more self-disclosing in the summary. For example, when discussing how the group was dealing with the concept of assuming responsibility for themselves, I noted that this is a stance difficult for anyone, certainly for myself, to assume completely. I disclosed my uneasiness in feeling that I am the only one heard when in fact there are others who are making equally helpful comments. I acknowledged how choked up and helpless I felt when one of the members was talking about her own personal crisis. Gradually it came about that the summaries for the patients resembled more closely the summaries I dictated for myself and my co-workers. This, of course, is a reflection of increased therapist self-disclosure. In a sense, then, the summary represents a rather subtle technique for dealing with a dependent group. It provides the therapist an opportunity to satisfy dependency needs and yet at the same time avoid infantilization of the group. He uses the group's overvaluation of him to plunge them into a more autonomous, independent form of group structure. After we started to use these structures, there were no further complaints about therapists who remained mysterious, did not answer questions, or never explained things to patients. At the same time the patients were increasingly able to challenge the therapists. Furthermore, the summaries helped patients assume the self-reflection that is so important for the interactional group therapy experience.

We have had considerable patient testimony about the value of the summaries. Members appreciated the work spent in preparing them, and some would reread them several times during the week. Members brought the summaries to the meeting to discuss parts they didn't fully understand or agree with. On a number of occasions members began the meeting by following up issues or hunches expressed in the summary.

Video Playback   Video playback is a structuring technique that, like others described earlier, has the potential to reduce anxiety. Every meeting was videotaped, and we started the following meeting by showing portions of the previous week's interaction. We tried several different formats. At times we played a section of the tape that we considered particularly important and then asked people to discuss what they were feeling but not saying during that session. At other times we would play particularly significant sections in which some patient was behaving in a way that we wished to reinforce. Or we played a section of the tape that we thought might help a patient view himself more accurately. At other times we selected a few sections (a total of approximately 15 minutes) and played them at the start of the meeting, without inviting comment from any of the patients during the playing. We never found an ideal format and, compared to the dictated summaries, the video playback provided only a modest amount of help for the group. It is an expensive procedure and may create distraction if the cameras or cameramen are visible or noisy.

An example of a constructive use of the playback occurred during a meeting when Mary was extremely upset about a turbulent love affair. When pressed by the group, she began to cry and suddenly ran out, not to return until the following week. Next meeting, we viewed the scene of her running away and the group's discussion of her after she had left. She had exited because of shame at her tears; she was convinced people would consider her stupid or silly for crying and even more so for running out of the meeting. It was a potent and constructive experience for her to observe herself and the other members discussing her after she had left. She was surprised and moved by their understanding and empathy. Another member who had probably been drinking spoke with noticeably slurred speech during a meeting, yet no one felt comfortable enough to comment upon it. We played that section back in the group and wondered what they were hearing then and what had prevented them from being honest with one another earlier. On a couple of occasions members came to view the whole tape of a meeting that they had missed so they could stay abreast of the group. One member, Arlene, came in on two occasions to review an entire meeting so that she would get a clearer idea of her behavior that had aroused so much antagonism.

Special Problems

Subgrouping Subgrouping, or extragroup socializing, may complicate the process of any therapy group, and is especially problematic in the group therapy of alcoholic patients. Most group therapists attempt either to discourage patients from meeting outside the group or to make it as clear as possible that it is important for patients to share with the rest of the group significant information obtained outside the group about other members. If such information is not shared it is likely that important subgroups will form, which may defeat the purpose of the primary therapy group.

Two basic principles provide useful guidelines. The first is that a subgroup can either strengthen or weaken the primary group, depending upon the subgroup's function and its norms. If the function of the subgroup overlaps that of the primary group and the norms conflict with the primary group norms, then it will weaken the larger group and be a disintegrative influence.

The second principle is that there is a distinction between primary task and secondary gratification in psychotherapy. The primary task in therapy is the fulfillment of the patient's implicit or explicit goals, such as relief of anguish and change of behavior. Secondary gratifications, of course, occur in all therapy formats, but they are especially marked in group therapy and may take many forms. For example, there is an inherent pleasure which derives from being dominant or influential, popular or admired, helpful to the others, or favored by the therapist. When the secondary gain becomes so marked that the patient loses sight of the primary task, then therapeutic work comes to a standstill and it is incumbent upon the therapist to intervene appropriately.

The members of the alcoholic group had an enormous amount of extragroup contact. They saw one another frequently at AA meetings or AA social functions. Some of the members had had a long-term relationship with one another before entering the group. A couple of them had sponsored other members of the group during their first contacts with AA. They regularly met after the group for lunch and frequently exchanged phone calls during the week. Two members of the group who were not AA members were often excluded from much of the outside socializing and gradually became irritated at their exclusion. Complications arose when some members who were closely involved with one another felt uneasy about discussing information confided in extragroup discussions. To do so would, in their opinion, "betray" the other individual. Furthermore, members often formed impressions of others from their observations outside the group or from information learned from other people about a specific member. They refrained from bringing up this material in the group because that too would have constituted a betrayal. This is an example of how a small group, either a dyad or triad, develops norms that conflict with the norms of the larger group. Members sense a stronger loyalty to the dyad or triad than they do to the primary group itself. The group suffers because important and very relevant information is withheld and unavailable for the work of the group. Because of his fear of betraying secrets and jeopardizing his friendship, a member does not speak to his friend in the group, and the two friends are of little value to each other in the therapeutic work. The secondary gratification that stems from friendship or companionship outside the group thus takes precedence over the primary task of therapy. The other members of the group usually become aware of extragroup contact between members and sense that secrets are being kept. The result is a global inhibition and lack of trust in the group process.

There was much information that members chose not to share with the group. For example, one knew that another member, during a period of heavy drinking, was also becoming addicted to Demerol; another knew that one of the members was involved in an extremely destructive extramarital relationship; two patients knew that one woman in the group had received an obscene phone call from one of the men in the group approximately a year before starting the group.

It is important that the therapist make as explicit as possible the fact that the members must, themselves, assume the responsibility for bringing up all pertinent information to the group. My experience has been that this is a much wiser course of action than any attempt to prevent extragroup socializing. Patients will inevitably meet outside of the group, and one does well not to lay down rules that will inevitably be broken and which patients will then attempt to conceal from the therapist and the rest of the group. Furthermore, it is helpful if the therapist explains why it is important for members to share this information in the group. We do this in our preparatory interviews and again, as the situation arises, both during the group and in the post-group summaries.

The Drinking Patient   The actively drinking member presented a major problem. It is more difficult to cope with drinking than with other forms of acting out, such as promiscuity or stealing, because the patient who comes into a therapy session intoxicated is in an altered state of mind, which makes it unlikely that he will be able to understand the feedback from others or to retain the experience. This, of course, makes the members extremely discouraged, since they recognize the futility of working with the inebriated patient and at the same time they cannot avoid dealing with him in the group. The drinking patient arouses "twelfth step call" reflexes from experienced AA members, who are strongly motivated to support and assist the drinking member and yet at the same time are aware that this "twelfth step reflex" is not the most effective way of involving themselves in the therapy process. In the AA tradition a "slip" is an extremely important event: it is an indelible entry into the record of the member and henceforth the AA member who has slipped at least once must always present himself as such. Consequently group members feel extraordinarily concerned and guilty should they perceive themselves as in any way having been responsible for the slip.

The problems surrounding a drinking member were exemplified in the case of Arlene who, as described, was criticized by some of the group and then came to the following meeting intoxicated. Her abrasive, maladaptive behavior was magnified; she monopolized the group, did not listen to other members, was contemptuous of several members, and refused to allow others to console her. Although it was obvious that she had been drinking, she patently denied it and in a long rambling monologue rationalized how useful alcohol was for her as an antidepressant. Despite the great sophistication and familiarity of the other members with alcohol, they accepted her statements and attempted to console her. Only after an hour of "punishment" did they first become discouraged and then openly confrontative, ordering Arlene to allow others to talk. They then refused to accept her rationalizations for drinking and absolved themselves of guilt when they learned that she had taken herself off Antabuse in preparation for drinking even before their attack at the previous meeting. Although this seemed like a disastrous meeting for Arlene, it eventually turned out to be a very significant incident in her therapy. She stopped drinking after leaving the meeting and as soon as possible resumed taking Antabuse. The meeting served as a "bottoming-out" point, and with the help of the summary and the videotape playback, she arrived at a penetrating awareness of the destructive nature of alcohol for her. She later stated that she realized she had no right to inflict this kind of punishment on a group of well-intentioned people. The summary helped her to retain and understand the comments made to her during the group, which she would have otherwise forgotten. As she put it, it provided her with a living record of the effects alcohol could have on herself and on her relationships with others. She has decided that when she is stronger she will see the whole meeting over again on videotape and asked us to save the tape for her.

The most thorny problem for the group was their feelings of responsibility for causing another to drink. We eventually effected some resolution of this issue within the larger context of personal responsibility. We helped members to realize that no one could make them drink; in the final analysis it was their responsibility and they could only *allow* someone to make them drink. No one could control them; they could only choose to allow others to control them. It was also important for the group members to make the distinction between short-term and long-term concerns. Immediate support is gratifying and is good to give and good to receive; but an even more substantial way of showing concern is to be more honest and direct with one's negative as well as one's positive feelings toward another. This is a long-term concern which, although somewhat unpleasant at first, may ultimately be more valuable to the other. For members to believe this, however, considerable faith in the therapist and in the therapeutic modality must be established.

Results

It is premature to comment on the results for each patient; this type of group therapy has ambitious goals and is a long-term process. With regard to some parameters the endeavor to establish a working therapy group has been "successful." The group has navigated past numerous dangerous shoals which have threatened to destroy it on several occasions. Despite many factors that we suspected would limit our success (no selection of patients, inclusion of many patients who appeared to be extremely high risks for group therapy, an infrequent, once-a-week format, some actively drinking members), the group developed into an effective working therapy group with high cohesion and excellent attendance.

PART 3

GROUP THERAPY WITH THE TERMINALLY ILL

Introduction

In recent years groups for patients facing life-threatening illness have become commonplace. Thousands of patients with cancer, AIDS, heart disease, and kidney disease attend support groups. Many publications, lay and professional, describe the groups; groups for breast cancer patients have had considerable national TV coverage. The article I reproduce here, "Group Therapy with the Terminally Ill," which I coauthored with Carlos Greaves, a psychiatric resident at the time, first appeared in the *American Journal of Psychiatry* (April 1977); it is, to the best of my knowledge, the first published description of a group for cancer patients.

During the late 1960s I grew increasingly interested in exploring existential sources of anxiety. These phenomena are deep, repressed, and difficult to discern in everyday psychotherapy patients, and gradually I turned to working with cancer patients whose illness forced them to confront more openly the issues of death, isolation, freedom, and meaning in life. After seeing a number of patients in a one-to-one setting, I met Katie Weers, a remarkable woman with advanced breast cancer, who acted as adviser and teacher to me. With her assistance I organized a group for patients with advanced cancer which first met in 1972. Meetings were held weekly in the psychiatric outpatient clinic with occasional meetings in the bedroom of a patient too ill to leave home. Most meetings were attended by four to seven patients. When the group grew larger, we broke it into two sections and had a joint session for the final fifteen minutes to review the events of both meetings. Over the first four years forty patients attended the group and twelve patients died. From its onset the group attracted considerable attention from students—professional caregivers from many disciplines—who observed the meetings through two-way mirrors. The group members welcomed observers: they felt they had learned much about life from their illness and they desired an opportunity to teach. Our clinical impression was that the group offered enormous support to the members and markedly improved their quality of life. Soon Dr. David Spiegel joined me in this work, and we formed other groups, which we based on the paradigm of the original cancer group and studied more systematically. Many years later Dr. Spiegel found that these supportive/expressive groups not only offered breast cancer patients valuable support but actually increased their survival time. His finding resulted in a flurry of new research and new applications of support groups for cancer patients.

Group Therapy with the Terminally Ill

with Carlos Greaves, M.D.

(excerpted from the *Am. J. of Psychiatry*, 134:4, Ap 1997, pp. 396–400)

During the past four years we have employed a group therapy format in the care of dying patients. Initially we assumed that the group members would profit from continued close contact with others facing the same tragic experience. We thought that sharing, open communication, and the opportunity to be helpful to others would be an antidote to the bitter isolation so many dying patients experience.

A second reason for organizing a therapy group for terminally ill patients was the conviction that such a group could teach us much about everyday psychotherapy with the living. Although it is common knowledge that a serious confrontation with death often triggers a profound reappraisal of one's basic relationship with oneself, others, and the world, it is uncommon for a concentrated contemplation of death to enter the psychotherapeutic dialogue. One important reason for this is that the psychotherapist's basic theories of anxiety (and hence his/her chief consideration in psychotherapy) rest not on the bedrock of the dread of nonbeing but on such derivative phenomena as separation, castration, and loss of ego boundaries. Another reason issues from the magnitude of the threat. Most psychotherapy patients and most therapists will not stare at death very long before they lower the blinds of denial. Psychotherapy groups occasionally deal with death when prodded by such stimuli as the death of someone close to one of the members or the departure of one of the members from the group. However, the focus is rarely sustained for more than a single session; depression, avoidance, and denial soon obstruct the work.

These considerations prodded us to organize a group of patients with terminal illnesses—patients who are so close to death that continual denial is not possible. We hoped to help them if we could, to learn from them, and to apply what we learned to the everyday therapy of the living.

Description of the Group

Four years ago, with the aid of a patient with metastatic cancer, we began a group for patients with metastatic carcinoma (breast carcinoma in most cases). Since then the group has met weekly for 90 minutes. The patients are all fully aware of the nature and prognosis of their illness. Our experience is that it is best to exclude patients who exhibit massive denial of their illness and its implications. We also exclude patients whose cancer has been contained and who have excellent prognoses. It is an open group; members come as often as their physical condition permits and as long as they continue to profit from the experience.

Course of the Group: Modes of Help

The therapeutic factor of altruism played an important role in the group. Not only did the patients help one another in quid pro quo (giving-receiving) fashion, but altruism, the act of giving, was intrinsically valuable to the members. As in any therapy group, the members themselves were the prime agents of help. In this group that fact took on an added dimension, since terminally ill patients are so imbued with a sense of powerlessness and uselessness. They dread nothing so much as helpless immobility, being not only personally burdensome but without value to another. Consequently, learning that they had much to offer others imbued many of the members with a renewed sense of worth.

Furthermore, being helpful to others brings patients out of a morbid self-absorption which, for many, had stripped life of its meaning. The more they are able to move out of themselves, to extend themselves to others, the more they experience a sense of fulfillment.

Members are able to be helpful in a number of ways. They telephone and visit members who are in despair. They share books and coping techniques that have been useful to them. For example, one of the members taught other members in the group the meditation techniques that had been useful to her in dealing with pain.

Another mode of offering help (and thus helping oneself) is to teach by sharing one's experiences with others. (The patients often thought before joining the group, "We are teachers but the students will not listen.") The patients are very willing to speak to medical students and to permit observation of the meetings through a one-way mirror. There is rarely a meeting without observers (for example, nurses, physical therapists, medical students, psychologists, oncologists, radiotherapists).

These patients are especially desirous of reaching and influencing the medical profession because, almost without exception, they have a complex and ambivalent set of feelings toward their doctors. At first, much anger was evident; in fact, the group's initial cohesiveness resulted at least in part from a common bond of enmity toward the medical profession. Some of this enmity was justified, some was irrational. Both types of anger were dealt with: the irrational by understanding and working through, the realistic by ventilation and development of adaptive coping strategies.

The irrational anger stems from the doctors' failure to meet extremely unrealistic demands. At deep, unconscious levels the members expected the doctors to be all-knowing and all-protecting. They put their faith in the doctor to the same degree that their ancestors had placed their faith in the hands of the priest. And, of course, the doctor could not be the ultimate rescuer. Patients are forced to confront limits and finiteness, and the ensuing anger and dread is often displaced to the physician.

However, much anger is justified. The surgeons and oncologists either lack the time or arrange their schedules in such a way that they cannot provide the kinds of support and information the patients crave.

The patients felt their physicians were too impersonal and too authoritarian. They resented not being kept fully informed and being excluded from important decisions regarding their own treatment. Many patients reported that physicians withdrew emotionally from them when metastasis occurred. They felt abandoned just at the time when they needed the most support.

Patients learn from one another what they can and cannot expect from their doctors. They compare notes and role-play methods of asking doctors questions. They come to grips with how much they really want to know—were the physicians concealing information, or were the patients asking questions in such a way that the physicians were merely complying with their wishes to avoid gaining the information they ostensibly wanted?

Over time it became abundantly clear in the group that the patients had a strong need for a sustaining relationship when their illness was no longer deemed curable and that many had physicians who were so threatened or discouraged that they could not provide the sheer presence the patients required. Presence was the overriding need and the chief commodity provided by the group. Almost without exception, patients facing death feel cut off and shunned by the living. We agree with Kübler-Ross that the question is not *whether* to tell the patient that his/her disease is one that has no cure, but *how* to tell the patient. The living, by a multitude of signals, always let the patient know that the illness is terminal. Nurses, paramedical personnel, and physicians cue the patient, often in the most subtle ways—a hushed shrinking away, a tendency to be less intimate, a slightly greater physical distance. One member commented that her doctor always ended his meetings with her by giving her a gentle pat on her fanny. When he became more solemn and, instead of patting her, shook her hand, she recognized the seriousness of her illness for the first time.

Not only are patients isolated because they are shunned by the living, but they increase their isolation by their reluctance to discuss their most central concerns with others. They fear that friends will be frightened and avoid them; they are reluctant to burden and depress their families further.

It became apparent that the most basic anxiety of many group members was not so much a fear of dying, of finiteness and nonbeing, but fear of the absolute utter loneliness that accompanies death. Obviously, basic existential loneliness cannot be allayed or taken away; it can only be appreciated and, in a curious way, shared through the sharing of it. The other kind of loneliness, secondary interpersonal loneliness that is a function both of the shunning of the dying person and of his/her self-imposed isolation, can be dealt with effectively in the group. First and most important, the group offers an arena in which all concerns can be aired and thoroughly discussed. There are no issues too deep or morbid to be discussed openly in the group. These issues include physical concerns (for example, loss of hair from chemotherapy, disfigurement from mutilating surgery), fear of the actual act of dying, fear of pain, the possibility of afterlife, the fear of becoming a "vegetable," the desire to have decision-making power concerning the time of death, euthanasia, the "living will," funeral arrangements, and so on. These concerns are foremost in the minds of many patients, but they are unable to discuss them with any living person. The group affords considerable relief by simply allowing patients to share these thoughts.

In this group, as in all therapy groups, one becomes ever more cognizant of the overarching need that people have for other people. The group spends much time and does much effective work with the patients who, because of characterological style or particular methods of coping with recent stress, have cut themselves off from others. For example, one patient never asked for any personal help from the group. For months she tended to speak in extremely concrete terms. When she was asked about herself, she responded by giving a long summary of her physical condition, her examinations by doctors, and her recent chemotherapeutic regimen. The therapist helped this patient by repeatedly asking her, when she had finished talking about her physical self, to respond again to the question, "How are *you?* How is the person feeling to whom all of these things are happening?" Gradually, she became more able to relate to others and to discuss her own needs. Although she could not easily discuss her feelings, she once reported to the group a dream of a poor injured kitten for whom she had wept. She was able to accept the interpretation offered by group members that she was the kitten and that she wept for herself. Later in the group she became more open to discussion of all affect; she even reported, after attending one member's funeral, the anger and fear that the sterility and impersonality of the service had aroused in her.

Another member had planned a large dinner party and learned from her physician that morning that her cancer had metastasized. Her chief concern at that point was less a fear of death than of isolation and abandonment. She feared that her illness would cause her so much pain that she would respond to it in a primitive, animalistic fashion and therefore be shunned by others. She held her party and kept her illness secret from friends. It was with much relief that she was able to discuss these concerns in the group and to hear how other members with more advanced disease had experienced and dealt with pain.

Another member began the group in bitter isolation. She was a widow who felt she had been isolated by all of her former friends and abandoned by her only child. The group at first empathized with her, and many members felt extremely angry toward her son, who had apparently behaved in an extremely ungrateful manner. Gradually some members became aware of the fact that neither the patient nor her son acted independently but were instead locked together in dynamic interaction. The patient had for years (long before her cancer) been an embittered and angry woman who had in effect driven her son away from her. With the help of the group she became softer, more open and responsive to others. Her son reciprocated and she became even more generous; eventually, before her death, she became a source of considerable strength for other members of the group.

A woman who was desperately ill with advanced leukemia came to the group for only one session. She spent the entire meeting discussing the fecklessness and coldness of her only child, a daughter, who was a psychologist and "should have known better." One of the other patients helped this woman appreciate the triviality of her charges against the daughter and suggested that she make the most of her remaining time by saying to her daughter, "You are the most important thing in the world to me, and I want us to be close before I die." The patient died only a few days after this meeting, but we learned from the nursing staff that she had followed the group's advice and had a final, deeply fulfilling meeting with her daughter.

The Therapist in the Group

The presence offered by the therapy group must, of course, include the therapist. One cannot effectively lead such a group by making a dichotomy between "us," the living therapists, and "them," the dying patients. Therapists lead effectively when they appreciate that it is "we" who face death; the leaders are members who must share in the group's anxiety. The anxiety that the leader must tolerate is considerable, and it has been our experience that a period of several months' apprenticeship is necessary for therapists to deal with their own dread of death so that they can work effectively. We found, for example, that when the group interaction was superficial, the therapists were often responsible. They considered certain topics too threatening for the patients to discuss, but ultimately they were protecting themselves. Given the opportunity, the group was willing to plunge deeply and meaningfully into any area.

Sometimes the therapist proceeded with extreme caution because he regarded the patient as too anguished to tolerate any additional anxiety. Not infrequently this spawned an overly conservative approach that merely enhanced the patient's sense of isolation. Victor Frankl once suggested that Boyle's law of gaseous expansion in a physical space could be applied to anxiety, in that anxiety expands to fill any space offered to it. Many people who are relatively unburdened find that trivial anxiety fills their life space completely. Thus, the absolute amount of anxiety in the dying patient is often no greater than that of patients facing a number of other life concerns. It seems that we get used to anything, even to dying. At times the group provided a type of desensitization experience, as patients repeatedly approached and palpated the most frightening issues. Laughter that was neither diversionary nor tension-spawned often occurred spontaneously. For example, during one meeting a member spoke about a seemingly healthy neighbor who had died suddenly during the night. One member stated that that was most regrettable since the woman had had no time to prepare either herself or her family for her death. Others disagreed, and one member said that that was precisely the way she would like to die, quipping, "I've always loved surprises."

At the same time, however, the therapist must learn to respect denial and to allow each patient to proceed at his/her own pace. Even though all of the group members are aware of their diagnosis and prognosis, they often shift their level of awareness, and the therapist renders the most help by respecting the patient's decision regarding what he/she chooses to know at that moment.

It is important to conceptualize the group as a group for living, not for dying. For one thing, physicians are more inclined to refer patients when the group's purpose is to improve the quality of life rather than to focus on dying. Even more important is the fact that an open confrontation with death allows many patients to move into a mode of existence that is richer than the one they experienced prior to their illness. Many patients report dramatic shifts in life perspective. They are able to trivialize the trivial, to assume a sense of control, to stop doing things they do not wish to do, to communicate more openly with families and close friends, and to live entirely in the present rather than in the future or the past. Many report that facing and mastering some of their fear of death dissolves many other fears, particularly fears of awkward interpersonal situations, rejection, or humiliation. We are not being ironic when we suggest that, in a grim fashion, cancer cures psychoneuroses. As one's focus turns from the trivial diversions of life, a fuller appreciation of the elemental factors in existence may emerge: the changing seasons, the falling leaves, the last spring, and especially, the loving of others. Over and over we hear our patients say (and this is a most compelling message for the psychotherapist), "Why did we have to wait till *now,* till we are riddled with cancer, to learn how to value and appreciate life?"

PART 4

GROUP THERAPY WITH THE BEREAVED

Bereavement groups, both professionally led (sponsored by hospitals, hospices, outpatient mental health agencies and churches) and self-help groups, have proliferated over the past three decades.

How effective are they? Should public mental health policy offer groups to all bereaved individuals? The existing research did not supply an answer to this question because virtually every study used a self-selected sample of bereaved individuals who sought help from professional caregivers or else responded to an invitation to join a research project.

Hence, in the mid-1980s my colleague Morton Lieberman and I designed a controlled study in which we offered a brief group experience to an unselected population of spousally bereaved individuals. This research had several goals: to develop appropriate specialized techniques for a bereavement group leader, to understand in depth the important issues faced by our members, to determine the outcome of a brief group intervention, and finally to test an observation I had made in individual therapy with the bereaved—namely, that an often forgotten facet of bereavement is that the death of the other confronts us with our own death and that part of the work of mourning is to integrate this confrontation.

Several papers were generated by this research. One, devoted to outcome, reported that although the groups were effective therapy groups, it was not possible to recommend them as routine prophylactic mental health practice because the control population also did extremely well: bereavement, in the great majority of instances, is a self limited process.[1]

Another paper documented that a significant number (approximately one-third) of the bereaved spouses *did* experience an existential confrontation that resulted in unexpected personal growth. For these individuals the end point of bereavement was not the reinstitution of function but a new and deeper level of maturity.² "Bereavement Groups: Techniques and Themes," which I coauthored with Sophia Vinogradov, was originally published in the *International Journal of Group Psychotherapy* (October 1988). The excerpt presented here explores the therapeutic techniques we employed in bereavement groups and clinical themes emerging in these groups.

Bereavement Groups: Techniques and Themes

with Sophia Vinogradov, M.D.
(*International J. of Group Therapy,* 38:4, Oct 1988)

The recently bereaved represent a large at-risk population, a fact indicated by persuasive clinical and research evidence. Bereavement groups constitute a particularly sensible approach to treating this population, as great numbers of clients may be reached in a systematic and cost-effective manner. Furthermore, the small group format specifically addresses and ameliorates the intense social isolation experienced by most bereaved spouses. Such groups represent excellent preventative mental health practice.

In this paper we will report on the technical and thematic considerations of four bereavement groups that met weekly for eight sessions. We contacted the spouses of all the patients who had died of cancer at two medical settings (Stanford Medical Center and the Palo Alto Medical Clinic) during a six-month time frame. Of the sample of 74 consecutive subjects, 63 (84 percent) agreed to participate. Fifteen were randomly assigned to a control condition: they were interviewed before the study, and one year later, but did not take part in the groups.

Techniques

General Principles   The general techniques we employed in the bereavement groups are those used by group therapists in most settings, and consisted essentially of establishing norms, of encouraging process review, and of making here-and-now interventions. In addition, since the life of the group was limited to eight sessions, and since issues of separation and loss were paramount for these members, we were careful to function as group timekeepers and to remind members of the number of remaining meetings.

First Meeting   After introductions, we began the opening session by briefly restating our expectations for the group. (We had already oriented each member in the individual intake sessions.) We hoped that the group would focus primarily on the future and would help each member learn to move forward despite the loss, the pain, and the major changes each had experienced. We stated, too, that although the group would explore painful issues surrounding bereavement, we would endeavor to ensure that such discussion be safe and gentle.

At this point, we invited the members to describe their bereavement and to share, in any way they chose, what they thought we should know about their current life situation. This go-round was, without exception, a moving and important part of the first meeting. Some members wept openly when describing the death of the spouse; others became tearful in sympathy, especially when hearing about the loss of a young spouse or about young children left without a parent. Invariably, the members were self-revealing and spontaneous, and the therapists' only task was to reaffirm the safety of the group by reminding members, when necessary, that one might say as little or as much as one chose. If a member became tearful, we might inquire, for example, if he or she wished to stop or whether questions from others would be welcomed.

Early Meetings   During the early meetings (sessions 2 to 4), the group discussed in greater depth many of the themes identified in the first meeting. If necessary, the therapists reminded the group of the salient issues and launched the discussion. These sessions were characterized by considerable energy and interaction, and members gave much explicit positive testimony about the group. For example, in one group, a young widow who had guiltily begun dating a man several months earlier received a great deal of support from other group members; after the third meeting, she decided to marry the man and thenceforth credited the group for enabling her to make this important decision. In all of the bereavement groups, members stated that they looked forward eagerly to meetings and that between meetings they did much thinking about each other.

An important norm that we attempted to shape early in the life of the groups was that the group accept responsibility for its own direction. We noted in one group, for example, that our request during the first meeting to have members list the expectations had not seemed productive or helpful, but no one had mentioned this. We raised questions about group norms. Was there an unwritten rule not to criticize the leaders? Does the group have the right to evaluate its own meetings?

This turned into a rather powerful intervention, as it evoked discussion of a theme that was to recur in all of the bereavement groups: the notion of "shoulds"—personal or perceived societal behavioral expectations. When we asked, "What are the 'shoulds' for behavior in this group?" it led many members to reflect on the yoke of "shoulds" they carry around in the outside life: One *should* grieve for a whole year, one *should* quickly give away all of the spouse's belongings, one *should* not be alone during the weekend. Identifying that invisible burden and recognizing their personal dominion over "shoulds" was a liberating experience for many members.

Seizing on this general theme, we took the opportunity to begin some gentle here-and-now work by asking different members to identify their "shoulds" for behavior in this group. For example, Mary, an orderly and shy woman who had always subordinated herself to her boisterous husband, felt concerned about taking up too much time in the group whenever she spoke. In contrast, Bob, a gregarious, self-made man, was burdened by the responsibility for keeping conversation going in the group. And more than one person was concerned about losing control and sobbing in front of everyone in a meeting. We obtained feedback for each of these members and helped decatastrophize weeping: the box of Kleenex often made rounds during the meetings.

We were careful to spend time in these early sessions and in the summaries on process review. Not only did this allow us to examine unfinished business or leftover feelings as early as the second meeting (for example, by asking what people had felt when they went home from the first session), but it permitted us to begin identifying and clarifying themes that we saw emerging and thus to begin to establish an agenda for later group work.

By the fourth meeting, the groups had developed considerable cohesiveness. Each individual member began to realize "I'm not alone." (One member offered a foxhole analogy: "There may be a lot of heavy bombardment and shelling going on out there, but I'm comforted by the presence of others in the foxhole who understand what I'm going through.") Likewise, members began to appreciate the ubiquity of pain.

At the end of the second meeting, we asked members to bring in photographs of themselves and their spouses—if possible, at least one early picture (perhaps a wedding portrait) and also a more recent picture. In the third meeting, members showed their pictures to the group and discussed them in any way they chose. We gave no further instructions, other than to express the hope that this would permit each person to be more fully known to the group.

The choice of pictures that were shown varied greatly. At one extreme were the formal memorial pictures or newspaper clippings brought in by widows who had idealized their husbands. At the other extreme was the honeymoon picture taken on Coney Island in the 1940s, where an ebullient bride and her young groom posed behind painted cardboard figures from the Old West. An 82-year-old widower who had been married for 53 years brought in five carefully chosen pictures, one from each decade of his marriage. There were stiff black-and-white photographs of young servicemen with their brides, favorite pictures of a wife or husband dressed up for some special occasion, and recent snapshots of families on vacation. Several people brought photos with particular poignancy, in which the spouse "must have had the cancer already, but we didn't know it yet." And several brought photographs in which the spouse was clearly ill, "but fighting it." Some members had a discussion with their children to help decide which pictures to bring, while a couple of others repeatedly "forgot" to bring in their pictures for several meetings.

The pictures not only increased the sense of group engagement, but also served as a vehicle for self-disclosure. The two members who initially forgot to bring in any photographs ultimately revealed through them some important and heretofore hidden aspects of their spouse and their marriage. One widower, who had found it difficult to tell the group about his wife's severe scoliosis, finally showed a photograph of her and only then shared a great deal about how his wife's physical handicap had placed considerable restrictions upon their activities as a couple. Another member, a young white man, had never mentioned to the group that his wife was black and that being part of an interracial couple had been a unique aspect of his marriage. Further, in the few years prior to her death she had, to his great displeasure, grown obese; it wasn't until he brought in pictures of her that this member was able to discuss his difficult, complex feelings about his marriage. A third widower, a young man in his thirties who repeatedly missed meetings, was very ambivalent about an affair he had started with his wife's best friend immediately after his wife's death from breast cancer. It was not until he showed the group a photograph of his wife together with her friend that he felt able to discuss his situation openly.

No group can be successfully led simply by stringing together a series of structured exercises, and the picture-showing exercise is a case in point. As powerful as it was, the success of this exercise varied widely. In one group, the members spent the entire session sharing their feelings about the photographs in great depth, while another group went through the entire exercise somewhat mechanically in five minutes. This latter group had, in general, been more reserved and, because of an early dropout and initial attendance problems, had developed cohesion more slowly. In retrospect, we should have waited until more trust developed in this group before introducing a task calling for such a high level of disclosure.

Later Meetings   By later meetings (sessions 5 to 7), the bereavement groups were cohesive, bonded, and hard working. As leaders, our most important task had become that of monitoring the time remaining in the group and of anticipating termination. We consistently and explicitly reminded the group of its limited life span, noting after the fourth session, for example, that the group was half over. We found it useful to link time-marking with the concept of anticipated regret: "What regrets can you anticipate experiencing after this group is over? What have you left unsaid or unasked? Would you be willing to act now to avoid having those regrets later?" This powerful technique helped to foster new behavior in the microcosm of the group and also stimulated members to examine the more global issue of bereavement and regrets in their outside lives.

The technique of "anticipated regret," combined with the impending end of the group, often provoked new self-disclosure, which now began to reflect the less idealized, more problematic areas of individual marriages: anger at the dead spouse and at oneself for things left unsaid in the marriage; resentment over fixed, restrictive roles; guilt about new or future relationships. For example, Nancy, a contentious woman in one of the groups, explicitly acknowledged her anger toward the insensitivity of the widowers in the group who protested too much, she thought, about the many single women who pursued them. Her anger in the group permitted her to reexperience and to express her anger toward her deceased husband for his neglect of her and for his relationships with other women. John, a proud self-made man, became deeply attached to the group, often referring to it as his family. At the final meeting, he made a high-risk disclosure: that he was an orphan, and that without his wife, the upcoming Christmas holidays were sure to evoke painful memories of his childhood spent in orphanages and foster homes.

These sorts of revelations provided the opportunity for some gentle here-and-now work in the group. As a general rule, group leaders can enhance the group work by considering not only the content but the *process* of deep self-disclosure—in other words, they can facilitate the exploration of metadisclosures, or disclosure about the act of disclosure. What was it like for John to reveal so much to us? What helped him decide to trust us today? Why was he usually so reticent about his background? How did the others respond to his revelation? What feelings did the men in group have when Nancy expressed anger toward them? In this fashion, we encouraged members to think about their usual mode of behaving in the group and to consider what part of their behavior might be shaped by preconceived expectations of other people's reactions.

Many of the members, as we shall discuss shortly, expressed concerns about their new identity as a widow or widower. They became aware, sometimes for the first time in 50 years, of being a single person, an "I" rather than a "we." They had had to relinquish old familiar roles—of husband or wife, of companion, of lover. We attempted to use some structured exercises that would help members to clarify and to explore this process. The first was a 30-minute exercise in meditative disidentification (a method suggested to me by James Bugental).[3] We asked each member to write an answer to the question "Who are you?" on seven cards, one answer per card (for example, answers might include "a wife" or "a teacher" or "someone who loves music"). At our instruction, members then arranged their seven cards from most peripheral to their sense of identity to most central. We then asked the members to meditate on each card, beginning with the most peripheral, and to imagine giving up that attribute. We served as timekeepers and after two minutes signaled the members to move on to the next card. We completed the exercise by reversing the procedure and reassuming each of these attributes.

A second, simpler exercise, but with the same purpose, consisted of asking members to pair up and then to spend several minutes having one person in each dyad repeatedly ask the question "Who are you?" while the other person supplied as many answers as possible. After several minutes, the roles were reversed. As with all structured exercises, the effectiveness of these two techniques was not in the tasks themselves but in the feelings and thoughts evoked and subsequently expressed during the discussion that followed each exercise.

In addition to concerns about their new identity, many members were experiencing a crisis of life meaning. Marriage and the marital relationship had heretofore supplied a major sense of purpose in life for most group members. The loss of that relationship left many with a sense of confusion and bewilderment about their values, goals, and life missions. We employed a simple structured exercise to focus the group's attention upon this issue. During the sixth or seventh session, we set aside 15 minutes and asked each member to consider the things for which he or she wished to be remembered and to compose his or her own obituary. The obituaries were then read and discussed in the group.

Termination   Groups have two tasks when termination approaches, and the leaders must ensure that the group attends to each task. The first is simply to deal with loss; this includes saying good-bye, acknowledging the ending of the group, and facing other feelings evoked by termination. The second task is to anticipate and prevent regret—regret over unfinished business and over work left undone in the group.

The first task—dealing with the termination of the group—raised several issues for the bereaved spouses. With termination, many members became aware of the importance of intimacy. They experienced a sense of relief from sharing their experiences with others during the group sessions, and thus they became persuaded of the necessity of developing a nourishing source of friends and potential confidants in their outside lives. For many, of course, termination re-evoked feelings related to the loss of their husband or wife. We reminded the group that grieving consists of a long sequence in which the feelings of painful loss must arise, again and again, be felt deeply, and then allowed to fade. To avoid this cyclical resurfacing of pain and grief—through distracting activity, through new relationships, or through workaholism or drugs—would, in our view, only result in a delayed or distorted recovery.

The second task of termination—the anticipation and avoidance of regret—is in fact a call to action and a call to the assumption of responsibility. By urging members to leave no work undone and no feelings or questions unexpressed, we urged them to take responsibility for making themselves feel better in the future. This technique also kept the groups working until the very last minute. Many members had considerable regret that they had left important sentiments unexpressed in their marriage. The group provided them with an opportunity to acknowledge and to change that behavior.

Every group hates to die, and the bereavement groups were no exception. Members exchanged phone numbers and made plans for a reunion or for continued leaderless meetings. In a therapy group, it is appropriate for the leaders to interpret such reunions as denial and an attempt to avoid the work of termination; in bereavement groups, however, there is evidence that long-term social involvement with other members is salutary.[4] Consequently, we supported and encouraged posttermination group meetings. All of the four groups had some subsequent socialization: one group scheduled a monthly evening meeting, which continued for seven months, a second arranged several group luncheons, and the others set up a reunion luncheon and occasional meetings or phone contact between members.

Themes

The leaders of bereavement groups must be familiar not only with specific therapeutic techniques, but also with the major problems in life facing the bereaved. Only then can they help their members to identify, explore, understand, and master the major tasks of bereavement. We observed that certain themes emerged again and again in each of the bereavement groups, common threads that stood out against the more complex background tapestry of the various idiosyncratic processes of each group and each member. Before we examine these themes, let us recall one common feature of our bereavement groups: every member's spouse had died of cancer. Thus, the spouse's death had generally been anticipated for at least several months, and in most cases, much anticipatory grieving had occurred by the time of death.

A basic assumption of our approach was that two fundamental stages occur during bereavement. The first—like the "fast pain" neurologists describe—consists of initial shock, denial, and numbness, followed by an acute sense of loss, a sharp, painful realization that one has lost a partner and best friend. This is followed by a stage of "slow pain," a more insidious and resistant discomfort related to the series of enforced changes the bereaved spouse must undergo: changes in lifestyle, in social role, in self-image. All of our group members had been bereaved from five to twelve months and were therefore struggling with this second stage of bereavement and with its monumental implications for their entire future life.

Loneliness and Aloneness   Every bereaved individual suffers from loneliness, and the members in our groups found themselves especially impaired by the loss of the intimate moments they had been used to sharing with their spouse. They noted that two levels of intimacy are suddenly lost upon the spouse's death. First, the small, daily intimacies of shared routines and private moments together disappear: one woman spoke of how much she missed the "silly little activity" of eating dinner in front of the TV and watching Monday Night Football with her husband. Second, there is the loss of the more obvious larger intimacies: family holidays, time spent with children and grandchildren, sexual and romantic closeness. The loss of these latter activities is so self-evident that the bereaved person is in a sense prepared for them ahead of time, but it is the small moments that are not anticipated and it is there that the loneliness appears unexpectedly. Another group member, for example, described her confrontation with a "5:00 to 7:00 syndrome," the time of day she had picked her husband up at the train station after work for the past fifteen years. C. S. Lewis gave an eloquent description of this phenomenon: "It is just at those moments when I feel least sorrow—getting into my morning bath is one of them—that H. rushes upon my mind in her full reality."[5]

In making the transition from "we" to "I," group members also confronted another kind of loneliness: that of no longer being the single most important person in someone's life, nor of having a single significant other with whom to share important experiences. For example, one widower described his inability, when alone, to derive any pleasure from a beautiful sunset or an entertaining movie; only in the prospect or process of sharing the event ("Wait till I tell . . . ") did the experience become fully realized. It was as if the memory of experience could become fastened to reality only if mediated through a significant other. Some found it devastatingly painful to realize that no one was thinking of them, observing them, aware of their leaving or entering their house. Other group members felt that much of their past history had died with their spouses. After all, they had each lost the one person who knew them over time, who shared the same memories.

Finally, being alone resulted in a radical change in social role for most of the widows or widowers in our groups. Individuals who had been part of a couple through most of adulthood were suddenly forced to adapt to life as a single person. One woman spoke of going to a party and with a flash realizing that she was single, that she could speak with whomever she wanted, that she could decide to leave the party at any time she pleased. The realization was bittersweet, for it was also clear that there was no one looking out for her at the party and that ultimately she would leave the party by herself.

This new single identity brought with it the sensation of being a fifth wheel. The bereaved learn that it's a "couples world." TV programs, travel excursions, restaurants, leisure activities are all oriented toward the couple, not the single person. The bereaved at first are issued many invitations to dinners and social functions, but gradually the invitations decline; even couples who are old friends of the family appeared to grow uncomfortable socializing with just one spouse. Many widows reported that married couples experienced the presence of a single woman as a threat to their marriage. Both widows and widowers found that others seemed awkward around them: friends didn't know what to say, and do-gooders were often intrusive. One member spoke of writing a book on her experiences entitled "Where Have All the People Gone?"

Freedom and Growth   If the loss of the "we" results in loneliness and disengagement from an established role and social network, the emergence of the "I" carries with it an awareness of freedom and the potential for change. Elsewhere we describe in detail the finding that approximately 25 percent of our subjects experience some type of personal growth. Some group members derived a sense of inner strength from the knowledge that they had faced deep loss and grief—and survived. Others grew to respect themselves for the courage they displayed during the illness and death of their spouses or in their ability to care for their children during the bereavement. Still others dealt admirably with the experience of loneliness and change in social role we have described above and gained strength from their ability to cope with such adversity.

Several widows also described a sense of liberation from a restrictive, stunting marriage. One woman marveled at the incredible feeling of independence and freedom she felt in deciding what to watch on TV: she could now watch all the PBS shows she wanted, something her husband had never permitted. Others described a sense of being liberated from schedules or tight routines. "I don't have to prepare full meals. I can have popcorn for dinner!" Or, "I can come home anytime I wish." One widower changed professions and took a job that his wife had always said he couldn't handle well. Many of our group members began to take first steps toward discovering their own autonomy and self-identity. They started asking themselves, "What is it that I do? What do I enjoy?" rather than "What should I be doing as a good wife?" or "What should we do as a couple?" For those members who had been part of a couple in which the deceased spouse had done all of the wishing or decision making in the family, there was a sudden new freedom of choice that came from having no one to please but oneself. Those members of a couple who had been the audience to a spouse who had been the "appreciator" (of art, music, natural beauty) had to undust and unpack long-unused sensory organs. This new sense of self, exhilarating as it was, also carried a bittersweet tinge for most members. Although there were several whose marriages had been so conflictual that they experienced unambivalent liberation, the overwhelming majority would have gladly exchanged this newfound freedom for the resumption of their old life with their spouse.

The Process of Change   The host of new responsibilities and roles forced upon the bereaved spouses obliged them to engage in behavior that, for many, encouraged a process of personal change. Men suddenly found themselves having to cook, clean, and care for a household; women were confronted with many financial decisions or mechanical repairs which their husbands used to manage. Many, for the first time, had to face decisions alone. Even minor decisions, like the purchase of a new toaster or television set, had far-reaching symbolic significance. Some members made major changes in lifestyle. Four moved into new homes, one to a new city, three began new jobs, and many embarked on various home redecorating projects.

The process of change for many of the group members influenced the decision to deal with the personal effects of the dead spouse. Painful choices had to be made about the disposal of mementos, clothes, and other personal belongings. For most of the widows and widowers, the ability to face these choices and to dispose of personal effects implied an acceptance of the spouse's death and acceptance of time's irreversibility. For a few others, it felt like an act that dismissed or betrayed the past.

Not surprisingly, a whole range of behaviors and reactions occurred around this process. Some group members made a clean break, moved into a new house soon after their spouse's death, and disposed of most personal items as quickly as possible. Others found the process painful, but after several months, usually with the help of children, were able to begin sorting through their spouse's belongings. Some derived special comfort in giving away cherished items to another family member or to a good friend who had known the spouse, while others experienced deep pain at seeing others wear their spouse's clothes. Four members, all with considerable unresolved grief, were completely unable to deal with their spouse's personal effects. One had not changed a single item in his house since his wife's funeral. Her favorite sheet music still stood at the piano; her purse, with its complete contents, still hung from the back of the same chair where she had placed it when she had come home from the hospital to die, eight months earlier.

Overall, members seemed to experience an inherent tension between the process of change and a sense of devotion or love for the deceased spouse. It was as if the very work of mourning, the letting go of one's old life, the putting behind, the facing forward, the detaching of emotional ties somehow represented a betrayal of the marital relationship.

The Theme of Time and Ritual   Much group discussion centered upon the proper length of time for the grieving process. Most members wisely concluded that each person has his or her own rhythm to grieving and recovery. Folk wisdom often posits one year as the proper time for grief, and although members rejected any prescribed limits to grief, many agreed that there was a kernel of truth in the one-year time frame. Over the course of the first year of bereavement, they knew they must face all of the major holidays and anniversaries without their spouse. After passing once through this annual cycle successfully, many described a sense of hope and survival: "If I made it through Christmas or through all those memories associated with our wedding anniversary, I can make it through anything." In addition, most members agreed that the rituals of a funeral or scheduled services proved helpful by providing structure and identifiable norms for behavior during the first painful weeks of bereavement.

The Theme of New Relationships   The formation of new relationships was an important theme in all of the groups. Members wondered when would be the proper time to begin seeking new relationships. How would society view this behavior? How does one enter the single world? The range of behavior among the members was very wide, ranging from one young widower who had started an affair several days after his wife's death to certain widows who declared that they could not imagine ever getting involved with anyone else. Overall the groups were deeply supportive to members who had formed new relationships and were effective in relieving guilt. Several members' responses to the issue of new relationships changed over the course of the group. One quiet and traditional woman who had vehemently said she could never be with another man announced at termination that she had shifted her stance and had informed all her friends of her readiness to begin dating.

The idea of loving someone new evoked a range of complex feelings in our bereavement groups. Many people agreed that the desire for a new intimate relationship signaled a kind of healing and a readiness to move forward in life. Others felt that a new love relationship represented a betrayal of their marriage, as if loving someone new might somehow diminish the love one had had for one's spouse. We often pointed out the fallacy of believing that love is a fixed commodity, of believing that only a specified amount of love is available for relationships. Finally, there were several members, all widowers, who frantically threw themselves into new romantic liaisons, as if trying to distract themselves from the depth of their loss.

The issues of dating and relationships created a major line of cleavage between the men and women in our groups. Almost without exception, the men were far more driven to form new relationships and seemed much less able to tolerate living alone. Seven of the ten men in the study had re-paired before the end of the study (approximately one-and-one-half years after bereavement), and two others were being actively pursued by women. The word "re-pair" is used here with double entendre: though they paired quickly, we sensed that many of these men had not truly repaired themselves. Some had formed relationships so quickly—two within the first few weeks of bereavement—that they had not yet accomplished the necessary work of mourning. In contrast, of the twenty-six widows in the groups, only three had paired before the end of the study. The widows in general were hesitant to become romantically involved with someone new too soon and seemed anxious about the idea of being pursued or, worse yet, being pursuers. The change in social mores that permits women to be more aggressive in dating was unsettling to many of the older widows, and many felt uncertain about how to behave on even a simple dinner date. Because widows outnumber eligible widowers, and because widowers have socioeconomic advantages and often a greater potential for future parenthood, the widows in our group generally felt quite disadvantaged and sometimes embittered as they faced future prospects for new relationships.

Existential Themes   Some of our members expressed considerable anger during group sessions. Often this anger was directed toward physicians, particularly physicians who had missed the diagnosis or who had been insensitive to the needs of the patient or the family. Others were aware of feeling angry toward their deceased spouse, generally because the spouse had shown persistent denial while ill or had refused to express feelings openly in the final stages of life.

But there was also considerable anger that could not be focused—anger at life, at destiny, at the unfairness of it all. Members became painfully aware of the fragility of their assumptions and worldviews, as they understood that the concept of justice, for example, is entirely human-made and human-serving. Many of the bereaved spouses reported realizing for the first time that there is no justice out there in nature, no rules that good will be rewarded and that working hard as a couple for decades to ensure a comfortable retirement places no mandate upon life to cooperate in such plans. Members struggled for some time with their recognition of the existential facts of life—of the indifference of the universe, of the random and contingent world into which we are thrown, of our own finiteness. For some, the dissolution of a belief in personal omnipotence was a startling revelation. One very articulate young woman described the experience of driving home from work and stopping at a stoplight. She mused about what it would be like if her husband were still alive; he could be crossing the street just in front of her. She entered a familiar reverie in which she was certain that she could will him back, that she could alter the past, and then suddenly reality struck her with a terrible thud: she realized, and it was as though she realized it for the first time, that time was irreversible, that all her wishing and willing was not going to bring him back.

The death of the spouse confronted nearly all of the subjects with their own mortality. A few members described increased fear—concern about personal safety, fear of being alone, ghost fear, hypochondriacal fears—but most used their increased awareness of personal death in a positive way. They stated that an awareness of life's brevity meant that they had to decide on what is important in life, what it means to seize the moment, to live fully, to appreciate each present moment and not be distracted by trivial concerns. Some described finally planning trips they had always wanted to take; others began to indulge their children and grandchildren, to buy things for themselves, to take up new hobbies. Now that they had learned the significance of words left unsaid or pleasurable experiences missed, members expressed their newfound desire to avoid future regrets and guilt for things not done or problems left unsolved. The death of their spouses served in this manner to teach them existential responsibility—that they, and only they, have ultimate responsibility for their life and their happiness.

Conclusion

In our view, the groups were highly successful: the members were deeply engaged, cohesion was high, many meetings were powerful, attendance was excellent (approximately one person absent per meeting), the groups displayed high levels of trust and self-disclosure, and only two members dropped out of the groups. At the one-year follow-up all but two members gave high testimonials to the group (one member, a religious zealot, felt the groups were too secular, while the other had remarried before the project began and considered many of the group meetings irrelevant to her life situation).

In conclusion, we found that our most important role as group leaders was to anticipate and facilitate a natural process of self-exploration and change, either by staying out of the way of the free-flowing currents of the bereavement groups or by serving as gentle midwives to themes and concerns that emerged almost spontaneously during the course of the group work. We believe that if one is able to live with the living, one can learn to live with the dead. Rather than dwelling on loss, pain, or emotional catharsis, we found ourselves concentrating on growth, self-knowledge, and existential responsibility. Rather than dealing with the silence and loneliness of bereavement, we found ourselves working where, in Tennyson's words, "the noise of life begins again."[6]

PART II

EXISTENTIAL
PSYCHOTHERAPY

CHAPTER 4

The Four Ultimate Concerns

INTRODUCTION

My text *Existential Psychotherapy* was four years in the writing. But before the writing I spent twice that long in the reading—all the while procrastinating and doubting whether the project was within my ability. I was jump-started one day while discussing my interminable reading program with a friend, Alex Comfort, who was prodigiously adept at starting and finishing books. (He wrote forty-five books, including novels; poetry; works of philosophy, medicine, and gerontology; and the highly successful *Joy of Sex*.) His advice was simple and liberating: *"Stop reading; start writing."* I put pencil to paper (in those precomputer days) the very next morning.

Existential Psychotherapy was a textbook for a course that did not yet exist, delineating a professional discipline that was both amorphous and controversial. The introduction to the book, part of which is included in the following selection, gives an overview of the book that defines and discusses the field in terms of four deep, ever-present, and clinically relevant ultimate concerns of human life.

EXISTENTIAL PSYCHOTHERAPY: THE INTRODUCTION

Once, several years ago, some friends and I enrolled in a cooking class taught by an Armenian matriarch and her aged servant. Since they spoke no English and we no Armenian, communication was not easy. She taught by demonstration; we watched (and diligently tried to quantify her recipes) as she prepared an array of marvelous eggplant and lamb dishes. But our recipes were imperfect; and, hard as we tried, we could not duplicate her dishes. "What was it," I wondered, "that gave her cooking that special touch?" The answer eluded me until one day, when I was keeping a particularly keen watch on the kitchen proceedings, I saw our teacher, with great dignity and deliberation, prepare a dish. She handed it to her servant, who wordlessly carried it into the kitchen to the oven and, without breaking stride, threw in handful after handful of assorted spices and condiments. I am convinced that those surreptitious "throw-ins" made all the difference.

That cooking class often comes to mind when I think about psychotherapy, especially when I think about the critical ingredients of successful therapy. Formal texts, journal articles, and lectures portray therapy as precise and systematic, with carefully delineated stages, strategic technical interventions, the methodical development and resolution of transference, analysis of object relations, and a careful, rational program of insight-offering interpretations. Yet I believe deeply that, when no one is looking, the therapist throws in the "real thing."

But what are these "throw-ins," these elusive, off-the-record extras? They exist outside of formal theory, they are not written about, they are not explicitly taught. Therapists are often unaware of them; yet every therapist knows that he or she cannot explain why many patients improve. The critical ingredients are hard to describe, even harder to define. Indeed, is it possible to define and teach such qualities as compassion, "presence," caring, extending oneself, touching the patient at a profound level, or—that most elusive one of all—wisdom?

One of the first recorded cases of modern psychotherapy is highly illustrative of how therapists selectively inattend to these extras.[1] (Later
descriptions of therapy are less useful in this regard because psychiatry
became so doctrinaire about the proper conduct of therapy that off-the-
record maneuvers were omitted from case reports.) In 1892, Sigmund
Freud successfully treated Fraulein Elisabeth von R., a young woman
who was suffering from psychogenic difficulties in walking. Freud explained his therapeutic success solely by his technique of abreaction, of
de-repressing certain noxious wishes and thoughts. However, in studying Freud's notes, one is struck by the vast number of his other therapeutic activities. For example, he sent Elisabeth to visit her sister's grave
and to pay a call upon a young man whom she found attractive. He
demonstrated a "friendly interest in her present circumstances"[2] by
interacting with the family in the patient's behalf: he interviewed the
patient's mother and "begged" her to provide open channels of communication with the patient and to permit the patient to unburden her
mind periodically. Having learned from the mother that Elisabeth had
no possibility of marrying her dead sister's husband, he conveyed that
information to his patient. He helped untangle the family financial tan-
gle. At other times Freud urged Elisabeth to face with calmness the fact
that the future, for everyone, is inevitably uncertain. He repeatedly con-
soled her by assuring her that she was not responsible for unwanted
feelings, and pointed out that her degree of guilt and remorse for these
feelings was powerful evidence of her high moral character. Finally, after the termination of therapy, Freud, hearing that Elisabeth was going
to a private dance, procured an invitation so he could watch her "whirl
past in a lively dance." One cannot help but wonder what really helped
Fraulein von R. Freud's extras, I have no doubt, constituted powerful
interventions; to exclude them from theory is to court error.

It is my purpose in this book to propose and elucidate an approach to
psychotherapy—a theoretical structure and a series of techniques
emerging from that structure—which will provide a framework for
many of the extras of therapy. The label for this approach, "existential
psychotherapy," defies succinct definition, for the underpinnings of the
existential orientation are not empirical but are deeply intuitive. I shall
begin by offering a formal definition, and then, throughout the rest of
this book, I shall elucidate that definition: *Existential psychotherapy is a*

dynamic approach to therapy which focuses on concerns that are rooted in
the individual's existence.

It is my belief that the vast majority of experienced therapists, regardless of their adherence to some other ideological school, employ many of the existential insights I shall describe. The majority of therapists realize, for example, that an apprehension of one's finiteness can often catalyze a major inner shift of perspective, that it is the relationship that heals, that patients are tormented by choice, that a therapist must catalyze a patient's "will" to act, and that the majority of patients are bedeviled by a lack of meaning in their lives.

But the existential approach is more than a subtle accent or an implicit perspective that therapists unwittingly employ. Over the past several years, when lecturing to psychotherapists on a variety of topics, I have asked, "Who among you consider yourselves to be existentially oriented?" A sizable proportion of the audience, generally over 50 percent, respond affirmatively. But when these therapists are asked, "What *is* the existential approach?" they find it difficult to answer. The language used by therapists to describe any therapeutic approach has never been celebrated for its crispness or simple clarity; but, of all the therapy vocabularies, none rivals the existential in vagueness and confusion. Therapists associate the existential approach with such intrinsically imprecise and apparently unrelated terms as "authenticity," "encounter," "responsibility," "choice," "humanistic," "self-actualization," "centering," "Sartrean," and "Heideggerian"; and many mental health professionals have long considered it a muddled, "soft," irrational, and romantic orientation which, rather than being an "approach," offers a license for improvisation, for undisciplined, woolly therapists to "do their thing." I hope to demonstrate that such conclusions are unwarranted, that the existential approach is a valuable, effective psychotherapeutic paradigm— as rational, as coherent, and as systematic as any other.

Existential Therapy: A Dynamic Psychotherapy

Existential psychotherapy is a form of dynamic psychotherapy. "Dynamic" is a term frequently used in the mental health field—as in "psychodynamics"; and if one is to understand one of the basic features of the existential approach, it is necessary to be clear about the meaning of dynamic therapy. "Dynamic" has both lay and technical meanings. In the lay sense "dynamic" (deriving from the Greek *dunasthi,* "to have strength or power") evokes energy and movement (a "dynamic" football player or politician, "dynamo," "dynamite"); but this is not its technical sense for, if it were, what therapist would own to being nondynamic—that is, slow, sluggish, stagnant, inert? No, the term has a specific technical use that involves the concept of "force." Freud's major contribution to the understanding of the human being is his dynamic model of mental functioning—a model that posits that there are forces in conflict within the individual, and that thought, emotion, and behavior, both adaptive and psychopathological, are the resultant of these conflicting forces. Furthermore—and this is important—*these forces exist at varying levels of awareness;* some, indeed, are entirely unconscious.

The psychodynamics of an individual thus include the various unconscious and conscious forces, motives, and fears that operate within him or her. The dynamic psychotherapies are therapies based upon this dynamic model of mental functioning.

So far, so good. Existential therapy, as I shall describe it, fits comfortably in the category of the dynamic therapies. But what if we ask, Which forces (and fears and motives) are in conflict? What is the *content* of this internal conscious and unconscious struggle? It is at this juncture that dynamic existential therapy parts company from the other dynamic therapies. Existential therapy is based on a radically different view of the specific forces, motives, and fears that interact in the individual.

The precise nature of the deepest internal conflicts is never easy to identify. The clinician working with a troubled patient is rarely able to examine primal conflicts in pristine form. Instead, the patient harbors an enormously complex set of concerns: the primary concerns are deeply buried, encrusted with layer upon layer of repression, denial, displacement, and symbolization. The clinical investigator must contend with a clinical picture of many threads so matted together that disentanglement is difficult. To identify the primary conflicts, one must use many avenues of access—deep reflection, dreams, nightmares, flashes of profound experience and insight, psychotic utterances, and the study of children. I shall, in time, explore these avenues, but for now a stylized schematic presentation may be helpful.

Existential Psychodynamics

The existential position emphasizes *a conflict that flows from the individual's confrontation with the givens of existence.* And I mean by "givens" of existence certain ultimate concerns, certain intrinsic properties that are a part, and an inescapable part, of the human being's existence in the world.

How does one discover the nature of these givens? In one sense the task is not difficult. The method is deep personal reflection. The conditions are simple: solitude, silence, time, and freedom from the everyday distractions with which each of us fills his or her experiential world. If we can brush away or "bracket" the everyday world, if we reflect deeply upon our "situation" in the world, upon our existence, our boundaries, our possibilities, if we arrive at the ground that underlies all other ground, we invariably confront the givens of existence, the "deep structures," which I shall henceforth refer to as "ultimate concerns." This process of reflection is often catalyzed by certain urgent experiences. These "boundary," or "border," situations, as they are often referred to, include such experiences as a confrontation with one's own death, some major irreversible decision, or the collapse of some fundamental meaning-providing schema.

This book deals with four ultimate concerns: death, freedom, isolation, and meaninglessness. The individual's confrontation with each of these facts of life constitutes the content of the existential dynamic conflict.

Death   The most obvious, the most easily apprehended ultimate concern is death. We exist now, but one day we shall cease to be. Death will come, and there is no escape from it. It is a terrible truth, and we respond to it with mortal terror. "Everything," in Spinoza's words, "endeavors to persist in its own being";[3] and a core existential conflict is the tension between the awareness of the inevitability of death and the wish to continue to be.

Freedom   Another ultimate concern, a far less accessible one, is freedom. Ordinarily we think of freedom as an unequivocally positive concept. Throughout recorded history has not the human being yearned and striven for freedom? Yet freedom viewed from the per-spective of ultimate ground is riveted to dread. In its existential sense "freedom" refers to the absence of external structure. Contrary to every-day experience, the human being does not enter (and leave) a well-struc-tured universe that has an inherent design. Rather, the individual is entirely responsible for—that is, is the author of—his or her own world, life design, choices, and actions. "Freedom," in this sense, has a terrify-ing implication: it means that beneath us there is no ground—nothing, a void, an abyss. A key existential dynamic, then, is the clash between our confrontation with groundlessness and our wish for ground and structure.

Existential Isolation   A third ultimate concern is isolation—not *in-terpersonal* isolation with its attendant loneliness, or *intrapersonal* isola-tion (isolation from parts of oneself), but a fundamental isolation—an isolation both from creatures and from world—which cuts beneath other isolation. No matter how close each of us becomes to another, there remains a final, unbridgeable gap; each of us enters existence alone and must depart from it alone. The existential conflict is thus the tension between our awareness of our absolute isolation and our wish for contact, for protection, our wish to be part of a larger whole.

Meaninglessness   A fourth ultimate concern, or given, of existence is meaninglessness. If we must die, if we constitute our own world, if each is ultimately alone in an indifferent universe, then what meaning does life have? Why do we live? How shall we live? If there is no preor-dained design for us, then each of us must construct our own meanings in life. Yet can a meaning of one's own creation be sturdy enough to bear one's life? This existential dynamic conflict stems from the dilemma of a meaning-seeking creature who is thrown into a universe that has no meaning.

The Existential Orientation: Strange but Oddly Familiar

A great deal of my material on the ultimate concerns will appear strange yet, in an odd way, familiar to the clinician. The material will appear strange because the existential approach cuts across common categories and clusters clinical observations in a novel manner. Furthermore, much of the vocabulary is different. Even if I avoid the jargon of the professional philosopher and use commonsense terms to describe existential concepts, the clinician will find the language psychologically alien. Where is the psychotherapy lexicon that contains such terms as "choice," "responsibility," "freedom," "existential isolation," "mortality," "purpose in life," "willing"? The medical library computers snickered at me when I requested literature searches in these areas.

Yet the clinician will find in them much that is familiar. I believe that the experienced clinician often operates implicitly within an existential framework: "in his bones" he appreciates a patient's concerns and responds accordingly. That response is what I meant earlier by the crucial "throw-ins." A major task of this book is to shift the therapist's focus, to attend carefully to these vital concerns and to the therapeutic transactions that occur on the periphery of formal therapy, and to place them where they belong—in the center of the therapeutic arena.

Another familiar note is that the major existential concerns have been recognized and discussed since the beginning of written thought, and that their primacy has been recognized by an unbroken stream of philosophers, theologians, and poets. That fact may offend our sense of pride in modernism, our sense of an eternal spiral of progress; but from another perspective, we may feel reassured to travel a well-worn path trailing back into time, hewed by the wisest and the most thoughtful of individuals.

These existential sources of dread are familiar, too, in that they are the experience of the therapist as Everyman; they are by no means the exclusive province of the psychologically troubled individual. Repeatedly, I shall stress that they are part of the human condition. How then, one may ask, can a theory of psychopathology* rest on factors that are experienced by every individual? The answer, of course, is that each person experiences the stress of the human condition in highly individualized fashion.

In fact, only the universality of human suffering can account for the

---

*In this discussion, as elsewhere, I refer to psychologically based disturbance, not to the major psychoses with a fundamental biochemical origin.

common observation that patienthood is ubiquitous. André Malraux, to cite one such observation, once asked a parish priest who had been taking confession for fifty years what he had learned about mankind. The priest replied, "First of all, people are much more unhappy than one thinks . . . and then the fundamental fact is that there is no such thing as a grown-up person."[4] Often it is only external circumstances that result in one person, and not another, being labeled a patient: for example, financial resources, availability of psychotherapists, personal and cultural attitudes toward therapy, or choice of profession—the majority of psychotherapists become themselves bona fide patients. The universality of stress is one of the major reasons that scholars encounter such difficulty when attempting to define and describe normality: the difference between normality and pathology is quantitative, not qualitative.

The contemporary model that seems most consistent with the evidence is analogous to a model in physical medicine that suggests that infectious disease is not simply a result of a bacterial or a viral agent invading an undefended body. Rather, disease is a result of a disequilibrium between the noxious agent and host resistance. In other words, noxious agents exist within the body at all times—just as stresses, inseparable from living, confront all individuals. Whether an individual develops clinical disease depends on the body's resistance (that is, such factors as immunological system, nutrition, and fatigue) to the agent: when resistance is lowered, disease develops, even though the toxicity and the virility of the noxious agent are unchanged. Thus, all human beings are in a quandary, but some are unable to cope with it: psychopathology depends not merely on the presence or the absence of stress but on the interaction between ubiquitous stress and the individual's mechanisms of defense.

The claim that the ultimate existential concerns never arise in therapy is entirely a function of a therapist's selective inattention: a listener tuned in to the proper channel finds explicit and abundant material. A therapist may choose, however, not to attend to the existential ultimate concerns precisely because they are universal experiences, and therefore nothing constructive can come from exploring them. Indeed, I have often noted in clinical work that when existential concerns are broached, the therapist and the patient are intensely energized for a short while;

but soon the discussion becomes desultory, and the patient and therapist seem to say tacitly, "Well that's life, isn't it! Let's move on to something neurotic, something we can do something about!"

Other therapists veer away from dealing with existential concerns not only because these concerns are universal but because they are too terrible to face. After all, neurotic patients (and therapists, too) have enough to worry about without adding such cheery items as death and meaninglessness. Such therapists believe that existential issues are best ignored, since there are only two ways to deal with the brutal existential facts of life—anxious truth or denial—and either is unpalatable. Cervantes voiced this problem when his immortal Don said, "Which would you have, wise madness or foolish sanity?"

An existential therapeutic position, as I shall attempt to demonstrate in later chapters, rejects this dilemma. Wisdom does not lead to madness, nor denial to sanity: the confrontation with the givens of existence is painful but ultimately healing. Good therapeutic work is always coupled with reality testing and the search for personal enlightenment; the therapist who decides that certain aspects of reality and truth are to be eschewed is on treacherous ground. Thomas Hardy's comment, "if a way to the Better there be, it exacts a full look at the Worst,"[5] is a good frame for the therapeutic approach I shall describe.

The Field of Existential Psychotherapy

Existential psychotherapy is rather a homeless waif. It does not really "belong" anywhere. It has no homestead, no formal school, no institution; it is not welcomed into the better academic neighborhoods. It has no formal society, no robust journal (a few sickly offspring were carried away in their infancy), no stable family, no paterfamilias. It does, however, have a genealogy, a few scattered cousins, and friends of the family, some in the old country, some in America.

Existential Philosophy: The Ancestral Home

"Existentialism is not easily definable." So begins the discussion of existential philosophy in philosophy's major contemporary encyclopedia.[6] Most other reference works begin in similar fashion and underscore the fact that two philosophers both labeled "existential" may disagree on every cardinal point (aside from their shared aversion to being so labeled). Most philosophical texts resolve the problem of definition by listing a number of themes relating to existence (for example, being, choice, freedom, death, isolation, absurdity), and by proclaiming that an existential philosopher is one whose work is dedicated to exploring them. (This is, of course, the strategy I use to identify the field of existential psychotherapy.)

There is an existential "tradition" in philosophy and a formal existential "school" of philosophy. Obviously the existential tradition is ageless. What great thinker has not at some point in both work and life turned his or her attention to life and death issues? The formal school of existential philosophy, however, has a clearly demarcated beginning. Some trace it to a Sunday afternoon in 1834, when a young Dane sat in a café smoking a cigar and mused upon the fact that he was on his way to becoming an old man without having made a contribution to the world. He thought about his many successful friends:

> . . . benefactors of the age who know how to benefit mankind by making life easier and easier, some by railways, others by omnibuses and steamboats, others by telegraph, others by easily apprehended compendiums and short recitals of everything worth knowing, and finally the true benefactors of the age who by virtue of thought make spiritual existence systematically easier and easier.[7]

His cigar burned out. The young Dane, Søren Kierkegaard, lit another and continued musing. Suddenly there flashed in his mind this thought:

> You must do something but inasmuch as with your limited capacities it will be impossible to make anything easier than it has become, you must, with the same humanitarian enthusiasm as the others, undertake to make something harder.[8]

He reasoned that when all combine to make everything easier, then there is a danger that easiness will be excessive. Perhaps someone is needed to make things difficult again. It occurred to him that he had discovered his destiny: he was to go in search of difficulties—like a new Socrates.[9] And which difficulties? They were not hard to find. He had only to consider his own situation in existence, his own dread, his choices, his possibilities and limitations.

Kierkegaard devoted the remainder of his short life to exploring his existential situation and during the 1840s published several important existential treatises. His work remained untranslated for many years and exerted little influence until after the First World War, when it found fertile soil and was taken up by Martin Heidegger and Karl Jaspers.

The relation of existential therapy to the existential school of philosophy is much like that of clinical pharmacotherapy to biochemical bench research. I shall frequently draw upon philosophical works to explicate, corroborate, or illustrate some of the clinical issues; but it is not my intention (nor within my range of scholarship) to discuss in a comprehensive fashion the works of any philosopher or the major tenets of existential philosophy. This is a book for clinicians, and I mean it to be clinically useful. My excursions into philosophy will be brief and pragmatic; I shall limit myself to those domains that offer leverage in clinical work. I cannot blame the professional philosopher who may liken me to the Viking raider who grabbed gemstones while leaving behind their intricate and precious settings.

As the education of the great majority of psychotherapists includes little or no emphasis on philosophy, I shall not assume any philosophical background in my readers. When I do draw upon philosophical texts, I shall attempt to do so in a straightforward, jargon-free fashion—not an easy task, incidentally, since professional existential philosophers surpass even psychoanalytic theoreticians in the use of turbid, convoluted language. The single most important philosophical text in the field, Heidegger's *Being and Time,* stands alone as the undisputed champion of linguistic obfuscation.

I have never understood the reason for the impenetrable deep-sounding language. The basic existential concepts themselves are not complex; they do not need to be uncoded and meticulously analyzed as much as they need to be uncovered. Every person, at some point in life, enters a "brown study" and has some traffic with existential ultimate concerns. What is required is not formal explication: the task of the philosopher, and of the therapist as well, is to de-repress, to reacquaint the individual with something he or she has known all along. This is precisely the reason that many of the leading existential thinkers (for example, Jean-Paul Sartre, Albert Camus, Miguel de Unamuno, Martin Buber) prefer literary exposition rather than formal philosophical argument. Above all, the philosopher and the therapist must encourage the individual to look within and to attend to his or her existential situation.

Existential Therapy and the Academic Community

Earlier I likened existential therapy to a homeless waif who was not permitted into the better academic neighborhoods. The lack of academic support from academic psychiatry and psychology has significant implications for the field of existential therapy, since academically dominated institutions control all the vital supply routes that influence the development of the clinical disciplines: the training of clinicians and academicians, research funding, licensure, and journal publication.

It is worth taking a moment to consider why the existential approach is so quarantined by the academic establishment. The answer centers primarily on the issue of the basis of knowledge—that is, how do we know what we know? Academic psychiatry and psychology, grounded in a positivist tradition, value empirical research as the method of validating knowledge.

Consider the typical career of the academician (and I speak not only from observation but from my own twenty-year academic career): the young lecturer or assistant professor is hired because he or she displays aptitude and motivation for empirical research, and later is rewarded and promoted for carefully and methodically performed research. The crucial tenure decision is made on the basis of the amount of empirical research published in refereed scientific journals. Other factors, such as teaching skills or nonempirical books, book chapters, and essays, are given decidedly secondary consideration.

It is extraordinarily difficult for a scholar to carve out an academic career based upon an empirical investigation of existential issues. The basic tenets of existential therapy are such that empirical research methods are often inapplicable or inappropriate. For example, the empirical research method requires that the investigator study a complex organism by breaking it down into its component parts, each simple enough to permit empirical investigation. Yet this fundamental principle negates a basic existential principle. A story told by Viktor Frankl is illustrative.[10]

Two neighbors were involved in a bitter dispute. One claimed that the other's cat had eaten his butter and, accordingly, demanded compensation. Unable to resolve the problem, the two, carrying the accused cat, sought out the village wise man for a judgment. The wise man asked the accuser, "How much butter did the cat eat?" "Ten pounds" was the response. The wise man placed the cat on the scale. Lo and behold! It weighed exactly ten pounds. "Mirabile dictu!" he proclaimed. "Here we have the butter. But where is the cat?"

Where is the cat? All the parts taken together do not reconstruct the creature. A fundamental humanistic credo is that "man is greater than the sum of his parts." No matter how carefully one understands the composite parts of the mind—for example, the conscious and the unconscious, the superego, the ego, and the id—one still does not grasp the central vital agency, the person whose unconscious (or superego or id or ego) it is. Furthermore, the empirical approach never helps one to learn the *meaning* of this psychic structure to the person who possesses it. Meaning can never be obtained from a study of component parts, because meaning is never caused; it is created by a person who is supraordinate to all his parts.

But there is in the existential approach a problem for empirical research even more fundamental than the one of "Where is the cat?" Rollo May alluded to it when he defined existentialism as "the endeavor to understand man by cutting below the cleavage between subject and object which has bedeviled Western thought and science since shortly after the Renaissance."[11] The "cleavage between subject and object"— let us take a closer look at that. The existential position challenges the traditional Cartesian view of a world full of objects and of subjects who perceive those objects. Obviously, this is the basic premise of the scientific method: there are objects with a finite set of properties that can be understood through objective investigation. The existential position cuts below this subject-object cleavage and regards the person not as a subject who can, under the proper circumstances, perceive external reality but as a consciousness who participates in the construction of reality. To emphasize this point, Heidegger always spoke of the human being as *dasein. Da* ("there") refers to the fact that the person is there, is a constituted object (an "empirical ego"), but at the same time constitutes the world (that is, is a "transcendental ego"). *Dasein* is at once the meaning giver and the known. Each *dasein* therefore constitutes its own world; to study all beings with some standard instrument as though they inhabited the same objective world is to introduce monumental error into one's observations.

It is important to keep in mind, however, that the limitations of empirical psychotherapy research are not confined to an existential orientation in therapy; it is only that they are more explicit in the existential approach. Insofar as therapy is a deeply personal, human experience, the empirical study of psychotherapy of any ideological school will contain errors and be of limited value. It is common knowledge that psychotherapy research has had, in its thirty-year history, little impact upon the practice of therapy. In fact, as Carl Rogers, the founding father of empirical psychotherapy research, sadly noted, not even psychotherapy researchers take their research findings seriously enough to alter their approach to psychotherapy.[12]

What is the alternative to an empirical approach? The proper method of understanding the inner world of another individual is the "phenomenological" one, to go directly to the phenomena themselves, to encounter the other without "standardized" instruments and presuppositions. So far as possible one must "bracket" one's own world perspective and enter the experiential world of the other. Such an approach to knowing another person is eminently feasible in psychotherapy: every good therapist tries to relate to the patient in this manner. That is what is meant by empathy, presence, genuine listening, nonjudgmental acceptance, or an attitude of "disciplined naïvety"—to use May's felicitous phrase.[13] Existential therapists have always urged that the therapist attempt to understand the private world of the patient rather than to focus on the way the patient has deviated from the "norms."

I have attempted to write this book in a style sufficiently lucid and free of jargon that it will be intelligible to the lay reader. However, the primary audience for whom I intend it is the student and the practicing psychotherapist. It is important to note that, even though I assume for my reader no formal philosophical education, I do assume some clinical background. I do not mean this to be a "first" or a complete psychotherapy text but expect the reader to be familiar with conventional clinical explanatory systems. Hence, when I describe clinical phenomena from an existential frame of reference, I do not always offer alternate modes of explanation for them. My task, as I view it, is to describe a coherent psychotherapy approach based on existential concerns which gives an explicit place to the procedures that the majority of therapists employ implicitly.

I do not pretend to describe *the* theory of psychopathology and psychotherapy. Instead, I present a paradigm, a psychological construct, that offers the clinician a system of explanation—a system that permits him or her to make sense out of a large array of clinical data and to formulate a systematic strategy of psychotherapy. It is a paradigm that has considerable explanatory power; it is parsimonious (that is, it rests on relatively few basic assumptions) and it is accessible (that is, the assumptions rest on experiences that may be intuitively perceived by every introspective individual). Furthermore, it is a humanistically based paradigm, consonant with the deeply human nature of the therapeutic enterprise.

But it is *a* paradigm, not *the* paradigm—useful for some patients, not for all patients; employable by some therapists, not by all therapists. The existential orientation is one clinical approach among other approaches. It repatterns clinical data but, like other paradigms, has no exclusive hegemony and is not capable of explaining all behavior. The human being has too much complexity and possibility to permit that it do so.

Existence is inexorably free and, thus, uncertain. Cultural institutions and psychological constructs often obscure this state of affairs, but confrontation with one's existential situation reminds one that paradigms are self-created, wafer-thin barriers against the pain of uncertainty. The mature therapist must, in the existential theoretical approach as in any other, be able to tolerate this fundamental uncertainty.

CHAPTER 5

—————

Death, Anxiety, and Psychotherapy

INTRODUCTION

Existential Psychotherapy is divided into four sections, each of which explores, from a clinical perspective, one of the core existential concerns—death, freedom, isolation, and meaning in life. This chapter excerpts what is perhaps the most fundamental and most important section of the work—the discussion of death and its implications for psychopathology and psychotherapy.

DEATH

[Let us explore] the role played by the concept of death in psychopathology and psychotherapy. The basic postulates I describe are simple:

1. The fear of death plays a major role in our internal experience; it haunts as does nothing else; it rumbles continuously under the

surface; it is a dark, unsettling presence at the rim of consciousness.

2. The child, at an early age, is pervasively preoccupied with death, and his or her major developmental task is to deal with terrifying fears of obliteration.

3. To cope with these fears, we erect defenses against death awareness, defenses that are based on denial, that shape character structure, and that, if maladaptive, result in clinical syndromes. In other words, psychopathology is the result of ineffective modes of death transcendence.

4. Lastly, a robust and effective approach to psychotherapy may be constructed on the foundation of death awareness.

LIFE, DEATH, AND ANXIETY

"Don't scratch where it doesn't itch," the great Adolph Meyer counseled a generation of student psychiatrists.[1] Is that adage not an excellent argument against investigating patients' attitudes toward death? Do not patients have quite enough fear and quite enough dread without the therapist reminding them of the grimmest of life's horrors? Why focus on bitter and immutable reality? If the goal of therapy is to instill hope, why invoke hope-defeating death? The aim of therapy is to help the individual learn how to live. Why not leave death for the dying?

These arguments demand a response, and I shall address them in this chapter by arguing that death itches all the time, that our attitudes toward death influence the way we live and grow and the way we falter and fall ill. I shall examine two basic propositions, each of which has major implications for the practice of psychotherapy:

1. Life and death are interdependent; they exist simultaneously, not consecutively; death whirs continuously beneath the membrane of life and exerts a vast influence upon experience and conduct.

2. Death is a primordial source of anxiety and, as such, is the primary fount of psychopathology.

Life-Death Interdependence

A venerable line of thought, stretching back to the beginning of written thought, emphasizes the interdigitation of life and death. It is one of life's most self-evident truths that everything fades, that we fear the fading, and that we must live, nonetheless, in the face of the fading, in the face of the fear. Death, the Stoics said, is the most important event in life. Learning to live well is to learn to die well; and conversely, learning to die well is to learn to live well. Cicero said, "To philosophize is to prepare for death,"[2] and Seneca: "No man enjoys the true taste of life but he who is willing and ready to quit it."[3] Saint Augustine expressed the same idea: "It is only in the face of death that man's self is born."[4]

It is not possible to leave death to the dying. The biological life-death boundary is relatively precise; but, psychologically, life and death merge into each other. Death is a fact of life; a moment's reflection tells us that death is not simply the last moment of life. "Even in birth we die; the end is there from the start," Manilius said.[5] Montaigne, in his penetrating essay on death, asked, "Why do you fear your last day? It contributes no more to your death than each of the others. The last step does not cause the fatigue, but reveals it."[6]

Virtually every great thinker (generally early in life or toward its end) has thought deeply and written about death; and many have concluded that death is inextricably a part of life, and that lifelong consideration of death enriches rather than impoverishes life. Although the physicality of death destroys man, the idea of death saves him.

This last thought is so important that it bears repeating: although the *physicality* of death destroys man, the *idea* of death saves him. But what precisely does this statement mean? How does the idea of death save man? And save him from what?

A brief look at a core concept of existential philosophy may provide clarification. Martin Heidegger, in 1926, explored how the idea of death may save man, and arrived at the important insight that the awareness

of our personal death acts as a spur to shift us from one mode of existence to a higher one. Heidegger believed that there are two fundamental modes of existing in the world: (1) a state of forgetfulness of being or
(2) a state of mindfulness of being.[7]

When one lives in a state of *forgetfulness of being,* one lives in the
world of things and immerses oneself in the everyday diversions of life:
One is "leveled down," absorbed in "idle chatter," lost in the "they."
One surrenders oneself to the everyday world, to a concern about the
way things are.

In the other state, the state of *mindfulness of being,* one marvels not
about the *way* things are but *that* they are. To exist in this mode means
to be continually aware of being. In this mode, which is often referred to
as the "ontological mode" (from the Greek *ontos,* meaning "existence"),
one remains mindful of being, not only mindful of the fragility of being
but mindful, too, of one's responsibility for one's own being. Since it
is only in this ontological mode that one is in touch with one's self-
creation, it is only here that one can grasp the power to change oneself.

Ordinarily one lives in the first state. Forgetfulness of being is the
everyday mode of existence. Heidegger refers to it as "inauthentic"—a
mode in which one is unaware of one's authorship of one's life and
world, in which one "flees," "falls," and is tranquilized, in which one
avoids choices by being "carried along by the nobody."[8] When, however,
one enters the second mode of being (mindfulness of being), one exists
authentically (hence, the frequent modern use of the term "authenticity" in psychology). In this state, one becomes fully self-aware—aware
of oneself as a transcendental (constituting) ego as well as an empirical
(constituted) ego; one embraces one's possibilities and limits; one faces
absolute freedom and nothingness—and is anxious in the face of them.

Now, what does death have to do with all this? Heidegger realized
that one doesn't move from a state of forgetfulness of being to a more
enlightened, anxious mindfulness of being by simple contemplation, by
bearing down, by gritting one's teeth. There are certain unalterable, ir-
remediable conditions, certain "urgent experiences" that jolt one, that
tug one from the first, everyday, state of existence to the state of mindfulness of being. Of these urgent experiences (Jaspers later referred to
them as "border" or "boundary" or "limit" situations),[9] death is the non-

pareil: *death is the condition that makes it possible for us to live life in an authentic fashion.*

This point of view—that death makes a positive contribution to life—is not one easily accepted. Generally we view death as such an unmitigated evil that we dismiss any contrary view as an implausible joke. We can manage quite well without the plague, thank you.

But suspend judgment for a moment and imagine life without any thought of death. Life loses something of its intensity. Life shrinks when death is denied. Freud, who for reasons I shall discuss shortly spoke little of death, believed that the transience of life augments our joy in it. "Limitation in the possibility of an enjoyment raises the value of the enjoyment." Freud, writing during the First World War, said that the lure of war was that it brought death into life once again. "Life has, indeed, become interesting again; it has recovered its full content."[10] When death is excluded, when one loses sight of the stakes involved, life becomes impoverished. It is turned into something, Freud wrote, "as shallow and empty as, let us say, an American flirtation, in which it is understood from the first that nothing is to happen, as contrasted with a continental love-affair in which both partners must constantly bear its serious consequences in mind."[11]

Many have speculated that the absence of the *fact* of death, as well as of the idea of death, would result in the same blunting of one's sensibilities to life. For example, Montaigne imagines a conversation in which Chiron, half-god, half-mortal, refuses immortality when his father, Saturn (the god of time and duration), describes the implications of the choice:

Imagine honestly how much less bearable and more painful to man would be an everlasting life than the life I have given him. If you did not have death, you would curse me incessantly for having deprived you of it. I have deliberately mixed with it a little bitterness to keep you, seeing the convenience of it, from embracing it too greedily and intemperately. To lodge you in the moderate state that I ask of you, of neither fleeing life nor fleeing back from death, I have tempered both of them between sweetness and bitterness.[12]

I do not wish to advocate a life-denying morbidity. But it must not be forgotten that our basic dilemma is that each of us is both angel and beast of the field; we are the mortal creatures who, because we are self-aware, know that we are mortal. A denial of death at any level is a denial of one's basic nature and begets an increasingly pervasive restriction of awareness and experience. The integration of the *idea* of death saves us; rather than sentence us to existences of terror or bleak pessimism, it acts as a catalyst to plunge us into more authentic life modes, and it enhances our pleasure in the living of life. As corroboration we have the testimony of individuals who have had a personal confrontation with death.

Confrontation with Death: Personal Change

Some of our greatest literary works have portrayed the positive effects on an individual of a close encounter with death.

Tolstoy's *War and Peace* provides an excellent illustration of how death may instigate a radical personal change.[13] Pierre, the protagonist, feels deadened by the meaningless, empty life of the Russian aristocracy. A lost soul, he stumbles through the first nine hundred pages of the novel searching for some purpose in life. The pivotal point of the book occurs when Pierre is captured by Napoleon's troops and sentenced to death by firing squad. Sixth in line, he watches the execution of the five men in front of him and prepares to die—only, at the last moment, to be unexpectedly reprieved. The experience transforms Pierre, who then spends the remaining three hundred pages of the novel living his life zestfully and purposefully. He is able to give himself fully in his relationships to others, to be keenly aware of his natural surroundings, to discover a task in life that has meaning for him, and to dedicate himself to it.

Tolstoy's story "The Death of Ivan Ilych" contains a similar message.[14] Ivan Ilych, a mean-spirited bureaucrat, develops a fatal illness, probably abdominal cancer, and suffers extraordinary pain. His anguish continues relentlessly until, shortly before his death, Ivan Ilych comes upon a stunning truth: *he is dying badly because he has lived badly*. In the few days remaining to him, Ivan Ilych undergoes a dramatic transformation that is difficult to describe in any other terms than personal growth. If Ivan Ilych were a patient, any psychotherapist would beam with pride at the changes in him: he relates more empathically to others; his chronic bitterness, arrogance, and self-aggrandizement disappear. In short, in the last few days of his life he achieves a far higher level of integration than he has ever reached previously.

This phenomenon occurs with great frequency in the world of the clinician. For example, interviews with six of the ten would-be suicides who leaped off the Golden Gate Bridge and survived indicate that, as a result of their leap into death, these six had changed their views of life.[15] One reported, "My will to live has taken over. . . . There is a benevolent God in heaven who permeates all things in the universe." Another: "We are all members of the Godhead—that great God humanity." Another: "I have a strong life drive now. . . . My whole life is reborn. . . . I have broken out of old pathways. . . . I can now sense other people's existence." Another: "I feel I love God now and wish to do something for others." Another:

> I was refilled with a new hope and purpose in being alive. It's beyond most people's comprehension. I appreciate the miracle of life—like watching a bird fly—everything is more meaningful when you come close to losing it. I experienced a feeling of unity with all things and a oneness with all people. After my psychic rebirth I also feel for everyone's pain. Everything was clear and bright.

Russell Noyes studied two hundred individuals who had near-death experiences (automobile accidents, drownings, mountain climbing falls, and so forth), and reported that a substantial number (23 percent) described, even years later, that as a result of their experience they possessed a

> strong sense of the shortness of life and the preciousness of it . . . a greater sense of zest in life, a heightening of perception and emotional responsivity to immediate surroundings . . . an ability to live in the moment and to savor each moment as it passes . . . a greater

awareness of life—awareness of life and living things and the urge to enjoy it now before it is too late.[16]

Many described a "reassessment of priorities," of becoming more compassionate and more human-oriented than they had been before.

Cancer: Confrontation with Death. The Chinese pictogram for "crisis" is a combination of two symbols: "danger" and "opportunity." Over my many years of work with terminally ill cancer patients, I have been struck by how many of them use their crisis and their danger as an opportunity for change. They report startling shifts, inner changes that can be characterized in no other way than "personal growth":

- A rearrangement of life's priorities: a trivializing of the trivial

- A sense of liberation: being able to choose not to do those things that they do not wish to do

- An enhanced sense of living in the immediate present, rather than postponing life until retirement or some other point in the future

- A vivid appreciation of the elemental facts of life: the changing seasons, the wind, falling leaves, the last Christmas, and so forth

- Deeper communication with loved ones than before the crisis

- Fewer interpersonal fears, less concern about rejection, greater willingness to take risks, than before the crisis.

An unusual confrontation with death afforded a turning point in the life of Arthur, an alcoholic patient. The patient had had a progressive downhill course. He had been drinking heavily for several years and had had no periods of sobriety sufficiently long to permit effective psychotherapeutic contact. He entered a therapy group and one day came to the session so intoxicated that he passed out. The group, with Arthur unconscious on the couch, continued their meeting, discussed what to do with Arthur, and finally carried him bodily from the session to the hospital.

Fortunately the session was videotaped; and later, when Arthur watched the videotape, he had a profound confrontation with death. Everyone had been telling him for years he was drinking himself to death; but until he saw the videotape, he never truly allowed that possibility to register. The videotape of himself stretched out on the couch, with the group surrounding his body and talking about him, bore an uncanny resemblance to the funeral of his twin brother who had died of alcoholism a year previously. He visualized himself at his own wake stretched out on a slab and surrounded by friends talking about him. Arthur was deeply shaken by the vision, embarked on the longest period of sobriety he had had in adult life, and for the first time committed himself to therapeutic work, which was ultimately of considerable benefit to him.

To summarize, the concept of death plays a crucial role in psychotherapy because it plays a crucial role in the life experience of each of us. Death and life are interdependent; though the physicality of death destroys us, the *idea* of death saves us. Recognition of death contributes a sense of poignancy to life, provides a radical shift of life perspective, and can transport one from a mode of living characterized by diversions, tranquilization, and petty anxieties to a more authentic mode. There are, in the examples of individuals undergoing significant personal change after confrontation with death, obvious and important implications for psychotherapy. What is needed are techniques to allow psychotherapists to mine this therapeutic potential with all patients, rather than be dependent upon fortuitous circumstances or the advent of a terminal illness.

Death and Anxiety

Anxiety plays such a central and obvious role in psychotherapy that there is little need to belabor the point. Therapists generally begin work with a patient by focusing on manifest anxiety, anxiety equivalents, or the defenses that the individual sets up in an attempt to protect himself or herself from anxiety. Though therapeutic work extends in many directions, therapists continue to use anxiety as a beacon or compass point: they work toward anxiety, uncover its fundamental sources, and attempt as their final goal to uproot and dismantle these sources.

Death Anxiety: An Influential Determinant of Human Experience and Behavior

The terror of death is ubiquitous and of such magnitude that a considerable portion of one's life energy is consumed in the denial of death. Death transcendence is a major motif in human experience—from the most deeply personal internal phenomena, our defenses, our motivations, our dreams and nightmares, to the most public macro-societal structures, our monuments, theologies, ideologies, slumber cemeteries, embalmings, our stretch into space, indeed our entire way of life—our filling time, our addiction to diversions, our unfaltering belief in the myth of progress, our drive to "get ahead," our yearning for lasting fame.

These social ramifications of the fear of death and the quest for immortality are widespread. Here I am primarily concerned with the effects of death anxiety on the internal dynamics of the individual. I shall argue that the fear of death is a primal source of anxiety. Although this position is simple and consonant with everyday intuition, its ramifications for theory and clinical practice are, as we shall see, extensive.

Death Anxiety: Definition

First, let me examine the meaning of "death anxiety." I shall use several terms interchangeably: "death anxiety," "fear of death," "mortal terror," "fear of finitude." Philosophers speak of the awareness of the "fragility of being" (Jaspers), of dread of "non-being" (Kierkegaard), of the "impossibility of further possibility" (Heidegger), or of ontological anxiety (Tillich). Many of these phrases imply a difference in emphasis, for individuals may experience the fear of death in very different ways. Can we be more precise? What exactly is it that we fear about death?

Researchers investigating this issue have suggested that the fear is a composite of a number of smaller, discrete fears. For example, James Diggory and Doreen Rothman asked a large sample (N = 563) drawn from the general population to rank-order several consequences of death. In order of descending frequency, these were the common fears about death:

1. My death would cause grief to my relatives and friends.

2. All my plans and projects would come to an end.

3. The process of dying might be painful.

4. I could no longer have any experiences.

5. I would no longer be able to care for my dependents.

6. I am afraid of what might happen to me if there is a life after death.

7. I am afraid of what might happen to my body after death.[17]

Of these fears, several seem tangential to personal death. Fears about pain obviously lie on this side of death; fears about an afterlife beg the question by changing death into a nonterminal event; fears about others are obviously not fears about oneself. The fear of personal extinction seems to be at the vortex of concern: "my plans and projects would come to an end" and "I could no longer have any experiences." It is this fear of ceasing to be (obliteration, extinction, annihilation), that seems more centrally the fear of death; and it is this fear to which I refer in this chapter.

Kierkegaard was the first to make a clear distinction between fear and anxiety (dread); he contrasted fear that is fear of *some* thing with dread that is a fear of *no* thing—"not," as he wryly noted, "a nothing with which the individual has nothing to do."[18] One dreads (or is anxious about) losing oneself and becoming nothingness. This anxiety cannot be located. As Rollo May says, "it attacks us from all sides at once."[19] A fear that can neither be understood nor located cannot be confronted and becomes more terrible still: it begets a feeling of helplessness which invariably generates further anxiety.

How can we combat anxiety? *By displacing it from nothing to something.* This is what Kierkegaard meant by "the nothing which is the object of dread becomes, as it were, more and more a something."[20] It is what Rollo May means by "anxiety seeks to become fear."[21] If we can transform a fear of nothing to a fear of something, we can mount some self-protective campaign—that is, we can either avoid the thing we fear, seek allies against it, develop magical rituals to placate it, or plan a systematic campaign to detoxify it.

Death Anxiety: Clinical Manifestations

The fact that anxiety seeks to become fear confounds the clinician's attempt to identify the primal source of anxiety. Primal death anxiety is rarely encountered in its original form in clinical work. Like nascent oxygen, it is rapidly transformed to another state. To ward off death anxiety, the young child develops protective mechanisms which are denial-based, pass through several stages, and eventually consist of a highly complex set of mental operations that repress naked death anxiety and bury it under layers of such defensive operations as displacement, sublimation, and conversion. Occasionally some jolting experience in life tears a rent in the curtain of defenses and permits raw death anxiety to erupt into consciousness. Rapidly, however, the unconscious ego repairs the tear and conceals once again the nature of the anxiety.

I can provide an illustration from my personal experience. While I was engaged in writing *Existential Psychotherapy,* I was involved in a head-on automobile collision. Driving along a peaceful suburban street, I suddenly saw, looming before me, a car out of control and heading directly at me. Though the crash was of sufficient force to demolish both automobiles, and though the other driver suffered severe lacerations, I was fortunate and suffered no significant physical injury. I caught a plane two hours later and was able that evening to deliver a lecture in another city. Yet, without question, I was severely shaken, I felt dazed, was tremulous, and could not eat or sleep. The next evening I was unwise enough to see a frightening movie (*Carrie*) which thoroughly terrified me, and I left before its end. I returned home a couple of days later with no obvious psychological sequelae aside from occasional insomnia and anxiety dreams.

Yet a strange problem arose. At the time I was spending a year as a fellow at the Center for Advanced Study in the Behavioral Sciences in Palo Alto, California. I enjoyed my colleagues and especially looked forward to the daily leisurely luncheon discussions of scholarly issues. Immediately after the accident I developed intense anxiety around these lunches. Would I have anything of significance to say? How would my colleagues regard me? Would I make a fool of myself? After a few days the anxiety was so extreme that I began to search for excuses to lunch elsewhere by myself.

I also began, however, to analyze my predicament, and one fact was abundantly clear: the luncheon anxiety appeared for the first time following the automobile accident. Furthermore, explicit anxiety about the accident, about so nearly losing my life, had, within a day or two, entirely vanished. It was clear that anxiety had succeeded in becoming fear. Considerable death anxiety had erupted immediately following the accident, and I had "handled" it primarily by displacement—by splitting it from its true source and riveting it to a convenient specific situation. My fundamental death anxiety thus had only a brief efflorescence before being secularized to such lesser concerns as self-esteem, fear of interpersonal rejection, or humiliation.

Although I had handled, or "processed," my anxiety, I had not eradicated it; and traces were evident for months afterward. Even though I had worked through my lunch phobia, a series of other fears emerged—fears of driving a car, of bicycling. Months later when I went skiing, I found myself so cautious, so frightened of some mishap that my skiing pleasure and ability were severely compromised. Still these fears could be located in space and time and could be managed in some systematic way. Annoying as they were, they were not fundamental, they did not threaten my being.

In addition to these specific fears, I noted one other change: the world seemed precarious. It had lost, for me, its hominess: danger seemed everywhere. The nature of reality had shifted, as I experienced what Heidegger called "uncanniness" (*unheimlich*)—the experience of "not being at home in the world," which he considered (and I can attest to it) a typical consequence of death awareness.[22]

One further property of death anxiety that has often created confusion in mental health literature is that the fear of death can be experienced at many different levels. One may, as I have discussed, worry about the act of dying, fear the pain of dying, regret unfinished projects, mourn the end of personal experience, or consider death as rationally and dispassionately as the Epicureans who concluded simply that death holds no terror because "where I am, death is not; where death is, I am not. Therefore death is nothing to me" (Lucretius). Yet keep in mind that these responses are adult conscious reflections on the phenomenon of death; by no means are they identical to the primitive dread of death that resides in the unconscious—a dread that is part of the fabric of being, that is formed early in life at a time before the development of precise conceptual formulation, a dread that is chilling, uncanny, and inchoate, a dread that exists prior to and outside of language and image.

The clinician rarely encounters death anxiety in its stark form: this anxiety is handled by conventional defenses (for example, repression, displacement, rationalization) and by some defenses specific only to it, which will be discussed later. Of course this situation should not overly trouble us: it prevails for every theory of anxiety. Primary anxiety is always transformed into something less toxic for the individual; that is the function of the entire system of psychological defenses. It is rare, to use a Freudian frame of reference, for a clinician to observe undisguised castration anxiety; instead, one sees some transformation of anxiety. For example, a male patient may be phobic of women, or fearful of competing with males in certain social situations, or inclined to obtain sexual gratification in some mode other than heterosexual intercourse.

A clinician who has developed the existential "set," however, will recognize the "processed" death anxiety and be astonished at the frequency and the diversity of its appearance. Let me give a clinical example. I recently saw a patient who sought therapy not because of existential anxiety but to solve commonplace, painful relationship problems.

Joyce was a thirty-year-old university professor who was in the midst of a painful divorce. She had first dated Jack when she was fifteen and married him at twenty-one. The marriage had obviously not gone well for several years, and they had separated three years previously. Although Joyce had formed a satisfying relationship with another man, she was unable to proceed with a divorce. In fact, her chief complaint when entering therapy was her uncontrollable weeping whenever she talked to Jack. An analysis of her weeping uncovered several important factors.

First, it was of the utmost importance that Jack continue to love her. Even though she no longer loved him or wanted him, she wanted very much that he think of her often and love her as he had never loved any other woman. "Why?" I asked. "Everyone wishes to be remembered," she replied. "It's a way of putting myself into posterity." She reminded me that the Jewish Kaddish ritual is built around the assumption that, as long as one is remembered by one's children, one continues to exist. When Jack forgot her, she died a little.*

Another source of Joyce's tears was her feeling that she and Jack had shared many lovely and important experiences. Without their union, these events, she felt, would perish. The fading of the past is a vivid reminder of the relentless rush of time. As the past disappears, so does the coil of the future shorten. Joyce's husband helped her to freeze time— the future as well as the past. Though she was not conscious of it, it was clear that Joyce was frightened of using up the future. She had a habit, for example, of never quite completing a task: if she was doing house-work, she always left one corner of the house uncleaned. She dreaded being "finished." She never started a book without another one on her night table awaiting its turn. One is reminded of Proust whose major literary corpus was devoted to escaping "the devouring jaws of time" by recapturing the past.

Still another reason why Joyce wept was her fear of failure. Life had until recently been an uninterrupted stairway of success. To fail in her marriage meant that she would be, as she often put it, "just like every-one else." Though she had considerable talent, her expectations were grandiose. She anticipated achieving international prominence, perhaps winning a Nobel prize for a research program upon which she was embarking. If that success did not occur within five years, she planned to

---

*Allen Sharp in *A Green Tree in Geddes* describes a small Mexican cemetery that is divided into two parts: the "dead" whose graves are still adorned with flowers placed there by the living, and the "truly dead" whose grave sites are no longer maintained—they are remembered by no living soul.[23] In a sense, then, when a very old person dies, many others die also; the dead person takes them along. All those recently dead who are remembered by no one else become, at that moment, "truly" dead.

turn her energies to fiction and write the *You Can't Go Home Again* of the 1970s—although she had never written any fiction. Yet she had reason for her sense of specialness: thus far she had not failed to accomplish every one of her goals. The failure of her marriage was the first interruption of her ascent, the first challenge to her solipsistic assumptive world. The failure of the marriage threatened her sense of specialness, which is one of the most common and potent death-denying defenses.

Joyce's commonplace problem, then, had roots stretching back to primal death anxiety. To me, an existentially oriented therapist, these clinical phenomena—the wish to be loved and remembered eternally, the wish to freeze time, the belief in personal invulnerability, the wish to merge with another—all served the same function for Joyce: to assuage death anxiety.

As she analyzed each one and came to understand the common source of these phenomena, Joyce's clinical picture improved remarkably. Most strikingly, as she gave up her neurotic needs for Jack, and stopped using him for all the death-defying functions he served, she was able to turn toward him for the first time in a truly loving fashion and re-establish the marriage on an entirely different basis.

The Inattention to Death in Psychotherapy Theory and Practice

All of the foregoing perspectives on death bear strong implications for psychotherapy. The incorporation of death into life enriches life; it enables individuals to extricate themselves from smothering trivialities, to live more purposefully and more authentically. The full awareness of death may promote radical personal change. Yet death is a primary source of anxiety; it permeates inner experience, and we defend against it by a number of personal dynamisms. Furthermore, as I shall discuss later, death anxiety dealt with maladaptively results in the vast variety of signs, symptoms, and character traits we refer to as "psychopathology."

Yet despite these compelling reasons, the dialogue of psychotherapy rarely includes the concept of death. Death is overlooked, and overlooked glaringly, in almost all aspects of the mental health field: theory, basic and clinical research, clinical reports, and all forms of clinical practice. The only exception lies in the area in which death cannot be ig-nored—the care of a dying patient. The sporadic articles dealing with death that do appear in the psychotherapy literature are generally in second- or third-line journals and are anecdotal in form. They are cu-riosities that are peripheral to the mainstream of theory and practice.

Clinical Case Reports

The omission of the fear of death in clinical case reports, to take one example, is so blatant that one is tempted to conclude that nothing less than a conspiracy of silence is at work. There are three major strategies for dealing with death in clinical case reports. First, the authors selec-tively inattend to the issue and report no material whatsoever pertain-ing to death. Second, authors may present copious clinical data related to death but ignore the material completely in their dynamic formula-tion of the case. Third, authors may present death-related clinical mate-rial but, in a formulation of the case, translate "death" into a concept compatible with a particular ideological school.

In a widely cited article, "The Attitudes of Psychoneurotics toward Death," published in a leading journal, two eminent clinicians, Walter Bromberg and Paul Schilder, present several case histories in which death plays a prominent role.[24] For example, one female patient devel-oped acute anxiety after the death of a woman friend for whom she had had some erotic longings. Although the patient stated explicitly that her personal fear of death was kindled by watching her friend die, the au-thors conclude that "her anxiety reaction was against the unconscious homosexual attachment with which she struggled ... her own death meant the reunion with the homosexual beloved who had departed ... to die means a reunion with the denied love object."

Another patient, whose father was an undertaker, described her se-vere anxiety: "I have always feared death. I was afraid I would wake up while they were embalming me. I have these queer feelings of immi-nent death. My father was an undertaker. I never thought of death while I was with corpses ... but now I feel I want to run. . . . I think of it steadily. . . . I feel as though I was fighting it off." The authors conclude that "the anxiety about death is the expression of a repressed wish to be passive and to be handled by the father-undertaker." In their view the patient's anxiety is the product of her self-defense against these dangerous wishes and of her desire for self-punishment because of her incest-uous wish. The other case histories in the same article provide fur-ther examples of translations of death into what the authors consider to be more fundamental fears: "death means for this boy final sado-masochistic gratification in a homosexual reunion with the father" or "death means for him separation from the mother and an end to expres-sion of his unconscious libidinal desires."

Obviously one cannot but wonder why there is such a press for trans-lation. If a patient's life is curtailed by a fear, let us say, of open spaces, dogs, radioactive fallout, or if one is consumed by obsessive ruminations about cleanliness or whether doors are locked, then it seems to make sense to translate these superficial concerns into more fundamental meanings. But, *res ipsa loquitur,* a fear of death may be a fear of death and not translatable into a "deeper" fear. Perhaps it is not translation that the neurotic patient needs; he or she may not be out of contact with reality but instead, through failing to erect "normal" denial defenses, may be too close to the truth.

The Clinical Practitioner

Some therapists state that death concerns are simply not voiced by their patients. I believe, however, that the real issue is that the therapist is not prepared to hear them. A therapist who is receptive, who inquires deeply into a patient's concerns, will encounter death continuously in his or her everyday work.

Patients, given the slightest encouragement, will bring in an extraor-dinary amount of material related to a concern about death. They dis-cuss the deaths of parents or friends, they worry about growing old, their dreams are haunted by death, they go to class reunions and are shocked by how much everyone else has aged, they notice with an ache the ascendancy of their children, they occasionally take note, with a start, that they enjoy old people's sedentary pleasures. They are aware of many small deaths: senile plaques, liver spots on their skin, gray hairs, stiff joints, stooped posture, deepening wrinkles. Retirement ap-proaches, children leave home, they become grandparents, their chil-dren take care of them, the life cycle envelops them. Other patients may speak of annihilation fears: the common horrifying fantasy of some murderous aggressors forcing entry into the home, or fearful reactions to television or cinematic violence. The termination work that occurs in the therapy of every patient is accompanied, if the therapist will only listen, by undercurrents of concern about death.

My personal clinical experience is highly corroborative of the ubiquity of death concerns. Throughout the writing of *Existential Psychotherapy* I have encountered considerable amounts of heretofore invisible clinical material. Undoubtedly to some extent I have cued patients to provide me with certain evidence. But it is my belief that, in the main, it was always there; I was simply not properly tuned in. Earlier, for example, I presented a patient, Joyce, who had commonplace clinical problems involving the establishment and the termination of interpersonal relationships. On deeper inquiry Joyce evinced much concern about existential issues which I would never have been able to recognize had I not had the appropriate psychological set.

Another example of "tuning in" is offered by a psychotherapist who attended a Saturday lecture I gave on the topic of death anxiety. A few days later she wrote in a letter:

> ... I did not expect the subject to come up in my work now, since I am a counselor at Reed College and our students are usually in good physical health. But my first appointment Monday morning was with a student who had been raped two months ago. She has been suffering from many disagreeable and painful symptoms since then. She made the comment, with an embarrassed laugh, "If I'm not dying of one thing, I'm dying of another." It was probably at least in part because of your remarks that the interview turned towards her fear of dying, and that being raped and dying used to be things she thought would happen only to other people. She now feels vulnerable and flooded with anxieties that used to be suppressed. She seemed to be relieved that it was all right to talk about being afraid to die, even if no terminal illness can be found in her body.[25]

Psychotherapy sessions following even some passing encounter with death often offer much clinical data. Dreams, of course, are especially fertile sources of material. For example, one thirty-year-old woman, the night following the funeral of an old friend, dreamed: "I'm sitting there watching TV. The doctor comes over and examines my lungs with a stethoscope. I get angry and ask him what right he has to do that. He said I was smoking like a smoke house. He said I have far advanced 'hourglass' disease of my lungs." The dreamer does not smoke, but her dead friend smoked three packs a day. Her association to "hourglass" disease of the lungs was "time is running out."[26]

Denial plays a central role in a therapist's selective inattention to death in therapy. Denial is a ubiquitous and powerful defense. Like an aura, it surrounds the affect associated with death whenever it appears. One joke from Freud's vast collection has it that a man says to his wife: "If one of us two dies before the other, I think I'll move to Paris."[27] Denial does not spare the therapist, and in the treatment process the denial of the therapist and the denial of the patient enter into collusion. Many therapists, though they have had long years of personal analysis, have not explored and worked through their personal terror of death; they phobically avoid the area in their personal lives and selectively inattend to obvious death-linked material in their psychotherapy practice.

DEATH AND PSYCHOPATHOLOGY

The range of psychopathology, the types of clinical picture with which patients present, is so broad that clinicians require some organizing principle that will permit them to cluster symptoms, behaviors, and characterological styles into meaningful categories. To the extent that clinicians can apply some structuring paradigm of psychopathology, they are relieved of the anxiety of facing an inchoate situation. They develop a sense of recognition or of familiarity and a sense of mastery which, in turn, engender in patients a sense of confidence and trust— prerequisites for a truly therapeutic relationship.

The paradigm that I shall describe here rests, as do most paradigms of psychopathology, on the assumption that psychopathology is a graceless, inefficient mode of coping with anxiety. An existential paradigm assumes that anxiety emanates from the individual's confrontation with the ultimate concerns in existence. I shall present a model of psychopathology based upon the individual's struggle with death anxiety and, in later chapters, models applicable to patients whose anxiety is more closely related to other ultimate concerns—freedom, isolation, and meaninglessness.* Though for didactic purposes I must discuss these concerns separately, all four represent strands in the cable of existence, and all must eventually be recombined into a unified existential model of psychopathology.

All individuals are confronted with death anxiety; most develop adaptive coping modes—modes that consist of denial-based strategies such as suppression, repression, displacement, belief in personal omnipotence, acceptance of socially sanctioned religious beliefs that "detoxify" death, or personal efforts to overcome death through a wide variety of strategies that aim at achieving symbolic immortality.

Either because of extraordinary stress or because of an inadequacy of available defensive strategies, the individual who enters the realm called "patienthood" has found insufficient the universal modes of dealing with death fear and has been driven to extreme modes of defense. These defensive maneuvers, often clumsy modes of dealing with terror, constitute the presenting clinical picture.

Psychopathology (in every system) is, by definition, an *ineffective* defensive mode. Even defensive maneuvers that successfully ward off severe anxiety prevent growth and result in a constricted and unsatisfying life. Many existential theorists have commented upon the high price exacted in the struggle to cope with death anxiety. Kierkegaard knew that man limited and diminished himself in order to avoid perception of the "terror, perdition and annihilation that dwell next door to any man."[28] Otto Rank described the neurotic as one "who refused the loan (life) in order to avoid the payment of the debt (death)."[29] Paul Tillich stated that "neurosis is the way of avoiding non-being by avoiding being."[30] Ernest Becker made a similar point when he wrote: "The irony of man's condition is that the deepest need is to be free of the anxiety of death and annihilation; but it is life itself which awakens it and so we

---

*The chapters referred to here constitute Parts II, III, and IV of *Existential Psychotherapy.*

must shrink from being fully alive."[31] Robert Jay Lifton used the term "psychic numbing" to describe how the neurotic individual shields himself from death anxiety.[32]

Naked death anxiety will not be easily apparent in the paradigm of psychopathology I shall describe. But that should not surprise us: primary anxiety in pristine form is rarely visible in any theoretical system. The defensive structures exist for the very purpose of internal camouflage: the nature of the core dynamic conflict is concealed by repression and other dysphoria-reducing maneuvers. Eventually the core conflict is deeply buried and can be inferred—though never wholly known— only after laborious analysis of these maneuvers.

To take one example: an individual may guard himself from the death anxiety inherent in individuation by maintaining a symbiotic tie with Mother. This defensive strategy may succeed temporarily, but as time passes, it will itself become a source of secondary anxiety; for example, the reluctance to separate from Mother may interfere with attendance at school or the development of social skills; and these deficiencies are likely to beget social anxiety and self-contempt which, in turn, may give birth to new defenses which temper dysphoria but retard growth and accordingly generate additional layers of anxiety and defense. Soon the core conflict is heavily encrusted with these epiphenomena, and the excavation of the primary anxiety becomes exceedingly difficult. Death anxiety is not immediately apparent to the clinician: it is discovered through a study of dreams, fantasies, or psychotic utterances or through painstaking analysis of the onset of neurotic symptoms.

The derivative, secondary forms of anxiety are nonetheless "real" anxiety. An individual may be brought down by social anxiety or by pervasive self-contempt; and, as we shall see, treatment efforts generally are directed toward derivative rather than toward primary anxiety. The psychotherapist, regardless of his or her belief system concerning the primary source of anxiety and the genesis of psychopathology, begins therapy at the level of the patient's concerns: for example, the therapist may assist the patient by offering support, by propping up adaptive defenses, or by helping to correct destructive interpersonal modes of interaction. Thus in the treatment of many patients the existential paradigm of psychopathology does not call for a radical departure from traditional therapeutic strategies or techniques.

Death Anxiety: A Paradigm of Psychopathology

A clinical paradigm that I believe to be of considerable practical and heuristic value issues from the child's mode of coping with death awareness. The two major bulwarks of the child's denial system are the archaic beliefs that one is either personally inviolable and/or protected eternally by an ultimate rescuer. These two beliefs are particularly powerful because they receive reinforcement from two sources: from the circumstances of early life, and from widespread culturally sanctioned myths involving immortality systems and the existence of a personal, observing deity.

The clinical expression of these two fundamental defenses became particularly clear to me one day when I saw two patients, whom I shall call Mike and Sam, in two successive hours. They provide a powerful study in the two modes of death denial; the contrast between the two is striking; and each, by illustrating the opposite possibility, sheds light on the dynamics of the other.

Mike, who was twenty-five years old and had been referred to me by an oncologist, had a highly malignant lymphoma, and though a new form of chemotherapy offered his only chance for survival, he refused to cooperate in treatment. I saw Mike only once (and he was fifteen minutes late for that meeting), but it was readily apparent that the guiding motif of his life was individuation. Early in life he had struggled against any form of control and developed remarkable skills at self-sufficiency. Since the age of twelve he had supported himself, and at fifteen he moved out of his parental home. After high school he went into contracting and soon mastered all aspects of the trade—carpentry, electrical work, plumbing, masonry. He built several houses, sold them at substantial profits, bought a boat, married, and sailed with his wife around the world. He was attracted to the self-sufficient individualistic culture that he had found in an underdeveloped country, and was preparing to emigrate when, four months before I saw him, his cancer was discovered.

The most striking feature of the interview was Mike's irrational attitude toward the chemotherapy treatment. True, the treatment was markedly unpleasant, causing severe nausea and vomiting, but Mike's fear exceeded all reasonable bounds: he could not sleep the night before treatment; he developed a severe anxiety state and obsessed about methods of avoiding treatment. What was it precisely that Mike feared about the treatment? He could not specify, but he did know that it had something to do with immobility and helplessness. He could not bear to wait while the oncologist prepared his medication for injection. (It could not be done in advance, since the dosage depended upon his blood count, which had to be examined before each administration.) Most terrible of all, however, was the intravenous: he hated the penetration of the needle, the taping, the sight of the drops entering his body. He hated to be helpless and restrained, to lie quietly on the cot, to keep his arm immobile. Though Mike did not consciously fear death, his fear of therapy was an obvious displacement of death anxiety. What was truly dreadful for Mike was to be dependent and static: these conditions ignited terror, they were death equivalents; and most of his life he had overcome them by a consummate self-reliance. He believed deeply in his specialness and his invulnerability and had, until the cancer, created a life that reinforced this belief.

I could do little for Mike except to suggest to his oncologist that Mike be taught to prepare his medications and to monitor and adjust his own intravenous. These suggestions helped, and Mike finished his course of treatment. He did not keep his next appointment with me but called to ask for a self-help muscle-relaxation cassette. He chose not to remain in the area for the oncological follow-up and decided to pursue his plans to emigrate. His wife so disapproved of his plan that she refused to go, and Mike set sail alone.

Sam was approximately the same age as Mike but resembled him in no other way. He came to see me in extremis following his wife's decision to leave him. Though he was not, like Mike, confronted with death in a literal sense, Sam's situation was similar on a symbolic level. His behavior suggested that he faced an extraordinarily severe threat to his survival: he was anxious to the point of panic, he wailed for hours on end, he could not sleep or eat, he longed for surcease at any cost and seriously contemplated suicide. As the weeks passed, Sam's catastrophic reaction subsided, but his discomfort lingered. He thought about his wife continuously. He did not, as he stated, "live in life" but slunk about outside life. "Passing time" became a conscious and serious proposition: crossword puzzles, television, newspapers, magazines were seen in their true nature—as vehicles for filling the void, for getting time over with as painlessly as possible.

Sam's character structure can be understood around the motif of "fusion"—a motif dramatically opposed to Mike's of "individuation." During the Second World War, Sam's family had, when he was very young, moved many times to escape danger. He had suffered many losses, including the death of his father when Sam was a preadolescent and the death of his mother a few years later. He dealt with his situation by forming close, intense ties: first with his mother and then with a series of relatives or adopted relatives. He was everyone's handyman and perpetual baby-sitter. He was an inveterate gift giver, bestowing generous amounts of time and money on a large number of adults. Nothing seemed more important to Sam than to be loved and cared for. In fact, after his wife left him, he realized that he felt he existed only if he were loved: in a state of isolation he froze, much like a terrified animal, into a state of suspended animation—not living but not dying either. Once when we talked about his pain following his wife's departure, he said, "When I'm sitting home alone, the most difficult thing is to think that no one really knows I'm alive." When alone, he scarcely ate or sought to satisfy any but the most primitive needs. He did not clean his house, he did not wash, he did not read; though he was a talented artist, he did not paint. There was, as Sam put it, no point in "expending energy unless I am certain it will be returned to me by another." He did not exist unless someone was there to validate his existence. When alone, Sam transformed himself into a spore, dormant until another person supplied life-restoring energy.

In his time of need Sam sought help from the elders in his life: he flew across the country for the solace of a few hours in the home of adopted relatives; he received support by simply standing outside the house he and his mother had once lived in for four years; he ran up astronomical phone bills soliciting advice and comfort; he received much support from his in-laws who, because of Sam's devotion to them, threw their lot (and love) in with Sam rather than with their daughter. Sam's efforts to help himself in his crisis were considerable but monothematic: he sought in a number of ways to reinforce his beliefs that some protective figure watched over and cared for him.

Despite his extreme loneliness, Sam was willing to take no steps to alleviate it. I made a number of practical suggestions about how he might meet friends: singles' events, church social activities, Sierra Club events, adult education courses, and so forth. My advice, much to my puzzlement, went completely unheeded. Gradually I understood: what was important for Sam was not, despite his loneliness, to be with others but to confirm his faith in an ultimate rescuer. He was explicit in his unwillingness to spend time away from his home on singles or dating activities. The reason? He was afraid of missing a phone call! One phone call from "out there" was infinitely more precious than joining dozens of social activities. Above all, Sam wanted to be "found," to be protected, to be saved *without* having to ask for help and without having to engineer his own rescue. In fact, at a deep level, Sam was made *more* uncomfortable by successful efforts to assume responsibility for helping himself out of his life predicament. I saw Sam over a four-month period. As he became more comfortable (through my support and through "fusion" with another woman), he obviously lost motivation for continued psychotherapeutic work, and we both agreed that termination was in order.

Two Fundamental Defenses Against Death

What do we learn from Mike and Sam? We see clearly two radically different modes of coping with fundamental anxiety. Mike believed deeply in his specialness and personal inviolability; Sam put faith in the existence of an ultimate rescuer. Mike's sense of self-sufficiency was hypertrophied, while Sam did not exist alone but strove to fuse with another. These two modes are diametrically opposed; and, though by no means mutually exclusive, they constitute a useful dialectic which permits the clinician to understand a wide variety of clinical situations.

In a crude, sweeping way, the two defenses constitute a dialectic—the human being either fuses or separates, embeds or emerges. He affirms his autonomy by "standing out from nature" (as Rank put it),[33] or seeks safety by merging with another force. Either he becomes his own father or he remains the eternal son. Surely this is what Fromm meant when he described man as either "longing for submission or lusting for power."[34]

This existential dialectic offers one paradigm that permits the clinician to "grasp" the situation. There are many alternate paradigms, each with explanatory power: Mike and Sam have character disorders—schizoid and passive-dependency, respectively. Mike can be viewed from the vantage points of a continued rebellious conflict with his parents, of counterdependency, of neurotic perpetuation of the Oedipal struggle, or of homosexual panic. Sam can be "grasped" from the vantage points of identification with Mother and unresolved grief, or of castration anxiety, or from a family dynamic perspective in which the clinician focuses attention on Sam's interaction with his wife.

The existential approach is, therefore, one paradigm among many, and its raison d'être is its clinical usefulness. This dialectic permits the therapist to comprehend data often overlooked in clinical work. The therapist may, for example, understand why Mike and Sam responded so powerfully and manneristically to their painful situations, or why Sam balked at the prospect of "improving" his situation by the assumption of responsibility for himself. This dialectic permits the therapist to engage the patient on the deepest of levels. It is based on an understanding of primary anxiety that exists in the immediate present: the therapist views the patient's symptoms as a response to death anxiety that currently threatens, not as a response to the evocation of past trauma and stress. Hence, the approach emphasizes awareness, immediacy, and choice—an emphasis that enhances the therapist's leverage.

I shall describe here these two basic forms of death denial and the types of psychopathology that spring from them. (Though many of the familiar clinical syndromes can be viewed and understood in terms of these basic denials of death, I make no pretense of an exhaustive classifying system—that would suggest greater precision and comprehensiveness than is the case.) Both beliefs, in specialness and in an ultimate rescuer, can be highly adaptive. Each, however, may be overloaded and stretched thin, to a point where adaptation breaks down, anxiety leaks through, the individual resorts to extreme measures to protect himself or herself, and psychopathology appears in the form of either defense breakdown or defense runaway.

For the sake of clarity I shall first discuss each defense separately. I shall then need to integrate them again because they are intricately interdependent: the great majority of individuals have traces of both defenses woven into their character structures.

Specialness

No one has ever described the deep irrational belief in our own specialness more powerfully or poignantly than Tolstoy who, through the lips of Ivan Ilych, says:

> In the depth of his heart he knew he was dying, but not only was he not accustomed to the thought, he simply did not and could not grasp it.
>
> The syllogism he had learnt from Kiezewetter's Logic: "Caius is a man, men are mortal, therefore Caius is mortal," had always seemed to him correct as applied to Caius, but certainly not as applied to himself. That Caius—man in the abstract—was mortal, was perfectly correct, but he was not Caius, not an abstract man, but a creature quite, quite separate from all others. He had been little Vanya, with a mamma and a papa, with Mitya and Volodya, with the toys, a coachman and a nurse, afterwards with Katenka and with all the joys, griefs, and delights of childhood, boyhood, and youth. What did Caius know of the smell of that striped leather ball Vanya had been so fond of? Had Caius kissed his mother's hand like that, and did the silk of her dress rustle so for Caius? Had he rioted like that at school when the pastry was bad? Had Caius been in love like that? Could Caius preside at a session as he did? "Caius really was mortal, and it was right for him to die; but for me, little Vanya, Ivan Ilyich, with all my thoughts and emotions, it's altogether a different matter. It cannot be that I ought to die. That would be too terrible."[35]

We all know that in the basic boundaries of existence we are no different from others. No one denies that at a conscious level. Yet deep, deep down each of us believes, as does Ivan Ilych, that the rule of mortality applies to others but certainly not to ourselves. Occasionally one is caught off guard when this belief pops into consciousness, and is surprised by one's own irrationality. Recently, for example, I visited my optometrist to complain that my eyeglasses no longer functioned as of yore. He examined me and asked my age. "Forty-eight," I said, and he replied, "Yep, right on schedule." From somewhere deep inside the thought welled up and hissed: "*What* schedule? *Who's* on schedule? You or others may be on a schedule, but certainly not I."

When an individual learns he or she has some serious illness—for example, cancer—the first reaction is generally some form of denial. The denial is an effort to cope with anxiety associated with the threat to life, but also it is a function of a deep belief in one's inviolability. Much psychological work must be done to restructure one's lifelong assumptive world. Once the defense is truly undermined, once the individual really grasps, "My God, I'm really going to die," and realizes that life will deal with him or her in the same harsh way as it deals with others, he or she feels lost and, in some odd way, betrayed.

In my work with terminally ill cancer patients I have observed that individuals vary enormously in their willingness to know about their deaths. Many patients for some time do not hear their physician tell them their prognosis. Much internal restructuring must be done to allow the knowledge to take hold. Some patients become aware of their deaths and face death anxiety in staccato fashion—a brief moment of awareness, brief terror, denial, internal processing, and then preparedness for more information. For others the awareness of death and the associated anxiety flood in with a terrible rush.

One of my patients, Pam, a twenty-eight-year-old woman with cervical cancer, had her myth of specialness destroyed in a striking fashion. After an exploratory laparotomy, her surgeon visited her and informed her that her condition was grave indeed, and that her life expectancy was in the neighborhood of six months. An hour later Pam was visited by a team of radiotherapists who had obviously not communicated with the surgeon, and who informed her that they planned to radiate her and that they were "going for a cure." She chose to believe her second visitors, but unfortunately her surgeon, unbeknownst to her, spoke with her parents in the waiting room and gave them the original message—namely, that she had six months to live.

Pam spent the next few months convalescing at her parents' home in the most unreal of environments. Her parents treated her as though she were going to be dead in six months. They insulated themselves and the world from her; they monitored her phone calls to screen out unsettling communications; in short, they made her "comfortable." Finally Pam confronted her parents and demanded to know what in God's name was going on. Her parents told her about their conversation with the surgeon; Pam referred them to the radiotherapist, and the misunderstanding was quickly cleared up.

Pam, however, was deeply shaken by the experience. The confrontation with her parents made her realize, in a way that a death sentence from the surgeon had not, that she was indeed veering toward death. Her comments at this time are revealing:

> I did seem to be getting better and it was a happier situation, but they began to treat me like I was not going to live and I was stung into this terrible feeling of realization *that they had already accepted my death*. Because of an error and a miscommunication I was already dead to my family, and I started being dead and it was a very hard way back to get myself to be alive. It was worse later on as I was getting better than it was when I was very sick because when the family suddenly realized that I was getting better then they left and went back to their daily chores and I was still left with being dead and I couldn't handle it very well. I'm still frightened and trying to cross the boundary line that seems to be in front of me—the boundary line of, am I dead or am I alive?

The point is that Pam truly understood what it meant to die not from anything her doctors told her but from the crushing realization that her parents would continue to live without her and that the world would go on as before—that, as she put it, the good times would go on without her.

Another patient with widespread metastatic cancer had arrived at the same point when she wrote a letter to her children instructing them how to divide some personal belongings of sentimental value. She had rather mechanically performed the other dreary administrative chores of dying—the writing of a will, the purchase of a burial plot, the appointment of an executor—but it was the personal letter to her children that made death real to her. It was the simple but dreadful realization that when her children read her letter she would no longer exist: neither to respond to them, to observe their reactions, to guide them; they would be there but she would be nothing at all.

Another patient, Jan, had breast cancer that had spread to her brain. Her doctors had forewarned her of paralysis. She heard their words but at a deep level felt smugly immune to this possibility. When the inexorable weakness and paralysis ensued, Jan realized in a sudden rush that her "specialness" was a myth. There was, she learned, no "escape clause." She said all this during a group therapy meeting and then added that she had discovered a powerful truth in the last week—a truth that made the ground shake under her. She had been musing to herself about her preferred life span—seventy would be about right, eighty might be too old—and then suddenly she realized, "When it comes to aging and when it comes to dying, *what I wish has absolutely nothing to do with it.*"

Perhaps these clinical illustrations begin to transmit something of the difference between knowing and truly knowing, between the everyday awareness of death we all possess and the full facing of "my death." Accepting one's personal death means facing a number of other unpalatable truths, each of which has its own force field of anxiety: that one is finite; that one's life really comes to an end; that the world will persist nonetheless; that one is one of many—no more, no less; that the universe does not acknowledge one's specialness; that all our lives we have carried counterfeit vouchers; and, finally, that certain stark immutable dimensions of existence are beyond one's influence. In fact, what one wishes "has absolutely nothing to do with it."

When an individual arrives at the discovery that personal specialness is mythic, he or she feels angry and betrayed by life. Surely this sense of betrayal is what Robert Frost had in mind when he wrote: "Forgive, O Lord, my little jokes on Thee/And I'll forgive Thy great big one on me."[36]

Many people feel that if they had only known, really known, earlier they would have lived their lives differently. They feel angry; yet the rage is impotent, for it has no reasonable object. (The physician is, incidentally, often a target for displaced anger, and especially for that of so many dying patients.)

The belief in personal specialness is extraordinarily adaptive and permits us to emerge from nature and to tolerate the accompanying dysphoria: the isolation; the awareness of our smallness and the awesomeness of the external world, of our parents' inadequacies, of our creatureliness, of the bodily functions that tie us to nature; and, most of all, the knowledge of the death which rumbles unceasingly at the edge of consciousness. Our belief in exemption from natural law underlies many aspects of our behavior. It enhances courage in that it permits us to encounter danger without being overwhelmed by the threat of personal extinction. Witness the psalmist who wrote, "A thousand shall fall at thy right hand, ten thousand at thy left, but death shall not come nigh thee." The courage thus generated begets what many have called the human being's "natural" striving for competence, effectance, power, and control. To the extent that one attains power, one's death fear is further assuaged and belief in one's specialness further reinforced. Getting ahead, achieving, accumulating material wealth, leaving works behind as imperishable monuments become a way of life which effectively conceals the mortal questions churning below.

Compulsive Heroism

For many of us, heroic individuation represents the best that man can do in light of his existential situation. The Greek writer Nikos Kazantzakis was such a spirit, and his Zorba was the quintessential self-sufficient man. (In his autobiography Kazantzakis cites the last words of the man who was his model for Zorba the Greek: ". . . if any priest comes to confess me and give me communion, tell him to make himself scarce, and may he give me his curse! . . . Men like me should live a thousand years.")[37] Elsewhere, through the lips of his Ulysses, Kazantzakis advises us to live life so completely that we leave death nothing but a "burned-out castle."[38] His own tombstone on the ramparts of Herakleion bears the simple heroic epitaph: "I want nothing, I fear nothing, I am free."

Push it a bit farther, though, and the defense becomes overextended: the heroic pose caves in on itself, and the hero becomes a compulsive hero who, like Mike, the young man with cancer, is driven to face danger in order to escape a greater danger within. Ernest Hemingway, the prototype of the compulsive hero, was compelled throughout his life to seek out and conquer danger as a grotesque way of proving there was no danger. Hemingway's mother reports that one of his first sentences was, "'Fraid of nothin'."[39] In an ironic way he was afraid of nothing precisely because he, like all of us, was afraid of nothingness. The Hemingway hero thus represents a runaway of the emergent, individualistic solution to the human situation. This hero is not choosing; his actions are driven and fixed; he does not learn from new experiences. Even the approach of death does not turn his gaze within or increase his wisdom. The Hemingway code contains no place for aging and diminishment, for they have the odor of ordinariness. In *The Old Man and the Sea,* Santiago meets his approaching death in a stereotyped way—the same way he faced every one of life's basic threats—by going out alone to search for the great fish.[40]

Hemingway himself could not survive the dissolution of the myth of his personal invulnerability. As his health and physical prowess declined, as his "ordinariness" (in the sense that he like everyone must face the human situation) became painfully evident, he grew bereft and finally deeply depressed. His final illness, a paranoid psychosis with persecutory delusions and ideas of reference, temporarily bolstered his myth of specialness. (All persecutory trends and ideas of reference flow from a core of personal grandiosity; after all, only a very special person would warrant that much attention, albeit malevolent attention, from his environment.) Eventually the paranoid solution failed; and, left with no defense against the fear of death, Hemingway committed suicide. Though it seems paradoxical that one would commit suicide because of a fear of death, it is not uncommon. Many individuals have said in effect that "I so fear death I am driven to suicide." The idea of suicide offers some surcease from terror. It is an active act; it permits one to control that which controls one. Furthermore, as Charles Wahl has noted, many suicides have a magical view of death and regard it as temporary and reversible.[41] The individual who commits suicide to express hostility or to generate guilt in others may believe in the continued existence of consciousness, so that it will be possible to savor the harvest of his or her death.

The Workaholic

The compulsive heroic individualist represents a clear, but not clinically common, example of the defense of specialness which is stretched too thin and fails to protect the individual from anxiety or degenerates into a runaway pattern. A commonplace example is the "workaholic"—the individual consumed by work. One of the most striking features of a workaholic is the implicit belief that he or she is "getting ahead," "progressing," moving up. Time is an enemy not only because it is cousin to finitude but because it threatens one of the supports of the delusion of specialness: the belief that one is eternally advancing. The workaholic must deafen himself or herself to time's message: that the past grows fatter at the expense of a shrinking future.

The workaholic life mode is compulsive and dysfunctional: the workaholic works or applies himself not because he wishes to but because he *has* to. The workaholic may push himself without mercy and without regard for human limits. Leisure time is a time of anxiety and is often frantically filled with some activity that conveys an illusion of accomplishment. Living, thus, becomes equated with "becoming" or "doing"; time not spent in "becoming" is not "living" but waiting for life to commence.

Culture, of course, plays an important role in the shaping of the individual's values. Regarding "activity," Florence Kluckholm suggests an anthropological classification of value orientations that postulates three categories: "being," "being-in-becoming," and "doing."[42] The "being" orientation emphasizes the activity rather than the goal. It focuses on the spontaneous natural expression of the "is-ness" of the personality. "Being-in-becoming" shares with the "being" orientation an emphasis on what a person is rather than on what the person can accomplish, but emphasizes the concept of "development." Thus, it encourages activity of a certain type—activity directed toward the goal of the development of all aspects of the self. The "doing" orientation emphasizes accomplishments measurable by standards outside of the acting individual.

Obviously contemporary conservative American culture, with its emphasis on "what does the individual do?" and "getting things done," is an extreme "doing" culture.

Still, in every culture there are wide ranges of individual variation. Something within the workaholic individual interacts with the cultural standard in a manner that breeds a hypertrophied and rigid internalization of the value system. It becomes difficult for individuals to assume a bird's-eye view of their culture and to view their value system as one among many possible stances. I had one workaholic patient who treated himself to a rare noonday walk (as a reward for some particularly important accomplishment) and was staggered by the sight of hundreds of people standing around simply sunning themselves. "What do they *do* all day? How can people live that way?" he wondered. A frantic fight with time may be indicative of a powerful death fear. Workaholic individuals relate to time precisely as if they were under the seal of imminent death and were scurrying to get as much completed as possible.

Embedded in our culture, we accept unquestioningly the goodness and rightness of getting ahead. Not too long ago I was taking a brief vacation alone at a Caribbean beach resort. One evening I was reading, and from time to time I glanced up to watch the bar boy who was doing nothing save languidly staring out to sea—much like a lizard sunning itself on a warm rock, I thought. The comparison I made between him and me made me feel very smug, very cozy. He was simply doing nothing—wasting time; I was, on the other hand, doing something useful, reading, learning. I was, in short, getting ahead. All was well, until some internal imp asked the terrible question: Getting ahead of what? How? And (even worse) why? Those questions were, and are still, deeply disquieting. What was brought home to me with unusual force was how I lull myself into a death-defeating delusion by continually projecting myself forward into the future. I do not exist as a lizard exists; I prepare, I become, I am in transit. John Maynard Keynes puts it this way: "What the 'purposeful' man is always trying to secure is a spurious and illusive immortality, immortality for his acts by pushing his interest in them forward in time. He does not love his cat, but his cat's kittens; nor, in truth the kittens, but only the kittens' kittens, and so on forward forever to the end of catdom."[43]

Tolstoy, in *Anna Karenina,* describes the collapse of the "upward spiral" belief system in the person of Alexey Alexandrovitch, Anna's husband, a man for whom everything has always ascended, a splendid career, a brilliant marriage. Anna's leaving him signifies far more than the loss of her: it is the collapse of a personal *Weltanschauung.*

> He felt that he was standing face to face with something illogical and irrational, and did not know what was to be done. Alexey Alexandrovitch was standing face to face with life, with the possibility of his wife's loving someone other than himself, and this seemed to him very irrational and incomprehensible because it was life itself. All his life Alexey Alexandrovitch had lived and worked in official spheres, having to do with the reflection of life. And every time he had stumbled against life itself he had shrunk away from it. Now he experienced a feeling akin to that of a man who, while calmly crossing a precipice by a bridge, should suddenly discover that the bridge is broken, and that there is a chasm below. That chasm was life itself, the bridge that artificial life in which Alexey Alexandrovitch had lived.[44]

"The chasm was life itself, the bridge that artificial life . . ." No one has said it more clearly. The defense, if successful, shields the individual from the knowledge of the chasm. The broken bridge, the failed defense, exposes one to a truth and a dread that an individual in midlife following decades of self-deception is ill equipped to confront.

The specialness mode of coping with death fear generates maladaptive forms of the individualistic or agentic solution. But there is another even more serious and intrinsic limitation to the defense of specialness. Many keen observers have noted that though great exhilaration may for some time accompany individualist expression and achievement, there comes a point where anxiety sets in. The person who "emerges from embeddedness" or "stands out from nature" must pay a price for his success. There is something frightening about individuation, about separating oneself from the whole, about going forward and living life as a separate isolated being, about surpassing one's peers and one's parents.

Many clinicians have written on the "success neurosis"—a curious condition where individuals on the point of the crowning success for which they have long striven develop not euphoria but a crippling dysphoria which often ensures that they do not succeed. Freud refers to the phenomenon as the "wrecked by success" syndrome.[45] Rank describes it as "life anxiety"[46]—the fear of facing life as a separate being. Maslow notes that we shrink away from our highest possibilities (as well as from our lowest), and terms the phenomenon the "Jonah complex," since Jonah like all of us could not bear his personal greatness and sought to avoid his destiny.[47]

How is one to explain this curious, self-negating human tendency? Perhaps it is a result of an entanglement of achievement and aggression. Some people use achievement as a method of vindictively surpassing others; they fear that others will become aware of their motives and retaliate when success becomes too great. Freud thought it had much to do with the fear of surpassing one's father and thereby exposing oneself to the threat of castration. Becker advances our understanding when he suggests that the terrible thing in surpassing one's father is not castration but the frightening prospect of becoming one's own father.[48] To become one's own father means to relinquish the comforting but magical parental buttress against the pain inherent in one's awareness of personal finiteness.

Thus the individual who plunges into life is doomed to anxiety. Standing out from nature, being one's own father or, as Spinoza put it, "one's own god," means utter isolation; it means standing alone without the myth of rescuer or deliverer and without the comfort of the human huddle. Such unshielded exposure to the isolation of individuation is too terrible for most of us to bear. When our belief in personal specialness and inviolability fails to provide the surcease from pain we require, we seek relief from the other major alternative denial system: the belief in a personal ultimate rescuer.

The Ultimate Rescuer

Ontogeny recapitulates phylogeny. In both the physical and the social development of the individual, the development of the species is mirrored. In no social attribute is this fact more clearly evident than in the human belief in the existence of a personal omnipotent intercessor: a force or being that eternally observes, loves, and protects us. Though it may allow us to venture close to the edge of the abyss, it will ultimately rescue us. Fromm characterizes this mythic figure as the "magic helper,"[49] and Masserman as the "omnipotent servant."[50] Like the belief in personal specialness, this belief system is rooted in events of early life when parents seemed eternally concerned and satisfied one's every need. Certainly humankind from the beginnings of written history has clung to the belief in a personal god—a figure that might be eternally loving, frightening, fickle, harsh, propitiated, or angered, but a figure that was always *there*. No early culture has ever believed that humans were alone in an indifferent world.

Some individuals discover their rescuer not in a supernatural being but in their earthly surroundings, either in a leader or in some higher cause. Human beings, for milleniums, have conquered their fear of death in this manner and have chosen to lay down their freedom, indeed their lives, for the embrace of some higher figure or personified cause.

The Rescuer Defense and Personality Restriction

Overall the ultimate rescuer defense is *less* effective than the belief in personal specialness. Not only is it more likely to break down but it is intrinsically restrictive to the person. Later I shall report on empirical research that demonstrates this ineffectiveness, but it is an insight that Kierkegaard arrived at intuitively over one hundred years ago. He has a curious statement contrasting the perils of "venturing" (emergence, individuation, specialness) and not venturing (fusion, embeddedness, belief in ultimate rescuer):

> ... it is dangerous to venture. And why? Because one may lose. Not to venture is shrewd. And yet, by not venturing, it is so dreadfully easy to lose that which it would be difficult to lose in even the most venturesome venture, ... one's self. For if I have ventured amiss—very well, then life helps me by its punishment. But if I have not ventured at all—who then helps me? And, moreover, if by not ven-

turing at all in the highest sense (*and to venture in the highest sense is precisely to become conscious of oneself*) I have gained all earthly advantages . . . and lose myself. What of that?[51]

To remain embedded in another, "not to venture," subjects one then to the greatest peril of all—the loss of oneself, the failure to have explored or developed the manifold potentials within oneself.

The Collapse of the Rescuer

Through much of life the belief in an ultimate rescuer provides considerable solace and functions smoothly and invisibly. Most individuals remain unaware of the structure of their belief system until it fails to serve its purpose; or until, as Heidegger put it, there is a "breakdown in the machinery."[52] There are many possibilities for breakdown and many forms of pathology associated with the collapse of the defense.

Fatal Illnesses.   Perhaps the severest test for the effectiveness of the ultimate rescuer delusion is presented by fatal illness. Many individuals, so stricken, channel a great deal of energy into bolstering their belief in the presence and power of a protector. As the obvious candidate for the role of rescuer is the physician, the patient-doctor relationship becomes charged and complex. In part, the robe of rescuer is thrust upon the physician by the patient's wish to believe; in part, however, the physician dons the robe gladly because playing God is the physician's method of augmenting his belief in his personal specialness. Either way, the result is the same: the doctor becomes larger than life, and the patient's attitude to him or her is often irrationally obeisant. Commonly, patients with a fatal illness dread angering or disappointing their physicians; these patients apologize for taking a physician's time and are so flustered in a physician's presence that they forget to ask the pressing questions they have prepared.

To patients it is so important that doctors retain their power that a patient will neither challenge nor doubt one. Many patients, in fact, in a highly magical way, permit physicians to maintain the role of the successful healer by concealing important information from them about their (the patients') psychological and even physical distress. Often, thus, the physician is the last to know about the depth of a patient's despair. A patient who is perfectly able to talk openly to nurses or social workers about his anguish maintains a cheery, plucky face toward the physician, who concludes that the patient is handling the situation as well as could be expected.

Individuals differ in the tenacity with which they cling to denial, but eventually all denial crumbles in the face of overwhelming reality. Kübler-Ross, for example, reports that in her long experience she has seen only a handful of individuals maintain denial to the moment of death. A patient's reaction to learning that no medical or surgical cure exists is catastrophic. He or she feels angry, deceived, and betrayed. At whom, however, can one be angry? At the cosmos? At fate? Many patients are angry at the doctor for failing them—not for failing medically but for failing to incarnate the patients' personal myth of an ultimate deliverer.

Depression.   In his study of psychotically depressed individuals, Silvano Arieti describes a central motif, a life ideology that precedes and "prepares the ground" for depression.[53] His patients lived a type of mediated existence; they lived not for themselves but for either the "dominant other" or the "dominant goal." Though the terminology differs, Arieti's description of these two ideologies coincides closely with the two defenses against the fear of death I have described. The individual who lives for the "dominant goal" is the individual who fashions his or her life around a belief in personal specialness and inviolability. As I discussed earlier, depression often ensues when the belief in an ever-ascending spiral ("dominant goal") collapses.

To live for the "dominant other" is to attempt to merge with another whom one perceives as the dispenser of protection and meaning in life. The dominant other may be one's spouse, mother, father, lover, therapist, or an anthropomorphization of a business or a social institution. The ideology may collapse for many reasons: the dominant other may die, leave, withdraw love and attention, or prove too fallible for the task.

When patients recognize the failure of their ideology, they are often overwhelmed; they may feel that they have sacrificed their lives for a currency that has proven counterfeit. Yet they have available no alternative strategy for coping.

The patient may attempt to re-establish the relationship or to search for another. If these attempts fail, the patient is without resources and feels both depleted and self-condemnatory. Restructuring a life ideology is beyond comprehension; and many patients, rather than question their basic belief system, conclude that they are too worthless or too bad to warrant the love and protection of the ultimate rescuer. Their depression is abetted, furthermore, by the fact that, unconsciously, suffering and self-immolation function as a last desperate plea for love. Thus, they are bereft because they have lost love, and they remain bereft in order to regain it.

Masochism.   I have described a cluster of behaviors associated with the hypertrophied belief in the ultimate rescuer: self-effacement, fear of withdrawal of love, passivity, dependency, self-immolation, refusal to accept adulthood, and depression at collapse of the belief system. When accented, each of these may produce a characteristic clinical syndrome. When self-immolation dominates, the patient is referred to as "masochistic."

Karen, a forty-year-old patient I treated for two years, taught me a great deal about the dynamics behind the urge to inflict pain on oneself. Karen entered therapy for a number of reasons: masochistic sexual propensities, an inability to achieve sexual pleasure with her "straight" boyfriend, depression, a pervasive inertia, and terrifying nightmares and hypnagogic experiences. In therapy she rapidly developed a powerful positive transference. She devoted herself to the project of eliciting care and concern from me. Her masturbatory fantasies consisted of her becoming very ill (either with a physical disease like tuberculosis, or a psychotic breakdown) and my feeding and cradling her. She delayed leaving my office so as to spend a few extra minutes with me; so as to have my signature, she saved her canceled checks with which she had paid my bills; she attempted to visit my lectures so as to catch sight of me. Nothing seemed to please her more than for me to be stern with her; in fact, if I expressed any irritation, she experienced sexual excitation in my office. In every way she made me bigger than life and selectively ignored all of my obvious flaws.

She responded similarly to signs of weakness or limitation in other important and powerful figures in her life. If her boyfriend became ill or evinced any sign of weakness, confusion, or indecision, she experienced much anxiety. She could not bear to see him falter. Once when he was severely injured in an auto accident, she became phobic about visiting his hospital room. She responded similarly to her parents and was sorely threatened by their increasing age and frailty. As a child, she had related to them through illness. "Being sick was the lie of my life," said Karen. She sought pain to get succor. On more than one occasion during her childhood, she spent weeks in bed with a fictitious disease. During adolescence she became anorexic, only too glad to exchange physical starvation for the attention and solicitude it incited.

Her sexuality joined in the pursuit for safety and deliverance: force, restraint, strength, and pain aroused her, while weakness, passivity, even tenderness repulsed her. To be punished was to be protected; to be bound, confined, or restricted was wonderful: it meant that limits were being set, and that some powerful figure was setting them. Her masochism was overdetermined: she sought survival not only through subjugation but also through the symbolic and magical value of suffering. A small death, after all, is better than the real thing.

Treatment was successful in alleviating the acute depression, the nightmares, the suicidal preoccupation; but there came a time when treatment with me seemed to impede further growth, since, to avoid losing me, Karen continued to immolate herself. I, therefore, set a termination date six months in the future and told her that after that time I would not see her again in treatment. Over the next few weeks we weathered the storm of a severe recrudescence of all symptomatology. Not only did her severe anxiety and nightmares return, but she had terrifying hallucinatory experiences consisting of gigantic swooping bats attacking her whenever she was alone.

This was a period of great fear and despair for Karen. Her delusion of the ultimate rescuer had always protected her against the terror of death and its removal left her overly exposed to dread. Wonderful poems she wrote in her journal (mailed to me after termination of therapy) describe her terror graphically.

> *With death in my mouth I speak to you*
> *And maggots eating at my heart.*
> *In the cacophony of bells*
> *My protests go unheard.*

Death is disappointment,
A bitter bread.
You cram it down my throat
To stifle my screams.

As the termination date approached, Karen pulled out all stops. She threatened suicide if I would not continue treating her. Another poem expressed her mood and her threat:

Death is no pretense.
It is as stark a reality,
as complete a presence as life itself,
the other ultimate choice.

I feel myself running into shadows,
clothing myself in cobwebs,
hiding from the reality you thrust at me.
I want to hold up my dark cloak, death,
and threaten you with it.

Do you understand?
I will wrap myself in this if you persist.

Though I felt frightened by Karen's threats and provided her as much support as possible, I decided not to budge from my stand and maintained that at the end of the six months I would not continue to see her regardless of how ill she was. Our termination was to be final and irrevocable; no degree of distress on her part could influence it. Gradually her efforts to merge with me subsided, and she turned toward the task at hand: how to use our final sessions as constructively as possible. It was only then, when she had relinquished all hope of my continued, eternal presence, that she could work truly effectively in therapy. She allowed herself to know and to make known her strengths and her growth. She rapidly obtained a full-time position commensurate with her talents and skills (she had procrastinated finding this work for four years!). She changed her demeanor and grooming radically from woebegone waif to mature, attractive woman.

Two years after termination she asked to see me again because of the death of a friend. I agreed to meet with her for a single session and learned that she not only had maintained her changes but had undergone considerably more growth. It seems that one important thing for patients to learn is that, though therapists can be helpful, there is a point beyond which they can offer nothing more. In therapy, as in life, there is an inescapable substrate of lonely work and lonely existence.

The Rescuer Defense and Interpersonal Difficulties.   The fact that some individuals avoid the fear of death through a belief in the existence of an ultimate rescuer offers the clinician a useful frame of reference for some baffling, interpersonal minuets. Consider the following examples of a common clinical problem: the patient who is enmeshed in a patently ungratifying, even destructive relationship and yet is unable to wrench free.

Bonnie was forty-eight years old, had a severe circulatory disorder (Buerger's disease), and after a twenty-year childless marriage, had been separated for ten years. Her husband, a fervent outdoorsman, appeared to be a highly insensitive, self-centered autocrat who finally left Bonnie when her poor health made it impossible for her to accompany him on hunting and fishing expeditions. He provided her no financial support during the ten years of separation, had affairs with numerous women (descriptions of which he did not fail to share with her), and visited Bonnie's home once every week or two to use the washing machine, to pick up recorded phone messages for the business phone he maintained there, and, once or twice a year, to have sexual relations with her. Bonnie, because of strong moral standards, refused to date other men while she was still married. She continued to be obsessed with her husband— at times enraged at the sight of him, at times enamored of him. Her life diminished, as she became ill, lonely, and tormented by his weekly washing machine visits. Yet she could neither divorce him, disconnect his phone, or terminate his laundry privileges.

Martha was thirty-one years old and desperate to marry and raise a family. For several years she had been involved with a man who belonged to a mystical religious sect that taught him that the fewer commitments an individual makes, the greater is his freedom. Consequently, though he enjoyed Martha, he refused to live with her or make any long-term commitment to her. He was alarmed by her need for him; and, the tighter she clutched, the less was he willing to promise. Martha was obsessed with binding him and was pained beyond description at his lack of commitment. Yet she felt addicted and was unable to wrench herself free; each time she broke with him, she suffered a painful state of withdrawal and finally in depression or panic reached for the telephone to call him. He, during times of separation, was maddeningly tranquil; he cared for her but could manage well without her. Martha was too consumed with him to search effectively for other relationships: her major project in life was to extract a commitment from him—a commitment that reason and experience strongly suggested was not to be forthcoming.

Each of these patients was involved in a relationship that was responsible for considerable anguish; each realized that continuing in the relationship was self-destructive. Each tried, in vain, to wrench herself free; in fact these futile attempts constituted the major theme of the therapy of each woman. What made disengagement so difficult? What welded each of them so tightly to another person? An obvious and a common thread runs through the concerns of the two patients, and it quickly became apparent when I asked each one to tell me what came to mind when she thought of separating from her mate.

Bonnie had a twenty-year marriage to a husband who had made every decision for her. He was a man who could do everything and "took care" of her. Of course, as she was to learn when she separated, "being taken care of" restricted her growth and self-sufficiency. But it was so comforting to know that someone was always there to protect and rescue her. Bonnie had a serious illness and doggedly continued to believe, even after ten years' separation, that her husband was "out there" taking care of her. Every time I urged her to reflect on life without his presence (and I speak here of symbolic presence; aside from the shared washing machine and a few mechanical coital acts, there had been no meaningful physical presence for years), she became very anxious. What would she do in an emergency? Whom would she call? Life would be unbearably lonely without him. Obviously he was a symbol that shielded her from confronting the harsh reality that there is no one "out there," that the "emergency" is inevitable and no person, symbolic or real, can obviate it.

Martha permitted her life to be governed by the future. Whenever I asked her to meditate on what it would be like to give up her relationship with her uncommitted boyfriend, she always responded that all she could think of was "eating alone at sixty-three." When I asked her for her definition of commitment, she replied, "It's the assurance I'll never have to live alone or die alone." The thought of dining alone or going to the movies alone filled her with shame and dread. What was it that she really wanted from a relationship? "Being able to get help without having to ask for it," she replied.

Martha was tyrannized by the always present, desperate fear that she would be alone in the future. Like many neurotic patients, she did not really live in the present, but instead attempted to find the past (that is, the comforting bond with mother) in the future. Martha's fear and her need were so great that they ensured that she would not establish a gratifying relationship with a man. She was too frightened of loneliness to give up her current unsatisfying relationship, and her need was so obviously frenzied that she frightened away prospective partners.

For each of these women, then, the bonding force was not the relationship per se but the terror of being alone; and what was especially fearful about being alone was the absence of that magical, powerful other who hovers about each of us, observing, anticipating our needs, providing each of us with a shield against the destiny of death.

Toward an Integrated View of Psychopathology

I have, for didactic purposes, focused separately on two major modes of coping with death anxiety and presented vignettes of patients who show extreme forms of one of these two basic defenses, but now it is time to integrate them. Most patients do not, of course, present with clear and monothematic clinical pictures. Generally one does not construct a single ponderous defense but instead uses multiple, interlaced defenses in an attempt to wall off anxiety. Most individuals defend against death anxiety through both a delusional belief in their own inviolability *and* a belief in the existence of an ultimate rescuer. Although I have thus far presented these two defenses as a dialectic, they are closely interdependent. *Because* we have an observing, omnipotent being or force continuously concerned with our welfare, we are unique and immortal and have the courage to emerge from embeddedness. *Because* we are unique and special beings, special forces in the universe are concerned with us. Though our ultimate rescuer is omnipotent, he is at the same time our eternal servant.

Otto Rank in a thoughtful essay entitled "Life Fear and Death Fear" posited a basic dynamic that illuminates the relationship between the two defenses.[54] Rank felt that there is in the individual a primal fear that manifests itself sometimes as a fear of life, sometimes as a fear of death. By "fear of life" Rank meant anxiety in the face of a "loss of connection with a greater whole." The fear of life is the fear of having to face life as an isolated being, it is the fear of individuation, of "going forward," of "standing out from nature." Rank believed that the prototypical life fear was "birth," the original trauma and the original separation. By "fear of death" Rank meant the fear of extinction, of loss of individuality, of being dissolved again into the whole.

Rank stated that "between these two fear possibilities, these poles of fear, the individual is thrown back and forth all his life." The individual attempts to separate himself, to individuate, to affirm his autonomy, to go forward, to fulfill his potential. Yet there comes a time when he develops fear in the face of life. Individuation, emergence—or, as I put it here, affirmation of specialness—are not duty-free: they entail a fearful, lonely sense of unprotectedness—a sense that the individual assuages by reversing direction: one goes "backward," relinquishes individuation, finds comfort in fusing, in dissolving oneself, in giving oneself up to another. Yet the comfort is unstable because this alternative evokes fear also—the fear of death: relinquishment, stagnation, and finally, inorganicity. Between these two poles of fear, *life fear* and *death fear,* the individual shuttles throughout life.

Though the paradigm I offer here of the dual defenses of specialness and the ultimate rescuer is not identical with Rank's life-fear, death-fear dialectic, they obviously overlap. Rank's poles of fear correspond closely to the inherent limits of the defenses I have described. "Life anxiety" emerges from the defense of specialness: it is the price one pays for standing out, unshielded, from nature. "Death anxiety" is the toll of fusion: when one gives up autonomy, one loses oneself and suffers a type of death. Thus one oscillates, one goes in one direction until the anxiety outweighs the relief of the defense, and then one moves in the other direction.

DEATH AND PSYCHOTHERAPY

The leap from theory to practice is not easy. In this section I shall transport us from metaphysical concerns about death to the office of the practicing psychotherapist and attempt to extract from those concerns what is relevant to everyday therapy.

The reality of death is important to psychotherapy in two distinct ways: death awareness may act as a "boundary situation" and instigate a radical shift in life perspective, and death is a primary source of anxiety. I shall discuss the application of each way, in turn, to the technique of therapy.

Death as a Boundary Situation

A "boundary situation" is an event, an urgent experience, that propels one into a confrontation with one's existential "situation" in the world. A confrontation with one's personal death ("my death") is the nonpareil boundary situation and has the power to provide a massive shift in the way one lives in the world. Death acts as a catalyst that can move one from one state of being to a higher one: from a state of wondering about *how* things are to a state of wonderment *that* they are. An awareness of death shifts one away from trivial preoccupations and provides life with depth and poignancy and an entirely different perspective.

Earlier I considered illustrative examples from literature and clinical records of individuals who, after a confrontation with death, have undergone a radical personal transformation. Tolstoy's Pierre in *War and Peace* and Ivan Ilych in "The Death of Ivan Ilych" are obvious instances of "personality change" or "personal growth." Another striking illustration is everyone's favorite miraculously transformed hero: Ebenezer Scrooge. Many of us forget that Scrooge's transformation was not simply the natural result of yule warmth melting his icy countenance. What changed Scrooge was a confrontation with his own death. Dickens's

Ghost of the Future (Ghost of the Christmas Yet to Come) used a powerful form of existential shock therapy: Scrooge was permitted to observe his own death, to overhear members of the community discuss his death and then dismiss it lightly, and to watch strangers quarreling over his material possessions, including even his bedsheets and nightshirt. Scrooge then witnessed his own funeral and, finally, in the last scene before his transformation, Scrooge knelt in the churchyard and examined the letters of his name inscribed on his tombstone.

Death Confrontation and Personal Change: Mechanism of Action

How does death awareness instigate personal change? What is the inner experience of the individual thus transformed? We have already discussed the type and the degree of positive change that some terminal cancer patients have undergone. Interviews with these patients provide insights into some of the mechanisms of change.

Cancer Cures Psychoneurosis.   One patient had disabling interpersonal phobias that almost miraculously dissolved after she developed cancer. When asked about this cure, she responded, "Cancer cures psychoneurosis." Although she tossed this statement off almost flippantly, there is an arresting truth in it: not the dismal truth that death eliminates life with all its attendant sorrows, but the optimistic truth that the anticipation of death provides a rich perspective for life concerns. When asked to describe her transformation, she stated that it was a simple process: having faced and, she felt, conquered her fear of death—a fear that had dwarfed all her other fears—she experienced a strong sense of personal mastery.

Existence Cannot Be Postponed.   Eva, forty-five years old and deeply depressed, had advanced ovarian cancer and was highly conflicted about whether she should take one last trip. In the midst of our therapeutic work she reported this dream:

> There was a large crowd of people. It looked something like a
> Cecil B. DeMille scene. I can recognize my mother in there. They
> were all chanting, "You can't go, you have cancer, you are ill." The
> chanting went on and on. Then I heard my dead father, a quiet
> reassuring voice, saying, "I know you have lung cancer like me, but

don't stay home and eat chicken soup, waiting to die like me. Go to Africa—live."

Eva's father had died many years ago of a lingering cancer. She last saw him several months before his death and had sorrowed not only at her loss but at the way he died. No one in the family had dared tell him about his cancer, and the symbol of staying home and eating chicken soup was apt: his remaining life and his death were unenlightened and unheroic. The dream bore powerful counsel; Eva heeded it well and altered her life dramatically. She confronted her physician and demanded all available information about her cancer and insisted that she share in the decisions made about her treatment. She re-established old friendships; she shared her fears with others and helped them share their grief with her. She did take that last journey to Africa which, though it was cut short by illness, did leave her with the satisfaction of having drunk deeply from life until the last draught.

The matter can be summed up simply: "Existence cannot be postponed." Many patients with cancer report that they live more fully in the present. They no longer postpone living until some time in the future. They realize that one can really live *only* in the present; in fact, one cannot outlive the present—it always keeps up with you. Even in the moment of looking back over one's life—even in the last moment—one is still there, experiencing, living. The present, not the future, is the eternal tense.

Another individual, a university professor, as a result of a serious bout with cancer, decided to enjoy the future in the immediate present. He discovered, with astonishment, that he could choose not to do those things he did not wish to do. When he recovered from his surgery and returned to work, his behavior changed strikingly: he divested himself of onerous administrative duties, immersed himself in the most exciting aspects of his research (eventually attaining national prominence), and—let this be a lesson to us all—never attended another faculty meeting.

Fran was chronically depressed and fearful and had for fifteen years been locked into a highly unsatisfying marriage which she could not bring herself to end. The final obstacle to separation was her husband's extensive home aquarium! She wished to remain in the house so that her children could keep their friends and remain in the same school; yet she could not undertake the two hours of time needed for the daily feeding of the fish. Nor could the huge aquarium be moved except at enormous expense. The problem seemed insoluble. (On such trifling issues is a life sacrificed.)

Fran then developed a malignant form of bone cancer which brought home to her the simple fact that this was her one and only life. She said that she suddenly realized that time's clock runs continuously, and that there are no "time-outs" when it stops. Though her illness was so severe that her need for her husband's physical and economic support were very great indeed, she nonetheless made the courageous decision to separate, a decision she had postponed for over a decade.

Death reminds us that existence cannot be postponed. And that there is still time for life. If one is fortunate enough to encounter his or her death and to experience life as the "possibility of possibility" (Kierkegaard)[55] and to know death as the "impossibility of further possibility" (Heidegger),[56] then one realizes that, as long as one lives, one has possibility—one can alter one's life until—but only *until* the last moment. If, however, one dies tonight, then all of tomorrow's intentions and promises die stillborn. That is what Ebenezer Scrooge learned; in fact, the pattern of his transformation consisted of a systematic reversal of his misdeeds of the previous day: he tipped the caroler he had cursed, he donated money to the charity workers he had spurned, he embraced the nephew he had scorned, he gave coal, food, and money to Cratchit whom he had tyrannized.

Count Your Blessings.   Another mechanism of change energized by a confrontation with death was well illustrated by a patient who had cancer that had invaded her esophagus. Swallowing became difficult; gradually she shifted to soft foods, then to puréed foods, then to liquids. One day in a cafeteria, after having been unable even to swallow some clear broth, she looked around at the other diners and wondered, "Do they realize how lucky they are to be able to swallow? Do they ever think of that?" She applied this simple principle to herself and became aware of what she *could* do and *could* experience: the elemental facts of life, the changing seasons, the beauty of her natural surroundings, seeing, listening, touching, and loving. Nietzsche expresses this principle in a beautiful passage:

> Out of such abysses, from such severe sickness one returns new-born, having shed one's skin, more ticklish and malicious, with a more delicate taste for joy, with a more tender tongue for all good things, with merrier senses, with a second dangerous innocence in joy, more childlike and yet a hundred times subtler than one has ever seen before.[57]

Count your blessings! How rarely do we benefit from that simple homily? Ordinarily what we *do* have and what we *can* do slips out of awareness, diverted by thoughts of what we lack or what we cannot do, or dwarfed by petty concerns and threats to our prestige or our pride systems. By keeping death in mind, one passes into a state of gratitude, of appreciation for the countless givens of existence. This is what the Stoics meant when they said, "Contemplate death if you would learn how to live."[58] The imperative is not, then, a call to a morbid death preoccupation but instead an urging to keep both figure and ground in focus so that being becomes conscious and life becomes richer. As Santayana put it: "The dark background which death supplies brings out the tender colors of life in all their purity."[59]

Disidentification. In everyday clinical work the psychotherapist encounters individuals who are severely anxious in the face of events that do not seem to warrant anxiety. Anxiety is a signal that one perceives some threat to one's continued existence. The problem is that the neurotic person's security is so tentative that he or she extends his or her defensive perimeter a long way into space. In other words, the neurotic not only protects his or her core but defends many other attributes (work, prestige, role, vanity, sexual prowess, or athletic ability) with the same intensity. Many individuals become inordinately stressed, therefore, at threats to their career or to any of a number of other attributes. They believe in effect, "I *am* my career," or "I *am* my sexual attractiveness." The therapist wishes to say, "No, you are not your career, you are not your splendid body, you are not mother or father or wise man or eternal nurse. You are your *self,* your core essence. Draw a line around it: the other things, the things that fall outside, they are not you; they can vanish, and you will still exist."

Unfortunately such self-evident exhortations, like all self-evident exhortations, are rarely effective in catalyzing change. Psychotherapists look for methods to increase the power of the exhortation. One such method I have used, with groups of cancer patients as well as in the classroom, is a structured "disidentification" exercise.* The procedure is simple and takes approximately thirty to forty-five minutes. I choose a quiet peaceful setting and ask the participants to list, on separate cards, eight important answers to the question "Who am I?" I then ask them to review their eight answers and to arrange their cards in order of importance and centricity: the answers closest to their core at the bottom, the more peripheral responses at the top. Then I ask them to study their top card and meditate on what it would be like to give up that attribute. After approximately two to three minutes I ask them (some quiet signal like a bell is less distracting) to go on to the next card and so on until they have divested themselves of all eight attributes. Following that, it is advisable to help the participants integrate by going through the procedure in reverse. This simple exercise generates powerful emotions. I once led three hundred individuals in an adult education workshop through it; and, even years afterward, participants gratuitously informed me how momentously important the procedure had been to them.

The individual with a chronic illness who copes well with his or her situation often spontaneously goes through this process of disidentification. One patient whom I remember well had always closely identified herself with her physical energy and activities. Her cancer gradually weakened her to the point where she could no longer backpack, ski, or hike, and she mourned these losses for a long time. Her range of physical activities inexorably diminished, but eventually she was able to transcend her losses. After months of work in therapy she was able to accept the limitations, to say "I cannot do it" without a sense of personal worthlessness and futility. Then she transmuted her energy into other forms of expression that were within her limits. She set feasible final

*Suggested to me by James Bugental.

projects for herself: completing personal and professional unfinished business, expressing unvoiced sentiments to other patients, friends, doctors, and children. Much later she was able to take another, major step—to disidentify even with her energy and impact and to realize that she existed apart from these, indeed apart from all other qualities.

Disidentification is an obvious and ancient mechanism of change— the transcendence of material and social accoutrements has long been embodied in ascetic traditions—but it is not easily available for clinical use. It is the awareness of death that promotes a shift in perspective and makes it possible for an individual to distinguish between core and accessory: to reinvest one and to divest the other.

Death Awareness in Everyday Psychotherapy

If we psychotherapists accept that awareness of personal death can catalyze a process of personal change, then it is our task to facilitate a patient's awareness of death. But how? Many of the examples I have cited are of individuals in an extraordinary situation. What about the psychotherapist treating the everyday patient—who does not have terminal cancer, or who is not facing a firing squad, or who has not had a near fatal accident?

Several of my cancer patients posed the same question. When speaking of their growth and what they had learned from their confrontation with death, they lamented, "What a tragedy that we had to wait till now, till our bodies were riddled with cancer, to learn these truths!"

There are many structured exercises that the therapist may employ to simulate an encounter with death. Some of these are interesting, and I shall describe them shortly. But the most important point I wish to make in this regard is that the therapist does not need to *provide* the experience; instead, the therapist needs merely to help the patient *recognize* that which is everywhere about him or her. Ordinarily we deny, or selectively inattend to, reminders of our existential situation; the task of the therapist is to reverse this process, to pursue these reminders, for they are not, as I have attempted to demonstrate, enemies but powerful allies in the pursuit of integration and maturity.

Consider this illustrative vignette. A forty-six-year-old mother takes the youngest of her four children to the airport where he departs for college. She has spent the last twenty-six years rearing her children and longing for this day. No more impositions, no more incessantly living for others, no more cooking dinners and picking up clothes, only to be reminded of her futile efforts by dirty dishes and a room in new disarray. Finally she is free.

Yet, as she says good-bye, she unexpectedly begins sobbing loudly, and on the way home from the airport a deep shudder passes through her body. "It is only natural," she thinks. It is only the sadness of saying good-bye to someone she loves very much. But it is more than that. The shudder persists and shortly turns into raw anxiety. What could it be? She consults a therapist. He soothes her. It is but a common problem: the "empty nest" syndrome. For so many years she has based her self-esteem on her performance as mother and housekeeper. Suddenly she finds no way to validate herself. Of course she is anxious: the routine, the structure of her life have been altered, and her life role and primary source of self-esteem have been removed. Gradually, with the help of Valium, supportive psychotherapy, an assertiveness training women's group, several adult education courses, a lover or two, and a part-time volunteer job, the shudder shrinks to a tremble and then vanishes altogether. She returns to her "premorbid" level of comfort and adaptation.

This patient, treated by a psychiatric resident some years ago, was part of a psychotherapy outcome research project. Her treatment results could only be described as excellent: on each of the measures used—symptom checklists, target problem evaluation, self-esteem—she had made considerable improvement. Even now, in retrospect, it seems clear that the psychotherapist fulfilled his function. Yet I also look upon this course of treatment as a "misencounter," as an instance of missed therapeutic opportunities.

I compare it with another patient I saw recently in almost precisely the same life situation. In the treatment of this patient I attempted to nurse the shudder rather than to anesthetize it. The patient experienced what Kierkegaard called "creative anxiety," and her anxiety led us into important areas. It *was* true that she had problems of self-esteem, she *did* suffer from "empty nest" syndrome, and she also was deeply troubled by her great ambivalence toward her child: she loved him but also resented and envied him for the chances in life she had never had (and, of course, she felt guilty because of these "ignoble" sentiments).

We followed her shudder, and it led us into important realms and raised fundamental questions. It was true enough that she could find ways to fill her time, but what was the *meaning* of the fear of the empty nest? She had always desired freedom but now, having achieved it, was terrified of it. Why?

A dream helped to illuminate the meaning of the shudder. Her son who had just left home for college had been an acrobat and a juggler in high school. Her dream consisted simply of herself holding in her hand a 35-millimeter photographic slide of her son juggling. The slide was peculiar, however, in that it was a slide in movement: it showed her son juggling and tumbling in a multitude of movements all at the same time. Her associations to the dream revolved around time. The slide captured and framed time and movement. It kept everything alive but made everything stand still. It froze life. "Time moves on," she said, "and there's no way I can stop it. I didn't want John to grow up. I really treasured those years when he was with us. Yet whether I like it or not, time moves on. It moves on for John and it moves on for me as well. It is a terrible thing to understand, to really understand."

This dream brought her own finiteness into clear focus, and rather than rush to fill time with distractions, she learned to wonder at and to appreciate time and life in richer ways than she previously had. She moved into the realm that Heidegger describes as authentic being: she wondered not at the *way* that things are but *that* things are. In my judgment, therapy helped the second patient more than the first. It would not be possible to demonstrate this conclusion on standard outcome measures; in fact, the second patient probably continued to experience more anxiety than the first did. But anxiety is a part of existence, and no individual who continues to grow and to create will ever be free of it. Nevertheless, such a value judgment evokes many questions about the therapist's role. Is the therapist not assuming too much? Does the patient engage his or her services as a guide to existential awareness? Or do not most patients say in effect, "I feel bad, help me feel better"; and if this is the case, why not use the speediest, most efficient means at one's disposal—for example, pharmacological tranquilization or behavioral modification? Such questions, which pertain to all forms of treatment based on self-awareness, cannot be ignored, and they will emerge here again and again.

In the treatment of every patient, situations arise that, if sensitively emphasized by the therapist, would increase the patient's awareness of the existential dimensions of his or her problems. The most obvious situations are the stark reminders of finiteness and the irreversibility of time. The death of someone close will, if the therapist persists, always lead to an increased death awareness. There are many components to grief—the sheer loss, the ambivalence and guilt, the disruption of a life plan—and all need to be thoroughly dealt with in treatment. But, as I stressed earlier, the death of another also brings one closer to facing one's own death; and this part of the grief work is commonly omitted. Some psychotherapists may feel that the bereaved is already too overwhelmed to accept the added task of dealing with his or her own finiteness. I think, however, that assumption is often an error: some individuals can grow enormously as a result of personal tragedy.

The Death of Another and Existential Awareness.   For many, the death of a close fellow creature offers the most intimate recognition one can have of one's own death. Paul Landsburg, discussing the death of a loved one, says:

> We have constituted an "us" with the dying person. And it is in this "us," it is through the specific power of this new and utterly personal being that we are led toward the living awareness of our own having to die. . . . My community with that person seems to be broken off; but this community in some degree was I myself, I feel death in the heart of my own existence.[60]

John Donne made the same point in his famous sermon: "And therefore never send to know for whom the bell tolls. It tolls for thee."[61]

The loss of a parent brings us in touch with our vulnerability; if our parents could not save themselves, who will save us? With parents gone nothing stands between ourselves and the grave. On the contrary, we become the barrier between our children and death. The experience of a colleague after the death of his father is illustrative. He had long been expecting his father's death and bore the news with equanimity. However, as he boarded an airplane to fly home for the funeral, he panicked. Though he was a highly experienced traveler, he suddenly lost faith in the plane's capacity to take off and land safely—as though his shield against precariousness had vanished.

The loss of a spouse often evokes the issue of basic isolation; the loss of the significant other (sometimes the dominant other) increases one's awareness that, try as hard as we may to go through the world two by two, there is nonetheless a basic aloneness that we must bear. No one can die one's own death with one or for one.

A therapist who attends closely to a bereaved patient's associations and dreams will discover considerable evidence of the latter's concern with his or her own death. For example, a patient reported this nightmare on the night after learning that his wife had inoperable cancer:

> I was living in my old house in _____. [A house that had been in
> the family for three generations.] A Frankenstein monster was
> chasing me through the house. I was terrified. The house was
> deteriorating, decaying. The tiles were crumbling and the roof
> leaking. Water leaked all over my mother. [His mother had died
> six months ago.] I fought with him. I had a choice of weapons. One
> had a curved blade with a handle, like a scythe. I slashed him and
> tossed him off the roof. He lay stretched out on the pavement
> below. But he got up and once again started chasing me through
> the house.

The patient's first association to the dream was: "I know I've got a hundred thousand miles on me." The symbolism of the dream seemed clear. His wife's impending death reminded him that his life, like his house, was deteriorating; he was inexorably pursued by death, personified, as in his childhood, by a monster who could not be halted.

The loss of a son or daughter is often the bitterest loss of all to us, and we simultaneously mourn our child and ourselves. Life seems to hit us, at such a time, on all fronts at once. Parents first rail at the injustice in the universe but soon begin to understand that what seemed injustice is, in reality, cosmic indifference. They also are reminded of the limit of their power: there is no time in life when they have greater motivation to act and yet are helpless; they cannot protect a defenseless child. As night follows day, the bitter lesson follows that we, in our turn, will not be protected.

The psychiatric grief literature does not emphasize this dynamic but instead often focuses on the guilt (thought to be associated with unconscious hostility) that parents experience at the death of a child. Richard Gardner[62] studied parental bereavement empirically by systematically interviewing and testing a large sample of parents whose children suffered from some type of fatal illness. Though he confirmed that many parents suffered considerable guilt, his data indicated that the guilt, rather than emanating from "unconscious hostility," was four times more commonly an attempt by the parent to assuage his or her own existential anxiety, to attempt to "control the uncontrollable." After all, if one is guilty about not having done something one should have done, then it follows that *there is something that could have been done*—a far more comforting state of affairs than the hard existential facts of life.

The loss of a child has another portentous implication for the parents. It signals the failure of their major immortality project: they will not be remembered, their seed will not take root in the future.

Milestones.   Anything that challenges the patient's permanent view of the world can serve as a fulcrum with which the therapist can wedge open the patient's defenses and permit him a view of life's existential innards. Heidegger emphasizes that only when machinery suddenly breaks down do we become aware of its functioning.[63] Only when defenses against death anxiety are removed do we become fully aware of what they shielded us from. Therefore, the therapist who looks may find existential anxiety lurking when any major event, especially an irreversible one, occurs in a patient's life. Marital separation and divorce are prime examples of such events. These experiences are so painful that therapists often make the error of focusing attention entirely on pain alleviation and miss the rich opportunity that reveals itself for deeper therapeutic work.

For some patients, the commitment to a relationship, rather than the termination of one, acts as a boundary situation. Commitment carries with it the connotation of finality, and many individuals cannot settle into a permanent relationship because that would mean "this is it," no more possibilities, no more glorious dreams of continued ascendancy.

The passage into adulthood is often particularly difficult. Individuals in their late teens and early twenties are often acutely anxious about death. In fact, a clinical syndrome in adolescents called the "terror of life" has been described: it consists of marked hypochondriasis and preoccupation with the aging of the body, with the rapid passage of time, and with the inevitability of death.[64]

Jaques, in his wonderful essay "Death and the Mid-Life Crisis," stresses that the individual in midlife is especially bedeviled by the thought of death.[65] This is the time of life when a person may become preoccupied with the thought, often unconscious, that he or she "has stopped growing up and has begun to grow old." Having spent the first half of life in the "achievement of independent adulthood," one may reach the prime of life (Jung called age forty the "noon of life")[66] only to become acutely aware that death lies beyond. As one thirty-six-year-old patient, who had become increasingly aware of death in his analysis, put it: "Up till now, life has seemed an endless upward slope with nothing but the distant horizon in view. Now suddenly I seemed to have reached the crest of the hill, and there stretching ahead is the downward slope with the end of the road in sight—far enough away, it's true—but there is death observably present at the end."

A threat to one's career or the fact of retirement (especially in individuals who had believed that life was an ever-ascending spiral) can be a particularly potent catalyst for increasing one's awareness of death. A recent study of individuals making a midlife radical career shift suggests that most of them had made the decision to "drop out" or to simplify their lives in the context of a confrontation with their existential situation.[67]

Simple milestones, such as birthdays and anniversaries, can be useful levers for the therapist. The pain elicited by these signs of the passage of time runs deep (and for that reason is generally dealt with by reaction formation, in the form of a joyous celebration). Sometimes mundane reminders of aging offer an opportunity for increased existential awareness. Even a penetrating look in the mirror can open the issue. One patient told me that she said to herself, "I'm just a little gnome. I'm the same little Isabelle inside, but outside I'm an old lady. I'm sixteen going on sixty. I know it's perfectly all right for others to age, but somehow I never thought it would happen to me." Even the recognition that one enjoys "old people's" pleasures—watching, walking, serene quiet times—may act as a spur to death awareness. The same may be said about looking at old photographs of oneself and noting how one resembles one's parents when they were considered old, or seeing friends after long intervals and noting how they have aged. The therapist who listens carefully will be able to use any of these everyday occurrences. Or the therapist may tactfully contrive such situations. Freud, for instance, had no qualms about requesting Fraulein Elisabeth to meditate at the site of her sister's grave.

A careful monitoring of dreams and fantasies will invariably provide material to increase death awareness. Every anxiety dream is a dream of death; frightening fantasies involving such themes as unknown aggressors breaking into one's home always, when explored, lead to the fear of death. Discussions of unsettling television shows, movies, or books may similarly lead to essential material.

Severe illness is such an obvious catalyst that no therapist should let this opportunity pass by unmined. Noyes studied two hundred patients who had had near-death experiences through sudden illness or accident and found that a substantial number (25 percent) had a new and powerful sense of death's omnipresence and nearness. One of his subjects commented, "I used to think death would never happen or, if it did, I would be eighty years old. But now I realize it can happen any time, any place, no matter how you live your life. A person has a very limited perception of death until he is confronted with it." Another described his death awareness in these terms: "I have seen death in life's pattern and affirmed it consciously. I am not afraid to live because I feel that death has a part in the process of my being." Though a few of Noyes's subjects reported an increased terror of death and a greater sense of vulnerability, the great majority reported that their increased death awareness had been a positive experience resulting in a greater sense of life's preciousness and a constructive reassessment of their life's priorities.[68]

Artificial Aids to Increase Death Awareness.   Though the naturally occurring reminders of death's presence are numerous, they are not, therapists often find, sufficiently potent to combat a patient's ever-vigilant denial. Consequently many therapists have sought vivid techniques to bring patients to face the fact of death. In the past, intentional and unintentional reminders of death were far more common than they are today. It was precisely for the purpose of reminding one of life's transiency that a human skull was a common furnishing in a medieval monk's cell. John Donne, the seventeenth-century British poet and clergyman, wore a funeral shroud when he preached "Look to eternity" to his congregation; and earlier, Montaigne, in his splendid essay "That to Philosophize Is to Learn How to Die," had much to say on the subject of intentional reminders of our finiteness:

> . . . we plant our cemeteries next to churches, and in the most frequented parts of town, in order (says Lycurgus) to accustom the common people, women and children, not to grow panicky at the sight of a dead man, and so that the constant sight of bones, tombs, and funeral processions should remind us of our condition. . . . To feasts, it once was thought, slaughter lent added charms/Mingling with foods the sight of combatants in arms,/And gladiators fell amid the cups, to pour/Onto the very tables their abundant gore. . . . And the Egyptians, after their feasts, had a large image of death shown to the guests by a man who called out to them: "Drink and be merry, for when you are dead you will be like this."
>
> So I have formed the habit of having death continually present, not merely in my imagination, but in my mouth. And there is nothing that I investigate so eagerly as the death of men: what words, what look, what bearing they maintained at that time; nor is there a place in the histories that I note so attentively. This shows in the abundance of my illustrative examples; I have indeed a particular fondness for this subject. If I were a maker of books, I would make a register, with comments, of various deaths. He who would teach men to die would teach them to live.[69]

Some encounter-group leaders have used a form of "existential shock" therapy by asking each member to write his or her own epitaph or obituary. "Destination" labs held for harried business executives commonly began with this structured exercise:

On a blank sheet of paper draw a straight line. One end of that line represents your birth; the other end, your death. Draw a cross to represent where you are now. Meditate upon this for five minutes.

This short, simple exercise almost invariably evokes powerful and profound reactions.

Interaction with the Dying.   There are many such exercises. As intriguing as many of them are, they nonetheless are make-believe. Though one can be drawn into such an exercise for a period of time, denial quickly sets in, and one reminds oneself that one still exists, that one is merely observing these experiences. It was precisely because of the persistence and ubiquity of denial to assuage dread that several years ago I started to treat individuals with a fatal illness, individuals who were continually in the midst of urgent experience and could not deny what was happening to them. My hope was not only to be useful to these patients but to be able to apply what I learned to the treatment of the physically healthy patient.

Group therapy sessions with terminal patients are often powerful with the evocation of much affect and the sharing of much wisdom. Many patients feel that they have learned a great deal about life but are frustrated in their efforts to be helpful to others. One patient put it, "I feel I have so much to teach, but my students will not listen." I have searched for ways to expose everyday psychotherapy patients to the wisdom and power of the dying and shall describe here my limited experience with one approach.

Observation of a Terminal Cancer Group by Everyday Psychotherapy Patients.   One patient who observed a meeting of the group of cancer patients was Karen, whom I discussed earlier. Karen's major dynamic conflict was her pervasive search for a dominant other—an ultimate rescuer—which took the form of psychic and sexual masochism. Karen would limit herself or inflict pain on herself, if necessary, to gain the attention and protection from some "superior" figure. The meeting she observed was particularly powerful. One patient, Eva, announced to the group that she had just learned she had a recurrence of cancer. She said that she had done something that morning that she had long postponed: she had written a letter to her children giving instructions about the division of minor sentimental items. In placing the letter in her safe-deposit box, she realized with a clarity she had never before attained that indeed she would cease to be. As I have described, she realized that when her children read that letter, she would not be there to observe or to respond to them. She wished, she said, that she had done her work on death in her twenties rather than waiting until now. Once one of her teachers had died (Eva was a school principal); and, rather than concealing the death from the students, she realized how right she had been to hold a memorial service and openly discuss death—the death of plants, animals, pets, and humans—with the children. Other group members, too, shared their moments of full realizations about their deaths, and some discussed the ways they had grown as a result of that realization.

An interesting debate developed as one member told about a neighbor who had been perfectly healthy and had died suddenly during the night. "That's the perfect death," she said. Another member disagreed and in a few moments had presented compelling reasons that that type of death was unfortunate: the dead woman had had no time to put her affairs in order, to complete unfinished business, to prepare her husband and her children for her death, to treasure the end of life as some of the members in the group had learned to do. "Just the same," the first quipped, "that's still the way I'd like to die. I've always loved surprises!"

Karen reacted strongly to the meeting she had observed. It was immediately thereafter that she arrived at many deep insights about herself. For example, she realized that because of her fear of death, she had sacrificed much of her life. She had so feared death that she had organized her life around the search for an ultimate rescuer; therefore, she had feigned illness during her childhood and stayed sick in adulthood to remain near her therapist. While observing the group, she realized with horror that she would have been willing to have cancer in order to be in that group and sit next to me, perhaps even hold my hand (the group ended with a hand-holding period of meditation). When I pointed out the obvious—that is, that no relationship is eternal, that I, as well as she, would die—she said that she felt that she would never be alone if she could die in my arms. The evocation and the subsequent working through of this material helped move Karen into a new phase of therapy, especially into a consideration of termination—an issue that previously she had never been willing to broach.

Another everyday therapy patient who observed the group was Susan, the wife of an eminent scientist who, when she was fifty, had sued her for divorce. In her marriage she had lived a mediated existence, serving him and basking in his accomplishments. Such a life pattern, not uncommon among wives of successful husbands in these days, had certain inevitable tragic consequences. First, she did not live her life; in her effort to build up credit with the dominant other she submerged herself, she lost sight of *her* wishes, her rights, and her pleasure. Second, because of the sacrifice of her own strivings, interests, desires, and spontaneity, she became a less stimulating partner and was considerably more at risk for divorce.

In our work Susan passed through a deep depression and gradually began to explore her *pro-active* feelings, not the reactive ones to which she had always limited herself. She felt her anger—deep, rich, and vibrant; she felt her sorrow—not at the loss of her husband but at the loss of herself all those years; she felt outraged at all the restrictions to which she had consented. (For example, to ensure that her husband had optimal working conditions at home, she was not permitted to watch television, to speak on the phone, to garden while he was home—his study looked out on the garden and her presence distracted him.) She ran the risk of being overcome with regret for so much wasted life, and the task of therapy was to enable her to revitalize the remainder of her life. After two months of therapy she watched a poignant meeting of the cancer group, was moved by the experience, and immediately plunged into productive work which finally permitted her to understand that the divorce might be salvation rather than requiem. After therapy she moved to another city and several months later wrote a debriefing letter which included:

> First of all, I've thought that those women with cancer need not be reminded of the inevitability of death; that the awareness of death helps them to see things and events in their proper proportions and corrects our ordinarily poor sense of time. The life ahead of me may be very short. Life is precious, don't waste it! Make the most of

every day in the ways you value! Reappraise your values! Check your priorities! Don't procrastinate! Do!

I, for one, have wasted time. Every once in a while in the past, I'd feel vividly that I was only a spectator or an understudy watching the drama of life from the wings, but always hoping and believing that one day I'd be on the stage myself. Sure enough there had been times of intense living, but more often than not life seemed just a rehearsal for the "real" life ahead. *But what if death comes before the "real" life has started?* It would be tragic to realize when it's too late, that one has hardly lived at all.

Death as a Primary Source of Anxiety

The concept of death provides the psychotherapist with two major forms of leverage. I have discussed the first: that death is of such momentous importance that it can, if properly confronted, alter one's life perspective and promote a truly authentic immersion in life. The second, to which I shall now turn my attention, is based on the premise that the fear of death constitutes a primary source of anxiety, that it is present early in life, is instrumental in shaping character structure, and continues throughout life to generate anxiety that results in manifest distress and in the erection of psychological defenses.

First, some general therapeutic principles. It is important to keep in mind that death anxiety, though it is ubiquitous and has pervasive ramifications, exists at the deepest levels of being, is heavily repressed, and is rarely experienced in its full sense. Death anxiety per se is not easily evident in the clinical picture of most patients; nor does it often become an explicit theme in the therapy, especially not in brief therapy, of most patients. Some patients are, however, suffused with overt death anxiety from the very onset of therapy. There are also life situations in which the patient has such a rush of death anxiety that the therapist, try as he or she might, cannot evade the issue. Furthermore, in long-term intensive therapy which explores deep levels of concern, explicit death anxiety is always to be found and must be considered in the therapeutic process.

Since death anxiety is so intimately tied to existence, it has a different connotation from "anxiety" in other frames of reference. Though the existential therapist hopes to alleviate crippling levels of anxiety, he or she does not hope to eliminate anxiety. Life cannot be lived nor can death be faced without anxiety. Anxiety is guide as well as enemy and can point the way to authentic existence. The task of the therapist is to reduce anxiety to comfortable levels and then to use this existing anxiety to increase a patient's awareness and vitality.

Another major point to keep in mind is that, even though death anxiety may not explicitly enter the therapeutic dialogue, a theory of anxiety based on death awareness provides the therapist with a frame of reference, an explanatory system, that may greatly enhance his or her effectiveness.

Repression of Death Anxiety

Earlier I described a head-on automobile collision where, had circumstances been less fortunate, I would have lost my life. My response to that accident serves as a transparent model for the workings of death anxiety in neurotic reactions. Recall that within a day or two I no longer experienced any explicit death anxiety but instead noted a specific phobia surrounding luncheon discussions. What happened was that I "handled" death anxiety by repression and displacement. I bound anxiety to a specific situation. Rather than being fearful of death or of nothingness, I became anxious about something. Anxiety is always ameliorated by becoming attached to a specific object or situation. Anxiety attempts to become fear. Fear is fear of some thing; it has a location in time and space; and, because it can be located, it can be tolerated and even "managed" (one may avoid the object or develop some systematic plan of conquering one's fear); fear is a current sweeping over one's surface—it does not threaten one's foundation.

I believe that this course of events is not uncommon. Death anxiety is deeply repressed and not part of our everyday experience. Gregory Zilboorg, in speaking of the fear of death, said: "If this fear were constantly conscious, we should be unable to function normally. It must be properly repressed to keep us living with any modicum of comfort."[70]

No doubt the repression, and subsequent invisibility, of death anxiety is the reason that many therapists neglect its role in their work. But surely the same state of affairs applies to other theoretical systems. The therapist always works with tracings of and defenses against primal anxiety. How often, for example, does an analytically oriented therapist encounter explicit castration anxiety? Another source of confusion is that the fear of death can be experienced at many different levels. One may, for example, consider death dispassionately and intellectually. Yet this adult perception is by no means the same as the dread of death that resides in the unconscious, a dread that is formed early in life at a time prior to the development of precise conceptual formulation, a dread that is terrible and inchoate and exists outside of language and image. The original unconscious nucleus of death anxiety is made more terrifying yet by the accretion of a young child's horrible misconceptions of death.

As a result of repression and transformation, existential therapy deals with anxiety that seems to have no existential referent. Later I shall discuss patients who have much overt death anxiety and also how layers of explicit death anxiety must always be reached through long and intensive therapy. But even in those courses of therapy where death anxiety never becomes explicit, the paradigm based on death anxiety may enhance the therapist's effectiveness.

The Therapist Is Provided with a Frame of Reference That Greatly Enhances His or Her Effectiveness.   As nature abhors a vacuum, we humans abhor uncertainty. One of the tasks of the therapist is to increase the patient's sense of certainty and mastery. It is a matter of no small importance that one be able to explain and order the events in our lives into some coherent and predictable pattern. To name something, to locate its place in a causal sequence, is to begin to experience it as under our control. No longer, then, is our internal experience or behavior frightening, alien, or out of control; instead, we behave (or have a particular inner experience) because of something we can name or identify. The "because" offers one mastery (or a sense of mastery that phenomenologically is tantamount to mastery). I believe that the sense of potency that flows from understanding occurs even in the matter of our basic existential situation: each of us feels less futile, less helpless, and less alone, even when, ironically, what we come to understand is the fact that each of us is basically helpless and alone in the face of cosmic indifference.

I've already discussed an explanatory system of psychopathology based on death anxiety. The importance of such an explanatory system is as important for the therapist as it is for the patient. Every therapist uses an explanatory system—some ideological frame of reference—to organize the clinical material with which he or she is faced.

The therapist's sense of certainty issuing from an explanatory system of psychopathology has a benefit for therapy which is curvilinear in nature. There is an optimal amount of therapist certainty: too little *and* too much are counterproductive. Too little certainty, for reasons already discussed, retards the formation of the necessary level of trust. Too *much* certainty, on the other hand, becomes rigidity. The therapist rejects or distorts data that will not fit into his system; furthermore, the therapist avoids facing, and helping the patient to face, one of the core concepts in existential therapy—that uncertainty exists, and that all of us must learn to coexist with it.

Interpretative Options: An Illustrative Case Study

Earlier I described some general existential dynamics underlying common clinical syndromes involving death anxiety. I shall present here specific interpretative options in a case of compulsive sexuality.

Bruce was a middle-aged male and had since adolescence been continually, as he put it, "on the prowl." He had had sexual intercourse with hundreds of women but had never cared deeply for any one of them. Bruce did not relate to a woman as to a whole person but as a "piece of ass." The women were more or less interchangeable. The important thing was bedding a woman—but, once orgasm was reached, he had no particular desire to remain with her. It was not unusual, therefore, once a woman had left, for him to go out searching for another, sometimes only minutes later. The compulsive quality of his behavior was so clear that it was evident even to him. He was aware often of "needing" or "having" to pursue a woman when he did not wish to.

Now Bruce could be understood from many perspectives, none of which had exclusive hegemony. The Oedipal overtones were clearly evident: he desired but feared women who resembled his mother. He was usually impotent with his wife. The closer he came in his travels to the city his mother inhabited, the stronger was his sexual desire. Furthermore, his dreams groaned with incestuous and castration themes. There was also evidence that his compulsive heterosexuality was powered by the need to handle the eruption of unconscious homosexual impulses. Bruce's self-esteem was severely impaired, and the successful seduction of women could be understood as an attempt to bolster his self-worth. Still another perspective: Bruce had both a need and a fear of closeness. The sexual encounter, at once closeness and caricature of closeness, honored both the need and the fear.

During more than eight years of analysis and several courses of therapy with competent therapists, all of these explanations, and many others besides, were explored fully, but without effect on his compulsive sexual drive.

During my work with Bruce I was struck by the rich, unmined existential themes. Bruce's compulsivity could be understood as a shield against confrontation with his existential situation. For example, it was apparent that Bruce was fearful of being alone. Whenever he was away from his family, Bruce took great pains to avoid spending an evening alone.

Anxiety can be a useful guide, and there are times when the therapist and patient must openly court anxiety. Accordingly, when Bruce had increased his ability to tolerate anxiety, I suggested that he spend an evening entirely alone and record his thoughts and feelings. What transpired that night was exceedingly important in his therapy. Raw terror is the best term for the experience. He encountered, for the first time since childhood, his fear of the supernatural. By sheer chance there was a brief power failure and Bruce grew terrified of the dark. He imagined that he saw a dead woman lying on the bed (resembling the old woman in the film *The Exorcist*); he imagined he saw a death's-head in the window; he feared that he might be touched by "something, perhaps a hand of a skeleton all dressed in rags." He gained enormous relief from the presence of a dog and for the first time realized the strong bond between some individuals and their pets: "What is needed," he said, "is not necessarily a human companion but something alive near you."

The terror of that evening was gradually, through the work of therapy, transformed into insight. Spending an evening alone made the function of sex abundantly clear. Without the protection of sex Bruce encountered massive death anxiety: the images were vivid—a dead woman, a skeleton's hand, a death's-head. How did sex protect Bruce from death? In a number of ways, each of which we analyzed in therapy. Sexual compulsivity, like every symptom, is overdetermined. For one thing sex was a form of death defiance. There was something frightening about sex for Bruce; no doubt sex was deeply entangled with buried incestuous yearnings and with fears of retaliatory castration—and by "castration" I mean not literal castration but annihilation. Thus the sexual act was counterphobic. Bruce stayed alive by jamming his penis into the vortex of life. Viewed in this way, Bruce's sexual compulsivity dovetailed with his other passions—parachuting, rock climbing, and motorcycling.

Sex also defeated death by reinforcing Bruce's belief in his personal specialness. Bruce stayed alive, in one sense, by being the center of his universe. Women revolved about him. All over the world women adored him. They existed for him alone. Bruce never thought of them as having independent lives. He imagined they remained in suspended animation for him; that, like Joseph K.'s flagellators in Kafka's *The Trial,* they were there for him every time he opened their doors, and that they froze into immobility when he did not call upon them. And of course sex served the function of preventing the conditions necessary for a true confrontation with death. Bruce never had to face the isolation that accompanies the awareness of one's personal death. Women were "something alive and near," much like the dog on the night of his terror. Bruce was never alone, he was always in the midst of coitus (a frenetic effort to fuse with a woman), searching for a woman, or just having left a woman. Thus, his search for a woman was not truly a search for sex, nor even a search powered by infantile forces, by "the stuff from which," as Freud liked to say, "sex will come,"[7] but instead it was a search to enable Bruce to deny and to assuage his fear of death.

Later in therapy an opportunity arose for him to go to bed with a beautiful woman who was the wife of his immediate boss. He deliberated about this chance and discussed it with a friend who counseled him against taking it because it might have destructive ramifications. Bruce also knew that the toll he would have to pay in anxiety and guilt would be prohibitive. Finally with a mighty wrench he, for the first time in his life, decided to forgo the sexual conquest. In our next therapy hour I agreed with him that he was acting indeed in his best interests.

His reaction to his decision was enlightening. He accused me of taking his life's pleasures away from him. He felt "done for," "finished." The following day, at a time when he could have had a sexual assignation, he read a book and sunbathed. "This is what Yalom wanted," he thought, "for me to grow old, sit in the sun and bleach like an old dog turd." He felt lifeless and depressed. That night he had a dream that illuminates better than any dream I have known the use of dream symbolism:

> I had a beautiful bow and arrow, I was proclaiming it as a great work of art that possessed magical qualities. You and X [a friend] differed and pointed out that it was just a very ordinary bow and arrow. I said, "No, it's magic, look at those features, and these!" [pointing at two protuberances]. You said, "No, it's very ordinary." And you proceeded to demonstrate to me how simply the bow was constructed, how simple twigs and bindings accounted for its shape.

What Bruce's dream illustrates so beautifully is another way that sex is death defeating. Death is connected with banality and ordinariness. The role of magic is to allow one to transcend the laws of nature, to transcend the ordinary, to deny one's creaturely identity—an identity that condemns one to biological death. His phallus was an enchanted bow and arrow, a magic wand lifting him above natural law. Each affair magically constituted a mini-life; although each of his affairs was a maze ending in a cul-de-sac, his affairs, all of them taken together, provided him with the illusion of a constantly lengthening lifeline.

As we worked through the material generated by his taking these two stands—spending time alone and *not* accepting a sexual invitation—a great deal of insight ensued to illuminate not only his sexual pathology but many other aspects of his life. For example, he had always related to others in a highly limited, sexual way. When his sexual compulsiveness waned, he began for the first time to confront the question, What are people for?—a question that launched a valuable exploration of Bruce's confrontation with existential isolation. Indeed, Bruce's course of therapy illustrates the interdependence of all the ultimate concerns. Bruce's decision, and his subsequent reluctance to accept that decision, to pass up a sexual invitation was the tip of the iceberg of another extraordinarily important existential concern, freedom, and especially of the issue of assuming responsibility. Lastly, Bruce's eventual relinquishment of his sexual compulsion confronted him with another ultimate concern—meaninglessness. With the removal of his major raison d'être, Bruce began to confront the problem of purpose in life.

Death Anxiety in Long-Term Therapy

Though brief courses of therapy often entirely circumvent any explicit consideration of death anxiety, any long-term intensive therapy will be incomplete without working through awareness and fear of death. As long as a patient continues to attempt to ward off death through an infantile belief that the therapist will deliver him or her from it, then the patient will not leave the therapist. "As long as I am with you, I will not die" is the unspoken refrain that so often emerges in late stages of therapy.

Death cannot be ignored in an extensive venture of self-exploration, because a major task of the mature adult is to come to terms with the reality of decline and diminishment. *The Divine Comedy,* which Dante wrote in his late thirties, may be understood on many allegorical levels, but certainly it reflects its author's concern about his personal death. The opening verses describe the fearful confrontation with one's own mortality that frequently occurs in midlife.

> In the middle of the course of our life, I came to myself within a dark wood, having lost the direct way. Ah, how difficult it is to describe what that wood was like, thick and savage and harsh, just the thought of which renews my fear.[72]

Individuals who have had significant emotional distress in their lives, and whose neurotic defenses have resulted in self-restriction, may encounter exceptionally severe difficulty in midlife, the time when aging and impending death must be recognized. The therapist who treats a patient in midlife must remind himself or herself that much psychopathology emanates from death anxiety. Jaques, in his essay on the midlife crisis, states this clearly:

A person who reaches midlife, either without having successfully established himself in marital and occupational life, or having established himself by means of manic activity and denial with consequent emotional impoverishment, is badly prepared for meeting the demands of middle age, and getting enjoyment out of his maturity. In such cases, the midlife crisis, and the adult encounter with the conception of life to be lived in the setting of an approaching personal death, will likely be experienced as a period of psychological disturbance and depressive breakdown. Or breakdown may be avoided by means of a strengthening of manic defenses, with a warding off of depression and persecution about aging and death, but with an accumulation of persecutory anxiety to be faced when the inevitability of aging and death eventually demands recognition.

The compulsive attempts, in many men and women reaching middle age, to remain young, the hypochondriacal concern over health and appearance, the emergence of sexual promiscuity in order to prove youth and potency, the hollowness and lack of genuine enjoyment of life, and the frequency of religious concern are familiar patterns. They are attempts at a race against time.[73]

Problems of Psychotherapy

Denial by Patient and Therapist

Despite the omnipresence of death and the vast number of rich opportunities available for exploring it, most therapists will find extraordinarily difficult the tasks of increasing the patient's death awareness and working through death anxiety. Denial confounds the process every step of the way. Fear of death exists at every level of awareness—from the most conscious, superficial, intellectualized levels to the realm of deepest unconsciousness. Often a patient's receptivity, at superficial levels, to the therapist's interpretation acts in the service of denial at deeper layers. A patient may be responsive to the therapist's suggestion that the patient examine his or her feelings about his or her finiteness, but gradually the session becomes unproductive, the material runs dry, and the discourse moves into an intellectualized discussion. It is important at these times that the therapist not leap to the erroneous conclusion that he or she is drilling a dry well. The blocking, the lack of associations, the splitting off of affect are all manifestations of resistance and should be treated accordingly. One of Freud's first discoveries in the practice of dynamic therapy was that the therapist repeatedly comes up against a psychological force in the patient that opposes the therapeutic work.

The Therapist Must Persevere.   The therapist must continue to collect evidence, to work with dreams, to persist in his or her observations, to make the same points, albeit with different emphases, over and over again. Observations about the existence of death may seem so banal, so overly obvious that the therapist feels fatuous in persisting to make them. Yet simplicity and persistence are necessary to overcome denial. One patient, a depressed, masochistic, suicidal individual, in a debriefing session some months after termination of therapy, described the most important comment I had made to her during therapy. She had frequently described her yearning for death and, at other times, the various things she would like to do in life. I had made, more than once, the embarrassingly simple observation that there is only one possible sequence for these events: experience first and death last.

The patient is not the only source of denial, of course. Frequently the denial of the therapist silently colludes with that of the patient. The therapist no less than the patient must confront death and be anxious in the face of it. Much preparation is required of the therapist who must in everyday work be aware of death. My co-therapist and I became acutely aware of this necessity while leading a group of patients with metastatic cancer. During the first months of the group the discussion remained superficial: much talk about doctors, medicines, treatment regimes, pain, fatigue, physical limitations, and so forth. We considered this superficiality to be defensive in nature—a signal of the depth of the patients' fear and despair. Accordingly, we respected the defense and led the group in a highly cautious manner.

Only much later did we learn that we therapists had played an active role in keeping the group superficial. When we could tolerate our anxiety and follow the patients' leads, then there was no subject too frightening for the group to deal with explicitly and constructively. The discussion was often extraordinarily painful for the therapists. The group was observed through a one-way mirror by a number of student mental health professionals, and on several occasions some had to leave the observation room to compose themselves. The experience of working with dying patients has propelled many therapists back for another course of personal therapy—often highly profitable for them, since many had not dealt with concerns about death in their first, traditional therapy experiences.

If a therapist is to help patients confront and incorporate death into life, he or she must have personally worked through these issues. An interesting parallel is to be found in the initiation rites of healers in primitive cultures, many of which have a tradition requiring that a shaman pass through some ecstatic experience that entails suffering, death, and resurrection. Sometimes the initiation is a true sickness, and the individual who hovers long between life and death is selected for shamanism. Generally the experience is a mystical vision. To take one, not atypical example, a Tungus (a Siberian tribe) shaman described his initiation as consisting of a confrontation with shaman ancestors who surrounded him, pierced him with arrows, cut off his flesh, tore out his bones, drank his blood, and then reassembled him.[74] Several cultures require that the novice shaman sleep on a grave or remain bound for several nights in a cemetery.[75]

Why Stir Up a Hornet's Nest?

Many therapists avoid discussions of death with a patient not because of denial but because of a deliberate decision based on the belief that the thought of death would aggravate that patient's condition. Why stir up a hornet's nest? Why plunge the patient deeply into a theme that can only increase anxiety and about which one can do nothing? Everyone must face death. Does not the neurotic patient have quite enough troubles without being burdened with reminders of the bitter quaff awaiting all humans?

It is one thing, these therapists feel, to excavate and examine neurotic problems; there at least they can be of some help. But to explore the real reality, the bitter, immutable facts of life, seems not only folly but antitherapeutic. The patient dealing with unreconciled Oedipal conflicts, for example, is hamstrung by phantasmal torments: some constellation of internal and external events that occurred long ago persists in the timeless unconscious and haunts the patient. The patient responds to current situations in distorted fashion: to the present as though it were the past. The therapist's mandate is clear: to illuminate the present, to expose and scatter the demons of the past, to help the patient detoxify events that are intrinsically benign but irrationally experienced as noxious.

But death? Death is not a ghost from the past. And it is not intrinsically benign. What can be done with it?

Increased Anxiety in Therapy.   First, it is true that the thought of our finitude has a force field of anxiety about it. To enter the field is to heighten anxiety. The therapeutic approach I describe here is dynamic and uncovering; it is not supportive or repressive. Existential therapy does increase the patient's discomfort. It is not possible to plunge into the roots of one's anxiety without, *for a period of time,* experiencing heightened anxiousness and depression.

Bugental, in his excellent discussion of the subject, refers to this phase of treatment as the "existential crisis"—an inevitable crisis which occurs when the defenses used to forestall existential anxiety are breached, allowing one to become truly aware of one's basic situation in life.[76]

Life Satisfaction and Death Anxiety:
A Therapeutic Foothold

From a conceptual standpoint the therapist does well to keep in mind that the anxiety surrounding death is *both* neurotic and normal. All human beings experience death anxiety, but some experience such excessive amounts of it that it spills into many realms of their experience and results in heightened dysphoria and/or a series of defenses against anxiety which constrict growth and often themselves generate secondary anxiety. Why some individuals are brought down by the conditions that all must face is a question I have already addressed: the individual, because of a series of unusual life experiences, is unduly traumatized by death anxiety and fails to erect the "normal" defenses against existential anxiety. What the therapist encounters is a failure of the homeostatic regulation of death anxiety.

One approach available to the therapist is to focus on the patient's current dynamics that alter that regulation. I believe that one particularly useful equation for the clinician is: *death anxiety is inversely proportional to life satisfaction.*

John Hinton reports some interesting and relevant research findings.[77] He studied sixty patients with terminal cancer and correlated their attitudes (including "sense of satisfaction or fulfillment in life") with their feelings and reactions during terminal illness. The sense of satisfaction in life was rated from interviews with the patient and the patient's spouse. The feelings and reactions during the terminal illness were measured by interviews with the patients and by rating scales completed by nurses and spouses. The data revealed that, to a highly significant degree, "when life had appeared satisfying, dying was less troublesome. . . . Lesser satisfaction with past life went with a more troubled view of the illness and its outcome." The lesser the life satisfaction, the greater was the depression, anxiety, anger, and overall concern about the illness and levels of satisfaction with the medical care.

These results seem counterintuitive because, on a superficial level, one might conclude that the unsatisfied and disillusioned might welcome the respite of death. But the opposite is true: a sense of fulfillment, a feeling that life has been well lived, mitigates against the terror of death. Nietzsche, in his characteristic hyperbole, stated: "What has become perfect, all that is ripe—wants to die. All that is unripe wants to live. All that suffers wants to live, that it may become ripe and joyous and longing—longing for what is further, higher, brighter."[78]

Surely this insight gives the therapist a foothold! If he can help the patient experience an increased satisfaction in life, he can allay excessive anxiety. Of course, there is a circularity about this equation since it is *because* of an excessive death anxiety that the individual lives a constricted life—a life dedicated more to safety, survival, and relief from pain than to growth and fulfillment.

Yet still there is a foothold. The therapist must not be overawed by the past. It is not necessary that one experience forty years of whole, integrated living to compensate for the previous forty years of shadow life. Tolstoy's Ivan Ilych, through his confrontation with death, arrived at an existential crisis and, with only a few days of life remaining, transformed himself and was able to flood, retrospectively, his entire life with meaning.

The less the life satisfaction, the greater the death anxiety. This principle is clearly illustrated by one of my patients, Philip, a fifty-three-year-old, highly successful business executive. Philip had always been a severe workaholic; he worked sixty to seventy hours a week, always lugged a briefcase brimming with work home in the evening, and during one recent two-year period worked on the East Coast and commuted weekends to his home on the West Coast. He had little life satisfaction: his work afforded safety, not pleasure; he worked not because he wanted to, but because he had to, to assuage anxiety. He hardly knew his wife and children. Years ago his wife had had a brief extramarital affair, and he had never forgiven her—not so much for the actual act, but because the affair and its attendant pain had been a major source of distraction from his work. His wife and children had suffered from the estrangement, and he had never dipped into this potential reservoir of love, life satisfaction, and meaning.

Then a disaster occurred that stripped Philip of all his defenses. Because of severe setbacks in the aerospace industry, his company failed and was absorbed by another corporation. Philip suddenly found himself unemployed and possibly, because of his age and high executive position, unemployable. He developed severe anxiety and at this point sought psychotherapy. At first his anxiety was entirely centered on his work. He ruminated endlessly about his job. Waking regularly at 4 A.M., he lay awake for hours thinking of work: how to break the news to his employees, how best to phase out his department, how to express his anger at the way he had been handled.

Philip could not find a new position, and as his last day of work approached, he became frantic. Gradually in therapy we pried loose his anxiety from the work concerns to which it adhered like barnacles to a pier. It became apparent that Philip had considerable death anxiety. Nightly he was tormented by a dream in which he circled the very edge of a "black pit." Another frightening recurrent dream consisted of his walking on the narrow crest of a steep dune on the beach and losing his balance. He repeatedly awoke from the dream mumbling, "I'm not going to make it." (His father was a sailor who drowned before Philip was born.)

Philip had no pressing financial concerns: he had a generous severance settlement, and a recent large inheritance provided considerable security. But the time! How was he going to use the time? Nothing meant very much to Philip, and he sank into despair. Then one night an important incident occurred. He had been unable to go to sleep and at approximately 3:00 A.M. went downstairs to read and drink a cup of tea. He heard a noise at the window, went over to it, and found himself face to face with a huge stocking-masked man. After his startle and the alarm had subsided, after the police had left and the search was called off, Philip's real panic began. A thought occurred to him, a jarring thought, that sent a powerful shudder through his frame: "Something might have happened to Mary and the children." When, during our therapy hour, he described this incident, his reaction, and his thought, I, rather than comfort him, reminded him that something *will* happen to Mary, to the children, and to himself as well.

Philip passed through a period of feeling wobbly and dazed. All of his customary denial structures no longer functioned: his job, his specialness, his climb to glory, his sense of invulnerability. Just as he had faced the masked burglar, he now faced, at first flinchingly and then more steadily, some fundamental facts of life: groundlessness, the inexorable passage of time, and the inevitability of death. This confrontation provided Philip with a sense of urgency, and he worked hard in therapy to reclaim some satisfaction and meaning in his life. We focused especially on intimacy—an important source of life satisfaction that he had never enjoyed.

Philip had invested so much in his belief in specialness that he dreaded facing (and sharing with others) his feelings of helplessness. I urged him to tell all inquirers the truth—that he was out of a job and having trouble finding another—and to monitor his feelings. He shrank away from the task at first but gradually learned that the sharing of vulnerability opened the door to intimacy. At one session I offered to send his résumé to a friend of mine, the president of a company in a related field, who might have a position for him. Philip thanked me in a polite, formal manner; but when he went to his car, he "cried like a baby" for the first time in thirty five years. We talked about that cry a great deal, what it meant, how it felt, and why he could not cry in front of me. As he learned to accept his vulnerability, his sense of communion, at first with me and then with his family, deepened; he achieved an intimacy with others he had never previously attained. His orientation to time changed dramatically: no longer did he see time as an enemy—to be concealed or killed. Now, with day after day of free time, he began to savor time and to luxuriate in it. He also became acquainted with other, long dormant parts of himself and for the first time in decades allowed some of his creative urges expression in both painting and writing. After eight months of unemployment, Philip obtained a new and challenging position in another city. In our last session he said, "I've gone through hell in the last few months. But, you know, as horrible as this has been, I'm glad I couldn't get a job immediately. I'm thankful I was forced to go through this." What Philip learned was that a life dedicated to the concealment of reality, to the denial of death, restricts experience and will ultimately cave in upon itself.

Death Desensitization

Another concept that offers a therapeutic foothold against death anxiety is "desensitization." "Desensitization to death"—a vulgar phrase, which is demeaning because it juxtaposes the deepest human concerns with mechanistic techniques. Yet it is difficult to avoid the phrase in a discussion of the therapist's techniques for dealing with death anxiety. It seems that, with repeated contact, one can get used to anything—even to dying. The therapist may help the patient deal with death terror in ways similar to the techniques that he uses to conquer any other form of dread. He exposes the patient over and over to the fear in attenuated doses. He helps the patient handle the dreaded object and to inspect it from all sides.

Montaigne was aware of this principle and wrote:

It seems to me, however, that there is a certain way of familiarizing ourselves with death and trying it out to some extent. We can have an experience of it that is, if not entire and perfect, at least not useless, and that makes us more fortified and assured. If we cannot reach it, we can approach it, we can reconnoiter it; and if we do not penetrate as far as its fort, at least we shall see and become acquainted with the approaches to it.[79]

In several years of working with groups of cancer patients, I have seen desensitization many times. Over and over a patient approaches his or her dread until gradually it diminishes through sheer familiarity. The model set by other patients and by the therapist—whether it be resoluteness, uneasy stoic acceptance, or equanimity—helps to detoxify death for many patients.

A basic principle of a behavioral approach to anxiety reduction is that the individual be exposed to the feared stimulus (in carefully calibrated amounts) in a psychological state and setting designed to retard the development of anxiety. The group approach employed this strategy. The group often began (and ended) with some anxiety-reducing meditational or muscle-relaxing exercise; each patient was surrounded by others with the same illness; they trusted one another and felt completely understood. The exposure was graduated in that one of the operating norms of the group was that each member be allowed to proceed at his or her own speed and that no pressure be placed on anyone to confront more than he or she wished to.

Another useful principle in anxiety management is dissection and analysis. One's feeling of organismic catastrophic dread generally includes many fearful components that can yield to rational analysis. It may be helpful to encourage the patient (both the everyday psychotherapy patient and the dying one) to examine his or her death and sort out all the various component fears. Many individuals are overwhelmed by a sense of helplessness in the face of death; and, indeed, the groups of dying patients I have worked with devoted much time to counteracting this source of dread. The major strategy is to separate ancillary *feelings* of helplessness from the true helplessness that issues from facing one's unalterable existential situation. I have seen dying patients regain a sense of potency and control by electing to control those aspects of their lives that were amenable to control. For example, a patient may change his mode of interacting with his physician: he may insist on being informed fully about his illness or on being included in important treatment decisions. Or he may change to another physician if he is dissatisfied with the current one. Other patients involve themselves in social action. Others develop a sense of choicefulness; they discover with exhilaration that they can elect not to do the things they do not wish to do.

There are other component fears: the pain of dying, afterlife, the fear of the unknown, concern for one's family, fear for one's body, loneliness, regression. In achievement-oriented Western countries death is curiously equated with failure. Each of these component fears, examined separately and rationally, is less frightening than the entire gestalt. Each is an obviously disagreeable aspect of dying; yet neither separately nor in concert do these fears need to elicit a cataclysmic reaction. It is significant, however, that many patients, when asked to analyze their death terrors, find that they correspond to none of these but to something primitive and ineffable. In the adult unconscious dwells the young child's irrational terror: death is experienced as an evil, cruel, mutilating force. These fantasies, no less than Oedipal or castration fears, are atavistic unconscious tags that disrupt the adult's ability to recognize reality and to respond appropriately. The therapist works with such fears as with any other distortions of reality: he attempts to identify, to illuminate, and to scatter these ghosts of the past.

Death is only one component of the human being's existential situation, and a consideration of death awareness illuminates only one facet of existential therapy. To arrive at a fully balanced therapeutic approach, we must examine the therapeutic implications of each of the other ultimate concerns. Death helps us understand anxiety, offers a dynamic structure upon which to base interpretation, and serves as a boundary experience that is capable of instigating a massive shift in perspective. Each of the other ultimate concerns contributes another segment of a comprehensive psychotherapy system: *freedom* helps us understand responsibility assumption, commitment to change, decision and action; *isolation* illuminates the role of relationship; whereas *meaninglessness* turns our attention to the principle of engagement.

PART III

ON WRITING

CHAPTER 6

Literature Informing Psychology

Literary Vignettes

INTRODUCTION

Histories of psychology often begin with the advent of scientific method and the pioneering experimental psychologists like Wundt and Pavlov. I have always considered this a shortsighted historical view: the discipline of psychology began long before, in the works of the great psychological thinkers who wrote about innermost human motivations: Sophocles, Aeschylus, Euripides, Epicurus, Lucretius, Shakespeare, and especially (for me) the great psychological novelists Dostoevsky, Tolstoy, and, later, Mann, Sartre, and Camus. Freud identified himself as a scientist, yet not a single one of his great insights was born of science: invariably they arose from his own intuition, his artistic imagination, and his deep knowledge of literature and philosophy.

I often turn to a great writer for a phrase or literary device that brings home an insight with power and clarity. Some examples follow.

Isolation.   There are many forms of isolation. *Interpersonal* isolation refers to the gulf between oneself and others. It is experienced as loneliness and may be ameliorated by a greater capacity to develop and sustain intimacy with others. *Intrapersonal* isolation refers to the lack of personal integration, to the existence of split-off parts of oneself. *Existential* isolation cuts deeper: it refers to an unbridgeable gulf not only between oneself and any other being but between oneself and the world. For the most part, existential isolation is concealed from us, but as this passage from *Existential Psychotherapy* illustrates, it is generally revealed by the imminence of death.

No one can take the other's death away from him.[1] Though we may be surrounded with friends, though others may die for the same cause, even though others may die at the same time (as in the ancient Egyptian practice of killing and burying servants with the pharaoh, or in suicide pacts), still at the most fundamental level dying is the most lonely human experience.

Everyman, the best-known medieval morality play, portrays in a powerful and simple manner the loneliness of the human encounter with death.[2] Everyman is visited by Death, who informs him that he must take his final pilgrimage to God. Everyman pleads for mercy, but to no avail. Death informs him that he must make himself ready for the day that "no man living may escape away." In despair Everyman hurriedly casts about for help. Frightened and, above all, isolated, he pleads to others to accompany him on his journey. The character Kindred refuses to go with him:

> Ye be a merry man:
> Take good heart to you and make no moan
> But one thing I warn you, by Saint Anne,
> As for me, ye shall go alone.

As does Everyman's cousin, who pleads that she is indisposed:

No, by our Lady! I have the cramp in my toe
Trust not to me. For so God me speed,
I will deceive you in your most need.

He is forsaken in the same way by each of the other allegorical characters in the play: Fellowship, Worldly Goods, and Knowledge. Even
his attributes desert him:

Beauty, strength and discretion.
When death bloweth his blast
They all run from me full fast.

Everyman is finally saved from the full terror of existential isolation
because one figure, Good Deeds, is willing to go with him even unto
death. And, indeed, that is the Christian moral of the play: good works
within the context of religion provide a buttress against ultimate isolation. Today's secular Everyman who cannot or does not embrace religious faith must indeed take the journey alone.

Isolation.   If we do not come to terms with existential isolation, we
tend to search for solace in our interpersonal relationships. Rather
than relate authentically, with caring, we use the other for a function.
In this passage from *Existential Psychotherapy,* I draw on Lewis Car
roll's work in my discussion of one such function: using the other to
verify our existence.

"The worst thing about being alone, the thought that drives me ba-
nanas, is that, at that moment, no one in the world may be thinking
about me." So declared a patient in a group session who had been hospitalized because of panic attacks when alone. There was, among the
other patients in this inpatient therapy group, instantaneous agreement
with this experience. One nineteen-year-old, who had been hospitalized
for slashing her wrists following the breakup of a romantic relationship,
said simply, "I'd rather be dead than alone!" Another said, "When I'm
alone, that's when I hear voices. Maybe my voices are a way not to be

alone!" (an arresting phenomenological explanation of hallucination). Another patient who, on several occasions, had mutilated herself stated that she had done so because of her despair about a highly unsatisfying relationship with a man. Yet she could not leave him because of her terror of being alone. When I asked her what terrified her about loneliness, she said with stark, direct, psychotic insight, "I don't exist when I'm alone."

The same dynamic speaks in the child's incessant plea, "Watch me," "Look at me"—the presence of the other is required to make reality real. (Here, as elsewhere, I cite the child's experience as anterior manifestation, not as cause, of an underlying conflict.) Lewis Carroll's *Through the Looking-Glass* wonderfully expressed the stark belief, held by many patients, that "I exist only so long as I am thought about." Alice, Tweedledee, and Tweedledum come upon the Red King sleeping:

"He's dreaming now," said Tweedledee, "and what do you think he's dreaming about?"

Alice said, "Nobody can guess that."

"Why, about *you!*" Tweedledee exclaimed, clapping his hands triumphantly. "And if he left off dreaming about you, where do you suppose you'd be?"

"Where I am now, of course," said Alice.

"Not you!" Tweedledee retorted contemptuously. "You'd be nowhere. Why, you're only a sort of thing in this dream!"

"If that there King was to wake," added Tweedledum, "you'd go out—bang!—just like a candle!"

"I shouldn't!" Alice exclaimed indignantly. "Besides, if *I'm* only a sort of thing in his dream, what are *you,* I should like to know?"

"Ditto," said Tweedledum.

"Ditto, ditto!" cried Tweedledee.

He shouted this so loud that Alice couldn't help saying, "Hush! You'll be waking him, I'm afraid, if you make so much noise."

"Well, it's no use *your* talking about waking him," said Tweedledum, "when you're only one of the things in his dream. You know very well you're not real."

"I *am* real!" said Alice, and began to cry.

"You won't make yourself a bit realer by crying," Tweedledee remarked. "There's nothing to cry about."

"If I wasn't real," Alice said—half laughing through her tears, it all seemed so ridiculous—"I shouldn't be able to cry."

"I hope you don't suppose those are real tears?" Tweedledum interrupted in a tone of great contempt.[3]

Love and freedom.   Subgrouping, especially romantic pairing, in psychotherapy groups is generally destructive to the group. But occasionally, if two romantically involved patients are highly committed to their therapy work and willing to analyze their relationship, considerable benefit may ensue. In a long vignette in *The Theory and Practice of Group Psychotherapy* I describe the tale of Jan and Bill, members of a long-term outpatient therapy group, who, for a brief time, became sexually involved and remained in the group to analyze what the relationship taught them about themselves. The following excerpt discussing Bill draws upon several ideas about love and freedom from Camus's novel *The Fall.*

For many sessions, the group plunged into the issues of love, freedom, and responsibility. Jan, with increasing directness, confronted Bill. She jolted him by asking exactly how much he cared for her. He squirmed and alluded both to his love for her and to his unwillingness to establish an enduring relationship with any woman. In fact, he found himself "turned off" by any woman who wanted a long-term relationship.

I was reminded of a comparable attitude toward love in the novel *The Fall,* where Camus expresses Bill's paradox with shattering clarity:

It is not true, after all, that I never loved. I conceived at least one great love in my life, of which I was always the object . . . sensuality alone dominated my love life. . . . In any case, my sensuality (to limit myself to it) was so real that even for a ten-minute adventure I'd have disowned father and mother, even were I to regret it bitterly. Indeed—especially for a ten-minute adventure and even more so if I were sure it was to have no sequel.[4]

The group therapist, if he was to help Bill, had to make certain that there was to be a sequel.

Bill did not want to be burdened with Jan's depression. There were women all around the country who loved him (and whose love made him feel alive), yet for him these women did not have an independent existence. He preferred to think that his women came to life only when he appeared to them. Once again, Camus spoke for him:

> I could live happily only on condition that all the individuals on earth, or the greatest possible number, were turned toward me, eternally in suspense, devoid of independent life and ready to answer my call at any moment, doomed in short to sterility until the day I should deign to favor them. In short, for me to live happily it was essential for the creatures I chose not to live at all. They must receive their life, sporadically, only at my bidding.[5]

Jan pressed Bill relentlessly. She told him that there was another man who was seriously interested in her, and she pleaded with Bill to level with her, to be honest about his feelings to her, to set her free. By now Bill was quite certain that he no longer desired Jan. (In fact, as we were to learn later, he had been gradually increasing his commitment to the woman with whom he lived.) Yet he could not allow the words to pass his lips—a strange type of freedom, then, as Bill himself gradually grew to understand: the freedom to take but not to relinquish. (Camus again: "Believe me, for certain men at least, not taking what one doesn't desire is the hardest thing in the world!")[6] He insisted he be granted the freedom to choose his pleasures, yet, as he came to see, he did not have the freedom to choose for himself. His choice almost invariably resulted in his thinking less well of himself. And the greater his self-hatred, the more compulsive, the less free, was his mindless pursuit of sexual conquests that afforded him only an evanescent balm.

Transference—that is, our proclivity to experience another in an irrational fashion—is particularly complex in therapy groups where patients not only must relate to the therapist, who holds a position of great authority in the group, but to the other members. In this selection from *The Theory and Practice of Group Psychotherapy* I draw from Tolstoy's *War and Peace* to illuminate the nature of transference.

Freud was very sensitive to the powerful and irrational manner in which group members view their leader, and made a major contribution by systematically analyzing this phenomenon and applying it to psychotherapy. Obviously, however, the psychology of member and leader has existed since the earliest human grouping, and Freud was not the first to note it. To cite only one example, Tolstoy in the nineteenth century was keenly aware of the subtle intricacies of the member-leader relationship in the two most important groups of his day: the church and the military. His insight into the overevaluation of the leader gives *War and Peace* much of its pathos and richness. Consider Rostov's regard for the tsar:

He was entirely absorbed in the feeling of happiness at the Tsar's being near. His nearness alone made up to him by itself, he felt, for the loss of the whole day. He was happy, as a lover is happy when the moment of the longed-for meeting has come. Not daring to look around from the front line, by an ecstatic instance without looking around, he felt his approach. And he felt it not only from the sound of the tramping hoofs of the approaching cavalcade, he felt it because as the Tsar came nearer everything grew brighter, more joyful and significant, and more festive. Nearer and nearer moved this sun, as he seemed to Rostov, shedding around him rays of mild and majestic light, and now he felt himself enfolded in that radiance, he heard his voice—that voice caressing, calm, majestic, and yet so simple. . . . And Rostov got up and went out to wander about among the campfires, dreaming of what happiness it would be to die—not saving the Emperor's life (of that he did not dare to dream), but simply to die before the Emperor's eyes. He really was in love with the Tsar and the glory of the Russian arms and the hope of coming victory. And he was not the only man who felt thus in those memorable days that preceded the battle of Austerlitz: nine-tenths of the men in the Russian army were at that moment in love, though less ecstatically, with their Tsar and the glory of the Russian arms.[7]

Indeed, it would seem that submersion in the love of a leader is a prerequisite for war. How ironic that more killing has probably been done under the aegis of love than of hatred!

Napoleon, that consummate leader of men, was, according to Tolstoy, not ignorant of transference, nor did he hesitate to utilize it in the service of victory. In *War and Peace,* Tolstoy had him deliver this dispatch to his troops on the eve of battle:

> Soldiers! I will myself lead your battalions. I will keep out of fire, if you, with your habitual bravery, carry defeat and disorder into the ranks of the enemy. But if victory is for one moment doubtful, you will see your Emperor exposed to the enemy's hottest attack, for there can be no uncertainty of victory, especially on this day, when it is a question of the honor of the French infantry, on which rests the honor of our nation.[8]

One of the fundamental sources of anxiety from an existential frame of reference is meaninglessness. We appear to be meaning-seeking creatures who are thrown into a universe and a world which lack intrinsic meaning. In the following selection from *Existential Psychotherapy* I draw upon passages from Sartre's play *The Flies* to illustrate several possible modes of creating a sense of life meaning.

Sartre, more than any other philosopher in this century, has been uncompromising in his view of a meaningless world. His position on the meaning of life is terse and merciless: "All existing things are born for no reason, continue through weakness and die by accident. . . . It is meaningless that we are born; it is meaningless that we die."[9] Sartre's view of freedom leaves one without a sense of personal meaning and with no guidelines for conduct; indeed, many philosophers have been highly critical of the Sartrean philosophical system precisely because it lacks an ethical component. Sartre's death in 1980 ended a prodigiously productive career, and his long-promised treatise on ethics will never be written.

However, in his fiction Sartre often portrayed individuals who discover something to live *for* and something to live *by*. Sartre's depiction of Orestes, the hero of his play *The Flies* (*Les Mouches*), is particularly illustrative.[10] Orestes, reared away from Argos, journeys home to find his sister Electra, and together they avenge the murder of their father (Agamemnon) by killing the murderers—their mother, Clytemnestra, and her husband, Aegisthus. Despite Sartre's explicit statements about life's meaninglessness, his play may be read as a pilgrimage to meaning. Let me follow Orestes as he searches for values on which to base his life. Orestes first looks for meaning and purpose in a return to home, roots, and comradeship:

> Try to understand I want to be a man who belongs to someplace, a
> man among comrades. Only consider. Even the slave bent beneath
> his load dropping with fatigue and staring dully at the ground and
> foot in front of him—why even that poor slave can say that he's in
> *his* town as a tree is in a forest or a leaf upon a tree. Argos is all
> around him, warm, compact, and comforting. Yes, Electra, I'd
> gladly be that slave and enjoy that feeling of drawing the city round
> me like a blanket and curling myself up in it.[11]

Later he questions his own life conduct and realizes that he has always done as they (the gods) wished in order to find peace within the status quo.

> So that is the right thing. To live at peace—always at perfect peace.
> I see. Always to say "excuse me," and "thank you." That's what's
> wanted, eh? The right thing. Their Right Thing.[12]

At this moment in the play Orestes wrenches himself away from his previous meaning system and enters his crisis of meaninglessness:

What a change has come on everything . . . until now I felt something warm and living round me, like a friendly presence. That
something has just died. What emptiness. What endless emptiness.[13]

Orestes, at that moment, makes the leap that Sartre made in his personal life—not a leap into faith (although it rests on no sounder argument than a leap of faith) but a leap into "engagement," into action, into
a project. He says good-bye to the ideals of comfort and security and
pursues, with crusader ferocity, his newfound purpose:

I say there is another path—my path. Can't you see it. It starts here
and leads down to the city. I must go down into the depths among
you. For you are living all of you at the bottom of a pit. . . . Wait.
Give me time to say farewell to all the lightness, the aery lightness
that was mine. . . . Come, Electra look at our city. . . . It fends me off
with its high walls, red roofs, locked doors. And yet it's mine for the
taking. I'll turn into an ax and hew those walls asunder. . . .[14]

Orestes' new purpose evolves quickly, and he assumes a Christlike burden:

Listen, all those people quaking with fear in their dark rooms—
supposing I take over all their crimes. Supposing I set out to win the
name of "guilt-stealer" and heap on myself all their remorse.[15]

Later Orestes, in defiance of Zeus, decides to kill Aegistheus. His decla-
ration at that time indicates a clear sense of purpose: he chooses justice,
freedom, and dignity and indicates that he knows what is "right" in life.

What do I care for Zeus. Justice is a matter between men and I have
no God to teach me it. It's right to stamp you out like the foul brute
you are, and to free the people from your evil influence. It is right to
restore to them their sense of human dignity.[16]

And glad he is to have found his freedom, his mission, and his path.
Though Orestes must carry the burden of being his mother's murderer,

it is better thus than to have *no* mission, no meaning, to wander pointlessly through life.

> The heavier it is to carry, the better pleased I shall be; for that bur-
> den is my freedom. Only yesterday I walked the earth haphazard;
> thousands of roads I tramped that brought me nowhere, for they
> were other men's roads. . . . Today I have one path only, and heaven
> knows where it leads. But it is *my* path.[17]

Then Orestes finds another and, for Sartre, an important meaning—
that there is no absolute meaning, that he is alone and must create his
own meaning. To Zeus he says:

> Suddenly, out of the blue, freedom crashed down on me and swept
> me off my feet. My youth went with the wind, and I know myself
> alone . . . and there was nothing left in heaven, no right or wrong,
> nor anyone to give me orders. . . . I am doomed to have no law but
> mine. . . . Every man must find his own way.[18]

When he proposes to open the eyes of the townspeople, Zeus protests
that, if Orestes tears the veils from their eyes, "they will see their lives as
they are: foul and futile." But Orestes maintains that they are free, that
it is right they face their despair, and utters the famous existential mani-
festo: "Human life begins on the far side of despair."[19]

One final purpose, self-realization, emerges when Orestes takes his
sister's hand to begin their journey. Electra asks, "Whither?" and
Orestes responds:

> Toward ourselves. Beyond the river and mountains are an Orestes
> and an Electra waiting for us, and we must make our patient way
> towards them.[20]

And so Sartre—the same Sartre who says that "man is a futile passion,"
and that "it is meaningless that we are born; it is meaningless that we
die"—arrived at a position in his fiction that clearly values the search for
meaning and even suggests paths to take in that search. These include

finding a "home" and comradeship in the world, action, freedom, rebellion against oppression, service to others, enlightenment, self-realization, and engagement—always and above all, engagement.

And *why* are there meanings to be fulfilled? On that question Sartre is mute. Certainly the meanings are not divinely ordained; they do not exist "out there," for there is no God, and nothing exists "out there" outside of man. Orestes simply says, "I *want* to belong," or "*It is right*" to serve others, to restore dignity to man, or to embrace freedom; or every man "*must*" find his own way, must journey to the fully realized Orestes who awaits him. The terms "want to" or "it is right" or "must" are purely arbitrary and do not constitute a firm basis for human conduct; yet they seem to be the best arguments Sartre could muster. He seems to agree with Thomas Mann's pragmatic position. "Whether that be so or not, it would be well for man to behave as if it were so."

What is important for both Sartre and Camus is that human beings recognize that one must invent one's own meaning (rather than discover God's or nature's meaning) and then commit oneself fully to fulfilling that meaning. This requires that one be, as Gordon Allport put it, "half-sure and whole-hearted"[21]—not an easy feat. Sartre's ethic requires a leap into engagement. On this one point most Western theological and atheistic existential systems agree: *it is good and right to immerse oneself in the stream of life.*

The secular activities that provide human beings with a sense of life purpose are supported by the same arguments that Sartre advanced for Orestes: they seem right; they seem good; they are intrinsically satisfying and need not be justified on the basis of any other motivation.

Decisions. Every psychotherapist deals frequently with patients who are tormented by decisions. In my discussion of the ultimate concern of freedom in *Existential Psychotherapy* I deal extensively with the impediments to wishing, willing, and deciding. John Gardner was a wonderful philosophical novelist and in this brief selection I use a passage from his novel *Grendel* to clarify one aspect of decision making.

There is something highly painful about unmade decisions. As I review my patients and attempt to analyze the meaning (and the threat) that decision has for them, I am struck first of all by the diversity of response. Decisions are difficult for many reasons: some obvious, some unconscious, and some, as we shall see, that reach down to the deepest roots of being.

Alternatives Exclude.   The protagonist of John Gardner's novel *Grendel* made a pilgrimage to an old priest to learn about life's mysteries. The wise man said, "The ultimate evil is that Time is perpetual perishing and being actual involves elimination." He summed up his meditations on life in two simple but terrible propositions, four devastating words: "Things fade: alternatives exclude."[22] I regard that priest's message as deeply inspired. "Things fade" refers to the fundamental pervasiveness of death anxiety, and "alternatives exclude" is one of the fundamental reasons that decisions are difficult.

CHAPTER 7

Psychology Informing Literature

"Ernest Hemingway: A Psychiatric View"

INTRODUCTION

"Ernest Hemingway: A Psychiatric View," which I wrote with my wife, Marilyn, was published in the *Archives of General Psychiatry* (June 1971). This article illustrates another facet of the interdependent relationship between literature and psychology. Here, we reverse the process: rather than drawing on insights of literature to illuminate psychology, we use psychodynamic expertise to illuminate an author's life and work. Such an approach is useful only for certain authors and for certain works of art. Psychodynamic insights have much to offer in understanding Ernest Hemingway who, though a stylistic genius, was (as a result of his personal torments) a narrow guide to life. This selection posits that Hemingway's inner conflicts informed, dominated, and perhaps hobbled his artistic vision as he struggled again and again in his fiction with the same set of personally unresolved issues.

ERNEST HEMINGWAY:
A PSYCHIATRIC VIEW

(Arch. Gen. Psychiatry, 24:485–494., 1971)

Ernest Hemingway died by suicide on July 2, 1961. Since then his bones have been stirred by hordes of journalists, critics, biographers, and eulogizers, all of them, and we too, attempting to appraise the Hemingway heritage. As scholars we gather around his historical and literary remains—Hemingway would have said like hyenas around carrion.

We join this congregation knowing that it is already overcrowded and realizing that we court the dead man's curse rather than his blessing. What do a psychiatrist and still another professor of literature have to add to the innumerable words which have already been published? It was perhaps the appearance of the long-awaited Baker biography[1] which convinced us that, despite the thoroughness of this useful encyclopedic work, some extremely important areas of Hemingway's inner world are still to be explored. Much as the psychiatrist tries to understand his patient, we shall undertake an examination of the major psychodynamic conflicts with which Hemingway struggled. We do not, of course, propose to explain or dissect his genius, but only to clarify the internal forces which so shaped the structure and substance of his work. Our data consist of the recorded events of Hemingway's life and his own writings. We have also been fortunate enough to have the counsel of Major General Charles T. (Buck) Lanham, one of Hemingway's closest friends, whose insightful memories and suggestions have been invaluable in the preparation of this manuscript.

To a psychiatrist, Hemingway is considerably more than another important writer, even more than the best-known American novelist of the century. When alive he was a public figure of the first magnitude, recognizable on sight to the literate of this country and most of Europe. His name was a synonym for an approach to life characterized by action, courage, physical prowess, stamina, violence, independence, and above all "grace under pressure"—attributes so well known that any of our readers could have compiled a comparable list. He was, in short, the heroic model of an age.

A popular hero is, to a large extent, a reflection, symbol, or symptom of the culture which creates him. The Hemingway image was of such vitality, however, that he not only mirrored his culture but helped to shape and perpetuate it. Wide exposure to Hemingway in multimedia imprinted his values into contemporary psychic life; he has been incorporated into the fabric of the character structure of a generation of Americans. Even those who did not read him were familiar with his famous cinema surrogates: Gary Cooper in *A Farewell to Arms* and *For Whom the Bell Tolls*, Humphrey Bogart in *To Have and Have Not*, Tyrone Power in *The Sun Also Rises*, Gregory Peck in *The Snows of Kilimanjaro*, Burt Lancaster in *The Killers*, and Spencer Tracy in *The Old Man and the Sea*.

Today Hemingway still has a large following, especially among adolescents and college students, though they have newer idols. While the young cannot deny him his literary position as the leader of a revolution in prose style, there are many indications that he is no longer an heroic model for a rising generation of culture makers. Those militantly committed to a national policy of peace find it hard to emulate a man who wrote that he did not believe in anything except that one should fight for one's country whenever necessary.[2] Young activists are disenchanted with the author who eschewed political and social involvement, for he was basically an apolitical man, drawn to battle less from ideological commitment than from the lure of danger and excitement. Unlike the socially minded writers of the 1930s who unsuccessfully attempted to activate him, he early lost any idealistic desire to change the world, as he humorously expressed in this 1924 verse:

> *I know monks masturbate at night*
> *That pet cats screw*
> *That some girls bite*
> *And yet*
> *What can I do*
> *To set things right?*[3]

In the retrospect of scarcely ten years, it appears to us that Hemingway's legacy is one more of form than of substance, that he will be remembered as a stylistic genius but as a very narrow guide to life. While

we appreciate the existential considerations generated by the Hemingway encounters with danger and death, we do not find the same mea
sure of universality and timelessness we associate with a Tolstoy or a
Conrad or a Camus. Why, we ask ourselves, is this so? Why is the
Hemingway worldview so restricted? We suspect that the limitations of
Hemingway's vision are related to his personal psychological restrictions. There are many questions he never raised about the universe.
There are even more he never dared to ask about himself. Just as there
is no doubt that he was an extremely gifted writer, there is also no doubt
that he was an extremely troubled man, relentlessly driven all his life,
who in a paranoid depressive psychosis killed himself at the age of 62.

During his training the psychiatrist is usually required to write for
each patient a report which attempts to "explain" the inner world of the
patient through an analysis of the past and current interpersonal and intrapersonal forces operating on him. This "dynamic formulation," as it
is labeled, is invariably the student's most difficult chore: generally he is
lost in a sea of information, multiple theoretical schools stream by like
so many sturdy transport ships, yet none seems capable of carrying the
entire cargo of clinical information available for each patient. The "reli-
ability" of the dynamic formulation is low, that is, many psychiatrists
with similar information will compose radically different formulations.
"Validity" fares no better, for the dynamic formulation has little corre-
lation with the diagnosis and clinical course of the patient.

The psychiatrist who gratuitously offers a dynamic formulation for
the patient he has never seen must be particularly humble. Ernest Hemingway resisted professional psychological introspection during his life
and now, posthumously, he remains uncooperative to clinical inquiry.
We nonetheless hope to suggest a frame of reference through which dis-
parate pieces of information may be organized into a coherent logical
schema, which may generate new hypotheses for future investigation.

Unlike the student psychiatrist struggling to make sense of an
avalanche of anamnestic interview data, fantasy, dream, and dream-
associated material as well as auxiliary information from concerned and
generally cooperative relatives and friends, we—the Hemingway for-
mulators—are obliged to rely on scanty and often unreliable data.
Hemingway's own statements offer little assistance: he was not celebrated for telling the truth about himself. World traveler and explorer,

he never purposefully and publicly embarked upon an inward journey and he opposed those psychologically oriented critics who attempted the journey on his behalf. The difference between his attitude to psychological inquiry and that of another major American writer was vividly demonstrated to one of us (I.Y.) by the following incident.

Several months ago, at a psychiatric meeting, I attempted to interview Howard Rome, the psychiatrist who treated Hemingway in his final depression. A friend pointed him out to me in a room crowded with colleagues, but as chance would have it, I approached the wrong man. After apologizing and explaining my interest in Hemingway, he remarked that, though he knew little about Hemingway, he had been Eugene O'Neill's psychiatrist! He continued by informing me that O'Neill had left him many personal effects, including letters and recorded conversations, and had encouraged him to write an in-depth account of his final years. It was not so with Hemingway. When I finally located Dr. Rome, he informed me, with a finger across his mouth, that before treating Hemingway, he had been obliged to promise that his lips would be forever sealed.

The reconstruction of the early formative years is a particularly vexing task. Baker's comprehensive and scholarly biography, exceeding 600 pages, devotes to Hemingway's first 17 years only 20 pages and much of that is prosaic factual material, which does not provide the kind of information useful for an investigation of the inner world. Other biographies, including the ones by Hemingway's brother Leicester[4] and his sister Marcelline[5] are considerably less helpful. Perhaps, though, we should not mourn the irretrievable loss of the early years. The reconstruction of the past and the subsequent use of this construct to comprehend the present (and the future) is an inferential, risky process. It has been well established by psychological research that recall of one's early life, especially of affect-laden events, is subject to considerable retrospective falsification.[6] The process of recall, in effect, tells us more about present psychological realities than about past events; present attitudes dictate which of the entire panoply of early life experiences we choose to remember and imbue with power. Common sense has it that the present is determined by the past and, yet, is not the converse equally true? The past becomes alive for us only as it is reexperienced through the filter of our present psychic apparatus. In different emotional states, in different stages of life, the past may assume a variety of hues. Mark Twain tells us that when he was 17 he thought his father was a damn fool, but when he was 21 he was surprised to see how much the old fool had learned!

We propose, then, a horizontal exploration rather than a vertical one. To understand an individual fully, one must understand all the conflicting internal forces operating on him at a point in time; the vertical or genetic exploration is, contrary to the lay conception of psychiatry, merely ancillary to the horizontal goal. We turn to the past only to explicate the present, much as a translator turns to history to elucidate an obscure text.[7] To aid us in our reconstruction of a psychological cross section, there is a not inconsiderable body of data from the middle and late years—anecdotal accounts by friends, a few recorded interviews, a large body of letters, and, most of all, the fiction itself. Hemingway's letters and notes corroborate the highly autobiographical nature of his writing. Baker cites a conversation with Irving Stone where Hemingway clearly said that his stories "could be called biographical novels rather than pure fictional novels because they emerged out of 'lived experience.'"[8] Like that of all latter-day romantics, his material is psychologically, if not factually, personal: Hemingway's loves, needs, desires, conflicts, values, and fantasies swarm nakedly across the written page.

Observe Hemingway at any point during his mature years and one meets a powerful, imposing figure—the Hemingway imago which he presented to others and to himself. "He was," said the poet John Pudney of Hemingway in 1944, "a fellow obsessed with playing the part of Ernest Hemingway!"[9] Whatever else we can see, always there is virility, strength, courage: he is the soldier searching out the eye of the battle storm; the intrepid hunter and fisherman compelled to pursue the greatest fish and stalk the most dangerous animal from the Gulf Stream to Central Africa; the athlete, swimmer, brawler, boxer; the hard drinker and hard lover who boasted that he had bedded every girl he wanted and some that he had not wanted;[10] the lover of danger, of the bullfight, of flying, of the wartime front lines; the friend of brave men, heroes, fighters, hunters, and matadors.

The list is so long, the image so powerful, that it obliges even the most naive observer of human nature to wonder whether a man firmly convinced of his identity would channel such a considerable proportion of his life energy into a search for masculine fulfillment. Since the earliest reviews of his works, a stream of Hemingway critics have pointedly noted his need to assert again and again a brute virility.[11]

Before we examine the image itself, let us test its boundaries. Was the Hemingway image a public image only, constructed by the author and his publisher, in secret complicity, to hoodwink the public and to increase revenue? Our research leads us to a most emphatic "No!" All available evidence suggests that the public and private Hemingways are merged: the Hemingway of private conversations, of letters, and of notebooks is identical with the Hemingway who careened across the pages of newspapers and journals and the many Hemingways who fought, loved, and challenged death in his novels and stories.

Although he was a well-known raconteur, Hemingway never laughed at himself, nor did he permit friends to question the Hemingway image. General Lanham, his closest friend for the last quarter of his life, once remarked to Hemingway's wife, Mary, that her husband was "frozen in adolescence." Hemingway learned of the remark, remembered it, and eventually rejoined: "Perhaps adolescence isn't such a bad place to be frozen."[12] On another occasion during World War II Lanham's 22nd infantry fought a hard battle to capture the town of Landrecies, ultimately ending up 60 miles ahead of the entire First Army. Lanham, scholar as well as soldier, sent Hemingway a bantering message paraphrasing Voltaire, which read, "Go hang thyself, brave Hemingstein. We have fought at Landrecies and you were not there."[13] Responding as if to a dare, Hemingway sped through 60 miles of German-infested territory, at great personal risk, in order to flourish his panache in front of Lanham.

Both publicly and privately Hemingway invested inordinate psychic energy in fulfilling his idealized image. The investment was not primarily a conscious, deliberate one, for many of Hemingway's life activities were overdetermined; he acted often not through free choice but because he was driven by some dimly understood internal pressure whose murky persuasiveness only shammed choice. He fished, hunted, and sought danger not only because he wanted to but because he had to, in order to escape some greater internal danger. In "The Snows of Kilimanjaro" Hemingway suggested that he needed to kill to stay alive.[14] The years following World War II were not generally good ones for the writer and man, and Hemingway complained of the emptiness and meaninglessness of his life without war.

Who does not have an idealized image? Who does not formulate a set of personal aspirations and self-expectations? But Hemingway's idealized image was more, much more. Rather than expectations, he forged a set of restrictive demands upon himself, a tyrannical and inexorable decalogue which pervaded all areas of his inner world. Many personality theorists have dealt with the construct of the idealized image, but none so cogently as Karen Horney. For a complete exposition of her personality theory we refer the reader to her last book, *Neurosis and Human Growth*.[15] To summarize drastically, a child suffers from basic anxiety, an extremely dysphoric state of being, if he has parents whose own neurotic conflicts prevent them from providing the basic acceptance necessary for the development of the child's autonomous being. During early life when the child regards the parents as omniscient and omnipotent, he can only conclude, in the face of parental disapproval and rejection, that there is something dreadfully wrong with him. To dispel basic anxiety, to obtain the acceptance, approval, and love he requires for survival, the child perceives he must become something else; he channels his energies away from the realization of his real self, from his own personal potential, and develops a construct of an idealized image—a way he must become in order to survive and to avoid basic anxiety. The idealized image may take many forms, all of which are designed to cope with a primitive sense of badness, inadequacy, or unlovability. Hemingway's idealized image crystallized around a search for mastery, for a vindictive triumph which would lift him above others.

The development at an early age of an idealized image and the channeling of energies away from fulfillment of one's actual potential has extremely far-reaching ramifications on the developing personality. The individual experiences great isolation as chasms arise between himself and others. He places increasingly severe demands upon himself (a process which Horney calls the "tyranny of the shoulds"), he develops a complete pride system that defines which feelings and attitudes he can permit and which he must squelch in himself. In short, he must shape himself according to a predesigned form rather than allow himself to unfold and to enjoy the experience of gradually discovering new and rich parts of himself.

When the idealized image is severe and unattainable, as it was for Hemingway, tragic consequences may result: the individual cannot in real life approximate the superhuman scope of the idealized image, reality eventually intrudes, and he realizes the discrepancy between what he wants to be and what he is in actuality. At this point he is flooded with self-hatred, which is expressed through a myriad of self-destructive mechanisms from subtle forms of self-torment (the tiny voice which whispers, "Christ, you're ugly!" when one gazes at a mirror) to total annihilation of the self.

Considering only the broad brush strokes of Hemingway's life, one might assume that he approximated his idealized image, that in every way he became what he most wanted to be. Yet throughout his life Hemingway judged himself, found himself wanting, and experienced recurrent cycles of extreme self-doubt and self-contempt.

Consider the quality of self-sufficiency upon which the Hemingway man is predicated: he must be true only to himself, to perhaps an elite cadre of friends, and impervious to the opinions of all others. Yet Hemingway was exceedingly dependent on praise from all quarters and highly sensitive to any critical judgment. He bore his critics vengeance and, in a paranoid way, considered anything but unqualified praise as conspiracy against him.[16] He was so tormented by adverse criticism of his writing that only a foolhardy friend would dare offer anything resembling authentic appraisal.

The lack of war decorations immediately following World War II was another ignominious affront to the Hemingway ego. He often lamented to Lanham that the Distinguished Service Cross, rightfully his for fighting in Rambouillet, was given to another. (Though Hemingway fought valiantly in the war, he was ineligible for citation as a soldier since he was a correspondent and not officially permitted to carry weapons in World War II.) In 1947 "he was glad enough to accept a Bronze Star . . . for 'meritorious service' as a war correspondent."[17] He wrote plaintively to Lanham of his fear that twenty years after his death "they" would deny he was in the war. Later this was shortened to "ten years" and finally to the fear that before his death "they'll" deny he ever saw action.

His relationship to Lanham was often highly inconsistent with the Hemingway image. The letters to Lanham reveal childlike admiration for the professional soldier, with whom Hemingway simultaneously compares himself unfavorably and attempts to identify. He wrote to Lanham that others were "always jealous" of people like them, that he "hurt" when Lanham "hurt," that *The Old Man and the Sea* had in it everything in which they both believed. He wrote also in a period of depression that he was just killing time wishing he were a soldier like Lanham instead of a "chickenshit writer." He demeaned his own accomplishments by suggesting that he would get into history only because of his close association with Lanham when Lanham commanded the 22nd infantry.[18]

In his relationship to the women in his life, Hemingway assumes a curiously paradoxical pose, scorning them as much as he loves them. He is at once the celebrated champion of romantic love and the misogynist. Yet to be written is the story of his innumerable love affairs and four marriages, wherein he undoubtedly demonstrated tenderness, sensitivity, and a capacity for caring, as well as the erotic feats of which he publicly and privately boasted. Baker's biography gives numerous examples of thoughtful attentions to his wives—Hadley, Pauline, Martha, and Mary. But despite Baker's tactful presentation of Hemingway the lover, there are numerous incidents of the unkindness, ugliness, and patent unfaithfulness which were invariably served to the Hemingway women; the ménages à trois to which Hadley and Pauline were subjected with their respective successors, and which Mary endured with younger rivals, are cases in point.[19] Lanham tells us that Hemingway was notoriously rude to his friends' wives, some of whom served as models for the "bitches" he described in his fiction. He rewarded Gertrude Stein, his early mentor and friend, with some vicious pages in *A Moveable Feast* (a not uncommon treatment of his fellow authors, whether they had befriended him or not). Hemingway once wrote that the things he loved were in the following order: "good soldiers, animals and women."[20]

In his fiction, which includes some of the most moving love stories in contemporary literature, there is scarcely a single example of a successful male-female egalitarian relationship.[21] *The Sun Also Rises* describes the relationship of an impotent man, Jake Barnes, with the seductive, promiscuous Brett Ashley. In *For Whom the Bell Tolls* the worldly American Robert Jordan and the young ingenuous Maria come together like teacher and pupil. This disparity is even more pronounced in *Across the River and Into the Trees,* where the 19-year-old girl Renata is called "daughter" by her lover, the 50-year-old Colonel Cantwell. In *To Have and Have Not* Harry's wife, Marie, is an unfeminine, blowsy ex-prostitute. In "The Snows of Kilimanjaro" Harry is married to a rich, intrusive woman who feeds on his vitality, and in "The Short Happy Life of Francis Macomber" the protagonist's wife infantilizes him until he begins to discover his authentic self, whereupon she manages to kill him by accident. The couple in *A Farewell to Arms* are perhaps Hemingway's most fulfilled lovers, yet their relationship appears unconvincing; Catherine Barkley, Frederick's former nurse, is an extraordinarily selfless, fleshless being who lives only for Frederick and dies rather pointlessly following childbirth by caesarian section (the novel, incidentally, was written immediately after Hemingway's second wife, Pauline, was delivered of his second child by caesarian section).

If Hemingway avoids depicting egalitarian male-female relationships, he is indeed inventive in creating alternatives. It is as though his attempts to portray a satisfying love-sex relationship are thwarted by a number of powerful counterforces, many of which Hemingway recognizes. Looming large in such works as "The Snows of Kilimanjaro," "The Short Happy Life of Francis Macomber," "Now I Lay Me," "The Three-Day Blow," "Mr. and Mrs. Elliot," "Out of Season," "Hills Like White Elephants," and "Cat in the Rain" is the danger of emasculation. Though the narrative varies, the outcome in each is the same—an enduring union with a woman results in a devitalized man. The father in "Now I Lay Me" observes, powerlessly, while his wife burns his treasured belongings. In "Hills Like White Elephants" another devitalized and dependent husband pleads with his pregnant wife to have an abortion because he cannot bear the thought of competition for her attention.

Even closer to home was the decline of Hemingway's own father from the able doctor and legendary huntsman immortalized in the Nick Adams stories to the wasted figure who visits his son some months before his death like a premature ghost whose life force had been absorbed by Hemingway's mother, looming beside him, "a picture of ruddy health."[22] Believing that his mother's aggressive bullying had driven his father to suicide, Hemingway modeled the parents of Robert Jordan in *For Whom the Bell Tolls* upon his own parents; like Ernest, Robert calls his father a coward because he did not resist his wife and finally resorted to suicide—the weakest act of all.

Throughout his life Hemingway considered love between man and woman as detrimental to other, truer types of relationships, such as friendship between males or man's communion with nature. When he fell in love with Hadley, he castigated himself for no longer caring about the two or three streams he had loved better than anything else in the world.[23] In "Cross Country Snow" the impending marriage of a young man threatens to destroy his deep relationship with a skiing comrade. The two speak wistfully of skiing again in the place to which one must move, but both know that "the mountains aren't much. . . . They're too rocky. There's too much timber and they're too far away."[24]

Another risk inherent in an adult love relationship is the potential rejection by the woman and the ensuing insult to one's narcissism. While recovering from his wound in the First World War, Hemingway fell deeply in love, probably for the first time, with Agnes von Kurowsky, one of the nurses who tended him. When Agnes finally chose another man, Hemingway was plunged into despair. That this emotional injury was profound and enduring is indicated by the fact that Hemingway returned to it in four separate works: "A Very Short Story," "The Snows of Kilimanjaro," *The Sun Also Rises,* and *A Farewell to Arms.*

To love another is to expose oneself to the risk of painful separation or loss, a risk against which Hemingway admonished in "In Another Country":[25]

"Why must not a man marry?"
"He cannot marry, he cannot marry," he said angrily.

"If he is to lose everything he should not place himself in a position to lose. He should find things he cannot lose."

Still another counterforce to mature love arose from a deeply based fear of women stemming from Oedipal conflicts. Literary critics are sometimes more intrepid than psychiatrists in offering highly inferential interpretations; Young, for example, in a study which Hemingway tried to block during his lifetime, suggested that Hemingway was psychologically crippled by castration anxiety, and that his major works derive from this source.[26] Freudian developmental theory holds that the male child in his early years experiences libidinal desires toward his mother; these libidinal impulses are, as Freud reminds us, not clearly sexual but of the stuff from which sex will come.[27] They beget conflicted feelings toward the father, at first competitive and then destructive, which may take the guise of stark death wishes; these hostile feelings rapidly evoke another constellation of feelings—fears of retribution which may assume the amorphous form of global annihilation or the specific form of castration. A successful resolution of this conflict involves identification with the father and repression or relinquishment of the incestuous desire for the mother.

If resolution does not occur, the child does not attain psychosexual maturity, and a number of adverse outcomes may ensue. Sexual encounters with women become symbolic recapitulations of the relationship with the mother, with its attendant feelings of desire, repulsion, and the anticipation and dread of catastrophe; sexual intercourse becomes an inchoate nightmare. Some methods of coping involve the abandonment of women as sexual objects, with the individual seeking refuge in alternative outlets. More common yet is the splitting of women into sexual and nonsexual categories; one avoids intercourse with "pure" women of one's age, intelligence, and class; one goes to bed with an unequal partner, a woman obviously inferior in education and social status.

The evidence that castration anxiety played an important role in Hemingway's conflicted attitude toward women is meager, and there are, as we have indicated, a number of other dynamics operating. Nevertheless, the theory of castration anxiety gains support as we consider Hemingway's reaction to significant physical trauma—one final area in which he experienced a marked discrepancy between his idealized and his real self. The idealized Hemingway courts danger and endures physical injury with little self-concern, heals quickly with no functional or psychological residue, and returns, untrammeled, to the fray. The real Hemingway did indeed court danger and did indeed suffer injury. The inventory of Hemingway's physical injuries rivals a list of his published works; it includes several spectacular plane and automobile crashes resulting in brain concussions, hemorrhages, multiple fractures, severe cuts, and burns, and a lifetime of minor accidents, many associated with hunting, fishing, boxing, and skiing. Lanham remarked that his body was crisscrossed with scars. Yet it seems that Hemingway's wounds seared his mind more harshly and more indelibly than they ever cauterized his flesh. Indeed, the big wound, the one suffered in Fossalta di Piave, Italy, in July 1918, may be regarded as the critical incident of his life.

During World War I, in which Hemingway served as an ambulance driver, he succeeded in getting closer to the fighting by distributing chocolates and cigarettes by bicycle to the front-line Italian troops at Fossalta. An enemy trench mortar shell exploded nearby, spewing scrap metal into Hemingway and three Italian soldiers. One soldier was killed outright, another severely wounded, and Hemingway absorbed hundreds of pieces of metal into his legs, scrotum, and lower abdomen. Nonetheless, with remarkable endurance and courage, he carried the wounded soldier 50 yards before he was hit in the leg by machine gun fire and then another 100 yards before he lost consciousness—a feat of bravery and fortitude of which any man would be proud. Young quotes Hemingway as saying, "I had been shot and I had been crippled and gotten away." We agree with Young who, aptly, wonders whether Hemingway truly got away and how far away he got.[28]

Hemingway was never to forget Fossalta and repetitively revisited it in person, in his conversation, letters, and, as we shall discuss, in his fiction; what happened that day was to be recounted in numerous variations for the fascination of tens of millions of Hemingway readers and moviegoers. Why could he not forget? Why could the wound not heal? Other men have suffered similar wounds without psychological sequelae.

Hemingway speculated that the wound haunted him so because it punctured the myth of his personal immortality. Through the lips of Colonel Cantwell in *Across the River and Into the Trees* he says:[29]

> He was hit three times that winter, but they were all gift wounds; small wounds in the flesh of the body without breaking bone, and he had become quite confident of his personal immortality since he knew he should have been killed in the heavy artillery bombardment that always preceded the attacks. Finally he did get hit properly and for good. No one of his other wounds had ever done to him what the first big one did. I suppose it is just the loss of the immortality, he thought. Well, in a way, that is quite a lot to lose.

The loss of his sense of immortality was indeed no small loss, for an important premise of Hemingway's assumptive world was that he was markedly different from others: he boasted that he had an unusually indestructible body, an extra thickness of skull, and was not subject to the typical biological limitations of man, being able, for example, to exist on "an average of two hours and 32 minutes sleep for 42 straight days."[30]

It is not unlikely, however, that the wound (and the subsequent convalescence, which involved falling in love with his nurse) had an additional significance for Hemingway. A serious and bloody injury to his legs and scrotum may have evoked terrifying, primitive fears of castration or annihilation. At some level of consciousness Hemingway realized this: the war wound inflicted upon his fictional counterpart in his first novel, *The Sun Also Rises,* rendered him physically, but not psychologically, impotent. In one of his letters he pens a ribald subtitle to *The Sun Also Rises,* adding "so does your cock if you happen to have one."[31]

In his posture toward the major areas we have considered—self-sufficiency, physical injury and integrity, women and mature love—Hemingway fell very short of his idealized goals. His failure took its toll; he was plagued by recurrent periods of self-hatred. Newton's third law of mechanics has its psychodynamic analogy: every force evoking an appreciable degree of dysphoria is countered by a psychological mechanism designed to guard the security of the individual. Hemingway employed a number of such mechanisms, each offering some temporary respite and all destined to fail in the final depressive cataclysm that culminated in his suicide.

Hemingway's anxiety and depression stemmed in large part from his failure to actualize his idealized self. Two factors were important in this failure: the image was so extreme that superhuman forces would have been required to satisfy it; second, a number of counterforces limited his available degree of adaptability. These secondary counterforces, for example, dependency cravings and Oedipal conflicts, were sources of anxiety in their own right and hampered the actualization of the idealized self.

Hemingway rejected the conventional source of help offered by psychotherapy; the suppliant, passive role of patient was anathema to the very core of the Hemingway ideal. He hated psychiatrists, openly mocked those he knew, and once told an army psychiatrist that he knew a lot about "fuck-offs" but little about brave men.[32] It seems more pathetic than ironic that he was forced into the role of psychiatric patient during the last weeks of his life—a role that, according to Lanham, Hemingway must have considered "the ultimate indignity." He said that his Corona typewriter was his analyst and one can hardly disagree with him.[33] We described the blow suffered by Hemingway when his nurse, Agnes, rejected his love. Hemingway attempted to work this through with his typewriter and relived the romance in four different works of fiction, each time capping it with an ending more satisfying to his pride than the real episode. In "A Very Short Story" the marriage for which Agnes leaves him does not materialize, and he rapidly forgets her, soon contracting gonorrhea from a casual sexual relationship with a salesgirl. One senses that he demeans Agnes by the banal circumstances of his next romantic encounter. In "The Snows of Kilimanjaro" the hero remembers writing, while intoxicated, an un-Hemingway, pleading letter to an Agnes surrogate; he regains his esteem immediately by making off with another man's woman after subduing his rival in a primitive brawl. Lieutenant Henry in *A Farewell to Arms* is, of course, not rejected by his nurse; on the contrary, it is she who contributes the greater love to their union, and she who dies during the delivery of his child. Brett Ashley, Jake Barnes's nurse in *The Sun Also Rises,* is meted out her dole by hopelessly loving the one man who is unable to satisfy her sexual needs. She laments, "That's my fault. Don't we pay for all the things we do, though ... when I think of the hell I've put chaps through. I'm paying for it all now."[34]

When his typewriter was called upon to help repair the trauma suffered at Fossalta, it seems to have been summoned in vain. He relived that injury often in his letters, conversation, and in his fiction. Not only does he revisit the site of the wound in real life but he makes a pilgrimage there in three works: *A Moveable Feast,* "A Way You'll Never Be," and *Across the River and Into the Trees.* In the latter (written over 30 years after the injury) Colonel Cantwell finds the exact site at Fossalta where the accident occurred, defecates there, and buries money in a ritualistic ceremony. (When Hemingway revisited Fossalta he was prevented from doing likewise only by the lack of privacy.) The big wound, in fact, was relived in every major piece of fiction, for each Hemingway protagonist receives a major injury, generally to an extremity. Jake Barnes's injury, of course, was to his genitals; Lieutenant Henry in *A Farewell to Arms* suffers Hemingway's exact wound; Robert Jordan, at the end of *For Whom the Bell Tolls,* fractures his leg and lies waiting for his death with "his heart pounding on the pine needle floor of the forest";[35] Harry in "The Snows of Kilimanjaro" dies from a gangrenous injury to his knee; Harry Morgan in *To Have and Have Not* suffered an injury which necessitated amputation of his arm; Colonel Cantwell in *Across the River and Into the Trees* had been badly wounded at Fossalta, which resulted in a limp and a badly misshapen hand; at the end of the novel he dies of a coronary; Santiago in *The Old Man and the Sea,* in addition to minor inflictions, endures the cruelest injury of all— old age.

Of what value is the fantasied or factual revisit to the site of injury? Does it not merely probe for pain in the same way that the tongue compulsively jars an aching tooth? Most psychiatric theoreticians agree that the deliberate revivification by a part of the psyche of a traumatic incident represents an attempt at mastery. When the terrifying event becomes familiar, it becomes detoxified, and indeed several psychotherapeutic techniques are based on this strategy. For example, during World War II narcosynthesis was introduced, which consisted of administering sodium pentothal (a powerful sedative) to the subject and then helping him (with accompanying simulated battle noises, if necessary) reexperience the traumatic battle incident. By reexperiencing the event with markedly less anxiety (because of medication and the knowledge, at some level of consciousness, that this time there is no "real" danger) the subject is gradually desensitized. Several other forms of therapy (for example, behavioral therapy) operate on similar assumptions, but, unassisted, the individual often does not desensitize himself to the trauma but merely freezes in his symptomatology and is doomed to be haunted by recurrent fantasies, nightmares, or disembodied waves of panic.

Hemingway attempted to heal his wound through counterphobic means and by forcing the incident, or its associated affect, from consciousness. By flaunting the danger, by recklessly reexposing oneself to a similar threat, one is, in effect, denying to oneself that danger exists. Inwardly the ego employs repression and denial; outwardly the individual seems compelled to face the very thing he fears the most. From his earliest years Hemingway roared in the face of danger; "'fraid a nothing" he shouted to his mother at the age of three,[36] and he maintained that pose for the rest of his life in real and imaginary combat. The concept of counterphobia by no means repudiates Hemingway's courage. The military board members awarding decorations do not take personal psychodynamics into consideration. When one draws a line under his name and totals up his deeds, no one can deny Hemingway was a brave man; Lanham, who was with Hemingway under fire during World War II, says he was the bravest man he ever knew.

But perhaps the most striking manner in which Hemingway dealt with trauma was by demonstrating in his fiction again and again that a maimed, crippled man could still be a man, could, *despite* his defects and injuries, function in the best tradition of the Hemingway code. In each of his major works an injured and noble hero reminds us that physical handicaps can be overcome. In *The Sun Also Rises* Jake Barnes, despite his impotence, still functions with dignity and grace. Indeed, he and Pedro, the matador, are the only heroic male figures in the book, and Pedro never more so than after a brutal beating. In *For Whom the Bell Tolls* Robert Jordan dies manfully despite a painfully broken leg, manifesting in the face of death the qualities of grace and courage which Hemingway most admired. In *To Have and Have Not* the one-armed Harry Morgan is a rugged hero, who, in one memorable scene, triumphs over his impairment by making love to his wife with the stump of his arm. In *Across the River and Into the Trees* Col. Cantwell also has a maimed hand which seems to aid rather than impede his romantic progress, since Renata during lovemaking wants to examine and caress his wound. In *The Old Man and the Sea* old age has assailed Santiago's entire body, yet he temporarily transcends his physical condition through an act of endurance praiseworthy in even a younger man.

Throughout his life Hemingway attempted to abolish the discrepancy between his real and idealized selves. No alterations could be made upon the idealized self; there is no evidence that Hemingway ever compromised or attenuated his self-demands. All the work had to be done upon his real self; he pushed himself to face more intense danger, to attempt physical feats which exceeded his capabilities, while at the same time he pruned and streamlined himself. All traces of traits not fitting his idealized image had to be eliminated or squelched. The softer feminine side, the fearful parts, the dependent cravings—all had to go.

Not infrequently Hemingway externalized undesired traits, that is, he saw in others those aspects he rejected in himself and often responded to the other person quite vitriolically. The mental mechanism of "projective identification" (the process of projecting parts of oneself to another and then forming an intense, irrational relationship with the other) has been given permanent literary embodiment by Dostoevsky in *The Double* and by Conrad in *The Secret Sharer,* to mention only the best of the modern authors who have intuitively understood this phenomenon. Projective identification was perhaps one of the major mechanisms behind Hemingway's extremely vituperative outbursts to innocent strangers and the unwarranted invective he frequently directed at friends and acquaintances.[37] At a time when most Americans felt compassion, if not admiration, for their wartime president, Hemingway scorned Roosevelt's physical infirmity, his sexlessness, and womanly appearance.[38] He disliked Jews because of their softness, passivity, and "wet-thinking," yet it was no accident that the Jew, Robert Cohn, in *The Sun Also Rises* was, like Hemingway, an expert boxer and dealt quite badly with unrequited love; nor is it an accident that Hemingway joked about his own mock Jewishness, very often referring to himself as Dr. Hemingstein.

Hard men drink hard. Hemingway joked and boasted about his

drinking in real life and glamorized it in his fiction. Yet there is no doubt that Hemingway, as the years went by, leaned more and more heavily on alcohol for respite from intense anxiety and depression. His wife, Mary, who tends to underplay Hemingway's flaws, notes that in the last few years of his life he obtained most of his nourishment from alcohol rather than from food.[39] Hemingway went into "training" when embarking upon serious writing for a new book. The training rules consisted of getting into good physical shape and abstaining from alcohol until noon (he did all of his writing in the morning). Lanham reports that when he visited him while he was in training for *The Old Man and the Sea,* Hemingway swam 80 laps in the morning in his very large pool. From time to time he would swim to the edge of the pool to look at his watch. At 11:00 A.M. his majordomo would come out of the house with what appeared to be a half-gallon pitcher of martinis. Hemingway would grin and say, "What the hell, Buck, it's noon in Miami," and that ended the swimming for the morning. Lanham could drink two of the powerful martinis, his wife about 1½. Hemingway finished the rest of the pitcher.[40] Toward the end of his life, as his health faltered and his hypertension increased, his internist attempted, with only moderate success, to prevent him from drinking.

The mechanisms employed to ward off dysphoria—alcohol, writing, intense physical feats—all the frenetic attempts to perpetuate the image he created, interlocked to form only a partially effective dam against an inexorable tide of anguish. Throughout his life, Hemingway suffered from recurrent bouts of depression. As early as 1926 he wrote to F. Scott Fitzgerald that he had been living in hell for nine months with plenty of insomnia to light the way around and assist him in the study of the terrain.[41] Time and again he gratuitously, and tongue-in-cheek, reassured his friends that he was no longer at the "bumping off" stage. It is not difficult to glean from any individual's life correspondence and conversation a series of melancholic comments, and to do so now proves only that hindsight is a sorry human faculty. Hemingway's fulsome preoccupation with death, melancholia, and suicide throughout his life, and especially in his later years, was, however, a source of concern to those who knew him well. After World War II the "black-ass" days (as Hemingway called his depressions) increased in frequency. Success offered only brief respite; he wrote Lanham in 1950 that *Across the River and Into the Trees* had sold 130,000 copies and that they could eat a share but that he had not much appetite.[42] A letter from Africa following his plane crashes contains the crossed-out statement that the wake of the boat looked very inviting.[43]

Of all the insults and injuries suffered by Hemingway, none was so grave, so irreparable to his psychic economy, as the somatic decline of his advancing years. He had no easy way of befriending old age; no slot existed for the old man in the Hemingway code. In *The Old Man and the Sea,* his final brilliant fantasy, Santiago triumphs over the receding power of the flesh through sheer strength of will. But the pathos of it! How many old men, after all, can transcend their years by taking to the sea in an open boat to catch the giant marlin? He tried, it seems, to find an old-age identity for himself as the counselor of the young, preferring to be called "Papa" by almost everyone, but he was not ready for the role of the wise old sage. When we read of the inappropriate antics of Hemingway at 60,[44] we feel compelled to cry out like Lear's fool: "Thou shouldst not have been old till thou hadst been wise."

There are the attempts to replenish his youth through associations with young women;[45] the impossibility of that rebirth is pathetically foreshadowed in *Across the River and Into the Trees,* where the love affair between Col. Cantwell and the nineteen-year-old Renata (whose name in Italian means "reborn") cannot delay his deterioration and early death. Hemingway in 1960 seemed finally overwhelmed by the inexorable advance of years and the equally relentless deterioration of his soma. The earlier rivulets of concern about his body soon swelled into a torrent of hypochondriasis; he magnified the significance of minor ailments and grew increasingly preoccupied with major ailments to the extent that his conscious thoughts, like the pages of his letters and the walls of his bathrooms, were plastered with meticulously kept charts of daily fluctuations in weight, blood pressure, blood sugar, and cholesterol. In 1960 Hemingway's mental health sharply deteriorated and he developed the signs and symptoms of a major psychological illness. The clinical picture of his final condition reflected a splitting asunder of the union of the ideal and the real Hemingway, a psychic system that, to survive, had become increasingly rigid and then, finally, brittle.

The expansive self in the end submerged from view but signalled its subterranean persistence through paranoid trends both tragic and grotesque. For example, Hemingway in his last year had many "ideas of reference," that is, he tended to refer circumstantial events in his environment to himself. Hotchner describes an episode in which Hemingway arrived in a town late at night, noted lights on at the bank, and expressed his conviction that the Internal Revenue Service had auditors working furiously on his tax statement. "When they want to get you they get you."[46] On another occasion Hemingway suddenly left a restaurant because he surmised that two men at the bar were FBI agents disguised as salesmen who had been assigned to keep him under surveillance.

Stark persecutory trends appeared, as Hemingway became convinced that the Immigration Bureau, as well as the FBI and the IRS, was after him for corrupting the morals of a minor. Soon friends were admonished not to write or use the phone or speak too loudly since he was constantly spied upon. His persecutory convictions were true delusions in that they were fixed, false beliefs impervious to logic. Gradually the delusional system expanded to include all those about him—nurses, doctors, friends, and, finally, his immediate family. An elaborate persecutory delusional system is the voice of a runaway decompensated grandiose self; if everyone in one's environment is preoccupied with plotting, watching, listening, then it can only be because one is an extremely special person. Every paranoid delusion has a center crystal of truth: Hemingway was a very special and important person but obviously not so special as to warrant the total energy of his environment.

Grandiosity does not occur de novo. It arises in response to an inner central identity experienced as worthless and bad. The grandiose or expansive solution allowed Hemingway to survive without crippling dysphoria; it permitted him to form a platform, albeit, as we have seen, an unsturdy one, on which to base his feelings of self-worth and regard. At the end, the union of the psychological central identity and the grandiose peripheral system fragmented: Hemingway's inner core, naked and vulnerable, pervaded his experiential world. Consumed with feelings of guilt and worthlessness, he sank deep into despair. Delusions of poverty plagued him; he externalized his sense of inner emptiness and developed the conviction that he had no material financial stores.

In 1960 the accompanying signs and symptoms of depression

anorexia, severe weight loss, insomnia, deep sadness, total pessimism, self-destructive trends—became so marked that hospitalization was required. At the Mayo Clinic two courses of electroconvulsive treatment were administered, but in vain. Electroconvulsive treatment is the treatment of choice for severe depressive illness but is frequently ineffective in the presence of strong accompanying paranoid trends. Finally Hemingway grew to regard his body and his life as a prison of despair from which there was only one exit—and that exit, suicide, the most ignoble one of all. It was the shameful "thing" that Robert Jordan's father and his own father and, later, his sister had to do. It was the act that no Hemingway hero had ever done. It was not the death that we would have wished for this man who, at the age of 20, wrote to his father, "... and how much better to die in all the happy period of undisillusioned youth, to go out in a blaze of light, than to have your body worn out and old and illusions shattered."[47]

CHAPTER 8

The Journey from Psychotherapy to Fiction

PATIENT VIGNETTES:
FIRST STEPS INTO NARRATIVE

My last three publications, a book of therapy tales and two novels, appear to represent a radical departure from my textbooks and empirically grounded research reports published in psychiatric journals. From professorial prose to storytelling—what a transformation! What happened?

The answer is less dramatic than the question. There was no sudden transformation, only a gradual patterned unfolding. I have loved the telling of stories since I was a child, certainly from my ninth year. I vividly remember my birthday that year; lying glumly in bed, swollen with mumps, greeting visiting relatives—mostly aunts (the uncles were entirely tied to grocery businesses). Each brought some small offering to me—a spinning top, a wondrous toy cannon that fired wooden bullets, a set of toy American soldiers (World War II was looming), a log cabin set containing tiny notched logs that fit together and a chimney, red shutters, and small cellophane windows (destined soon to be shot out with wooden bullets). But no gift was as intriguing as my Aunt Leah's copy of *Treasure Island,* with a glossy, light-blue cardboard cover picturing a scowling Long John Silver—parrot on shoulder—and his pirates rowing toward an island, their treasure chest visible in the bow of the boat.

As soon as she left I leafed through the book, looted the illustrations, and then started reading. Within minutes I forgot all about my painfully swollen jaws; I floated away from my small bed wedged into a corner of the dining room of our roach-infested apartment above my father's grocery store on First and Seaton Place in Washington, D.C., and entered the magical world of Robert Louis Stevenson.

I liked that world; I moved in and hated to leave it. No sooner had I finished the book than I turned back to page one and began all over again. Since then I have read fiction continuously; I have never not been immersed in a novel. Every night before going to sleep (indeed, it has long been a prerequisite for sleep) I enter some alternate fictional world. By midadolescence I was aware of my enormous gratitude to the creators of these enchanted worlds—Dickens, Steinbeck, Thomas Wolfe, James Farrell, Thomas Hardy, Kipling, Sir Walter Scott, Melville, Hawthorne. What gifts they had left—for me, for all the world. And then, a couple of years later, when I entered the incomparable worlds of Dostoevsky and Tolstoy, I developed the powerful conviction, one I still hold with almost religious tenacity, that the finest thing a person can do in life is to write a good novel.

During my entire childhood and adolescence my parents, Ben and Ruth (or Beryl and Rifke), Jewish immigrants from a small *shtetl* in Russia, worked side by side fourteen hours a day in their dusty grocery store. When they obtained a license to sell liquor, the hours grew even longer, since the store remained open till midnight on Fridays and Saturdays. I never saw either of them read a book (they had neither the time nor any secular education), but it always seemed to give them pleasure to see me reading. They nodded their heads in approval; sometimes my father would come up to stroke my hair and glance, for only an instant, at my book. Once my Uncle Sam (in reality a distant cousin, but all the relatives were "uncles" and "aunts") told me that in his youth my father wrote wonderful poems. I often imagined him sitting atop a grain loft in the Russian countryside scribbling poetry. Even today I conjure up that delicious image. I love to think that, through me, his dreams have been realized.

My father's grocery store lay in the midst of a poor black neighborhood so unsafe that I dared not wander far. Hence I spent much of my early childhood alone. The large Sunday gathering of my parents' clan— fifteen to twenty friends or relatives who had emigrated from the same *shtetl*—partly attenuated my isolation but exacted a high price: encasement, conformity, a narrow paranoid ghetto mentality. I felt smothered. I wanted out and I knew the way. Week after week, year after year, I bicycled regularly, saddlebags bursting with novels, to and from the main library at Seventh and K Streets.

But years later, when the time came to choose a profession, I did not escape my milieu. My professional choices were limited—at least I perceived them as limited—and the idea of writing as a profession never presented itself as a possibility: all the bright young men of my background either went into business with their fathers, went to medical school, or, failing that, to dental school. I had a premonition that a medical career might be a wrong turn but nonetheless medical school—and especially psychiatry—was closer to Tolstoy and Dostoevsky than was my father's grocery business. And so off I went into years of total immersion in a scientific medical curriculum.

Once I entered psychiatry, my love for storytelling gradually awoke from its slumber and insisted upon a voice. For example, the therapy approach I ultimately developed is closely linked to the creative process, to the reading and writing of fiction: *reading* in that I always listen for the unique, fascinating story in each patient's life; *writing* in that I believe, with Jung, that therapy is a creative act and the effective therapist must invent a new therapy for each patient.

In my professional texts I indulged my passion for storytelling by smuggling mini-tales into the text via the form of the case vignette: sometimes a brief paragraph, sometimes a page or two. Students who have studied these texts know what I mean. How many times have I heard teachers say they like to use my texts because the students enjoy reading them?

Students have informed me about several appealing features of my professional writing. They appreciate the absence of professional jargon. (I have a great abhorrence of professional jargon: whether psychiatric, psychoanalytic, philosophic, poststructuralist, deconstructionist, or New Age, all such jargon is equally obfuscating and creates distance between the student and true understanding.) Students have told me they appreciate my clarity. Throughout my career I have made a point of never writing anything I myself do not completely understand. That may not seem a remarkable trait, yet the professional literature is full of contributions in which authors ranging from Sullivan, Lacan, Fenichel, and Klein to Boss and Binswanger make the murky assumption that linguistic clarity is not essential, that it is possible to communicate directly from the writer's unconscious to that of the reader. I have never believed a word of this. If an intelligent, diligent reader cannot understand the text, it is the author's failing, not the reader's.

But beyond clarity and the absence of jargon, I believe that the short clinical stories I have woven into my texts contribute heavily to their success. Students are willing to pay the price of wading through theory and research if they know that an engaging story lies waiting for them just around the bend, in perhaps a page or two.

The four patient vignettes presented here illustrate various problems of technique in group and individual therapy.

Group therapy is particularly well suited to narcissistic patients. Although a healthy love of oneself is essential to the development of self-respect and self-confidence, excessive self-love creates a variety of interpersonal problems, as we see in this excerpt from *The Theory and Practice of Group Psychotherapy*.

The narcissistic patient generally has a stormier but more productive course in group than in individual therapy. In fact, the individual format provides so much gratification that the core problem emerges much more slowly: the patient's every word is listened to; every feeling, fantasy, and dream is examined; everything is given to and little demanded from the patient.

In the group, however, the patient is expected to share time, to understand, to empathize with and to help other patients, to form relationships, to be concerned with the feelings of others, to receive constructive but sometimes critical feedback. Often narcissistic patients feel alive when onstage: they judge the group's usefulness to them on the basis of how many minutes of the group's and the therapist's time they have obtained at a meeting. They guard their specialness fiercely and often object when anyone points out similarities between themselves and other members. For the same reason, they also object to being included with the other members in mass group interpretations.

"Vicky"

One patient, Vicky, frequently criticized the group format by commenting on her preference for the one-to-one format. She often supported her position by citing psychoanalytic literature critical of the group therapy approach. She felt bitter at having to share time in the group. For example, one day three-fourths of the way through a meeting, the therapist remarked that he perceived Vicky and John to be under much pressure. They both admitted that they needed and wanted time in the meeting that day. After a moment's awkwardness, John gave way, saying he thought his problem could wait until the next session. Vicky consumed the rest of the meeting and, at the following session, continued where she left off. When it appeared that she had every intention of using the entire meeting again, one of the members commented that John had been left hanging in the last session. But there was no easy transition, since, as the therapist pointed out, only Vicky could entirely release the group, and she gave no sign of doing so graciously (she had lapsed into a sulking silence).

Nonetheless, the group turned to John, who was in the midst of a major life crisis. John presented his situation, but no good work was done. At the very end of the meeting, Vicky began weeping silently. The group members, thinking that she wept for John, turned to her.

But she wept, she said, for all the time that was wasted on John — time that she could have used so much better. What Vicky could not appreciate for at least a year in the group was that this type of incident did not indicate that she would be better off in individual therapy. Quite the contrary: the fact that such difficulties arose in the group was precisely the reason that the group format was especially indicated for her.

Self-disclosure is an essential part of successful group psychotherapy, and the therapist must be prepared to deal with all aspects of it—how to encourage it, how to minimize the risks of disclosure, how to steer the group into useful, therapeutic disclosure. This excerpt from *The Theory and Practice of Group Psychotherapy* illustrates some principles of therapeutic response to self-disclosure in therapy.

The group member who has just disclosed a great deal faces a moment of vulnerability and requires support from the members and/or the therapist. Regardless of the circumstances, no patient should be attacked for important self-disclosure. A clinical vignette will illustrate.

"Joe"

Five members were present at a meeting of a year-old group. (Two members were out of town, and one was ill.) Joe, the protagonist of this episode, began the meeting with a long, rambling statement about feeling uncomfortable in a smaller group. Ever since Joe had started the group, his style of speaking had turned members off. Everyone found it hard to listen to him and longed for him to stop. But no one had really dealt honestly with these vague, unpleasant feelings about Joe until this meeting when, after several minutes, Betsy interrupted him: "I'm going to scream—or burst! I can't contain myself any longer! Joe, I wish you'd stop talking. I can't bear to listen to you. I don't know who you're talking to—maybe the ceiling, maybe the floor, but I know you're not talking to me. I care about everyone else in this group. I think about them. They mean a lot to me. I hate to say this, but for some reason, Joe, you don't matter to me."

Stunned, Joe attempted to understand the reason behind Betsy's feelings. Other members agreed with Betsy and suggested that Joe never said anything personal. It was all filler, all cotton candy—he never revealed anything important about himself; he never related personally to any of the members of the group. Spurred, and stung, Joe took it upon himself to go around the group and describe his personal feelings toward each of the members.

I thought that, even though Joe revealed more than he had previously, he still remained in comfortable, safe territory. I asked, "Joe, if you were to think about revealing yourself on a ten-point scale, with 'one' representing cocktail party stuff and 'ten' representing the most you could ever imagine revealing about yourself to another person, how would you rank what you did in the group over the last ten minutes?" He thought about it for a moment and said he guessed he would give himself "three" or "four." I asked, "Joe, what would happen if you were to move it up a rung or two?"

He deliberated for a moment and then said, "If I were to move it up a couple of rungs, I would tell the group that I was an alcoholic."

This was a staggering bit of self-disclosure. Joe had been in the group for a year, and no one—not me, my co-therapist, nor the group members—had known of this. Furthermore, it was vital information. For weeks, for example, Joe had bemoaned the fact that his wife was pregnant and had decided to have an abortion rather than have a child by him. The group was baffled by her behavior and over the weeks became highly critical of his wife—some members even questioned why Joe stayed in the marriage. The new information that Joe was an alcoholic provided a crucial missing link. Now his wife's behavior made sense!

My initial response was one of anger. I recalled all those futile hours Joe had led the group on a wild-goose chase. I was tempted to exclaim, "Damn it, Joe, all those wasted meetings talking about your wife! Why didn't you tell us this before?" But that is just the time to bite your tongue. The important thing is not that Joe did not give us this information earlier but that he did tell us today. Rather than be-

ing punished for his previous concealment, he should be reinforced for having made a breakthrough and been willing to take an enormous risk in the group. The proper technique consisted of supporting Joe and facilitating further "horizontal" disclosure, that is disclosure about the process of his disclosure.

Earlier I discussed the modification of group therapy technique to meet the specialized clinical situation. A crucial step in that modification is the construction of a set of reasonable, achievable goals. This vignette from *Inpatient Group Psychotherapy* describes an important goal of the inpatient psychotherapy group.

The duration of therapy in the inpatient therapy group is far too brief to allow patients to work through problems. But the group can efficiently help patients spot problems that they may, with profit, work on in ongoing individual therapy, both during their hospital stay and in their posthospital therapy. The therapy group points patients toward the areas where work needs to be done. By providing a discrete focus for therapy, inpatient groups increase the efficiency of other therapies.

It is important that the groups identify problems with some therapeutic handle—problems that the patient perceives as circumscribed and malleable (not some generalized problem, such as depression or suicidal inclinations, which the patient is very aware of having and which offers no handhold for therapy). The group is most adept at helping patients identify problems in their mode of relating to other people. I mentioned earlier that group therapy is not an effective format to reduce anxiety or to ameliorate psychotic thinking or profound depression, but *it is the therapy setting nonpareil in which to learn about maladaptive interpersonal behavior.* Emily's story is a good illustration of this point.

"Emily"

Emily was an extremely isolated young woman. She complained that she was always in the position of calling others for a social engagement. She never received invitations: she had no close girlfriends who sought her out. Her dates with men always turned into one-night stands. She attempted to please them by going to bed with them, but they never called for a second date. People seemed to forget her as soon as they met her. During the three group meetings she attended, the group gave her consistent feedback about the fact that she was always pleasant and always wore a gracious smile and always seemed to say what she thought would be pleasing to others. In this process, however, people soon lost track of who Emily was. What were her own opinions? What were her own desires and feelings? Her need to be eternally pleasing had a serious negative consequence: people found her boring and predictable.

A dramatic example occurred in her second meeting, when I forgot her name and apologized to her. Her response was, "That's all right, I don't mind." I suggested that the fact that she didn't mind was probably one of the reasons I had forgotten her name. In other words, had she been the type of person who would have minded or made her needs more overt, then most likely I would not have forgotten her name. In her three group meetings, Emily identified a major problem that had far-reaching consequences for her social relationships outside: her tendency to submerge herself in a desperate but self-defeating attempt to capture the affection of others.

Assumption of responsibility—for life as well as for therapy—is a fundamental step in the process of psychotherapy. This vignette from *Existential Psychotherapy* describes some aspects of the therapy work with a patient who adamantly resisted such a step.

A therapist who has a sense of being heavily burdened by a patient, who is convinced that nothing useful will transpire in the hour unless he or she brings it to pass, has allowed that patient to shift the burden of responsibility from his or her own shoulders to those of the therapist. Therapists may deal with this process in a number of ways. Most therapists choose to reflect upon it. The therapist may comment that the patient seems to dump everything in his or her (the therapist's) lap, or that he or she (the therapist) does not experience the patient as actively collaborating in therapy. Or the therapist may comment upon his or her sense of having to carry the entire load of therapy. Or the therapist may find that there is no more potent mode of galvanizing a sluggish patient into action than by simply asking, "Why do you come?"

There are several typical resistances on the part of patients to these interventions, and they center on the theme of "I don't know what to do," or "If I knew what to do, I wouldn't need to be here," or "That's why I'm coming to see you," or "Tell me what I have to do." The patient feigns helplessness. Though insisting that he or she does not know what to do, the patient has in fact received many explicit and implicit guidelines from the therapist. But the patient does not disclose his or her feelings; the patient cannot remember dreams (or is too tired to write them down, or forgets to put paper and pencil by the bed); the patient prefers to discuss intellectual issues or to engage the therapist in a never-ending discussion of how therapy works. The problem, as every experienced therapist knows, is not that the patient does not know what to do. Each of these gambits reflects the same issue: the patient refuses to accept responsibility for change just as, outside the therapy hour, he or she refuses to accept responsibility for an uncomfortable life predicament.

"Ruth"

Ruth, a patient in a therapy group, illustrates this point. She avoided responsibility in every sphere of her life. She was desperately lonely, she had no close women friends, and all of her relationships with males had failed because her dependency needs were too great for her partners. More than three years of individual therapy had proved ineffective. Her individual therapist reported that Ruth seemed like a "lead weight" in therapy: she produced no material aside from circular rumination about her dilemmas with men, no fantasies, no transference material, and, over a three-year span, not a single dream. In despera-

tion, her individual therapist had referred her to a therapy group. But in the group Ruth merely recapitulated her posture of helplessness and passivity. After six months she had done no work in the group and made no progress.

In one crucial meeting she bemoaned the fact that she had not been helped by the group, and announced that she was wondering whether this was the right group or the right therapy for her.

THERAPIST: *Ruth, you do here what you do outside the group. You wait for something to happen. How can the group possibly be useful to you if you don't use the group?*

RUTH: *I don't know what to do. I come here every week and nothing happens. I get nothing out of therapy.*

THERAPIST: *Of course you get nothing out of it. How can something happen until you make it happen?*

RUTH: *I feel "blanked out" now. I can't think of what to say.*

THERAPIST: *It seems important for you never to know what to say or do.*

RUTH: (crying) *Tell me what you want me to do. I don't want to be like this all my life. I went camping this weekend—all the other campers were in seventh heaven, everything was in bloom, and I spent the whole time in complete misery.*

THERAPIST: *You want me to tell you what to do, even though you have a good idea of how you can work better in the group.*

RUTH: *If I knew, I'd do it.*

THERAPIST: *On the contrary! It seems very frightening for you to do what you can do for yourself.*

RUTH: (sobbing) *Here I am again in the same shitty place. My mind is scrambled eggs. You're irritated with me. I feel worse, not better in this group. I don't know what to do.*

At this point the rest of the group joined in. One of the members resonated with Ruth, saying he was in the same situation. Two others expressed their annoyance at her eternal helplessness. Another commented, accurately, that there had been endless discussions in the group about how members could participate more effectively. (In fact, a long segment of the previous meeting had been devoted to that very *issue.) She had innumerable options, another told her. She could talk about her tears, her sadness, or about how hurt she was. Or about what a stern bastard the therapist was. Or about her feelings toward any of the other members. She knew, and everyone knew that she knew, these options. "Why," the group wondered, "did she need to maintain her posture of helplessness and pseudo dementia?"*

Thus galvanized, Ruth said that for the last three weeks during her commuting to the group she had made a resolution to discuss her feelings toward others in the group, but always reneged. Today she said she wanted to talk about why she never attended any of the postgroup coffee klatches. She had wanted to participate but had not done so because she was reluctant to get any closer to Cynthia (another member of the group) lest Cynthia, whom she saw as exceptionally needy, would begin phoning her in the middle of the night for help. Following an intense interaction with Cynthia, Ruth openly showed her feelings about two other members of the group and by the end of the session had done more work than in the six previous months combined. What is worth underlining in this illustration is that Ruth's lament, "Tell me what you want me to do," was a statement of responsibility avoidance. When sufficient leverage was placed upon her, she knew very well what to do in therapy. But she did not want to know what to do! She wanted help and change to come from outside. To help herself, to be her own mother, was frightening; it brought her too close to the frightening knowledge that she was free, responsible, and fundamentally alone.

EVERY DAY GETS A LITTLE CLOSER: AN EXPERIMENT IN THERAPY AND NARRATIVE

Despite the many opportunities to smuggle narrative into my professional writing, I longed to express my creative impulses more fully and more openly. The opportunity to do so presented itself one day in 1974 when Ginny Elkins (a *nom de plume*) walked into my office. Ginny was a gifted creative writer—a Stegner fellow at Stanford—who suffered from massive inhibition. Not only was she blocked in her writing but so blocked in her expressiveness that she could make little use of the group therapy I offered.

She had decided to leave group therapy—her fellowship had ended and she could no longer afford it—when I proposed an unusual experiment. I offered to see her in individual therapy and suggested that, in lieu of payment, she write a free-flowing, uncensored summary following each therapy hour; in other words I asked her to express in writing all the feelings and thoughts she had not verbalized during our session. I, for my part, proposed to do exactly the same. Further, I suggested that we would each hand in our weekly reports in sealed envelopes to my secretary, and that every few months we would review each other's notes.

My proposal was overdetermined: I had multiple motives for this unusual request. First, it was taking seriously the dictum of creating a new therapy for each patient. I hoped that the writing assignment might not only unblock my patient's writing but encourage her to express herself more freely in therapy. Perhaps, also, her reading my notes might improve our relationship. I intended to write uncensored notes in which I would disclose my own experiences during the hour—pleasures, frustrations, distractions. It was possible that if Ginny could see me more realistically, she could begin to de-idealize me and relate to me on a more human basis.

But let's be honest. I had another, more self-serving motive: this device afforded me an unusual writing exercise, an opportunity to break my professional shackles, to liberate my voice, to free associate on paper, to write anything that came to mind in the ten minutes after each hour.

The exchange of notes every few months was highly instructive. Whenever participants in a relationship study their own interaction (that is, examine their own "process"), they are plunged more deeply into their encounter. When Ginny and I read each other's summaries, that was precisely what happened: on each reading, therapy was catalyzed.

The notes provided a Rashomon experience: although we had lived through the same hour, we *experienced* the hour very differently. For one thing, we valued very different parts of the session. My elegant and brilliant interpretations? She never even heard them. She valued instead the small personal acts that I barely noticed: my complimenting her clothing or appearance or writing, my awkward apologies for arriving a couple of minutes late, my chuckling at her satire, my teasing her when she role-played, my teaching her how to relax.

Later, when using our session summaries in my psychotherapy classes, I was struck by the students' intense interest in the sequence of summaries. My wife, a literary scholar and an excellent editor, thought that the summaries read like an epistolary novel. She suggested the notes be published as a book, and volunteered to edit them. (The editing of the notes of the sixty sessions consisted of pruning and clarification. Nothing was added: they remain very much as they were first written.)

Ginny was enthusiastic about the project; we agreed that we would each contribute a foreword and afterword and share the royalties equally. The book was published in 1974 under the title *Every Day Gets a Little Closer.* In retrospect the subtitle, *A Twice-Told Therapy,* would have been more apt, but Ginny loved the old Buddy Holly song and had always wanted it played at her wedding. Despite the unfortunate title, the book won a small but faithful audience and for the next twenty years regularly sold approximately two to three copies a day. It has been translated into several languages and in 1994 it was released in paperback and began a new life.

This excerpt consists of my foreword, Ginny's foreword, our notes from the third session, and the final paragraphs of my afterword.

Doctor Yalom's Foreword

It always wrenches me to find old appointment books filled with the half-forgotten names of patients with whom I have had the most tender experiences. So many people, so many fine moments. What has happened to them? My many-tiered file cabinets, my mounds of tape recordings often remind me of some vast cemetery: lives pressed into clinical folders, voices trapped on electromagnetic bands mutely and eternally playing out their dramas. Living with these monuments imbues me with a keen sense of transience. Even as I find myself immersed in the present, I sense the specter of decay watching and waiting—a decay which will ultimately vanquish lived experience and yet, by its very inexorability, bestows a poignancy and beauty. The desire to relate my experience with Ginny is a very compelling one; I am intrigued by the opportunity to stave off decay, to prolong the span of our brief life together. How much better to know that it will exist in the mind of the reader rather than in the abandoned warehouse of unread clinical notes and unheard electromagnetic tapes.

The story begins with a phone call. A thready voice told me that her name was Ginny, that she had just arrived in California, that she had been in therapy for several months with a colleague of mine in the East who had referred her to me. Having recently returned from a year's sabbatical in London, I had still much free time and scheduled a meeting with Ginny two days later.

I met her in the waiting room and ushered her down the hall into my office. I could not walk slowly enough; like a Japanese wife she followed a few noiseless steps behind. She did not belong to herself, nothing went with anything else—her hair, her grin, her voice, her walk, her sweater, her shoes, everything had been flung together by chance, and there was the immediate possibility of all—hair, walk, limbs, tattered jeans, G.I. socks, everything—flying asunder. Leaving what? I wondered. Perhaps just the grin. Not pretty, no matter how one arranged the parts! Yet curiously appealing. Somehow, in only minutes, she managed to let me know that I could do everything and that she completely delivered herself up into my hands. I did not mind. At the time it did not seem a heavy burden.

She spoke, and I learned that she was twenty-three years old, the daughter of a onetime opera singer and a Philadelphia businessman. She had a sister four years younger and a gift for creative writing. She had come to California because she had been accepted, on the basis of some short stories, into a one-year creative writing program at a nearby college.

Why was she now seeking help? She said that she needed to continue the therapy she had begun last year, and, in a confusing unsystematic fashion, gradually recounted her major difficulties in living. In addition to her explicit complaints, I recognized during the course of the interview several other major problem areas.

First, her self-portrait—related quickly and breathlessly with occasional fetching metaphors punctuating the litany of self-hatred. She is masochistic in all things. All her life she has neglected her own needs and pleasures. She has no respect for herself. She feels she is a disembodied spirit—a chirping canary hopping back and forth from shoulder to shoulder, as she and her friends walk down the street. She imagines that only as an ethereal wisp is she of interest to others.

She has no sense of herself. She says, "I have to prepare myself to be with people. I plan what I am going to say. I have no spontaneous feelings—I do, but within some little cage. Whenever I go outside I feel fearful and must prepare myself." She does not recognize or express her anger. "I am full of pity for people. I am that walking cliché: 'If you can't say anything nice about people, don't say anything at all.'" She remembers getting angry only once in her adult life: years ago she yelled at a coworker who was insolently ordering her around. She trembled for hours afterward. She has no rights. It doesn't occur to her to be angry. She is so totally absorbed with making others like her that she never thinks of asking herself whether she likes others.

She is consumed with self-contempt. A small voice inside endlessly taunts her. Should she forget herself for a moment and engage life spontaneously, the pleasure-stripping voice brings her back sharply to her casket of self-consciousness. In the interview she could not permit herself a single prideful sentiment. No sooner had she mentioned her creative writing program than she rushed to remind me that she had come by it through sloth; hearing about this program through gossip, she had applied for it only because it required no formal application other than sending in some stories she had written two years previously. Of course, she did not comment on the presumably high quality of the stories. Her literary output had gradually waned and she was now in the midst of a severe writing block.

All of her problems in living were reflected in her relationships with men. Though she desperately wanted a lasting relationship with a man, she had never been able to sustain one. At the age of twenty-one she leapt from nubile sexual innocence to sexual intercourse with several men (she had no right to say "No!") and lamented that she had hurled herself through the bedroom window without even entering the adolescent antechamber of dating and petting. She enjoys being physically close to a man but cannot release herself sexually. She has experienced orgasm through masturbation, but the internal taunting voice makes quite certain that she rarely approaches orgasm in sexual intercourse.

Ginny rarely mentioned her father, but her mother's presence was very large. "I am my mother's pale reflection," she put it. They have always been unusually close. Ginny told her mother everything. She remembers how she and her mother used to read and chuckle over

Ginny's love letters. Ginny was always thin, had many food aversions, and for over a year in her early teens vomited so regularly before breakfast that her family grew to consider it as part of her routine morning toilet. She always ate a great deal, but when she was very young she could swallow only with much difficulty. "I would eat a whole meal and at the end still have it all in my mouth. I would try then to swallow it all at once."

By the end of the hour, I felt considerable alarm about Ginny. Despite many strengths—a soft charm, deep sensitivity, wit, a highly developed comic sense, a remarkable gift for verbal imagery—I found pathology wherever I turned: too much primitive material, dreams which obscured the reality-fantasy border, but above all a strange diffuseness, a blurring of "ego boundaries." She seemed incompletely differentiated from her mother, and her feeding problems suggested a feeble and pathetic attempt at liberation. I experienced her as feeling trapped between the terrors of an infantile dependency which required a relinquishment of selfhood—a permanent stagnation—and, on the other hand, an assumption of an autonomy which, without a deep sense of self, seemed stark and unbearably lonely.

I rarely trouble myself excessively with diagnosis. But I knew that she was seriously troubled and that therapy would be long and chancy. I was at that moment forming a therapy group which my students were to observe as part of their training program, and since my experience in group therapy with individuals who have problems similar to Ginny's has been good, I decided to offer her a place in the group. She accepted the recommendation a bit reluctantly; she liked the idea of being with others but feared that she would become a child in the group and never be able to express her intimate thoughts. This is a typical expectation of a new patient in group therapy, and I reassured her that, as her trust in the group developed, she would be able to share her feelings with the others. Unfortunately, as we shall see, her prediction of her behavior proved all too accurate.

Aside from the practical consideration of my forming a group and searching for patients, I had reservations about treating Ginny individually. In particular, I felt some disquiet at the depth of her admiration for me, which, like some ready-made mantle, was thrust over me as soon as she entered my office. Consider her dream dreamt the night before our first meeting. "I had severe diarrhea and a man was going to buy me some medicine that had Rx's written on it. I kept thinking I should have Kaopectate because it was cheaper, but he wanted to buy me the most expensive medicine possible." Some of the positive feelings for me stemmed from her previous therapist's high praise of me, some from my professorial title, the rest from parts unknown. But the overevaluation was so extreme that I suspected it would prove an impediment in individual therapy. Participation in group therapy, I reasoned, would allow Ginny the opportunity to view me through the eyes of many individuals. Furthermore, the presence of a co-therapist in the group should allow her to obtain a more balanced view of me.

During the first month of the group, Ginny did very poorly. Terrifying nightmares interrupted her sleep nightly. For example, she dreamt that her teeth were glass and her mouth had turned to blood. Another dream reflected some of her feelings about sharing me with the group. "I was lying prostrate on the beach, and was picked up and carried away to a doctor who was to perform an operation on my brain. The doctor's hands were held and so guided by two of the group members that he accidentally cut a part of the brain he hadn't intended to." Another dream involved her going to a party with me and our rolling on the grass together in sexual play.

Ginny attended the group religiously, rarely missing a meeting even when after one year she moved to San Francisco, which necessitated a long inconvenient commute via public transportation. Though Ginny received enough support from the group to hold her own during this time, she made no real progress. In fact, few patients would have shown the perseverance to continue so long in the group with so little benefit. There was reason to believe that Ginny continued in the group primarily to continue her contact with me. She persisted in her conviction that I, and perhaps only I, had the power to help her. Repeatedly the therapists and the group members made this observation; repeatedly they noted that Ginny was fearful of changing, since improvement would mean that she would lose me. Only by remaining fixed in her helpless state could she insure my presence. But there was no movement. She remained tense, withdrawn and often noncommunicative in the group. The other members were intrigued by her; when she did speak, she was often perceptive and helpful to others. One of the men in the group fell deeply in love with her, and others vied for her attention. But the thaw never came; she remained frozen with terror and never was able to express her feelings freely or to interact with the others.

During the period of her group therapy, Ginny searched for other methods to escape from the dungeon of self-consciousness she had constructed for herself. She frequently attended Esalen and other local growth centers. The leaders of these programs designed a number of crash-program confrontational techniques to change Ginny instantaneously: nude marathons to overcome her reserve and hiddenness, psychodrama techniques and psychological karate to alter her meekness and unassertiveness, and vaginal stimulation with an electric vibrator to awake her slumbering orgasm. All to no avail! She was an excellent actress and could easily assume another role onstage. Unfortunately, when the performance was over, she shed her new role quickly and left the theater clad as she had entered it.

Ginny's fellowship at college ended, her savings dwindled, and she had to find work. Finally, a part-time job provided an irreconcilable scheduling conflict, and Ginny, after agonized weeks of deliberation, served notice that she would have to leave the group. At approximately the same time my co-therapist and I had concluded that there was little likelihood of her benefiting from the group. I met with her to discuss future plans. It was apparent that she required continued therapy; though her grasp on reality was more firm, the monstrous night and waking dreams had abated, she was living with a young man, Karl (of whom we shall hear more later), and she had formed a small group of friends, she enjoyed life still with only a small fraction of her energies. Her internal demon, a pleasure-stripping small voice, tormented her relentlessly, and she continued to live her life against a horizon of dread and self-consciousness. The relationship to Karl, the closest she had ever experienced, was a particular source of agony. Though she cared deeply for him, she was convinced that his feelings toward her were so conditional that any foolish word or false move would tip the balance against her. Consequently, she derived little pleasure from the creature comforts she shared with Karl.

I considered referring Ginny for individual therapy to a public clinic in San Francisco (she could not afford to see a therapist in private practice), but many doubts nagged me. The waiting lists were long, the therapists sometimes inexperienced. But the compelling factor was that Ginny's great faith in me colluded with my rescuer fantasy to convince me that only I could save her. Besides all this, I have a very stubborn streak; I hate to give up and admit that I cannot help a patient.

So I did not surprise myself when I offered to continue treating Ginny. I wanted, however, to break the set. A number of therapists had failed to help her and I looked for an approach which would not repeat the errors of the others and would at the same time permit me to capitalize, for therapeutic benefit, on Ginny's powerful positive transference to me. I describe in some detail my therapeutic plan and the theoretical rationale underlying my approach in the Afterword. For now, I need only comment on one aspect of the approach, a bold procedural ploy which has resulted in the following pages. I asked Ginny, in lieu of financial payment, to write an honest summary of each session, containing not only her reactions to what transpired, but also a depiction of the subterranean life of the hour, a note from the underground—all the thoughts and fantasies that never emerged into the daylight of verbal intercourse. I thought the idea, innovative to the best of my knowledge in psychotherapeutic practice, was a happy one; Ginny was then so inert that any technique demanding effort and motion seemed worth trying. Ginny's total writing block, which deprived her of an important source of positive self-regard, made a procedure requiring mandatory writing even more appealing.

I was intrigued by a potentially powerful exercise in self-disclosure. Ginny could not disclose herself to me, or anyone, in a face-to-face encounter. She regarded me as infallible, omniscient, untroubled, perfectly integrated. I imagined her sending me, in a letter if you will, her unspoken wishes and feelings toward me. I imagined her reading my own personal and deeply fallible messages to her. I could not know the precise effects of the exercise, but I felt certain that the plan would release something powerful.

I knew that our writing would be inhibited if we were conscious of the other's immediate perusal; so we agreed not to read the other's reports for several months and my secretary would store them for us. Artificial? Contrived? We would see. I knew that the arena of therapy and of change would be the relationship existing between us. I believed that if we could, one day, replace the letters with words immediately spoken to each other, that if we could relate in an honest, human fashion, then all other desired changes would follow.

Ginny's Foreword

I was an A student in high school in New York. Even though I was creative, that was just a sideline to being mostly stunned, as though I had been hit on the head by a monster shyness. I went through puberty with my eyes shut and my head migrained. Fairly early in my college life I put myself out to pasture academically. Although I did occasional "great" work, I liked nothing better than to be a human sundial, a curled up outdoor nap. I was scared of boys and didn't have any. My few later affairs were all surprises. As part of my college education, I spent some time in Europe working and studying and compiling a dramatic résumé that was really all anecdotes and friends, not progress. What passed for bravery was a form of nervous energy and inertia. I was scared to come home.

After I graduated from college, I returned to New York. I couldn't find a job, in fact had no direction. My qualifications dripped like Dali's watch, as I was tempted toward everything and nothing. By chance, I got a job teaching small children. Actually none of the children (and there were only about eight) were pupils; they were kindred spirits and what we did was play for a year.

While in New York I took classes in acting on how to howl and breathe and read lines so they sounded like they were hooked up to a real bloodstream. There was a stillness to my life, though, no matter how much I rushed through classes and friends.

Even when I didn't know what I was doing, I smiled a great deal. One friend, feeling himself pressed up against Pollyanna, said, "What have you got to be so happy about?" In fact, with my few great friends (I've always had them), I could be happy; my faults seemed only minor distractions compared to how natural and easy life was. However, my grin was stifling. My mind was filled with a jangling carousel of words that rotated constantly around moods and aromas, only occasionally dropping out into my voice or onto paper. I was not too good when it came to facts.

I lived alone in New York. My contact with the outside world, except for classes and letters, was minimal. I began to masturbate for the first time, and found it frightening, just because it was something private happening in my life. The transparent quality of my fears and happiness had always made me feel light and silly. A friend said, "I can read you like a book." I was someone like Puck, who didn't need any responsibility; who never did anything more serious than vomit. And suddenly I was starting to act differently. Quickly I began to immerse myself in therapy.

The therapist was a woman and in the five months I was with her, twice a week, she tried to make my grin go away. She was convinced that my whole objective in therapy was to get her to like me. In the sessions she pounded away at my relationship with my parents. It had always been ridiculously loving and open and ironic.

I was afraid in therapy because I was sure there was some horrible secret that my mind was withholding from me. Some explanation of why my life felt like one of those children's drawing boards: when you lift up the paper, the easy funny faces, the squiggly lines, are all erased, leaving no traces. At that time no matter how much I did, how many best friends I loved, I was dependent on others to give me my setting and pulse. I was both vibrant and dead. I needed their push; I could never be self-starting. And my memory was mostly deadly and derogatory.

I was progressing in therapy to the point where both me and my feelings were sitting in the same leather chair. Then an unusual circumstance changed my life, or at least my location. I had applied on a whim to a writing program in California and was accepted. My therapist in New York was not happy with the news; in fact, was against my going. She said I was stuck, took no responsibility for my life, and no amount of fellowship was going to get me out. However, I could not act adult about it and write to the grant people saying, "Please postpone my miraculous stipend while I try to find my emotions and feel confident and human." No, as with everything else, I waded into the new environment, even though I was afraid that my therapist's words were correct and that I was just leaving at the beginning, risking my life for a guaranteed year of sun. But I could not refuse experience, since that was my alibi, my backdrop for feeling, my way of thinking, of moving. Always the scenic view rather than the serious, thoughtful route.

My therapist in the end gave me her blessing, convinced that I could get excellent help from a psychiatrist she knew in California. I left New York, and as always there was something thrilling about leaving. No matter how many valuables you have left behind, you still have your energy and your eyes, and right before I left, my grin, like a permanent logo, came back, with the exhilaration of getting out. I gambled that the psychological pot would still be waiting for me when I arrived in California, and I wouldn't have to start from scratch as a child star.

Because of the intensive and heroic work I had done in New York with acting, therapy, and loneliness, I made it to California with all my limited, padded feelings still intact. It was a great time in my life because I had a guaranteed future, plus no men whom I had to try and stretch myself for and be judged by. I hadn't had any boyfriend since college. I found a small cottage, with an orange tree in front; I never even thought of picking the oranges off the tree till a friend said I could. I substituted tennis for acting. And made my usual quota of one great girlfriend. At the college I did okay, though I acted like an ingenue.

I went from one therapist to another in coming from New York to Mountain View.

In a teetering frame of mind, teething on Chekhov and Jacques Brel and other sweet and sour sadnesses, I first went to see Dr. Yalom. Expectations, which are an important part of my lot, were great, since he had been recommended by my New York therapist. As I went into his room vulnerable and warm, maybe even Bela Lugosi could have done the trick, but I doubt it. Dr. Yalom was special.

That first interview with him, my soul became infatuated. I could talk straight; I could cry, I could ask for help and not be ashamed. There were no recriminations waiting to escort me home. All his questions seemed to penetrate past the mush of my brain. Coming into his room I seemed to have license to be myself. I trusted Dr. Yalom. He was Jewish—and that day, I was too. He seemed familiar and natural without being a Santa Claus psychiatrist type.

Dr. Yalom suggested I join his group therapy that he conducted with another doctor. It was like signing up for the wrong course—I wanted Poetry and Religion on a one-to-one visitation and instead I got beginning bridge (and with no good chocolate mix either). He sent me to the co-leader of the group. In my preliminary interview with the other doctor there were no tears, no truths, just the subtext of an impersonal tape recorder breathing.

Group therapy is really hard. Especially if the table is stacked with inertia as ours was. The group of about seven patients plus two doctors met at a round table with a microphone dangling from the ceiling; on one side there was a wall of mirrors like a glassy web where my face would get caught every once in a while looking at itself. A group of resident doctors sat on the other side and looked in the window mirror. It really didn't bother me. Although I am shy, I am also a little exhibitionist, and I removed myself accordingly and "acted" like a stuffed Ophelia. The table and chair put you in a posture where it was difficult to get going.

Many of us had the same problems—an inability to feel, unjelled anger, love troubles. There were a few miraculous days when one or the other of us caught fire and something would happen. But the time boundaries on either side of the hour and a half usually doused any big breakthroughs. And by the next week we had subsided into our usual psychological rigor mortis.

I was beginning to feel lifeless again and pretentious, so I sought artificial respiration from encounter groups, which were indigenous to the area. They were held in people's lush forest homes—on rugs, on straw mats, in Japanese baths, at midnight. I enjoyed the milieu even more than the content. Physicists, dancers, middle-aged people, boxers would show up with their skills and problems. There would be stage lights and Bob Dylan coaching from the corner of a hi-fi, you *know* something is happening, but you don't know what it is.

This form of theater with your soul auditioning appealed to me. There were tears and screaming and laughter and silence—all energizing. Fear, real hits on the back, and friendships staggered up out of the midnight slime. Marriages dissolved before your eyes; white-collar jobs were slashed. I gladly signed up for these judgment days and resurrections since I'd had nothing like it in my life.

Sometimes you would only be brought down though, without any upward sweep and salvation. You were supposed to be able to follow a certain ritual rhythm and beat, from fear and panic to howling insight, confession, and acclamation. And if that failed you were supposed to be able to say, "Well, I'm a schmuck, I'm hopeless, so what? I'm going to go on from there," and dance out your stomach cramps.

Eventually, though, I realized I was straddling two opposite salvations—the impacted, solid, sluggish, constant, patient group therapy which was just like my life; and the medieval carnivals of the mind and heart of the psychodramas. I knew Dr. Yalom disapproved of my encounters, especially one particular group leader who was inspired and brilliant but with no credentials other than magic. I never really chose my side but continued both forms of therapy, diminishing all the while. Finally in group therapy I got to feel as though I dragged my cocoon in, fastened it onto the chair each week, held on for an hour and a half, and left. Refusing to be born.

I was bloated from the many months of group therapy, but was making no move to get out of the situation. My life was happy and yet as usual I felt somewhat submerged and foggy. Through friends I'd met a boyfriend named Karl who was intelligent and dynamic. He had his own book business, which I helped him with, learning no skills but managing to ply him with my jokes and getting stirred up inside. I was at first, however, not naturally attracted to him, which worried me. There was something about his eyes that seemed a little fierce and alien. But I enjoyed being with him even though I had some doubts, because unlike my few other loves, Karl was not an immediate crush, not someone I would have chosen from afar.

After a few terrific weeks of dalliance, we settled into a livable nonchalance. One day, almost as an aside, he told me there was an apartment he knew of where we could live together, and I moved from Mountain View into the city. Karl once said, holding me, that I brought humanity into his life, but he wasn't given to many love declarations.

We began living together easily and enjoying ourselves. It was the beginning of our life together and there were plenty of new green shoots—movies, books, walks, talks, embraces, meals, making our friends mutual and giving up some. I remember I had a physical around then at a free clinic and they wrote: "A twenty-five-year-old white female in excellent health."

I had left psychodrama by then, and the group therapy was just a habit that I dared not give up. I was waiting as usual to see what would happen in therapy rather than choose my own fate. One day Dr. Yalom called and asked if I would like to have private, free therapy with him on condition that we would both write about it afterward. It was one of those wonderful calls from out of the blue that I am susceptible to. I said yes, overjoyed.

When I began therapy as a private patient with Dr. Yalom, two years had gone by since my first fertile interview with him. I had replaced acting with tennis, looking for someone with being with someone, experiencing loneliness with trying to recall it. Inside I had a feeling that I had skipped out on my problems and that they would all be waiting for me at the ambush of night, some night. The critics, such as my New York therapist, and loves, whom I carried around with me, would have said that there was hard work to be done. That I had succeeded too easily without deserving it, and that Karl, who had started calling me "babe," really didn't know my name. I tried to get him to call me by my name—Ginny—and whenever he did, my life flowed. Sometimes, though, in deference to my blond hair and nerves, he called me the Golden Worrier.

Eighteen months of hibernation in group therapy had left me groggy and soiled. I began private therapy with only vague anxieties.

THIRD SESSION
Dr. Yalom's Notes

Better today. What was better? I was better. In fact, I was very good today. It's almost as though I am performing in front of an audience. The audience that will read this. No, I guess that isn't completely true—now I'm doing the very thing I accuse Ginny of doing, which is to negate the positive aspects of myself. I was being good for Ginny today. I worked hard and I helped her get at some things, although I wonder if I wasn't just trying to impress her, trying to make her fall in love with me. Good Lord! Will I never be free of that? No, it's still there, I have to keep an eye on it—the third eye, the third ear. What do I want her to love me for? It's not sexual—Ginny doesn't stir sexual feelings in me—no, that's not completely true—she does, but that's not really important. Is it that I want to be known by Ginny as the person who cultivated her talent? There is some of that. At one point I caught myself hoping that she would notice that some of the books in my bookcases were nonpsychiatric ones, O'Neill plays, Dostoevsky. Christ, what a cross to bear! The ludicrousness of it. Here I am trying to help Ginny with survival problems and I'm still burdened down with my own petty vanities.

Think of Ginny—how was she? Pretty sloppy today. Her hair uncombed, not even a straight part, worn-out jeans, shirt patched in a couple of places. She started off by telling me what a bad night she had had last week when she was unable to achieve orgasm, and then couldn't sleep the entire night because she feared rejection from Karl. And then she started to go back to the image of herself as the same body of a little girl who used to lie awake all night when she was in junior high school, hearing the same bird crying at three in the morning, and suddenly there I was again with Ginny, back in a hazy, clouded, mystical magical world. How fetching it all is, how much I would like to stroll around in that pleasant mist for a while, but . . . contraindicated. That would really be selfish of me. So, I tackled the problem. We went back to the sexual act with her boyfriend and talked about some obvious factors that prevent her from reaching orgasm. For example, there are some clear things that Karl could do to help arouse her to reach climax, but she is unable to ask him, and then we went into her inability to ask. It was all so obvious that I almost feel Ginny was doing it on purpose to allow me to demonstrate how perceptive and helpful I can be.

So, too, with the next problem. She described how she had met two friends on the street and how she had made, as usual, a fool of herself. I analyzed that with her, and we got into some areas that perhaps Ginny hadn't quite expected. She behaved with them in a chance meeting on the street in such a way, she says, as to leave them walking away saying, "Poor pathetic Ginny." So I asked, "What could you have said that would have made them feel you were rather hearty?" In fact, I proved to her there were some constructive things she could have mentioned. She's trying out for an improvisational acting group, she has done some writing, she has a boyfriend, she spent an interesting summer in the country, but she can never say anything positive about herself since it would not call forth the response "Poor pathetic Ginny," and there is a strong part of her that wants just that reaction.

She does the same thing with me in the session, as I pointed out to her. For example, she had never really conveyed to me the fact that she is good enough to work with a professional acting troupe. Her self-effacing behavior is a pretty pervasive theme, going back to her behavior in the group. I shocked her a bit by telling her that she looked intentionally like a slob, that some day I'd like to see her looking nice, even to the extent of putting a comb through her hair. I tried to de-reflect her self-indulgent inner gaze by suggesting that maybe her core isn't in the midst of her vast inner emptiness, that maybe her core is as much outside of herself, even with other people. I also pointed out to her that although it is necessary for her to look inside to write, sheer introspection without writing or some other form of creation is often a barren exercise. She did say that she has done considerably more writing during the last week. That makes me very happy. It may be that she is just giving me a gift, something to keep me anticipating improvement.

I tried to get her to discuss her notion of my expectations for her, since this is a genuine blind spot for me. I suspect I have great expectations for Ginny; am I really exploiting her writing talent so that she will produce something for me? How much of my asking her to write instead of paying is sheer altruism? How much is selfish? I want to keep urging her to talk about what she thinks I'm expecting of her; I must keep this in focus—the Almighty God "Countertransference"—the more I worship it the less I give to Ginny. What I must not do is try to fill her sense of inner void with my own Pygmalion expectations.

She's a fetching, likable soul, Ginny is. Though a doctor's dilemma. The more I like her as she is, the harder it will be for her to change; yet for change to occur, I have to show her that I like her, and at the same time convey the message that I also want her to change.

THIRD SESSION
Ginny's Notes

Something might happen if I were more natural looking. So I left my glasses on. Something might not happen though.

I spoke about that bad Tuesday night which turned out to have had a bad Tuesday beginning. The idea of a hearty, robust me, which you suggested and asked for, was very encouraging. My usual register of "success" is how much I have been released and done difficult things, like crying or thinking straight without fantasizing. And you pushed me in that direction.

I had fun at the session and before that could disturb me I enjoyed the sensation, the buoyancy. I seemed to see alternatives to my way of acting. This lasted even when I went on the campus afterwards. Though during the session and later I was obviously questioning this optimistic feeling. Surely happiness must be harder? Could I end it as a hearty wench?

I was looking at your way of treating me, like an adult. I wonder if you think I am pathetic or, if not, a hypocrite, or just an old magazine that you read in a doctor's office. Your methods are very comforting and absurd. You still seem to think that you can ask me questions that I will answer helpfully or with insight. You treat me with interest.

I think during the session that I am bragging, trying to show myself off good. I am dropping little self-indulgent hints and facts, like me being pretty (a real static fact), like the acting group, like the good sentence I wrote (treading water in front of your face). I know these are a waste of time since they don't do me any good and are things that go through my head every day with or without you. Even when you say, "I don't quite understand," that is a kind of flattery to my worst old habits of being elusive in word and deed. And inside me I don't understand either. God knows, I know the difference between the things I say and the things I feel. And my sayings are not satisfying most times. The few times in therapy when I react in a fashion not predestined by my mind, I feel alive in an eternal way.

So yesterday's experience was strange. I usually distrust the things that are said. Parent pep talk. I give it to myself regularly.

But I didn't feel down when the session was over, or let down. It was funny to hear you talk about my hair and dress. Kind of like my father but not quite. Of course maybe you think Franny dressed good. To me she looked attractive but always seemed an arm's length away. I look like a badly bent hanger with the clothes slipping off. I like to look heroic, like I've just done something. Though I wish I didn't have such an uncanny burlesque instinct in dressing. Sometimes I try and still look schleppy.

The night after the session I couldn't sleep at all. There was such a rush of blood in my chest and stomach and I could feel my heart beating all night. Was it because there was no release in the session or that I couldn't wait for a new day to begin? I was raring to go. I am saying this now 'cause I don't want to say it in the next session.

I think it is wrong in therapy for me to be too self-conscious, to say things like "I am feeling something in my leg." Those are probably cheap asides left over from sensory awareness afternoons that stop the direction you are heading me in. You must get sick of them, infliction, indulgence.

It was funny when you said I couldn't make a career out of schizophrenia. (I still think catatonia is right up my sleeve.) In a sense this takes away a lot of the romance I have been flirting with. I feel awkward and lacking and can't connect in social situations. There must be another way. With Dr. M.—I think he thought the things I said were "far-out," weird, and that they should be recorded for their nuances. I think you know they're shit. I was always watching him write down things. I'm not aware of your face too much except that it seems to be sitting over there waiting for something. And you seem to have a lot of patience. I don't like to look at your face 'cause I know I haven't said anything. If it did light up at the wrong places, I'd begin to distrust you.

In these first few sessions I think I can be as bad as I want, so later the transition will seem lovely.

Excerpt from Dr. Yalom's Afterword

. . . So much for the theory behind my therapy with Ginny, for the techniques and their rationale. I have delayed as long as I can. What about the therapist, me, the other actor in this drama? In my office I hide behind my title, interpretations, my Freudian beard, penetrating gaze, and posture of ultimate helpfulness; in this book, behind my explanations, my thesaurus, my reportorial and belletristic efforts. But this time I have gone too far. If I do not step gracefully out of my sanctum sanctorum, almost certainly my analytic colleagues and reviewers will yank me out.

The issue, of course, is countertransference. During our life together Ginny often related to me irrationally, on the basis of a very unrealistic appraisal of me. But what of my relationship to her? To what extent did my own unconscious or barely conscious needs dictate my perception of Ginny and my behavior toward her?

It is not entirely true that she was the patient and I the therapist. I first discovered that a few years ago when I spent a sabbatical year in London. I had no claims on my time and had planned to do nothing but work on a book on group therapy. Apparently that was not enough; I grew depressed, restless, and finally arranged to treat two patients—more for my sake than for theirs. Who was the patient and who the therapist? I was more troubled than they and, I think, benefited more than they from our work together.

For over fifteen years, I have been a healer; therapy has become a core part of my self-image; it provides me meaning, industry, pride, mastery. Thus, Ginny helped me by allowing me to help her. But I had to help her a great deal, a very great deal. I was Pygmalion, she my Galatea. I had to transform her, to succeed where others had failed, and to succeed in an astonishingly brief period of time. (Though the notes of our sessions may seem lengthy, sixty hours is a relatively short course of therapy.) The miracle worker. Yes, I own that, and the need was not silent in therapy: I pressured her relentlessly, I gave voice to my frustration when she rested or consolidated for even a few hours, I improvised continuously. "Get well," I shouted at her, "get well for your sake, not for your mother's sake or for Karl's—get well for yourself." But, very softly, I also said, "Get well for me, help me be a healer, a rescuer, a miracle worker." Did she hear me? I scarcely heard myself.

In still another more evident way the therapy was for me. I became Ginny and treated myself. She was the writer I always wanted to become. The pleasure I obtained from reading her sentences transcended sheer aesthetic appreciation. I struggled to unlock her, to unlock myself. How many times during therapy did I go back twenty-five years to my high school English class, to old frayed Miss Davis who read my compositions aloud to the class, to my embarrassing notebooks of verse, to my never-begotten Thomas Wolfe-ian novel. She took me back to a crossroad, to a path I never dared take for myself. I tried to take it through her. "If only Ginny could have been deeper," I said to myself. "Why did she have to be content with satire and parody? What I could have done with that talent!" Did she hear me?

The healer-patient, the rescuer, Pygmalion, the miracle worker, the great unrealized writer. Yes, all these. And there is more. Ginny developed a strong positive transference toward me. She overvalued my wisdom, my potency. She fell in love with me. I tried to work with that transference, to "work through" it, to resolve it in a therapeutically beneficial way. But I had to work against myself as well. I *want* to appear wise and omnipotent. It is important that attractive women fall in love with me. And so in my office we were many patients sitting in many chairs. I struggled against parts of myself, trying to ally with parts of Ginny in the conflict against other parts. I had to monitor myself continuously. How many times did I silently ask myself, "Was that for me or for Ginny?" Often I caught myself engaging or about to engage in a seduction that would do nothing but foster Ginny's exaltation of me. How many times did I elude my own watchful eye?

I became far more important to Ginny than she to me. It is so with every patient, how could it be otherwise? A patient has only one therapist, a therapist many patients. And so Ginny dreamt about me, held imaginary conversations with me during the week (just as I used to converse with my analyst, old Olive Smith—bless her staunch heart), or imagined I was there at her elbow watching her every action. And yet there is more to it. True, Ginny rarely entered my fantasy life. I did not think about her between sessions, I never dreamt about her, yet I know that I cared deeply about her. I think I did not permit myself full knowledge of my feelings and so I must awkwardly deduce these things about myself. There were many clues: my jealousy toward Karl; my disappointment when Ginny missed a session; my snug, cozy feelings when we were together ("snug" and "cozy" are just the right words—not clearly sexual but by no means ethereal). All these are self-evident, I expected and recognized them, but what was unexpected was the eruption of my feelings when my wife, editor of our notes, moved into my relationship with Ginny. Earlier I described our social meeting in California after the end of therapy. When Ginny left I was morose, diffusely irritated, and sullenly refused my wife's invitations to talk about our meeting. Though my phone conversations with Ginny were generally brief and impeccably professional, I was invariably uneasy at my wife's presence in the room. It is even possible that I invited, ambivalently, my wife into our relationship to help me with my countertransference. (I am not sure, though; my wife generally edits my work.) All these reactions become explicable if one concludes that I was in the midst of a heavily sublimated affair with Ginny.

Ginny's positive transference complicated therapy in many ways. I wrote earlier that she was in therapy in large part to be with me. To get well was to say good-bye. "And so she remained suspended in a great selfless wasteland, not so well as to lose me, not so sick as to drive me away in frustration." And I? What did I do to prevent Ginny from leaving me? Our book has insured that Ginny never will become a half-forgotten name in my old appointment book or a lost voice on an electromagnetic band. In both a real and symbolic sense we have defeated termination. Would it be going too far to say that our affair has been consummated in this shared work?

Add, then, Lothario, lover, to the list of healer-patient, rescuer, Pygmalion, unborn writer, and still there is more which I cannot or will not see. Countertransference was always present, like a gauzed veil through which I attempted to see Ginny. To the best of my ability I tugged at it,

I stared through it, I refused, as best I could, to allow it to obstruct our work. I know that I did not always succeed, nor am I convinced that the total subjugation of my irrational side, needs, and wishes would have promoted therapy; in a bewildering fashion countertransference supplied much of the energy and humanity that made our venture a successful one.

Was therapy successful? Has Ginny undergone substantial change? Or do we see "a transference cure," she having merely learned how to behave differently, how to appease and please the now-internalized Dr. Yalom? The Readers shall have to judge for themselves. I feel satisfied with our work and optimistic about Ginny's progress. There are remaining areas of conflict, yet I regard them with equanimity; I have long ago lost the sense that I as the therapist have to do it all. What is important is that Ginny is unfrozen and can take an open posture to new experiences. I have confidence in her ability to continue changing, and my view is supported by most objective measures.

She has now terminated a relationship with Karl which, with retrospective wisdom, was growth retarding for both parties; she is actively writing and, for the first time, functioning well in a responsible and challenging job (a far cry from the playground worker or the placard-carrying traffic guard); she has established a social circle and a more satisfying relationship with a new man. Gone are the night panics, the frightening dreams of disintegration, the migraines, the petrifying self-consciousness and self-effacement.

But I would have been satisfied even without these observable measures of outcome. I wince as I confess that, since I have devoted much of my professional career to a rigorous, quantifiable study of the outcome of psychotherapy. It is a paradox hard to embrace, even harder to banish. The "art" of psychotherapy has for me a dual meaning: "art" in that the execution of therapy requires the use of intuitive faculties not derivable from scientific principles and "art" in the Keatsian sense, in that it establishes its own truth transcending objective analysis. The truth is a beauty that Ginny and I experienced. We knew each other, touched each other deeply, and shared splendid moments not easily come by.

LOVE'S EXECUTIONER:
CASE HISTORIES INTO SHORT STORIES

After *The Theory and Practice of Group Psychotherapy* was published in 1970, I joined the ranks of textbook writers who find, much to their surprise, that they have enlisted for a lifetime mission. I learned that the demands on a textbook writer are severe: I kept current with the professional literature, allowing no significant group therapy article to escape my purview; I continued my own group therapy research; I kept a record of illuminating episodes from my own clinical practice; and I spent many years preparing revisions—a second, third, fourth edition.

The job description of a university professor and academician calls for staying abreast of one's field and continuing to contribute significantly to it. I knew how to do that in the area of group psychotherapy: it was a matter of continuing my clinical research and revising my group therapy textbook. But how was I to contribute to my second field of interest, existential psychotherapy? That was far more problematic for a number of reasons. (Lack of desire was never a factor: although I was very visible in the large field of group therapy, I always considered the world of existential therapy as my true home.) A major reason was that the standard activity of medical academicians—the empirical investigative study—was not available because the subject matter of an existential approach does not lend itself to empirical investigation.

Another reason was my uncertainty concerning how to write about existential therapy. Long after my text *Existential Psychotherapy* was published, I continued to search for a deeper understanding of existential ideas and for methods of applying them more effectively in my everyday therapy practice. I read widely in relevant philosophical texts. I audited philosophy and religious studies courses at Stanford. I co-taught courses with colleagues in the philosophy and English departments. I centered my clinical practice on patients who faced existential issues: life-threatening illness, bereavement, midlife crisis, separation, divorce.

I considered revising *Existential Psychotherapy* but in the end rejected that plan—there was no tradition of an evolving literature, no research to update and review. Besides, it seemed silly to update a book that purported to deal with timeless elements of the human condition.

Nor did the prospect of writing some other professional text seem attractive. More and more I had begun to feel that formal psychiatric or philosophic prose was hopelessly inadequate to describe the true existential dilemma, the human, all-too-human, flesh-and-blood, deeply subjective experience. Ever since Freud posited psychoanalysis as a science subject to the same rules of procedure and observation as the natural sciences, the field of psychiatry has struggled to fit itself into that framework. But case histories written in precise, frosty scientific language simply fail to communicate the complexity, the passion, and the pain of the emotional dilemmas facing each human being.

So I began searching in earnest for a more evocative method of communicating these sentiments. My quest rendezvoused quickly with my storytelling inclinations, and it was not long before I began experimenting with a frankly literary conveyance. Of course, I'm hardly the first to employ this method. There exists a long skein of existential thinkers who decided that the deep experience they wished to depict was better done through literature than through formal philosophical prose—think of Camus, Sartre, Unamuno, Kierkegaard, Nietzsche, Ortega y Gasset, de Beauvoir. In psychiatry there exist no similar models, aside from some of Freud's own cases and Robert Lindner's collection of tales about hypnotherapy, *The Fifty-Minute Hour,* published over forty years before.

All these considerations informed the shape and the meter of my next project, *Love's Executioner.* I had two purposes in writing *Love's Executioner:* to teach the fundamentals of a clinical existential approach and to express my literary aspirations. I decided that, in this book, I would reverse my earlier strategy of smuggling illustrative stories into the midst of theoretical material: *instead I would give the story center stage* and allow theoretical material to emanate from it.

I had an abundance of material. From the beginning of my psychiatric career I have kept a journal of illuminating therapy events—epiphanies in a Joycean sense, that is, clarifying moments of luminous insight, some event, phrase, or dream that contains a preternatural amount of information about the essence, the "whatness" or "whyness," of a state of being. I write these notes immediately after therapy sessions and have always scheduled fifteen or twenty minutes between patients (instead of the traditional five or ten) expressly for this purpose.

My first plan for *Love's Executioner* was based on the model of Lewis Thomas's *The Lives of a Cell*. That book, a thoughtful, graceful work, is a series of three- to four-page essays, each consisting of a description of an arresting biological phenomenon followed by a brief discussion of the broader implications of the phenomenon for human behavior. I hoped, then, to do something analogous for psychotherapy: I would describe a therapy event in a page or two and then, in the next few pages, explore its implications for the understanding of psychotherapy. A collection of thirty or forty of these brief expositions would constitute a book-length manuscript.

And so off I went on a year-long round-the-world sabbatical with a laptop and my notes. The first vignette involved a purse snatching that traumatized an elderly widow, Elva, and confronted her with her own or-dinariness. Although Elva had lost her husband eighteen months before, she had never really come to terms with his death. To shield herself from the full impact of her loss, she had wrapped herself in denial and dwelled in an in-between state in which she knew he was dead, but at the same time also believed in his continued existence and ability to pro-tect her from life's unpleasantness. And then came the shattering purse-snatching experience, which confronted her with the reality of both her husband's death and her own personal finiteness.

That was the essential part of the story. I wrote a three-page vignette followed by a discussion of some relevant aspects of grief; for example, how the death of the other serves, if it is not resisted, to confront one with one's own finiteness. I wrote also about the major psychological devices we employ in the service of death denial, including, in Elva's case, the be-lief in some ultimate rescuer, embodied in her husband, Albert: in life he had been a fixer, and in death, a pervasive presence watching over her, protecting her, always there to pull her back from the edge of the abyss.

When I reread the story I felt unsatisfied. Elva was a flat character and demanded more roundness, but the more I gave, the more she de-manded. Even when she seemed fully realized, the story itself seemed truncated and demanded a more complete resolution. So I stitched to it another journal vignette—an interaction with Elva that occurred a few weeks after the purse snatching. I had been bantering with her about car-rying such a large purse and suggested she would soon have to put wheels on it to carry it around. She insisted she needed everything in it. I challenged that statement and then, heads bent close together, we emptied her purse and examined every item of its contents. This process turned out to be an extraordinarily intimate act; it drew us more closely together and ultimately persuaded Elva that she had not lost her capacity for intimacy—even in a world without her husband.

The odd language I've just used—*Elva demanded more roundness . . . the story demanded . . .* —accurately reflects my experience. I had, from the start, planned that the stories should be organic: in other words, they should evolve as they were being written. Thus the story had one foot in fact, another in fiction. Was it historically correct? For example, did I accurately describe the contents of her purse? I hardly remember. What difference does it make?

Even the *selection* of stories was organic. I began the book with no preconception of which of my many vignettes I would use, nor in which order. Nor, when writing one story, did I know which I would select next. I had the remarkable writerly experience of my unconscious taking over. As I was approaching the end of one story, I would find another unaccountably wafting into my mind: it was as though I didn't choose the story—the story chose me. In fact, the process soon reversed itself in an odd manner—*the first appearance of the next story in my mind informed me that the present one was nearing its end.*

The word "organic" thus denotes that the story grew in nondetermined ways, autonomously, as if it were writing itself. But even more striking examples of literary organicity were in store for me. Again and again I created characters—partly based on patients but largely fictionalized to disguise identity—who were willful, rebellious, who took on a life of their own and would not comply with my scheme for the story.

Although these phrases—"the story demanded," "the story chose me," "the characters took on a life of their own"—may appear fanciful or precious, they describe a well-known phenomenon. E. M. Forster noted: "The characters arrive when evoked, but full of the sense of mutiny . . . they 'run away,' they 'get out of hand': they are creations within a creation and often inharmonious towards it; if they are given complete freedom they kick the book to pieces, and if they are kept too sternly in check, they revenge themselves by dying, and destroy it by intestinal decay."[1]

A story is told of the nineteenth-century novelist Thackeray, who emerged from his studio one day, weary from long hours of writing. His wife asked him how the day had gone and he replied, "Terrible. Pendennis [one of his fictional characters] made a fool of himself and there was nothing I could do to stop him."

Although Elva was resistive, I managed, nonetheless, to close her story ("I Never Thought It Would Happen to Me") in eight pages (rather than the three or four I had originally planned). But with each succeeding story, closure became more difficult. Soon I was forced to jettison the idea of writing thirty or forty short pieces: each story demanded more and more space. Ten stories added up to a book-length manuscript.

It was also part of my original plan to write a theoretical afterword to each story in *Love's Executioner*. But each afterword I wrote seemed stilted and unnecessary. I kept two of the afterwords and eliminated the other eight—these I would incorporate into a lengthy theoretical foreword to the book.

But the publisher vehemently disagreed. Phoebe Hoss, my long-term editor at Basic Books, insisted that the stories were sufficient and that less was more. We had a lengthy battle: each time I sent a prologue she, with remarkable consistency, red-penciled out 70 to 80 percent of it. Ultimately I understood that I could not give just lip service to the idea that literature could convey powerful, otherwise inexpressible, thoughts: I had to pack all I wanted to say within the narrative and save nothing for a separate pedagogical overview. Eventually *Love's Executioner* was published with an eight-page prologue and no afterword. It took me fourteen months to write the three hundred pages of my ten stories; I struggled over the ten-page prologue for *four months*. But it was a watershed personal struggle that permitted me to abandon the didactic mode and let the story speak for itself.

In the following pages, the prologue and the second story, "If Rape Were Legal . . . ," are reproduced.

Love's Executioner: The Prologue

Imagine this scene: three to four hundred people, strangers to one another, are told to pair up and ask their partner one single question, "What do you want?" over and over and over again.

Could anything be simpler? One innocent question and its answer. And yet, time after time, I have seen this group exercise evoke unexpectedly powerful feelings. Often, within minutes, the room rocks with emotion. Men and women—and these are by no means desperate or needy, but successful, well-functioning, well-dressed people who glitter as they walk—are stirred to their depths. They call out to those who are forever lost—dead or absent parents, spouses, children, friends: "I want to see you again." "I want your love." "I want to know you're proud of me." "I want you to know I love you and how sorry I am I never told you." "I want you back—I am so lonely." "I want the childhood I never had." "I want to be healthy—to be young again. I want to be loved, to be respected. I want my life to mean something. I want to accomplish something. I want to matter, to be important, to be remembered."

So much wanting. So much longing. And so much pain, so close to the surface, only minutes deep. Destiny pain. Existence pain. Pain that is always there, whirring continuously just beneath the membrane of life. Pain that is all too easily accessible. Many things—a simple group exercise, a few minutes of deep reflection, a work of art, a sermon, a personal crisis, a loss—remind us that our deepest wants can never be fulfilled: our wants for youth, for a halt to aging, for the return of vanished ones, for eternal love, protection, significance, for immortality itself.

It is when these unattainable wants come to dominate our lives that we turn for help to family, to friends, to religion—sometimes to psychotherapists.

In this book I tell the stories of ten patients who turned to therapy, and in the course of their work struggled with existence pain. This was not the reason they came to me for help; on the contrary, all ten were suffering the common problems of everyday life: loneliness, self-contempt, impotence, migraine headaches, sexual compulsivity, obesity, hypertension, grief, a consuming love obsession, mood swings, depression. Yet somehow (a "somehow" that unfolds differently in each story), therapy uncovered deep roots of these everyday problems—roots stretching down to the bedrock of existence.

"I want! I want!" is heard throughout these tales. One patient cried, "I want my dead darling daughter back," as she neglected her two living sons. Another insisted, "I want to fuck every woman I see," as his lymphatic cancer invaded the crawlspaces of his body. And another pleaded, "I want the parents, the childhood I never had," as he agonized over three letters he could not bring himself to open. And another declared, "I want to be young forever," as she, an old woman, could not relinquish her obsessive love for a man thirty-five years younger.

I believe that the primal stuff of psychotherapy is always such existence pain—and not, as is often claimed, repressed instinctual strivings or imperfectly buried shards of a tragic personal past. In my therapy with each of these ten patients, my primary clinical assumption—an assumption on which I based my technique—is that basic anxiety emerges from a person's endeavors, conscious and unconscious, to cope with the harsh facts of life, the "givens" of existence.

I have found that four givens are particularly relevant to psychotherapy: the inevitability of death for each of us and for those we love; the freedom to make our lives as we will; our ultimate aloneness; and, finally, the absence of any obvious meaning or sense to life. However grim these givens may seem, they contain the seeds of wisdom and redemption. I hope to demonstrate, in these ten tales of psychotherapy, that it is possible to confront the truths of existence and harness their power in the service of personal change and growth.

Of these facts of life, death is the most obvious, most intuitively apparent. At an early age, far earlier than is often thought, we learn that death will come, and that from it there is no escape. Nonetheless, "everything," in Spinoza's words, "endeavors to persist in its own being." At one's core there is an ever-present conflict between the wish to continue to exist and the awareness of inevitable death.

To adapt to the reality of death, we are endlessly ingenious in devising ways to deny or escape it. When we are young, we deny death with the help of parental reassurances and secular and religious myths; later, we personify it by transforming it into an entity, a monster, a sandman, a demon. After all, if death is some pursuing entity, then one may yet find a way to elude it; besides, frightening as a death-bearing monster may be, it is less frightening than the truth—that one carries within the spores of one's own death. Later, children experiment with other ways to attenuate death anxiety: they detoxify death by taunting it, challenge it through daredevilry, or desensitize it by exposing themselves, in the reassuring company of peers and warm buttered popcorn, to ghost stories and horror films.

As we grow older, we learn to put death out of mind; we distract ourselves; we transform it into something positive (passing on, going home, rejoining God, peace at last); we deny it with sustaining myths; we strive for immortality through imperishable works, by projecting our seed into the future through our children, or by embracing a religious system that offers spiritual perpetuation.

Many people take issue with this description of death denial. "Nonsense!" they say. "We don't deny death. Everyone's going to die. We know that. The facts are obvious. But is there any point to dwelling on it?"

The truth is that we know but do not know. We know *about* death, intellectually we know the facts, but we—that is, the unconscious portion of the mind that protects us from overwhelming anxiety—have split off, or dissociated, the terror associated with death. This dissociative process is unconscious, invisible to us, but we can be convinced of its existence in those rare episodes when the machinery of denial fails and death anxiety breaks through in full force. That may happen only rarely, sometimes only once or twice in a lifetime. Occasionally it happens during waking life, sometimes after a personal brush with death, or when a loved one has died; but more commonly death anxiety surfaces in nightmares.

A nightmare is a failed dream, a dream that, by not "handling" anxiety, has failed in its role as the guardian of sleep. Though nightmares differ in manifest content, the underlying process of every nightmare is the same: raw death anxiety has escaped its keepers and exploded into consciousness. The story "In Search of the Dreamer" offers a unique backstage view of the escape of death anxiety and the mind's last-ditch attempt to contain it: here, amidst the pervasive, dark death imagery of Marvin's nightmare, is one life-promoting, death-defying instrument— the glowing white-tipped cane with which the dreamer engages in a sexual duel with death.

The sexual act is seen also by the protagonists of other stories as a talisman to ward off diminishment, aging, and approaching death: thus, the compulsive promiscuity of a young man in the face of his killing cancer ("If Rape Were Legal . . . "); and an old man's clinging to yellowing thirty-year-old letters from his dead lover ("Do Not Go Gentle").

In my many years of work with cancer patients facing imminent death, I have noted two particularly powerful and common methods of allaying fears about death, two beliefs, or delusions, that afford a sense of safety. One is the belief in personal specialness; the other, the belief in an ultimate rescuer. While these are delusions in that they represent "fixed false beliefs," I do not employ the term *delusion* in a pejorative sense: these are universal beliefs which, at some level of consciousness, exist in all of us and play a role in several of these tales.

Specialness is the belief that one is invulnerable, inviolable—beyond the ordinary laws of human biology and destiny. At some point in life, each of us will face some crisis: it may be serious illness, career failure, or divorce; or as happened to Elva in "I Never Thought It Would Happen to Me," it may be an event as simple as a purse snatching, which suddenly lays bare one's ordinariness and challenges the common assumption that life will always be an eternal upward spiral.

While the belief in personal specialness provides a sense of safety from within, the other major mechanism of death denial—*belief in an ultimate rescuer*—permits us to feel forever watched and protected by an outside force. Though we may falter, grow ill, though we may arrive at the very edge of life, there is, we are convinced, a looming, omnipotent servant who will always bring us back.

Together these two belief systems constitute a dialectic—two diametrically opposed responses to the human situation. The human being either asserts autonomy by heroic self-assertion or seeks safety through fusing with a superior force: that is, one either emerges or merges, separates or embeds. One becomes one's own parent or remains the eternal child.

Most of us, most of the time, live comfortably by uneasily avoiding the glance of death, by chuckling and agreeing with Woody Allen when he says, "I'm not afraid of death. I just don't want to be there when it happens." But there is another way—a long tradition, applicable to psychotherapy—that teaches us that full awareness of death ripens our wisdom and enriches our life. The dying words of one of my patients (in "If Rape Were Legal . . . ") demonstrate that though the *fact*, the physicality, of death destroys us, the *idea* of death may save us.

Freedom, another given of existence, presents a dilemma for several of these ten patients. When Betty, an obese patient, announced that she had binged just before coming to see me and was planning to binge again as soon as she left my office, she was attempting to give up her freedom by persuading me to assume control of her. The entire course of therapy of another patient (Thelma in "Love's Executioner") revolved around the theme of surrender to a former lover (and therapist) and my search for strategies to help her reclaim her power and freedom.

Freedom as a given seems the very antithesis of death. While we dread death, we generally consider freedom to be unequivocally positive. Has not the history of Western civilization been punctuated with yearnings for freedom, even driven by it? Yet freedom from an existential perspective is bonded to anxiety in asserting that, contrary to everyday experience, we do not enter into, and ultimately leave, a well-structured universe with an eternal grand design. Freedom means that one is responsible for one's own choices, actions, one's own life situation.

Though the word *responsible* may be used in a variety of ways, I prefer Sartre's definition: to be responsible is to "be the author of," each of us being thus the author of his or her own life design. We are free to be anything but unfree: we are, Sartre would say, condemned to freedom. Indeed, some philosophers claim much more: that the architecture of the human mind makes each of us even responsible for the structure of external reality, for the very form of space and time. It is here, in the idea of self-construction, where anxiety dwells: we are creatures who desire structure, and we are frightened by a concept of freedom which implies that beneath us there is nothing, sheer groundlessness.

Every therapist knows that the crucial first step in therapy is the patient's assumption of responsibility for his or her life predicament. As long as one believes that one's problems are caused by some force or agency outside oneself, there is no leverage in therapy. If, after all, the problem lies out there, then why should one change oneself? It is the outside world (friends, job, spouse) that must be changed—or exchanged. Thus, Dave (in "Do Not Go Gentle"), complaining bitterly of being locked in a marital prison by a snoopy, possessive wife—warden, could not proceed in therapy until he recognized how he himself was responsible for the construction of that prison.

Since patients tend to resist assuming responsibility, therapists must develop techniques to make patients aware of how they themselves create their own problems. A powerful technique, which I use in many of these cases, is the here-and-now focus. Since patients tend to re-create *in the therapy setting* the same interpersonal problems that bedevil them in their lives outside, I focus on what is going on at the moment between a patient and me rather than on the events of his or her past or current life. By examining the details of the therapy relationship (or, in a therapy group, the relationships among the group members), I can point out on the spot how a patient influences the responses of other people. Thus, though Dave could resist assuming responsibility for his marital problems, he could not resist the immediate data he himself was generating in group therapy: that is, his secretive, teasing, and elusive behavior was activating the other group members to respond to him much as his wife did at home.

In similar fashion, Betty's ("Fat Lady") therapy was ineffective as long as she could attribute her loneliness to the flaky, rootless California culture. It was only when I demonstrated how, in our hours together, her impersonal, shy, distancing manner re-created the same impersonal environment in therapy that she could begin to explore her responsibility for creating her own isolation.

While the assumption of responsibility brings the patient into the vestibule of change, it is not synonymous with change. And it is change that is always the true quarry, however much a therapist may court insight, responsibility assumption, and self-actualization.

Freedom not only requires us to bear responsibility for our life choices but also posits that change requires an act of will. Though *will* is a concept therapists seldom use explicitly, we nonetheless devote much effort to influencing a patient's will. We endlessly clarify and interpret, assuming (and it is a secular leap of faith, lacking convincing empirical support) that understanding will invariably beget change. When years of interpretation have failed to generate change, we may begin to make direct appeals to the will: "Effort, too, is needed. You have to try, you know. There's a time for thinking and analyzing but there's also a time for action." And when direct exhortation fails, the therapist is reduced, as these stories bear witness, to employing any known means by which one person can influence another. Thus, I may advise, argue, badger, cajole, goad, implore, or simply endure, hoping that the patient's neurotic worldview will crumble away from sheer fatigue.

It is through willing, the mainspring of action, that our freedom is enacted. I see willing as having two stages: a person initiates through wishing and then enacts through deciding.

Some people are wish-blocked, knowing neither what they feel nor what they want. Without opinions, without impulses, without inclinations, they become parasites on the desires of others. Such people tend to be tiresome. Betty was boring precisely because she stifled her wishes, and others grew weary of supplying wish and imagination for her.

Other patients cannot decide. Though they know exactly what they want and what they must do, they cannot act and, instead, pace tormentedly before the door of decision. Saul, in "Three Unopened Letters," knew that any reasonable man would open the letters; yet the fear they invoked paralyzed his will. Thelma ("Love's Executioner") knew that her love obsession was stripping her life of reality. She *knew* that she was, as she put it, living her life eight years ago; and that, to regain it, she would have to give up her infatuation. But that she could not, or would not, do, and she fiercely resisted all my attempts to energize her will.

Decisions are difficult for many reasons, some reaching down into the very socket of being. John Gardner, in his novel *Grendel,* tells of a wise man who sums up his meditations on life's mysteries in two simple but terrible postulates: "Things fade: alternatives exclude." Of the first postulate, death, I have already spoken. The second, "alternatives exclude," is an important key to understanding why decision is difficult. Decision invariably involves renunciation: for every yes there must be a no, each decision eliminating or killing other options (the root of the word *decide* means "slay," as in *homicide* or *suicide*). Thus, Thelma clung to the infinitesimal chance that she might once again revive her relationship with her lover, renunciation of that possibility signifying diminishment and death.

Existential isolation, a third given, refers to the unbridgeable gap between self and others, a gap that exists even in the presence of deeply gratifying interpersonal relationships. One is isolated not only from other beings but, to the extent that one constitutes one's world, from the world as well. Such isolation is to be distinguished from two other types of isolation: interpersonal and intrapersonal isolation.

One experiences *interpersonal* isolation, or loneliness, if one lacks the social skills or personality style that permits intimate social interactions. *Intrapersonal* isolation occurs when parts of the self are split off, as when one splits off emotion from the memory of an event. The most extreme, and dramatic, form of splitting, the multiple personality, is relatively rare (though growing more widely recognized); when it does occur, the therapist may be faced, as was I in the treatment of Marge ("Therapeutic Monogamy"), with the bewildering dilemma of which personality to cherish.

While there is no solution to existential isolation, therapists must discourage false solutions. One's efforts to escape isolation can sabotage one's relationships with other people. Many a friendship or marriage has failed because, instead of relating to, and caring for, each other, one person uses another as a shield against isolation.

A common, and vigorous, attempt to solve existential isolation, which occurs in several of these stories, is fusion—the softening of one's boundaries, the melting into another. The power of fusion has been demonstrated in subliminal perception experiments in which the message "Mommy and I are one," flashed on a screen so quickly that the subjects cannot consciously see it, results in their reporting that they feel better, stronger, more optimistic—and even in their responding better than other people to treatment (with behavioral modification) for such problems as smoking, obesity, or disturbed adolescent behavior.

One of the great paradoxes of life is that self-awareness breeds anxiety. Fusion eradicates anxiety in a radical fashion—by eliminating self-awareness. The person who has fallen in love, and entered a blissful state of merger, is not self-reflective because the questioning lonely *I* (and the attendant anxiety of isolation) dissolve into the *we*. Thus one sheds anxiety but loses oneself.

This is precisely why therapists do not like to treat a patient who has fallen in love. Therapy and a state of love-merger are incompatible because therapeutic work requires a questioning self-awareness and an anxiety that will ultimately serve as guide to internal conflicts.

Furthermore, it is difficult for me, as for most therapists, to form a relationship with a patient who has fallen in love. In the story "Love's Executioner," Thelma would not, for example, relate to me: her energy was completely consumed in her love obsession. Beware the powerful exclusive attachment to another; it is not, as people sometimes think, evidence of the purity of the love. Such encapsulated, exclusive love—feeding on itself, neither giving to nor caring about others—is destined to cave in on itself. Love is not just a passion spark between two people; there is infinite difference between falling in love and standing in love. Rather, love is a way of being, a "giving to," not a "falling for"; a mode of relating at large, not an act limited to a single person.

Though we try hard to go through life two by two or in groups, there are times, especially when death approaches, that the truth—that we are born alone and must die alone—breaks through with chilling clarity. I have heard many dying patients remark that the most awful thing about dying is that it must be done alone. Yet, even at the point of death, the willingness of another to be fully present may penetrate the isolation. As a patient said in "Do Not Go Gentle," "Even though you're alone in your boat, it's always comforting to see the lights of the other boats bobbing nearby."

Now, if death is inevitable, if all of our accomplishments, indeed our entire solar system, shall one day lie in ruins, if the world is contingent (that is, if everything could as well have been otherwise), if human beings must construct the world and the human design within that world, then what enduring meaning can there be in life?

This question plagues contemporary men and women, and many seek therapy because they feel their lives to be senseless and aimless. We are meaning-seeking creatures. Biologically, our nervous systems are organized in such a way that the brain automatically clusters incoming stimuli into configurations. Meaning also provides a sense of mastery: feeling helpless and confused in the face of random, unpatterned events, we seek to order them and, in so doing, gain a sense of control over them. Even more important, meaning gives birth to values and, hence, to a code of behavior: thus the answer to *why* questions (Why do I live?) supplies an answer to *how* questions (How do I live?).

There are, in these ten tales of psychotherapy, few explicit discussions of meaning in life. The search for meaning, much like the search for pleasure, must be conducted obliquely. Meaning ensues from meaningful activity: the more we deliberately pursue it, the less likely are we to find it; the rational questions one can pose about meaning will always outlast the answers. In therapy, as in life, meaningfulness is a by-product of engagement and commitment, and that is where therapists must direct their efforts—not that engagement provides the rational answer to questions of meaning, but it makes these questions not matter.

This existential dilemma—a being who searches for meaning and certainty in a universe that has neither—has tremendous relevance for the profession of psychotherapist. In their everyday work, therapists, if they are to relate to their patients in an authentic fashion, experience considerable uncertainty. Not only does a patient's confrontation with unanswerable questions expose a therapist to these same questions, but also the therapist must recognize, as I had to in "Two Smiles," that the experience of the other is, in the end, unyieldingly private and un-knowable.

Indeed, the capacity to tolerate uncertainty is a prerequisite for the profession. Though the public may believe that therapists guide patients systematically and sure-handedly through predictable stages of therapy to a foreknown goal, such is rarely the case: instead, as these stories bear witness, therapists frequently wobble, improvise, and grope for direc-tion. The powerful temptation to achieve certainty through embracing an ideological school and a tight therapeutic system is treacherous: such belief may block the uncertain and spontaneous encounter necessary for effective therapy.

This encounter, the very heart of psychotherapy, is a caring, deeply human meeting between two people, one (generally, but not always, the patient) more troubled than the other. Therapists have a dual role: they must both observe and participate in the lives of their patients. As ob-server, one must be sufficiently objective to provide necessary rudimen-tary guidance to the patient. As participant, one enters into the life of the patient and is affected and sometimes changed by the encounter.

In choosing to enter fully into each patient's life, I, the therapist, not only am exposed to the same existential issues as are my patients but must be prepared to examine them with the same rules of inquiry. I must assume that knowing is better than not knowing, venturing than not venturing; and that magic and illusion, however rich, however alluring, ultimately weaken the human spirit. I take with deep seriousness Thomas Hardy's staunch words "If a way to the Better there be, it exacts a full look at the Worst."

The dual role of observer and participant demands much of a therapist and, for me in these ten cases, posed harrowing questions. Should I, for example, expect a patient, who asked me to be the keeper of his love letters, to deal with the very problems that I, in my own life, have avoided? Was it possible to help him go further than I have gone? Should I ask harsh existential questions of a dying man, a widow, a bereaved mother, and an anxious retiree with transcendent dreams— questions for which I have no answers? Should I reveal my weakness and my limitations to a patient whose other, alternative personality I found so seductive? Could I possibly form an honest and caring relationship with a fat lady whose physical appearance repelled me? Should I, under the banner of self-enlightenment, strip away an old woman's irrational but sustaining and comforting love illusion? Or forcibly impose my will on a man who, incapable of acting in his best interests, allowed himself to be terrorized by three unopened letters?

Though these tales of psychotherapy abound with the words *patient* and *therapist,* do not be misled by such terms: these are everyman, everywoman stories. Patienthood is ubiquitous; the assumption of the label is largely arbitrary and often dependent more on cultural, educational, and economic factors than on the severity of pathology. Since therapists, no less than patients, must confront these givens of existence, the professional posture of disinterested objectivity, so necessary to scientific method, is inappropriate. We psychotherapists simply cannot cluck with sympathy and exhort patients to struggle resolutely with their problems. We cannot say to them *you* and *your* problems. Instead, we must speak of *us* and *our* problems, because our life, our existence, will always be riveted to death, love to loss, freedom to fear, and growth to separation. We are, all of us, in this together.

"If Rape Were Legal . . . "

"Your patient is a dumb shit and I told him so in the group last night— in just those words." Sarah, a young psychiatric resident, paused here and glared, daring me to criticize her.

Obviously something extraordinary had occurred. Not every day does a student charge into my office and, with no trace of chagrin—indeed, she seemed proud and defiant—tell me she has verbally assaulted one of my patients. Especially a patient with advanced cancer.

"Sarah, would you sit down and tell me about it? I've got a few minutes before my next patient arrives."

Struggling to keep her composure, Sarah began, "Carlos is the grossest, most despicable human being I have ever met!"

"Well, you know, he's not my favorite person either. I told you that before I referred him to you." I had been seeing Carlos in individual treatment for about six months and, a few weeks ago, referred him to Sarah for inclusion in her therapy group. "But go on. Sorry for stopping you."

"Well, as you know, he's been generally obnoxious—sniffing the women as though he were a dog and they bitches in heat, and ignoring everything else that goes on in the group. Last night, Martha—she's a really fragile borderline young woman, who has been almost mute in the group—started to talk about having been raped last year. I don't think she's ever shared that before—certainly not with a group. She was so scared, sobbing so hard, having so much trouble saying it, that it was incredibly painful. Everyone was trying to help her talk and, rightly or wrongly, I decided it would help Martha if I shared with the group that I had been raped three years ago."

"I didn't know that, Sarah."

"No one else has known either!"

Sarah stopped here and dabbed her eyes. I could see it was hard for her to tell me this—but at this point I couldn't be sure what hurt worse: telling me about her rape, or how she had excessively revealed herself to her group. (That I was the group therapy instructor in the program must have complicated things for her.) Or was she most upset by what she had still to tell me? I decided to remain matter-of-fact about it.

"And then?"

"Well, that's when your Carlos went into action."

My Carlos? Ridiculous! I thought. As though he's my child and I have to answer for him. (Yet it was true that I had urged Sarah to take him on: she had been reluctant to introduce a patient with cancer into her group. But it was also true that her group was down to five, and she needed new members.) I had never seen her so irrational—and so challenging. I was afraid she'd be very embarrassed about this later, and I didn't want to make it worse by any hint of criticism.

"What did he do?"

"He asked Martha a lot of factual questions—when, where, what, who. At first that helped her talk, but as soon as I talked about my attack, he ignored Martha and started doing the same thing with me. Then he began asking us both for more intimate details. Did the rapist tear our clothing? Did he ejaculate inside of us? Was there any moment when we began to enjoy it? This all happened so insidiously that there was a time lag before the group began to catch on that he was getting off on it. He didn't give a damn about Martha and me, he was just getting his sexual kicks. I know I should feel more compassion for him—but he is such a creep!"

"How did it end up?"

"Well, the group finally wised up and began to confront him with his insensitivity, but he showed no remorse whatsoever. In fact, he became more offensive and accused Martha and me (and all rape victims) of making too much of it. 'What's the big deal?' he asked, and then claimed he personally wouldn't mind being raped by an attractive woman. His parting shot to the group was to say that he would welcome a rape attempt by any woman in the group. That's when I said, 'If you believe that, you're fucking ignorant!'"

"I thought your therapy intervention was calling him a dumb shit?" That reduced Sarah's tension, and we both smiled.

"That, too! I really lost my cool."

I stretched for supportive and constructive words, but they came out more pedantic than I'd intended. "Remember, Sarah, often extreme situations like this can end up being important turning points *if* they're worked through carefully. Everything that happens is grist for the mill in therapy. Let's try to turn this into a learning experience for him. I'm meeting with him tomorrow, and I'll work on it hard. But I want you to be sure to take care of yourself. I'm available if you want someone to talk to—later today or anytime this week."

Sarah thanked me and said she needed time to think about it. As she left my office, I thought that even if she decided to talk about her own issues with someone else, I would still try to meet with her later when she settled down to see if we could make this a learning experience for *her* as well. That was a hell of a thing for her to have gone through, and I felt for her, but it seemed to me that she had erred by trying to bootleg therapy for herself in the group. Better, I thought, for her to have worked on this first in her personal therapy and then, even if she still chose to talk about it in the group—and that was problematic—she would have handled it better for all parties concerned.

Then my next patient entered, and I turned my attention to her. But I could not prevent myself from thinking about Carlos and wondering how I should handle the next hour with him. It was not unusual for him to stray into my mind. He was an extraordinary patient; and ever since I had started seeing him a few months earlier, I thought about him far more than the one or two hours a week I spent in his presence.

"Carlos is a cat with nine lives, but now it looks as if he's coming to the end of his ninth life." That was the first thing said to me by the oncologist who had referred him for psychiatric treatment. He went on to explain that Carlos had a rare, slow-growing lymphoma which caused problems more because of its sheer bulk than its malignancy. For ten years the tumor had responded well to treatment but now had invaded his lungs and was encroaching upon his heart. His doctors were running out of options: they had given him maximum radiation exposure and had exhausted their pharmacopeia of chemotherapy agents. How honest should they be? they asked me. Carlos didn't seem to listen. They weren't certain how honest he was willing to be with himself. They did know that he was growing deeply depressed and seemed to have no one to whom he could turn for support.

Carlos was indeed isolated. Aside from a seventeen-year-old son and daughter—dizygotic twins, who lived with his ex-wife in South America—Carlos, at the age of thirty-nine, found himself virtually alone in the world. He had grown up, an only child, in Argentina. His mother had died in childbirth, and twenty years ago his father succumbed to the same type of lymphoma now killing Carlos. He had never had a male friend. "Who needs them?" he once said to me. "I've never met anyone who wouldn't cut you dead for a dollar, a job, or a cunt." He had been married only briefly and had had no other significant relationships with women. "You have to be crazy to fuck any woman more than once!" His aim in life, he told me without a trace of shame or self-consciousness, was to screw as many different women as he could.

No, at my first meeting I could find little endearing about Carlos's character—or about his physical appearance. He was emaciated, knobby (with swollen, highly visible lymph nodes at elbows, neck, behind his ears) and, as a result of the chemotherapy, entirely hairless. His pathetic cosmetic efforts—a wide-brimmed Panama hat, painted-on eyebrows, and a scarf to conceal the swellings in his neck—succeeded only in calling additional unwanted attention to his appearance.

He was obviously depressed—with good reason—and spoke bitterly and wearily of his ten-year ordeal with cancer. His lymphoma, he said, was killing him in stages. It had already killed most of him—his energy, his strength, and his freedom (he had to live near Stanford Hospital, in permanent exile from his own culture).

Most important, it had killed his social life, by which he meant his sexual life: when he was on chemotherapy, he was impotent; when he finished a course of chemotherapy, and his sexual juices started to flow, he could not make it with a woman because of his baldness. Even when his hair grew back, a few weeks after chemotherapy, he said he still couldn't score: no prostitute would have him because they thought his enlarged lymph nodes signified AIDS. His sex life now was confined entirely to masturbating while watching rented sadomasochistic videotapes.

It was true—he said, only when I prompted him—that he was isolated and, yes, that did constitute a problem, but only because there were times when he was too weak to care for his own physical needs. The idea of pleasure deriving from close human (nonsexual) contact seemed alien to him. There was one exception—his children—and when Carlos spoke of them real emotion, emotion that I could join with, broke through. I was moved by the sight of his frail body heaving with sobs as he described his fear that they, too, would abandon him: that their mother would finally succeed in poisoning them against him, or that they would become repelled by his cancer and turn away from him.

"What can I do to help, Carlos?"

"If you want to help me—then teach me how to hate armadillos!"

For a moment Carlos enjoyed my perplexity, and then proceeded to explain that he had been working with visual imaging—a form of self-healing many cancer patients attempt. His visual metaphors for his new chemotherapy (referred to by his oncologists as BP) were giant *B*'s and *P*'s—Bears and Pigs; his metaphor for his hard cancerous lymph nodes was a bony-plated armadillo. Thus, in his meditation sessions, he visualized bears and pigs attacking the armadillos. The problem was that he couldn't make his bears and pigs be vicious enough to tear open and destroy the armadillos.

Despite the horror of his cancer and his narrowness of spirit, I was drawn to Carlos. Perhaps it was generosity welling out of my relief that it was he, and not I, who was dying. Perhaps it was his love for his children or the plaintive way he grasped my hand with both of his when he was leaving my office. Perhaps it was the whimsy in his request: "Teach me how to hate armadillos."

Therefore, as I considered whether I could treat him, I minimized potential obstacles to treatment and persuaded myself that he was more *un*socialized than malignantly antisocial, and that many of his noxious traits and beliefs were soft and open to being modified. I did not think through my decision clearly and, even after I decided to accept him in therapy, remained unsure about appropriate and realistic treatment goals. Was I simply to escort him through this course of chemotherapy? (Like many patients, Carlos became deathly ill and despondent during chemotherapy.) Or, if he were entering a terminal phase, was I to commit myself to stay with him until death? Was I to be satisfied with offering sheer presence and support? (Maybe that would be sufficient. God knows he had no one else to talk to!) Of course, his isolation was his own doing, but was I going to help him to recognize or to change that? Now? In the face of death, these considerations seemed immaterial. Or did they? Was it possible that Carlos could accomplish something more "ambitious" in therapy! No, no, no! *What sense does it make to talk about "ambitious" treatment with someone whose anticipated life span may be, at best, a matter of months?* Does anyone, do I, want to invest time and energy in a project of such evanescence?

Carlos readily agreed to meet with me. In his typical cynical mode, he said that his insurance policy would pay ninety percent of my fee, and that he wouldn't turn down a bargain like that. Besides, he was a person who wanted to try everything once, and he had never before spoken to a psychiatrist. I left our treatment contract unclear, aside from saying that having someone with whom to share painful feelings and thoughts always helped. I suggested that we meet six times and then evaluate whether treatment seemed worthwhile.

To my great surprise, Carlos made excellent use of therapy; and after six sessions, we agreed to meet in ongoing treatment. He came to every hour with a list of issues he wanted to discuss—dreams, work problems (a successful financial analyst, he had continued to work throughout his illness). Sometimes he talked about his physical discomfort and his loathing of chemotherapy, but most of all he talked about women and sex. Each session he described all of his encounters with women that week (often they consisted of nothing more than catching a woman's eye in the grocery store) and obsessing about what he might have done in each instance to have consummated a relationship. He was so preoccupied with women that he seemed to forget that he had a cancer that was actively infiltrating all the crawlspaces of his body. Most likely that was the point of his preoccupation—that he might forget his infestation.

But his fixation on women had long predated his cancer. He had always prowled for women and regarded them in highly sexualized and demeaning terms. So Sarah's account of Carlos in the group, shocking as it was, did not astonish me. I knew he was entirely capable of such gross behavior—and worse.

But how should I handle the situation with him in the next hour? Above all, I wished to protect and maintain our relationship. We were making progress, and right now I was his primary human connection. But it was also important that he continue attending his therapy group. I had placed him in a group six weeks ago to provide him with a community that would both help to penetrate his isolation and also, by identifying and urging him to alter some of his most socially objectionable behavior, help him to create connections in his social life. For the first five weeks, he had made excellent use of the group but, unless he changed his behavior dramatically, he would, I was certain, irreversibly alienate all the group members—if he hadn't done so already!

Our next session started uneventfully. Carlos didn't even mention the group but, instead, wanted to talk about Ruth, an attractive woman he had just met at a church social. (He was a member of a half dozen churches because he believed they provided him with ideal pickup opportunities.) He had talked briefly to Ruth, who then excused herself because she had to go home. Carlos said good-bye but later grew convinced that he had missed a golden opportunity by not offering to escort her to her car; in fact, he had persuaded himself that there was a fair chance, perhaps a ten to fifteen percent chance, he might have married her. His self-recriminations for not having acted with greater dispatch continued all week and included verbal self-assaults and physical abuse—pinching himself and pounding his head against the wall.

I didn't pursue his feelings about Ruth (although they were so patently irrational that I decided to return to her at some point) because I thought it was urgent that we discuss the group. I told him that I had spoken to Sarah about the meeting. "Were you," I asked, "going to talk about the group today?"

"Not particularly, it's not important. Anyway, I'm going to stop that group. I'm too advanced for it."

"What do you mean?"

"Everyone is dishonest and playing games there. I'm the only person there with enough guts to tell the truth. The men are all losers—they wouldn't be there otherwise. They're jerks with no *cojones*, they sit around whimpering and saying nothing."

"Tell me what happened in the meeting from your perspective."

"Sarah talked about her rape, she tell you that?"

I nodded.

"And Martha did, too. That Martha. God, that's one for you. She's a mess, a real sickie, she is. She's a mental case, on tranquilizers. What the hell am I doing in a group with people like her anyway? But listen to me. The important point is that they talked about their rapes, both of them, and everyone just sat there silently with their mouths hanging open. At least I responded. I asked them questions."

"Sarah suggested that some of your questions were not of the helpful variety."

"Someone had to get them talking. Besides, I've always been curious about rape. Aren't you? Aren't all men? About how it's done, about the rape victim's experience?"

"Oh, come on, Carlos, if that's what you were after, you could have read about it in a book. These were real people there—not sources of information. There was something else going on."

"Maybe so, I'll admit that. When I started the group, your instructions were that I should be honest in expressing my feelings in the group. Believe me, I swear it, in the last meeting I was the only honest person in the group. I got turned on, I admit it. It's a fantastic turn-on to think of Sarah getting screwed. I'd love to join in and get my hands on those boobs of hers. I haven't forgiven you for preventing me from dating her." When he had first started the group six weeks ago, he talked at great length about his infatuation with Sarah—or rather with her breasts—and was convinced she would be willing to go out with him. To help Carlos become assimilated in the group, I had, in the first few meetings, coached him on appropriate social behavior. I had persuaded him, with difficulty, that a sexual approach to Sarah would be both futile and unseemly.

"Besides, it's no secret that men get turned on by rape. I saw the other men in the group smiling at me. Look at the porno business! Have you ever taken a good look at the books and videotapes about rape or bondage? Do it! Go visit the porno shops in the Tenderloin—it'd be good for your education. They're printing those things for somebody—there's gotta be a market out there. I'll tell you the truth, *if rape were legal, I'd do it*—once in a while."

Carlos stopped there and gave me a smug grin—or was it a poke-in-the-arm leer, an invitation to take my place beside him in the brotherhood of rapists?

I sat silently for several minutes trying to identify my options. It was easy to agree with Sarah: he *did* sound depraved. Yet I was convinced part of it was bluster, and that there was a way to reach something better, something higher in him. I was interested in, grateful for, his last few words: the "once in a while." Those words, added almost as an afterthought, seemed to suggest some scrap of self-consciousness or shame.

"Carlos, you take pride in your honesty in the group—but were you really being honest? Or only part honest, or easy honest? It's true, you were more open than the other men in the group. You did express some of your real sexual feelings. And you do have a point about how widespread these feelings are: the porno business must be offering something which appeals to impulses all men have.

"But are you being completely honest? What about all the other feelings going on inside you that you *haven't* expressed? Let me take a guess about something: when you said 'big deal' to Sarah and Martha about their rapes, is it possible you were thinking about your cancer and what you have to face all the time? It's a hell of a lot tougher facing something that threatens your life *right now* than something that happened a year or two ago.

"Maybe you'd like to get some caring from the group, but how can you get it when you come on so tough? You haven't yet talked about having cancer." (I had been urging Carlos to reveal to the group that he had cancer, but he was procrastinating: he said he was afraid he'd be pitied, and didn't want to sabotage his sexual chances with the women members.)

Carlos grinned at me. "Good try, Doc! It makes a lot of sense. You've got a good head. But I'll be honest—the thought of my cancer never entered my mind. Since we stopped chemotherapy two months ago, I go days at a time without thinking of the cancer. That's goddamn good, isn't it—to forget it, to be free of it, to be able to live a normal life for a while?"

Good question! I thought. Was it good to forget? I wasn't so sure. Over the months I had been seeing Carlos, I had discovered that I could chart, with astonishing accuracy, the course of his cancer by noting the things he thought about. Whenever his cancer worsened and he was actively facing death, he rearranged his life priorities and became more thoughtful, compassionate, wiser. When, on the other hand, he was in remission, he was guided, as he put it, by his pecker and grew noticeably more coarse and shallow.

I once saw a newspaper cartoon of a pudgy lost little man saying, "Suddenly, one day in your forties or fifties, everything becomes clear. . . . And then it goes away again!" That cartoon was apt for Carlos, except that he had not one, but *repeated* episodes of clarity—and they always went away again. I often thought that if I could find a way to keep him continually aware of his death and the "clearing" that death effects, I could help him make some major changes in the way he related to life and to other people.

It was evident from the specious way he was speaking today, and a couple of days ago in the group, that his cancer was quiescent again, and that death, with its attendant wisdom, was far out of mind.

I tried another tack. "Carlos, before you started the group I tried to explain to you the basic rationale behind group therapy. Remember how I emphasized that whatever happens in the group can be used to help us work in therapy?" He nodded.

I continued, "And that one of the most important principles of groups is that the group is a miniature world—whatever environment we create in the group reflects the way we have chosen to live? Remember that I said that each of us establishes *in* the group the *same kind of social world we have in our real life?*"

He nodded again. He was listening.

"Now, look what's happened to you in the group! You started with a number of people with whom you might have developed close relationships. And when you began, the two of us were in agreement that you needed to work on ways of developing relationships. That was why you began the group, remember? But now, after only six weeks, all the members and at least one of the co-therapists are thoroughly pissed at you. And it's your own doing. You've done *in* the group what you do *outside* of the group! I want you to answer me honestly: Are you satisfied? Is this what you want from your relationships with others?"

"Doc, I understand completely what you're saying, but there's a bug in your argument. I don't give a shit, not one shit, about the people in the group. They're not real people. I'm never going to associate with losers like that. Their opinion doesn't mean anything to me. I don't *want* to get closer to them."

I had known Carlos to close up completely like this on other occasions. He would, I suspected, be more reasonable in a week or two, and under ordinary circumstances I would simply have been patient. But unless something changed quickly, he would either drop out of the group or would, by next week, have ruptured beyond repair his relationships with the other members. Since I doubted very much, after this charming incident, whether I'd ever be able to persuade another group therapist to accept him, I persevered.

"I hear those angry and judgmental feelings, and I know you really feel them. But, Carlos, try to put brackets around them for a moment and see if you can get in touch with anything else. Both Sarah and Martha were in a great deal of pain. What other feelings did you have about them? I'm not talking about major or predominant feelings, but about any other flashes you had."

"I know what you're after. You're doing your best for me. I want to help you, but I'd be making up stuff. You're putting feelings into my mouth. Right here, this office, is the one place I can tell the truth, and the truth is that, more than anything else, what I want to do with those two cunts in the group is to fuck them! I meant it when I said that if rape were legal, I'd do it! And I know just where I'd start!"

Most likely he was referring to Sarah, but I did not ask. The last thing I wanted to do was enter into that discourse with him. Probably there was some important Oedipal competition going on between the two of us which was making communication more difficult. He never missed an opportunity to describe to me in graphic terms what he would like to do to Sarah, as though he considered that we were rivals for her. I know he believed that the reason I had earlier dissuaded him from inviting Sarah out was that I wanted to keep her to myself. But this type of interpretation would be totally useless now: he was far too closed and defensive. If I were going to get through, I would have to use something more compelling.

The only remaining approach I could think of involved that one burst of emotion I had seen in our first session—the tactic seemed so contrived and so simplistic that I could not possibly have predicted the astonishing result it would produce.

"All right, Carlos, let's consider this ideal society you're imagining and advocating—this society of legalized rape. Think now, for a few minutes, about your daughter. How would it be for her living in the community—being available for legal rape, a piece of ass for whoever happens to be horny and gets off on force and seventeen-year-old girls?"

Suddenly Carlos stopped grinning. He winced visibly and said simply, "I wouldn't like that for her."

"But where would she fit, then, in this world you're building? Locked up in a convent? You've got to make a place where she can live: that's what fathers do—they build a world for their children. I've never asked you before—what do you really want for her?"

"I want her to have a loving relationship with a man and have a loving family."

"But how can that happen if her father is advocating a world of rape? If you want her to live in a loving world, then it's up to you to construct that world—and you have to start with your own behavior. You can't be outside your own law—that's at the base of every ethical system."

The tone of the session had changed. No more jousting or crudity. We had grown deadly serious. I felt more like a philosophy or religious teacher than a therapist, but I knew that this was the proper trail. And these were things I should have said before. He had often joked about his own inconsistency. I remember his once describing with glee a dinner-table conversation with his children (they visited him two or three times a year) when he informed his daughter that he wanted to meet and approve any boy she went out with. "As for *you,*" he said, pointing to his son, "*you* get all the ass you can!"

There was no question now that I had his attention. I decided to increase my leverage by triangulation, and I approached the same issue from another direction:

"And, Carlos, something else comes to my mind right now. Remember your dream of the green Honda two weeks ago? Let's go back over it."

He enjoyed working on dreams and was only too glad to apply himself to this one and, in so doing, to leave the painful discussion about his daughter.

Carlos had dreamed that he went to a rental agency to rent a car, but the only ones available were Honda Civics—his least favorite car. Of several colors available, he selected red. But when he got out to the lot, the only car available was green—his least favorite color! The most important fact about a dream is its emotion, and this dream, despite its benign content, was full of terror: it had awakened him and flooded him with anxiety for hours.

Two weeks ago we had not been able to get far with the dream. Carlos, as I recall, went off on a tangent of associations about the identity of the female auto rental clerk. But today I saw the dream in a different light. Many years ago he had developed a strong belief in reincarnation, a belief that offered him blessed relief from fears about dying. The metaphor he had used in one of our first meetings was that dying is simply trading in your body for another one—like trading in an old car. I reminded him now of that metaphor.

"Let's suppose, Carlos, that the dream is more than a dream about cars. Obviously renting a car is not a frightening activity, not something that would become a nightmare and keep you up all night. I think the dream is about death and future life, and it uses your symbol of comparing death and rebirth to a trade of cars. If we look at it that way, we can make more sense of the powerful fear the dream carried. What do you make of the fact that the only kind of car you could get was a green Honda Civic?"

"I hate green and I hate Honda Civics. My next car is going to be a Maserati."

"But if cars are dream symbols of bodies, why would you, in your next life, get the body, or the life, that you hate above all others?"

Carlos had no option but to respond: "You get what you deserve, depending on what you've done or the way you've lived your present life. You can either move up or down."

Now he realized where this discussion was leading, and began to perspire. The dense forest of crassness and cynicism surrounding him had always shocked and dissuaded visitors. But now it was his turn to be shocked. I had invaded his two innermost temples: his love for his children and his reincarnation beliefs.

"Go on, Carlos, this is important—apply that to yourself and to your life."

He bit off each word slowly. "The dream is saying that I'm not living right."

"I agree, I think that *is* what the dream is saying. Say some more on your thoughts about living right."

I was going to pontificate about what constitutes a good life in any religious system—love, generosity, care, noble thoughts, pursuit of the good, charity—but none of that was necessary. Carlos let me know I had made my point: he said that he was getting dizzy, and that this was a lot to deal with in one day. He wanted time to think about it during the week. Noting that we still had fifteen minutes left, I decided to do some work on another front.

I went back to the first issue he had raised in the hour: his belief that he had missed a golden opportunity with Ruth, the woman he had met briefly at a church social, and his subsequent head pounding and self-recrimination for not having walked her to her car. The function that this irrational belief served was patent. As long as he continued to believe that he was tantalizingly close to being desired and loved by an attractive woman, he could buttress his belief that he was no different from anyone else, that there was nothing seriously wrong with him, that he was not disfigured, not mortally ill.

In the past I hadn't tampered with his denial. In general, it's best not to undermine a defense unless it is creating more problems than solutions, and unless one has something better to offer in its stead. Reincarnation is a case in point: though I personally consider it a form of death denial, the belief served Carlos (as it does much of the world's population) very well; in fact, rather than undermine it, I had always supported it and in this session buttressed it by urging that he be consistent in heeding all the implications of reincarnation.

But the time had come to challenge some of the less helpful parts of his denial system.

"Carlos, do you really believe that if you had walked Ruth to her car you'd have a ten to fifteen percent chance of marrying her?"

"One thing could lead to another. There was something going on between the two of us. I felt it. I know what I know!"

"But you say that every week—the lady in the supermarket, the receptionist in the dentist's office, the ticket seller at the movie. You even felt that with Sarah. Look, how many times have you, or any man, walked a woman to her car and *not* married her?"

"O.K., O.K., maybe it's closer to a one percent or half percent chance, but there was still a chance—if I hadn't been such a jerk. I didn't even *think* of asking to walk her to the car!"

"The things you pick to beat yourself up about! Carlos, I'm going to be blunt. What you're saying doesn't make any sense at all. All you've told me about Ruth—you only talked to her for five minutes—is that she's twenty-three with two small kids and is recently divorced. Let's be very realistic—as you say, this is the place to be honest. What are you going to tell her about your health?"

"When I get to know her better, I'll tell her the truth—that I've got cancer, that it's under control now, that the doctors can treat it."

"And?"

"That the doctors aren't sure what's going to happen, that there are new treatments discovered every day, that I may have recurrences in the future."

"What did the doctors say to you? Did they say *may* have recurrences?"

"You're right—*will* have recurrences in the future, unless a cure is found."

"Carlos, I don't want to be cruel, but be objective. Put yourself in Ruth's place—twenty-three years old, two small children, been through a hard time, presumably looking for some strong support for herself and her kids, having only a layman's knowledge and fear of cancer—do you represent the kind of security and support she's looking for? Is she going to be willing to accept the uncertainty surrounding your health? To risk placing herself in the situation where she might be obligated to nurse you? What really are the chances she would allow herself to know you in the way you want, to become involved with you?"

"Probably not one in a million," Carlos said in a sad and weary voice.

I was being cruel, yet the option of *not* being cruel, of simply humoring him, of tacitly acknowledging that he was incapable of seeing reality, was crueler yet. His fantasy about Ruth allowed him to feel that he could still be touched and cared for by another human. I hoped that he would understand that my willingness to engage him, rather than wink behind his back, was my way of touching and caring.

All the bluster was gone. In a soft voice Carlos asked, "So where does that leave me?"

"If what you really want now is closeness, then it's time to take all this heat off yourself about finding a wife. I've been watching you beat yourself up for months about this. I think it's time to let up on yourself. You've just finished a difficult course of chemotherapy. Four weeks ago you couldn't eat or get out of bed or stop vomiting. You've lost a lot of weight, you're regaining your strength. Stop expecting to find a wife right now, it's too much to ask of yourself. Set a reasonable goal—you can do this as well as I. Concentrate on having a good conversation. Try deepening a friendship with the people you already know."

I saw a smile begin to form on Carlos's lips. He saw my next sentence coming: *"And what better place to start than in the group?"*

Carlos was never the same person after that session. Our next appointment was the day following the next group meeting. The first thing he said was that I would not believe how good he had been in the group. He bragged that he was now the most supportive and sensitive member. He had wisely decided to bail himself out of trouble by telling the group about his cancer. He claimed—and, weeks later, Sarah was to corroborate this—that his behavior had changed so dramatically that the members now looked to him for support.

He praised our previous session. "The last session was our best one so far. I wish we could have sessions like that every time. I don't remember exactly what we talked about, but it helped me change a lot."

I found one of his comments particularly droll.

"I don't know why, but I'm even relating differently to the men in the group. They are all older than me but, it's funny, I have a sense of treating them as though they were my own sons!"

His having forgotten the content of our last session troubled me little. Far better that he forget what we talked about than the opposite possibility (a more popular choice for patients)—to remember precisely what was talked about but to remain unchanged.

Carlos's improvement increased exponentially. Two weeks later, he began our session by announcing that he had had, during that week, two major insights. He was so proud of the insights that he had christened them. The first, he called (glancing at his notes) "Everybody has got a heart." The second was "I am not my shoes."

First, he explained "Everybody has got a heart." "During the group meeting last week, all three women were sharing a lot of their feelings, about how hard it was being single, about loneliness, about grieving for their parents, about nightmares. I don't know why, but I suddenly saw them in a different way! They were like me! They were having the same problems in living that I was. I had always before imagined women sitting on Mount Olympus with a line of men before them and sorting them out—this one to my bedroom, this one not!

"But that moment," Carlos continued, "I had a vision of their naked hearts. Their chest wall vanished, just melted away, leaving a square blue-red cavity with rib-bar walls and, in the center, a liver-colored glistening heart thumping away. All week long I've been seeing everyone's heart beating, and I've been saying to myself, 'Everybody has got a heart, everybody has got a heart.' I've been seeing the heart in every-one—a misshapen hunchback who works in reception, an old lady who does the floors, even the men I work with!"

Carlos's comment gave me so much joy that tears came to my eyes. I think he saw them but, to spare me embarrassment, made no comment and hurried along to the next insight: "I am not my shoes."

He reminded me that in our last session we had discussed his great anxiety about an upcoming presentation at work. He had always had great difficulty speaking in public: excruciatingly sensitive to any criticism, he had often, he said, made a spectacle of himself by viciously counterattacking anyone who questioned any aspect of his presentation.

I had helped him understand that he had lost sight of his personal boundaries. It is natural, I had told him, that one should respond adversely to an attack on one's central core—after all, in that situation one's very survival is at stake. But I had pointed out that Carlos had stretched his personal boundaries to encompass his work and, consequently, he responded to a mild criticism of any aspect of his work as though it were a mortal attack on his central being, a threat to his very survival.

I had urged Carlos to differentiate between his core self and other, peripheral attributes or activities. Then he had to "disidentify" with the non-core parts: they might represent what he liked, or did, or valued—but they were not *him,* not his central being.

Carlos had been intrigued by this construct. Not only did it explain his defensiveness at work, but he could extend this "disidentification" model to pertain to his body. In other words, even though his body was imperiled, he himself, his vital essence, was intact.

This interpretation allayed much of his anxiety, and his work presentation last week had been wonderfully lucid and nondefensive. Never had he done a better job. Throughout his presentation, a small mantra wheel in his mind had hummed, "I am not my work." When he finished and sat down next to his boss, the mantra continued, "I am not my work. Not my talk. Not my clothes. None of these things." He crossed his legs and noted his scuffed and battered shoes: "And I'm not my shoes either." He began to wiggle his toes and his feet, hoping to attract his boss's attention so as to proclaim to him, "I am not my shoes!"

Carlos's two insights—the first of many to come—were a gift to me and to my students. These two insights, each generated by a different form of therapy, illustrated, in quintessential form, the difference between what one can derive from group therapy, with its focus on communion *between,* and individual therapy, with its focus on communion *within.* I still use many of his graphic insights to illustrate my teaching.

In the few months of life remaining to him, Carlos chose to continue to give. He organized a cancer self-help group (not without some humorous crack about this being the "last stop" pickup joint) and also was the group leader for some interpersonal skills groups at one of his churches. Sarah, by now one of his greatest boosters, was invited as a guest speaker to one of his groups and attested to his responsible and competent leadership.

But, most of all, he gave to his children, who noted the change in him and elected to live with him while enrolling for a semester at a nearby college. He was a marvelously generous and supportive father. I have always felt that the way one faces death is greatly determined by the model one's parents set. The last gift a parent can give to children is to teach them, through example, how to face death with equanimity—and Carlos gave an extraordinary lesson in grace. His death was not one of the dark, muffled, conspiratorial passings. Until the very end of his life, he and his children were honest with one another about his illness and giggled together at the way he snorted, crossed his eyes, and puckered his lips when he referred to his "lymphooooooooooooomma."

But he gave no greater gift than the one he offered me shortly before he died, and it was a gift that answers for all time the question of whether it is rational or appropriate to strive for "ambitious" therapy in those who are terminally ill. When I visited him in the hospital he was so weak he could barely move, but he raised his head, squeezed my hand, and whispered, "Thank you. Thank you for saving my life."

CHAPTER 9

The Teaching Novel

In a manner I could never have anticipated, my unconscious played a key role in the writing of *Love's Executioner:* as I approached the end of each of the first nine stories, the next one mysteriously wafted into my mind, as though I had unknowingly constructed in advance an outline and table of contents. While I worked on the ending of the tenth story, "In Search of the Dreamer," another surprise was in store for me: I found myself unaccountably thinking not of another clinical tale, but of Friedrich Nietzsche. I began rereading, with fascination, Nietzsche's work as well as several biographies of Nietzsche. Soon, even before *Love's Executioner* was fully edited, I began work on a novel about Nietzsche and his relationship to psychotherapy.

I never regarded the writing of *Love's Executioner* as a radical departure from my role as an academician. I was simply fulfilling the job description—making a contribution to the professional literature of my field. I meant *Love's Executioner* to be a pedagogical device, a collection of teaching tales to be used in psychotherapy training programs; that the book became a best-seller surprised no one more than me.

It was with that same sentiment that I began *When Nietzsche Wept*.

My intention was to teach and my target audience was still the professional community—student and practicing psychotherapists. I planned, through the use of a new pedagogical device, a teaching novel, to expose students to a fictionalized account of the conception and birth of existential therapy.

The novel invites students to engage in a number of thought experiments involving psychotherapy. They are asked, for example, *to imagine what type of psychotherapy might have evolved if Freud had never lived.* Or, in a more complex experiment: *Suppose Freud had lived and left us only his topographical model of the mind (that is, his posited structure of the psyche, encompassing the dynamic unconscious and the mechanisms of defense) without his psychoanalytic content—without the idea of anxiety issuing from the vagaries of psychosexual development? And imagine, further, the nature of psychotherapy if the content were based on an existential model—that is, that anxiety issues from a confrontation with the terrifying facts of life inherent in existence?*

I knew I wanted to write fiction, but a special kind of fiction: fiction that would serve a rhetorical, pedagogical purpose. While thinking about the nature of this writing, I encountered a phrase in a novel by André Gide, *Lafcadio's Adventures* (also translated as *The Vatican Swindle* and *The Vatican Cellars*). "History," Gide said, "is fiction that did happen. Whereas fiction is history that might have happened."

Fiction is history that might have happened. Perfect! That was precisely what I wanted to write. I wanted to describe a genesis of psychotherapy that might have happened, if history had rotated only slightly on its axis. I wanted the events of *When Nietzsche Wept* to have had a possible existence.

So although the novel is fiction, it is not, I think, an improbable account of how Friedrich Nietzsche might have invented psychotherapy. Moreover, Nietzsche's relationship to therapy might well have been more than that of sheer creator: he lived much of his life in deep despair and could well have used therapy. Ultimately, I fashioned a plot that consists of this central thought experiment:

Suppose that Nietzsche were placed in a historical situation that would have enabled him to invent a psychotherapy, derived from his own published writings, that could have been used to heal Nietzsche himself.

But why Nietzsche? First, the basic tenets of much of my thinking about existential psychotherapy and the meaning of despair are to be found in Nietzsche's writings. It is not that I read Nietzsche and deliberately set about to develop clinical applications for his insights. I've never thought or worked in that manner. Instead, my ideas about existential therapy emerged from my clinical work; I then turned to philosophy as a way of confirming and deepening this work.

In the process of writing the textbook *Existential Therapy,* I immersed myself for years in the work of the great existential philosophers—Sartre, Heidegger, Camus, Jaspers, Kierkegaard, Nietzsche. Of these thinkers, I found Nietzsche to be the most creative, the most powerful, and the most relevant for psychotherapy.

The idea of Nietzsche as a therapist may seem jarring to many of us because we so often think of Nietzsche as a destroyer or nihilist. After all, did he not describe himself as the philosopher who does philosophy with a hammer? But Nietzsche, full of contradictions, revered destruction only as a stage in the process of creation—often he said that one can build a new self only on the ashes of the old.

Many philosophers—the "gentle Nietzscheans"—have considered Nietzsche not as a destroyer but as a healer, a man who aspired to be a physician to his entire epoch. And the disease he hoped to treat? Nihilism—the post-Darwinian nihilism that was creeping over Europe in the late nineteenth century. In the wake of Darwin all the old traditional religious values were crumbling. God was dead and a new secular humanism squatted in the temple ruins. Nietzsche—Nietzsche the creator, the seeker, not Nietzsche the destroyer—sought to use the death of God as an opportunity to create a new set of values. Over a century ago he said, "If we have our own 'why' of life we shall get along with almost any 'how.'"[1] But Nietzsche wanted the new "why," the new set of values, to be based not on supernatural values but on human experience, and on *this* life rather than on the illusion of some afterlife.

Nietzsche's relevance for contemporary psychotherapy makes more sense when one reviews the many ways in which Nietzsche anticipated

Freud. For example, consider Nietzsche's concept of the truly evolved individual (the *Übermensch, superman,* or *overman*). Nietzsche believed that the path to becoming an *Übermensch* lay *not* in the conquest or subjugation of others but in a *self-overcoming.* The truly powerful man never inflicts pain or suffering but, like the prophet Zarathustra, overflows with power and wisdom that he offers freely to others. His offer emanates from a personal abundance, never from a sense of pity—that would represent a kind of scorn. So the overman, then, is a life affirmer, one who loves his fate, one who says yes to life.

In his life-celebratory stand, Nietzsche was much at odds with his first hero, Socrates, who, just before taking his fatal draught of hemlock, said, "I owe Asclepius a rooster." Why would Socrates owe the god of medicine a rooster—a fee the Greeks offered a doctor when he cured a patient? Apparently Socrates meant that he was now cured of the disease of life and its inherent, inescapable suffering. Nietzsche was at odds also with the Buddhist view that life was suffering and that relief from suffering lay in the giving up of attachments. According to this view the final goal of life is the detachment from individual consciousness, the end of the cyclical wheel of individual ego, the attainment of Nirvana.

But not so for Nietzsche, who once said, "Was that life? Well, then, once more!"[2] Nietzsche's overman is one who, if offered the opportunity to live life in precisely the same way, again and again and again, and for all eternity, is able to say, "Yes, yes, give it to me. I'll take that life and I'll live it again in precisely the same way." The Nietzschean overman loves his fate, embraces his suffering, and turns it into art and into beauty. And he is also a person who, in Nietzsche's view, overcomes the narcotic need for some supernaturally imposed purpose. Once a man can do that, Nietzsche said, he becomes an *Übermensch,* a philosophical soul, one of those who represent the next stage of human evolution.

So Nietzsche urged us not to strive toward the conquest of others but toward an interior, self-actualizing process, toward the realization of our potential. Nietzsche's words were not lost to history: in the 1960s they found expression again in the human potential movement. He offered a new, nonsupernatural, humanistically-oriented purpose in life, namely, that we are a bridge to something higher, that each of us is in the process of becoming something more. Our task in life, Nietzsche said, is to perfect nature and our own nature. And he offered instruction for the necessary inner work: his first "granite sentence" was—*Become who you are.*

Despite Nietzsche's focus on the deep inner work of the individual, many of his words were twisted into Nazi slogans about world-conquering Aryan supermen during World War II. To understand that phenomenon one must draw a careful distinction between what Nietzsche really wrote and the vulgarized version of Nietzsche's philosophy that was disseminated by his sister, Elisabeth, one of the great villainesses of intellectual history.

Elisabeth, who ultimately became Nietzsche's literary executor, had strong protofascist, anti-Semitic leanings, whereas Nietzsche vigorously rejected these sentiments. He had a deeply ambivalent relationship to his sister, at times closely attached to her, at times dismissing her as "an anti-Semitic goose."[3] Much dismayed by her marriage in 1885 to Bernhard Förster, a professional anti-Semitic agitator, Nietzsche was not altogether sorry to see her emigrate with her husband to Paraguay to found Nueva Germania, an Aryan colony built on soil "uncontaminated" by Jewish presence.

Ultimately, due to Förster's ineptness and grandiosity, the Paraguay project floundered. Bernhard Förster was accused of embezzlement and ultimately committed suicide. Elisabeth, after an unsuccessful attempt to salvage the colony, returned home to Europe just in time to take over her ailing brother's estate. Seizing her one great chance to attain political prominence, she set about distorting Nietzsche's writings in order to promulgate her Wagnerian-fascist ideas. So effectively did she do this that it has taken a generation of scholars to separate Nietzsche's golden grain from Elisabeth's chaff.

Nietzsche recoiled from the building of great philosophic systems, like that of Hegel. He was more a brilliant gadfly whose remarkable insights even now, a century later, continue to fuel philosophic investigations. Employing a penetrating, intuitive style, he preferred quick dips into the cold pool of truth, which he mostly described aphoristically. He even wrote an aphorism about aphorisms: "*A good aphorism is too hard for the tooth of time and is not consumed by all millennia, although it serves every time for nourishment: thus it is the great paradox of literature, the intransitory amid the changing, the food that always remains esteemed, like salt, and never loses its savor, as even that does.*"[4]

Many fields—aesthetics, philosophy, ethics, history, philology, politics, music—have profited from Nietzsche's sparkling ideas. One of my intentions in *When Nietzsche Wept* was to underscore the relevance of Nietzsche's psychological insights to contemporary psychotherapy.

In many places he stressed the importance of coming to terms with one's destiny, destiny in the deepest sense, not just an individualistic developmental destiny but the very condition of being human. It was the task of the evolved human being, Nietzsche held, to look deeply into this destiny. Looking deeply often incurs pain, he knew, but he believed that we must train ourselves to bear the suffering of truth. Staring at the truth is not easy, Nietzsche wrote: "It makes one strain one's eyes all the time, and in the end one finds more than one might have wished."[5] Ultimately suffering becomes the great liberator that permits us to plumb our deepest depths. Nietzsche's second granite sentence was: *That which does not kill me makes me stronger.*

Nietzsche's ability to stare unflinchingly at the truth, to break illusion, was remarkable. "One must pay dearly for immortality," he said. "One has to die several times while still alive."[6] In other words, if one is to become enlightened and worthy of immortality, one must face down the terror of death and plunge into the vision of one's own dying many times while still alive.

Although Nietzsche never explicitly addressed the field of medicine or psychiatry, he nonetheless had thoughts about the training of healers:

Physician help thyself: thus you help your patients too. Let this be his best help—that he, the patient, may behold with his eyes the man who heals himself.[7]

You shall build over and beyond yourself, but first you must be built yourself, perpendicular in body and soul. You shall not only reproduce yourself, but produce something higher.[8]

Obviously these aphorisms, written a century ago, argue for the position (to which almost all contemporary teachers of psychotherapy ascribe) that a personal therapy is a sine qua non of the training of therapists. But another aphorism adds a moderating note: "Some cannot loosen their own chains and can nonetheless redeem their friends."[9] In other words, even though personal exploration and insight are needed, total enlightenment (that is, a full personal self-overcoming) may not be necessary because therapists can take their patients farther than they themselves have gone. Even the wounded therapist can still point the way to the patient—therapists are guides, not conveyor belts.

Nietzsche wrote on the nature of the healing relationship:

Here and there on earth we may encounter a kind of confirmation of love in which this possessive craving of two people for each other gives way to a new desire—a shared higher thirst for an ideal above them. But who knows such love? Who has experienced it? Its right name is friendship.[10]

"A shared higher thirst for an ideal above them . . . its right name is friendship." It might also be called psychotherapy—an authentic relationship, sharing a thirst for an ideal above, which emerges when all possessive cravings and transference distortions have dissipated.

How close a relationship? How distant? In a light piece of verse Nietzsche advises that it be neither too distant nor too enmeshed. Perhaps the best role for the healer is as a participant-observer:

Do not stay in the field
nor climb out of sight
the best view of the world
is from a medium height.[11]

As I planned my novel I had to imagine what kind of therapist Nietzsche might have been. Ambitious, resolute, and uncompromising, I believe. He would have made no concessions, would have expected his clients to face the truth about themselves and their "situation" in existence. I grew convinced he would have been disdainful of simple symptom relief or the limited goals of behavioral-cognitive modes. Listen:

I am a railing by the torrent: let those who can, grasp me. A crutch, however, I am not![12]

Or again:

> *For that is what I am through and through: reeling in, raising up, raising, a raiser, cultivator, and disciplinarian, who once counseled himself, not for nothing: Become who you are!*[13]

Given even these few glimpses into Nietzsche's relevance for contemporary psychotherapy, we may turn to the question of whether Nietzsche has taken his deserved place in the history, theory, or practice of psychotherapy. The answer is "absolutely not." Turn to history of psychiatry or psychotherapy textbooks and you will find no mention of his name.

Why not? After all, Nietzsche lived in the right place at the right time, that is, in the crucible of psychotherapy: central Europe, mid-nineteenth century (he was born in 1844, twelve years before Freud). To answer the question of why Nietzsche's name has been ignored in the psychotherapy literature, we must turn to the relationship between Nietzsche and Freud. I refer, of course, to the intellectual relationship: the two men never met.

Nietzsche would not have known of Freud. By 1889, which marks the end of Nietzsche's intellectual career, Freud had published nothing in the field of psychiatry. (His first published article in psychiatry appeared in 1893, and his first book, *Studies in Hysteria,* in 1895.) But did Freud know Nietzsche's work? Here the record is contradictory. Sometimes Freud flatly denied he had ever read Nietzsche; at other times he appeared to be intimately familiar with Nietzsche's writings.

Was it possible that Freud was ignorant of Nietzsche's work? How prominent was Nietzsche at the end of the nineteenth century? During his productive lifetime Nietzsche's writings were not well known. *Thus Spake Zarathustra*, his best-known book and a standard undergraduate text for later generations, sold only one hundred copies in its first year of publication. In fact, so few copies of any of his books sold that Nietzsche once claimed to know the owner of every copy. Yet Nietzsche's name was not unknown during his lifetime; throughout Western Europe there was an active underground Nietzsche appreciation movement, and many artists and intellectuals were aware of his genius.

Nietzsche's death was no less remarkable than his life: in effect, he died twice—in 1889 and eleven years later in 1900. In 1889 he suffered a cataclysmic dementia and his great mind was gone forever. Most medical historians have concluded that he suffered from tertiary syphilis—paresis (general paralysis of the insane), a common incurable condition of the era. After 1889 Nietzsche remained broken for the rest of his life, unable to think clearly, barely able to formulate a coherent sentence. His vacant husk lingered on for eleven more years until his corporeal death in 1900.

How Nietzsche ever contracted syphilis remains a puzzle for historians, since he was believed to have led a chaste life. Unfounded speculations abound, ranging from contact with the cigars of wounded soldiers when Nietzsche served in an ambulance corps in the Franco-Prussian War, to liaisons with prostitutes in Cologne, to medically prescribed romps with Southern Italian peasant women, to (Jung's theory) visits to gay brothels in Genoa.

When Nietzsche was incapacitated, his sister, Elisabeth, moved in to take care of him and of his writings. A great self-promoter, she made the most of her one possible vehicle for fame, her brother's philosophy, for the rest of her life. Her political pandering was so successful that Hitler funded her Nietzsche Archive at Weimar, visited her on her ninetieth birthday bearing a huge bouquet of roses, and, a few years later, attended her funeral and placed a laurel wreath on her casket.

Although Nietzsche was little known before his first death in 1889, Elisabeth was to change that dramatically in the next ten years. As a result of her promotion, all of Nietzsche's work was republished. Before long, copies of his books by the tens of thousands cascaded from the great presses of Europe.

It is conceivable that Freud may have been unfamiliar with Nietzsche's writings during Nietzsche's productive lifetime, but it is highly improbable that he (or any educated middle European) would have been unaware of the deluge of Nietzsche's books printed after 1900. We know, also, that some of Freud's university friends (for example, Joseph Paneth) became early devotees of Nietzsche in the 1870s and early 1880s and wrote to Freud concerning their opinions of Nietzsche. And of course there was Freud's intimate twenty-six-year relationship with Lou Salomé who, as I shall discuss shortly, had previously been intimate with

Nietzsche. We know, too, that Otto Rank gave Freud a complete set of Nietzsche's writings bound in white leather. Freud prized these books. When the gestapo forced him to abandon most of his library and exit Vienna hastily, he took care to keep his Nietzsche collection with him.

The detailed minutes of the Psychoanalytic Society in Vienna inform us that two entire meetings in 1908 were devoted to Nietzsche. In these minutes Freud acknowledged that Nietzsche's intuitional method had reached insights amazingly similar to those reached through the laboriously systematic scientific efforts of psychoanalysis. The Psychoanalytic Society explicitly credited Nietzsche as being the first to discover the significance of abreaction, of repression, of forgetting, of flight into illness, of illness as an excessive sensitivity to the vicissitudes of life, and of the instincts in mental life—both the sexual and sadistic instincts. Freud, in fact, went so far as to point out the two or three ways in which he thought Nietzsche had *not* anticipated psychoanalysis. Obviously, in order to do that, Freud must have known the many ways in which Nietzsche *did* anticipate the discipline.

Although Freud said at times that he had not read Nietzsche, he did say at other times that he had tried to read Nietzsche but was too lazy— an odd statement, considering Freud's legendary diligence and energy. (A perusal of his daily schedule, often consisting of ten to twelve clinical hours before he sat down to write, always leaves me gasping for breath.) On still other occasions (and here, I believe, we move closer to the truth) Freud said he tried to read Nietzsche but got dizzy because Nietzsche's pages were so crammed with insights uncomfortably close to his own. Thus to read Nietzsche was to deprive himself of the satisfaction of making an original discovery: in other words, Freud had to remain ignorant of Nietzsche's work lest he, as he put it, be forced to view himself as a "verifying drudge."

Elsewhere he explicitly acknowledged that Schopenhauer and Nietzsche so precisely described and anticipated the theory of repression that it was only because he (Freud) was not well read that he had the chance to make a great discovery. And making a great discovery was extraordinarily important to Freud, who realized early in life that a university career would be closed to him because of the anti-Semitism rampant in *fin-de-siècle* Vienna. Private practice was the only venue available to him, and the great independent discovery was the only route to the fame he so craved. The idea of himself as an original thinker making independent discoveries was thus crucially important to Freud, whose creative energy depended on this romantic image of himself. "Even Einstein," Freud said, "had the advantage of a long line of predecessors from Isaac Newton forward, whereas I had to hack every step of my own way alone through a tangled jungle."

Grounded in classical philosophy, especially the earliest Western philosophers, the pre-Socratic Greeks, Nietzsche had a very different attitude toward priority. "Am I called upon," Nietzsche asked, "to discover new truths? There are far too many old ones as it is." He believed that the past was always embodied in the great man and sought only "to put history in balance again." Never a modest man, Nietzsche predicted that "a thousand secrets of the past will crawl out of their hiding places into my sunshine."[14]

Thus there is evidence that Freud knew and admired Nietzsche's work. According to his biographer Ernest Jones, Freud placed several great men in a pantheon and said he could never achieve their rank.[15] In this group were Goethe, Kant, Voltaire, Darwin, Schopenhauer—and Nietzsche. Perhaps some of Freud's confused feelings toward Nietzsche issued from his ambivalence toward the entire discipline of philosophy. At times Freud derided philosophy for its lack of a scientific methodology. Yet at other times he yearned to settle into pure philosophic and historical speculation, and considered his entire medical career as a detour, a false turn from his true calling as a *Lebens*-philosopher, an unraveler of the mystery of how man came to be what he is.

Hence there is unfinished business between Nietzsche and the field of psychotherapy: although Nietzsche was prescient about the field of psychotherapy and although he exercised considerable influence upon Freud, Freud never acknowledged that debt. The entire field of psychotherapy has followed Freud's lead and ignored Nietzsche's contributions. One of my intentions in *When Nietzsche Wept* is to address this oversight and to begin to harvest, more explicitly, Nietzsche's psychological insights.

There is still another reason to write about Nietzsche—the extraordinary drama of his life makes him an intriguing novelistic subject. He was born in 1844 into a family of modest means. His father, a Lutheran minister, died when Nietzsche was five. His genius noted at an early age, Nietzsche was awarded a scholarship to one of the best schools in Germany. At the age of twenty-four, before he matriculated from a graduate university program in philology, he was offered, and he accepted, the chair in classical philology at the University of Basel. While there, he was tormented by an illness that first appeared in his adolescence and was destined to plague him all his life. The illness was not the syphilis that ultimately was to kill him, but almost certainly a severe migraine condition.

His migraine so incapacitated him—according to Stefan Zweig, sometimes he was ill more than two hundred days in a given year—that at the age of thirty, Nietzsche had to resign his professorship. As he put it, he kicked the dust of the German-speaking world from his shoes and departed to Italy, where he spent the rest of his life traveling mostly in Southern Italy and Switzerland, going from one modest hotel to another, in search of the climate and atmospheric conditions that would grant him health enough to think and to write for two or three consecutive days.

Where, then, the drama? From the perspective of external events, Nietzsche's life might seem unusually uneventful. Yet from the internal perspective there is great drama in the lonely life of this man, one of the great courageous spirits of history, wandering from one unassuming inn to another in Italy and Switzerland and, all the while, unflinchingly confronting the harshest facts of human existence. And Nietzsche always pursued his task starkly, without material comfort (he lived on a small university pension), without a home (he referred to himself as a tortoise—the steamer trunk he lugged from hotel to hotel contained all his possessions), without a family (save for a distant mother and the problematic Elisabeth). He lived without the touch of a loving friend, without a professional community (he never again held a university position), without a country (because of his anti-German sentiments he gave up his German passport and never stayed in one place long enough to obtain another). He had little public recognition (his publishers, he said, should have worked at political intrigue—they were skilled at keeping secrets and his books were their greatest secret) and no professional acclaim or students.

Perhaps the lack of acclaim troubled Nietzsche so little because he had an unswerving belief in his ultimate place in history. In his preface to one of his later books (*The Antichrist*) he says, "This book belongs to the very few. Perhaps none of them is even living today. Only the day after tomorrow belongs to me. Some are born posthumously." (I liked the phrase "born posthumously" so well that for a time I considered using it for my book's title.)

During these years Nietzsche suffered a great deal from the effects of the debilitating migraine, as well as from isolation and the sheer task of living a life devoid of illusion. He often said that despair is the price one pays for self-awareness, and wondered how much truth a man could stand. Perhaps, also, the despair issued from some kind of presentiment of his percolating disease—the ticking bomb that would burst his brain at the seams when he was forty-five.

Let us return now to the basic thought experiment that constitutes the spine of my novel: *Suppose that Nietzsche were placed in a historical situation where he would have been enabled to invent a psychotherapy, derived from his own published writings, that could have been used to heal Nietzsche himself.*

In which way could a psychotherapeutic experience have helped Nietzsche? Through insight? Unlikely. Recall that Freud said Nietzsche was a man who had more insight about himself than any man who ever lived. More than insight would have been needed. What Nietzsche needed was a therapeutic encounter, a meaningful relationship. Nietzsche experienced himself as desperately isolated. His letters bulge with references to his loneliness: "Neither among the living nor the dead is there anyone with whom I feel kinship"; "No one who had any sort of God to keep him company ever reached my level of loneliness."[16]

But Nietzsche in psychotherapy? Is it conceivable that Nietzsche would have made himself so vulnerable to another? And would Nietzsche's grandiose, arrogant self have permitted the self-disclosure required for successful therapy? Obviously the plot called for some device that would have permitted Nietzsche to be in therapy and yet, at the same time, in control of his therapy procedure.

And when should the story be set? Nietzsche was in despair much of his life. Would there have been a particularly propitious time for a therapeutic encounter? Ultimately, I settled on the autumn of 1882: Nietzsche was thirty-eight and, after the breakup of a brief, passionate (but chaste) love affair, had slumped into such a state of despair that his letters were full of suicidal ideation. The woman, Lou Salomé, a young and remarkable Russian, would go down in history as a writer, critic, disciple of Freud, practicing psychoanalyst, and friend and lover to several eminent men of the late nineteenth century, including the poet Rainer Maria Rilke.

One of the most striking aspects of Nietzsche's depression in 1882 was his rapid recovery: though he was suicidal in the autumn of 1882, it was only a few months later, in the spring of 1883, that he began energetically writing *Thus Spake Zarathustra.* He completed the first three parts in only ten days, writing in a frenzy, writing as no philosopher had ever before written, as though he were in a trance, as though he were a medium through whom *Thus Spake Zarathustra* was released.

Furthermore, *Thus Spake Zarathustra* is a life-affirming, life-celebrating work. How was Nietzsche able to transport himself from such despair to such life affirmation in only a few months? Wouldn't it have been reasonable, and wonderful, for Nietzsche to have had a successful therapy encounter at the end of 1882?

But who would be Nietzsche's therapist? That was a vexing problem. In 1882 there were no professional psychotherapists. There was no such thing as dynamic psychotherapy: Freud was twenty-seven years old and had yet to enter the field of psychiatry. If Nietzsche had seen a contemporary physician for his despair, he might have been told there was no medical treatment for his condition, or he might have been sent to Baden-Baden, Marienbad, or one of the other central European spas for a water cure, or perhaps he might have been referred to the church for religious counseling. There were no practicing secular therapists. Although A. A. Liebault and Hippolyte Bernheim had a school of hypnotherapy in Nancy, France, they offered no psychotherapy per se, only hypnotic symptom-removal.

If only I could have set the novel a decade later; by then Freud would have been developing psychoanalytic methods and a Freud-Nietzsche encounter would have made an interesting story. This, however, was not possible: by 1892 Nietzsche had already lapsed into irreversible dementia. No, all things pointed toward 1882 as the most propitious historical moment.

Unable to identify a psychotherapist in 1882, I decided to invent one. I began sketching a fictional Jesuit priest-therapist (a lapsed priest, because of Nietzsche's anticlerical sentiments). Then it suddenly dawned on me that there *was,* after all, right under my nose, one therapist alive in 1882—Josef Breuer, Freud's friend and mentor, who was the first person to employ dynamic theory and methods in the psychotherapy of a patient. (I knew Breuer's work particularly well because, for a decade, I had taught a Freud appreciation course in which I discussed the contributions of Breuer.) Although the full case history of the patient, Bertha Pappenheim (whom Breuer gave the pseudonym Anna O.), was not published until 1893, in a psychiatric journal, and would reappear in 1895 in Freud's and Breuer's *Studies in Hysteria,* Breuer had actually treated Bertha Pappenheim many years earlier, in 1881.

Once I had selected Breuer as Nietzsche's therapist, the rest of the plot quickly fell into place. In the early 1880s Nietzsche had consulted a great many central European physicians because of his deteriorating health. Breuer was not a psychiatrist but was a superb medical diagnostician and the personal physician to many of the eminent figures of his era. It would have been historically plausible for Nietzsche to have sought consultation with Breuer.

I chose Lou Salomé as the instrument to bring Nietzsche and Breuer together. Feeling guilty about her role in Nietzsche's depression, she asks Breuer to meet with Nietzsche. In this regard Lou Salomé's behavior is indeed fictional, since the historical evidence paints her as a free spirit unlikely to be burdened by a heavy conscience.

But she was undoubtedly a woman of considerable beauty, charm, and persuasiveness. Although Breuer first takes the position that there is no medical treatment for lovesick despair, Lou Salomé urges him to improvise and reminds him that, until he invented it, there was also no treatment for Anna O.'s hysteria. (Although the case had not yet been published in 1882, I suggest that Lou Salomé might have heard about it from her brother, Jenia, who, by the sheerest chance and good fortune for the historical consistency of my plot, happened to be a medical student in Vienna in 1882 and might have studied with Breuer.)

Breuer reluctantly agrees and fashions a plan (in consultation with the young Freud, who, in 1882, was a medical intern and a frequent visitor to the Breuer household) to consult with Nietzsche about his physical health and then, slowly and subtly, to redirect attention to his psychological distress. Nietzsche, however, whose personal definition of hell might have been a situation where he disclosed his vulnerability to a stranger, powerfully resists all Breuer's attempts to engage him in therapy and, after two medical consultations, sharply breaks off contact.

Before he can leave Vienna, however, Nietzsche is stricken with a cardiac arrhythmia and a severe migraine requiring Breuer's treatment. For a short period, while desperately ill, Nietzsche appears more vulnerable and amenable to a psychological investigation, but twenty-four hours later, when he recovers, he reverts to his distant, concealed persona. Late at night Breuer, while trudging home from his consultation with Nietzsche, ponders his options and suddenly has an inspired idea:

> Breuer gave up. He stopped thinking. His legs took over and he continued walking toward a warm, well-lit home, toward his children, and his loving, unloved Mathilde. He concentrated only on breathing in the cold, cold air, warming it in the cradle of his lungs, and releasing it in steamy clouds. He listened to the wind, to his steps, to the bursting of the fragile icy crust of snow underfoot. And suddenly he knew a way— the only way!
>
> His pace quickened. All the way home, he crunched the snow and, with every step, chanted to himself, "I know a way! I know a way!"

In the following excerpt, one of the pivotal chapters, Breuer launches his scheme to ensnare Nietzsche in a therapeutic contract.

When Nietzsche Wept: Chapter 12

On Monday morning, Nietzsche came to Breuer's office for the final stages of their business together. After carefully studying Breuer's itemized bill to be sure nothing had been omitted, Nietzsche filled out a bank draft and handed it to Breuer. Then Breuer gave Nietzsche his clinical consultation report and suggested he read it while still in the office in case he had any questions.

After scrutinizing it, Nietzsche opened his briefcase and placed it in his folder of medical reports.

"An excellent report, Doctor Breuer, comprehensive and comprehensible. And unlike many of my other reports, it contains no professional jargon, which, though offering the illusion of knowledge, is in reality the language of ignorance. And now, back to Basel. I have taken too much of your time."

Nietzsche closed and locked his briefcase. "I leave you, Doctor, feeling more indebted to you than to any man ever before. Ordinarily, leavetaking is accompanied by denials of the permanence of the event: people say, 'Auf Wiedersehen'—until we meet again. They are quick to plan for reunions and then, even more quickly, forget their resolutions. I am *not* one of those. I prefer the truth—which is that we shall almost certainly not meet again. I shall probably never return to Vienna, and I doubt you will ever be in such want of a patient like me as to track me down in Italy."

Nietzsche tightened his grip on his briefcase and started to get up.

It was a moment for which Breuer had prepared carefully. "Professor Nietzsche, please, not just yet! There is another matter I wish to discuss with you."

Nietzsche tensed. No doubt, Breuer thought, he has been expecting another plea to enter the Lauzon Clinic. And dreading it.

"No, Professor Nietzsche, it's not what you think, not at all. Please relax. It is quite another matter. I've been procrastinating in raising this issue for reasons that will soon be apparent."

Breuer paused and took a deep breath.

"I have a proposition to make you—a rare proposition, perhaps one never before made by a doctor to a patient. I see myself delaying. This is hard to say. I'm not usually at a loss for words. But it's best simply to say it.

"I propose a professional exchange. That is, I propose that for the next month I act as physician to your body. I will concentrate only on your physical symptoms and medications. And you, in return, will act as physician to my mind, my spirit."

Nietzsche, still gripping his briefcase, seemed puzzled, then wary. "What do you mean—your mind, your spirit? How can I act as physician? Is this not but another variation of our discussion last week—that you doctor me and I teach you philosophy?"

"No, this request is entirely different. I do not ask you to teach me, but to *heal* me."

"Of what, may I ask?"

"A difficult question. And yet I pose it to my patients all the time. I asked it of *you,* and now it is my turn to answer it. I ask you to heal me of despair."

"Despair?" Nietzsche relaxed his hold on his briefcase and leaned forward. "What kind of despair? I see no despair."

"Not on the surface. *There* I seem to be living a satisfying life. But, underneath the surface, despair reigns. You ask what kind of despair? Let us say that my mind is not my own, that I am invaded and assaulted by alien and sordid thoughts. As a result, I feel self-contempt, and I doubt my integrity. Though I care for my wife and children, I don't *love* them! In fact, I resent being imprisoned by them. I lack courage: the courage either to change my life or to continue living it. I have lost sight of *why* I live—the point of it all. I am preoccupied with aging. Though every day I grow closer to death, I am terrified of it. Even so, suicide sometimes enters my mind."

On Sunday, Breuer had rehearsed this answer often. But today it had been—in a strange way, considering the underlying duplicity of the plan—*sincere*. Breuer knew he was a poor liar. Though he had to conceal the big lie—that his proposal was a ploy to engage Nietzsche in treatment—he had resolved to tell the truth about everything else. Hence, in his speech, he presented the truth about himself in slightly exaggerated form. He also tried to select concerns that might in some way interlace with some of Nietzsche's own, unspoken concerns.

For once, Nietzsche appeared truly astounded. He shook his head slightly, obviously wanting no part of this proposal. Yet he was having difficulty formulating a rational objection.

"No, no, Doctor Breuer, this is impossible. I cannot do this, I've no training. Consider the risks—everything might be made worse."

"But, Professor, there is no such thing as training. Who is trained?

To whom can I turn? To a physician? Such healing is not part of the medical discipline. To a religious leader? Shall I take the leap into religious fairy tales? I, like you, have lost the knack for such leaping. You, a *Lebens*-philosopher, spend your life contemplating the very issues that confound my life. To whom can I turn if not to you?"

"Doubts about yourself, wife, children? What do *I* know about these?"

Breuer responded at once. "And aging, death, freedom, suicide, the search for purpose—you know as much as anyone alive! Aren't these the precise concerns of your philosophy? Aren't your books entire treatises on despair?"

"I can't cure despair, Doctor Breuer. I study it. Despair is the price one pays for self-awareness. Look deeply into life, and you will always find despair."

"I know that, Professor Nietzsche, and I don't expect cure, merely relief. I want you to advise me. I want you to show me how to tolerate a life of despair."

"But I don't know how to show such things. And I have no advice for the singular man. I write for the race, for humankind."

"But, Professor Nietzsche, you believe in scientific method. If a race, or a village, or a flock has an ailment, the scientist proceeds by isolating and studying a single prototypic specimen and then generalizing to the whole. I spent ten years dissecting a tiny structure in the inner ear of the pigeon to discover how pigeons maintain their equilibrium! I could not work with pigeonkind. I had to work with individual pigeons. Only later was I able to generalize my findings to all pigeons, and then to birds and mammals, and humans as well. That's the way it has to be done. You can't conduct an experiment on the whole human race."

Breuer paused, awaiting Nietzsche's rebuttal. None came. He was rapt in thought.

Breuer continued. "The other day you described your belief that the specter of nihilism was stalking Europe. You argued that Darwin has made God obsolete, that just as we once created God, we have all now killed him. And that we no longer know how to live without our religious mythologies. Now I know you didn't say this directly—correct me if I'm mistaken—but I believe you consider it your mission to demonstrate that out of disbelief one can create a code of behavior for man, a new morality, a new enlightenment, to replace one born out of superstition and the lust for the supernatural." He paused.

Nietzsche nodded for him to continue.

"I believe, though you may disagree with my choice of terms, that your mission is to save humankind from both nihilism and illusion?"

Another slight nod from Nietzsche.

"Well, save *me!* Conduct the experiment with *me!* I'm the perfect subject. I have killed God. I have no supernatural beliefs, and am drowning in nihilism. I don't know *why* to live! I don't know *how* to live!"

Still no response from Nietzsche

"If you hope to develop a plan for all mankind, or even a select few, try it on me. Practice on me. See what works and what doesn't—it should sharpen your thinking."

"You offer yourself as an experimental lamb?" Nietzsche replied. "*That* would be how I repay my debt to you?"

"I'm not concerned about risk. I believe in the healing value of talking. Simply to review my life with an informed mind like yours—that's what I want. That cannot fail to help me."

Nietzsche shook his head in bewilderment. "Do you have a specific procedure in mind?"

"Only this. As I proposed before, you enter the clinic under an assumed name, and I observe and treat your migraine attacks. When I make my daily visits, I shall first attend to you. I shall monitor your physical condition and prescribe any medication that may be indicated. For the rest of our visit, you become the physician and help me talk about my life concerns. I ask only that you listen to me and interject any comments you wish. That is all. Beyond that, I don't know. We'll have to invent our procedure along the way."

"No." Nietzsche shook his head firmly. "It is impossible, Doctor Breuer. I admit your plan is intriguing, but it is doomed from the onset. I am a writer, not a talker. And I write for the few, not the many."

"But your books are not for the few," Breuer quickly responded. "In fact, you express scorn for philosophers who write only for one another, whose work is removed from life, who do not *live* their philosophy."

"I don't write for other philosophers. But I do write for the few who represent the future. I am not meant to mingle, to live *among*. My skills for social intercourse, my trust, my caring for others   these have long atrophied. If, indeed, such skills were ever present. I have always been alone. I shall always remain alone. I accept that destiny."

"But, Professor Nietzsche, you want more. I saw sadness in your eyes when you said that others might not read your books until the year two thousand. You *want* to be read. I believe there is some part of you that still craves to be with others."

Nietzsche sat still, rigid in his chair.

"Remember that story you told me about Hegel on his deathbed?" Breuer continued. "About the only one student who understood him being one who *mis*understood him—and ended by saying that, on your own deathbed, you couldn't claim even one student. Well, why wait for the year two thousand? Here I am! You have your student right here, right now. And I'm a student who will listen to you, because my life depends on understanding you!"

Breuer paused for breath. He was very pleased. In his preparation the day before, he had correctly anticipated each of Nietzsche's objections and countered each of them. The trap was elegant. He could hardly wait to tell Sig.

He knew he should stop at this juncture—the first object being, after all, to ensure that Nietzsche did not take the train to Basel today—but could not resist adding one further point. "And, Professor Nietzsche, I remember how you said the other day that nothing disturbed you more than to be in debt to another with no possibility of equivalent repayment."

Nietzsche's response was quick and sharp. "You mean that you do this for *me*?"

"No, that's just the point. Even though my plan might in some way serve you, that is *not* my intention! My motivation is entirely self-serving. I need help! Are you strong enough to help me?"

Nietzsche stood up from his chair.

Breuer held his breath.

Nietzsche took a step toward Breuer and extended his hand. "I agree to your plan," he said.

Friedrich Nietzsche and Josef Breuer had struck a bargain.

Letter from Friedrich Nietzsche to Peter Gast

4 December 1882

My dear Peter,

A change of plans. Again. I shall be in Vienna for an entire
month and, hence, must, with regret, postpone our Rapallo visit.
I will write when I know my plans more precisely. A great deal
has happened, most of it interesting. I am having a slight attack
(which would have been a two-week monster were it not for the
intervention of your Dr. Breuer) and am too weak now to do
more than give you a précis of what has transpired. More to
follow.

Thank you for finding me the name of this Dr. Breuer—he is
a great curiosity—a thinking, *scientific* physician. Is that not
remarkable? He is willing to tell me what he knows about my
illness and—even *more* remarkable—what he does *not* know!

He is a man who greatly wishes to dare and I believe is
attracted to my daring to dare greatly. He has dared to offer me a
most unusual proposition, and I have accepted it. For the next
month he proposes to hospitalize me at the Lauzon Clinic, where
he will study and treat my medical illness. (And all this to be at
his expense! This means, dear friend, that you need not concern
yourself about my subsistence this winter.)

And I? What must I offer in return? I, who none believed
would ever again be gainfully employed, I am asked to be Dr.
Breuer's personal philosopher for one month to provide personal
philosophic counsel. His life is a torment, he contemplates
suicide, he has asked me to guide him out of the thicket of
despair.

How ironic, you must think, that your friend is called upon to
muffle death's siren call, the same friend who is so enticed by
that rhapsody, the very friend who wrote you last saying that the
barrel of a gun seemed not an unfriendly sight!

Dear friend, I tell you this about my arrangement with Dr.
Breuer in *total* confidence. This is for no one else's ear, not even

Overbeck. You are the *only one* I entrust with this. I owe the good doctor total confidentiality.

Our bizarre arrangement evolved to its present form in a complex manner. First he offered to counsel *me* as part of my medical treatment! What a clumsy subterfuge! He pretended that he was interested only in my welfare, his only wish, his only reward, to make *me* healthy and whole! But we know about those priestly healers who project their weakness into others and then minister to others only as a way of increasing their own strength. We know about "Christian charity"!

Naturally, I saw through it and called it by its true name. He choked on the truth for a while—called me blind and base. He swore to elevated motives, mouthed fake sympathy and comical altruisms, but finally, to his credit, he found the strength to seek strength openly and honestly from me.

Your friend, Nietzsche, in the marketplace! Are you not appalled by the thought? Imagine my *Human, All Too Human,* or my *The Gay Science,* caged, tamed, housebroken! Imagine my aphorisms alphabetized into a practicum of homilies for daily life and work! At first, I, too, was appalled! But no longer. The project intrigues me—a forum for my ideas, a vessel to fill when I am ripe and overflowing, an opportunity—indeed, a laboratory, to test ideas on an individual specimen before positing them for the species (that was Dr. Breuer's notion).

Your Dr. Breuer, incidentally, seems a superior specimen, with the perceptiveness and the desire to stretch upward. Yes, he has the desire. And he has the head. But does he have the eyes—and the heart—to see? We shall see!

So today I convalesce and think quietly about *application*—a new venture. Perhaps I was in error to think that my sole mission was truth finding. For the next month, I shall see if my wisdom will enable another to live through despair. Why does he come to *me?* He says that after tasting my conversation and nibbling a bit of *Human, All Too Human,* he has developed an appetite for my philosophy. Perhaps, given the burden of my physical disease, he thought that I must be an expert on survival.

Of course he doesn't know the half of my burden. My friend, the Russian bitch-demon, that monkey with false breasts, continues her course of betrayal. Elisabeth, who says Lou is living with Rée, is campaigning to have her deported for immorality.

Elisabeth also writes that friend Lou has moved her hate-and-lie campaign to Basel, where she intends to imperil my pension. Cursed be that day in Rome when I first saw her. I have often said to you that every adversity—even encounters with pure evil—makes me stronger. But if I can turn *this* shit into gold, I shall . . . I shall . . . —we shall see.

I have not the energy to make a copy of this letter, dear friend. Please return it to me.

Yours,
F.N.

This section, elaborating upon the fluid, shifting relationship between therapist and patient, was a great delight to write. I have lost sight of the precise moment of inspiration, but I do know that several relevant stories about the basic nature of the patient-therapist relationship have rattled about in my mind for many years. In one way or another, the echoes of these tales ring throughout the pages of *When Nietzsche Wept.*

The Story of the Two Healers

Herman Hesse, in his novel *Magister Ludi,* tells a tale about two hermits who were powerful healers. The two worked in different ways, one through offering sagacious advice, and the other through quiet and in-spired listening. They never met but worked as rivals for many years until the younger healer grew spiritually ill and fell into despair. He was un-able to heal himself with his own therapeutic methods and ultimately, in desperation, set out on a long journey to seek help from Dion, his rival healer.

While on his pilgrimage he fell into a conversation with an older traveler to whom he described the purpose and goal of his journey. Imagine his astonishment when the older man informed him that he was Dion, the very man he sought.

Without hesitation the older healer invited his younger rival into his cave, where they lived and worked together for many years, first as student and teacher, then as full colleagues. Years later the older man fell ill and on his deathbed called his young colleague to him. "I have a great secret to tell you," he said, "a secret that I have long kept. Do you remember that night we met when you told me you were on your way to see me?"

The younger man replied that he could never forget that night, the turning point of his entire life.

The dying man took the hand of his younger colleague and revealed the secret: that he, too, had been in despair and on the night of their meeting was journeying to seek help from him.

Hesse's moving tale strikes deep into the very heart of the therapy relationship. It is an illuminating statement about giving and receiving help, about honesty and duplicity, and about the relationship between the healer and patient. For years after reading it I found it so compelling that I never wanted to tamper with it. Yet recently I have been drawn to the idea of composing variations on its basic theme. Consider, for example, how each man received help. The younger healer was nurtured, nursed, taught, mentored, and parented. The older healer, on the other hand, received help in a different manner—through serving another, through obtaining a disciple from whom he received filial love, respect, and salve for his isolation.

But often I have wondered whether these two wounded healers took advantage of the best therapy available to them. Perhaps they missed the opportunity for something deeper, something more powerfully mutative. Perhaps the real therapy occurred at the deathbed scene when they moved into honesty with the admission that both were burdened with simple human frailty. Although it may have been helpful to keep a secret for twenty years, it may also have prevented a more profound kind of help. What would have happened, what manner of growth might have taken place, if their revelation had occurred twenty years earlier?

A Wounded Healer: *Emergency*

Thirty-five years ago I read a fragment of a play, *Emergency,* by Helmuth Kaiser, published in a psychiatric journal (and later in *Effective Psychotherapy,* a volume of Kaiser's collected papers).[17] Although I've never seen a reference to it or, until recently, reread it, Kaiser's delicious plot has stayed in my mind all these years. It begins with a woman visiting a therapist to plead with him to help her husband, also a therapist, who was deeply depressed and likely to kill himself.

The therapist replied that he, of course, would be glad to help and advised her to tell her husband to call for an appointment. The woman responded that therein lay the problem: her husband denied that he was troubled and rejected all suggestions that he obtain help. The therapist wondered how he could be of service. How could he help anyone unwilling to see him?

"I have a plan," the woman said. She suggested that he should pretend to be a patient, enter into treatment with her husband, and through a gradual role reversal, smuggle help for her husband into their meetings.

The rest of the play fragment is poorly executed and fails to fulfill its promise. But the central conceit—the patient becoming the therapist—seemed a gorgeous idea, and I yearned to finish that play someday.

Turning the Tables—Another Version

When I first came to Stanford in 1962, Don Jackson, a highly gifted therapist, offered a weekly teaching seminar in which he demonstrated interview techniques. He had an innovative, intuitive interviewing style and never failed to use some unexpected, quirky (and effective) approach.

In one conference he interviewed a highly delusional, three-hundred-fifty-pound Hawaiian chronic patient who believed he was the celestial emperor of the ward and dressed accordingly, in magenta trousers and a long flowing purple cape. Every day, perched imperiously on his velvet-draped chair, regarding patients and staff alike as supplicants and vassals, he held court on the ward. After a few minutes of exposure to the patient's regal demeanor, Jackson suddenly fell to his knees, bowed his head to the ground, took his keys out of his pocket, and, arms outstretched, offered them to the patient, saying, "Your Highness, *you,* not I, should possess the keys to this ward."

The patient, his left eye twitching, pulled his cape about him and stared hard at the genuflecting psychiatrist. For a moment, just for a moment, he appeared perfectly sane as he said, "Mistah, one of us here is very, very crazy."

Note, incidentally, that I could have made this point using professional psychiatric prose by describing Don Jackson's technique of creating a therapeutic alliance by entering a patient's delusional system and undermining the delusion by a reductio ad absurdum approach. But dramatization—that is, fictionalization (I did not personally witness this incident, which took place forty years ago)—conveys the information more vividly and memorably. This is precisely the reason I chose to use the novel as a pedagogical device.

Who Is the Patient? Who Is the Therapist?

Harry Stack Sullivan, one of the most influential American psychiatric theorists, defined psychotherapy as a discussion of personal issues between two people, one of them more anxious than the other. And if the therapist develops more anxiety than the patient, Sullivan went on, *he* becomes the patient and the patient the therapist.

Or consider Jung's view that only the wounded doctor can truly heal. Jung went so far as to suggest that an ideal therapeutic situation occurs when the patient brings the perfect salve for the therapist's lesion.

Or consider how often it happens that therapists begin a therapy session with a heavy heart, with anxiety that exceeds that of their patient. I certainly have. And often I have finished a therapy session feeling much better. In fact, like Dion, the older healer in the *Magister Ludi* story, I may have profited as much as my patient. How so? How did I receive benefit without explicitly addressing my discomfort? Perhaps as a by-product of altruistic behavior—that is, I was helped through the act of helping others. Or through feeling better about myself because of my effectiveness as a therapist—that is, I reminded myself that I am good at what I do. Or perhaps I felt better because I dipped into the healing waters of an intimate relationship that I myself helped to construct.

I have found this to be particularly true in my group therapy practice. Many times I have started a therapy group session feeling troubled about some personal issue and finished the meeting feeling considerably relieved. The intimate healing ambiance of a good therapy group is almost tangible. Scott Rutan, an eminent group therapist, once compared the therapy group to a bridge built during a battle. Although there may be some casualties sustained during the building (that is, group therapy dropouts), the bridge, once in place, can transport a great many people to a better place.

Most of these themes are played out, in one way or another, in the Nietzsche-Breuer relationship. At first Breuer improvised a therapeutic approach that seemed to be the only possible way to engage Nietzsche in therapy. Yet this therapeutic relationship, much like that between the healers in *Magister Ludi,* was conceived in duplicity. From this point forward the focus of the novel is upon the gradual transformation of this dishonest relationship into an authentic one ultimately redemptive to both. Both characters are at once patient and therapist. Sometimes giving and receiving help takes place explicitly; at other times it must be smuggled into the relationship. Their relationship goes through many stages—from manipulation to care, from distrust to love, from subject and object to I and thou.

The first major sign of the relationship's evolution is Breuer's perception that therapy is more powerful than he had expected; soon he is unable to resist becoming a genuine patient. What kind of patient? I have posited a midlife crisis for Breuer manifested by a powerful obsessive countertransferential love entanglement with his former patient Bertha Pappenheim. Although Breuer's professional work is well known, little is known of the personal Breuer. Is my fictionalization of Breuer's inner life plausible? There is some historical basis for my suppositions: generations of analysts have speculated about the mysterious and explosive ending to Breuer's treatment of Bertha Pappenheim, and many, including Freud, have posited that Breuer had fallen in love with his beautiful and talented patient.

In this phase of their relationship Nietzsche applies himself diligently to the task of inventing a therapy to help Breuer examine his life in general and free himself from his obsession with Bertha in particular. Several chapters follow a similar structure: Nietzsche and Breuer spend an hour in which Nietzsche invents a number of methods to lay bare the existential roots of Breuer's despair. At times he accedes to Breuer's request for more direct help and experiments with behavioral methods. Following each session the reader sees the private therapy notes that both Nietzsche and Breuer have written—a format suggested by my earlier book, *Every Day Gets a Little Closer*.

Nietzsche continues to invent, employ, and discard a number of existential therapy approaches until finally, in the following excerpt, he offers Breuer his mightiest thought, eternal recurrence—the great and terrible idea that was percolating in Nietzsche's mind in 1882 and which he was to develop in his next book, *Thus Spake Zarathustra*.

The scene is set in a cemetery where Nietzsche has accompanied Breuer on a visit to his parents' grave. They have been conversing congenially about their dead fathers.

For both men, the cemetery visit opens old childhood wounds; as they stroll, they reminisce. Nietzsche recounts a dream (an actual, non-fictional dream) he remembers from when he was six, a year after his father had died.

When Nietzsche Wept: Chapter 20

"It's as vivid today as if I'd dreamed it last night. A grave opens and my father, dressed in a shroud, arises, enters a church, and soon returns carrying a small child in his arms. He climbs back into his grave with the child. The earth closes on top of them, and the gravestone slides over the opening.

"The truly horrible thing was that shortly after I had that dream, my younger brother was taken ill and died of convulsions."

"How ghastly!" Breuer said. "How eerie to have had such a prevision! How do you explain it?"

"I can't. For a long time, the supernatural terrified me, and I said my prayers with great earnestness. Over the last few years, however, I've begun to suspect that the dream was unrelated to my brother, that it was *me* my father had come for, and that the dream was expressing my fear of death."

At ease with one another in a way they had not been before, both men continued to reminisce. Breuer recalled a dream of some calamity occurring in his old home: his father standing helplessly, praying and rocking, wrapped in his blue-and-white prayer shawl. And Nietzsche described a nightmare in which, entering his bedroom, he saw, lying in his bed, an old man dying, a death rattle in his throat.

"We both encountered death very early," said Breuer thoughtfully, "and we both suffered a terrible early loss. I believe, speaking for myself, I've never recovered. But you, what about *your* loss? What about having had no father to protect you?"

"To protect me—or to *oppress* me? Was it a loss? I'm not so sure. Or it may have been a loss for the child, but not for the man."

"Meaning?" Breuer asked.

"Meaning that I was never weighed down by carrying my father on my back, never suffocated by the burden of his judgment, never taught that the object of life was to fulfill his thwarted ambitions. His death may well have been a blessing, a liberation. His whims never became my law. I was left alone to discover my own path, one not trodden before. Think about it! Could I, the Antichrist, have exorcised false beliefs and sought new truths with a parson-father wincing with pain at my every achievement, a father who would have regarded my campaigns against illusion as a personal attack against *him*?"

"But," Breuer rejoined, "if you had had his protection when you needed it, would you have *had* to be the Antichrist?"

Nietzsche did not respond, and Breuer pressed no further. He was learning to accommodate to Nietzsche's rhythm: any truth-seeking inquiries were permissible, even welcomed; but added force would be resisted. Breuer took out his watch, the one given him by his father. It was time to turn back to the fiacre, where Fischmann awaited. With the wind at their backs, the walking was easier.

"You may be more honest than I," speculated Breuer. "Perhaps my father's judgments weighed me down more than I realized. But most of the time I miss him a great deal."

"What do you miss?"

Breuer thought about his father and sampled the memories passing before his eyes. The old man, yarmulke on head, chanting a blessing before he tasted his supper of boiled potatoes and herring. His smile as he sat in the synagogue and watched his son wrapping his fingers in the tassels of his prayer shawl. His refusal to let his son take back a move in chess: "Josef, I cannot permit myself to teach you bad habits." His deep baritone voice, which filled the house as he sang passages for the young students he was preparing for their bar mitzvah.

"Most of all, I think I miss his attention. He was always my chief audience, even at the very end of his life, when he suffered considerable confusion and memory loss. I made sure to tell him of my successes, my diagnostic triumphs, my research discoveries, even my charitable donations. And even after he died, he was still my audience. For years I imagined him peering over my shoulder, observing and approving my achievements. The more his image fades, the more I struggle with the feeling that my activities and successes are all evanescent, that they have no real meaning."

"Are you saying, Josef, that if your successes could be recorded in the ephemeral mind of your father, *then* they would possess meaning?"

"I know it's irrational. It's much like the question of the sound of a tree falling in an empty forest. Does unobserved activity have meaning?"

"The difference is, of course, that the tree has no ears, whereas it is you, yourself, who bestows meaning."

"Friedrich, you're more self-sufficient than I—more than anyone I've known! I remember marveling, in our very first meeting, at your ability to thrive with no recognition whatsoever from your colleagues."

"Long ago, Josef, I learned that it is easier to cope with a bad reputation than with a bad conscience. Besides, I'm not greedy; I don't write for the crowd. And I know how to be patient. Perhaps my students are not yet alive. Only the day after tomorrow belongs to me. Some philosophers are born posthumously!"

"But, Friedrich, believing you will be born posthumously—is that *so* different from my longing for my father's attention? You can wait, even until the day after tomorrow, but you, too, yearn for an audience."

A long pause. Nietzsche nodded finally and then said softly, "Perhaps. Perhaps I have within me pockets of vanity yet to be purged."

Breuer merely nodded. It did not escape his notice that this was the first time one of his observations had been acknowledged by Nietzsche. Was this to be a turning point in their relationship?

No, not yet! After a moment, Nietzsche added, "Still, there is a difference between coveting a parent's approval and striving to elevate those who will follow in the future."

Breuer did not respond, though it was obvious to him that Nietzsche's motives were not purely self-transcendent; he had his own back-alley ways of courting remembrance. Today it seemed to Breuer as if *all motives,* his and Nietzsche's, sprang from a single source—the drive to escape death's oblivion. Was he growing too morbid? Maybe it was the effect of the cemetery. Maybe even one visit a month was too frequent.

But not even morbidity could spoil the mood of this walk. He thought of Nietzsche's definition of friendship: two who join together in a search for some higher truth. Was that not precisely what he and Nietzsche were doing that day? Yes, they were friends.

That was a consoling thought, even though Breuer knew that their deepening relationship and their engrossing discussion brought him no closer to relief from his pain. For the sake of friendship, he tried to ignore his disturbing idea.

Yet, as a friend, Nietzsche must have read his mind. "I like this walk we take together, Josef, but we must not forget the raison d'être of our meetings—your psychological state."

Breuer slipped and grabbed a sapling for support as they descended a hill. "Careful, Friedrich, this shale is slick." Nietzsche gave Breuer his hand, and they continued their descent.

"I've been thinking," Nietzsche continued, "that, though our discussions appear to be diffuse, we, nonetheless, steadily grow closer to a solution. It's true that our direct attacks on your Bertha obsession have been futile. Yet in the last couple of days we have found out *why:* because the obsession involves not Bertha, or not only her, but a series of meanings folded into Bertha. We agree on this?"

Breuer nodded, wanting to suggest politely that help was not going to come by way of such intellectual formulations. But Nietzsche hurried on. "It's clear now that our primary error has been in considering Bertha the target. *We have not chosen the right enemy.*"

"And that is—?"

"*You* know, Josef! Why make *me* say it? The right enemy is the underlying *meaning* of your obsession. Think of our talk today—again and again, we've returned to your fears of the void, of oblivion, of death. It's there in your nightmare, in the ground liquefying, in your plunge downward to the marble slab. It's there in your cemetery dread, in your concerns about meaninglessness, in your wish to be observed and remembered. The paradox, *your* paradox, is that you dedicate yourself to the search for truth but cannot bear the sight of what you discover."

"But you, too, Friedrich, must be frightened by death and by godlessness. From the very beginning, I have asked, 'How do you bear it? How have *you* come to terms with such horrors?'"

"It may be time to tell you," Nietzsche replied, his manner becoming portentous. "Before, I did not think that you were ready to hear me."

Breuer, curious about Nietzsche's message, chose, for once, not to object to his prophet voice.

"I do not teach, Josef, that one should 'bear' death, or 'come to terms' with it. That way lies life-betrayal! Here is my lesson to you: *Die at the right time!*"

"Die at the right time!" The phrase jolted Breuer. The pleasant afternoon stroll had turned deadly serious. "Die at the right time? What do you mean? Please, Friedrich, I can't stand it, as I tell you again and again, when you say something important in such an enigmatic way. Why do you do that?"

"You pose two questions. Which shall I answer?"

"Today, tell me about dying at the right time."

"Live when you live! Death loses its terror if one dies when one has consummated one's life! If one does not live in the right time, then one can never die at the right time."

"What does *that* mean?" Breuer asked again, feeling ever more frustrated.

"Ask yourself, Josef: *Have you consummated your life?*"

"You answer questions with questions, Friedrich!"

"You ask questions to which you know the answer," Nietzsche countered.

"If I knew the answer, why would I ask?"

"To avoid knowing your own answer!"

Breuer paused. He knew Nietzsche was right. He stopped resisting and turned his attention within. "Have I consummated my life? I have achieved a great deal, more than anyone could have expected of me. Material success, scientific achievement, family, children—but we've gone over all that before."

"Still, Josef, you avoid my question. Have you lived your life? Or been lived by it? Chosen it? Or did it choose you? Loved it? Or regretted it? That is what I mean when I ask whether you have consummated your life. Have you used it up? Remember that dream in which your father stood by helplessly praying while something calamitous was happening to his family? Are you not like him? Do you not stand by helplessly, grieving for the life you never lived?"

Breuer felt the pressure mounting. Nietzsche's questions bore down on him; he had no defense against them. He could hardly breathe. His chest seemed about to burst. He stopped walking for a moment and took three deep breaths before answering.

"These questions—you know the answer! No, I've not chosen! No, I've not lived the life I've wanted! I've lived the life assigned me. I—the real I—have been encased in my life."

"And *that,* Josef, is, I am convinced, the primary source of your *Angst.* That precordial pressure—it's because your chest is bursting with unlived life. And your heart ticks away the time. And time's covetousness is forever. Time devours and devours—and gives back nothing. How terrible to hear you say that you lived the life assigned to you! And how terrible to face death without ever having claimed freedom, even in all its danger!"

Nietzsche was firmly in his pulpit, his prophet's voice ringing. A wave of disappointment swept over Breuer; he knew now that there was no help for him.

"Friedrich," he said, "these are grand-sounding phrases. I admire them. They stir my soul. But they are far, far away from my life. What does claiming freedom mean to my everyday situation? How can I be free? It's not the same as you, a young single man giving up a suffocating university career. It's too late for me! I have a family, employees, patients, students. It's far too late! We can talk forever, but I cannot change my life—it is woven too tight with the thread of other lives."

There was a long silence, which Breuer broke, his voice weary. "But I cannot sleep, and now I cannot stand the pain of this pressure in my chest." The icy wind pierced his greatcoat; he shivered and wrapped his scarf more tightly around his neck.

Nietzsche, in a rare gesture, took his arm. "My friend," he whispered, "I *cannot* tell you how to live differently because, if I did, you would *still* be living another's design. But, Josef, there is something I *can* do. I can give you a gift, the gift of my mightiest thought, my thought of thoughts. Perhaps it may already be somewhat familiar to you, since I sketched it briefly in *Human, All Too Human.* This thought will be the guiding force of my next book, perhaps of all my future books."

His voice had lowered, assuming a solemn, stately tone, as if to signify the culmination of everything that had gone before. The two men walked arm in arm. Breuer looked straight ahead as he awaited Nietzsche's words.

"Josef, try to clear your mind. Imagine this thought experiment! What if some demon were to say to you that this life—as you now live it and have lived it in the past—you will have to live once more, and innumerable times more; and there will be nothing new in it, but every pain and every joy and everything unutterably small or great in your life will return to you, all in the same succession and sequence—even this wind and those trees and that slippery shale, even the graveyard and the dread, even this gentle moment and you and I, arm in arm, murmuring these words?"

As Breuer remained silent, Nietzsche continued, "Imagine the eternal hourglass of existence turned upside down again and again and again. And each time, also turned upside down are you and I, mere specks that we are."

Breuer made an effort to understand him. "How is this—this—this fantasy—"

"It's more than a fantasy," Nietzsche insisted, "more really than a thought experiment. Listen only to my words! Block out everything else! Think about infinity. Look behind you—imagine looking infinitely far into the past. Time stretches backward for all eternity. And, if time infinitely stretches backward, must not everything that *can* happen have *already* happened? Must not all that passes *now* have passed this way before? Whatever walks here, mustn't it have walked this path before? And if everything has passed before in time's infinity, then what do you think, Josef, of *this* moment, of our whispering together under this arch of trees? Must not *this,* too, have come before? And time that stretches back infinitely, must it not also stretch ahead infinitely? Must not we, in this moment, in every moment, recur eternally?"

Nietzsche fell silent, to give Breuer time to absorb his message. It was midday, but the sky had darkened. A light snow began to fall. The fiacre and Fischmann loomed into sight.

On the ride back to the clinic, the two men resumed their discussion. Nietzsche claimed that, though he had termed it a thought experiment, his assumption of eternal recurrence could be scientifically proven. Breuer was skeptical about Nietzsche's proof, which was based on two metaphysical principles: that time is infinite, and force (the basic stuff of the universe) is finite. Given a finite number of potential states of the world and an infinite amount of time that has passed, it follows, Nietzsche claimed, that all possible states must have already occurred; and that the present state must be a repetition; and, likewise, the one that gave birth to it and the one that arises out of it and so on, backward into the past and forward into the future.

Breuer's perplexity grew. "You mean that through sheer random occurrences this precise moment would have occurred previously?"

"Think of time that has always been, time stretching back forever. In such infinite time, must not recombinations of all events constituting the world have repeated themselves an infinite number of times?"

"Like a great dice game?"

"Precisely! The great dice game of existence!"

Breuer continued to question Nietzsche's cosmological proof of eternal recurrence. Though Nietzsche responded to each question, he eventually grew impatient and finally threw up his hands.

"Time and time again, Josef, you have asked for concrete help. How many times have you asked me to be relevant, to offer something that can change you? *Now* I give you what you request, and you ignore it by picking away at details. Listen to me, my friend, listen to my words— this is the most important thing I will ever say to you: *let this thought take possession of you, and I promise you it will change you forever!*"

Breuer was unmoved. "But how can I believe without proof? I cannot conjure up belief. Have I given up one religion simply to embrace another?"

"The proof is extremely complex. It is still unfinished and will require years of work. And now, as a result of our discussion, I'm not sure I should even bother to devote the time to working out the cosmological proof—perhaps others, too, will use it as a distraction. Perhaps they, like you, will pick away at the intricacies of the proof and ignore the important point—the psychological *consequences* of eternal recurrence."

Breuer said nothing. He looked out the window of the fiacre and shook his head slightly.

"Let me put it another way," Nietzsche continued. "Will you not grant me that eternal recurrence is *probable*? No, wait, I don't need even that! Let us say simply that it is *possible,* or *merely* possible. That is enough. Certainly it is more possible and more provable than the fairy tale of eternal damnation! What do you have to lose by considering it a possibility? Can you not think of it, then, as 'Nietzsche's wager'?"

Breuer nodded.

"I urge you, then, to consider the *implications* of eternal recurrence for your life—not abstractly, but now, *today,* in the most concrete sense!"

"You suggest," said Breuer, "that every action I make, every pain I experience, will be experienced through all infinity?"

"Yes, eternal recurrence means that every time you choose an action you must be willing to choose it *for all eternity.* And it is the same for every action *not* made, every stillborn thought, every choice avoided. And all unlived life will remain bulging inside you, unlived through all eternity. And the unheeded voice of your conscience will cry out to you forever."

Breuer felt dizzy; it was hard to listen. He tried to concentrate on Nietzsche's mammoth mustache pounding up and down at each word. Since his mouth and lips were entirely obscured, there was no forewarning of the words to come. Occasionally his glance would catch Nietzsche's eyes, but they were too sharp, and he shifted his attention down to the fleshy but powerful nose, or up to the heavy overhanging eyebrows which resembled ocular mustaches.

Breuer finally managed a question: "So, as I understand it, eternal recurrence promises a form of immortality?"

"No!" Nietzsche was vehement. "I teach that life should never be modified, or squelched, because of the promise of some other kind of life in the future. What is immortal is *this* life, *this* moment. There is no afterlife, no goal toward which this life points, no apocalyptic tribunal or judgment. *This moment exists forever,* and you, alone, are your only audience."

Breuer shivered. As the chilling implications of Nietzsche's proposal grew more clear, he stopped resisting and, instead, entered a state of uncanny concentration.

"So, Josef, once again I say, let this thought take possession of you. Now I have a question for you: *Do you hate the idea? Or do you love it?*"

"*I hate it!*" Breuer almost shouted. "To live *forever* with the sense that I have *not* lived, have *not* tasted freedom—the idea fills me with horror."

"*Then,*" Nietzsche exhorted, "*live in such a way that you love the idea!*"

"All that I love *now,* Friedrich, is the thought that I have fulfilled my duty toward others."

"Duty? Can duty take precedence over your love for *yourself* and for your own quest for unconditional freedom? If you have not attained yourself, then 'duty' is merely a euphemism for using others for your own enlargement."

Breuer summoned the energy for one further rebuttal. "There *is* such a thing as a duty to others, and I have been faithful to that duty. There, at least, I have the courage of my convictions."

"Better, Josef, far better, to have the courage to *change* your convictions. Duty and faithfulness are shams, curtains to hide behind. Self-liberation means a sacred *no,* even to duty."

Frightened, Breuer stared at Nietzsche.

"You want to become *yourself,*" Nietzsche continued. "How often have I heard you say that? How often have you lamented that you have never known your freedom? Your goodness, your duty, your faithfulness—these are the bars of your prison. You will perish from such small virtues. You must learn to know your wickedness. You cannot be *partially* free: your instincts, too, thirst for freedom; your wild dogs in the cellar—they bark for freedom. Listen harder, can't you hear them?"

"But I *cannot* be free," Breuer implored. "I have made sacred marriage vows. I have a duty to my children, my students, my patients."

"To build children you must first be built yourself. Otherwise, you'll seek children out of animal needs, or loneliness, or to patch the holes in yourself. Your task as a parent is to produce not another self, another Josef, but something higher. It's to produce a creator.

"And your wife?" Nietzsche went on inexorably. "Is she not as imprisoned in this marriage as you? Marriage should be no prison, but a garden in which something higher is cultivated. *Perhaps the only way to save your marriage is to give it up.*"

"I have made sacred vows of wedlock."

"Marriage is something large. It is a large thing to always be two, to remain in love. Yes, wedlock *is* sacred. And yet . . ." Nietzsche's voice trailed off.

"And yet?" Breuer asked.

"Wedlock *is* sacred. Yet"—Nietzsche's voice was harsh—"*it is better to break wedlock than to be broken by it!*"

Breuer closed his eyes and sank into deep thought. Neither man spoke for the remainder of their journey.

Friedrich Nietzsche's Notes on Dr. Breuer, 16 December 1882

A stroll that began in sunlight and ended darkly. Perhaps we journeyed too far into the graveyard. Should we have turned back earlier? Have I given him too powerful a thought? Eternal recurrence is a mighty hammer. It will break those who are not yet ready for it.

No! A psychologist, an unriddler of souls, needs hardness more than anyone. Else he will bloat with pity. And his student drown in shallow water.

Yet at the end of our walk, Josef seemed sorely pressed, barely able to converse. Some are not born hard. A true psychologist, like an artist, must love his palette. Perhaps more kindness, more patience was needed. Do I strip before teaching how to weave new clothing? Have I taught him "freedom from" without teaching "freedom for"?

No, a guide must be a railing by the torrent, but he must not be a crutch. The guide must lay bare the trails that lie before the student. But he must not choose the path.

"Become my teacher," he asks. "Help me overcome despair." Shall I conceal my wisdom? And the student's responsibility? He must harden himself

to the cold, his fingers must grip the railing, he must lose himself many times on wrong paths before finding the right one.

In the mountains alone, I travel the shortest way—from peak to peak. But students lose their way when I walk too far ahead. I must learn to shorten my stride. Today, we may have traveled too fast. I unraveled a dream, separated one Bertha from another, reburied the dead, and taught dying at the right time. And all of this was but the overture to the mighty theme of recurrence.

Have I pushed him too deep into misery? Often he seemed too upset to hear me. Yet what did I challenge? What destroy? Only empty values and tottering beliefs! That which is tottering, one should also push!

Today I understood that the best teacher is one who learns from his student. Perhaps he is right about my father. How different my life would be had I not lost him! Can it be true that I hammer so hard because I hate him for dying? And hammer so loud because I still crave an audience?

I worry about his silence at the end. His eyes were open, but he seemed not to see. He scarcely breathed.

Yet I know the dew falls heaviest when the night is most silent.

CHAPTER 10

━━━━━━

The Psychological Novel

P. D. James, the fine British writer, begins her novels with a vision of place from which her plot and characters emerge. Other novelists begin with plot or with characters. I know a writer who was unable to finish one novel but managed to lift the characters, still talking to one another, and plunk them down into an entirely different book.

My novel *Lying on the Couch,* like *When Nietzsche Wept,* is neither place-driven, nor plot-driven, nor character-driven. Instead, it is idea-driven. I intended *When Nietzsche Wept* to be an inquiry into the existential approach to psychotherapy. In *Lying on the Couch* I meant to explore some fundamental ideas about the therapeutic relationship.

Every investigation of the nature of the therapeutic relationship sooner or later leads to Carl Rogers's dictum: *it is the relationship that heals.* That notion, perhaps psychotherapy's most fundamental axiom— and "axiom" is not too strong a term—posits that the mutative force in the process of personal change is the nature, the texture, of the relationship between patient and therapist. Other considerations (for example, the ideological school to which the therapist belongs, the actual *content* of the therapy discussion, or the techniques employed, such as free association, or reconstruction of childhood or psychodrama) are quite secondary.

Not only did Carl Rogers demonstrate the centrality of the therapeutic relationship, but he also identified the *specific characteristics* of the successful relationship—namely, that the effective therapist relates to the patient in a genuine, unconditionally supportive, and accurately empathic manner.

These findings, central to psychotherapy practice for decades, appear beyond dispute—not only because they are supported by so much empirical evidence, but because they seem so right, so self-evident. Yet let us pluck the variables off the research rating scales and consider their appearance in vivo. Picture the psychotherapy hour. Heads bowed together, a therapist and patient converse about important matters. The patient reveals intimate material. The therapist responds with empathy, support, clarifications, interpretations. Is this a *genuine* relationship?

In the past it was easier to identify genuineness, or at least the *absence* of genuineness. The archaic blank screen analyst did not relate *genuinely*. But most therapists today, fortunately, eschew such a role and instead interact directly with their patients, revealing more of themselves. Hence the determination of genuineness in contemporary practice becomes more complex and subtle. How do genuine, or "authentic," therapists behave? Do they shuck the trappings of their professional role and become "real" in the therapy situation? As real *in* the hour as out of the hour? What about payment? Is therapy merely purchased friendship? Should self-revealing and the attachment go both ways? Do therapists feel deeply about their clients? Love their clients? Profit themselves, psychologically, from the therapy they offer to others?

TRANSPARENCY

In an irreverent and playful manner *Lying on the Couch* explores these vexing problems. It attempts to illuminate core aspects of the patient-therapist relationship through a sustained focus on therapist transparency. There is an ongoing debate in the field about therapists' self-revelation. Should therapists share their feelings openly in therapy? Feelings about themselves? Their own lives? Feelings toward their patients? The theme of transparency is introduced in one of the opening paragraphs of *Lying on the Couch.* Here Ernest Lash, the protagonist, pays homage to his psychotherapy ancestors.

> "Thank you, thank you," Ernest would chant. He thanked them all—all the healers who had ministered to despair. First, the ur-ancestors, their empyreal outlines barely visible: Jesus, Buddha, Socrates. Below them, somewhat more distinct— the great progenitors: Nietzsche, Kierkegaard, Freud, Jung. Nearer yet, the grandparent therapists: Adler, Horney, Sullivan, Fromm, and the sweet smiling face of Sandor Ferenczi.

Note the last phrase. Why the extra tip of the hat to Sandor Ferenczi? Precisely because of Ernest's fascination with therapist transparency. Sandor Ferenczi (1873–1933), a Hungarian psychoanalyst, was a member of Freud's inner circle and probably Freud's closest professional and personal confidant. Basically pessimistic about therapy, Freud was not heavily committed to experimentation with therapy technique. By nature he was more drawn to speculative questions about the application of psychoanalysis to understanding the origins of culture. Of all the analysts in the inner circle, it was Sandor Ferenczi who was most relentless and bold in the search for improved therapist technique.

Never was he more bold than in a radical 1932 transparency experiment where he pushed therapist self-disclosure to the limit. This experiment, which he referred to as "mutual analysis," consisted of his analyzing a patient one hour and the patient analyzing him the next.[1] Ferenczi's experiment failed, shipwrecked on some treacherous reefs of early analysis. There were, for example, complications around the issue of free association and confidentiality: Ferenczi found that he could not free-associate to one patient without having to share thoughts about his other analysands. And Ferenczi fretted about billing: who should pay whom? Ultimately he grew discouraged and abandoned the experiment. His disappointed patient believed Ferenczi was unwilling to continue because he feared having to acknowledge that he was in love with her. Ferenczi held a contrary opinion: that he was unwilling to express the fact that he hated her.

For a while I considered using Ferenczi as a character in the novel and alternating the action between the present and 1932. In preparation, I read all the fiction I could locate that was set in two time periods, but I eventually abandoned the idea because I never found a satisfactory novelistic device to bind the two eras together. (Such standard devices as an old manuscript discovered and read in another era or characters from a different era inhabiting the same house seemed too frail to support a novel on psychotherapy.) Finally I built Ferenczi's idea, not his person, into the plot by having my protagonist reenact Ferenczi's experiment in contemporary times.

Lying on the Couch opens with a therapy session in which Ernest Lash faces a dilemma about his degree of transparency. For five long years he has treated Justin, who originally came in requesting help in leaving a horrendous marriage. For months Ernest dispassionately investigated the dynamics of the marriage: Justin's passive aggressiveness, his role in the marital discord, his instigation of his wife's irrational behavior, his original choice of a mate, and his unwillingness to leave the marriage. After an exhaustive exploration Ernest eventually came to agree with Justin—this was, indeed, a marriage from hell. Thereafter, for a period of two years, Ernest did everything a person could do to persuade another to take action: he advised Justin, encouraged, exhorted, analyzed resistance. But nothing worked, and the discouraged Ernest gave up. "This man is immobile," he declared, "he is passive, hopelessly stuck, a deadweight, rooted to the ground; he will never leave this marriage." And so Ernest lowered his goals and resigned himself to more supportive "containing" therapy.

Later in the opening chapter, Justin saunters in for a therapy hour and almost *en passant* tells Ernest, "Oh, yes, I left my wife last night." Naturally Ernest has mixed feelings: on the one hand, he is pleased his patient has taken the long-delayed step of liberation; on the other hand, he is vexed to be informed of it so casually. And even more vexed a few minutes later when Justin tells him that the day before the young woman with whom he has been having an affair said to him, "It's time, Justin, to leave your wife." And so he did, that very evening.

Despite himself, Ernest thinks, "*Here I, one of the premier therapists of San Francisco, have been breaking my ass for five years to persuade him to leave his marriage and this little teenage twit merely says, 'It's time,' and Justin jumps to it.*" And Ernest is jangled even more when

Justin goes on to muse about how much more convenient life would be if he could afford to buy a condo—if only he still had the eighty thousand dollars he has spent for therapy over the last few years.

Justin senses Ernest's mood quite accurately and confronts him about not being pleased with the positive steps his patient has taken. In an attempt to protect himself and to preserve the therapeutic alliance, Ernest self-righteously denies Justin's observation. Later that evening, as he reviews the therapy hour, he realizes that he had just disconfirmed his patient's accurate perception of an event. If a goal of therapy is to improve a patient's reality-testing, Ernest muses, then it is difficult to escape the conclusion that he had just been engaged, not in therapy, but in *countertherapy*.

After further brooding upon his duplicitous behavior, Ernest resolves to be more honest in his relationships with his patients. He decides on a course of full, even radical, self-disclosure: he will run Ferenczi's 1932 transparency experiment with the next new patient who enters his office. But he will set more sensible, less heroic, conditions: rather than alternate hours of free association with the patient, he will be consistently honest in every transaction during each therapy hour. Ernest's trial-and-error experiment proceeds throughout the novel and teaches him a great deal about the consequences—both positive and negative—of greater therapist transparency.

Despite the burlesque sequences in many sections of *Lying on the Couch,* my attitude toward transparency is entirely serious and the rules of therapist self-disclosure that Ernest stumbles upon are meant to be useful guidelines to the practicing clinician. I have always felt that openness in therapy enhances the efficacy of treatment. Too often therapists deliberately embrace an opaque posture in their work—either to conform to Freud's blank-screen mandate (a rule that Freud did not follow in his own analytic work) or to protect themselves from too much self-exposure, involvement, or fatigue. Other therapists remain opaque because they take seriously the words of Dostoevsky's Grand Inquisitor, who insisted that human beings really want magic, mystery, and authority. Accordingly, these therapists attempt to heal through authority and employ age-old authoritarian techniques: placebos; Latin prescriptions; the robes, incantations, and rituals of medical cure.

I have always believed that psychotherapy is an intrinsically robust process that need not rest upon the accoutrements of authority. In fact, insofar as therapy is conceptualized as a process of personal growth and enlightenment, I consider the appeal to authority counterproductive.

Often therapists are alarmed at the idea of transparency and reject it out of hand because they assume it demands that they reveal a great deal about their personal life—both past and present. As Ernest discovers, however, *there are other levels of self-disclosure that are far more crucial to therapeutic success.* In the novel I focus particularly upon two: (1) transparency concerning the therapy procedure itself and (2) transparency concerning the therapist's here-and-now experience.

The process of being transparent about the *therapy procedure* begins even before the first hour with the preparation for therapy. Some of my early research demonstrated that a systematic preparation for group therapy (which includes a lucid discussion of the rationale and mechanics of therapy) significantly influences the efficacy of group therapy. Others have demonstrated that preparation has the same beneficial effect in the individual therapy setting.

Therapists who are transparent about their here-and-now *experience* reveal their immediate feelings to the patient in the moment. They may say that they feel distant or close to the patient; or moved, shut out, criticized at every turn; or elevated, idealized, or avoided by the patient. There are examples of this on almost every page of *Lying on the Couch*. I take therapist transparency very seriously and have, throughout my career, experimented with a series of techniques designed to encourage and enhance transparency. I shall describe a few of these.

One transparency technique I've used is "multiple therapy." In an article discussing this teaching format, I described how a colleague and I and several trainees met with a single patient and worked together as a group, focusing at times upon the patient and at other times upon the group process (that is, upon the nature of the relationship between the group members). Our openness demonstrated to both students and patients that obfuscation and mystification were unnecessary.[2]

Another transparency exercise I've employed is the open group rehash. In most group therapy training programs students observe therapy groups through two-way mirrors or TV and discuss the meeting after its completion. Group therapy members permit the observation but generally resent it, since it raises their discomfort and self-consciousness.

Yet, by being willing to increase their transparency, therapists can transform observation from a limited teaching device into an integral part of therapy. I have long made a practice of inviting the *group members to observe the student rehash of the group meeting*—sometimes students and group members simply switch rooms for the postsession. In my experience such a format invariably energizes both the therapy and the teaching.[3]

In my model of inpatient therapy groups I use a similar approach: toward the end of the meeting we adopt a "fishbowl" format—the student observers and the group leaders form an inner circle and review the group session in the presence of the group members for ten minutes.[4] Then, in the final ten minutes, the group members discuss their feelings about this review. Very frequently the rehash raises so many issues and so much affect that the members consider the final ten minutes of the session to be the most profitable part of the meeting.

Another benefit of such teaching formats is that patients gain respect for the therapeutic enterprise if they observe the therapist and student therapists personally engaging in the same honest discourse they encourage in their therapy.

Earlier in this volume, in a paper on alcoholics in group therapy, I described my practice of mailing summaries of each outpatient group meeting to the members before the next session. Among other purposes, the summaries serve to provide a vehicle for therapist transparency: I include comments about my personal feelings and observations of the meeting. I review the interventions I made—those that I considered important, those I wished I had made in the session but did not, and those I regretted making.

Generally in therapy groups there is a particularly clear mandate for therapists to be more interactive and transparent. This is necessary for two reasons: first, because group leaders are lightning rods for so many powerful feelings that they must work through their relationships with many of the group members; second, because the leaders' behavior— through the mechanism of modeling—is instrumental in shaping the norms of the group.

Although much of my writing has centered on group therapy, I believe that transparency is no less important in the individual therapy setting, where therapists must be willing to be open about the mechanisms of therapy and about their own here-and-now feelings. *Nothing the therapist does takes precedence, in my view, over building a trusting relationship with the patient.* I have long believed that other activities in therapy—for example, exploration of the past and the construction of a unified life narrative—are valuable only insofar as they keep therapist and patient bound together in some mutually valued, interesting endeavor while the real healing force, the therapeutic relationship, germinates and takes root.

My own self-disclosure, especially about here-and-now feelings, almost invariably has deepened the therapeutic relationship; to the best of my knowledge the opposite has never occurred—therapy has never been impaired by my revealing too much. Very frequently in my practice I see patients who have had some prior unsatisfactory therapy. Over and over again I hear them voice the same complaint: their therapist was too impersonal, too uninvolved, too wooden. I have almost never heard a patient criticize a therapist for being too open, honest, or interactive.

The salubrious effect of therapist transparency is the very core of *Lying on the Couch,* as Ernest doggedly pursues the experiment that, unknown to him, is played out in the most unfavorable possible circumstance—in the therapy of a patient committed to duplicity.

THERAPEUTIC BOUNDARIES

Another major therapist-patient theme I explore in *Lying on the Couch* is the question of appropriate *boundaries.* Can a relationship be genuine and yet at the same time be sharply and formally limited? Do the strict time limits, the formality, and the exchange of money corrode the genuineness of the relationship? Is the therapist a friend? Is there love between therapist and patient? Should caring therapists ever touch or hold their patients? What are the appropriate sexual, social, business, financial boundaries of a therapeutic relationship?

These contemporary concerns are not only crucial and complex: they are also highly inflammatory. With so many lawsuits, so many cases of reported abuse by therapists (and priests, teachers, physicians, police officers, employers, supervisors, gurus—by anyone involved in a power imbalance), it seemed distinctly risky to discuss boundaries in an irreverently comic novel. I attempted to maintain a balanced perspective—on the one hand, to address the alarming incidence of abuse suffered by patients, and on the other hand, to confront the equally alarming legalistic backlash that threatens the very fabric of the therapy relationship.

What is one to think, for example, of articles in professional journals that seriously propose that *all* therapy hours be videotaped with a continuously running security patrol camera to protect the patient from sexual abuse by the therapist and the therapist from false charges by the patient? How is one to respond to the sanctimonious, patronizing official guidelines prescribing appropriate behavior that so many professional organizations mail to therapists? These publications warn that attorneys assume that smoke means fire and, accordingly, instruct practitioners to err on the far side of formality: one must wear neckties; avoid sweaters, first names, or social chitchat; not offer coffee or tea; end sessions very punctually; and (for male therapists) not schedule a female patient for the last hour of the day. (Soon one becomes wary of scheduling *anyone* for the last hour of the day.)

All these factors have resulted in a new defensive psychotherapy. The legal profession has so invaded the intimacy of the therapy hour that administrators don't stop to consider the extent to which a security TV camera would destroy the heart of the therapy enterprise. Practitioners conduct therapy hours with the perceived presence of a tort attorney occupying a third chair in the office. Students are taught to write progress notes in charts as though a hostile attorney were reading them. Therapists who have been wrongfully sued—an ever-growing cohort—become less open, less trusting.

I know a competent, dedicated psychiatrist—let us call her Dr. Robertson—who treated a depressed man successfully with antidepressants for a year. The patient refused to engage in psychotherapy or to come for appointments more than once monthly. The patient's depression broke through after a year and Dr. Robertson unsuccessfully tried other medications. She repeatedly urged the patient to come in more frequently and to enter psychotherapy, but the patient refused to see her or anyone else in therapy. More than once, Dr. Robertson sought consultation from colleagues. Over a period of months the patient collected a

cache of sleeping pills and eventually took a fatal overdose; he left a suicide note for his wife with detailed instructions about the family financial
affairs. The last line of the note: "Sue Robertson!"

The family sued and was ultimately offered a small settlement by the
malpractice insurance company, which wished to expedite the process
and save legal fees. Even though Dr. Robertson was cleared of any
wrongdoing, the two-year legal process left her depleted and disillusioned; she even considered changing professions. She tells me that,
when interviewing prospective new clients, a question now invariably
comes to mind: "Will this person sue me?"

In *Lying on the Couch* I wanted to explore therapist-patient boundary
issues in all their complexity: the risks and temptations, the desires of the
therapist, the modes of avoiding pitfalls, the dangers to the exploited patient. Most of all, I strove for a full understanding of each two-person
drama: I wanted to explore the deep subjective experience of each participant without rushing to blame or to lynch. If psychotherapists will not
attempt to understand behavior and motivation in the therapy situation,
who will?

Hence *Lying on the Couch* examines many controversial questions,
even, for example, the delicate one of whether, if the relationship is a
genuine one, there may be a legitimate role for sexual energy (not sexual
behavior) in successful therapy. A dream a patient describes to her therapist in the novel is illustrative:

> I dreamt you and I were attending a conference together at a
> hotel. At some point you suggested I get a room adjoining
> yours so we could sleep together. So I went to the desk and
> arranged for my room to be moved. Then a little later you
> change your mind and say it's not a good idea. So then I go
> back to the desk to cancel the transfer. Too late. All of my
> things had been moved to the new room. But it turns out that
> the new room is a much nicer room—larger, higher, better
> view. And better, too, numerologically: the room number,
> 929, was a far more propitious number for me.

This dream (an actual dream of one of my clients) suggests that, for some clients, sexual energy may play an important role in the therapeutic process. The dream suggests that the intense intimacy of the relationship (catalyzed by the illusion of ultimate sexual union) results in considerable personal growth for the client (her new room is larger, nicer, with a better view, and is numerologically more advantageous). By the time she understands the illusory nature of her hopes for union, it is too late to revert: the positive changes have been set in place.

Although I am persuaded there is a role for great intimacy, even love, in the therapeutic relationship, and though I am candid and graphic in my discussion of the risks and temptations from the therapist's perspective, I do not mean to minimize or excuse sexual exploitation and violations on the part of the therapist. A careless reading of *Lying on the Couch* may lead the reader to conclude that I am offering an apologia for the offending therapist. Absolutely not. I am convinced that, almost invariably, a sexual relationship between patient and therapist is highly destructive for the patient and equally destructive for the therapist at the level of conscience, self-worth, and integrity.

DREAMS

Another therapy theme explored in *Lying on the Couch* is the relevance and use of dreams. Too many contemporary psychotherapists neglect dreams in their work. Many of my students avoid even asking their patients to relate dreams (as well as fantasies). To some extent, they may be responding to the emphasis health maintenance organizations give to brief therapy, but many new therapists who have less formal training than the past generation of therapists are, I believe, awed and intimidated by the voluminous, arcane literature on dream interpretation.

Accordingly, I have made a deliberate attempt to demonstrate a pragmatic approach to dream work in *Lying on the Couch*. I try to show that dreams are useful not because of astonishing deep insights that emerge from exhaustive dream analysis but simply because the patients' associations to dreams lead them to unexpected memories, reflections, and disclosures.

I have never been able to invent convincing dreams in my fiction.

Every attempt lacks the requisite mysterious, uncanny, well . . . *dreamy* quality. Consequently, all the dreams in *Lying on the Couch* are real. Some of them are my own dreams, like this one (which I give to the protagonist, Ernest):

> *I was walking with my parents and my brother in a mall and then we decided to go upstairs. I found myself on an elevator alone. It was a long, long ride. When I got off, I was by the seashore. But I couldn't find my family. I looked and looked for them. Though it was a lovely setting . . . the seashore is always paradise for me . . . I began to feel pervasive dread. Then I started to put on a nightshirt which had a cute, smiling face of Smokey the Bear. That face then became brighter, then brilliant . . . soon the face became the entire focus of the dream—as though all the energy of the dream was transferred onto that cute grinning little Smokey the Bear face.*

There was no mystery for me about the source of this dream. I dreamt it immediately after spending most of the night sitting with a dying friend. His death hurled me into a confrontation with my own death (represented in the dream by pervasive dread, by my separation from my family, and by my long elevator ascent to a heavenly seashore).

I put my sentiments into Ernest's words:

> *How annoying, Ernest thought, that his own dream-maker had bought into the fairy tale of an ascent to paradise! But what could he do? The dream-maker was its own master, formed in the dawn of consciousness, and was obviously shaped more by popular culture than by volition.*

The power of the dream resided in the nightshirt adorned by the gleaming Smokey the Bear emblem. I could see through that symbol: after my friend's death and before calling the funeral parlor, his widow and I had discussed how to dress him—how does one clothe a corpse for a cremation? Smokey the Bear represented cremation! I was certain of it. Eerie, but instructive. Recall Freud's insight that a primary function of dreams is to preserve sleep. In this instance, frightening thoughts—death and cremation—are transformed into something more benign and pleasing: the cunning figure of Smokey the Bear. But the dream mechanism was only partially successful: it enabled me to continue sleeping, but it could not prevent death anxiety from seeping out into the dream.

Most of the dreams in my fiction are my patients' dreams. Obtaining their permission was instructive in a number of ways. One powerful dream in *Lying on the Couch* came from a patient who dreamt of walking along the Big Sur coast and coming upon a river which, remarkably, flowed backward, *away* from the sea. He followed the river inland and discovered his father and then his grandfather standing in front of caves.

The river flowing backward was a poignant image of the wish to break time, to reverse its inexorable flow, to resuscitate his dead father and grandfather. Originally, eighteen months previously when we had worked on the dream, it had led us to deep and dark realms—his fears of aging and death; his belief that he, like the other men in his family, would have to face the end of life alone; his deep regret at having turned his back on his family of origin.

When I requested his permission to cite the dream in my novel, he appeared baffled and denied that he had ever dreamt such a dream. I asked him to read my notes of that therapy session, but still the dream appeared entirely alien to him. Such an amnesiac response to a potent dream is a good demonstration of the power of repression. Not only do we find it difficult to recall dreams in the first place, but even after having recalled them, we often repress them once again.

Incidentally, the notes of that session eighteen months before contained not only the dream but several other important observations about his relationship to ambition and to authority. When the patient read those notes, his therapy was immediately catalyzed—he realized how much he had changed in his attitudes toward authority, and realized, as well, how much work still remained. The process of psychotherapy may be thought of as "cyclotherapy": we return again and again to rework, at deeper and deeper levels, the same themes.

I have often been asked whether clients object to my writing about them. Almost always it is the clients *not* written about who have expressed concern, wondering whether they are not interesting or special enough to warrant inclusion in my work. Without exception, clients have gladly permitted me to cite their dreams. I always give them the opportunity to approve the final document before publication, but none have ever asked to change any part of the dream.

Consider this curious incident involving a dream in *Love's Executioner*. A patient whom I had not seen for many years called me for an appointment after the publication of the book. She entered my office, sat down, and with a somber voice told me that she knew she was not Thelma, the protagonist of the first story, yet one of Thelma's dreams strangely resembled a dream she had once described to me.

I was immediately alarmed at being confronted by an unhappy patient who was apparently accusing me of taking something from her without permission. The dream in question involved a woman dancing with a man and then lying on the dance floor with him and having sex. Just before orgasm she whispered in his ear, "Kill me."

I knew that this dream did not belong to Thelma. I had heard the dream long ago from someone else, though I had forgotten whom, and, in the service of making it a better story, had stitched it onto Thelma. As I spoke to the patient I recalled that it was indeed her dream, and apologized profusely for having forgotten and, consequently, for not having obtained her permission.

She brushed that off. I had misunderstood her, she said. Ownership of the dream was not her concern; what troubled her was the thought that her imagination could be so banal that another client would dream the same dream. She left my office much reassured about her creativity and the uniqueness of her dreams.

Thus far, we have been discussing the use of clients' dreams in therapy. In *Lying on the Couch* I describe a variation: Ernest dreams about Carolyn, his client, and takes the radical step of sharing *his* dream with her:

> *I am rushing through an airport. I spot you amidst a throng of passengers. I am glad to see you and I run up and try to give you a big hug but you keep your purse in the way, making it a bulky and unsatisfactory hug.*

The ensuing discussion of the dream proves fruitful in therapy. Several possible meanings are aired. Ernest suggests that the dream depicts his attempt to develop a close therapeutic relationship with her, an attempt that is foiled by her interjecting into the therapy her demands for sexuality (represented by the symbol of the purse, which so often signifies the vagina) and thus preventing true intimacy from evolving. His patient, Carolyn, counters with a simpler, more parsimonious interpretation, namely, that the purse simply represents the exchange of money and that his desire to have a *real* relationship (that is, a man woman sexual encounter) is frustrated by their professional contract. Ernest suggests yet another meaning:

> *"Another thought I had, Carolyn, was about the contents of the purse. Of course, as you suggest, money immediately comes to mind. But what else could be stuffed in there that gets in the way of our intimacy?"*
>
> *"I'm not sure what you mean, Ernest."*
>
> *"I mean that perhaps you may not be seeing me as I really am because of some preconceived ideas or biases getting in the way. Maybe you're toting some old baggage that's blocking our relationship—for example, wounds from your past relationships with other men, your father, your brother, your husband. Or perhaps expectations from another era: think, for example, of your former therapist, Ralph Cooke, and of how often you've said to me: 'Be like Ralph Cooke . . . be my lover-therapist.' In a sense, Carolyn, you're saying to me: Don't be you, Ernest, be something or someone else."*

Which interpretation is true? The patient's sexualization of the relationship? The therapist's regret that he could not have a romantic, nonprofessional relationship with his client? The client's transference-based distortion of the real relationship? In the pragmatic spirit of William James, the truth is what works. And what works in the novel *and* the real-life situation in which this dream (my own dream) occurred is the acknowledgment by both therapist and client that there is truth in each of these interpretations: taken together they are instrumental in deepening the authenticity of the relationship and the therapeutic work.

THE HERE-AND-NOW

Earlier in this volume I have emphasized the key role that the here-and-now plays in group psychotherapy. One of my goals in *Lying on the Couch* is to demonstrate that it is no less important in individual therapy.

There is a long tradition in individual therapy of focusing on transference, that is, examining distortions in the patient-therapist relationship in order to shed light on other relationships, particularly parental relationships. Generations of analysts have used the information gleaned from the study of transference to inform their interpretations. Their aim has been to use here-and-now material to facilitate the patient's recall and understanding of earlier formative relationships. In recent years new progressive analytic schools have broadened the transference focus and have reversed the emphasis: that is, they now explore the past in order to understand *present* relationships. But often the goal remains insight, and the therapy relationship is used primarily as an investigative tool.

I attempt to demonstrate in *Lying on the Couch* that a focus on the here-and-now has implications beyond transference clarification— namely, that *the relationship to the patient is important in its own right* and that forces more powerful than insight are at play in therapy, forces that can be enhanced by focusing on and enriching the "in-betweenness" of therapist and patient. The therapeutic act of establishing a deeply intimate and authentic relationship, *in itself,* is healing. Such a relationship can become an antidote to loneliness and offer an internal reference point for patients, who learn that such intimacy is rewarding *and* that they are capable of attaining it. Furthermore the work of creating and sustaining an authentic relationship with the therapist is often excellent modeling for the formation of future relationships in a patient's life.

A therapy group generates so much data about interpersonal relationships that it is not difficult to maintain the entire focus of the group in the here-and-now. Many individual therapists neglect the here-and-now focus because they mistakenly believe that the insularity of the individual therapy precludes the development of rich here-and-now data. *Lying on the Couch* demonstrates how the therapist can focus on the here-and-now in the individual therapy hour. Ernest, my protagonist, makes a conscious effort to focus on process (that is, the nature of the relationship between therapist and patient) several times each session.

Sometimes the here-and-now inquiry may be a simple process check: for example, such questions as "How are you and I doing today?" or "What about the space in between us today? Far? Near?" or "The hour is almost over: are there feelings about the way we are relating that we should examine before we stop?"

Every aspect of the hour provides data—patients' arrival and departure, their punctuality, their payment of bills. One patient, for example, enters my office tentatively and apologizes when my faulty latch prevents the door from closing satisfactorily. She apologizes again when, taking a piece of tissue to clean her glasses, she moves the Kleenex box a few inches. And then she begins the hour by apologizing for not having made more progress in therapy.

My office is a cottage in the midst of a large garden. Some patients ignore the garden; others never fail to comment upon it, especially during the spring bloom. Another patient characteristically chooses to comment on the mud on the path or the construction noise in the neighborhood. This same patient elected to read *Lying on the Couch* but not to pay for it: he read it in snatches standing in the back of various bookstores. His reason: "I gave at the office." An exploration of this here-and-now data proved invaluable in helping this patient explore his fear of exploitation and his deep anger at me and any other authority figure. A mild, gentle man externally, he has deeply ingrained passive-aggressive trends, which take the form of severe procrastination and have persistently gotten him into serious difficulty with supervisors.

Another patient never tells me the end of stories. He may be on the brink of some bold act—sending his novel to an agent, confronting his boss to protest a salary cut, or demanding that a former girlfriend tell him why she broke off their relationship—and then he never lets me know the outcome. Why not? Does he think I am not curious, that I have no concern for him? Is he ashamed of the outcome? Does he consider himself so uninteresting that I would have little curiosity about him? Or does he simply never think about the wishes or needs of the other? Does he treat other people this way too? Perhaps this here-and-now behavior contains a clue about his inability, in general, to maintain intimate relationships.

The process of therapy is an alternating sequence of affect evocation and affect integration. Strong affects are experienced in the session—irritation, fear, arousal, hatred—and then examined by the patient and therapist. Even if the affect has little to do with the therapist—for example, grief over a past loss—it is still profitable for the therapist to ask how the patient feels about expressing strong emotions in the presence of another. One may inquire, simply, "How did it feel to cry in front of me, to let me see your sadness?"

THE LEAP INTO PURE FICTION

When Nietzsche Wept and Lying on the Couch are both novels of ideas that address fundamental questions about the nature of psychotherapy. There are, however, significant differences between the two books. Since my first publications in the 1960s, my writing has been gradually moving away from a home base of academic psychiatry to the domain of pure fiction. When Nietzsche Wept was a move in that direction; Lying on the Couch was a more radical step.

When Nietzsche Wept is fiction, yes, but a safe and structured fiction. It is, I believe, a complex book from the perspective of the philosophic themes explored, but from the standpoint of novelistic technique it is not a giant step away from my previous writing. In some ways it is fiction-writing with training wheels.

For one thing, there was much in When Nietzsche Wept that I did not have to fictionalize. Many of the characters are historical figures: Friedrich Nietzsche, Josef Breuer, Sigmund Freud, Bertha Pappenheim (Anna O.), and Lou Salomé. Of course, we know little about their psychological concerns (with the exception of Freud's), and I had to fictionalize each interior life. But in general, I stayed as close as possible to the actual recorded events of the lives of my characters in 1882 and then proceeded to insert a fictional thirteenth month into the winter of that year.

Once I had selected the year and the place (Vienna and Venice), I set about creating many of my visual details with the help of old photographs and an 1885 Baedeker guide of Vienna. I could also draw upon my visual memory, since I had once spent several months at the Vienna campus of Stanford University (teaching Freud to undergraduates). And, of course, much of the intellectual content of the novel is not fictional but is drawn from the body of Nietzsche's pre–1882 philosophical writings.

Lying on the Couch was a far riskier project, not only because it would discuss vexing and controversial issues but also because it was to be pure fiction. Ever since my adolescence I had wanted to write a novel. I had suppressed that desire, sublimated it, dreamt of it, viewed it from afar, paced around it, and now, finally, I took the plunge.

Earlier I referred to *When Nietzsche Wept* as a teaching novel. Did I also intend *Lying on the Couch* to be a teaching novel? I was ambivalent about that. On the one hand, the psychotherapy practitioner and trainee constituted my secret audience during the writing, and nothing would please me more than for *Lying on the Couch* to be assigned in therapy training programs. On the other hand, I longed to be a real novelist, and whenever I faced a decision point in writing *Lying on the Couch*, I opted each time for literary considerations—for the book to be entertaining rather than didactic. Over and over I sacrificed juicy opportunities to insert a pedagogical aside.

Nonetheless, I did not, and do not, experience the freedom of most novelists. For one thing, I am restrained by knowing that the patients in my practice read my novels. Moreover, I have much visibility in the field as a professor of psychiatry at Stanford and as an author of textbooks used in many psychotherapy training programs. It is important for me that my students not confuse my professional writing with my psychotherapy fiction. Whenever possible, I emphasize that my fiction is fictional, that I do not endorse all the behavior of the therapists I write about, and that the plot of each book and inner life of each character are pure invention. Still, there are questions raised as to whether my novels are indeed fiction. In my defense, I have noted that Robert Ludlum's novels reek of murder and mayhem, yet no one accuses him of being a serial killer; nor is Philip Roth, who writes incessantly of diverse and bizarre sexual practices, dismissed as a pervert.

My fears were realized in the first review of the book, which questioned whether the novel was truly fiction or whether, like *Love's Executioner*, it represented a personal confessional. Another reviewer posited that the novel questioned the relevance of psychotherapy. My intentions, however, were quite different. I have never doubted the relevance nor

the power of psychotherapy, and although I satirize some aspects of contemporary therapeutic practice, my protagonist, Ernest Lash, is meant to
be a man of integrity. Despite his lust, his bumbling, his struggles with his
primitive appetites, he remains totally committed to his patients and to
his vision of the continuing possibility of human growth.

IS FICTION FICTIONAL? TRUTH TRUE?

Writing *Lying on the Couch* felt like a radical departure from my previous
professional writing, an adventurous plunge into the realm of "pure fiction." But what is "pure fiction"? Recent years have witnessed considerable readjustment of the boundary between fiction and nonfiction.
Consider the development in psychotherapy of the view that an accurate
reconstruction of an individual's life is, to a great extent, illusory. The
psychotherapeutic goal has become a *construction* and not a reconstruction; we search to provide some plausible satisfying life narrative—even
a fiction—that can provide coherence and understanding. Or consider
the new research on implanted memories, which indicates that false
memories may be implanted easily and that individuals are often unable
to differentiate them from "real" memories of actual events. The old sure
distinctions between truth and fiction grow increasingly blurred.

Nietzsche, perhaps more than any other thinker, has contributed to
the blurring. He compared truth to discarded snakeskins shed as their
owners grew larger and older. His perspectivistic view of truth posits that
there is no truth, there is only interpretation: truth is a convenience,
"truth is the kind of error without which a certain species of life could
not survive."[5]

Truth blends with fiction in the writing of *Lying on the Couch;* a great
many scenes have some kind of relationship to reality: they are *drawn
from, based on,* or *inspired by* actual events. For example, chapter 7
takes place in a psychoanalytic institute meeting in which a revered but
maverick psychoanalyst is expelled from the institute. Although the
scene is meant to be comic and fantastical, it is inspired by an actual
event—the expulsion, twenty-five years ago, of Masud Khan from the
British Psychoanalytic Institute (as related to me by Dr. Charles Rycroft
and described in Judy Cooper's biography of Masud Khan).[6]

In the prologue to *Lying on the Couch*, Seymour Trotter, a patriarch of the profession and a past president of the American Psychiatric Association, is a composite of at least three figures: a therapist who, years before, had sexually abused one of my patients; an eminent figure in Boston psychoanalytic circles; and Jules Masserman, a past president of the American Psychiatric Association and the American Psychoanalytic Association, who was indicted for sexually abusing patients after drugging them with sodium pentothal.

The plot of the prologue was partially inspired by a story that floated around when I was a resident in psychiatry. In one of the first major malpractice settlements, a prominent New York analyst was found guilty of sexual abuse, and a huge insurance settlement was awarded to his young female patient. Months later, so the story went, they were seen strolling arm in arm on a beach near Rio de Janeiro. Is this tale true or apocryphal? I don't know. I only know that it remained dormant in my mind for almost forty years and then found expression in the novel.

Thus fiction is not wholly fictional in that real incidents and individuals are often incorporated into the narrative. The following incident depicts how fiction and memory may meld in less obvious ways.

In *When Nietzsche Wept*, Nietzsche, while wandering in the cemetery and reflecting upon the gravestones, composes a little ditty:

> *till stone is laid on stone*
> *and though none can hear*
> *and none can see*
> *each sobs softly: remember me, remember me.*

These lines of doggerel (preceded by several others which did not make the final cut in the novel) came to me quickly, and I wrote them with a flush of pleasure—my first published verse. About a year later, when I was changing offices, my secretary found a large sealed manila envelope, yellowed with age, which had fallen behind the file cabinet. It contained a large packet of poetry I had written in my late adolescence and had not seen for decades. Among the verses were the identical lines, word for word, which I thought I had freshly composed in the novel. I had written them in 1954, forty years before, at the time of my fiancée's father's death. I had plagiarized myself.

A somewhat similar incident involves one of the Beatles, George Harrison, who was sued by a musician claiming that Harrison's song "My Sweet Lord" had plagiarized the musician's earlier song, "He's So Fine." Expert musicologists agreed that the scores were remarkably similar and the court ordered Harrison to pay damages. Harrison hardly needed to plagiarize another musician's work; instead, what probably occurred was that he had heard the song, repressed it, and then reinvented it.

These incidents are testimony to the existence of the unconscious. I think of such stories whenever I hear neuropsychologists proclaim that no research evidence documents the existence of the unconscious. At such times the neurophysiologist Sherrington's comment comes to mind: "If you teach an Airedale to play the violin, you don't need a string quartet to prove it."

When Nietzsche Wept blurred boundaries between fiction and truth by placing real historical characters in a fictional setting. This postmodern blurring of literary boundaries—between biography, autobiography, and fiction—has been slowly evolving for the past twenty years. Recall, for example, the playwright Tom Stoppard's 1966 *Rosencrantz and Guildenstern Are Dead,* in which minor characters from *Hamlet* become protagonists of their own play, or his 1974 *Travesties,* which describes a fictional meeting between Joyce, Lenin, and Tristan Tzara. In my book *Love's Executioner,* I had already experimented with blurring the boundaries between case history and fiction.

In psychotherapy the boundary between fiction and personal history has *always* been unclear. It is only recently, perhaps because of Donald Spence's landmark book, *Narrative Truth and Historical Truth,* that therapists have become appreciative of their own narrative-constructive (as opposed to *reconstructive*) efforts in psychotherapy. Therapists and analysts no longer consider themselves, as Freud did, psychological archaeologists striving to excavate the real historical truth of a life: we have all become Nietzschean perspectivists. We understand that the truth changes according to the perspective of the observer and, in the case of therapy, truth's form is vastly influenced by the nature of the therapeutic relationship.

Leslie Farber provides an illustrative vignette of psychotherapy perspectivism in an essay entitled "Lying on the Couch" which appeared in his 1976 book, *Lying, Despair, Jealousy, Envy, Sex, Suicide, Drugs, and the Good Life.* Early in his career, while being analyzed in an office in his analyst's home, he had been frequently disturbed by the discordant sounds of her son practicing on the violin elsewhere in the house. When he finally complained, his analyst immediately accommodated him by leaving the office and silencing her son.

Soon afterward his analytic hours were flooded with memories of playing the violin during his own childhood. Since he had been a precocious musician, his father had harbored great hopes of seeing him become a concert violinist. When he "outgrew" the violin in his adolescence, his father was wounded and disappointed: the rift between them required months, years, to heal.

Only much later did Farber realize that he had "lied on the couch" and succumbed to a romanticization of his youth. Although he had indeed played the violin when young, he was a mediocre musician and no one had ever raised the question of a musical career. Certainly the violin had never caused a rift with his father, with whom he had always remained on good terms. Yet during his analysis the narrative had been wonderfully satisfying to him and ultimately prompted him to explore more deeply his transference to his analyst.

Incidentally, the title of Farber's essay, "Lying on the Couch," provides an illustration of the difficulty of ascertaining attribution: I have no doubt I took the name of my novel from this essay, yet I have no memory of "deciding" to use it. I had not reread or even laid eyes on Farber's book since 1976, but as I was plotting my novel, the title simply appeared in my mind and I knew instantaneously that it was the right one.

So, too, for the story fragments I described in my essay on *When Nietzsche Wept* (Herman Hesse's story of the two healers, and Helmuth Kaiser's play fragment, *Emergency*). Did I methodically use these tales in my plot construction? Was it really true, as I have suggested elsewhere, that these tales had "rattled about in my mind for many years" and that "their echoes ring throughout the pages"? Or is that a fiction, a romanticized version of the sense-providing narrative we so often construct in therapy and in life?

Alas, I simply do not remember! The computer has made original jottings and first drafts obsolete. As far as I can recall, it was months *after* the completion of *When Nietzsche Wept,* while preparing a lecture on the process of writing a psychotherapy novel, that the possible influence of these tales first occurred to me. Whether the stories consciously or un-consciously influenced the novel, or whether I simply recalled them later for the purpose of inventing a coherent linear narrative suitable for a lec-ture, is something I shall never know.

Farber's fiction of the violin virtuoso reminds us that memory may be too often conceptualized as trauma-based—that is, the experience of trauma is instrumental in what we choose to remember and to forget. Memory may also be influenced by an aesthetic drive—by the desire to make an artistic product of one's life.

The satisfying life narrative the patient constructs during therapy often changes as new data emerge. Sometimes one may develop alternating narratives that are brought into play to meet the demands of a particular situation. I can personally attest to two guiding life narratives that be-came evident to me during my personal analysis.

I described one of these narratives earlier—that of myself as a young storyteller, a novelist manqué, who knew that the most marvelous thing one could do in life was to write a fine novel, but who, because of cul-tural pressures, chose a medical career and only decades later was able to return to his true calling.

This romantic narrative has served me well. It was always there in the background, available when needed, comforting me when I was over-come with doubts about my professional research or my therapy prac-tice. Now, as I distance myself from a remedicalized field of psychiatry, it has moved more into the foreground. Whenever I open an issue of the *American Journal of Psychiatry* and flip through page after page of re-ports on psychopharmacological or brain imaging research hoping, in vain, to find even one article I can understand, one article dealing with the human concerns of patients, I draw this narrative more closely around me, saying, "I don't belong in medicine or even psychiatry; I'm a writer—that's where I really live."

A second, alternate core narrative that unfolded in my analysis had its inception when I was thirteen. On a cold November night, at about three in the morning, my father suffered a serious coronary, and we (my mother, father, and I) awaited the arrival of our family physician, Dr.

Manchester. My mother was distraught and, as she habitually did in times of stress, looked around for someone to blame. As usual, her gaze fell upon me.

"It's your fault," she shouted, "you did this—all the aggravation, all the grief you gave him—you did this to him. You. You." We waited for the doctor's arrival, my mother weeping, my father groaning with pain, and I shivering abjectly by his bed, holding his hand, hating my mother and pondering whether there was truth in her accusation. Finally Dr. Manchester arrived. Never before in my life had I heard a more beautiful, more terror-allaying sound than the tires of his big Buick crunching the autumn leaves piled by the curb.

He was wonderful. Miraculous. He eased my father's pain with an injection. He calmed my mother with reassurances. He affectionately tousled my hair and let me hold his stethoscope. He waited with us till the ambulance arrived and followed it to the hospital. So grateful was I that, then and there (as I remember it), I resolved to be a physician and to pass on to others what Dr. Manchester had given me.

This narrative has carried me through most of my life. My primary identity has been that of a physician or healer, and I have never allowed anything to take precedence over my commitment to patients. Even in recent years, as I have become a more dedicated writer, it is difficult to release my grip upon the "doctor" life narrative. I know that I resist cutting down my therapy practice; once I hear the particulars of an individual's despair I have great difficulty refusing to take the patient into treatment.

And, of course, whenever I am bruised by negative book reviews, I run back into the arms of my identity as a physician and soothe myself by saying: "I'm not a writer; I'm a physician. Always have been."

LYING AND PSYCHOTHERAPY

The double entendre of the title *Lying on the Couch* raises yet another aspect of the boundary between fiction and nonfiction. When do patients lie and when do they tell the truth? Many years ago, during my military service, a sergeant was admitted to my ward exhibiting a strange set of symptoms. He was only a few weeks short of completing thirty years of service (which would have provided him with a handsome lifelong pension) when he was arrested for sexually abusing a young boy. He immediately fell into an amnesiac, confused state in which he answered all questions incorrectly but in such a manner as to indicate that he knew the correct answers: for example, five times four is nineteen, six times three is seventeen, a horse has three legs.

His officers suspected malingering. How convenient for the sergeant, they said, to develop a psychosis just in time to avoid responsibility for a criminal act that would incur a dishonorable discharge and loss of his military pension. Even the near-miss way he answered questions suggested lying. But a lie has intention and a birth: there must have been a time when he invented the lie, and a place in his mind where he knew he was lying. Where was that place, that time? I could never find it. No matter how deep I went with prolonged interviews, hypnosis, or sodium pentothal, I never found the seam of the lie.

Eventually he prevailed and got what everyone thought he wanted: a medical discharge with his pension intact. I lost touch with him after that; I was far too busy in the army to follow up discharged patients. (Later in my life I would never miss out on the end of such a story.) Most likely, however, his was a Pyrrhic victory: usually individuals exhibiting his symptoms (the formal diagnosis used to be Ganser syndrome, also known as the syndrome of approximate answers) wind up, to everyone's surprise, living out much of their life in psychosis.

Overt lying is part of everyday business in forensic psychiatry or any situation where some third party—the law, an employer, an insurance company, a spouse—intrudes into the therapy situation. But in the traditional therapy relationship, where patients pursue greater personal comfort, self-understanding, and personal growth, lying takes the far more subtle forms of concealment, exaggeration, omission, and distortion.

Even though we depth psychotherapists appreciate that there is a basic unknowability to the other, we never stop struggling to bridge the gap separating us from the client. In retrospect, I now understand that many of my experiments with therapy technique have been motivated by this desire. I reveal more and more of myself in an effort to encourage patients to reciprocate. I tap into dreams and fantasies. I encourage patients to hold nothing back. I have (far too rarely, incidentally) visited their homes in order to learn more about them. I ask them to bring in pictures of their past and present families. I asked Ginny (of *Every Day Gets a Little Closer*) to reveal in her written reports what she had concealed in our meetings. Even in my fiction I asked Nietzsche and Breuer to write reports of their secret unexpressed feelings about their meetings.

I often lead therapy groups of my own individual patients and marvel at how much everyone conceals. Clients commonly withhold from the group much that they have revealed in the individual hours. Sometimes I look around the group and think, "Everyone is lying"—concealing both vital parts of themselves and their feelings toward the other members. I have known patients who have refused to reveal their enormous wealth, abused backgrounds, criminal convictions, sexual paraphilias, or extramarital affairs. Recently I had two psychotherapists in therapy groups who, despite my urgings, refused to reveal their profession to the group (one for fear that his words would be given undue weight, the other for fear of being judged as an unfit therapist because of her personal psychological problems). Almost everyone conceals some of their stronger feelings toward other members—envy, attraction, lust, fear, repulsion. Often I feel like a Magus, knowing so much more than is overt in the group. Indeed, one of the vexing problems for therapists doing combined therapy (individual and group) is to know how to handle their privileged knowledge.

Consider Leslie Farber's tale of having been a young violin prodigy. Was he explicitly lying? Or unconsciously romanticizing his life by reshaping his memory according to the demands of the two-person situation? Was he so desirous of winning approval from his analyst that his memory was reforged? Perhaps he was competing with his analyst's son and hoped to win her admiration by alluding to his superior musical skill. Or he may have been grateful to her for silencing her son and rewarded her with a flood of derepressed delectable memories.

Memory's unreliability is incontestable. Nietzsche was fully appreciative of its malleability when he wrote, "'I have done that,' says my memory. 'I cannot have done that,' says my pride, and remains inexorable. Eventually—memory yields."[7] Over and again memory yields, and there is no objective perch from which one may view the yielding. As he grew older, Mark Twain said, his memory of events that never happened grew more vivid.

Case histories in the nonfiction textbook are far less true than is generally known. Publishers are so threatened by the current litigation epidemic that most published case histories in the contemporary psychotherapy literature are almost entirely fictionalized. But is that a legitimate pedagogical concern? Is "realness" equivalent to historical accuracy? I've often found fictional characters to be more "real" than historical characters. Because novelists know their characters fully, they have a distinct advantage over psychotherapists who collude with their subjects to keep their secrets. Thus my fictional characters—Ernest Lash, Josef Breuer, or Friedrich Nietzsche—may be more *real,* that is, *fully known,* than some of the real-life characters described in my nonfiction work, such as the vignettes in my textbooks and the case histories in *Love's Executioner.*

Much the same may be said for another practitioner of nonfiction, the professional biographer, who, like the psychotherapist, attempts to re-create a life. But is biographical nonfiction *real*? Consider how greatly biographers are limited by their sources. If psychotherapists, who spend countless hours listening to intimate details of lives, marvel at how little they really know their patients, imagine how far biographers are from the mark. Consider how much of your own essence would be captured in a biography based only on your papers or E-mail, or on published reminiscences of acquaintances. Even if biographers write about a contemporary figure, still they are greatly limited by what they—or the subject—choose to make public.

A biographer of Samuel Beckett once commented that Beckett began their interviews with a characteristic greeting: "Here is the person who is going to show the world what an empty fraud I am." What a delicious quote, I thought. If I were writing the biography, I would have made it a centerpiece. Yet when I asked the biographer about how she used this material in her writing, she responded that she could never write about that: it was confidential—a private joke between the two of them.

This quirky perspective of biography as fiction and fiction as life is wonderfully summed up in Thornton Wilder's comment: "If historical characters—Queen Elizabeth, Frederick the Great, or Ernest Hemingway, for example—were to read their biographies, they would exclaim, 'Ah—my secret is still safe.' But if Natasha Rostov were to read *War and Peace*, she would cry out, as she covered her face with her hands, 'How did he know? How did he know?'"

The prologue of *Lying on the Couch*, reproduced in the following pages, takes place several years before the rest of the novel and may be read as a freestanding story. Seymour Trotter, who is being questioned about sexual misconduct with a young female patient, is a wounded healer, part sham, part wizard; he is a falling giant who, in his descent, offers a gift to Ernest. Seymour's story is meant as a cautionary tale, a dark backdrop against which the rest of the novel will be played out.

Lying on the Couch: The Prologue

Ernest loved being a psychotherapist. Day after day his patients invited him into the most intimate chambers of their lives. Day after day he comforted them, cared for them, eased their despair. And in return, he was admired and cherished. And paid as well, though, Ernest often thought, if he didn't need the money, he would do psychotherapy for nothing.

Lucky is he who loves his work. Ernest felt lucky, all right. More than lucky. Blessed. He was a man who had found his calling—a man who could say, I am precisely where I belong, at the vortex of my talents, my interests, my passions.

Ernest was not a religious man. But when he opened his appointment book every morning and saw the names of the eight or nine dear people with whom he would spend his day, he was overcome with a feeling that he could only describe as religious. At these times he had the deepest desire to give thanks—to someone, to something—for having led him to his calling.

There were mornings when he looked up, through the skylight of his Sacramento Street Victorian, through the morning fog, and imagined his psychotherapy ancestors suspended in the dawn.

"Thank you, thank you," he would chant. He thanked them all—all the healers who had ministered to despair. First, the ur-ancestors, their empyreal outlines barely visible: Jesus, Buddha, Socrates. Below them, somewhat more distinct—the great progenitors: Nietzsche, Kierkegaard, Freud, Jung. Nearer yet, the grandparent therapists: Adler, Horney, Sullivan, Fromm, and the sweet smiling face of Sandor Ferenczi.

A few years ago, they answered his cry of distress when, after his residency training, he fell into lockstep with every ambitious young neuropsychiatrist and applied himself to neurochemistry research—the face of the future, the golden arena of personal opportunity. The ancestors knew he had lost his way. He belonged in no science laboratory. Nor in a medication-dispensing psychopharmacological practice.

They sent a messenger—a droll messenger of power—to ferry him to his destiny. To this day Ernest did not know *how* he decided to become a therapist. But he remembered *when*. He remembered the day with astonishing clarity. And he remembered the messenger, too: Seymour Trotter, a man he saw only once, who changed his life forever.

Six years ago Ernest's department chairman had appointed him to serve a term on the Stanford Hospital Medical Ethics Committee, and Ernest's first disciplinary action was the case of Dr. Trotter. Seymour Trotter was a seventy-one-year-old patriarch of the psychiatric community and a former president of the American Psychiatric Association. He had been charged with sexual misconduct with a thirty-two-year-old female patient.

At that time Ernest was an assistant professor of psychiatry just four years out of residency. A full-time neurochemistry researcher, he was completely naive about the world of psychotherapy—far too naive to know he had been assigned this case because no one else would touch it: every older psychiatrist in Northern California greatly venerated and feared Seymour Trotter.

Ernest chose an austere hospital administrative office for the interview and tried to look official, watching the clock while waiting for Dr. Trotter, the complaint file on the desk in front of him, unopened. To remain unbiased, Ernest had decided to interview the accused with no previous knowledge and thus hear his story with no preconceptions. He would read the file later and schedule a second meeting, if necessary.

Presently he heard a tapping noise echoing down the hallway. Could

Dr. Trotter be blind? No one had prepared him for that. The tapping, followed by shuffling, grew closer. Ernest rose and stepped into the hallway.

No, not blind. Lame. Dr. Trotter lurched down the hall, balanced uneasily between two canes. He was bent at the waist and held the canes widely apart, almost at arm's length. His good, strong cheekbones and chin still held their own, but all softer ground had been colonized by wrinkles and senile plaques. Deep folds of skin hung from his neck, and puffs of white hairy moss protruded from his ears. Yet age had not vanquished this man—something young, even boyish, survived. What was it? Perhaps his hair, gray and thick, worn in a crew cut, or his dress, a blue denim jacket covering a white turtleneck sweater.

They introduced themselves in the doorway. Dr. Trotter staggered a couple of steps into the room, suddenly raised his canes, twisted vigorously, and, as though by the sheerest chance, pirouetted into his seat.

"Bull's-eye! Surprised you, eh?"

Ernest was not to be distracted. "You understand the purpose of this interview, Dr. Trotter—and you understand why I'm tape-recording it?"

"I've heard that the hospital administration is considering me for the Worker of the Month award."

Ernest, staring unblinking through his large goggle spectacles, said nothing.

"Sorry, I know you've got your job to do, but when you've passed seventy, you'll smile at good cracks like that. Yeah, seventy-one last week. And you're how old, Dr. . . . ? I've forgotten your name. Every minute," he said as he tapped his temple, "a dozen cortical neurons buzz out like dying flies. The irony is, I've published four papers on Alzheimer's—naturally I forget where, but good journals. Did you know that?"

Ernest shook his head.

"So you never knew and I've forgotten. That makes us about even. Do you know the two good things about Alzheimer's? Your old friends become your new friends, and you can hide your own Easter eggs."

Despite his irritation Ernest couldn't help smiling.

"Your name, age, and school of conviction?"

"I'm Dr. Ernest Lash, and perhaps the rest isn't germane just now, Dr. Trotter. We've got a lot of ground to cover today."

"My son's forty. You can't be more than that. I know you're a graduate of the Stanford residency. I heard you speak at grand rounds last year. You did well. Very clear presentation. It's all psychopharm now, isn't it? What kind of psychotherapy training you guys getting now? Any at all?"

Ernest took off his watch and put it on the desk. "Some other time I'll be glad to forward you a copy of the Stanford residency curriculum, but for now, please, let's get into the matter at hand, Dr. Trotter. Perhaps it would be best if you tell me about Mrs. Felini in your own way."

"Okay, okay, okay. You want me to be serious. You want me to tell you my story. Sit back, *boychik,* and I'll tell you a story. We'll start at the beginning. It was about four years ago—at least four years ago . . . I've misplaced all of my records on this patient . . . what was the date according to your charge sheet? What? You haven't read it. Lazy? Or trying to avoid unscientific bias?"

"Please, Dr. Trotter, continue."

"The first principle of interviewing is to forge a warm, trusting environment. Now that you've accomplished that so artfully, I feel a great deal freer to talk about painful and embarrassing material. Oh—*that* got to you. Gotta be careful of me, Dr. Lash, I've had forty years reading faces. I'm very good at it. But if you've finished the interruptions, I'll start. Ready?

"Years ago—let's say about four years—a woman, Belle, walks into, or I should say drags herself into, my office—or bedraggles herself in—bedraggles, that's better. Is *bedraggle* a verb? About mid-thirties, from a wealthy background—Swiss-Italian—depressed, wearing a long-sleeved blouse in the summertime. A cutter, obviously—wrists scarred up. If you see long sleeves in the summertime, perplexing patient, always think of wrist cutting and drug injections, Dr. Lash. Good-looking, great skin, seductive eyes, elegantly dressed. Real class, but on the verge of going to seed.

"Long self-destructive history. You name it: drugs, tried everything, didn't miss one. When I first saw her she was back to alcohol and doing a little heroin chipping. Yet not truly addicted. Somehow she didn't have the knack for it—some people are like that—but she was working on it. Eating disorder, too. Anorexia mainly, but occasional bulimic purging. I've already mentioned the cutting, lots of it up and down both arms and wrists—liked the pain and blood; that was the only time she felt alive. You hear patients say that all the time. A half-dozen hospitalizations—brief. She always signed out in a day or two. The staff would cheer when she left. She was good—a true prodigy—at the game of Uproar. You remember Eric Berne's *Games People Play*?

"No? Guess it's before your time. Christ, I feel old. Good stuff—Berne wasn't stupid. Read it—shouldn't be forgotten.

"Married, no kids. She refused to have them—said the world was too ghastly a place to inflict on children. Nice husband, rotten relationship. He wanted kids badly, and there was lots of fighting about that. He was an investment banker like her father, always traveling. A few years into the marriage, his libido shut off or maybe got channeled into making money—he made good money but never really hit the big time like her father. Busy busy busy, slept with the computer. Maybe he fucked it, who knows? He certainly didn't fuck Belle. According to her, he had avoided her for years, probably because of his anger about not having children. Hard to say what kept them married. He was raised in a Christian Science home and consistently refused couples therapy, or any other form of psychotherapy. But she admits she has never pushed very hard. Let's see. What else? Cue me, Dr. Lash.

"Her previous therapy? Good. Important question. I always ask that in the first thirty minutes. Nonstop therapy—or attempts at therapy—since her teens. Went through all the therapists in Geneva and for a while commuted to Zurich for analysis. Came to college in the U.S.—Pomona—and saw one therapist after another, often only for a single session. Stuck it out with three or four of them for as long as a few months, but never really took with anyone. Belle was—and is—very dismissive. No one good enough, or at least no one right for her. Something wrong with every therapist: too formal, too pompous, too judgmental, too condescending, too business-oriented, too cold, too busy with diagnosis, too formula-driven. Psych meds? Psychological testing? Behavioral protocols? Forget it—anyone suggest those and they were scratched immediately. What else?

"How'd she choose me? Excellent question, Dr. Lash—focuses us and quickens our pace. We'll make a psychotherapist of you yet. I had that feeling about you when I heard your grand rounds. Good, incisive mind. It showed as you presented your data. But what I liked was your case presentation, especially the way you let patients affect you. I saw you had all the right instincts. Carl Rogers used to say, 'Don't waste your time training therapists—time is better spent in *selecting* them.' I always thought there was a lot to that.

"Let's see, where was I? Oh, how she got to me: her gynecologist, whom she adored, was a former patient of mine. Told her I was a regular guy, no bullshit, and willing to get my hands dirty. She looked me up at the library and liked an article I wrote fifteen years ago discussing Jung's notion of inventing a new therapy language for each patient. You know that work? No? *Journal of Orthopsychiatry*. I'll send you a reprint. I took it even farther than Jung. I suggested we invent a new therapy for each patient, that we take seriously the notion of the uniqueness of each patient and develop a unique psychotherapy for each one.

"Coffee? Yeah, I'll have some. Black. Thanks. So that's how she got to me. And the next question you should ask, Dr. Lash? *Why then?* Precisely. That's the one. Always a high-yield question to ask a new patient. The answer: dangerous sexual acting out. Even she could see it. She had always done some of this stuff, but it was getting very heavy. Imagine, driving next to vans or trucks on the highway—high enough for the driver to see in—and then pulling up her skirt and masturbating—at eighty miles an hour. Crazy. Then she'd take the next exit and if the driver followed her off, she'd stop, climb into his cabin, and give him a blow job. Lethal stuff. And lots of it. She was so out of control that when she was bored, she'd go into some seedy San Jose bar, sometimes Chicano, sometimes black, and pick someone up. She got off on being in dangerous situations surrounded by unknown, potentially violent men. And there was danger not only from the men but from the prostitutes who resented her taking their business. They threatened her life and she had to keep moving from one place to another. And AIDS, herpes, safe sex, condoms? Like she never heard of them.

"So that, more or less, was Belle when we started. You get the picture? You got any questions or shall I just go on? Okay. So, somehow, in our first session I passed all her tests. She came back a second time and a third and we began treatment, twice, sometimes three times a week. I spent a whole hour taking a detailed history of her work with all her previous therapists. That's always a good strategy when you're seeing a difficult patient, Dr. Lash. Find out how they treated her and then try to avoid their errors. Forget that crap about the patient not being ready for therapy! *It's the therapy that's not ready for the patient.* But you have to be bold and creative enough to fashion a new therapy for each patient.

"Belle Felini was not a patient to be approached with traditional technique. If I stay in my normal professional role—taking a history, reflecting, empathizing, interpreting—poof, she's gone. Trust me. *Sayonara. Auf Wiedersehen.* That's what she did with every therapist she ever saw—and many of them with good reputations. You know the old story: the operation was a success, but the patient died.

"What techniques did I employ? Afraid you missed my point. *My technique is to abandon all technique!* And I'm not just being smart-assed, Dr. Lash—that's the first rule of good therapy. And that should be your rule, too, if you become a therapist. I tried to be more human and less mechanical. I don't make a systematic therapy plan—you won't either after forty years of practice. I just trust my intuition. But that's not fair to you as a beginner. I guess, looking back, the most striking aspect of Belle's pathology was her impulsivity. She gets a desire—bingo, she has to act on it. I remember wanting to increase her tolerance for frustration. That was my starting point, my first, maybe my major, goal in therapy. Let's see, how did we start? It's hard to remember the beginning, so many years ago, without my notes.

"I told you I lost them. I see the doubt in your face. The notes are gone. Disappeared when I moved offices about two years ago. You have no choice but to believe me.

"The main recollections I have are that in the beginning things went far better than I could have imagined. Not sure *why,* but Belle took to me immediately. Couldn't have been my good looks. I had just had cataract surgery and my eye looked like hell. And my ataxia did not improve my sex appeal . . . this is familial cerebellar ataxia, if you're curious. Definitely progressive . . . a walker in my future, another year or two, and a wheelchair in three or four. *C'est la vie.*

"I think Belle liked me because I treated her like a person. I did exactly what you're doing now—and I want to tell you, Dr. Lash, I appreciate your doing it. I didn't read any of her charts. I went into it blind, wanted to be entirely fresh. Belle was *never* a diagnosis to me, not a borderline, not an eating disorder, not a compulsive or antisocial disorder. That's the way I approach all my patients. And I hope I will never become a diagnosis to you.

"What, do I think there's a place for diagnosis? Well, I know you guys graduating now, and the whole psychopharm industry, live by diagnosis. The psychiatric journals are littered with meaningless discussions about nuances of diagnosis. Future flotsam. I know it's important in some psychoses, but it plays little role—in fact, a negative role—in everyday psychotherapy. Ever think about the fact that it's easier to make a diagnosis the first time you see a patient and that it gets harder the better you know a patient? Ask any experienced therapist in private—they'll tell you the same thing! In other words, certainty is inversely proportional to knowledge. Some kind of science, huh?

"What I'm saying to you, Dr. Lash, is not just that I didn't *make* a diagnosis on Belle; I didn't *think* diagnosis. I still don't. Despite what's happened, despite what she's done to me, I still don't. And I think she knew that. We were just two people making contact. And I liked Belle. Always did. Liked her a lot! And she knew that, too. Maybe *that's* the main thing.

"Now Belle was not a good talking-therapy patient—not by anyone's standard. Impulsive, action-oriented, no curiosity about herself, nonintrospective, unable to free-associate. She always failed at the traditional tasks of therapy—self-examination, insight—and then felt worse about herself. *That's* why therapy had always bombed. And that's why I knew I had to get her attention in other ways. That's why I had to invent a new therapy for Belle.

"For example? Well, let me give you one from early therapy, maybe the third or fourth month. I'd been focusing on her self-destructive sexual behavior and asking her about what she really wanted from men, including the first man in her life, her father. But I was getting nowhere. She was real resistive to talking about the past—done too much of that with other shrinks, she said. Also she had a notion that poking in the ashes of the past was just an excuse to evade personal responsibility for our actions. She had read my book on psychotherapy and cited me saying that very thing. I hate that. When patients resist by citing your own books, they got you by the balls.

"One session I asked her for some early daydreams or sexual fantasies and finally, to humor me, she described a recurrent fantasy from the time she was eight or nine: a storm outside, she comes into a room cold and soaking wet, and an older man is waiting for her. He embraces her, takes off her wet clothes, dries her with a large warm towel, gives her hot chocolate. So I suggested we role-play: I told her to go out of the office and enter again pretending to be wet and cold. I skipped the undressing part, of course, got a good-sized towel from the washroom, and dried her off vigorously—staying nonsexual, as I always did. I 'dried' her back and her hair, then bundled her up in the towel, sat her down, and made her a cup of instant hot chocolate.

"Don't ask me why or how I chose to do this at that time. When you've practiced as long as I have, you learn to trust your intuition. And the intervention changed everything. Belle was speechless for a while, tears welled up in her eyes, and then she bawled like a baby. Belle had never, never cried in therapy. The resistance just melted away.

"What do I mean by her resistance melting? I mean that she trusted me, that she believed we were on the same side. The technical term, Dr. Lash, is 'therapeutic alliance.' After that she became a real patient. Important material just erupted out of her. She began to live for the next session. Therapy became the center of her life. Over and over she told me how important I was to her. And this was after only three months.

"Was I *too* important? No, Dr. Lash, the therapist can't be too important early in therapy. Even Freud used the strategy of trying to replace a psychoneurosis with a transference neurosis—that's a powerful way of gaining control over destructive symptoms.

"You look puzzled by this. Well, what happens is that the patient becomes obsessed with the therapist—ruminates powerfully about each session, has long fantasy conversations with the therapist between sessions. Eventually the symptoms are taken over by therapy. In other words, the symptoms, rather than being driven by inner neurotic factors, begin to fluctuate according to the exigencies of the therapeutic relationship.

"No, thanks, no more coffee, Ernest. But you have some. You mind if I call you Ernest? Good. So to continue, I capitalized on this development. I did all I could to become even more important to Belle. I answered every question she asked me about my own life, I supported the positive parts of her. I told her what an intelligent, good-looking woman she was. I hated what she was doing to herself and told her so very directly. None of this was hard: all I had to do was tell the truth.

"Earlier you asked what my technique was. Maybe my best answer is simply: *I told the truth*. Gradually I began to play a larger role in her fantasy life. She'd slip into long reveries about the two of us—just being together, holding each other, my playing baby games with her, my feeding her. Once she brought a container of Jell-O and a spoon into the office and asked me to feed her—which I did, to her great delight.

"Sounds innocent, doesn't it? But I knew, even at the beginning, that there was a shadow looming. I knew it then, I knew it when she talked about how aroused she got when I fed her. I knew it when she talked about going canoeing for long periods, two or three days a week, just so she could be alone, float on the water, and enjoy her reveries about me. I knew my approach was risky, but it was a calculated risk. I was going to allow the positive transference to build so that I could use it to combat her self-destructiveness.

"And after a few months I had become so important to her that I could begin to lean on her pathology. First, I concentrated on the life-or-death stuff: HIV, the bar scene, the highway-angel-of-mercy blow jobs. She got an HIV test—negative, thank God. I remember waiting the two weeks for the results of the HIV test. Let me tell you, I sweated that one as much as she did.

"You ever work with patients when they're waiting for the results of the HIV test? No? Well, Ernest, that waiting period is a window of opportunity. You can use it to do some real work. For a few days patients come face-to-face with their own death, possibly for the first time. It's a time when you can help them to examine and reshuffle their priorities, to base their lives and their behavior on the things that really count. *Existential shock therapy*, I sometimes call it. But not Belle. Didn't faze her. Just had too much denial. Like so many other self-destructive patients, Belle felt invulnerable at anyone's hand other than her own.

"I taught her about HIV and about herpes, which, miraculously, she didn't have either, and about safe-sex procedures. I coached her on safer places to pick up men if she absolutely had to: tennis clubs, PTA meetings, bookstore readings. Belle was something—what an operator! She could arrange an assignation with some handsome total stranger in five or six minutes, sometimes with an unsuspecting wife only ten feet away. I have to admit I envied her. Most women don't appreciate their good fortune in this regard. Can you see men—especially a pillaged wreck like me—doing that at will?

"One surprising thing about Belle, given what I've told you so far, was her absolute honesty. In our first couple of sessions, when we were deciding to work together, I laid out my basic condition of therapy: *total honesty*. She had to commit herself to share every important event of her life: drug use, impulsive sexual acting out, cutting, purging, fantasies—everything. Otherwise, I told her, we were wasting her time. But if she leveled with me about everything, she could absolutely count on me to see this through with her. She promised and we solemnly shook hands on our contract.

"And, as far as I know, she kept her promise. In fact, this was part of my leverage because if there were important slips during the week—if, for example, she scratched her wrists or went to a bar—I'd analyze it to death. I'd insist on a deep and lengthy investigation of what happened just before the slip. 'Please, Belle,' I'd say, 'I must hear everything that preceded the event, everything that might help us understand it: the earlier events of the day, your thoughts, your feelings, your fantasies.' That drove Belle up the wall—she had other things she wanted to talk about and hated using up big chunks of her therapy time on this. That alone helped her control her impulsivity.

"Insight? Not a major player in Belle's therapy. Oh, she grew to recognize that more often than not her impulsive behavior was preceded by a feeling state of great deadness or emptiness and that the risk taking, the cutting, the sex, the bingeing, were all attempts to fill herself up or to bring herself back to life.

"But what Belle didn't grasp was that these attempts were futile. Every single one backfired, since they resulted in eventual deep shame and then more frantic—and more self-destructive—attempts to feel alive. Belle was always strangely obtuse at apprehending the idea that her behavior had consequences.

"So insight wasn't helpful. I had to do something else—and I tried every device in the book, and then some—to help her control her impulsivity. We compiled a list of her destructive impulsive behaviors, and she agreed not to embark on any of these before phoning me and allowing me a chance to talk her down. But she rarely phoned—she didn't want to intrude on my time. Deep down she was convinced that my commitment to her was tissue-thin and that I would soon tire of her and dump her. I couldn't dissuade her of this. She asked for some concrete memento of me to carry around with her. It would give her more self-control. Choose something in the office, I told her. She pulled my handkerchief out of my jacket. I gave it to her, but first wrote some of her important dynamics on it:

"'I feel dead and I hurt myself to know I'm alive. I feel deadened and must take dangerous risks to feel alive. I feel empty and try to fill myself with drugs, food, semen. But these are brief fixes. I end up feeling shame—and even more dead and empty.'

"I instructed Belle to meditate on the handkerchief and the messages every time she felt impulsive.

"You look quizzical, Ernest. You disapprove? Why? Too gimmicky? Not so. It seems gimmicky, I agree, but desperate remedies for desperate conditions. For patients who seem never to have developed a definitive sense of object constancy, I've found some possession, some concrete reminder, very useful. One of my teachers, Lewis Hill, who was a genius at treating severely ill schizophrenic patients, used to breathe into a tiny bottle and give it to his patients to wear around their necks when he left for vacation.

"You think that's gimmicky too, Ernest? Let me substitute another word, the proper word: *creative*. Remember what I said earlier about creating a new therapy for every patient? This is exactly what I meant. Besides, you haven't asked the most important question.

"Did it work? Exactly, exactly. That's the proper question. The *only* question. Forget the rules. Yes, it worked! It worked for Dr. Hill's patients and it worked for Belle, who carried around my handkerchief and gradually gained more control over her impulsivity. Her 'slips' became less frequent and soon we could begin to turn our attention elsewhere in our therapy hours.

"What? Merely a transference cure? Something about this is really getting to you, Ernest. That's good—it's good to question. You have a sense for the real issues. Let me tell you, you're in the wrong place in your life—you're not meant to be a neurochemist. Well, Freud's denigration of 'transference cure' is almost a century old. Some truth to it, but basically it's wrong.

"Trust me: if you can break into a self-destructive cycle of behavior—no matter *how* you do it—you've accomplished something important. The first step has *got to be* to interrupt the vicious circle of self-hate, self-destruction, and then more self-hate from the shame at one's behavior. Though she never expressed it, imagine the shame and self-contempt Belle must have felt about her degraded behavior. It's the therapist's task to help reverse that process. Karen Horney once said. . . . Do you know Horney's work, Ernest?

"Pity, but that seems to be the fate of the leading theoreticians of our field—their teachings survive for about one generation. Horney was one of my favorites. I read all of her work during my training. Her best book, *Neuroses and Human Growth,* is over fifty years old, but it's as good a book about therapy as you'll ever read—and not one word of jargon. I'm going to send you my copy. Somewhere, perhaps in that book, she made the simple but powerful point: 'If you want to be proud of yourself, then do things in which you can take pride.'

"I've lost my way in my story. Help me get started again, Ernest. My relationship with Belle? Of course, that's what we're really here for, isn't it? There were many interesting developments on that front. But I know that the development of most relevance for your committee is physical touching. Belle made an issue of this almost from the start. Now, I make a habit of physically touching all of my patients, male and female, every session—generally a handshake upon leaving, or perhaps a pat on the shoulder. Well, Belle didn't much care for that: she refused to shake my hand and began making some mocking statement like, 'Is that an APA-approved shake?' or 'Couldn't you try to be a little more formal?'

"Sometimes she'd end the session by giving me a hug—always

friendly, not sexual. The next session she'd chide me about my behavior, about my formality, about the way I'd stiffen up when she hugged me. And 'stiffen' refers to my body, not my cock, Ernest—I saw that look. You'd make a lousy poker player. We're not yet at the lascivious part. I'll cue you when we arrive.

"She'd complain about my age-typing. If she were old and wizened, she said, I'd have no hesitation about hugging her. She's probably right about that. Physical contact was extraordinarily important for Belle: she insisted that we touch and she never stopped insisting. Push, push, push. Nonstop. But I could understand it: Belle had grown up touch-deprived. Her mother died when she was an infant, and she was raised by a series of remote Swiss governesses. And her father! Imagine growing up with a father who had a germ phobia, never touched her, always wore gloves in and out of the home. Had the servants wash and iron all his paper currency.

"Gradually, after about a year, I had loosened up enough, or had been softened up enough by Belle's relentless pressure, to begin ending the sessions regularly with an avuncular hug. Avuncular? It means 'like an uncle.' But whatever I gave, she always asked for more, always tried to kiss me on the cheek when she hugged me. I always insisted on her honoring the boundaries, and she always insisted on pressing against them. I can't tell you how many little lectures I gave her about this, how many books and articles on the topic I gave her to read.

"But she was like a child in a woman's body—a knockout woman's body, incidentally—and her craving for contact was relentless. Couldn't she move her chair closer? Couldn't I hold her hand for a few minutes? Couldn't we sit next to each other on the sofa? Couldn't I just put my arm around her and sit in silence, or take a walk, instead of talking?

"And she was ingeniously persuasive. 'Seymour,' she'd say, 'you talk a good game about creating a new therapy for each patient, but what you left out of your articles was "as long as it's in the official manual" or "as long as it doesn't interfere with the therapist's middle-aged bourgeois comfort."' She'd chide me about taking refuge in the APA's guidelines about boundaries in therapy. She knew I had been responsible for writing those guidelines when I was president of the APA, and she accused me of being imprisoned by my own rules. She'd criticize me for not reading my own articles. 'You stress the honoring of each patient's uniqueness, and then you pretend that a single set of rules can fit all patients in all situations. We all get lumped together,' she'd say, 'as if all patients were the same and should be treated the same.' And her chorus was always, 'What's more important: Following the rules? Staying in your armchair comfort zone? Or doing what's best for your patient?'

"Other times she'd rail about my 'defensive therapy': 'You're so terrified about being sued. All you humanistic therapists cower before the lawyers, while at the same time you urge your mentally ill patients to grab hold of their freedom. Do you really think I would sue you? Don't you know me yet, Seymour? You're saving my life. And I love you!'

"And, you know, Ernest, she was right. She had me on the run. I *was* cowering. I was defending my guidelines even in a situation where I knew they were antitherapeutic. I was placing my timidity, my fears about my little career, before her best interests. Really, when you look at things from a disinterested position, there *was* nothing wrong with letting her sit next to me and hold my hand. In fact, every time I did this, without fail, it charged up our therapy: she became less defensive, trusted me more, had more access to her inner life.

"What? Is there any place at all for firm boundaries in therapies? Of course there is. Listen on, Ernest. My problem was that Belle railed at all boundaries, like a bull and a red flag. Wherever—*wherever*—I set the boundaries she pushed and pushed against them. She took to wearing skimpy clothes or see-through blouses with no brassiere. When I commented on this, she ridiculed me for my Victorian attitudes toward the body. I wanted to know every intimate contour of her mind, she'd say, yet her skin was a no-no. A couple of times she complained about a breast lump and asked me to examine her—of course, I didn't. She'd obsess about sex with me for hours on end, and beg me to have sex with her just once. One of her arguments was that one-time sex with me would break her obsession. She'd learn that it was nothing special or magical and then be freed to think about other things in life.

"How did her campaign for sexual contact make me feel? Good question, Ernest, but is it germane to this investigation?

"You're not sure? What seems to be germane is what I *did*—that's what I'm being judged for—not what I felt or thought. Nobody gives a shit about that in a lynching! But if you turn off the tape recorder for a couple of minutes, I'll tell you. Consider it instruction. You've read Rilke's *Letters to a Young Poet,* haven't you? Well, consider this my letter to a young therapist.

"Good. Your pen, too, Ernest. Put it down, and just listen for a while. You want to know how this affected me? A beautiful woman obsessed with me, masturbating daily while thinking of me, begging me to lay her, talking on and on about her fantasies about me, about rubbing my sperm over her face or putting it into chocolate chip cookies—how do you *think* it made me feel? Look at me! Two canes, getting worse, ugly—my face being swallowed up in my own wrinkles, my body flabby, falling apart.

"I admit it. I'm only human. It began to get to me. I thought of her when I got dressed on the days we had a session. What kind of shirt to wear? She hated broad stripes—made me look too self-satisfied, she said. And which aftershave lotion? She liked Royall Lyme better than Mennen, and I'd vacillate each time over which one to use. Generally I'd splash on the Royall Lyme. One day at her tennis club, she met one of my colleagues—a nerd, a real narcissist who's always been competitive with me—and as soon as she heard he had some connection to me, she got him to talk about me. His connection to me turned her on, and she immediately went home with him. Imagine, this schnook gets laid by this great-looking woman and doesn't know it's because of me. And I can't tell him. Pissed me off.

"But having strong feelings about a patient is one thing. Acting on them is another. And I fought against it—I analyzed myself continually, I consulted with a couple of friends on an ongoing basis, and I tried to deal with it in the sessions. Time after time I told her there was no way in hell I would ever have sex with her, that I wouldn't ever again be able to feel good about myself if I did. I told her that she needed a good, caring therapist much more than she needed an aging, crippled lover. But I did acknowledge my attraction to her. I told her I didn't want her sitting so close to me because the physical contact stimulated me and rendered me less effective as a therapist. I took an authoritarian posture: I insisted that my long-range vision was better than hers, that I knew things about her therapy that she couldn't yet know.

"Yes, yes, you can turn the recorder back on. I think I've answered your question about my feelings. So, we went along like this for over a year, struggling against outbreaks of symptoms. She'd have many slips, but on the whole we were doing well. I knew this was no cure. I was only 'containing' her, providing a holding environment, keeping her safe from session to session. But I could hear the clock ticking; she was growing restless and fatigued.

"And then one day she came in looking all worn out. Some new, very clean stuff was on the streets, and she admitted she was very close to scoring some heroin. 'I can't keep living a life of total frustration,' she said. 'I'm trying like hell to make this work, but I'm running out of steam. I know me, I know me, I know how I operate. You're keeping me alive and I want to work with you. I think I can do it. But *I need some incentive!* Yes, yes, Seymour, I know what you're getting ready to say: I know your lines by heart. You're going to say that I already have an incentive, that my incentive is a better life, feeling better about myself, not trying to kill myself, self-respect. But that stuff is not enough. It's too far away. Too airy. I need to touch it. I need to touch it!'

"I started to say something placating, but she cut me off. Her desperation had escalated and out of it came a desperate proposition. 'Seymour, work with me. My way. I beg you. If I stay clean for a year—really clean, you know what I mean: no drugs, no purging, no bar scenes, no cutting, no *nothing*—then *reward me!* Give me some incentive! Promise to take me to Hawaii for a week. And take me there as man and woman—not shrink and sap. Don't smile, Seymour, I'm serious—dead serious. I need this. Seymour, for once, put *my* needs ahead of the rules. Work with me on this.'

"Take her to Hawaii for a week! You smile, Ernest; so did I. Preposterous! I did as you would have done: I laughed it off. I tried to dismiss it as I had dismissed all of her previous corrupting propositions. But this one wouldn't go away. There was something more compelling, more ominous in her manner. And more persistent. She wouldn't let go of it. I couldn't move her off it. When I told her it was out of the question, Belle started negotiating: she raised the good-behavior period to a year and a half, changed Hawaii to San Francisco, and cut the week first to five and then to four days.

"Between sessions, despite myself, I found myself thinking about

Belle's proposition. I couldn't help it. I toyed with it in my mind. A year and a half—*eighteen months*—of good behavior? Impossible. Absurd. She could never do it. Why were we wasting our time even talking about it?

"But *suppose*—just a thought experiment, I told myself—suppose that she was really able to change her behavior for eighteen months? Try out the idea, Ernest. Think about it. Consider the possibility. Wouldn't you agree that if this impulsive, acting-out woman were to develop controls, behave more ego-syntonically for eighteen months, off drugs, off cutting, off all forms of self-destruction, *she'd no longer be the same person*?

"What? 'Borderline patients play games'? That what you said? Ernest, you'll never be a real therapist if you think like that. That's exactly what I meant earlier when I talked about the dangers of diagnosis. There are borderlines and there are borderlines. Labels do violence to people. You can't treat the label; you have to treat the person behind the label. So again, Ernest, I ask you: Wouldn't you agree that this person, not this label, but this Belle, this flesh and blood person, would be intrinsically, radically changed, if she behaved in a fundamentally different fashion for eighteen months?

"You won't commit yourself? I can't blame you—considering your position today. And the tape recorder. Well, just answer silently, to yourself. No, let me answer for you: I don't believe there's a therapist alive who wouldn't agree that Belle would be a vastly different person if she were no longer governed by her impulse disorder. She'd develop different values, different priorities, a different vision. She'd wake up, open her eyes, see reality, maybe see her own beauty and worth. And she'd see me differently, see me as you see me: a tottering, moldering, old man. Once reality intrudes, then her erotic transference, her necrophilia, would simply fade away and with it, of course, all interest in the Hawaiian incentive.

"What's that, Ernest? Would I miss the erotic transference? Would that sadden me? Of course! Of course! I love being adored. Who doesn't? Don't you?

"Come on, Ernest. *Don't you?* Don't you love the applause when you finish giving grand rounds? Don't you love the people, especially the women, crowding around?

"Good! I appreciate your honesty. Nothing to be ashamed of. Who doesn't? Just the way we're built. So to go on, I'd miss her adoration, I'd feel bereft: but that goes with the territory. That's my job: to introduce her to reality, to help her grow away from me. Even, God save us, to forget me.

"Well, as the days and the weeks went on, I grew more and more intrigued with Belle's wager. *Eighteen months of being clean,* she offered. And remember that was still an early offer. I'm a good negotiator and was sure I could probably get more, increase the odds, provide even more room. Really cement the change. I thought about other conditions I could insist upon: some group therapy for her, perhaps, and a more strenuous attempt to get her husband into couples therapy.

"I thought about Belle's proposition day and night. Couldn't get it out of my mind. I'm a betting man, and the odds in my favor looked fantastic. If Belle lost the bet, if she slipped—by taking drugs, purging, cruising bars, or cutting her wrists—*nothing would be lost*. We'd merely be back to where we were before. Even if I got only a few weeks or months of abstinence, I could build on that. And if Belle won, she'd be so changed that she would never collect. This was a no-brainer. Zero risk downside and a good chance upside that I could save this woman.

"I've always liked action, love the races, bet on anything—baseball, basketball. After high school I joined the navy and put myself through college on my shipboard poker winnings; in my internship at Mount Sinai in New York I spent many of my free nights in a big game on the obstetrics unit with the on-call Park Avenue obstetricians. There was a continuous game going on in the doctors' lounge next to the labor room. Whenever there was an open hand, they called the operator to page 'Dr. Blackwood.' Whenever I heard the page, 'Dr. Blackwood wanted in the delivery room,' I'd charge over as fast as I could. Great docs, every one of them, but poker chumps. You know, Ernest, interns were paid almost nothing in those days, and at the end of the year all the other interns were in deep debt. Me? I drove to my residency at Ann Arbor in a new De Soto convertible, courtesy of the Park Avenue obstetricians.

"Back to Belle. I vacillated for weeks about her wager and then, one day, I took the plunge. I told Belle I could understand her needing incentive, and I opened serious negotiation. I insisted on two years. She was so grateful to be taken seriously that she agreed to all my terms, and we quickly fashioned a firm, clear contract. Her part of the deal was to stay entirely clean for two years: no drugs (including alcohol), no cutting, no purging, no sex pickups in bars or highways or any other dangerous sex behavior. Urbane sexual affairs were permitted. And no illegal behavior. I thought that covered everything. Oh, yes, she had to start group therapy and promise to participate with her husband in couples therapy. My part of the contract was a weekend in San Francisco: all details, hotels, activities were to be her choice—carte blanche. I was to be at her service.

"Belle treated this very seriously. At the finish of negotiation, she suggested a formal oath. She brought a Bible to the session and we each swore on it that we would uphold our part of the contract. After that we solemnly shook hands on our agreement.

"Treatment continued as before. Belle and I met approximately two times a week—three might have been better, but her husband began to grumble about the therapy bills. Since Belle stayed clean and we didn't have to spend time analyzing her 'slips,' therapy went faster and deeper. Dreams, fantasies—everything seemed more accessible. For the first time I began to see seeds of curiosity about herself; she signed up for some university extension courses on abnormal psychology, and she began writing an autobiography of her early life. Gradually she recalled more details of her childhood, her sad search for a new mother among the string of disinterested governesses, most of whom left within a few months because of her father's fanatical insistence on cleanliness and order. His germ phobia controlled all aspects of her life. Imagine: until she was fourteen she was kept out of school and educated at home because of his fear of her bringing home germs. Consequently she had few close friends. Even meals with friends were rare; she was forbidden to dine out and she dreaded the embarrassment of exposing her friends to her father's dining antics: gloves, hand washing between courses, inspections of the servants' hands for cleanliness. She was not permitted to borrow books—one beloved governess was fired on the spot because she permitted Belle and a friend to wear each other's dresses for a day. Childhood and daughterhood ended sharply at fourteen, when she was sent to boarding school at Grenoble. From then on, she had only perfunctory contact with her father, who soon remarried. His new wife was a beautiful woman but a former prostitute—according to a spinster aunt, who said the new wife was only one of many whores her father had known in the previous fourteen years. Maybe, Belle wondered—and this was her very first interpretation in therapy—*he* felt dirty, and that was why he was always washing and why he refused to let his skin touch hers.

"During these months Belle raised the topic of our wager only in the context of expressing her gratitude to me. She called it the 'most powerful affirmation' she'd ever gotten. She knew that the wager was a gift to her: unlike 'gifts' she had received from other shrinks—words, interpretations, promises, 'therapeutic caring'—this gift was real and palpable. Skin to skin. It was tangible proof that I was entirely committed to helping her. And proof to her of my love. Never before, she said, had she ever been loved like that. Never before had anyone put her ahead of his self-interests, ahead of the rules. Certainly not her father, who never gave her an ungloved hand and until his death ten years ago sent her the same birthday present every year: a bundle of hundred-dollar bills, one for every year of her age, each bill freshly washed and ironed.

"And the wager had another meaning. She was tickled by my willingness to bend the rules. What she loved best about me, she said, was my willingness to take chances, my open channel to my own shadow. 'There's something naughty and dark about you, too,' she'd say. 'That's why you understand me so well. In some ways I think we are twin brains.'

"You know, Ernest, that's probably why we hit it off so quickly, why she knew immediately that I was the therapist for her—just something mischievous in my face, some irreverent twinkle in my eyes. Belle was right. She had my number. She was a smart cookie.

"And you know, I knew exactly what she meant—exactly! I can spot it in others the same way. Ernest, just for a minute, turn off the recorder. Good. Thanks. What I wanted to say is that I think I see it in you. You and I, we sit on different sides of this dais, this judgment table, but we have something in common. I told you, I'm good at reading faces. I'm rarely wrong about such things.

"No? C'mon! You know what I mean! Isn't it precisely for this reason that you listen to my tale with such interest? More than interest! Do

I go too far if I call it *fascination*? Your eyes are like saucers. Yes, Ernest, you and me. You could have been me in my situation. My Faustian wager.could have been yours as well.

"You shake your head. Of course! But I don't speak to your head. I aim straight at your heart, and the time may come when you open yourself to what I say. And more—perhaps you will see yourself not only in me but in Belle as well. The three of us. We're not so different from one another! Okay, that's all—let's get back to business.

"Wait! Before you turn the recorder back on, Ernest, let me say one more thing. You think I give a shit about the ethics committee? What can they do? Take away hospital admitting privileges? I'm seventy, my career is over, I know that. So why do I tell you all this? In the hope that some good will come of it. In the hope that maybe you'll allow some speck of me into you, let me course in your veins, let me teach you. Remember, Ernest, when I talk about your having an open channel to your shadow, I mean that *positively*—I mean that you may have the courage and largeness of spirit to be a great therapist. Turn the recorder back on, Ernest. Please, no reply is necessary. When you're seventy, you don't need replies.

"Okay, where were we? Well, the first year passed with Belle definitely doing better. No slips whatsoever. She was absolutely clean. She placed fewer demands on me. Occasionally she asked to sit next to me, and I'd put my arm around her and we'd spend a few minutes sitting like that. It never failed to relax her and make her more productive in therapy. I continued to give her fatherly hugs at the end of sessions, and she usually planted a restrained, daughterly kiss on my cheek. Her husband refused couples therapy but agreed to meet with a Christian Science practitioner for several sessions. Belle told me that their communication had improved, and both of them seemed more content with their relationship.

"At the sixteen-month mark, all was still well. No heroin—no drugs at all—no cutting, bulimia, purging, or self-destructive behavior of any sort. She got involved with several fringe movements—a channeler, a past-lives therapy group, an algae nutritionist—typical California flake stuff, harmless. She and her husband had resumed their sexual life, and she did a little sexual acting out with my colleague—that jerk, that asshole, she met at the tennis club. But at least it was safe sex, a far cry from the bar and highway escapades.

"It was the most remarkable therapy turnabout I've ever seen. Belle said it was the happiest time of her life. I challenge you, Ernest: plug her into any of your outcome studies. She'd be the star patient! Compare her outcome with any drug therapy: Risperidone, Prozac, Paxil, Effexor, Wellbutrin—you name it—my therapy would win hands down. The best therapy I've ever done, and yet I couldn't publish it. Publish it? I couldn't even tell anyone about it. Until now! You're my first real audience.

"At about the eighteen-month mark, the sessions began to change. It was subtle at first. More and more references to our San Francisco weekend crept in, and soon Belle began to speak of it at every session. Every morning she'd stay in bed for an extra hour daydreaming about what our weekend would be like: about sleeping in my arms, phoning for breakfast in bed, then a drive and lunch in Sausalito, followed by an afternoon nap. She had fantasies of our being married, of waiting for me in the evenings. She insisted that she could live happily the rest of her life if she knew that I'd come back home to her. She didn't need much time with me; she'd be willing to be a second wife, to have me next to her for only an hour or two a week—she could live healthy and happy with that forever.

"Well, you can imagine that by this time I was growing a little uneasy. And then a lot uneasy. I began to scramble. I did my best to help her face reality. Practically every session I talked about my age. In three or four years I'd be in a wheelchair. In ten years I'd be eighty. I asked her how long she thought I would live. The males in my family die young. At my age my father had been in his coffin for fifteen years. She would outlive me at least twenty-five years. I even began exaggerating my neurological impairment when I was with her. Once I staged an intentional fall—that's how desperate I was growing. And old people don't have much energy, I repeated. Asleep at eight-thirty, I'd tell her. Been five years since I'd been awake for the ten o'clock news. And my failing vision, my shoulder bursitis, my dyspepsia, my prostate, my gassiness, my constipation. I even thought of getting a hearing aid, just for the effect.

"But all this was a terrible blunder. One hundred eighty degrees wrong! It just whetted her appetite even more. She had some perverse infatuation with the idea of my being infirm or incapacitated. She had fantasies of my having a stroke, of my wife leaving me, of her moving in to care for me. One of her favorite daydreams involved nursing me: making my tea, washing me, changing my sheets and my pajamas, dusting me with talcum powder, and then taking off her clothes and climbing under the cool sheets next to me.

"At the twenty-month mark, Belle's improvement was even more pronounced. On her own she had gotten involved with Narcotics Anonymous and was attending three meetings a week. She was doing volunteer work at ghetto schools to teach teenage girls about birth control and AIDS, and had been accepted in an MBA program at a local university.

"What's that, Ernest? How did I know she was telling me the truth? You know, I never doubted her. I know she has her character flaws but truth telling, at least with me, seemed almost a compulsion. Early in our therapy—I think I mentioned this before—we established a contract of mutual and absolute truth telling. There were a couple of times in the first few weeks of therapy when she withheld some particularly unseemly episodes of acting out, but she couldn't stand it; she got into a frenzy about it, was convinced that I could see inside her mind and would expel her from therapy. In each instance she could not wait till the next session to confess but had to phone me—once after midnight—to set the record straight.

"But your question is a good one. Too much was riding on this to simply take her word for it, and I did what you would have done: I checked all possible sources. During this time I met with her husband a couple of times. He refused therapy but agreed to come in to help accelerate the pace of Belle's therapy, and he corroborated everything she said. Not only that but he gave me permission to contact the Christian Science counselor—who, ironically enough, was getting her Ph.D. in clinical psychology and was reading my work—and who also corroborated Belle's story: working hard on her marriage, no cutting, no drugs, community volunteer work. No, Belle was playing it straight.

"So what would you have done in this situation, Ernest? What?

Wouldn't have been there in the first place? Yeah, yeah, I know. Facile answer. You disappoint me. Tell me, Ernest, if you wouldn't have been there, where *would* you have been? Back in your lab? Or in the library? You'd be safe. Proper and comfortable. But where would the patient be? Long gone, that's where! Just like Belle's twenty therapists before me—they all took the safe route, too. But I'm a different kind of therapist. A saver of lost souls. I refuse to quit on a patient. I will break my neck, I'll put my ass on the line, I'll try anything to save the patient. That's been true my whole career. You know my reputation? Ask around. Ask your chairman. He knows. He's sent me dozens of patients. I'm the therapist of last resort. Therapists send me the patients they give up on. You're nodding? You've heard that about me? Good! It's good you know I'm not just some senile schnook.

"So consider my position! What the hell could I do? I was getting jumpy. I pulled out all the stops: I began to interpret like mad, in a frenzy, as if my life depended on it. I interpreted everything that moved.

"And I got impatient with her illusions. For example, take Belle's loony fantasy of our being married and her putting her life on hold waiting all week, in suspended animation, for an hour or two with me. 'What kind of life is that and what kind of relationship?' I asked her. It was not a relationship—it was shamanism. Think of it from my point of view, I'd say: What did she imagine I'd get out of such an arrangement? To have her healed by an hour of my presence—it was unreal. Was this a relationship? No! We weren't being real with each other; she was using me as an icon. And her obsession with sucking me and swallowing my sperm. Same thing. Unreal. She felt empty and wanted me to fill her up with my essence. Couldn't she see what she was doing, couldn't she see the error in treating the symbolic as if it were concrete reality? How long did she think my thimbleful of sperm would fill her up? In a few seconds her gastric hydrochloric acid would leave nothing but fragmented DNA chains.

"Belle gravely nodded at my frenetic interpretations—and then returned to her knitting. Her Narcotics Anonymous sponsor had taught her to knit, and during the last weeks she worked continuously on a cable-stitched sweater for me to wear during our weekend. I found no way to rattle her. Yes, she agreed that she might be basing her life on fantasy. Maybe she was searching for the wise old man archetype. But was that so bad? In addition to her MBA program, she was auditing a course in anthropology and reading *The Golden Bough*. She reminded me that most of mankind lived according to such irrational concepts as totems, reincarnation, heaven, and hell, even transference cures of therapy, and the deification of Freud. 'Whatever works works,' she said, 'and the thought of our being together for the weekend works. This has been the best time in my life; it feels just like being married to you. It's like waiting and knowing you'll be coming home to me shortly; it keeps me going, it keeps me content.' And with that she turned back to her knitting. That goddamned sweater! I felt like ripping it out of her hands.

"By the twenty-two-month mark, I hit the panic button. I lost all composure and began wheedling, weaseling, begging. I lectured her on love. 'You say you love me, but love is a relationship, love is caring about the other, caring about the growth and the being of the other. Do you ever care about me? How *I* feel? Do you ever think about my guilt, my fear, the impact of this on my self-respect, knowing that I've done something unethical? And the impact on my reputation, the risk I'm running—my profession, my marriage?'

"'How many times,' Belle responded, 'have you reminded me that we are two people in a human encounter—nothing more, nothing less? You asked me to trust you, and I trusted you—I trusted for the first time in my life. Now I ask *you* to trust *me*. This will be our secret. I'll take it to my grave. No matter what happens. Forever! And as for your self-respect and your guilt and your professional concerns, well, what's more important than the fact that you, a healer, are healing me? Will you let rules and reputation and ethics take precedence over that?' You got a good answer for that, Ernest? I didn't.

"Subtly, but ominously, she alluded to the potential effects of my welshing on the wager. She had lived for *two years* for this weekend with me. Would she ever trust again? Any therapist? Or *anyone,* for that matter? *That,* she let me know, would be something for me to feel guilty about. She didn't have to say very much. I knew what my betrayal would mean to her. She had not been self-destructive for over two years, but I had no doubt she had not lost the knack. To put it bluntly, I was convinced that if I welshed, Belle would kill herself. I still tried to escape from my trap, but my wing beats grew more feeble.

"'I'm seventy years old—you're thirty-four,' I told her. 'There's something unnatural about us sleeping together.'

"'Chaplin, Kissinger, Picasso, Humbert Humbert and Lolita,' Belle responded, not even bothering to look up from her knitting.

"'You've built this up to grotesque levels,' I told her; 'it's all so inflated, so exaggerated, so removed from reality. This whole weekend cannot fail to be a downer for you.'

"'A downer is the best thing that could happen,' she replied. 'You know—to break down my obsession about you, my "erotic transference," as you like to call it. This is a no-loser for our therapy.'

"I kept weaseling. 'Besides, at my age, potency wanes.'

"'Seymour,' she chided me, 'I'm surprised at you. You still haven't gotten it, still haven't gotten that potency or intercourse is of no concern. What I want is you to be with me and hold me—as a person, a woman. Not as a patient. Besides, Seymour,' and here she held the half-knitted sweater in front of her face, coyly peeked over, and said, 'I'm going to give you the fuck of your life!'

"And then time was up. The twenty-fourth month arrived and I had no choice but to pay the devil his due. If I welshed, I knew the consequences would be catastrophic. If, on the other hand, I kept my word? Then, who knows? Perhaps she was right, perhaps it *would* break the obsession. Perhaps, without the erotic transference, her energies would be freed to relate better to her husband. She'd maintain her faith in therapy. I'd retire in a couple of years, and she'd go on to other therapists. Maybe a weekend in San Francisco with Belle would be an act of supreme therapeutic agape.

"What, Ernest? My countertransference? Same as yours would have been: gyrating wildly. I tried to keep it out of my decision. I didn't act on my countertransference—I was convinced I had no other rational choice. And I'm convinced of that still, even in the light of what has happened. But I'll cop to being more than a little enthralled. There I was, an old man facing the end, with cerebellar cortical neurons croaking daily, eyes failing, sexual life all but over—my wife, who's good at giving things up, gave sex up long ago. And my attraction toward Belle? I won't deny it: I adored her. And when she told me she was going to give me the fuck of my life, I could hear my worn-out gonadal engines cranking up and turning over again. But let me say to you—and the tape recorder, let me say it as forcefully as I can—*that's not why I did it!* That may not be important to you or the ethics board, but it's of life-or-death importance to me. I never broke my covenant with Belle. I never broke my covenant with any patient. I never put my needs ahead of theirs.

"As for the rest of the story, I guess you know it. It's all in your chart there. Belle and I met in San Francisco for breakfast at Mama's in North Beach on Saturday morning and stayed together till Sunday dusk. We decided to tell our spouses that I had scheduled a weekend marathon group for my patients. I do such groups for ten to twelve of my patients about twice a year. In fact, Belle had attended such a weekend during her first year of therapy.

"You ever run groups like that, Ernest? No? Well let me tell you that they are powerful ... accelerate therapy like mad. You should know about them. When we meet again—and I'm sure we will, under different circumstances—I'll tell you about these groups; I've been doing them for thirty-five years.

"But back to the weekend. Not fair to bring you this far and not share the climax. Let's see, what can I tell you? What do I *want* to tell you? I tried to keep my dignity, to stay within my therapist persona, but that didn't last long—Belle saw to that. She called me on it as soon as we had checked into the Fairmont, and very soon we were man and woman and everything, everything that Belle had predicted came to pass.

"I won't lie to you, Ernest. I loved every minute of our weekend, most of which we spent in bed. I was worried that all my pipes were rusted shut after so many years of disuse. But Belle was a master plumber, and after some rattling and clanging everything began to work again.

"For three years I had chided Belle for living in illusion and had imposed my reality on her. Now, for one weekend, I entered her world and found out that life in the magic kingdom wasn't so bad. She was my fountain of youth. Hour by hour I grew younger and stronger. I walked better, I sucked in my stomach, I looked taller. Ernest, I tell you, I felt like bellowing. And Belle noticed it. 'This is what you needed, Seymour. And this is all I ever wanted from you—to be held, to hold, to give my love. Do you understand that this is the first time in my life I have given love? Is it so terrible?'

"She cried a lot. Along with all other conduits, my lachrymal ducts, too, had unplugged, and I cried too. She gave me so much that weekend. I spent my whole career giving, and this was the first time it came back, really came back, to me. It's like she gave for all the other patients I've ever seen.

"But then real life resumed. The weekend ended. Belle and I went back to our twice-weekly sessions. I never anticipated losing that wager, so I had no contingency plans for the postweekend therapy. I tried to go back to business as usual, but after one or two sessions I saw I had a problem. A big problem. It is almost impossible for intimates to return to a formal relationship. Despite my efforts, a new tone of loving playfulness replaced the serious work of therapy. Sometimes Belle insisted on sitting in my lap. She did a lot of hugging and stroking and groping. I tried to fend her off, I tried to maintain a serious work ethic, but, let's face it, it was no longer therapy.

"I called a halt and solemnly suggested we had two options: either we try to go back to serious work, which meant returning to a nonphysical and more traditional relationship, or we drop the pretense that we're doing therapy and try to establish a purely social relationship. And 'social' didn't mean sexual: I didn't want to compound the problem. I told you before, I helped write the guidelines condemning therapists and patients having posttherapy sexual relationships. I also made it clear to her that, since we were no longer doing therapy, I would accept no more money from her.

"Neither of those options were acceptable to Belle. A return to formality in therapy seemed a farce. Isn't the therapy relationship the one place where you don't play games? As for not paying, that was impossible. Her husband had set up an office at home and spent most of his time around the house. How could she explain to him where she was going for two regular hours a week if she was not regularly writing checks for therapy?

"Belle chided me for my narrow definition of therapy. 'Our meetings together—intimate, playful, touching, sometimes making good love, real love, on your couch—that *is* therapy. And good therapy, too. Why can't you see that, Seymour?' she asked. 'Isn't effective therapy good therapy? Have you forgotten your pronouncements about the "one important question in therapy"—*Does it work?* And isn't my therapy working? Aren't I continuing to do well? I've stayed clean. No symptoms. Finishing grad school. I'm starting a new life. You've changed me, Seymour, and all you have to do to maintain the change is continue to spend two hours a week being close to me.'

"Belle was a smart cookie, all right. And growing smarter. I could marshal no counterargument that such an arrangement was not good therapy.

"Yet I knew it couldn't be. I enjoyed it too much. Gradually, much too gradually, it dawned on me that I was in big trouble. Anyone looking at the two of us together would conclude that I was exploiting the transference and using this patient for my own pleasure. Or that I was a high-priced geriatric gigolo!

"I didn't know what to do. Obviously I couldn't consult with anyone—I knew what they would advise and I wasn't ready to bite the bullet. Nor could I refer her to another therapist—she wouldn't go. But to be honest, I didn't push that option hard. I worry about that. Did I do right by her? I lost a few nights' sleep thinking about her telling another therapist all about me. You know how therapists gossip among themselves about the antics of previous therapists—and they'd just love some juicy Seymour Trotter gossip. Yet I couldn't ask her to protect me—keeping that kind of secret would sabotage her next therapy.

"So my small-craft warnings were up but, even so, I was absolutely unprepared for the fury of the storm when it finally broke. One evening I returned home to find the house dark, my wife gone, and four pictures of me and Belle tacked to the front door: one showed us checking in at the registration desk of the Fairmont Hotel; another showed us, suitcases in hand, entering our room together; the third was a close-up of the hotel registration form—Belle had paid cash and registered us as Dr. and Mrs. Seymour. The fourth showed us locked in an embrace at the Golden Gate Bridge scenic overlook.

"Inside, on the kitchen table, I found two letters: one from Belle's husband to my wife, stating that she might be interested in the four enclosed pictures portraying the type of treatment her husband was offering his wife. He said he had sent a similar letter to the state board of medical ethics and ended with a nasty threat suggesting that if I ever saw Belle again, a lawsuit would be the least important thing the Trotter family would have to worry about. The second letter was from my wife—short and to the point, asking me not to bother to explain. I could do my talking to her lawyer. She gave me twenty-four hours to pack up and move out of the house.

"So, Ernest, that brings us up to now. What else can I tell you?

"How'd he get the pictures? Must've hired a private eye to tail us. What irony—that her husband chose to leave only when Belle had improved! But, who knows? Maybe he'd been looking for an escape for a long time. Maybe Belle had burned him out.

"I never saw Belle again. All I know is hearsay from an old buddy of mine at Pacific Redwood Hospital—and it ain't good hearsay. Her husband divorced her and ultimately skipped the country with the family assets. He had been suspicious of Belle for months, ever since he had spotted some condoms in her purse. That, of course, is further irony: it was only because therapy had curbed her lethal self-destructiveness that she was willing to use condoms in her affairs.

"The last I heard, Belle's condition was terrible—back to ground zero. All the old pathology was back: two admissions for suicidal attempts—one cutting, one a serious overdose. She's going to kill herself. I know it. Apparently she tried three new therapists, fired each in turn, refuses further therapy, and is now doing hard drugs again.

"And you know what the worst thing is? I know I could help her, even now. I'm sure of it, but I'm forbidden to see her or speak to her by court order and under the threat of severe penalty. I got several phone messages from her, but my attorney warned me that I was in great jeopardy and ordered me, if I wanted to stay out of jail, not to respond. He contacted Belle and informed her that by court injunction I was not permitted to communicate with her. Finally she stopped calling.

"What am I going to do? About Belle, you mean? It's a tough call. It kills me not to be able to answer her calls, but I don't like jails. I know I could do so much for her in a ten-minute conversation. Even now. Off the record—shut off the recorder, Ernest. I'm not sure if I'm going to be able to just let her sink. Not sure if I could live with myself.

"So, Ernest, that's it. The end of my tale. Finis. Let me tell you, it's not the way I wanted to end my career. Belle is the major character in this tragedy, but the situation is also catastrophic for me. Her lawyers are urging her to ask for damages—to get all she can. They will have a feeding frenzy—the malpractice suit is coming up in a couple of months.

"Depressed! Of course I'm depressed. Who wouldn't be? I call it an appropriate depression: I'm a miserable, sad old man. Discouraged, lonely, full of self-doubts, ending my life in disgrace.

"No, Ernest, not a drug-treatable depression. Not that kind of depression. No biological markers: psychomotor symptoms, insomnia, weight loss—none of that. Thanks for offering.

"No, not suicidal, though I admit I'm drawn to darkness. But I'm a survivor. I crawl into the cellar and lick my wounds.

"Yes, very much alone. My wife and I had been living together by habit for many years. I've always lived for my work; my marriage has always been on the periphery of my life. My wife always said I fulfill all my desires for closeness with my patients. And she was right. But that's not why she left. My ataxia's progressing fast, and I don't think she relished the idea of becoming my full-time nurse. My hunch is that she welcomed the excuse to cut herself loose from that job. Can't blame her.

"No, I don't need to see anyone for therapy. I told you I'm not clinically depressed. I appreciate your asking, Ernest, but I'd be a cantankerous patient. So far, as I said, I'm licking my own wounds and I'm a pretty good licker.

"It's fine with me if you phone to check in. I'm touched by your offer. But put your mind at ease, Ernest. I'm a tough son of a bitch. I'll be all right."

And with that, Seymour Trotter collected his canes and lurched out of the room. Ernest, still sitting, listened to the tapping grow fainter.

When Ernest phoned a couple of weeks later, Dr. Trotter once again refused all offers of help. Within minutes he switched the conversation to

Ernest's future and again expressed his strong conviction that, whatever Ernest's strengths as a psychopharmacologist, he was still missing his calling: he was a born therapist and owed it to himself to fulfill his destiny. He invited Ernest to discuss the matter further over lunch, but Ernest refused.

"Thoughtless of me," Dr. Trotter had responded without a trace of irony. "Forgive me. Here I am advising you about a career shift and at the same time asking you to jeopardize it by being seen in public with me."

"No, Seymour." For the first time Ernest called him by first name. "That is absolutely not the reason. The truth is, and I am embarrassed to say this to you, I'm committed already to serve as an expert witness at your civil suit trial for malpractice."

"Embarrassment is not warranted, Ernest. It's your duty to testify. I would do the same, precisely the same, in your position. Our profession is vulnerable, threatened on all sides. It is our to duty to protect it and to preserve standards. Even if you believe nothing else about me, believe that I treasure this work. I've devoted my entire life to it. That's why I told you my story in such detail—I wanted you to know it is not a story of betrayal. I acted in good faith. I know it sounds absurd, yet even to this moment I think I did the right thing. Sometimes destiny pitches us into positions where the right thing is the wrong thing. I never betrayed my field, nor a patient. Whatever the future brings, Ernest, believe me. I believe in what I did: I would never betray a patient."

Ernest did testify at the civil trial. Seymour's attorney, citing his advanced age, diminished judgment, and infirmity, tried a novel, desperate defense: he claimed that Seymour, not Belle, had been the victim. But their case was hopeless, and Belle was awarded two million dollars—the maximum of Seymour's malpractice coverage. Her lawyers would have gone for more but there seemed little point to it since, after his divorce and legal fees, Seymour's pockets were empty.

That was the end of the public story of Seymour Trotter. Shortly after the trial he silently left town and was never heard from again, aside from a letter (with no return address) that Ernest received a year later.

Ernest had only a few minutes before his first patient. But he couldn't resist inspecting, once again, the last trace of Seymour Trotter.

Dear Ernest,

You, alone, in those demonizing witch hunt days, expressed concern for my welfare. Thank you—it was powerfully sustaining. Am well. Lost, but don't want to be found. I owe you much—certainly this letter and this picture of Belle and me. That's her house in the background, incidentally: Belle's come into a good bit of money.

Seymour

Ernest, as he had so many times before, stared at the faded picture. On a palm-studded lawn, Seymour sat in a wheelchair. Belle stood behind him, forlorn and gaunt, fists clutching the handles of the wheelchair. Her eyes were downcast. Behind her a graceful colonial home, and beyond that the gleaming milky-green water of a tropical sea. Seymour was smiling—a big, goofy, crooked smile. He held on to the wheelchair with one hand; with the other, he pointed his cane jubilantly toward the sky.

As always, when he studied the photograph, Ernest felt queasy. He peered closer, trying to crawl into the picture, trying to discover some clue, some definitive answer to the real fate of Seymour and Belle. The key, he thought, was to be found in Belle's eyes. They seemed melancholy, even despondent. Why? She had gotten what she wanted, hadn't she? He moved closer to Belle and tried to catch her gaze. But she always looked away.

Notes

[Numbers in brackets refer to the note number of the original complete citation of a reference in each chapter.]

CHAPTER 1. THE THERAPEUTIC FACTORS

1. H. Feifel and J. Eells, "Patients and Therapists Assess the Same Psychotherapy," *Journal of Consulting and Clinical Psychology* 27 (1963): 310–18.

2. J. Schaffer and S. Dreyer, "Staff and Inpatient Perceptions of Change Mechanisms in Group Therapy," *American Journal of Psychiatry* 139 (1982): 127–28; J. Flora-Tastado, "Patient and Therapist Agreement on Curative Factors in Psychotherapy," *Dissertation Abstracts International* 42 (1981): 371-B; S. Bloch and J. Reibstein, "Perceptions by Patients and Therapists of Therapeutic Factors in Group Therapy," *British Journal of Psychiatry* 137 (1980): 274–78. R. Cabral and A. Paton, "Evaluation of Group Therapy: Correlations Between Clients' and Observers' Assessments," *British Journal of Psychiatry* 126 (1975): 475–77; and C. Glass and D. Arnkoff, "Common and Specific Factors in Client Descriptions and Explanations for Change," *Journal of Integrative and Eclectic Psychotherapy* 7 (4 [winter 1988]): 427–40.

3. T. Butler and A. Fuhriman, "Level of Functioning and Length of Time in Treatment Variables Influencing Patients' Therapeutic Experience in Group Psychotherapy," *International Journal of Group Psychotherapy* 33 (4 [October 1983]): 489–504.

4. J. Maxmen, "Group Therapy as Viewed by Hospitalized Patients," *Archives of General Psychiatry* 28 (March 1973): 404–8; T. Butler and A. Fuhriman, "Patient Perspective on the Curative Process: A Comparison of Day Treatment and Outpatient Psychotherapy Groups," *Small Group Behavior* 11 (4 [November 1980]): 371–88; T. Butler and A. Fuhriman, "Curative Factors in Group Therapy: A Review of the Recent Literature," *Small Group Behavior* 14 (2 [May 1983]): 131–42; M. Leszcz, I. Yalom, and M. Norden, "The Value of Inpatient Group Psychotherapy: Patients' Perceptions," *International Journal of Group Psychotherapy* 35 (1985): 411–35; and E. Rynearson and S. Melson, "Short-term Group Psychotherapy for Patients with Functional Complaint," *Postgraduate Medical Journal* 76 (1984): 141–50.

5. B. Corder, L. Whiteside, and T. Haizlip, "A Study of Curative Factors in Group Psychotherapy with Adolescents," *International Journal of Group Psychotherapy* 31 (3 [July 1981]): 345–54; N. Macaskill, "Therapeutic Factors in Group Therapy with Borderline Patients," *International Journal of Group Psychotherapy* 32 (1 [January 1982]): 61–73; and S. Colijn et al., "A Comparison of Curative Factors in Different Types of Group Psychotherapy," *International Journal of Group Psychotherapy* 41 (3 [July 1991]): 365–78.

6. M. Lieberman and L. Borman, *Self-Help Groups for Coping with Crisis* (San Francisco: Jossey-Bass, 1979); M. Lieberman, "Comparative Analyses of Change Mechanisms in Group," in *Advances in Group Therapy,* edited by R. Dies and K. R. MacKenzie (New York: International Universities Press, 1983); and S. Bloch and E. Crouch, *Therapeutic Factors in Group Therapy* (Oxford: Oxford University Press, 1985), pp. 25–67.

7. F. Taylor, *The Analysis of Therapeutic Groups* (Oxford: Oxford University Press, 1961); and B. Berzon and R. Farson, "The Therapeutic Event in Group Psychotherapy: A Study of Subjective Reports by Group Members," *Journal of Individual Psychology* 19 (1963): 204–12.

8. T. Kaul and R. Bednar, "Experiential Group Research: Can the Cannon Fire?" in *Handbook of Psychotherapy and Behavioral Change: An Empirical Analysis,* 4th ed., edited by S. Garfield and A. Bergin (New York: John Wiley, 1994), pp. 201–3; A. P. Goldstein, *Therapist-Patient Expectancies in Psychotherapy* (New York: Pergamon Press, 1962); S. Bloch et al., "Patients' Expectations of Therapeutic Improvement and Their Outcomes," *American Journal of Psychiatry* 133 (1976): 1457–59; J. Frank and J. Frank, *Persuasion and Healing: A Comparative Study of Psychotherapy*, 3d ed. (Baltimore: Johns Hopkins University Press, 1991), pp. 132–54; J. Connelly et al., "Premature Termination in Group Psychotherapy: Pretherapy and Early Therapy Predictors," *International Journal of Group Psychotherapy* 36 (2 [1986]): 145–52; A. Rabin et al., "Factors Influencing Continuation," *Behavioral Therapy* 23 (1992): 695–98; H. Hoberman et al., "Group Treatment of Depression: Individual Predictors of Outcome," *Journal of Consulting and Clinical Psychology* 56 (3 [1988]): 393–98; M. Pearson and A. Girling, "The Value of the Claybury Selection Battery in Predicting Benefit from Group Therapy," *British Journal of Psychiatry* 157 (1990): 384–88; and W. Piper, "Client Variables," in *Handbook of Group Psychotherapy*, edited by A. Fuhriman and G. Burlingame (New York: John Wiley, 1994).

9. Goldstein, *Therapist-Patient Expectancies* [8], pp. 35–53; Kaul and Bednar, "Experiential Group Research" [8], pp. 229–63; E. Uhlenhuth and D. Dun-

can, "Some Determinants of Change in Psychoneurotic Patients," *Archives of General Psychiatry* 18 (1968): 532–40; and J. Frank and J. Frank, *Persuasion and Healing* [8], pp. 154–67.

10. Lieberman and Borman, *Self-Help Groups* [6]; and G. Goodman and M. Jacobs, "The Self-Help Mutual Support Group," in *Handbook of Group Psychotherapy* [8].

11. J. Moreno, "Group Treatment for Eating Disorders," in *Handbook of Group Psychotherapy* [8].

12. S. Goldsteinberg and M. Buttenheim, "'Telling One's Story' in an Incest Survivors' Group," *International Journal of Group Psychotherapy* 43 (2 [April 1993]): 173–89; F. Mennen and D. Meadow, "Process to Recovery: In Support of Long-Term Groups for Sexual Abuse Survivors," *International Journal of Group Psychotherapy* 43 (1 [January 1993]): 29–44; and M. Schadler, "Brief Group Therapy with Adult Survivors of Incest," in *Focal Group Therapy*, edited by Matthew McKay and Kim Paleg (Oakland, Calif.: New Harbinger Publications, 1992), pp. 292–322.

13. P. Tsui and G. Schultz, "Ethnic Factors in Group Process," *American Journal of Orthopsychiatry* 58 (1988): 136–42.

14. M. Galanter, "Zealous Self-Help Groups as Adjuncts to Psychiatric Treatment: A Study of Recovery, Inc.," *American Journal of Psychiatry* 143 (1988): 1248–53; M. Galanter, "Cults and Zealous Self-Help Movements," *American Journal of Psychiatry* 145 (1990): 543–51; and C. Gartner, "A Self-Help Organization for Nervous and Former Mental Patients—Recovery, Inc., Chicago," *Hospital and Community Psychiatry* 42 (1991): 1055–56.

15. A. Low, *Mental Health Through Will Training* (Boston: Christopher Publishing House, 1950).

16. Lieberman and Borman, *Self-Help Groups* [6], pp. 194–234; Goodman and Jacobs, "The Self-Help Mutual Support Group," in *Handbook of Group Psychotherapy* [8]; and D. Salem, E. Seidman, and J. Rappaport, "Community Treatment of the Mentally Ill: The Promise of Mutual Help Organizations," *Social Work* 33 (1988): 403–408.

17. S. Tenzer, "Fat Acceptance Therapy: A Non-Dieting Group Approach to Physical Wellness, Insight, and Self-Acceptance," *Women and Therapy* 8 (1989): 39–47.

18. Moreno, "Group Treatment for Eating Disorders," in *Handbook of Group Psychotherapy* [8]; J. Mitchel et al., "A Comparison Study of Antidepressants and Structured Intensive Group Therapy in the Treatment of Bulimia Nervosa," *Archives of General Psychiatry* 47 (1990): 149–57; J. Laube, "Why

Group for Bulimia?" *International Journal of Group Psychotherapy* 40 (2 [April 1990]): 169–88; D. Franko, "The Use of a Group Meal in the Brief Group Therapy of Bulimia Nervosa," *International Journal of Group Psychotherapy* 43 (2 [April 1993]): 237–42; R. Bogdaniak and F. Piercy, "Model for the Group Treatment of Eating Disorders," *International Journal of Group Psychotherapy* 37 (4 [October 1987]): 589–602; and J. Brisman and M. Siegel, "The Bulimia Workshop: A Unique Integration of Group Treatment Approaches," *International Journal of Group Psychotherapy* 35 (4 [October 1985]): 585–602.

19. M. Kalb, "The Effects of Biography on the Divorce Adjustment Process," *Sexual and Marital Therapy* 2 (1987): 53–64; and D. Grenvold and G. Welch, "Structured Short-Term Group Treatment of Postdivorce Adjustment," *International Journal of Group Psychotherapy* 29 (1979): 347–58.

20. L. Gallese and E. Treuting, "Help for Rape Victims Through Group Therapy," *Journal of Psychosocial Nursing and Mental Health Services* 19 (1981): 20–21.

21. R. Kris and H. Kramer, "Efficacy of Group Therapy with Postmastectomy Self-Perception, Body Image, and Sexuality," *Journal of Sex Research* 23 (1986): 438–51.

22. E. Herman and S. Baptiste, "Pain Control: Mastery Through Group Experience," *Pain* 10 (1981): 79–86.

23. A. Beckett and J. Rutan, "Treating Persons with ARC and AIDS in Group Psychotherapy," *International Journal of Group Psychotherapy* 40 (1 [January 1990]): 19–30.

24. F. Fromm-Reichman, *Principles of Intensive Psychotherapy* (Chicago: University of Chicago Press, 1950).

25. Frank and Frank, *Persuasion and Healing* [8], p. 119; and J. Frank, "Emotional Reactions of American Soldiers to an Unfamiliar Disease," *American Journal of Psychiatry* 102 (1946): 631–40.

26. J. Frank et al., "Behavioral Patterns in Early Meetings of Therapy Groups," *American Journal of Psychiatry* 108 (1952): 771–78; C. Peters and H. Brunebaum, "It Could Be Worse: Effective Group Therapy with the Help-Rejecting Complainer," *International Journal of Group Psychotherapy* 27 (1977): 471–80; and E. Berne, *Games People Play* (New York: Grove Press, 1964).

27. J. Rubin and K. Locasio, "A Model for Communication Skills Group Using Structured Exercises and Audiovisual Equipment," *International Journal of Group Psychotherapy* 35 (1985): 569–84.

28. J. Flowers, "The Differential Outcome Effects of Simple Advice, Alternatives, and Instructions in Group Psychotherapy," *International Journal of Group Psychotherapy* 29 (1979): 305–15.

29. Frank and Frank, *Persuasion and Healing* [8].

30. V. Frankl, *The Will to Meaning* (Cleveland: World Publishing, 1969).

31. S. Barlow, W. Hansen, et al., "Leader Communication Style: Effects on Members of Small Groups," *Small Group Behavior* 13 (1982): 513–81; E. Lineham and J. O'Toole, "Effects of Subliminal Stimulation of Symbiotic Fantasies on College Student Self-Disclosure in Group Counseling," *Journal of Counseling Psychology* 29 (1982): 151–57; and S. Borgers, "Uses and Effects of Modeling by the Therapist in Group Therapy," *Journal for Specialists in Group Work* 8 (1983): 133–39.

32. P. Van der Linden, "Individual Values in Therapeutic Communities," *International Journal of Therapeutic Communities* 11 (1990): 43–51; and D. Fram, "Group Methods in the Treatment of Substance Abusers," *Psychiatric Annals* 20 (1990): 385–88.

33. A. Bandura, E. Blanchard, and B. Ritter, "The Relative Efficacy of Desensitization and Modeling Approaches for Inducing Behavioral, Affective, and Attitudinal Changes," *Journal of Personality and Social Psychology* 13 (1969): 173–99; and A. Bandura, D. Ross, and S. Ross, "Vicarious Reinforcements and Imitative Learning," *Journal of Abnormal and Social Psychology* 67 (1963): 601–7.

34. J. Moreno, "Psychodramatic Shock Therapy," *Sociometry* 2 (1939): 1–30.

35. S. Colijn et al., "A Comparison of Curative Factors."

36. J. Breuer and S. Freud, *Studies on Hysteria,* vol. 2 of *The Standard Edition of the Complete Psychological Works of Sigmund Freud,* edited by James Strachey (London: Hogarth Press, 1955).

37. M. Lieberman, I. Yalom, and M. Miles, *Encounter Groups: First Facts* (New York: Basic Books, 1973).

38. S. Freedman and J. Hurley, "Perceptions of Helpfulness and Behavior Groups," *Group* 4 (1980): 51–58.

39. M. McCallum, W. Piper, and H. Morin, "Affect and Outcome in Short-Term Group Therapy for Loss," *International Journal of Group Psychotherapy* 43 (1993): 303–19.

40. I. Yalom, J. Tinklenberg, and M. Gilula, "Curative Factors in Group Therapy," unpublished study, Department of Psychiatry, Stanford University, 1968.

41. M. Smith, G. Glass, and T. Miller, *The Benefits of Psychotherapy* (Baltimore: Johns Hopkins University Press, 1980), p. 87.

42. Kaul and Bednar, "Experiential Group Research" [8]; D. Orlinski and K. Howard, "Process and Outcome in Psychotherapy," in *Handbook of Psychotherapy and Behavioral Change,* 3d ed., edited by S. Garfield and A. Bergin

(New York: John Wiley, 1986); R. Dies, "Practical, Theoretical, and Empirical Foundations for Group Psychotherapy," in *The American Psychiatric Association Annual Review*, vol. 5, edited by A. Frances and R. Hales (Washington, D.C.: American Psychiatric Press, 1986); C. Tillitski, "A Meta-analysis of Estimated Effect Sizes for Group vs. Individual Effect Sizes for Group versus Individual vs. Control Treatments," *International Journal of Group Psychotherapy* 40 (1990): 215–24; and R. Toseland and M. Siporin, "When to Recommend Group Therapy: A Review of the Clinical and Research Literature," *International Journal of Group Psychotherapy* 36 (1986): 171–201.

43. A. Bergin, "The Effects of Psychotherapy: Negative Results Revisited," *Journal of Counseling Psychology* 10 (1963): 244–50; H. Strupp, S. Hadley, and B. Gomes-Schwartz, *Psychotherapy for Better or Worse: The Problem of Negative Effects* (New York: Jason Aronson, 1977); and M. Lambert and A. Bergin, "The Effectiveness of Psychotherapy," in *Handbook of Psychotherapy and Behavioral Change,* 4th ed. [8], pp. 176–80. Luborsky et al. raise a dissenting voice: in their study they found little evidence of negative psychotherapy effects: L. Luborsky, P. Crits-Christoph, J. Mintz, and A. Auerbach, *Who Will Benefit from Psychotherapy?* (New York: Basic Books, 1988).

44. A. Horvath, L. Gaston, and L. Luborsky, "The Therapeutic Alliance and Its Measures," in *Dynamic Psychotherapy Research*, edited by N. Miller, L. Luborsky, and J. Docherty (New York: Basic Books, 1993); and L. Gaston, "The Concept of the Alliance and Its Role in Psychotherapy: Theoretical and Empirical Considerations," *Psychiatry* 27 (1990): 143–53.

45. D. Orlinsky and K. Howard, "The Relation of Process to Outcome in Psychotherapy," in *Handbook of Psychotherapy and Behavioral Change,* 4th ed. [8], pp. 308–76; H. Strupp, R. Fox, and K. Lessler, *Patients View Their Psychotherapy* (Baltimore: Johns Hopkins University Press, 1969); P. Martin and A. Sterne, "Post-hospital Adjustment as Related to Therapists' In-therapy Behavior," *Psychotherapy: Theory, Research, and Practice* 13 (1976): 267–73; G. Barrett-Lennard, "Dimensions of Therapist Response as Causal Factors in Therapeutic Change," *Psychological Monographs* 76, 43 (whole, 562 [1962]); A. Gurman and A. Razin, *Effective Psychotherapy: A Handbook for Research* (New York: Pergamon Press, 1977); M. Parloff, I. Waskow, and B. Wolfe, "Research on Therapist Variables in Relation to Process and Outcome," in *Handbook of Psychotherapy and Behavioral Change: An Empirical Analysis,* 2d ed., edited by S. Garfield and A. Bergin (New York: John Wiley, 1978), pp. 233–82; and P. Buckley et al., "Psychodynamic Variables as Predictors of Psychotherapy Outcome," *American Journal of Psychiatry* 141 (6 [June 1984]): 742–48.

46. A. Horvath and B. Symonds, "Relation Between Working Alliance

and Outcome in Psychotherapy: A Meta-analysis," *Journal of Consulting Psychology* 38 (1991): 139–49; F. Fiedler, "Factor Analyses of Psychoanalytic, Non-Directive, and Adlerian Therapeutic Relationships," *Journal of Consulting Psychology* 15 (1951): 32–38; F. Fiedler, "A Comparison of Therapeutic Relationships in Psychoanalytic, Non-Directive and Adlerian Therapy," *Journal of Consulting Psychology* 14 (1950): 436–45; and Lieberman, Yalom, and Miles, *Encounter Groups* [37].

47. R. DeRubeis and M. Feeley, "Determinants of Change in Cognitive Therapy for Depression," *Cognitive Therapy and Research* 14 (1990): 469–80; B. Rounsaville et al., "The Relation Between Specific and General Dimension: The Psychotherapy Process in Interpersonal Therapy of Depression," *Journal of Consulting and Clinical Psychology* 55 (1987): 379–84; A. Bergin and M. Lambert, "The Evaluation of Therapeutic Outcomes," in *Handbook of Psychotherapy and Behavioral Change,* 2d ed. [45], pp. 150–70; Gurman and Razin, *Effective Psychotherapy* [45]; and R. Sloane, F. R. Staples, A. H. Cristol, N. J. Yorkston, and K. Whipple, *Short-Term Analytically Oriented Psychotherapy vs. Behavior Therapy* (Cambridge: Harvard University Press, 1975).

48. Kaul and Bednar, "Experiential Group Research" [8].

49. Bloch and Crouch, *Therapeutic Factors in Group Psychotherapy* [6], pp. 99–103; and N. Evans and P. Jarvis, "Group Cohesion: A Review and Reevaluation," *Small Group Behavior* 2 (1980): 359–70.

50. For an in-depth discussion of research methodology and instrumentation, see: Kaul and Bednar, "Experiential Group Research" [8]; S. Drescher, G. Burlingame, and A. Fuhriman, "Cohesion: An Odyssey in Empirical Understanding," *Small Group Behavior* 16 (1985): 3–30; and G. Burlingame, J. Kircher, and S. Taylor, "Methodological Considerations in Group Therapy Research: Past, Present, and Future Practices," in *Handbook of Group Psychotherapy* [8].

51. D. Cartwright and A. Zander, eds., *Group Dynamics: Research and Theory* (Evanston, Ill.: Row, Peterson, 1962), p. 74.

52. J. Frank, "Some Determinants, Manifestations, and Effects of Cohesion in Therapy Groups," *International Journal of Group Psychotherapy* 7 (1957): 53–62.

53. Bloch and Crouch, *Therapeutic Factors in Group Psychotherapy* [6].

54. Researchers either have had to depend on members' subjective ratings of attraction to the group or critical incidents or, more recently, have striven for greater precision by relying entirely on raters' evaluations of global climate or such variables as fragmentation versus cohesiveness, withdrawal versus involvement, mistrust versus trust, disruption versus cooperation, abusiveness

versus expressed caring, unfocused versus focused. See S. Budman et al., "Preliminary Findings on a New Instrument to Measure Cohesion in Group Psychotherapy," *International Journal of Group Psychotherapy* 37 (1987): 75–94.

55. D. Kivlighan and D. Mullison, "Participants' Perceptions of Therapeutic Factors in Group Counseling," *Small Group Behavior* 19 (1988): 452–68; L. Braaten, "The Different Patterns of Group Climate: Critical Incidents in High and Low Cohesion Sessions of Group Psychotherapy," *International Journal of Group Psychotherapy* 40 (1990): 477–93; and S. Budge, "Group Cohesiveness Reexamined," *Group* 5 (1981): 10–18.

56. R. MacKenzie and V. Tschuschke, "Relatedness, Group Work, and Outcome in Long-Term Inpatient Psychotherapy Groups," *Journal of Psychotherapy Practice and Research* 2 (1993): 147–56.

57. Frank, "Some Determinants" [52].

58. H. Grunebaum and L. Solomon, "Peer Relationships, Self-Esteem, and the Self," *International Journal of Group Psychotherapy* 37 (1987): 475–513.

59. J. Frank, "Some Values of Conflict in Therapeutic Groups," *Group Psychotherapy* 8 (1955): 142–51.

60. H. Sullivan, *The Interpersonal Theory of Psychiatry* (New York: W. W. Norton, 1953); and H. Sullivan, *Conceptions of Modern Psychiatry* (New York: Norton, 1940).

61. P. Mullahy, *The Contributions of Harry Stack Sullivan* (New York: Hermitage House, 1952), p. 10.

62. H. S. Sullivan, "Psychiatry: Introduction to the Study of Interpersonal Relations," *Psychiatry* 1 (1938): 121–34.

63. Sullivan, *Conceptions* [60], p. 207.

64. Ibid., p. 237.

CHAPTER 2: THE THERAPIST WORKING IN THE HERE-AND-NOW

1. Y. Agazarian, "Contemporary Theories of Group Psychotherapy: A Systems Approach to the Group-as-a-Whole," *International Journal of Group Psychotherapy* 42 (1992): 177–204.

2. M. Lieberman, I. Yalom, and M. Miles, *Encounter Groups: First Facts* (New York: Basic Books, 1973).

3. L. Ormont, "The Leader's Role in Resolving Resistances to Intimacy in the Group Setting," *International Journal of Group Psychotherapy* 38 (1988): 29–47.

4. M. Berger, "Nonverbal Communications in Group Psychotherapy," *International Journal of Group Psychotherapy* 8 (1958): 161–78.

5. J. Flowers and C. Booraem, "The Effects of Different Types of Interpretation on Outcome in Group Therapy," *Group* 14 (1990): 81–88.

6. O. Rank, *Will Therapy and Truth and Reality* (New York: Alfred A. Knopf, 1950); R. May, *Love and Will* (New York: W. W. Norton, 1969); S. Arieti, *The Will to Be Human* (New York: Quadrangle Books, 1972), L. Farber, *The Ways of the Will* (New York: Basic Books, 1966); A. Wheelis, "Will and Psychoanalysis," *Journal of the Psychoanalytic Association* 4 (1956): 285–303; and I. Yalom, *Existential Psychotherapy* (New York: Basic Books, 1983).

7. Yalom, *Existential Psychotherapy* [6], pp. 286–350.

8. Farber, *Ways of the Will* [6].

9. T. Aquinas, quoted in *The Encyclopedia of Philosophy*, edited by P. Edwards, vol. 7 (New York: Free Press, 1967), p. 112.

10. J. Frank and J. Frank, *Persuasion and Healing: A Comparative Study of Psychotherapy*, 3d ed. (Baltimore: Johns Hopkins University Press, 1991), pp. 21–51.

11. D. Spence, *Narrative Truth and Historical Truth* (New York: W. W. Norton, 1982).

CHAPTER 3: GROUP THERAPY WITH SPECIALIZED GROUPS

1. M. Lieberman and I. D. Yalom, "Brief Group Therapy with the Spousally Bereaved: A Controlled Study," *International Journal of Group Psychotherapy* 42 (1992): 1–18.

2. I. D. Yalom and M. Lieberman, "Bereavement and Heightened Existential Awareness," *Psychiatry* 54 (1991): 334—45.

3. I. D. Yalom, *Existential Psychotherapy* (New York: Basic Books, 1980), p. 164.

4. M. A. Lieberman and L. Videka-Sherman, "The Impact of Self-Help Groups on the Mental Health of Widows and Widowers," *American Journal of Orthopsychiatry* 56 (1986):435–49.

5. C. S. Lewis, "A Grief Observed," in *The Oxford Book of Death,* edited by D. J. Enright (Oxford: Oxford University Press, 1983), p. 110.

6. A. Tennyson, "In Memoriam A.H.H.," in *The Oxford Book of Death,* p. 105.

CHAPTER 4: THE FOUR ULTIMATE CONCERNS

1. J. Breuer and S. Freud, *Studies on Hysteria,* vol. 2 of *The Standard Edition of the Complete Psychological Works of Sigmund Freud,* edited by James Strachey (London: Hogarth Press, 1955; originally published 1895), pp. 135–83.

2. Ibid., p. 158.

3. B. Spinoza, cited by M. de Unamuno, *The Tragic Sense of Life,* translated by J. E. Flitch (New York: Dover, 1954), p. 6.

4. A. Malraux, cited in P. Lomas, *True and False Experience* (New York: Taplinger, 1973), p. 8.

5. T. Hardy, "In Tenebris," *Collected Poems of Thomas Hardy* (New York: Macmillan, 1926), p. 154.

6. *The Encyclopedia of Philosophy,* edited by P. Edwards, vol. 3 (New York: Free Press, 1967), p. 147.

7. S. Kierkegaard, "How Johannes Climacus Became an Author," in *A Kierkegaard Anthology,* edited by R. Bretall (Princeton, N.J.: Princeton University Press, 1946), p. 193.

8. Ibid.

9. W. Barrett, *What Is Existentialism?* (New York: Grove Press, 1954), p. 21.

10. V. Frankl, oral communication, 1974.

11. R. May, E. Angel, and H. Ellenberger, *Existence* (New York: Basic Books, 1958), p. 11.

12. C. Rogers, cited in D. Malan, "The Outcome Problem in Psychotherapy Research," *Archives of General Psychiatry* 29 (1973): 719–29.

13. Personal communication, 1978.

CHAPTER 5: DEATH, ANXIETY, AND PSYCHOTHERAPY

1. A. Meyer, cited by J. Frank, oral communication, 1979.

2. Cicero, cited in M. Montaigne, *The Complete Essays of Montaigne,* translated by Donald Frame (Stanford: Stanford University Press, 1965), p. 56.

3. Seneca, cited ibid., p. 61.

4. Saint Augustine, cited ibid., p. 63.

5. Manilius, cited ibid., p. 65.

6. Ibid., p. 67.

7. M. Heidegger, *Being and Time,* translated by J. Macquarrie and E. Robinson (New York: Harper & Row, 1962, pp. 210–24.

8. Ibid., passim.

9. K. Jaspers, cited in J. Choron, *Death and Western Thought* (New York: Collier Books, 1963), p. 226.

10. S. Freud, "Thoughts for the Times on War and Death," in vol. 14 of *The Standard Edition of the Complete Psychological Works of Sigmund Freud*

(hereafter cited as *Standard Edition*), edited by James Strachey (London: Hogarth Press, 1957; originally published in 1915), p. 291.

11. Ibid., p. 290.

12. Montaigne, *Complete Essays* [2], p. 67.

13. L. Tolstoy, *War and Peace* (New York: Modern Library, 1931), p. 57.

14. L. Tolstoy, *The Death of Ivan Ilych and Other Stories* (New York: Signet Classics, 1960).

15. D. Rosen, "Suicide Survivors," *Western Journal of Medicine* 122 (April 1975): 289–94.

16. R. Noyes, "Attitude Changes Following Near-Death Experiences," *Psychiatry* 43 (1980): 234–242.

17. J. Diggory and D. Rothman, "Values Destroyed by Death," *Journal of Abnormal and Social Psychology* 63 (1961): 205–10.

18. S. Kierkegaard, *The Concept of Dread* (Princeton, N.J.: Princeton University Press, 1957), p. 55.

19. R. May, *The Meaning of Anxiety,* rev. ed. (New York: W. W. Norton, 1977), p. 207.

20. Kierkegaard, *Concept of Dread* [18], p. 55.

21. May, *Meaning of Anxiety* [19], p. 207.

22. Heidegger, *Being and Time* [7], p. 223.

23. A. Sharp, *A Green Tree in Geddes* (New York: Walker, 1968).

24. W. Bromberg and P. Schilder, "The Attitudes of Psychoneurotics Toward Death," *Psychoanalytic Review* 23 (1936): 1–28.

25. A. Witt, personal communication, September 1978.

26. Personal communication from a friend.

27. Freud, "Thoughts for the Times" [10], p. 298.

28. S. Kierkegaard, cited in E. Becker, *The Denial of Death* (New York: Free Press, 1973), p. 70.

29. O. Rank, *Will Therapy and Truth and Reality* (New York: Alfred A. Knopf, 1945), p. 126.

30. P. Tillich, *The Courage to Be* (New Haven and London: Yale University Press, 1952), p. 66.

31. Becker, *Denial of Death* [28], p. 66.

32. R. Lifton, "The Sense of Immortality: On Death and the Continuity of Life," in *Explorations of Psychohistory,* edited by R. Lifton and E. Olson (New York: Simon & Schuster, 1974), p. 282.

33. Rank, *Will Therapy* [29], p. 124.

34. E. Fromm, *Escape from Freedom* (New York: Holt, Rinehart & Winston, 1941), p. 6.

35. L. Tolstoy, *Death of Ivan Ilych* [14], pp. 131–32.

36. R. Frost, *In the Clearing* (New York: Holt, Rinehart & Winston, 1962), p. 39.

37. N. Kazantzakis, *Report to Greco,* translated by P. A. Bien (New York: Simon & Schuster, 1965), p. 457.

38. N. Kazantzakis, *The Odyssey: A Modern Sequel,* translated by Kimon Friar (New York: Simon & Schuster, 1958).

39. C. Baker, *Ernest Hemingway: A Life Story* (New York: Charles Scribner, 1969), p. 5.

40. E. Hemingway, *The Old Man and the Sea* (New York: Charles Scribner, 1961).

41. C. Wahl, "Suicide as a Magical Act," *Bulletin of Menninger Clinic* 21 (May 1957): 91–98.

42. F. Kluckholm and F. Stroedbeck, *Variations in Value Orientations* (New York: Harper & Row, 1961), p. 15.

43. J. M. Keynes, cited in Norman Brown, *Life Against Death* (New York: Vintage Books, 1959), p. 107.

44. L. Tolstoy, *Anna Karenina* (New York: Modern Library, 1950), p. 168.

45. S. Freud, *Some Character Types Met with in Psychoanalytic Work,* vol. 14 of *Standard Edition* [10], pp. 316–31.

46. Rank, *Will Therapy* [29], p. 119.

47. A. Maslow, *The Further Reaches of Human Nature* (New York: Viking, 1971), p. 35.

48. Becker, *Denial of Death* [28], pp. 35–39.

49. Fromm, *Escape from Freedom* [34], pp. 174–79.

50. J. Masserman, *The Practice of Dynamic Psychiatry* (London: W. B. Saunders, 1955), pp. 476–81.

51. S. Kierkegaard, cited in May, *Meaning of Anxiety* [19], p. 38.

52. Heidegger, *Being and Time* [7], p. 105.

53. S. Arieti, "Psychotherapy of Severe Depression," *American Journal of Psychiatry* 134 (1977): 864–68.

54. Rank, *Will Therapy* [29], pp. 119–34.

55. S. Kierkegaard, cited in May, *Meaning of Anxiety* [19], p. 37.

56. Heidegger, *Being and Time* [7], p. 294.

57. F. Nietzsche, *The Gay Science,* translated by Walter Kaufman (New York: Vintage Books, 1974), p. 37.

58. Cited in Montaigne, *Complete Essays* [2], p. 65.

59. G. Santayana, cited in K. Fisher, "Ultimate Goals in Psychotherapy," *Journal of Existentialism* 7 (winter 1966–67): 215–32.

60. P. Landsburg, cited in Choron, *Death and Western Thought* [9], p. 16.

61. J. Donne, *Complete Poetry and Selected Prose* (New York: Modern Library, 1952), p. 332.

62. R. Gardner, "The Guilt Reaction of Parents of Children with Severe Physical Disease," *American Journal of Psychiatry* 126 (1969): 82–90.

63. Heidegger, *Being and Time* [7], p. 105.

64. S. Golburgh and C. Rotman, "The Terror of Life: A Latent Adolescent Nightmare," *Adolescence* 8 (1973): 569–74.

65. E. Jaques, "Death and the Mid-Life Crisis," *International Journal of Psychoanalysis* 46 (1965): 502–13.

66. C. Jung, cited in D. Levinson, *The Seasons of a Man's Life* (New York: Alfred A. Knopf, 1978), p. 4.

67. D. Krantz, *Radical Career Change: Life Beyond Work* (New York: Free Press, 1978).

68. Noyes, "Attitude Changes" |16|.

69. Montaigne, *Complete Essays* [2], p. 62.

70. G. Zilboorg, "Fear of Death," *Psychoanalytic Quarterly* 12 (1943): 465–75.

71. S. Freud, *Three Essays on the Theory of Sexuality,* vol. 7 of *Standard Edition* [10], pp. 125–231.

72. Dante Alighieri, *La Divina Commedia* (Florence, Italy: Casa Editrice Nerbini, n.d.); translation by John Freccero, 1980.

73. Jaques, "Death and the Mid-Life Crisis" [66].

74. M. Eliade, *Shamanism: Archaic Techniques of Ecstasy* (Princeton, N.J.: Princeton University Press, 1964), p. 43.

75. Ibid., p. 45.

76. J. Bugental, *The Search for Authenticity* (New York: Holt, Rinehart & Winston, 1965), p. 167.

77. J. Hinton, "The Influence of Previous Personality on Reactions to Having Terminal Cancer," *Omega* 6 (1975): 95–111.

78. F. Nietzsche, cited in N. Brown, *Life Against Death* (New York: Vintage Books, 1959), p. 107.

79. Montaigne, *Complete Essays* [2], p. 268.

CHAPTER 6: LITERATURE INFORMING PSYCHOLOGY: LITERARY VIGNETTES

1. M. Heidegger, *Being and Time,* translated by J. Macquarrie and E. Robinson (New York: Harper & Row, 1962), p. 284.

2. *Everyman,* in *The Norton Anthology of English Literature,* edited by M. Abrams et al., vol. 1 (New York: W. W. Norton, 1962), pp. 281–303. R. Bollendorf, unpublished doctoral dissertation, Northern Illinois University, 1976.

3. L. Carroll, cited in J. Solomon, "Alice and the Red King," *International Journal of Psychoanalysis* 44 (1963): 64–73.

4. A. Camus, *The Fall* (New York: Vintage Books, 1956), p. 58.

5. Ibid., p. 68.

6. Ibid., p. 63.

7. L. Tolstoy, *War and Peace* (New York: Modern Library, 1931), p. 231.

8. Ibid., p. 245.

9. J. P. Sartre, cited in R. Hepburn, "Questions about the Meaning of Life," *Religious Studies* 1 (1965): 125–40.

10. J. P. Sartre, *No Exit and Three Other Plays* (New York: Vintage Books, 1955).

11. Ibid., p. 91.

12. Ibid., p. 92.

13. Ibid.

14. Ibid., p. 94.

15. Ibid.

16. Ibid., p. 105.

17. Ibid., p. 108.

18. Ibid., pp. 121–22.

19. Ibid., p. 123.

20. Ibid., p. 124.

21. G. Allport, cited in V. Frankl, *The Will to Meaning* (Cleveland: New American Library, 1969), p. 66.

22. J. Gardner, *Grendel* (New York: Ballantine Books, 1971), p. 115.

CHAPTER 7: PSYCHOLOGY INFORMING LITERATURE

1. C. Baker, *Ernest Hemingway: A Life Story* (New York: Charles Scribner's Sons, 1969).

2. E. Hemingway to Charles T. Lanham, letter, 27 November 1947.

3. E. Hemingway, "The Earnest Liberal's Lament," *Der Querschnitt,* autumn 1924.

4. L. Hemingway, *My Brother, Ernest Hemingway* (Cleveland: World Publishing, 1962).

5. M. H. Sanford, *At the Hemingways: A Family Portrait* (Boston: Little, Brown, 1962).

6. I. D. Yalom, *The Theory and Practice of Group Psychotherapy* (New York: Basic Books, 1970), pp. 121–23.

7. C. Rycroft, *Psychoanalysis Observed* (London: Constable & Company, 1966), p. 18.

8. Baker, *Ernest Hemingway* [1], p. 268.

9. Ibid., p. 392.

10. Ibid., p. 465.

11. R. P. Weeks, ed., introduction to *Hemingway: A Collection of Critical Essays* (Englewood Cliffs, N.J.: Prentice-Hall, 1962), pp. 1–16.

12. C. T. Lanham, written communication, 22 August 1967.

13. Ibid.

14. E. Hemingway, "The Snows of Kilimanjaro: A Long Story," *Esquire* 6, no. 27 (1936): 194–201.

15. K. Horney, *Neurosis and Human Growth* (New York: W. W. Norton, 1950).

16. Baker, *Ernest Hemingway* [1].

17. Ibid., p. 461.

18. E. Hemingway to Charles T. Lanham, letters, 20 April 1945, 7 August 1949, 18 June 1952, and 18 December 1952.

19. Baker, *Ernest Hemingway* [1].

20. E. Hemingway to Charles T. Lanham, letter, 22 September 1950.

21. Bickford Sylvester, unpublished observations.

22. Marcelline Sanford, cited in Baker, *Ernest Hemingway* [1], p. 193.

23. Ibid., p. 79.

24. E. Hemingway, "Cross Country Snow," in *The Short Stories of Ernest Hemingway* (New York: Charles Scribner's Sons, 1966).

25. E. Hemingway, "In Another Country," ibid.

26. P. Young, *Ernest Hemingway: A Reconsideration* (University Park: Pennsylvania State University Press, 1952).

27. S. Freud, *Three Contributions to the Theory of Sex* (New York: E. P. Dutton, 1962).

28. Young, *Ernest Hemingway* [25] p. 165.

29. E. Hemingway, *Across the River and Into the Trees* (New York: Charles Scribner's Sons, 1950), p. 33.

30. C. T. Lanham, written communication, 22 August 1967.

31. E. Hemingway to F. Scott Fitzgerald, letter, December 1926.

32. Baker, *Ernest Hemingway* [1], p. 642.

33. C. T. Lanham, oral communication, April 1967.

34. E. Hemingway, *The Sun Also Rises* (New York: Charles Scribner's Sons, 1950), p. 26.

35. E. Hemingway, *For Whom the Bell Tolls* (New York: Charles Scribner's Sons, 1940), p. 471.

36. Baker, *Ernest Hemingway* [1], p. 5.

37. Ibid.

38. Ibid., pp. 315 and 477.

39. O. Fallaci, ed., "Interview with Mary Hemingway: My Husband, Ernest Hemingway," *Look* 30 (1966): 62–68.

40. C. T. Lanham, written communication, 22 August 1967.

41. Baker, *Ernest Hemingway* [1], p. 175.

42. E. Hemingway to Charles T. Lanham, letter, 11 September 1950.

43. C. T. Lanham, written communication, 22 August 1967.

44. Baker, *Ernest Hemingway* [1], pp. 545–48.

45. Ibid., pp. 476 and 547.

46. A. E. Hotchner, *Papa Hemingway* (New York: Random House, 1966), p. 268.

47. Baker, *Ernest Hemingway* [1], p. 552.

CHAPTER 8: THE JOURNEY FROM PSYCHOTHERAPY TO FICTION

1. E. M. Forster, *Aspects of the Novel* (San Diego, Calif.: Harcourt, Brace, 1927), p. 66.

CHAPTER 9: THE TEACHING NOVEL

1. *Portable Nietzsche,* edited by Walter Kaufman (New York: Viking Press, 1954), p. 468.

2. Ibid., p. 430.

3. F. Nietzsche to Malwida Von Mesenburg, letter, May 1884.

4. F. Nietzsche, *Human, All Too Human,* translated by Erich Heller (Cambridge: Cambridge University Press, 1986), p. 250.

5. F. Nietzsche, *The Gay Science*, translated by Walter Kaufman (New York: Vintage Books, 1974), p. 198.

6. Ibid., p. 321.

7. *Portable Nietzsche* [1], p. 189.

8. Ibid., p. 181.

9. Ibid., p. 169.

10. Nietzsche, *Gay Science* [5], p. 89.

11. Ibid., p. 43.

12. *Portable Nietzsche* [1], p. 152.

13. Ibid., p. 351.

14. Nietzsche, *Gay Science* [5], p. 104.

15. E. Jones, *The Life and Work of Sigmund Freud,* 3 vols. (New York: Basic Books, 1953–57).

16. F. Nietzsche to F. Overbeck, letter, 5 August 1986, in P. Fuss and H. Shapiro, eds., *Nietzsche, a Self-Portrait from His Letters* (Cambridge: Harvard University Press, 1971), pp. 87 and 90.

17. H. Kaiser, *Effective Psychotherapy: The Contribution of Helmuth Kaiser,* edited by L. Fierman (New York: Free Press, 1965).

CHAPTER 10: THE PSYCHOLOGICAL NOVEL

1. S. Ferenczi, *The Clinical Journals of Sandor Ferenczi* (Cambridge: Harvard University Press, 1988).

2. I. D. Yalom and J. Handlon, "The Use of Multiple Therapists in the Teaching of Psychiatric Residents," in *Journal of Nervous and Mental Disorders* 141 (1966): 684-92.

3. I. D. Yalom, *The Theory and Practice of Group Psychotherapy,* 4th ed. (New York: Basic Books, 1995), pp. 514-15.

4. I. D. Yalom, *Inpatient Group Psychotherapy* (New York: Basic Books, 1983), pp. 259-74.

5. F. Nietzsche, *The Will to Power,* edited by Walter Kaufman (New York: Vintage Books, 1968), p. 272.

6. J. Cooper, *Speak of Me as I Am: The Life and Work of Masud Khan* (London: Karnac Books, 1993).

7. F. Nietzsche, *Beyond Good and Evil* (New York: Vintage Books, 1989), p. 80.

Index